At the Mercy of Tiberius

by Augusta J. Evans

Copyright © 1/28/2016
Jefferson Publication

ISBN-13: 978-1523750269

Table of Contents

CHAPTER I.

"You are obstinate and ungrateful. You would rather see me suffer and die, than bend your stubborn pride in the effort to obtain relief for me. You will not try to save me."

The thin, hysterically unsteady voice ended in a sob, and the frail wasted form of the speaker leaned forward, as if the issue of life or death hung upon an answer.

The tower clock of a neighboring church began to strike the hour of noon, and not until the echo of the last stroke had died away, was there a reply to the appeal.

"Mother, try to be just to me. My pride is for you, not for myself. I shrink from seeing my mother crawl to the feet of a man, who has disowned and spurned her; I cannot consent that she should humbly beg for rights, so unnaturally withheld. Every instinct of my nature revolts from the step you require of me, and I feel as if you held a hot iron in your hand, waiting to brand me."

"Your proud sensitiveness runs in a strange groove, and it seems you would prefer to see me a pauper in a Hospital, rather than go to your grandfather and ask for help. Beryl, time presses, and if I die for want of aid, you will be responsible; when it is too late, you will reproach yourself. If I only knew where and how to reach my dear boy, I should not importune you. Bertie would not refuse obedience to say wishes."

The silence which followed was so prolonged that a mouse crept from its covert in some corner of the comfortless garret room, and nibbled at the fragments of bread scattered on the table.

Beryl stood at the dormer window, holding aside the faded blue cotton curtain, and the mid-day glare falling upon her, showed every curve of her tall full form; every line in the calm, pale Sibylline face. The large steel gray eyes were shaded by drooping lids, heavily fringed with black lashes, but when raised in a steady gaze the pupils appeared abnormally dilated; and the delicately traced black brows that overarched them, contrasted conspicuously with the wealth of deep auburn hair darkened by mahogany tints, which rolled back in shining waves from her blue veined temples. While moulding the figure and features upon a scale almost heroic, nature had jealously guarded the symmetry of her work, and in addition to the perfect proportion of the statuesque outlines, had bestowed upon the firm white flesh a gleaming smoothness, suggestive of fine grained marble highly polished. Majesty of mien implies much, which the comparatively short period of eighteen years rarely confers, yet majestic most properly describes this girl, whose archetype Veleda read runic myths to the Bructeri in the twilight of history.

Beryl crossed the room, and with her hands folded tightly together, came to the low bed, on which lay the wreck of a once beautiful woman, and stood for a moment silent and pre-occupied. With a sudden gesture of surrender, she stooped her noble head, as if assuming a yoke, and drew one long deep breath. Did some prophetic intuition show her at that instant the Phicean Hill and its dread tenant, which sooner or later we must all confront?

"Dear mother, I submit. Obedience to your commands certainly ought not to lead me astray; yet I feel that I stand at the cross-roads, longing to turn and flee from the way whither your finger points. I have no hope of accomplishing any good, and nothing but humiliation can result from the experiment; but I will go. Sometimes I believe; that fate maliciously hunts up the things we most bitterly abhor, and one by one sets them down before us—labelled Duty. When do you wish me to start?"

"To-night, at nine o'clock. In the letter which you will take to father, I have told him our destitution; and that the money spent for your railway ticket has been obtained by the sacrifice of the diamonds and pearls, that were set around my mother's picture; that cameo, which he had cut in Rome and framed in Paris. Beryl so much depends on the impression you make upon him, that you must guard your manner against haughtiness. Try to be patient, my daughter, and if he should seem harsh, do not resent his words. He is old now, and proud and bitter, but he once had a tender love for me. I was his idol, and when my child pleads, he will relent."

Mrs. Brentano laid her thin hot fingers on her daughter's hands, drawing her down to the edge of the bed; and Beryl saw she was quivering with nervous excitement.

"Compose yourself, mother, or you will be so ill that I cannot leave you. Dr. Grantlin impressed upon us, the necessity of keeping your nervous system quiet. Take your medicine now, and try to sleep until I come back from Stephen & Endicott's."

"Do not go to-day."

"I must. Those porcelain types were promised for a certain day, and they should be packed in time for the afternoon express going to Boston."

"Beryl."

"Well, mother?"

"Come nearer to me. Give me your hand. My heart is so oppressed by dread, that I want you to promise me something, which I fancy will lighten my burden. Life is very uncertain, and if I should die, what would become of my Bertie? Oh, my boy! my darling, my first born! He is so impulsive, so headstrong; and no one but his mother could ever excuse or forgive his waywardness. Although younger, you are in some respects, the strongest; and I want your promise that you will always be patient and tender with him, and that you will shield him from evil, as I have tried to do. His conscience of course, is not sensitive like yours—because you know, a boy's moral nature is totally different from a girl's; and like most of his sex, Bertie has no religious instincts bending him always in the right direction. Women

4

generally have to supply conscientious scruples for men, and you can take care of your brother, if you will. You are unusually brave and strong, Beryl, and when I am gone, you must stand between him and trouble. My good little girl, will you?"

The large luminous eyes that rested upon the flushed face of the invalid, filled with a mist of yearning compassionate tenderness, and taking her mother's hands, Beryl laid the palms together, then stooping nearer, kissed her softly.

"I think I have never lacked love for Bertie, though I may not always have given expression to my feelings. If at times I have deplored his reckless waywardness, and expostulated with him, genuine affection prompted me; but I promise you now, that I will do all a sister possibly can for a brother. Trust me, mother; and rest in the assurance that his welfare shall be more to me than my own; that should the necessity arise, I will stand between him and trouble. Banish all depressing forebodings. When you are strong and well, and when I paint my great picture, we will buy a pretty cottage among the lilacs and roses, where birds sing all day long, where cattle pasture in clover nooks; and then Bertie, your darling, shall never leave you again."

"I do trust you, for your promise means more than oath and vows from other people, and if occasion demand, I know you will guard my Bertie, my high-strung, passionate, beautiful boy! Your pretty cottage? Ah, child! when shall we dwell in Spain?"

"Some day, some day; only be hopeful, and let me find you better when I return. Sleep, and dream of our pretty cottage. I must hurry away with my pictures, for this is pay day."

Tying the strings of her hat under one ear, and covering her face with a blue veil, Beryl took a pasteboard box from a table, on which lay brushes and paints, and leaving the door a-jar, went down the narrow stairs.

At the window of a small hall on the next floor, a woman sat before her sewing-machine, bending so close to her work that she did not see the tall form, which paused before her, until a hand was laid on the steel plate.

"Mrs. Emmet, will you please be so good as to go up after a while, and see if mother needs anything?"

"Certainly, Miss, if I am here, but I have some sewing to carry home this afternoon."

"I shall not be absent more than two hours. To-night I am going South, to attend to some business; and mother tells me you have promised to wait upon her, and allow your daughter Maggie to sleep on a pallet by her bed, while I am gone. I cannot tell you how grateful I shall be for any kindness you may show her, and I wish you would send the baby often to her room, as he is so sweet and cunning, and his merry ways amuse her."

"Yes, I will do all I can. We poor folks who have none of this world's goods, ought to be rich at least in sympathy and pity for each other's suffering, for it is about all we have to share. Don't you worry and fret, for I will see your ma has what she needs. I was mothered by the best woman God ever made, and since she died, every sick mother I see has a sort of claim on my heart."

Pausing an instant to adjust the tucker of her machine, Mrs. Emmet looked up, and involuntarily the women shook hands, as if sealing a compact.

It was a long walk to the building whither Beryl directed her steps, and as she passed through the rear entrance of a large and fashionable photograph establishment, she was surprised to find that it was half-past two o'clock.

The Superintendent of the department, from whom she received her work, was a man of middle-age, of rather stern and forbidding aspect; and as she approached his desk, he pointed to the clock on the mantel-piece.

"Barely time to submit those types for inspection, and have them packed for the express going East. They are birthday gifts, and birthdays have an awkward habit of arriving rigidly on time."

He unrolled the tissue paper, and with a magnifying glass, carefully examined the pictures; then took from an envelope in the box, two short pieces of hair, which he compared with the painted heads before him.

"Beautifully done. The lace on that child's dress would bear even a stronger lens than my glass. Here Patterson, take this box, and letter to Mr. Endicott, and if satisfactory, carry them to the packing counter. Shipping address is in the letter. Hurry up, my lad. Sit down, Miss Brentano."

"Thank you, I am not tired. Mr. Mansfield, have you any good news for me?"

"You mean those etchings; or the designs for the Christmas cards? Have not heard a word, pro or con. Guess no news is good news; for I notice 'rejected' work generally travels fast, to roost at home."

"I thought the awards were made last week, and that to-day you could tell me the result."

"The awards have been made, I presume, but who owns the lucky cards is the secret that has not yet transpired. You young people have no respect for red tape, and methodical business routine. You want to clap spurs on fate, and make her lower her own last record? 'Bide awee. Bide awee'."

"Winning this prize means so much to me, that I confess I find it very hard to be patient. Success would save me from a painful and expensive journey, upon which I must start to-night; and therefore I hoped so earnestly that I might receive good tidings to-day. I am obliged to go South on an errand, which will necessitate an absence of several days, and if you should have any news for me, keep it until I call again. If unfavorable it would depress my mother, and therefore I prefer you should not write, as of course she will open any letters addressed to me. Please save all the work you can for me, and I will come here as soon as I get back home."

"Very well. Any message, Patterson?"

"Mr. Endicott said, 'All right; first-rate;' and ordered them shipped."

"Here is your money, Miss Brentano. Better call as early as you can, as I guess there will be a lot of photographs ready in a few days. Good afternoon."

"Thank you. Good-bye, sir."

From the handful of small change, she selected some pennies which she slipped inside of her glove, and dropping the remainder into her pocket, left the building, and walked on toward Union Square. Absorbed in grave reflections, and oppressed by some vague foreboding of impending ill, dim, intangible and unlocalized—she moved slowly along the crowded sidewalk—unconscious of the curious glances directed toward her superb form, and stately graceful carriage, which more than one person turned and looked back to admire, wondering when she had stepped down from some sacred Panathenaic Frieze.

Near Madison Square, she paused before the window of a florist's, and raising her veil, gazed longingly at the glowing mass of blossoms, which Nineteenth Century skill and wealth in defiance of isothermal lines, and climatic limitations force into perfection, in, and out of season. The violet eyes and crocus fingers of Spring smiled and quivered, at sight of the crimson rose heart, and flaming paeony cheeks of royal Summer; and creamy and purple chrysanthemums that quill their laces over the russet robes of Autumn, here stared in indignant amazement, at the premature presumption of snowy regal camellias, audaciously advancing to crown the icy brows of Winter. All latitudes, all seasons have become bound vassals to the great God Gold; and his necromancy furnishes with equal facility the dewy wreaths of orange flowers that perfume the filmy veils of December brides—and the blue bells of spicy hyacinths which ring "Rest" over the lily pillows, set as tribute on the graves of babies, who wilt under August suns.

From early childhood, an ardent love of beauty had characterized this girl, whose covetous gaze wandered from a gorgeous scarlet and gold orchid nodding in dreams of its habitat, in some vanilla scented Brazilian jungle, to a bed of vivid green moss, where skilful hands had grouped great drooping sprays of waxen begonias, coral, faint pink, and ivory, all powdered with gold dust like that which gilds the heart of water-lilies.

Such treasures were reserved for the family of Dives; and counting her pennies, Beryl entered the store, where instantaneously the blended breath of heliotrope, tube-rose and mignonette wafted her across the ocean, to a white-walled fishing village on the Cornice, whose gray rocks were kissed by the blue lips of the Mediterranean.

"What is the price of that cluster of Niphetos buds?"

"One dollar."

"And that Auratum—with a few rose geranium leaves added?"

"Seventy-five cents. You see it is wonderfully large, and the gold bands are so very deep."

She put one hand in her pocket and fingered a silver coin, but poverty is a grim, tyrannous stepmother to tender aestheticism, and prudential considerations prevailed.

"Give me twenty-five cents worth of those pale blue double violets, with a sprig of lemon verbena, and a fringe of geranium leaves."

She laid the money on the counter, and while the florist selected and bound the blossoms into a bunch, she arrested his finishing touch.

"Wait a moment. How much more for one Grand Duke jasmine in the centre?"

"Ten cents, Miss."

She added the dime to the pennies she could ill afford to spare from her small hoard, and said: "Will you be so kind as to sprinkle it? I wish it kept fresh, for a sick lady."

Dusky shadows were gathering in the gloomy hall of the old tenement house, when Beryl opened the door of the comfortless attic room, where for many months she had struggled bravely to shield her mother from the wolf, that more than once snarled across the threshold.

Mrs. Brentano was sitting in a low chair, with her elbows on her knees, her face hidden in her palms; and in her lap lay paper and pencil, while a sealed letter had fallen on the ground beside her. At the sound of the opening door, she lifted her head, and tears dripped upon the paper. In her faded flannel dressing-gown, with tresses of black hair straggling across her shoulders, she presented a picture of helpless mental and physical woe, which painted itself indelibly on the panels of her daughter's heart.

"Why did you not wait until I came home? The exertion of getting up always fatigues you."

"You staid so long—and I am so uncomfortable in that wretchedly hard bed. What detained you?"

"I went to see the Doctor, because I am unwilling to start away, without having asked his advice; and he has prescribed some new medicine which you will find in this bottle. The directions are marked on the label. Now I will put things in order, and try my hands on that refractory bed."

"What did the Doctor say about me?"

"Nothing new; but he is confident that you can be cured in time, if we will only be patient and obedient. He promised to see you in the morning."

She stripped the bed of its covering, shook bolster and pillows; turned over the mattress, and beat it vigorously; then put on fresh sheets, and adjusted the whole comfortably.

"Now mother, turn your head, and let me comb and brush and braid all this glossy black satin, to keep it from tangling while I am away. What a pity you did not dower your daughter with part of it, instead of this tawny mane of mine, which is a constant affront to my fastidious artistic instincts. Please keep still a moment."

She unwrapped the tissue paper that covered her flowers, and holding her hands behind her, stepped in front of the invalid.

"Dear mother, shut your eyes. There—! of what does that remind you? The pergola—with great amber grape clusters—and white stars of jasmine shining through the leaves? All the fragrance of Italy sleeps in the thurible of this Grand-Duke."

"How delicious! Ah, my extravagant child! we cannot afford such luxuries now. The perfume recalls so vividly the time when Bertie—"

A sob cut short the sentence. Beryl pinned the flowers at her mother's throat, kissed her cheek, and kneeling before her, crossed her arms on the invalid's lap, resting there the noble head, with its burnished crown of reddish bronze braids.

"Mother dear, humor my childish whim. In defiance of my wishes and judgment, and solely in obedience to your command, I am leaving you for the first time, on a bitterly painful and humiliating mission. To-night, let me be indeed your little girl once more. My heart brings me to your knees, to say my prayers as of yore, and now while I pray, lay your dear pretty hands on my head. It will seem like a parting benediction; a veritable Nunc dimmitas."

6

CHAPTER II.

"I do not want a carriage. If the distance is only a mile and a half, I can easily walk. After leaving town is there a straight road?"

"Straight as the crow flies, when you have passed the factory, and cemetery, and turned to the left. There is a little Branch running at the foot of the hill, and just across it, you will see the white palings, and the big gate with stone pillars, and two tremendous brass dogs on top, showing their teeth and ready to spring. There's no mistaking the place, because it is the only one left in the country that looks like the good old times before the war; and the Yankees would not have spared it, had it not been such comfortable bombproof headquarters for their officers. It's our show place now, and General Darrington keeps it up in better style, than any other estate I know."

"Thank you. I will find it."

Beryl walked away in the direction indicated, and the agent of the railway station, leaning against the door of the baggage room, looked with curious scrutiny after her.

"I should like to know who she is. No ordinary person, that is clear. Such a grand figure and walk, and such a steady look in her big solemn eyes, as if she saw straight through a person, clothes, flesh and all. Wonder what her business can be with the old general?"

From early childhood Beryl had listened so intently to her mother's glowing descriptions of the beauty and elegance of her old home "Elm Bluff," that she soon began to identify the land-marks along the road, after passing the cemetery, where so many generations of Darringtons slept in one corner, enclosed by a lofty iron railing; exclusive in death as in life; jealously guarded and locked from contact with the surrounding dwellers in "God's Acre."

The October day had begun quite cool and crisp, with a hint of frost in its dewy sparkle, but as though vanquished Summer had suddenly faced about, and charged furiously to cover her retreat, the south wind came heavily laden with hot vapor from equatorial oceanic caldrons; and now the afternoon sun, glowing in a cloudless sky, shed a yellowish glare that burned and tingled like the breath of a furnace; while along the horizon, a dim dull haze seemed blotting out the boundary of earth and sky.

A portion of the primeval pine forest having been preserved, the trees had attained gigantic height, thrusting their plumy heads heavenward, as their lower limbs died; and year after year the mellow brown carpet of reddish straw deepened, forming a soft safe nidus for the seeds that sprang up and now gratefully embroidered it with masses of golden rod, starry white asters, and tall, feathery spikes of some velvety purple bloom, which looked royal by the side of a cluster of belated evening primroses.

Pausing on the small but pretty rustic bridge, Beryl leaned against the interlacing cedar boughs twisted into a balustrade, and looked down at the winding stream, where the clear water showed amber hues, flecked with glinting foam bubbles, as it lapped and gurgled, eddied and sang, over its bed of yellow gravel. Unacquainted with "piney-woods' branches," she was charmed by the novel golden brown wavelets that frothed against the pillars of the bridge, and curled caressingly about the broad emerald fronds of luxuriant ferns, which hung Narcissus-like over their own graceful quivering images. Profound quiet brooded in the warm, hazy air, burdened with balsamic odors; but once a pine burr full of rich nutty mast crashed down through dead twigs, bruising the satin petals of a primrose; and ever and anon the oboe notes of that shy, deep throated hermit of ravines—the russet, speckled-breasted lark—thrilled through the woods, like antiphonal echoes in some vast, cool, columned cloister.

The perfect tranquillity of the scene soothed the travel-weary woman, as though nestling so close to the great heart of nature, had stilled the fierce throbbing, and banished the gloomy forebodings of her own; and she walked on, through the iron gate, where the bronze mastiffs glared warningly from their granite pedestal—on into the large undulating park, which stretched away to meet the line of primitive pines. There was no straight avenue, but a broad smooth carriage road curved gently up a hillside, and on both margins of the graveled way, ancient elm trees stood at regular intervals, throwing their boughs across, to unite in lifting the superb groined arches, whose fine tracery of sinuous lines were here and there concealed by clustering mistletoe—and gray lichen masses—and ornamented with bosses of velvet moss; while the venerable columnar trunks were now and then wreathed with poison-oak vines, where red trumpet flowers insolently blared defiance to the waxen pearls of encroaching mistletoe.

On the other side, the grounds were studded with native growth, as though protective forestry statutes had crossed the ocean with the colonists, and on this billowy sea of varied foliage Autumn had set her illuminated autograph, in the vivid scarlet of sumach and black gum, the delicate lemon of wild cherry—the deep ochre all sprinkled and splashed with intense crimson, of the giant oaks—the orange glow of ancestral hickory—and the golden glory of maples, on which the hectic fever of the dying year kindled gleams of fiery red;—over all, a gorgeous blazonry of riotous color, toned down by the silver gray shadows of mossy tree-trunks, and the rich, dark, restful green of polished magnolias.

Half a dozen fine Cotswold ewes browsed on the grass, and the small bell worn by a staid dowager tinkled musically, as she threw up her head and watched suspiciously the figure moving under the elm arches. Beneath the far reaching branches of a patriarchal cedar, a small herd of Jersey calves had grouped themselves, as if posing for Landseer or Rosa Bonheur; and one pretty fawn-colored weanling ran across the sward to meet the stranger, bleating a welcome and looking up, with unmistakable curiosity in its velvety, long-lashed eyes.

As the avenue gradually climbed the ascent, the outlines of the house became visible; a stately, typical southern mansion, like hundreds, which formerly opened hospitably their broad mahogany doors, and which, alas! are becoming traditional to this generation—obsolete as the brave chivalric, warm-hearted, open-handed, noble-souled, refined southern gentlemen who built and owned them. No Mansard roof here, no pseudo "Queen Anne" hybrid, with lowering, top-heavy projections like scowling eyebrows over squinting eyes; neither mongrel Renaissance, nor feeble, sickly, imitation Elizabethan facades, and Tudor towers; none of the queer, composite, freakish impertinences of architectural style, which now-a-day do duty as the adventurous vanguard, the aesthetic vedettes "making straight the way," for the coming cohorts of Culture.

The house at "Elm Bluff" was built of brick, overcast with stucco painted in imitation of gray granite, and its foundation was only four feet high, resting upon a broad terrace of brickwork; the latter bounded by a graceful wooden balustrade, with pedestals for vases, on either

7

side of the two stone steps leading down from the terrace to the carriage drive. The central halls, in both stories, divided the space equally into four rooms on each side, and along the wide front, ran a lofty piazza supporting the roof, with white smooth round pillars; while the upper broad square windows, cedar-framed, and deeply embrasured, looked down on the floor of the piazza, where so many generations of Darringtons had trundled hoops in childhood—and promenaded as lovers in the silvery moonlight, listening to the ring doves cooing above them, from the columbary of the stucco capitals. This spacious colonnade extended around the northern and eastern side of the house, but the western end had formerly been enclosed as a conservatory—which having been abolished, was finally succeeded by a comparatively modern iron veranda, with steps leading down to the terrace. In front of the building, between the elm avenue and the flower-bordered terrace, stood a row of very old poplar trees, tall as their forefathers in Lombardy, and to an iron staple driven into one of these, a handsome black horse was now fastened.

Standing with one foot on the terrace step, close to the marble vases where heliotropes swung their dainty lilac chalices against her shoulder, and the scarlet geraniums stared unabashed, Beryl's gaze wandered from the lovely park and ancient trees, to the unbroken facade of the gray old house; and as, in painful contrast she recalled the bare bleak garret room, where a beloved invalid held want and death at bay, a sudden mist clouded her vision, and almost audibly she murmured: "My poor mother! Now, I can realize the bitterness of your suffering; now I understand the intensity of your yearning to come back; the terrible home-sickness, which only Heaven can cure."

What is presentiment? The swaying of the veil of futurity, under the straining hands of our guardian angels? Is it the faint shadow, the solemn rustle of their hovering wings, as like mother birds they spread protecting plumes between blind fledglings, and descending ruin? Will theosophy ever explain and augment prescience?

"It may be—
The thoughts that visit us, we know not whence,
Sudden as inspiration, are the whispers
Of disembodied spirits, speaking to us
As friends, who wait outside a prison wall,
Through the barred windows speak to those within."

With difficulty Beryl resisted an inexplicable impulse to turn and flee; but the drawn sword of duty pointed ahead.

Striking her hands together, as if thereby crushing her reluctance to enter, she waited a moment, with closed eyes, while her lips moved in silent prayer; then ascending the terrace, she crossed the stone pavement, walked up the stops and slowly advanced to the threshold. The dark mahogany door was so glossy, that she dimly saw her own image on its polished panels, as she lifted and let fall the heavy silver knocker, in the middle of an oval silver plate, around the edges of which were raised the square letters of the name "Darrington." The clanging sound startled a peacock, strutting among the verbena beds, and his shrill scream was answered by the deep hoarse bark of some invisible dog; then the heavy door swung open, and a gray-headed negro man, who wore a white linen apron over his black clothes, and held a waiter in one hand, stood before her.

"I wish to see Mr. Darrington."

"I reckon you mean Gin'l Darrington, don't you? Mr. Darrington, Marse Prince Darrington, is in Yurope."

"I mean Mr. Luke Darrington, the owner of this place."

"Jess so; Gin'l Luke Darrington. Well, you can't see him."

"Why not? I must see him, and I shall stay here until I do."

"'Cause he is busy with his lie-yer, fixin' of some papers; and when he tells me not to let nobody else in I'de ruther set down in a yaller jacket's nest than to turn the door knob, after he done shut it. Better leave your name and call ag'in."

"No, I will wait until he is at leisure. I presume my sitting on the steps here will not be a violation of your orders."

"To be shore not. But them steps are harder than the stool of repentance, and you had better walk in the drawing-room, and rest yourself. There's pictures, and lots and piles of things there, you can pass away the time looking at."

He waved his waiter toward a long, dim apartment, on the left side of the hall.

"Thank you, I prefer to sit here."

She seated herself on the top of the stone steps, and taking off her straw hat, fanned her heated brow, where the rich waving hair clung in damp masses.

"What name, miss, must I give, when the lie-yer finishes his bizness?"

"Say that a stranger wishes to see him about an important matter."

"Its mighty uncertain how long he will tarry; for lie-yers live by talking; turning of words upside down, and wrong side outards, and reading words backards, and whitewashing black things, and smutting of white ones. Marse Lennox Dunbar (he is our lie-yer now, since his pa took paralsis) he is a powerful wrastler with justice. They do say down yonder, at the court house, that when he gets done with a witness, and turns him aloose, the poor creetur is so flustrated in his mind, that he don't know his own name, on when he was born, or where he was born, or whether he was ever born at all."

Curiosity to discover the nature of the stranger's errand had stimulated the old man's garrulity, but receiving no reply, he finally retreated, leaving the front door open. By the aid of a disfiguring scar on his furrowed cheek, Beryl recognized him as the brave, faithful, family coachman, Abednego, (abbreviated to "Bedney")—who had once saved his mother's life at the risk of his own. Mrs. Brentano had often related to her children, an episode in her childhood, when having gone to play with her dolls in the loft of the stable, she fell asleep on the hay; and two hours later, Bedney remembering that he had heard her singing there to her dolls, rushed into the burning building, groped through the stifling smoke of the loft, and seizing the sleeping child, threw her out upon a pile of straw. When he attempted to jump after her, a falling rafter struck him to the earth, and left an honorable scar in attestation of his heroism.

Had she yielded to the promptings of her heart, the stranger would gladly have shaken hands with him, and thanked him, in the name of those early years, when her mother's childish feet made music on the wide mahogany railed stairs, that wound from the lower hall to the one above; but the fear of being denied an audience, deterred her from disclosing her name.

Educated in the belief that the utterance of the abhorred name of Brentano, within the precincts of "Elm Bluff," would produce an effect very similar to the ringing of some Tamil Pariah's bell, before the door of a Brahman temple, Beryl wisely kept silent; and soon forgot her forebodings, in the contemplation of the supreme loveliness of the prospect before her.

The elevation was sufficient to command an extended view of the surrounding country, and of the river, which crossed by the railroad bridge north of the town, curved sharply to the east, whence she could trace its course as it gradually wound southward, and disappeared behind the house; where at the foot of a steep bluff, a pretty boat and bath house nestled under ancient willow trees. At her feet the foliage of the park stretched like some brilliant carpet, before whose gorgeous tints, ustads of Karman would have stood in despair; and beyond the sea-green, undulating line of pine forest she saw the steeple of a church, with its gilt vane burning in the sunshine, and the red brick dome of the ante bellum court house.

Time seemed to have fallen asleep on that hot, still afternoon, and Beryl was roused from her reverie by the sound of hearty laughter in the apartment opposite the drawing-room—followed by the tones of a man's voice.

"Thank you, General. That is my destination this afternoon, and I shall certainly expect you to dance at my wedding."

Quick, firm steps rang on the oil-cloth-covered floor of the hall, and Beryl rose and turned toward the door.

With a cigar in one hand, hat and riding-whip in the other, the attorney stepped out on the colonnade, and pausing involuntarily, at sight of the stranger, they looked at each other. A man, perhaps, more, certainly not less than thirty years old, of powerful and impressive physique; very tall, athletic, sinewy, without an ounce of superfluous flesh to encumber his movements, in the professional palaestra; with a large finely modeled head, whose crisp black hair closely cut, was (contrary to the prevailing fashion) parted neither in the middle, nor yet on the side, but brushed straight back from the square forehead, thereby enhancing the massiveness of its appearance.

Something in this swart, beardless face, with its brilliant inquisitorial dark blue eyes, handsome secretive mouth veiled by no mustache—and boldly assertive chin deeply cleft in the centre—affected Beryl very unpleasantly, as a perplexing disagreeable memory; an uncanny resemblance hovering just beyond the grasp of identification. A feeling of unaccountable repulsion made her shiver, and she breathed more freely, when he bowed slightly, and walked on toward his horse. Upon the attorney her extraordinary appearance produced a profound impression, and in his brief scrutiny, no detail of her face, figure, or apparel escaped his keen probing gaze.

Glancing back as he untied his bridle rein, his unspoken comment was: "Superb woman; I wonder what brings her here? Evidently a stranger—with a purpose."

He sprang into the saddle, stooped his head to avoid the yellow poplar branches, and disappeared under the elm arches.

"Gin'l Darrington's compliments; and if your bizness is pressin' you will have to see him in his bedcharmber, as he feels poorly to-day, and the Doctor won't let him out. Follow me. You see, ole Marster remembers the war by the game leg he got at Sharpsburg, and sometimes it lays him up."

The old servant led Beryl through a long room, fitted up as a library and armory, and pausing before an open door, waved her into the adjoining apartment. One swift glance showed her the heavy canopied bedstead in one corner, the arch-shaped glass door leading out upon the iron veranda; and at an oblong table in the middle of the floor, the figure of a man, who rose, taller and taller, until he seemed a giant, drawn to his full height, and resting for support on the hand that was rested upon the table. Intensity of emotion arrested her breath, as she gazed at the silvered head, piercing black eyes, and spare wasted framp of the handsome man, who had always reigned as a brutal ogre in her imagination. The fire in his somewhat sunken eyes, seemed to bid defiance to the whiteness of the abundant hair, and of the heavy mustache which drooped over his lips; and every feature in his patrician face revealed not only a long line of blue-blooded ancestors, but the proud haughtiness which had been considered always as distinctively characteristic of the Darringtons as their finely cut lips, thin nostrils, small feet and unusual height.

Unprepared for the apparition that confronted him, Luke Darrington bowed low, surveyed her intently, then pointed to a chair opposite his own.

"Walk in, Madam; or perhaps it may be Miss? Will you take a seat, and excuse the feebleness that forces me to receive visits in my bed-room?"

As he reseated himself, Beryl advanced and stood beside him, but for a moment she found it impossible to utter the words, rehearsed so frequently during her journey; and while she hesitated, he curiously inspected her face and form.

Her plain, but perfectly fitting bunting dress, was of the color, popularly dominated "navy-blue," and the linen collar and cuffs were scarcely whiter than the round throat and wrists they encircled. The burnished auburn hair clinging in soft waves to her brow, was twisted into a heavy coil, which the long walk had shaken down till it rested almost on her neck; and though her heart beat furiously, the pale calm face might have been marble, save for the scarlet lines of her beautiful mouth, and the steady glow of the dilated pupils in her great gray eyes.

"Pray be seated; and tell me to whom I am indebted for the pleasure of this visit?"

"I am merely the bearer of a letter which will explain itself, and my presence, in your house."

Mechanically he took the preferred letter, and with his eyes still lingering in admiration upon the classic outlines of her face and form, leaned back comfortably against the velvet lining of his armchair.

"Are you some exiled goddess travelling incognito? If we lived in the 'piping days of Pan' I should flatter myself that 'Ox-eyed Juno' had honored me with a call, as a reward for my care of her favorite bird."

Receiving no reply he glanced at the envelope in his hand, and as he read the address—"To my dear father, Gen'l Luke Darrington"—the smile on his face changed to a dark scowl and he tossed the letter to the floor, as if it were a red-hot coal.

9

"Only one living being has the right to call me father—my son, Prince Darrington. I have repeatedly refused to hold any communication with the person who wrote that letter."

Beryl stooped to pick it up, and with a caressing touch, as though it were sentient, held it against her heart.

"Your daughter is dying; and this is her last appeal."

"I have no daughter. Twenty-three years ago my daughter buried herself in hopeless disgrace, and for her there can be no resurrection here. If she dreams that I am in my dotage, and may relent, she strangely forgets the nature of the blood she saw fit to cross with that of a beggarly foreign scrub. Go back and tell her, the old man is not yet senile and imbecile; and that the years have only hardened his heart. Tell her, I have almost learned to forget even how she looked."

His eyes showed a dull reddish fire, like those of some drowsy caged tiger, suddenly stirred into wrath, and a grayish pallor—the white heat of the Darringtons—settled on his face.

Twice Beryl walked the length of the room, but each time the recollection of her mother's tearful, suffering countenance, and the extremity of her need, drove her back to the chair.

"If you knew that your daughter's life hung by a thread, would you deliberately take a pair of shears and cut it?"

He glared at her in silence, and leaning forward on the table, pushed roughly aside a salver, on which stood a decanter and two wine glasses.

"I am here to tell you a solemn truth; then my responsibility ends. Your daughter's life rests literally in your hands; for unless you consent to furnish the money to pay for a surgical operation, which may restore her health, she will certainly die. I am indulging in no exaggeration to extort alms. In this letter is the certificate of a distinguished physician, corroborating my statement. If you, the author of her being, prefer to hasten her death, then your choice of an awful revenge must be settled between your hardened conscience and your God."

"You are bold indeed, to beard me in my own house, and tell me to my face what no man would dare to utter."

His voice was an angry pant, and he struck his clenched hand on the table with a force that made the glasses jingle, and the sherry dance in the decanter.

"Yes, you scarcely realize how much bravery this painful errand demands; but the tender love in a woman's heart nerves her to bear fiery ordeals, that vanquish a man's courage."

"Then you find that age has not drawn the fangs from the old crippled Darrington lion, nor clipped his claws?"

The sneer curved his white mustache, until she saw the outline of the narrow, bloodless underlip.

"That king of beasts scorns to redden his fangs, or flesh his claws, in the quivering body of his own offspring. Your metaphor is an insult to natural instincts."

She laid the letter once more before him, and looked down on him, with ill-concealed aversion.

"Who are you? By what right dare you intrude upon me?"

"I am merely a sorrowful, anxious, poverty-stricken woman, whose heart aches over her mother's sufferings and vho would never have endured the humiliation of this interview, except to deliver a letter in the hope of prolonging my mother's life."

"You do not mean that you are—my—"

"I am nothing to you, sir, but the bearer of a letter from your dying daughter."

"You cannot be the child of—of Ellice?"

After the long limbo of twenty-three years, the name burst from him, and with what a host of memories its echo peopled the room, where that erring daughter had formerly reigned queen of his heart.

"Yes, Ellice is my dear mother's name."

He stared at the majestic form, and at the faultless face looking so proudly down upon him, as from an inaccessible height; and she heard him draw his breath, with a labored hissing sound.

"But—I thought her child was a boy?"

"I am the youngest of two children."

"It is impossible that you are the daughter of that infernal, low-born, fiddling foreign vagabond who—"

"Hush! The dead are sacred!"

She threw up her hand, with an imperious gesture, not of deprecation, but of interdict; and all the stony calm in her pale face seemed shivered by a passionate gust, that made her eyes gleam like steel under an electric flash.

"I am the daughter of Ignace Brentano, and I love, and honor his memory, and his name. No drop of your Darrington blood runs in my veins; I love my dear mother—but I am my father's daughter—and I want no nobler heritage than his name. Upon you I have no shadow of claim, but I am here from dire necessity, at your mercy—a helpless, defenseless pleader in my mother's behalf—and as such, I appeal to the boasted southern chivalry, upon which you pride yourself, for immunity from insult while I am under your roof. Since I stood no taller than your knee, my mother has striven to inculcate a belief in the nobility, refinement, and chivalric deference to womanhood, inherent in southern gentlemen; and if it be not all a myth, I invoke its protection against abuse of my father. A stranger, but a lady, every inch, I demand the respect due from a gentleman."

For a moment they eyed each other, as gladiators awaiting the signal, then General Darrington sprang to his feet, and with a bow, stately and profound as if made to a duchess, replied:

"And in the name of southern chivalry, I swear you shall receive it."

"Read your daughter's letter; give me your answer, and let us cut short an interview—which, if disagreeable to you, is almost unendurable to me."

Turning away, she began to walk slowly up and down the floor; and smothering an oath under his heavy mustache, the old man sank back in his chair, and opened the letter.

CHAPTER III.

Holding in leash the painful emotions that struggled for utterance, Beryl was unconscious of the lapse of time, and when her averted eyes returned reluctantly to her grandfather's face, he was slowly tearing into shreds the tear-stained letter, freighted with passionate prayers for pardon, and for succor. Rolling the strips into a ball, he threw it into the waste-paper basket under the table; then filled a glass with sherry, drank it, and dropped his head wearily on his hand. Five leaden minutes crawled away, and a long, heavy sigh quivered through Gen'l Darrington's gaunt frame. Seizing the decanter, he poured the contents into two glasses, and as he raised one to his lips, held the other toward his visitor.

"You must be weary from your journey; let me insist that you drink some sherry."

"Thank you, I neither wish nor require it."

"I find your name is Beryl. Sit down here, and answer a few questions." He drew a chair near his own.

She shook her head:

"If you will excuse me, I prefer to stand."

In turning, so as to confront her fully, his elbow struck from the table, a bronze paper-weight which rolled just beyond his reach. Instinctively she stooped to pick it up, and in restoring it, her fingers touched his. Leaning suddenly forward he grasped her wrists ere she was aware of his intention, and drew her in front of him.

"Pardon me; but I want a good look at you."

His keen merciless eyes searched every feature, and he deliberately lifted and examined the exquisitely shaped strong, white hands, the dainty nails, and delicately rounded wrists with their violet tracery of veins. It cost her an effort, to abstain from wrenching herself free; but her mother's caution: "So much depends on the impression you make upon father," girded her to submit to his critical inspection.

A grim smile crossed his face, as he watched her.

"Blood often doubles, like a fox; sometimes 'crops back,' but never lies. You can't play out your role of pauper; and you don't look a probable outcome of destitution and hard work. Your hands would fit much better in a metope of the Elgin Marbles, than in a wash-tub, or a bake-oven."

Drawing away quickly, she put them behind her, and felt her palms tingle.

"It is expected I should believe that for some time past, you have provided for your own, and your mother's wants. In what way?"

"By coloring photographs; by furnishing designs for Christmas and Easter cards, and occasionally (not often), by selling drawings used for decorating china, and wallpaper. At one time, I had regular pay for singing in a choir, but diphtheria injured my throat, and when I partly recovered my voice, the situation had been given to another person."

"I am informed also that before long, you intend to astonish the world with a wonderful picture, which shall distance such laggards as Troyon, Dore, and Ary Scheffer?"

She was looking, not at him, but out through the glass door, at the glowing western sky, where distant pine trees printed their silhouettes. Now her gaze came back to his face, and he noted a faint quiver in her full throat.

"If God will mercifully spare my mother to me, my loftiest and holiest ambition shall be to distance the wolfish cares and woes that have hunted her, ever since she became a widow. Any and all honest labor that can contribute to her comfort, will be welcome and sweet to me."

"The laws of heredity must be occult and complex. The offspring of a rebellious and disobedient child, is certainly entitled to no filial instincts; and some day the strain will tell, and you will overwhelm your mother with ingratitude, black as that which she showed me."

"When I do, may God eternally forsake me!"

A brief silence ensued, and the old man drummed on the table, with the fingers of his right hand.

"Who educated you?"

"My dear father."

"It seems there are two of you. Where is your brother?"

"At present, I do not know exactly where he is, but I think in the far West; possibly in Montana—probably in Canada."

"How does he earn his bread? By daubing, or fiddling?"

"Since he earns it honestly, that is his own affair. We have not heard from him for some months."

"I thought so! He inherits the worthless vagabond strain of—"

"He is his mother's idol, and she glories in his resemblance to you, sir; and to your father; hence his name—Robert L. Darrington."

"Then she must have one handsome child! I am not surprised that he is the favorite."

"Bertie certainly is her darling, and he is very handsome; not in the very least degree like me."

For the first time, their eyes met in a friendly glance, and a covert smile stirred the General's lips; but as he put out his hand toward her, she moved a step beyond his reach.

"Beryl, you consider me a dreadful, cruel old tyrant?"

She made no reply.

"Answer me."

"You are my mother's father; and that word—father, means so much to me, that it shall shield even you, from the shadow of disrespect."

"Oh! very dutiful indeed, but dead as the days when daughters obeyed, and honored their fathers! Beggarly foreign professors wiped all that out of the minds of wealthy girls at boarding schools—just as they changed their backwoods pronunciation of French and Italian. Don't evade my question."

"I did not come here, sir, to bandy words; and I ended my mission by delivering the letter intrusted to me."

"You regard me as a vindictive old bear?"

"I had heard much of the Darringtons; I imagined a great deal more; but now, like the Queen of Sheba, I must testify—'Behold, the half was not told me.'"

He threw back his lion-like head, and laughed.

"That will do. Shake hands, child."

"No, thank you."

"And you will not sit down?"

"Frankly, I prefer not. I long to get away."

"You shall certainly be gratified, but there are a few things which I intend you shall hear. Of course you know that your mother was my only child, and an heiress; but you are ignorant probably of the fact that when she returned to boarding school for the last session, she was engaged in marriage to the son of my best friend—a man in every respect desirable, and thoroughly acceptable to me."

"So my mother told me."

"Indeed? She should blush to remember it. While she wore his engagement ring, she forgot her promise to him, her duty to me, her lineage, her birth, her position—and was inveigled by a low adventurer who—"

"Who was my own precious father—poor, but noble, and worthy of any princess! Unless you can refer to him respectfully, name him not at all, in his child's presence."

She suddenly towered over him, like some threatening fate, and her uplifted arm trembled from the intensity of her indignation.

"At least—you are loyal to your tribe!"

"I am, to my heart's core. You could pay me no higher compliment."

"Ellice wrote that she had bestowed her affections on—on—the 'exiled scion of a noble house,' who paid his board bill by teaching languages and music in the school; and who very naturally preferred to marry a rich fool, who would pay them for him. I answered her letter, which was addressed to her own mother—then quite ill at home—and I told her precisely what she might expect, if she persisted in her insane folly. As soon as my wife convalesced sufficiently to render my departure advisable, I started to bring my daughter home; but she ran away, a few hours before my arrival, and while, hoping to rescue Ellice, I was in pursuit of the precious pair, my wife relapsed and died—the victim of excitement brought on by her child's disgrace. I came back here to a desolate, silent house;—bereft of wife and daughter; and in the grave of her mother, I buried every atom of love and tenderness I ever entertained for Ellice. When the sun is suddenly blotted out at noon, and the world turns black—black, we grope to and fro aimlessly; but after awhile, we accommodate ourselves to the darkness;—and so, I became a different man—very hard, and I dare say very bitter. The world soon learned that I would tolerate no illusion to my disgrace, and people respected my family cancer, and prudently refrained from offering me nostrums to cure it. My wife had a handsome estate of her own right, and every cent of her fortune I collected, and sent with her jewelry to Ellice. Did you know this?"

"I have heard only of the jewels."

"As I supposed, the money was squandered before you could recollect."

"I know that we were reduced to poverty, by the failure of some banking house in Paris. I was old enough when it occurred, to remember ever afterward, the dismay and distress it caused. My father no doubt placed my mother's money there for safety."

"I wrote one long, final letter when I sent the checks for the money, and I told Ellice I wished never to see, never to hear from her again. I told her also, I had only one wish concerning her, and that was, that I might be able to forget her so completely, that if we should meet in the Last Judgment, I could not possibly know her. I assured her she need expect nothing at my death; as I had taken good care that my estate should not fall into the clutches of—her—'exiled scion of a noble house.' Now do you consider that she has any claim on me?"

"You must not ask me to sit in judgment on my parents."

"You shall decide a question of business facts. I provided liberally for her once; can you expect me to do so again? Has she any right to demand it?"

"Having defied your parental wishes, she may have forfeited a daughter's claim; but as a heart-broken sufferer, you cannot deny her the melancholy privilege of praying for your help, on her death-bed."

The proud clear voice trembled, and Beryl covered her face with her hands.

"Then we will ignore outraged ties of blood, and treat on the ground of mere humanity? Let me conclude, for it is sickening and loathsome to a man of my age, to see his long silent household graves yawn, and give up uncalled—their sheeted dead. For some years the money sent, was a quietus, and I was left in peace. I was lonely; it was, hard work to forget, because I could never forgive; and the more desolate the gray ruin, the more nature yearns to cover it close with vines and flowers; so after a time, I married a gentle, pure hearted woman, who made the best of what was left of me. We had no children, but she had one son of a former marriage, who proved a noble trustworthy boy; and by degrees he crept into my heart, and raked together the cinders of my dead affections, and kindled a feeble flame that warmed my shivering old age. When I felt assured that I was not thawing another serpent to sting me for my pains, I adopted Thorton Prince, and with the aid of a Legislative enactment, changed his name to Prince Darrington. Only a few months elapsed, before his mother, of whom I was very fond, died of consumption and my boy and I comforted each other. Then I made my second and last will, and took every possible precaution to secure my estate of every description to him. He is my sole heir, and I intend that at my death he shall receive every cent I possess. Did you know this?"

"I did, because your last endorsement on a letter of my mother's returned unopened to her, informed her of the fact."

"Why? Because in violation of my wishes she had persisted in writing, and soon began to importune me for money. Then I made her understand that even at my death, she would receive no aid; and since that endorsement, I have returned or destroyed her letters unread. My Will is so strong—has been drawn so carefully—that no contest can touch it; and it will stand forever between your mother and my property."

As he uttered these words, he elevated his voice, which had a ring of savage triumph in its harsh excited tones. Just then, a muffled sound attracted his attention, and seizing his gold-headed cane, he limped with evident pain to the threshold of the adjoining room.

"Bedney."

Receiving no reply, he closed the door with a violence that jarred the whole room; and came slowly back to the table, where he stood leaning heavily on his stick.

"At least we will have no eavesdropping at this resurrection of my dead. That Ellice is now a miserable woman, I have no doubt; for truly: 'Quien se casa por amores, ha de vivir con dolores.' Of course you understand Spanish?"

"No, sir; but no matter; I take it for granted that you intend some thrust at my mother, and I have heard quite enough."

"Don't know Spanish? Why I fancied your—your 'exiled scion of a noble house'—taught all the languages under the sun; including that used by the serpent in beguiling Eve! Well, the wise old adage means: 'Who marries for love, lives with sorrow.' Ellice made her choice, and she shall abide by it; and you—being unluckily her daughter—will share the punishment. If 'fathers WILL eat sour grapes, the children's teeth MUST be set on edge.' I repudiate all claims on my parental treasury, save such as I have given to my son Prince. To every other draft I am bankrupt; but merely as a gentleman, I will now for the last time, respond to the petition of a sick woman, whose child is so loyal as to arouse my compassion. Ellice has asked for one hundred dollars. You shall have it. But first, tell me why she did not go to the hospital, and submit to the operation which she says will cure her?"

"Because I could not be with her there, and I will never be separated from her. The aneurism has grown so alarmingly, that I became desperate, and having no one to aid us, I reluctantly obeyed my mother's requirement that I should come here. I could not summon my brother, because I have no idea where a letter would reach him; and with no friend—but the God of the friendless—I am before you. There is one thing I ought to tell you; I have terrible forebodings of the result of the operation, from which the Doctor encourages her to hope so much. She will not be able to take anesthetics, at least not chloroform, because she has a weak heart, and—"

"Yes—a very weak heart! It was never strong enough to hold her to her duty."

"If you could see her now, I think even your vindictive hatred would be sufficiently gratified. So wasted, so broken!—and with such a ceaseless craving for a kind word from you. One night last week pain made her restless, and I heard her sob. When I tried to relieve the suffering, she cried bitterly: 'It is not my poor body alone—it is the gnawing hunger to see father once more. He loved me so fondly once and if I could crawl to his feet, and clasp his knees in my arms, I could at least die in peace. I am starving for just one sight of him—one touch.' My poor darling mother! My beautiful, bruised, broken flower."

Through the glittering mist of unshed tears, her eyes shone, like silver lamps; and for a moment Gen'l Darrington covered his face with one hand.

"If you could realize how bitterly galling to my own pride and self respect is this appeal to a man who hates and spurns all whom I love, I think, sir, that even you would pity me so heartily, that your hardened heart would melt into one last farewell message of forgiveness to your unfortunate daughter. I would rather carry her one word of love than all your fortune."

"No—I come of a flinty race. We never forgive insults; never condone wrongs; and expecting loyalty in our own blood, we cannot live long enough to pardon its treachery. Once, I made an idol of my beautiful, graceful, high-bred girl; but she stabbed my pride, dragged my name through the gutters, broke her doting mother's heart; and now, I tell you, she is as dead to me as if she had lain twenty-three years in her grave. I have only one message. Tell her she is reaping the tares her own hand sowed. I know her no more as child of mine, and my son fills her place so completely, I do not even miss her. That is the best I can say. No doubt I am hard, but at least I am honest; and I will not feign what I cannot feel."

He limped across the floor, to a recess on one side of the chimney, where a square vault with an iron door had been built into the wall. Leaning on his cane, he took from his pocket a bunch of keys, fitted one into the lock, and pushing the bolt, the door slid back into a groove, instead of opening on hinges. He lifted a black tin box from the depths of the vault, carried it to the table, sat down, and opened it. Near the top, were numerous papers tied into packages with red tape, and two large envelopes carefully sealed with dark-green wax. In removing the bundles, to find something beneath them, these envelopes were laid on the table; and as one was either accidentally or intentionally turned, Beryl saw the endorsement written in bold black letters, and heavily underscored in red ink: "Last Will and Testament of Robert Luke Darrington." Untying a small chamois bag, the owner counted out five twenty-dollar gold pieces, closed the bag, and replaced it in the box.

"Hold out your hand. Your mother asked fur one hundred dollars. Here is the exact amount. Henceforth, leave me in peace. I am an old man, and I advise you to 'let sleeping dogs lie.'"

If he had laid a red-hot iron on her palm, it would scarcely have been more scorching than the touch of his gold, and only the vision of a wan and woeful face in that far off cheerless attic room, restrained her impulse to throw it at his feet.

An almost intolerable humiliation dyed her pale cheeks a deep purplish crimson, and she proudly drew herself to her utmost height.

"Because I cannot now help myself, I accept the money—not as a gift, but as a loan for my mother's benefit; and so help me God! I will not owe it to you one moment longer than by hard labor I can earn and return it. Goodbye, Gen'l Darrington."

She turned toward the closed door leading to the library, but raising his cane, he held it out, to intercept her.

13

"Wait a moment. There is one thing more."

He took from the tin box an oblong package, wrapped in letter paper, yellowed by age, and carefully sealed with red wax. As he held it up, she read thereon: "My last folly." He tore off the paper, lifted an old fashioned morocco case, and attempted to open it, but the catch was obstinate, or rusty, and several ineffectual efforts were made, ere he succeeded in moving the spring. The once white velvet cushion, had darkened and turned very yellow, but time had robbed in no degree, the lustre of the magnificent sapphires coiled there; and the blue fires leaped out, as if rejoicing in the privilege of displaying their splendor. "This set of stones was intended as a gift to your mother, when she was graduated at boarding-school. The time fixed for the close of the session was only one month later than the day on which she eloped with that foreign fraud, who should never have been allowed in the school. My wife had promised that if your mother won the honor of valedictorian, she should have the handsomest present ever worn at a commencement. These costly sapphires were my poor wife's choice. Poor Helena! how often she admired them!" His voice faltered, and he bit his under lip to still its quiver.

Was there some necromancy in the azure flames, that suddenly revealed the beloved face of the wife of his youth, and the lovely vision of their only child? His eagle eyes were dim with tears, and his hand shook; but, as if ashamed of the weakness, he closed the jewel case with a snap, and held it out.

"Here—take them. I had intended to give them as a bridal present to my son's wife, when he marries to suit me—as he certainly will; but somehow, such a disposal seems hard on my dear Helena's wishes, and for her sake, I don't feel quite easy about leaving them to Prince's bride. Your mother never saw them, never knew of their existence. They are very valuable, and the amount they will bring must relieve all present necessities. Tell Ellice the sight of the case disturbs me, like a thorn in the flesh, so I send them away, to rid myself of an annoyance. She must not thank me; they come from her—dead mother."

"A knowledge of their history would give her infinitely more pain than the proceeds of their sale could bring comfort. I would not stab her aching heart for twenty times the value of the jewels."

"Then sell them, or do as you like. It matters not what becomes of them, if I am spared in future all reminders of the past. Put them in your pocket. What? The case is too large? Where is your trunk—your baggage?"

"I have none, except my basket and shawl."

She picked them up from the carpet near the library door, and dropped the case into her basket.

"You are a brave, and a loyal woman, and you appear to deserve far better parents than fell to your lot. Before you go, let me offer you a glass of wine, and a biscuit."

"Thank you—no. I could not possibly accept it."

"Well, we shall never meet again. Good-bye. Shake hands."

"I will very gladly do so if you will only give me just one gentle, forgiving kind word to comfort mother."

He set his teeth, and shook his head.

"Good-bye, Gen'l Darrington. When you lie down to die, I hope God will be more merciful to your poor soul, than you have shown yourself to your suffering child."

He bowed profoundly.

Her hand was on the knob of the door, when he pointed to the western veranda.

"You are going back to town? Then, if you please, be so good as to pass out through that rear entrance, and close the glass door after you. A side path leads to the lawn; and I prefer that you should not meet the servants, who pry and tattle."

When she stood on the veranda, and turned to close the wide arched glass door, whence the inside red silk curtain had been looped back, her last view of the gaunt, tall figure within, showed him leaning on his stick, with the tin box held in his left hand, and the dying sunlight shining on his silver hair and furrowed face.

Along the serpentine path which was bordered with masses of brilliant chrysanthemums, Beryl walked rapidly, feeling almost stifled by the pressure of contending emotions. Recollecting that these spice censers of Autumn were her mother's favorite flowers, she stooped and broke several lovely clusters of orange and garnet color, hoping that a lingering breath of perfume from the home of her girlhood, might afford at least a melancholy pleasure to the distant invalid.

Advancing into the elm avenue, she heard a voice calling, and looking back, saw the old negro man, Bedney, waving his white apron and running toward her; but at that moment his steps were arrested by the sudden, loud and rapid ringing of a bell. He paused, listened, wavered; then threw up his hands, and hurried back to the house, whence issued the impatient summons.

The sun had gone down in the green sea of far-off pine tops, but the western sky glowed like some vast altar of topaz, whereon zodiacal fires had kindled the rays of vivid rose, that sprang into the zenith and cooled their flush in the pale blue of the upper air. Under the elms, swift southern twilight was already filling the arches with purple gloom, and when the heavy iron gate closed with a sullen clang behind her, Beryl drew a long deep breath of relief. On the sultry atmosphere broke the gurgling andante music of the "branch," as it eddied among the nodding ferns, and darted under the bridge; and the weary, thirsty woman knelt on the mossy margin, dipped up the amber water in her palms, drank, and bathed her burning face which still tingled painfully.

Having learned from the station agent, who had already sold her a return ticket, that the north bound railway train, by which she desired to travel home, would not depart until 7.15, she was beguiled by the brilliance of the sky into the belief that she had ample time, to comply with her mother's farewell request. Mrs. Brentano had tied with a scrap of ribbon the bouquet of flowers, bought by her daughter on the afternoon of her journey south, and asked her to lay them on her mother's grave.

Anxious to accomplish this sacred mission Beryl took the faded blossoms from her basket, added a cluster of chrysanthemums, a frond of fern from the "branch" border, and hurried on to the cemetery. When she reached the entrance, the gate was locked, but unwilling to return without having gratified her mother's wish, she climbed into a spreading cedar close by the low brick wall, and swung herself easily down inside the enclosure.

14

Some time was lost in finding the Darrington lot, but at last she stood before a tall iron railing, that bristled with lance-like points, between the dust, of her ancestors and herself. In one corner rose a beautiful monument, bearing on its front, in gilt letters, the inscription "Helena Tracy, wife of R. L. Darrington."

Thrusting her hand through a space in the railing, Beryl dropped her mother's withered Arkja tribute on the marble slab. Her dress was caught by a sharp point of iron, and while endeavoring to disengage it, she heard the shrill whistle of the R. R. engine. Tearing the skirt away, she ran to the wall, climbed over, after some delay, and finding herself once more in the open road, darted on as fast as possible through the dusk, heedless of appearances, fearful only of missing the train. How the houses multiplied, and what interminable lengths the squares seemed, as she neared the brick warehouse and office of the station! The lamps at the street corners beckoned her on, and when panting for breath she rushed around the side of the tall building that fronted the railway, there was no train in sight.

Two or three coal cars stood on a siding, near a detached engine, where one man was lighting the lamp before the reflector of the headlight, and another, who whistled merrily, burnished the brass and copper platings. In the door of the ticket office the agent lounged, puffed his cigar, and fanned himself with his hat.

"What time is it?" cried Beryl.

"Seven-forty-five."

"Oh! do not tell me I have missed the train."

"You certainly have. I told you it left at 7:15 sharp. It was ten minutes behind time on account of hot boxes, but rolled out just twenty minutes ago. Did you get lost hunting 'Elm Bluff,' and miss your train on that account?"

"No, I had no difficulty in finding the place, but having no watch, I was forced to guess at the time. Only twenty minutes too late!"

"Did you see the old war-horse?"

Beryl did not answer, and after a moment the agent added:

"That is Gen'l Darrington's nick-name all over this section."

"When will the next train leave here?"

"Not until 3:05 A.M."

Beryl sat down on the edge of a baggage truck, and pondered the situation. She knew that her mother, who had carefully studied the railway schedule, was with feverish anxiety expecting her return by the train, now many miles away; and she feared that any unexplained detention would have an injurious effect on the sick woman's shattered nerves.

Although she could ill afford the expense, she resolved to allay all apprehension, by the costly sedative of a telegram.

Only a wall separated the ticket office from that of the "telegraph," and approaching the operator, Beryl asked for a blank form, on which she wrote her mother's address, and the following message:

"Complete success required delay. All will be satisfactory. Expect me Saturday. B. B."

When she had paid the operator, there remained in her purse, exclusive of the gold coins received that afternoon, only thirty-eight cents. Where could she spend the next seven hours? Interpreting the perplexed expression of her face, the agent, who had curiously noted her movements, said courteously:

"There is a hotel a few blocks off, where you can rest until train time."

"I prefer to remain here."

"We generally lock up this office about half-past eight, and re-open at half-past two, which gives passengers ample accommodation for the 3:05 train."

"Would you violate regulations by leaving the waiting-room open to-night?"

"Not exactly; as of course we are obliged to keep open for delayed trains; but it will be lonesome waiting, for no one stays here, except the Night Train Despatcher, and the switch watchman. Still if it will oblige you, miss, I will not lock up, and you can doze away the time by spreading your shawl on two chairs. I am going to supper now, and shall turn down the lights. One burner will be sufficient."

"Thank you very much. Where can I find some water?"

"In the cooler in the ladies' dressing-room. It is most unaccountably hot tonight, and I never knew anything like it in October. There must be a cyclone brewing somewhere not far off."

He lifted his hat, as he passed her, and disappeared; and the tired girl seated herself near a window and stirred the dense, impure air by fanning herself with her straw hat. Gradually the few stragglers loitering about the station wandered away; the engineer stepped upon the locomotive; a piercing whistle broke suddenly on the silence settling down over the whilom busy precincts, and as the rhythmic measure of the engine bell rang farewell chimes, a pyramid of sparks leaped high, and the mighty mechanism fled down the track, hunting its own echoes. The man in charge of the express office came out, looked up and down the street; yawned, lighted his pipe, and after locking the office, wended his way homeward.

From the adjoining room came the slow monotonous clicking of the telegraph wires, as messages passed to other stations, and only the switch watchman was visible, sitting on an inverted tub, and playing snatches from "Mascotte" and "Olivette" upon a harmonicon.

Heat seemed radiating from the brick pavement outside, from the inner walls of the waiting-room; and Beryl, finding the atmosphere almost stifling, went out under the stars. Up and down she paced, until weary of the dusty thoroughfare, she turned into the street which, earlier in the day, had conducted her toward the suburbs. She knew that a full moon had climbed above the horizon, and some malign Morgana lured her on, with visions of cool pine glades paved with silver mosaics, and balmy with breath of balsam; where through vast forest naves echoed the melodious monody chanted by the reddish gold wavelets of the "branch." In the eastern sky the florid face of a hunter's moon looked down, from the level line of a leaden cloud, which striped the star emblazoned shield of night, like a bar sinister; and the white lustre of her rays was dimmed to a lurid dulness solemn and presageful.

As Beryl crossed the common near the station, and entered the pillared aisles of the pines, the air was less oppressive, but a dun haze seemed on every side to curtain the horizon, and the stars looked bleared and tired in the breathless vault above her. A man driving two cows toward town, stared at her; then a wagon drawn by four horses rattled along, bearing homeward a gay picnic party of young people, who made the woods ring with the echoes of "Hold the Fort." The grandeur of towering pines, the mysterious dimness of illimitable arcades, and the peculiar resinous odor that stole like lingering ghosts of myrrh, frankincense and onycha through the vaulted solitude of a deserted hoary sanctuary, all these phases of primeval Southern forests combined to weave a spell that the stranger could not resist.

After a while, fearful of straying too far, the weary woman threw her shawl on the brown straw, and sat down quite near the road. She leaned her bare head against the trunk of a pine, listened to the katydids gossiping in a distant oak that shaded the "branch," to the quavering strident song of a locust; and she intended, after resting for a few moments, to return to the station-house; but unexpected drowsiness overpowered her. Suddenly aroused from a sound sleep, she heard the clatter of galloping hoofs, and as she sprang up, the horse, startled by her movement, shied and reared within a few feet of the spot where she stood. The moon shone full on the glossy black animal, and upon his powerful rider, and Beryl recognized the massive head, swarthy face and keen eyes of the attorney, Lennox Dunbar. He leaned forward and said, as he patted the erect ears of his horse:

"Madam, you seem a stranger. Have you lost your way?"

"No, sir."

"Pardon me; but having seen you this afternoon at 'Elm Bluff,' I thought it possible you had missed the road."

Standing so straight and tall, with the sheen of the moon on her faultless features, he thought she looked the incarnation of some prescient Norn, fit for the well of Urda.

She made no reply; and he touched his hat, and rode rapidly away in the direction of the town, carrying an indelible impression of the mysterious picture under the pines.

The sky had changed; the face of the moon had cleared, but tatters and scuds of smoke-colored cloud fled northward, as if scourged by a stormy current too high to stir the sultry stagnation of the lower atmospheric stratum. From its vaporous lair somewhere in the cypress and palm jungles of the Mexican Gulf borders, the tempest had risen, and before its breath the shreds of cloud flew like avant couriers of disaster. Already the lurid glare of incessant sheet lightning fought with the moon for supremacy, and from a leaden wall along the southeastern sky, came the long reverberating growl of thunder, that told where the electric batteries had opened fire. A vague foreboding, which for several days had haunted Beryl's mind, now pressed so heavily upon her, that she hurried back to the station, which was near the edge of the town; and more than once she started nervously at sight of grotesque shadows cast by the trees across the sandy road.

The streets were deserted, and lights gleamed only in upper windows of apartments, where sick sufferers tossed, or tender mothers sang soft lullabys to restless babies crooning in their cribs. Now and then a sudden gust of wind shook the yellow berries from the china trees, that bordered the pavements, and very soon the moonshine faded, then flashed fitfully, and finally vanished, as the blackening cloud swept over the face of earth and sky. The watchman dozed on his post of observation; a porter slept on a baggage truck under the awning, and as Beryl peeped into the telegraph office, she heard the snoring of the operator, whose head rested upon the table close to the silent instrument. She listened to the ticking of a clock in the ticket office, but could not see its face; wondered how late it was, and how long she had been absent. Feeling very lonely and restless she closed the door, and sat down in the deserted waiting-room, glad of the companionship of a tortoise-shell cat which was curled up on a chair next her own.

Gradually the storm approached, and she thought that an hour had elapsed, when the dust-tainted smell of rain came with the rush of cold air. There was no steady gale, but the tempest broke in frantic spasmodic gusts, as though it had lost its reckoning, and simultaneously assaulted all the points of the compass; while the lightning glared almost continuously, and the roar of the thunder was uninterrupted. Now and then a vivid zig-zag flash gored the intense darkness with its baleful blue death-light, followed by a crash, appalling as if the battlements of heaven had been shattered. Once the whole air seemed ablaze, and the simultaneous shock of the detonation was so violent, that Beryl involuntarily sank on her knees, and hid her eyes on a chair. The rain fell in torrents, that added a solemn sullen swell to the diapason of the thunder fugue, and by degrees a delicious coolness crept into the cisterns of the night.

When the cloud had wept away its fury, and electric fires burned low in the far west, a gentle shower droned on the roof, and lulled by its cadence Beryl fell asleep, still kneeling on the floor, with her head resting on the chair where the cat lay coiled.

In dreams, she wandered with her father and brother upon a Tuscan hillside draped with purple fruited grape vines, and Bertie was crushing a luscious cluster against her thirsty lips, when some noise startled her. Wide awake, she sprang to her feet, and listened.

"There ain't no train till daylight, 'cepting it be the through freight."

"When is that due?"

"Pretty soon; it's mighty nigh time now, but it don't stop here; it goes on to the water tank, whar it blows for the railroad bridge."

"How far is the bridge?"

"Only a short piece down the track, after you pass the tank."

Beryl had rushed to the window, and looked out, but no one was visible. She could scarcely mistake that peculiar voice, and was so assured of its identity, that she ran out under the awning and looked up and down the platform in front of the station buildings. The rain had ceased, but drops still pattered from the tin roof, and a few stars peeped over the ragged ravelled edge of slowly drifting clouds. By the light of a gas lamp, she saw an old negro man limping away, who held a stick over his shoulder, on which was slung a bundle wrapped in a red handkerchief; and while she stood watching, he vanished in some cul de sac. With her basket in her hand, and her shawl on her arm, she sped down the track, looking to right and left.

"Bertie! Bertie!"

Once she fancied she discerned a form flying ahead of her, leaping from cross tie to cross tie to avoid the water, but when she called vehemently, only the sound of her own voice broke the silence.

Was it merely an illusion born of her vivid dream of her brother; and while scarcely awake, had she confounded the tones of a stranger, with those so long familiar? She could not shake off the conviction that Bertie had really spoken only a few yards from her, and while she stood irresolute, puzzling over the problem, the through freight train dashed by the station and left a trail of sparks and cinders. To avoid it she sprang on a pile of cross ties beside the track, and when the fiery serpent wound out of sight, she reluctantly retraced her steps. How long the night seemed! Would day never dawn again? She heard the telegraph operator whistling at his work, and as she re-entered the waiting-room, she saw the ticket agent standing in his office.

"What time is it?"

"Half-past two o'clock. I might as well have locked up as usual, for after all, you did not stay here."

"Yes I did."

He eyed her suspiciously.

"I came back from supper, and brought a pitcher of cold tea, thinking you might relish it, but you were not here. I waited nearly an hour; then I went home."

"It was so hot, I walked about outside. What a frightful storm."

"Yes, perfectly awful. Were you exposed to the worst of it?"

"No, I was here."

He shook his head, smiled, and went into the next room, knowing that when he returned to unlock his office she was not in the building, and that he had seen her coming up the railway track. The bustle of preparation soon began; the baggage wagons thundered up to the platform, porters called to one another; passengers collected in the waiting-room, carriages and omnibuses dashed about; then at 2:50 the long train of north bound cars swept in. With her shawl and basket in one hand, and the odorous bunches of chrysanthemums clasped in the other, Beryl stepped upon the platform. She found a seat at an open window, and made herself comfortable; placing her feet upon the basket which contained the jewels that constituted her sole earthly fortune. The bell rang, the train glided on, and as it passed the office door, she saw the agent watching her, with a strangely suspicious expression.

The cars wound around a curve, and she sank back and shut her eyes, rejoicing in the belief that her mission to "Elm Bluff," and its keen humiliation, were forever ended.

CHAPTER IV.

"I concede that point. Your lover is amply endowed with brains, and moreover has a vast amount of shrewdness, all that is requisite to secure success and eminence in his profession; but to-day, it seems as much a matter of astonishment to me—as it certainly was six months ago, when first you told me of your engagement—that you, Leo Gordon, could ever fancy just such a man as Lennox Dunbar."

"I am very sorry, Aunt Patty, that he finds no favor in your eyes, and I think he is aware of the fact that he is not in your good graces. You both look so vaguely uncomfortable when thrown into each other's presence; but for my sake you must try to like Lennox."

Miss Gordon bent her pretty head over a square of ruby velvet, whereon she was embroidering a wreath of pansies, and the delicate flush on her fair face, deepened to a vivid carnation.

"My likes or dislikes are a matter of moonshine, in comparison with your happiness. Because you are an orphan, I feel a sort of responsibility; and sometimes I am not exactly easy over the account of my stewardship I must render to my poor dead Marcia. The more I see of your lover, the more I dread your marriage. A man who makes no profession of religious belief, is an unsafe guardian of any woman's peace of mind. You who have been reared almost in the shadow of the altar, accustomed to hearing grace at your meals, to family prayers, to strict observance of our ritual, will feel isolated indeed, when transplanted to the home of a godless man, who rarely darkens the door of the sanctuary. 'Be ye not unequally yoked together with unbelievers.'"

Miss Patty Dent took off her spectacles, wiped them with the string of her white muslin cap, and adjusting them firmly on her nose, plucked nervously at the fluted lace ruffles around her wrists.

"Auntie, you are scarcely warranted in using such strong language. Because a man refrains from the public avowal of faith, incident to church membership, he is not necessarily godless; nor inevitably devoid of true religious feeling. Mr. Dunbar has a strong, reticent nature, habituated to repression of all evidences of emotion, but of the depth and earnestness of his real feeling, I entertain no doubt."

"I fear your line and plummet will never sound his depth. You often speak of his strength; but, Leo, hardness is not always strength; and he is hard, hard. I never saw a man with a chin like his, who was not tyrannical, and idolatrous of his own will. My dear, such men are as uncomfortable to live in the same house with, as a smoky chimney, or a woman with shattered nerves, or creaking doors, or draughty windows. They are a sort of everlasting east wind that never veers, blowing always to the one point, attainment of their own ends, mildewing all else. Ugh!"

Miss Patty shivered, and her companion smiled.

"What a grewsome picture, Auntie dear! Fortunately human taste is as diverse and catholic as the variety of human countenances. For example: Clara Morse raves over Mr. Dunbar's 'clear-cut features, so immensely classical'; and she pronounces his offending 'chin simply perfect! fit for a Greek God!'"

"A very thin and gauzy partition divides Clara Morse's brains from idiocy. In my day, all such feeble watery minds as hers were regarded as semi-imbecile, pitied as intellectual cripples, and wisely kept in the background of society; but, bless me! in this generation they skip and prance to the very edge of the front, pose in indecent garments without starch, or crinoline, or even the protection of pleats and gathers; and insult good, sound, wholesome common sense with the sickening affectations they are pleased to call 'aesthetics.' Don't waste your time, and dilute your own mind by quoting the silly twaddle of a poor girl who was turned loose too early on society, who falls on her knees in ecstasies before a hideous broken-nose tea-pot from some filthy hovel in Japan; and who would not dare to admire the loveliest bit of Oiron pottery, or precious old Chelsea claret-colored china in Kensington Museum, until she had turned it upside down, and hunted the potter's mark with a microscope. I say Mr. Dunbar has a domineering and tyrannical chin, and five years hence, if you do not agree with me, it will be because 'Ephraim is joined to his idols'—clay feet and all."

"Then follow the Bible injunction to 'let him alone.' I see Lennox through neither Clara's rosy lenses, nor your jaundiced glasses; and these circular discussions are as fruitless as they are unpleasant. Let us select some more agreeable topic. I gave you Leighton's letter. What think you of his scheme?"

"That it is admirable, worthy of the brain that conceived it. What a wonderful man he is, considering his age? Such a devout and fervent spirit, and withal such a marvel of executive ability. Ah! happy the woman who can command his wise guardianship, and renew her aspirations after holiness, in his spiritual society. I honor, even more than I love, Leighton Douglass."

"So do I, Aunt Patty. He is quite my ideal pastor, and when he marries, I hope his wife will be worthy of him in every respect. Only a very noble woman would suit my cousin."

A bright spot burned on Miss Dent's wrinkled cheek, and she knitted her brows, and shook her head.

"He is so absorbed in his holy work that he has no leisure for such trifles as love-making; but if he should ever honor a woman by the offer of his consecrated hand, it must be one of large fortune, who will dedicate herself and her money to the accomplishment of his ecclesiastical schemes."

The corners of Miss Gordon's mouth twitched mutinously, but she contrived to throw much innocent surprise and questioning into the handsome brown eyes, which she lifted from her gold-hearted pansies, to her Aunt's face.

"Could you possibly associate mercenary motives with any step which he might take? Such a supposition would be totally incompatible with my estimate of his character."

"When a man dedicates himself to a solemn mission, he is lifted far above the ordinary plane, can dispense with sentimental conventionalities, and must learn to regard all human relations as merely means to an end. Want of money has palsied many an arm lifted to advance the good of the Church; and zeal without funds, accomplishes as little as rusty machinery stiff from lack of oil. If Dr. Douglass could only control even a hundred thousand dollars, what shining monuments he would leave to immortalize him! Indeed, it passes my comprehension how persons who could so easily help him, deliberately turn a deaf ear to the 'cry from Macedonia'."

"There is far more eclat in trips to Macedonia, but the God of recompense does not forget the steady, tireless help and sympathy extended to the needy, who dwell within sight of our own doors. Organized society work is good, but individual self-sacrifice and labor are much better; and if every unit did full duty, co-operative systems would not be so necessary; still, Leighton's scheme commends itself to every woman's heart, and when I answered his letter, I expressed cordially my approbation."

"Did you prove your faith by your works, and send him a large check?"

"Auntie, dear, do you expect me to stultify all your training, both your example and precept—for lo! these many years—by setting my left hand to gossip about my right? I am very sure."

"Well, Andrew, what is it?"

"A boy from Mr. Dunbar's office has just galloped up, and says I am to tell you he can't ride to the Falls to-day, as he expected, because of some pressing business; and he wants to know if the Judge will come into town right away? Mr. Dunbar will explain when he comes late this evening."

"Very well. Tell Daniel I shall not want 'Rebel' saddled; and say to the messenger that my Uncle is not at home. Aunt Patty, do you know where he has gone?"

"Doubtless to his office; where else should he be? He said he had a pile of tiresome papers to examine to-day."

Miss Gordon folded up her work, laid it away in a dainty basket lined with blue satin and flounced with lace; and after pausing a moment to pet her Aunt's white Maltese cat which lay dozing In the sunshine, walked away toward a Small hot-house, built quite near the dining-room, and connected with it by an arcade, covered in summer by vines, in winter by glass.

Twenty-four years before that day, when a proud, fond young mother puffed and tucked the marvel of lace and linen cambric, which was intended as a christening robe for her baby, and laid it away with spicery of rose leaves and sachet of lavender and deer tongue, to wait until a "furlough" allowed the child's father to be present at the baptism, she had supposed that its delicate folds would one day adorn a dimpled rosy-faced infant, for whom the name Aurelia Gordon had long been selected. Fate cruelly vetoed all the details of the programme, carefully arranged by maternal affection; and the lurid sun that set in clouds of smoke on one of the most desperate battles of the Confederacy, saw Colonel Gordon's brave, patriotic soul released on that long "furlough" which glory granted her heroes; saw his devoted wife a wailing widow. The red burial of battle had precluded the solemnization of baptismal rites at the sacred marble font; and when four days after Colonel Gordon's death, his frail young wife welcomed the summons to an everlasting re-union, she laid her cold hands on her baby's golden head, and died, as she whispered:

"Name her Leo, for her father."

So it came to pass, that the clergyman who read the burial service beside the mother's coffin, lifted the cooing infant in the midst of a weeping funeral throng, and with a faltering voice baptized her, in the presence of the dead, Leo Gordon.

To the care of her sister Patty, and of her widowed brother, Judge Dent, Mrs. Gordon had consigned her child; and transplanted so early to her uncle's house, the orphan knew no other home.

When the problem of vast numerical preponderance had solved itself in accordance with the rules of avoirdupois, and history—fond like all garrulous old crones of repeating even her inglorious episodes—had triumphantly inscribed on her bloody tablets, that once more the Few were throttled and trampled by the Many, then the fabled "Ragnarok" of the Sagas described only approximately the doom of the devastated South. In the financial and social chaos that followed the invasion by "loyal" hordes, rushing under "sealed orders" on the mission of "Reconstruction," and eminently successful in "reconstructing" their individual fortunes, an anomaly presented itself for the consideration of political economists. The wealthy classes of ante bellum days were the most destitute paupers that the newly-risen Union sun shone upon.

The French Revolution and its subsequent eruptions of Communism failed to destroy the value of land; and the emancipation of Russian serfs may have stimulated agricultural activity, but that political and social Communism which the Pandora of "reconstruction" let loose throughout the conquered States of the South, accomplished all that the victors could have desired.

Abandoned by the laborers God had fitted to endure toil under climatic conditions peculiar to the soil, vast silent fields of weeds stared blankly, and the richer a man found himself in ancestral acres, the more hopelessly was he manacled by taxes. "Reconstructionists" most thoroughly inoculated with "Loyal" rabies, held in lofty disdain the claims of widows and orphans, and the right of minors was as dead as that of secession. In the general maelstrom, Colonel Gordon's large estate went to pieces; but after a time, Judge Dent took lessons from his new political masters in the science of wrecking, and by degrees, as fragments and shreds stranded, he collected and secreted them. Certain mining interests were protected, and some valuable plantations in distant sugar belts, were secured. As guardian of his sister's daughter, he changed, or renewed investments in stocks which rapidly increased in value, until an unusually large fortune had accumulated: and verifying figures justified his boast, that his niece and ward was the wealthiest heiress in the State.

Reared in a household which consisted of an elderly uncle and aunt, and a middle-aged governess, Leo Gordon had never known intimate association with younger people; and while her nature was gentle and tranquil, she gradually imbibed the grave and rather prim ideas which were in vogue when Miss Patty was the reigning belle of her county. Although petted and indulged, she had not been spoiled, and remained singularly free from the selfishness usually developed in the character of an only child, nurtured in the midst of mature relatives. When eighteen years old, Leo, accompanied by her governess, Mrs. Eldridge, had been sent to New York and Boston for educational advantages, which it was supposed that her own section of the country could not supply; and subsequently the two went abroad, gleaning knowledge in the great centres of European Art. During their sojourn in Munich, Mrs. Eldridge died after a very brief illness; and returning to her southern home, Leo found herself the object of social homage.

Thoroughly well-bred, accomplished, graceful and pretty, she commanded universal admiration; yet her manner was marked by a quiet, grave dignity, and a peculiar reticence, at variance with the prevailing type of young ladyhood, now alas! too dominant; whose premature emancipation from home rule, and old-fashioned canons of decorum renders "American girlhood" synonymous with flippant pertness. Moulded by two women who were imbued with the spirit of Richter's admonition: "Girls like the priestesses of old, should be educated only in sacred places, and never hear, much less see, what is rude, immoral or violent"; the pate tendre of Leo's character showed unmistakably the potter's marks.

She shrewdly surmised that the knowledge of her unusual wealth contributed to swell the number of her suitors, and she was twenty-four years old when Lennox Dunbar, for whom she had long secretly cherished a partiality, succeeded in placing his ring on her fair, slender hand. In character they differed widely, and the deep and tender love that filled her heart, found only a faint echo in his cold and more selfish nature, which had carefully calculated all the advantages derivable from this alliance.

He cordially admired and esteemed his brown-eyed fair-haired fiancee, considered her the personification of feminine refinement and delicacy; and congratulated himself warmly on his great good fortune in winning her affection; but tender emotions found little scope for exercise in his intensely practical, busy life, which was devoted to the attainment of eminence in his profession; and the merely dynamic apparatus which did duty as his heart, had never been disturbed by any feeling sufficiently deep to quicken his calm, steady pulse.

There were times, when Leo wondered whether all accepted lovers were as undemonstrative as her own, and she would have been happier had he occasionally forgotten professional aspirations, in the charm of her presence; but her confidence in the purity and fidelity of his affection was unshaken, even by the dismal predictions of Miss Patty, who found it impossible to reconcile herself to the failure of her darling scheme, that Leo should marry her second cousin, Leighton Douglass, D.D., and devote her fortune to the advancement of his church.

To-day, as she sought pleasant work in arranging the ferns and carnations of her conservatory, her thoughts reverted to the previous evening, which Mr. Dunbar had spent with her; and she could not avoid indulging regret, that he should have allowed business affairs to interfere with their engagement for horseback riding, but her reverie was speedily interrupted by the excited tones of her aunt's voice.

"Leo! Leo! Where do you hide yourself?"

"Here, Auntie, in the conservatory."

"Oh! my child, such dreadful news! Such a frightful tragedy!"

Pale and panting, Miss Patty ran down the arcade, and stumbled over a barricade of potted plants on the threshold of the door.

"What is the matter? Is it my Uncle, or—or Lennox?"

Leo sprang to her feet, and caught her aunt's arm.

"Horrible! horrible! General Darrington was robbed, and then most brutally murdered last night!"

"Murdered! Can it be possible? Murdered—by whom?"

"How should I know? The whole town is wild about it. My brother is at Elm Bluff, with the body, and I shall take the carriage and drive over there at once. Dear me; I am so nervous I can't stand still, and my teeth chatter like a pair of castanets."

"Perhaps there may be some mistake. How did you hear it?"

"Your Uncle Mitchell sent a boy to tell me why he was detained. There has been a coroner's inquest, and of course, as an old and intimate friend of General Darrington's, Mitchell feels he must do all he can. Poor old gentleman! So proud and aristocratic! To be murdered in his own house, like any common pauper! Positively it makes me sick. May the Lord have mercy on his soul."

"Amen!" murmured Leo.

"Will you go with me to Elm Bluff?"

"Oh, no! Not for worlds. Why should I? Women will only be in the way; and who could desire to contemplate so horrible a spectacle? It will merely harrow your feelings, Aunt Patty, and you can do no good."

"It is my Christian duty as a neighbor; and I was always very fond of the first Mrs. Darrington, Helena Tracey. What is this wicked world coming to? Robbery and murder stalking bare-faced through the land. It will be a dreadful blow to Mitchell, because he and Luke Darrington have been intimate all their lives. I see the carriage coming round, so I must get my bonnet and wrap."

"I presume Mr. Dunbar is engaged in the same melancholy details which occupy my uncle."

"Doubtless he is, because his father was General Darrington's attorney until his health failed; and Lennox is now his lawyer and business agent. It is a thousand pities that Prince is away in Europe."

Two hours after the carriage had disappeared on the road leading to Elm Bluff, Leo crossed the grassy lawn, and sat down near the gate, on a rustic bench under a cluster of tall lilacs, which gave their name to her uncle's home.

A keen north wind whistling through neighboring walnut tree tops, drove the dying leaves like frightened flocks before it, and ever and anon the ripened nuts pattered down, hiding themselves under the drift of yellow foliage, that had sheltered them in cool greenery during summer heats. Overhead a red squirrel barked and frisked, and across the pale-blue sky, feathered nomads, teal or mallard, moved swiftly en echelon, their quivering pinions flashing like silver, as they fled southward. On a distant hillside cattle browsed, and sheep wandered; and the drowsy tinkle of bells, as the herd wended homeward, seemed a nocturne of rest, for the closing day.

How serene, harmonious and holy all nature appeared; and yet a few miles distant, into what a fierce seething whirlpool of conflicting passions, of hatred and bloodthirsty vengeance, had human crime plunged an entire community. We plume ourselves upon nineteenth century civilization, upon ethical advancement, upon Christian progress; we adorn our cathedrals, build temples for art treasures, and museums for science, and listen to preludes of the "music of the future;" and we shudder at the mention of vice, as at the remembrance of the tortures of Regulus, but will the Cain type ever become extinct, like the dodo, or the ichthyosaurus? When will the laws of heredity, and the by-laws of agnation result in an altruism, where human bloodshed is an unknown horror?

The apostles of Evolution tell us, that in the genealogical ages during which man has struggled upward, from the lower stages of vertebrate and mammal to the genus of catarrhine apes, he has gradually thrown off bestial instincts, and that the tiger taint will ultimately be totally eliminated; that "original sin is neither more nor less than the brute inheritance which every man carries with him, and that Evolution is an advance toward true salvation." Meanwhile what becomes of the "Survival of the Fittest", which is only a euphemism for the strangling of the feeble by the strong? We can understand how perfection, or permanence of type, individual and national, demands carnage, and entails all the dire catalogue of human woes, but wherein is altruism evolved? How many aeons shall we wait, to behold the leopard and the lamb pasturing together in peace?

Pondering this problem, as he rode along the public road outside the boundary of Judge Dent's lawn, Mr. Dunbar caught a glimpse of his betrothed, sitting behind the hedge of lilacs, and he lifted his hat, hoping that she would meet him at the entrance; but although she bowed in recognition, he was forced to open the gate and admit himself. Throwing the bridle rein over one of the iron spikes of the fence, and taking off his gloves, he approached the bench.

"Dare I flatter myself, that my queen deigns to meet me half way?"

He took her outstretched hand, and kissed it softly, while his glance noted every detail of her handsome fawn-colored dress, with its jabot of creamy lace, and the cluster of crimson carnations in her belt. The touch of his lips on her fingers, deepened the flush in her cheeks, and, making room for him beside her, she replied:

"Sit down, and tell me if this dreadful news about General Darrington be indeed true? I have hoped there might be some mistake, some exaggeration."

"Some horrors exceed the possibility of verbal exaggeration, and last night's tragedy is one of that class. General Darrington was most brutally murdered."

"Poor old gentleman! How incredible it seems that such awful crimes can be committed in our quiet neighborhood? who could have been so guilty; and what motive could have prompted such a fiendish act?"

"The one all-powerful evil passion of mankind—greed of gold; lust of filthy lucre. He was first robbed, then murdered by the thief, to avoid detection and punishment. There is unmistakable evidence that the General was chloroformed while asleep; but he must have awakened in time to discover the robber, with whom he struggled desperately, and by whom he was struck down. The coroner's inquest developed some startling facts."

"Has any clue been discovered which would indicate the murderer?"

"A handful of clues."

"Then you have a theory concerning the person who perpetrated this awful crime?"

"My dear Leo, not a theory, but a conviction; I might almost say an absolute knowledge."

"Would it be pardonable for me to ask whom you suspect; would it be a violation of professional etiquette for you to tell me?"

"Certainly, my dearest, you can ask me anything, only—" he paused a moment; and she put her hand quickly on his arm.

"I see. Do not tell me mere suspicions; they might cruelly wrong an innocent person; and I ought not to have asked the question."

"My hesitation arose from a totally different source, and I was merely wondering whether you, my sweet saint, could believe that a woman committed the bloody deed."

"Oh, Mr. Dunbar, impossible! A woman guilty of taking that old man's life? The supposition is as horrible as the crime itself."

Passing his hand lightly over her crimped fair hair, and looking down into her eyes, as brown as the back of a thrush, her lover replied:

"I find that the nobler and purer a woman's heart is, the less she credits the existence of vice and the possibility of crime among her own sex. You doubtless consider the Brinvilliers, Fredegonds, Fulvias and Faustinas, quite as fabulous as Centaurs, Sirens and Were-wolves;

and I feel as reluctant to shake your fair faith in womanhood, as to dash the dew from a rose-bud, or rudely brush the bloom a cluster of tempting grapes; but the grim truth must be told, that our old friend was robbed and murdered by a woman."

"One of his servants? They all seemed devotedly attached to him."

"No, by his granddaughter, a young and very beautiful woman; Beryl Brentano, the child of General Darrington's daughter Ellice, whom he had disowned on account of her wretched marriage with a foreigner, who taught her music and the languages. Of course you have heard from your aunt and uncle all the details of that family episode. Yesterday this girl Beryl suddenly presented herself at Elm Bluff, and demanded money from her grandfather; alleging that her mother's life was in danger for want of it. I learn there was a stormy interview, part of the conversation having been overheard by two persons; and the General, who was as vindictive as a Modoc, or a Cossack, drove the young lady through a door leading down to the rosery. This occurred in the afternoon, immediately after I left Elm Bluff, where I went to obtain his signature to a deed to some lands recently sold in Texas. I saw the girl sitting on the front steps, and when she rose and looked at me, her superb physique impressed me powerfully. She is as beautiful and stately as some goddess stepping out of the Norse 'Edda', and altogether a remarkable looking person. It will appear in evidence, that the General harshly refused her pleadings, and made a point of assuring her that his will, already prepared, would forever debar her mother and herself from any inheritance at his death; as he had bequeathed his entire estate to his adopted son Prince. Unfortunately, she learned where the will was kept, as during the interview, persons in the next room distinctly heard the peculiar noise made by the sliding door of the iron vault, where General Darrington kept all his valuable papers. She disappeared from Elm Bluff about sunset, going toward town; and last night at ten o'clock, when I left you and rode home, I saw her lurking in the pine woods not very far from the bridge over the branch, near the park gate. She was evidently hiding, as she sat on the ground half screened by a tree; but my horse shied and plunged badly, and when she rose, the full moon showed her face and figure distinctly. There was something so mysterious in her movements, that I asked her if she had lost her way; to which she curtly replied that she had not. I learn from Burk, the station agent, that her actions aroused his suspicion, and that instead of leaving town, as she said she intended, by the 7:15 train, she hung about the station, and finally took the 3:05 express this morning. He said she had begged permission to stay in the waiting-room, but that at 2:30 A.M., when he went back to open the ticket office, she was nowhere to be found; and that later, he saw her coming down the railroad track. She must have gone back to Elm Bluff after I passed her on the road, and effected an entrance through the window on the front piazza, as it was found open; and the awful work of robbery and murder was accomplished during the storm, which you know was so frightful that it drowned all minor sounds. This morning when the General did not ring for his hot water at the usual time, it was supposed that he was sleeping late, but finally old Bedney knocked. Unable to arouse his master, he opened the door, and found our old friend lying on the floor, near the fireplace. He had been dead for hours, and close to his head was a heavy brass andiron, which evidently had been snatched from the hearth by the murderess, who must have dealt the fatal blow with it, as there was a dark spot on his temple, and also on the left side near the heart. The room was in disorder, and two glass vases on the mantel were shivered, as though some missile had struck them—probably a heavy ledger which was found on the floor."

"How horrible! But no woman could have overpowered a man like General Darrington."

"Physically, his granddaughter was more than a match for him, especially since his last illness; and I assure you she looks like some daughter of the Vikings. She certainly is a woman of grand proportions, and wonderfully symmetrical."

"What is her age?"

"About eighteen, I should think; though her size and a certain majestic bearing might convey the impression that she was older."

"How can you connect so dreadful a crime with a young and beautiful woman, of whom you know absolutely nothing?"

"My theory is, that she intended merely to get possession of the will, the contents of which had been made known to her—and of the money, that she knew or surmised was kept in the vault. When the effect of the chloroform wore off, and the General waked to find her at the vault; a struggle evidently took place, and in desperation at the thought of being detected, she killed him. You do not understand all the bearings of even slight circumstances in a case like this, but we who make a study of such sad matters, know the significance of the disappearance of the will; the destruction of which could benefit only her mother and herself. The vault was open; the gold, silver, some valuable jewelry, and the will are missing from the tin box. All the other papers were left, even a package of bonds, amounting to thousands of dollars. She seemed to know that the bonds might lead to detection, hence she did not take them. On the floor, and in the bottom of the tin box were found two twenty-dollar gold pieces. We are collecting all the evidence, and it constitutes a powerful array of proof."

"We? Do you mean that you are hunting down a woman?"

Miss Gordon withdrew her hand from her lover's, and instinctively moved farther from him.

"I am most diligently hunting down the author of a foul and awful crime; and it is my duty to my friend and client to use every possible exertion, in discovering and bringing to punishment the person who robbed and murdered him—be it man, woman or child. Feminine youth and beauty are no aegis against the barbed javelins of justice and the District Solicitor (Mr. Churchill) and I, have no doubt of the guilt of the woman, who will soon be put on trial here for her monstrous and unnatural crime."

CHAPTER V.

In a deep, narrow "railway cut," through Virginia hills, a south-bound freight train had been so badly wrecked in consequence of a "washout," that the southern passenger express going north was detained fourteen hours; thereby missing connection at Washington City, where the passengers were again delayed nearly twelve hours. Tired and very hungry, having eaten nothing but a sandwich and a cup of coffee for three days, Beryl felt profoundly thankful when the cars rolled into Jersey City. In the bustle and confusion incident to arrival in that Babel, she did not observe the scrutiny to which she was subjected by a man genteelly dressed, who gave her his hand as she stepped down from the train, and kept by her side while she hastened in the direction of the ferry.

Reaching the slip where the boat awaited passengers, she was vexed to see it backing out into the stream, and leaned against the chain which barred egress until the next trip.

"You have only five minutes to wait for the boat. You seem to have had a long and trying journey, madam?"

Glancing at him for the first time, Beryl perceived that he held a slip of yellow paper from which he looked now and then to her face. His features were coarse and heavy, but his eyes were keen as a ferret's; and without answering his question, she turned away and looked across the water which teemed with craft of every description, laden with freight animate and inanimate, passing to and from the vast city, whose spires, domes and forest of masts rose like a gray cloud against the sky, etching there their leaden outlines.

"You live at No.—West—Street, between 8th and 9th Avenue?"

"You are a stranger, and your questions are offensive and impertinent."

As she turned and confronted him haughtily, he stepped closer to her, threw back his blue overcoat, and pointed to the metal badge on his breast.

"I am an officer of the law, and have a warrant for your arrest. You are Beryl Brentano."

"I am Beryl Brentano, yes; but there is some blunder, some mistake. How dare you annoy me? Arrest me? Me!"

"Do not make a scene. My instructions are to deal with you as gently as possible. Better come quietly into the station near, and I will read you the warrant, otherwise I shall be obliged to use force. You see I have two assistants yonder."

"Arrested for what? By whom?"

"I am ordered to arrest you for the murder of General Darrington."

"Murder! General Darrington is alive and well. I have just left him. Stand back! Do not touch me. I will call on the police to protect me."

Laying his fingers firmly on her arm, he beckoned to two men clad in police uniform, who promptly approached.

"You see resistance is worse than useless, and since there is no escape, come quietly."

"You are insulting me, under some frightful mistake. I am a lady. Do I look like a criminal?"

"General Darrington has been robbed and murdered, and I have telegraphic orders to arrest and hold a woman named Beryl Brentano, who corresponds in every respect with the description of the person suspected of having committed the crime."

Hitherto she had attributed the insult of the interview to some question of mistaken identity, but as she slowly comprehended the possibility that she was the person accused, and intended for arrest, a sickening horror seized and almost paralyzed her, blanching her face and turning her to stone. As he led her along the street, she staggered from the numbness that possessed her, and her eyes stared blankly, like those of a somnambulist. When she had been ushered into a room where several policemen were lounging and smoking, the intolerable sense of shame and indignation shook off her apathy.

"This is a cruel and outrageous wrong, and only base cowards could wantonly insult an unprotected and innocent woman. You call yourselves men? Have you no mothers, no sisters, whose memory can arouse some reverence, some respect for womanhood in your brutal souls?"

Electric lamps set in the sockets of some marble face, might perhaps resemble the blaze that leaped up in her eyes, as she wrenched her arm from the officer's profaning touch, and her voice rang like the clash of steel.

"Madam, we are allowed no discretion; we are only the blind and deaf machines that obey orders. Read the warrant, and you will understand that our duty is imperative."

Again and again she read the paper, in which the sheriff of the county where Elm Bluff is situated, demanded her arrest and return to X——, on the charge of robbery and murder committed during the night which she had spent at the station. Then several telegrams were placed before her. The description of herself, her dress, even of the little basket and shawl, was minutely accurate; and by degrees the horror of her situation, and her utter helplessness, became frightfully distinct. The papers fell from her nerveless fingers, and one desperate cry broke from her white lips:

"O just God! Will you permit such a shameful, cruel outrage? Save me from this horrible injustice and disgrace!"

Seeing neither the men, nor the room, her strained gaze seemed in her great agony fixed upon the face of Him, who, silvering the lilies of the field and watching the flight of sparrows, has tender care for all who trust Him. Even in this terrible trial, the girl's first thought was of her mother; and of the disastrous effect that the misfortune would produce upon the invalid.

"I am sorry to tell you, that we are required to search all persons arrested under similar charges, and in the next room a female detective will receive and retain every thing in your possession, except your clothing. You are suspected of having secreted money, jewelry and some very valuable papers."

"Suspected of being a common thief! I am as innocent as any angel beside the throne of Christ! Save me at least from the degradation of being searched. Here is my basket, and here is my purse."

She handed him the worn leather pocket-book, which contained only the few pennies reserved to pay her passage across the ferry, and turned the pocket of her dress inside cut.

At the tap of a hand-bell, a tall, angular woman opened the door of an adjoining room.

"Mrs. Foster, you will very carefully examine the prisoner, and search her clothing for papers, as well as valuables."

"Spare me at least this indignity!" cried the shuddering girl.

"Come with me, madam. We have no choice."

When the door closed behind her, the constable walked up and down the floor.

"How deceitful appearances are! That woman looks as pure and innocent as an angel, and I half believed her protestations; but here in the basket, sure enough, hidden at the bottom, are the jewelry and the gold. No sign of the papers, but she may have destroyed them.

"Thief or not, she is a grand beauty; and if her heart was not in that prayer she put up just now, she is a grand actress also. This is a beastly trade of ours, hunting down and trapping the unwary. Sometimes I feel no better than a sleuth-hound, and that girl's eyes went through and through me a while ago like a two-edged dirk."

As he vented his views of his profession, one of the policemen lighted his pipe and puffed vigorously.

Mrs. Foster came back, followed by her victim.

"I find absolutely nothing secreted on the prisoner."

"No papers of any description?"

"None, sir."

"Madam, your basket contains the missing jewelry and money, at least a portion of it, and I shall place it in the hands of the sheriff."

"The money and jewels are not mine. They belong to my mother, to whom they were given by her father; and she needs the money at this moment—"

"Let me advise you to say as little as possible for your own sake; because your words will be weighed against you."

"I speak only the truth, and it will, it must, vindicate me. What papers are you searching for?"

"General Darrington's will. It was stolen with the money. Here is yesterday's paper, with an account of the whole affair, telegraphed from X——. If you need to learn anything, you will understand when you read it."

The sight of the capital letters in the Telegraphic Despatches, coupling her name with a heinous and revolting crime, seemed to stab her eyes with red-hot thrusts; and shivering from head to foot, she slowly realized the suspicious significance of the disappearance of the will, which was the sole obstacle that debarred her from her grandfather's wealth. Although sustained by an unfaltering trust in the omnipotence of innocence, she was tormented by a dread spectre that would not "down" at her bidding; how could she prove that the money and jewels had been given to her? Would the shock of the tidings of her arrest kill her mother? Was there any possible way by which she might be kept in ignorance of this foul disgrace?

Beryl hid her face in her hands, and tried to think, but the whole universe appeared spinning into chaos. She had opposed the trip South so steadily and vehemently; had so sorrowfully and reluctantly yielded at last to maternal solicitation, and had been oppressed with such dire forebodings of some resultant evil. So bitter was her repugnance to the application to her grandfather, that she had set out on her journey feeling as though it were a challenge to fate; and this was the answer? The vague distrust, the subtle sombre presentiment, the haunting shadow of an inexplicable ill, had all meant this; this bloody horror, dragging her fair name down to the loathsome mire of the slums of crime. Had some merciful angel leaned from the parapets of heaven and warned her; or did her father's spirit, in mysterious communion of deathless love and prescient guardianship, stir her soul to oppose her mother's scheme? Sceptical and heedless Tarquins are we all, whom our patient Sibylline intuitions finally abandon to the woes which they sought to avert.

In the maddening rush and whirl of Beryl's reflections, her mother's image was the one centre around which all things circled; and at length, rallying her energies, she turned to her captor.

"You intend to take me to prison?"

"I am obliged to detain and deliver you to the officer who has come from X——with the warrant, and who will carry you back there for trial. He knew from the detentions along the route, that he could easily overhaul you here, so he went straight to Trenton with a requisition from the Governor of his State upon Governor Mansfield, for your surrender. It is but a short run to the Capital, and he expects to get here in time to catch the train going South to-day. We had a telegram a while ago, saying the papers were all right, and that he would meet us at the train, as there will be only a few moments to spare."

"But I must first see my mother. I must give her the money and explain—"

"The money will be claimed by the officer who takes charge of you."

"Have you no mercy? My mother is ill, destitute; and she will die unless I can go to her. Oh! I beg of you, for the sake of common humanity, carry me home, if only for five minutes! Just let me see mother, let me speak to her!"

In the intensity of her dread, she fell upon her knees, and lifted her hands imploringly; and the anguish in her white quivering face was so piteous that the man turned his head away.

"I would oblige you if I could, but it is impossible. The law is cruel, as you say, but it is intended as a terror to evil-doers. Things look awfully black for you, but all the same I am sorry for you, if your mother is to suffer for your deeds. If you wish to write to her, I will see that she receives your note; but you have very little time left."

"O God! how hard! What a foul, horrible wrong inflicted upon the innocent!"

She cowered on the floor, unconscious that she still knelt; seeing only the suffering woman in that dreary attic across the river, where sunken feverish eyes watched for her return.

Accidentally Beryl's gaze fell on the bunch of faded chrysanthemums which had dropped unnoticed on the floor, and snatching them she buried her face in their petals. Their perfume was the potent spell that now melted her to tears, and the tension of her overtaxed nerves gave way in a passionate burst of sobs. When she rose a few moments later, the storm had passed; the face regained its stony rigidity, and henceforth she fronted fate with an unnatural calmness.

"Will you give me some paper and a pen?"

"You can write here at the desk."

Mrs. Foster approached her, and said hesitatingly:

"Would it comfort you at all, for me to go and see your mother and explain why you could not return to her? I am very sorry for you, poor thing."

"Thank you, but—you could not explain, and the sight of a stranger would startle her. In one way you can help me; do you know Dr. Grantlin of New York?"

"Only by reputation; but I can find him."

"Will you deliver into his hand the note I am writing?"

"I certainly will."

"How soon?"

"Before nine o'clock to-night."

"Thank you—a thousand times."

After a while she folded a sheet containing these words:

"DEAR DR. GRANTLIN:

"In the extremity of my distress, I appeal to you as a Christian gentleman, as a true physician, a healer of the suffering, and under God, the guardian of my mother's life. You know why I went to my grandfather. He gave me the money, one hundred dollars, and some valuable jewels. When in sight of home, I have been arrested on the charge of having murdered my grandfather, and stolen his will. Need I tell you that I am as innocent as you are? The thought of my mother is the bitterest drop in my cup of shame and sorrow. You can judge best, how much it may be expedient to tell her, and you can devise the kindest method of breaking the truth, if she must know it. Have her removed to the hospital, and do not postpone the operation. O Doctor! be pitiful, be tender to her, and do not let her need any little comforts. Some day I will pay you for all expenses incurred in her behalf, but at present I have not a dollar, as the money has been seized. I am sure you will not deny my prayer, and may God reward and bless you, for your mercy to my precious mother.

"In grateful trust,

"BERYL BRENTANO.

"P.S.—If you approve, deliver the enclosed note."

On a separate sheet she wrote:

"MY DARLING MOTHER:

"Finding it necessary to return to X——, I have requested Dr. Grantlin to take particularly good care of you for a few days. Your father will never forgive, never receive you, but he kindly complied with your request and gave me one hundred dollars. Try to be patient until I can come and tell you everything, and believe that God will not forsake us. With these hurried lines, I send you a few chrysanthemums—your favorite flowers—which I gathered in the rose garden of your old home. When you smell them, think of your little girl who loves you better than her own life, and who will hasten home at the earliest possible moment, to take you in her arms. Mother, pray for me, and may God be very merciful to you, my dearest, and to—

"Your devoted child,

"BERYL."

She had bound the withered flowers together with a strip of fringe from her shawl, and now, with dry eyes and firm white lips, she kissed them twice, pinned the last note around them and laid the whole in Mrs. Foster's hand.

"I trust you to deliver them in person to Dr. Grantlin before you sleep to-night; and if I survive this awful outrage, perpetrated under the name of law, I will find you some day, and thank you."

Looking at the lovely face, pure in its frozen calm, as some marble lily in the fingers of a monumental effigy, Mrs. Foster felt the tears dimming her own vision and said earnestly:

"Keep as silent as possible. The less you say, the safer you will be; and run no risk of contradicting your own statements."

"I appreciate your motive, but I have nothing to conceal."

Beryl laid her hand on her shawl, then drew back.

"Am I allowed the use of my shawl?"

"Oh, certainly, madam."

The officer would have opened and put it around her, but with an indescribable movement of proud repulsion, she shook it out, then wrapped it closely about her, and sat down, keeping her eyes fixed on the face of the clock ticking over the fireplace. After a long and profound silence, the man who had arrested her, said gravely and gently:

"Time is up. I must deliver you to Officer Gibson at the train. Come with me."

She rose, gave her hand to Mrs. Foster, and stooping suddenly touched with her lips the withered flowers, then followed silently.

In subsequent years, when she attempted to recall consecutively the incidents of the ensuing forty-eight hours, they eluded her, like the flitting phantasmagoria that throng delirium; yet subtle links fastened the details upon her brain, and sometimes most unexpectedly, that psychic necromancer—association of ideas—selected some episode from the sombre kaleidoscope of this dismal journey, and set it in lurid light before her, as startling and unwelcome as the face of an enemy long dead. Life and personality partook in some degree of duality; all that she had been before she saw Elm Bluff, seemed a hopelessly distinct existence, yet irrevocably chained to the mutilated and blackened Afterward, like the grim and loathsome unions enforced by the Noyades of Nantes.

The sun did not forget to shine, nor the moon to keep her appointment with the throbbing stars that signalled all along her circuit. Men whistled, children laughed; the train thundered through tunnels, and flew across golden stubble fields, where grain shocks and hay stacks crowded like tents of the God of plenty, in the Autumnal bivouac; and throughout the long days and dreary lagging nights. Beryl was fully conscious of a ceaseless surveillance, of an ever-present shadow, which was tall and gaunt, wore a drab overcoat and slouched hat, and was redolent of tobacco. As silent as two mummies in the crypts of Karnac they sat side by side; and twice when the officer touched her arm and asked if she would take some refreshments, she merely shook her head, and tightened the folds of her veil; shrinking closer to the window against which she leaned. Not until they approached X——, and she recognized some features of the landscape, were her lips unsealed:

"What persons are responsible for my arrest?"

"Our District Solicitor, Mr. Churchill, and Mr. Dunbar, the lawyer, who made the affidavit under which the warrant was issued. I am only a deputy, acting under orders from the sheriff."

"You are taking me to prison?"

"Perhaps not; it depends on the result of the preliminary examination, and you may be allowed bail."

A ray of hope silvered the shrouding gloom; there was a possibility of escaping the stain of incarceration.

"When will the examination take place?"

"About noon to-day. You will have time to eat something and freshen up a little. Here we are. What a crowd to welcome us! Don't stir. We will just wait a while, and I will get you into a carriage as quietly as possible."

He whispered some directions to the conductor of the train, and standing in the aisle with his arm across the seat, screened her from the gaze of a motley crew of men and boys who rushed in to stare at the prisoner, whose arrival had been impatiently expected. On the railway platform and about the station house surged a sea of human heads, straining now in the direction of the first passenger coach; and when in answer to some question, the conductor pointed to the sleeping car which was at the rear of the train, the mass swayed down the track.

"Quick! Now is our time!"

The deputy sheriff hurried her out, almost lifted her from the steps, and pushing her forward, turned a corner of the street, and handed her into a carriage which awaited them.

CHAPTER VI.

To Beryl many hours seemed to have crept away, since she had been left alone in a small dusty apartment, adjoining the office where the chief magistrate of X——-daily held court. Too restless to sit still, she paced up and down the floor, trying to collect her thoughts, and at last knelt by the side of a table, and laid her weight of dread and peril before the Throne of the God she trusted. The Father of the fatherless and Friend of the friendless, would surely protect her in this hour of intolerable degradation.

"O, Thou that hearest prayer; unto Thee shall all flesh come."

The door opened, and a venerable, gray-haired man approached the table, where her head was bent upon her crossed arms. When she lifted her white face, with the violet circles under her dry eyes, making them appear preternaturally large and luminous, and the beautiful mouth contracted by a spasm of intense pain, a deep sigh of compassion passed the stranger's lips.

"I am Mitchell Dent, an old friend of General Darrington's, and of your mother, who has often sat upon my knee. Because of my affection for your grandfather, I have asked permission to see you for a few moments. If you are unjustly accused, I desire to befriend you, and offer you some advice. I am told you assert your innocence of the great crime of which you are suspected. I hope you can prove it; but for your own sake I advise you to waive an examination, and await the action of the Grand Jury, as you have had no opportunity of consulting counsel, or preparing your defence."

"You knew my mother? Then you should require no other proof that her child is not a criminal. I am innocent of every offence against General Darrington, except that of being my father's daughter; and my unjustifiable arrest is almost as foul a wrong as his murder."

She drew herself proudly to her full height, and as his eyes dwelt in irrepressible admiration upon her, his manhood did homage to her grace and dignity, and he took off his hat.

"I earnestly hope so; and the law holds every person innocent until her guilt be fully proved and established."

"Of the significance of law terms I know nothing; and of the usages of courts I am equally ignorant. If, as you suggest, I should waive an examination, should I escape imprisonment?"

"No."

"Then I must be tried at once; because I want to hurry back to my mother who is ill, and needs me."

"But you have no counsel as yet, and delay is your best policy."

"Delay might cost my mother's life. I have no money to pay a lawyer to stand up and mystify matters, and my best policy is to defend myself, by telling the simple truth."

Again Judge Dent sighed. Could guilt be masked by this fair semblance of childlike guilelessness?

"Can you summon any witnesses to prove that you were not at Elm Bluff on the night of the storm?"

"Yes, the ticket agent knows I was in the waiting-room during that storm."

He shook his gray head.

"He will be one of the strongest witnesses against you."

"Then I have no witnesses except—God, and my conscience."

The door opened, and with his watch in his hand the deputy sheriff entered.

"Sorry to shorten your interview, Judge, but you know we have a martinet in yonder, a regular Turk, and he splits seconds into fractions."

As Judge Dent withdrew, Beryl realized that her hour of woe had arrived, and she began to pin her veil tightly over her face.

"Come along—You can't keep your veil on. Try to be as non-committal as possible when they ask you crooked questions. Of course I want justice done, and I hope I am a faithful servant of the law; but if you are as innocent as a flock of ring-doves, the lawyers will try to confuse you."

He attempted to lead her, but she drew back.

"I will follow you; but please do not hold my arm; do not touch me."

A moment later, a door opened and closed, a glare of light showed her a crowded room; a monotonous hum like the swell of the sea fell on her ear; then stifled ejaculations, to which succeeded a sudden, deathlike hush. The officer placed a chair for her in front of the platform where the magistrate sat, and retired to the rear of the room. With some difficulty Judge Dent made his way through the throng of spectators, and seated himself beside Mr. Dunbar.

"Well, sir, how did the prisoner impress you?" asked the latter, as he folded up a paper.

"Dunbar, you have made a mistake. I have spent the best of my life in the study of criminals; and if that woman yonder is not innocent, I am in my dotage."

"Pardon me, Judge, if I dispute both propositions. I made no mistake; and you are merely, in the goodness of your heart, and the fervor of your chivalry, dazzled momentarily by the glamour of extraordinary beauty and touching youth."

When Beryl recovered in some degree from the shock of finding herself actually on trial, she endeavored to collect her faculties; but the violent palpitation of her heart was almost suffocating, and in her ears the surging as of an ocean tide, drowned the accents of the magistrate. At first the words were as meaningless as some Sanskrit formula, but gradually her attention grasped and comprehended. In a strident incisive voice he read from a paper on the desk before him:

"At an inquisition held at X——, T——county, on the twenty-seventh day of October, before me, Jeremiah Bateman, Coroner of said county, on the body of Robert Luke Darrington, there lying dead, by the jurors whose names are hereto subscribed; the said jurors upon their oath do say that Robert Luke Darrington came to his death on the night of Thursday, October twenty-sixth, by a murderous assault committed upon him by means of a heavy brass andiron. And from all the evidence brought before them, the jury believe that the fatal blow was feloniously given by the hand of his granddaughter, Beryl Brentano.

"In testimony whereof, the said jurors have hereunto set their hands, this twenty-seventh day of October, A.D., 18—.

"Signed————

"Attest,

"JEREMIAH BATEMAN, Coroner."

"In consequence of this verdict, and by virtue of a warrant issued at the request of the District Solicitor, Governor Glenbeigh made a prompt requisition for the arrest and detention of the said Beryl Brentano, who has been identified and returned to this city, to answer the charges brought against her. The prisoner will unveil and stand up.

"Beryl Brentano, you are charged with the murder of Robert Luke Darrington, by striking him with a brass andiron. Are you guilty, or not guilty?"

"Not guilty." Her voice was unsteady, but the words were distinct.

Mr. Dunbar, Mr. Burk, and a middle-aged woman lean as Cassius, came nearer to the platform, and after a leisurely survey of the girl's face and figure, pronounced her the person whom they had severally accused of the crime of causing the death of General Darrington.

The canons that govern psychical phenomena are as occult as the abstraction of the "fourth division of space"; and they defy the realism of common-place probability, mock all analysis, and annihilate distance. When Beryl had first met the keen scrutiny of Mr. Dunbar's glittering blue eyes, their baleful influence made her shiver slightly; and now at the instant in which he approached, and inspected her closely, she forgot that she was on trial for her life, became temporarily oblivious of her dismal entourage, and stood once more before a marble image in the Vatican, where the light streamed full on the cold face, that for centuries has been the synonym of blended beauty and cruelty. In her ears rang again the words her father had rend aloud at her side, while she sketched: "But he does not inspire confidence, by the smile that would like to express goodness. The finely cut underlip that rises from the strongly marked hollow over the chin ought to sharpen with a dash of contempt the conscious superiority that lies upon his broad, magnificent forehead. His smile is in strong contrast with the cold gaze of the large open eyes; a gaze that hesitates not, but without mercy verifies a judgment fixed in advance, that gives up every one to condemnation."

The dusty crowded court-room appeared to swim in the rich aroma distilled from the creamy hearts of Roman hyacinths; and the velvet lips of purple Roman violets suddenly babbled out the secret of the mysterious repulsion which had puzzled her, from the hour in which she first looked into Mr. Dunbar's face; his strange resemblance to the Chiaramonti Tiberius, which she had studied and copied so carefully. In days gone by, the subtle repose, the marvelous beauty of that marble face, where as yet the demon of destruction had cast no stain, possessed a singular fascination for her; and now the haunting likeness which had perplexed her at Elm Bluff, became associated inseparably with old Bedney's description of Mr. Dunbar's merciless treatment of witnesses, and Beryl realized with alarming clearness that in her grandfather's lawyer she had met the incarnation of her cruel fate.

Standing quite near her, he gravely related, with emphatic distinctness and careful detail, his first meeting with the prisoner on the piazza at Elm Bluff, and the vivid impression she left on his mind; his return to Elm Bluff about half-past nine the same evening, in order to get a deed which he had forgotten to put into his pocket at the first visit. Learning that General Darrington had not yet retired for the night, he sent in to ask for the deed, and was summoned "to come and get it himself." On entering the bedroom, he found his client wrapped in a cashmere dressing-gown, and sitting in an easy chair by the window, which opened on the north or front piazza. He appeared much perturbed and harassed, and in reply to inquiries touching his health, answered that he was "completely shaken up, and unnerved, by a very stormy and disagreeable interview held that afternoon with the child of his wayward daughter Ellice." "When witness asked: "Did not the great beauty of the embassadress accomplish the pardon and restoration of the erring mother?" General Darrington had struck his cane violently on the floor, and exclaimed: "Don't talk such infernal nonsense! Did you ever hear of my pardoning a wrong against my family name and honor? Does any man live, idiotic enough to consider me so soft-hearted? No, no. On the contrary, I was harsh to the girl; so harsh that she turned upon me, savage as a strong cub defending a crippled helpless dam. They know now that the last card has been played, and the game ended; for I gave her distinctly to understand that at my death, Prince would inherit every iota of my estate, and that my will had cut them off without a cent. I meant it then, I mean it now. I swear that lowborn fiddler's brood shall never darken these doors; but somehow, I am unable to get rid of the strange, disagreeable sensation the girl left behind her, as a farewell legacy. She stood there at that glass door, and raised her hand like a prophetess. 'General Darrington, when you lie down to die, may God have more mercy on your poor soul than you have shown to your suffering child.'"

Witness advised him to go to bed, and sleep off the unpleasant recollections of the day, but he said it was so oppressively hot, he wanted to sit at the window, which was wide open. Witness having secured the deed, which was on the table in the room, bade his client good-night, and left the house.

He was riding toward town, and thought it was about ten o'clock, when he saw the prisoner sitting under a pine tree near the road, and not more than a half a mile from the bridge over the "Branch" that runs at the foot of Elm Bluff. His horse had shied and plunged at sight of her, and, the moonlight being bright as day, witness easily recognized her as the same person he had seen earlier in the afternoon. Thinking her appearance there at that hour was rather mysterious, he asked her if she had lost her way; to which she replied "No, sir." On the following morning, when the mournful news of the murder of General Darrington had convulsed the entire community with grief and horror, witness had smothered his reluctance to proceed against a woman, and a solemn sense of duty forced him to bring these suspicious circumstances to the knowledge of the District Solicitor.

While he gave his testimony, Mr. Dunbar watched her closely for some trace of emotion, but she met his gaze without the movement of a muscle, and he detected not even a quiver of the jet lashes that darkened her proud gray eyes.

Antony Burk next testified that he had given the accused instructions about the road to Elm Bluff, when she arrived at X—; and that after buying her return ticket, she told him it was necessary she should take the 7:15 train, and that she would be sure to catch it. The train was a few minutes late, but had pulled out of the station twenty minutes before the prisoner came back, when she appeared much annoyed at having missed it.

Then she had sent a telegram (a copy of which was in the possession of the Solicitor), and requested him to allow her to remain in the ladies' waiting-room until the next train at 3:05. He had directed her to a hotel close by, but she declined going there. Thinking she was fatigued and might relish it, he had, after supper, carried a pitcher of iced tea to the waiting-room, but though he remained there until nine o'clock she was nowhere visible. He went home and went to sleep, but the violence of the storm aroused him; and when he took his lantern and went back to unlock the ticket office, he searched the whole place, and the prisoner was not in the building. This was at half-past two A.M., and the pitcher of tea remained untouched where he had placed it. It was not raining when he returned, and a few minutes after he had hunted for the prisoner, he was standing in the door of his office and he saw her coming down the railway track, from the direction of the water tank and the bridge. She was breathing rapidly as if she had been running, and witness noticed that her clothes were damp, and that some drops of water fell from the edge of her hat. A lamp-post stood in front of the station, and he saw her plainly; asked her why she did not stay in the room, which he had left open for her? Prisoner said she had remained there. Witness told her he knew better; that she was not there at nine nor yet at half-past two o'clock. The accused did not appear inclined to talk, and gave no explanation, but got aboard the 3:05 train. Witness considered her actions so suspicious, that he had related all he knew to Mr. Dunbar, who had summoned him before the magistrate. He (witness) was very loath to think evil of a woman, especially one so beautiful and noble looking, and if he wronged her, he hoped God would forgive him; but he never dodged telling the truth.

Here the female Cassius rose, and gave her name as Angeline Dobbs.

"She had for several years attended to the sewing and mending at Elm Bluff, being summoned there whenever her services were required. On the afternoon previous to General Darrington's death she was sitting at her needlework in the hall of the second story of his house. As the day was very hot, she had opened the door leading out to an iron balcony, which projected just over the front hall door downstairs; and since the piazza was open from the roof to the floor, she had peeped over, and seen the prisoner when she arrived and had watched her while she sat on the steps, waiting to be admitted. After the accused had been inside the house some time, she (witness) recollected that she had seen a hole in one of the lace curtains in the library downstairs, and thought this would be such a nice time to darn it. The library was opposite the drawing room, and adjoined General Darrington's bed-room. The door was open and witness heard what she supposed was a quarrel, as General Darrington's voice was loud and violent; and she distinctly heard him say: 'My will is so strong, no contest can touch it! and it will stand forever between your mother and my property.' Soon after, General Darrington had slammed the door, and though she heard loud tones for some time, she could not make out the words. The impression left on witness's mind was that the prisoner was very impudent to the old gentleman; and not long afterward she saw accused standing in the rose garden, pretending to gather some flowers, but really looking up and down at the front windows. Witness knew the prisoner saw the vault where the General kept his papers, because she heard it opened while she was in the bed-room. The door of the vault or safe did not open on hinges, but was iron, and slid on a metal rod, which made a very peculiar squeaking sound. When she heard the noise she thought that General Darrington was so enraged that he got the will to show prisoner it was all fixed forever, against her and her mother."

When Miss Dobbs sat down, a lame man, disfigured by a scar on his cheek, learned upon a stick and testified:

"My name is Belshazzar Tatem. Was an orderly sergeant attached to General Darrington's staff dtiring the war; but since that time have been a florist and gardener, and am employed to trim hedges and vines, and transplant flowers at Elm Bluff." On the afternoon of the prisoner's visit there, he was resetting violet roots on a border under the western veranda, upon which opened the glass door leading out from the General's bed-room. He had heard an angry altercation carried on between General Darrington and some one, and supposed he was scolding one of the servants. He went to a shed in the barn yard to get a spade he needed, and when he came back he saw the prisoner walk down the steps, and thought it singular a stranger should leave the house that way. Wondered whom she could be, and wondered also that the General had quarrelled with such a splendid looking lady. Next morning when he went back to his work, he noticed the glass door was shut, but the red curtain inside was looped back. He thought it was half-past eight o'clock, when he heard a loud cry in the bed-room, and very soon after, somebody screamed. He ran up the steps, but the glass door was locked on the inside, and when he went around and got into the room, the first thing he saw was General Darrington's body lying on the floor, with his feet toward the hearth, and his head almost on a line with the iron vault built in the wall. The servants were screaming and wringing their hands, and he called them to help him lift the General, thinking that he had dropped in a fit; but he found him stone cold and stiff. There was no sign of blood anywhere, but a heavy, old-fashioned brass andiron was lying close to the General's head, and he saw a black spot like a bruise on his right temple. General Darrington wore his night clothes, and the bed showed he had been asleep there. Some broken vases were on the floor and hearth, and the vault was wide open. The tin box was upside down on the carpet, and some papers in envelopes were scattered about.

Witness had picked up a leather bag carefully tied at the top with red tape, drawn into hard knots; but in one side he found a hole which had been cut with a knife, and at the bottom of the bag was a twenty-dollar gold piece. Two more coins of the same value were discovered on the floor, when General Darrington's body was lifted; and on the bolster of the bed lay a bottle containing chloroform. Witness immediately sent off for some of General Darrington's friends, and also notified the coroner; and he did not leave the room again until the inquest was held. The window on the front piazza was open, and witness had searched the piazza and the grounds for tracks, but discovered no traces of the burglar and murderer, who had escaped before the rain ceased, otherwise the tracks would have been found. Witness was positive that the prisoner was the same person whom he had seen coming out of the bed-room, and with whom General Darrington had quarrelled.

The sheriff here handed to the magistrate, the gold pieces found on the floor at Elm Bluff, by the last witness; then the little wicker basket which had been taken from the prisoner when she was arrested. The coins discovered therein were taken out, and careful comparison showed that they corresponded exactly with those picked up after the murder. The case of sapphires was also shown, and Mr. Dunbar rose to say, that "The prosecution would prove by the attorney who drew up General Darrington's will, that these exceedingly valuable stones had been bequeathed by a clause in that will to Prince Darrington, as a bridal present for whomsoever he might marry."

A brief silence ensued, during which the magistrate pulled at the corner of his tawny mustache, and earnestly regarded the prisoner. She stood, with her beautiful white hands clasped before her, the slender fingers interlaced, the head thrown proudly back. Extreme pallor had given place to a vivid flush that dyed her cheeks, and crimsoned her delicate lips; and her eyes looking straight into space, glowed with an unnatural and indescribable lustre. Tadmor's queen Bath Zabbai could not have appeared more regal in her haughty pose, amid the exulting shouts that rent the skies of conquering Rome. The magistrate cleared his throat, and addressed the accused.

"You are Beryl Brentano, the granddaughter of General Darrington?"

"I am Beryl Brentano."

"You have heard the charges brought against you. What have you to say in defence?"

"That I am innocent of every accusation."

"By what witnesses will you prove it?"

"By a statement of the whole truth in detail, if I may be allowed to make it."

Here the Solicitor, Mr. Churchill, rose and said:

"While faithfully discharging my official duties, loyalty to justice does not smother the accents of human sympathy; and before proceeding any further, I hope your Honor will appoint some counsel to confer with and advise the prisoner. Her isolation appeals to every noble instinct of manhood, and it were indeed puerile tribute to our lamented General Darrington, to bring his granddaughter before this tribunal, without the aid and defence of legal advisers. Justice itself would not be welcome to me, if unjustly won. My friend, Mr. Hazelton, who is present, has expressed his desire to defend the prisoner; and while I am aware that your Honor is under the impression she refuses to accept counsel, I trust you will nevertheless commit her, until she can confer with him."

Mr. Hazelton rose and bowed, in tacit approval.

Beryl advanced a few steps, and her clear pure voice thrilled every heart in the crowded room.

"I need no help to tell the truth, and I want to conceal nothing. Time is inexpressibly valuable to me now, for a human life more precious than my own is at stake; and if I am detained here, my mother may die. May I speak at once, and explain the circumstances which you consider so mysterious as to justify the shameful indignity put upon me?"

"Since you assume the responsibility of your own defence, you may proceed with your statement. Relate what occurred from the hour you reached Elm Bluff, until you left X——next morning."

"I came here to deliver in person a letter written by my mother to her father, General Darrington, because other letters sent through the mail, had been returned unread. It contained a request for one hundred dollars to pay the expense of a surgical operation, which we hoped would restore her health. When I reached Elm Bluff, I waited on the steps, until General Darrington's attorney finished his business and came out; then I was led by an old colored man to the bed-room where General Darrington sat. I gave no name, fearing he might refuse to admit me, and he was very courteous in his manner until I laid the letter before him. He immediately recognized the handwriting, and threw it to the floor, declaring that no human being had the right to address him as father, except his son Prince. I picked up the letter, and insisted he should at least read the petition of a suffering, and perhaps dying woman. He was very violent in his denunciation of my parents, and his voice was loud and angry. So painful was the whole interview, that it was a bitter trial to me to remain in his presence, but knowing how absolutely necessary it was that mother should obtain the money, I forced myself to beg him to read the letter. Finally he consented, read it, and seemed somewhat softened; but he tore it into strips and threw it from him. He drank several glasses of wine from a decanter on the table, and offered me some, expressing the opinion that I must be tired from my journey. I declined it. General Darrington then questioned me about my family, my mode of living; and after a few moments became very much excited, renewing his harsh invectives against my parents. It was at this stage of the interview that he uttered the identical words quoted by the witness: 'My Will is so strong, no contest can touch it, and it will stand forever between your mother and my property.'

28

"Immediately after, he went to the door leading into the library and called 'Bedney!' No one answered, and he shut the door, kicking it as it closed. When he came back to his chair, he said very bitterly: 'At least we will have no eavesdroppers at this resurrection of my dead.' He told me all the story of my mother's girlhood; of her marriage, which had infuriated him; that he had sent her a certain proportion of property, and then disowned and disinherited her. Afterward he described his lonely life, his second marriage which was very happy, and his adoption of his wife's son, who, he repeatedly told me, had usurped my mother's place in his affections. Finally he said:

"'Your mother has asked for one hundred dollars. You shall have it; not because I recognize her as child of mine, but because a sick woman appeals to a Southern gentleman.'

"He took a bunch of keys from his pocket, and with one of them opened a safe or iron closet on the wall near the chimney, and from that vault he brought a square black tin box to the table, where he opened it. He took out a leather bag, and counted into my hand five gold pieces of twenty dollars each. The money was given so ungraciously that I told him I would not accept it, save as a loan for mother's benefit; and that as soon as I could earn it I would return the amount to him. I was so anxious to get away, I started toward the library door, but he called me back, and gave me the morocco case which contains the sapphires. He said my mother's mother had bought them as a gift for her daughter, to be worn when she was graduated at school; but as she married and left school without his knowledge, the jewels had never been seen by her. He told me he had intended to give them to his son Prince, for his bride, but that now he would send them to mother, who could sell them for a handsome sum, because they were valuable. He showed so much sorrow at this time, that I begged him to give me some message of pardon and affection, which she would prize infinitely more than money or jewels; but he again became angry and bitter, and so I left him. I came away by the door leading out on the iron veranda, because he directed me to do so, saying that he did not wish me to meet the servants, who would pry and tattle. When I closed the glass door I saw him standing in the middle of the room, leaning on his cane, and he had the black tin box in his hand. The sun was setting then, and now—"

She ceased speaking for some seconds, then raised her hands toward heaven, and with uplifted eyes that seemed in their strained gaze to pierce beyond the veil, she added with solemn emphasis:

"I call God to witness, that was the last and only time I ever saw General Darrington. That was the last and only visit I ever made to Elm Bluff."

There was a general movement among the spectators, and audible excitement, which was promptly quelled by the magistrate.

"Silence there in front, or I shall order the room cleared."

Turning toward Beryl, he said:

"If you left Elm Bluff at sunset, why did you not take the 7:15 train?"

"I tried to do so, but missed it because I desired to obey my mother's injunctions as strictly as possible. She gave me a small bunch of flowers, and asked me to be sure to lay them for her on her mother's grave. When I reached the cemetery, which you know is in sight of the road from Elm Bluff, the gate was locked, and it required some time to enable me to climb over the wall and find the monument. It was growing dark, and when I arrived at the station, I learned the train had just gone."

"Why did you not go to a hotel, as you were advised to do?"

"Because after sending the telegram to my mother, I had no money to pay for lodging; and I asked permission to stay in the ladies' waiting-room."

"State where and how you spent the night."

"It was very hot and sultry in that room, and as there was a bright moon shining, I walked out to get some fresh air. The pine woods had appeared so pretty and pleasant that afternoon, that I went on and on toward them, and did not realize how far they were. I met people passing along the road, and it did not seem lonely. The smell of the pines was new to me, and to enjoy it, I sat down on the straw. I was tired, and must have fallen asleep at once, for I remember nothing till some noise startled me, and there I saw the same man on horseback in the road, whom I had met at Elm Bluff. He asked me if I had misled my way, and I answered 'No, sir.' The height of the moon showed me it was late, and as I was frightened at finding myself alone in the woods, I almost ran back to the railway station, where I saw no one, except a telegraph operator, who seemed to be asleep in his chair. I cannot say what time it was, because I could not see the clock. Soon after, it began to thunder, and all through that terrible storm I was alone in the waiting-room. So great was my relief when the wind and lightning ceased, that I went to sleep, and dreamed of a happy time when I lived in Italy, and of talking with one very dear to me. Just then I awoke with a start, and heard a voice talking outside, which seemed very familiar. There were two persons; one, a negro, said:

"'There ain't no train 'till daylight, excepting the through freight.'

"The other person asked: 'When is it due?' The negro answered:

"'Pretty soon, but it don't stop here; it goes to the water tank where it blows for the railroad bridge; and that is only a short distance up the track.'

"I think I must have been only half awake, and with my mind fixed on my dream, I ran out in front of the station house. An old negro man limping down the street was the only person visible, and while I watched him he suddenly vanished. I went along the track for some distance but saw no one; and when I came back, the ticket agent was standing in the door of his office. I cannot explain to you the singular impulse which carried me out, when I heard the dialogue, because it is inexplicable to myself, save by the supposition that I was still dreaming; and yet I saw the negro man distinctly. There was a lamp-post near him, and he had a bundle on his shoulder. When the 3:05 train came, I went aboard and left X——."

A smile parted Mr. Dunbar's lips, and his handsome teeth glittered as he whispered to Judge Dent:

"Even your chivalrous compassion can scarcely digest this knotty solution of her movements that night. As a fabrication, it does little credit to her ingenuity."

"Her statement impresses me differently. She is either entirely innocent, or she had an accomplice, whose voice she recognized; and this clue should be investigated."

The District Solicitor rose and bowed to the Magistrate.

"With your Honor's permission, I should like to ask the prisoner whom she expected to see, when she recognized the voice?"

"A person who is very dear to me, but who is not in the United States."

"What is the name of that person?"

Her lips moved to pronounce his name, but some swift intuitive warning restrained the utterance. Suddenly a new horror, a ghastly possibility, thrust itself for the first time before her, and she felt as though some hand of ice clutched her heart.

Those who watched her so closely, saw the blood ebb from cheeks and lips; noted the ashy pallor that succeeded, and the strange groping motion of her hands. She staggered toward the platform, and when the Magistrate caught her arm, she fell against him like some tottering marble image, entirely unconscious.

So prolonged and death-like was the swoon, and so futile the usual methods of restoration, that the prisoner was carried into the small ante-room, and laid upon a wooden bench; where a physician, who chanced to be in the audience, was summoned to attend her. Finding restoratives ineffectual, he took out his lancet:

"This is no ordinary fainting fit."

He attempted to roll up one of her sleeves, but seeing this was impracticable, would have unfastened her dress, had not Judge Dent arrested his hand.

"No, doctor; cut out the sleeve if necessary, but don't touch her otherwise."

"Let me assist you; I can easily bare the arm."

As he spoke, Mr. Dunbar knelt beside the bench, and with a small, sharp pen-knife ripped the seam from elbow to shoulder, from elbow to wrist, swiftly and deftly folding back the sleeve, and exposing the perfect moulding of the snowy arm.

"Just hold the hand, Dunbar, so as to keep it steady."

Clasping closely the hand, which the physician laid in his palm the attorney noted the exquisite symmetry of the slender fingers and oval nails. He bent forward and watched the frozen face. When the heavily lashed lids quivered and lifted, and she looked vacantly at the grave compassionate countenances leaning over her, a certain tightening of the hold upon her fingers, drew her attention. Her gaze fastened on the lawyer's blue eyes as if by a subtle malign fascination. The veil that shrouded consciousness was rent, not fully raised; and as in some dream the solemn eyes appeared to search his. A strange shivering thrill shot along his nerves, and his quiet, well regulated heart so long the docile obedient motor, fettered vassal of his will, bounded, strained hard on the steel cable that held it in thrall.

"You feel better now?" asked the physician, who was stanching the flow of blood.

Still her gaze seemed to penetrate the inmost recesses of the lawyer's nature, calling into sudden revolt dormant elements that amazed and defied him.

A shadowy smile curved her pale lips.

"At the mercy of Tiberius. At the mercy of Tiberius."

Those present looked inquiringly at each other.

"Her mind wanders a little. Sheriff, give her some of that brandy. She is as weak as a baby."

Judge Dent raised her head, and the officer held the tumbler to her mouth; while the former said gently:

"My poor girl, drink a little, it will strengthen you."

With a gesture of loathing, she rejected it; and as she attempted to raise herself, all the dire extremity of her peril rushed back upon her mind, like a black overwhelming tide from the sea of the past.

"Lie still, until I have bandaged your arm. Here, Dunbar, you acquitted yourself so dexterously with your knife, just lend a hand. Hold the arm until I secure the bandage."

To find herself surrounded by men, helpless in the grasp of strangers, with no womanly touch or glance to sustain her, served to intensify her misery; and wrenching herself free, she struggled into a sitting posture, then staggered to her feet. The heavy coil of hair loosened when they bore her from the court-room, now released itself from restraining pins, and fell in burnished waves to her knees, clothing her with a glory, such as the world's great masters in art reserve for the beatified. Had all the blood that fed her heart been drained, she would not have appeared more deadly pale, and in her wide eyes was the desperate look of a doomed animal, that feels the hot fangs of the hounds, and the cold steel of the hunters.

"Be persuaded for your own sake, to swallow some stimulant, of which you are sadly in need. You will require all your strength, and, as a physician, I insist upon your taking my prescription."

"If I might have some water. Just a little water."

Some one brought a brown stone pitcher, and she drank long and thirstily; then looked for a moment at the faces of those who crowded about her.

"What will be done now?"

Every eye fell to the floor, and after a painful silence Judge Dent said very gently:

"For the present, the Magistrate will retain you in custody, until the action of the Grand Jury. Should they fail to indict you, then you will at once be released."

"I am to go to prison? I am to be thrust among convicts, vile criminals! I—? My father's Beryl? O, righteous God! Where is Thy justice? O, Christ! Is Thy mercy a mockery?"

She stood, with her chin resting on her clenched hands, and twice a long violent shudder shook her from head to foot.

"I hope your imprisonment will be only temporary. The Grand Jury will be in session next week. Meantime diligent search may discover the persons whose conversation you overheard at the station; and if you be innocent, we are all your friends, and the law, which now seems so stern, will prove your strongest protector and vindicator."

Judge Dent stood close beside her, as he essayed these words of comfort, and saw that she caught her breath as though in mortal agony. Her face writhed, and she shut her eyes, unable to contemplate some hideous apparition. He suspected that she was fighting desperately an impulse that suggested succor; and he was sure she had strangled it, when her hands fell nerveless at her side, and she raised her bowed head. If the finger of paralysis had passed over her features, they would not have appeared more hopelessly fixed. Mechanically she twisted and coiled her hair, and took the hat and shawl which the officer held out to her.

"If I can assist you in any way, you have only to send for me."

She looked at Judge Dent intently, for an instant, then shook her head.

"No one can help me now."

She tied her veil over her face, and silently followed the deputy sheriff to a carriage, that stood near the pavement.

When he would have assisted her, she haughtily repelled him.

"I will follow you, because I must; but do not put your hands on me."

CHAPTER VII.

In ante bellum days, when States' Rights was a sacred faith, a revered and precious palladium, State pride blossomed under Southern skies, and State coffers overflowed with the abundance wherewith God blessed the land. During that period, when it became necessary to select a site for a new Penitentiary, the salubrity and central location of X——had so strongly commended it, that the spacious structure was erected within its limits, and regarded as an architectural triumph of which the State might justly boast. Soon after this had been completed, the old county jail, situated on the border of the town, was burned one windy March night; then the red rain of war deluged the land, and when the ghastly sun of "Reconstruction" smiled upon the grave of States' Rights, Municipal money disappeared in subterranean channels. Thus it came to pass, that with the exception of a small "lockup" attached to Police Headquarters, X——had failed to rebuild its jail, and domiciled its dangerous transgressors in the great stone prison; paying therefor to the State an annual amount per capita.

Built of gray granite which darkened with time and weather stains, its massive walls, machicolated roof, and tall arched clock-tower lifted their leaden outlines against the sky, and cast a brooding shadow over the town, lying below; a grim perpetual menace to all who subsequently found themselves locked in its reformatory arms. Separated from the bustling mart and busy traffic, by the winding river that divided the little city into North and South X——, it crested an eminence on the north; and the single lower story flanking the main edifice east and west, resembled the trailing wings of some vast bird of prey, an exaggerated simulacrum of a monstrous gray condor perched on a "coigne of vantage," waiting to swoop upon its victims. Encircled by a tall brick wall, which was surmounted by iron spikes sharp as bayonets, that defied escalade, the grounds extended to the verge of the swift stream in front, and stretched back to the border of a heavily timbered tract of pine land, a bit of primeval forest left to stare at the encroaching armies of Philistinism.

Within the precincts of the yard, the tender conservatism of our great-hearted mother Nature, gently toned the savage stony features; and even under the chill frown of iron barred windows, golden sunshine bravely smiled, soft grasses wove their emerald velvet tapestries starred and flushed with dainty satin petals, which late Autumn roses showered in munificent contribution, to the work of pitying love.

In a comfortably furnished room situated in the second story of the main building, sat a woman apparently thirty-five years old, who was singing to a baby lying face downward on her lap, while with one hand she rocked the wicker cradle beside her, where a boy of four years was tossing. Her hazel eyes were full of kindly light, the whole face eloquent with that patient, limitless tenderness, which is the magic chrism of maternity, wherewith Lucina and Cuba abundantly anoint Motherhood. The blessed and infallible nepenthe for all childhood's ills and aches, mother touch, mother songs, soon held soothing sway; and when the woman laid the sleeping babe on her own bed, and covered her with a shawl, she saw her husband leaning against the partly open door.

"Come here, Susie. The kids are snug and safe for the present, and I want you."

"For shame, Ned! To call our darlings such a beastly name. Kids, indeed! My sweetest, loveliest lambs!"

"There! Hear yourself! If I can see any choice of respectability between kids and lambs, may I turn to a thoroughbred Southdown, and take the blue ribbon at the next Fair. Beasts of the field, all of them. The always-wide-awake-contrariness of womankind is a curious and fearful thing. If I had called our beloved towheads, lambs, you would have sworn through blue ruin that they were the cutest, spryest pair of spotted kids, that ever skipped over a five-railed fence!"

"So much the worse for you, Ned Singleton, that you are such a hopeless heathen; you do not even know where the Elect are appointed to stand, at that great day when the sheep come up on the right hand of the Lord, and the goats go down to the left. If you read your Bible more, I should have less to teach you."

"Oh! but let me tell you, I thought of all that before I made up my mind to marry the daughter of a Presbyterian preacher. I knew your dear little blue-nose would keep the orthodox trail; and being one of the Elect you could not get the points of the celestial compass mixed. Don't you forget, that it is part of the unspoken marriage contract, that the wife must not only keep her own soul white, but bleach her husband's also; and no matter what a reprobate a man may be, he always expects his better-half, by hook or by crook, to steer him into heaven."

He put his hands on his wife's shoulders, shook her, in token of mastery, and kissed her.

"What do you want of my 'always-wide-awake-contrariness'? I have half a mind not to help you out of your scrape; for of course you have mired somewhere. What is the matter now, Ned?"

"Yes—stuck hard and fast; so my dear little woman, don't you go back on your wedding-day promises, but just lend a helping hand. I don't know what is to be done with that poor young woman in No. 19. One of the under-wardens, Jarvis, sleeps this week right under her cell, and he tells me that all night long she tramps up and down, without cessation, like some caged animal. This is her third day in, and she has not touched a morsel; though at Judge Dent's request I ordered some extras given her. Jarvis said she was not sullen, but he thought it proper to report to me that she seemed to act very strangely; so I went up to see after her. When I opened the door she was walking up and down the floor, with her hands locked at the back of her head, and I declare, Susie, she looks five years older than when she came here. There are great dark hollows under her eyes, and two red spots like coals of fire on her cheeks. I said: 'Are you sick, that you reject your meals?' To which she replied: 'Don't trouble yourself to send me food; I cannot eat!' Then I told her I understood that she was restless at night, and I advised her to take a mixture which would quiet her nerves. She shook her head, and I could not bear to look at her; the eyes seemed so like a wounded fawn's, brimful of misery. I asked her if there was anything I could do, to make her more comfortable; or if she needed medicine. All this time she kept up her quick walk to and fro, and she answered: 'Thank you. I need nothing—but death; and that will come soon.' Now what could I say? I felt such a lump in my throat, that if Solomon had whispered to me some kind speech, I could not have uttered it, so I got out of the room just as fast as possible, to dry the tears that somehow would blur my eyes. When they are surly, or snappish, or violent, or insolent, I know exactly what to do, and have no trouble; but hang me, if I can cope with this lady—there it is out! She is a lady every inch, and as much out of place here as I should be in Queen Victoria's drawing-room. Men are clumsy brutes, even in kid gloves, and bruise much oftener than they heal. Whenever I am in that girl's presence, I have a queer feeling that I am walking on eggs, and tip-toe as I may, shall smash things. If something is not done, she will be ill on our hands, and a funeral will balk the bloodhounds."

"O, hush, Ned! You give me the shivers. My heart yearns toward that beautiful young creature, and I believe she is as innocent as my baby. It is a burning shame to send her here, unless there is no doubt of her guilt. Judge Dent is too shrewd an old fox to be baited with chaff, and I am satisfied from what he told you, that he believes her statement. There is nothing I would not do to comfort her, but I would rather have my ears boxed than witness her suffering. The day I carried to her a change of clothes, until her own could be washed, and sewed up her dress sleeve. I did nothing but cry. I could not help it, when she moaned and wrung her hands, and said her mother's heart would break. I have heard all my life that justice is blind; I have learned to believe it, for it stumbles, and gropes, and lays iron claws on the wrong person. As for the lawyers? They are fit pilots: and the courts are little better than blind man's buff. Don't stand chewing your mustache, Ned. Tell me what you want me to do, while baby is asleep. She has a vexatious habit of taking cat naps."

"Little woman, I turn over the case to you. Just let your heart loose, and follow it."

"If I do, will you endorse me?"

"Till the stars fall."

"Can you stay here awhile?"

"Yes, if you will tell Jarvis where he can find me."

"Mind you, Ned, you are not to interfere with me?"

"No—I swear I won't. Hurry up, or there will be much music in this bleating fold; and you know I am as utterly useless with a crying child, as a one-armed man in a concert of fiddlers."

The cell assigned to the new prisoner was in the centre of a line, which rose tier above tier, like the compartments in a pigeon house, or the sombre caves hewn out of rock-ribbed cliffs, in some lonely Laura. Iron stairways conducted the unfortunates to these stone cages, where the dim cold light filtered through the iron lattice-work of the upper part of the door, made a perpetual crepuscular atmosphere within. The bare floor, walls, and low ceiling were spotlessly clean and white; and an iron cot with heavy brown blankets spread smoothly and a wooden bench in one corner, constituted the furniture. Scrupulous neatness reigned everywhere, but the air was burdened with the odor of carbolic acid, and even at mid-day was chill as the breath of a tomb. Where the doors were thrown open, they resembled the yawning jaws of rifled graves; and when closed, the woful inmates peering through the black lattice seemed an incarnation of Dante's hideous Caina tenants.

When Mrs. Singleton stopped in front of No. 19, and looked through the grating, Beryl was standing at the extremity of the cell, with her face turned to the wall, and her hands clasping the back of her neck. The ceiling was so low she could have touched it, had she lifted her arms, and she appeared to have retreated as far in the gloomy den as the barriers allowed. Thinking that perhaps the girl was praying, the warden's wife waited some minutes, but no sound greeted her; and so motionless was the figure, that it might have been only an alto rilievo carved on the wall. Pushing the door open, Mrs. Singleton entered, and deposited on the iron bed a waiter covered with a snowy napkin. At the sound, Beryl turned, and her arms fell to her side, but she shrank back against the wall, as if solitude were her only solace, and human intrusion an added torture.

Mrs. Singleton took both hands, and held them firmly:

"Do you believe it right to commit suicide?"

"I believe in everything but human justice, and Divine mercy."

"Your conscience tells you that—"

"Am I allowed a conscience? What ghastly mockery! Thieves and murderers are not fit tenements for conscience, and I—I—am accused of stealing, and of bloodshed. Justice! What a horrible sham! We—her victims—who adored the beneficent and incorruptible attribute of God Himself—we are undeceived, when Justice—the harpy—tears our hearts out with her hideous, foul, defiling claws."

She spoke through set teeth, and a spasm of shuddering shook her from head to feet.

"Listen to me. Suspicion is one thing, proof something very different. You are accused, but not convicted, and—"

"I shall be. Justice must be appeased, and I am the most convenient and available victim. An awful crime has been committed, and outraged law, screaming for vengeance, pounces like a hungry hawk on an innocent and unsuspecting prey. Does she spare the victim because it quivers, and dies hard?"

32

"Hush! You must not despair. I believe in your innocence; I believe every word you uttered that day was true, and I believe that our merciful God will protect you. Put yourself in His hands, and His mercy will save, for 'it endureth forever.'"

"I don't ask mercy! I claim justice—from God and man. The wicked grovel, and beg for mercy; but innocence lays hold upon the very throne of God, and clutches His sword, and demands justice!"

"I understand how you feel, and I do not wonder; but for your own sake, in order to keep your mind clear and strong for your vindication, you certainly ought to take care of your health. Starvation is the surest leech for depleting soul and body. Do you want to die here in prison, leaving your name tarnished, and smirched with suspicion of crime, when you can live to proclaim your innocence to the world? Remember that even if you care nothing for your life, you owe something to your mother. You have two chances yet; the Grand Jury may not find a true bill—"

"Yes, that tiger-eyed lawyer will see that they do. He knows that the law is a cunning net for the feet of the innocent and the unwary. He set his snare dexterously, and will not fail to watch it."

"You mean Mr. Dunbar? Yes, you certainly have cause to dread him; but even if you should be indicted, you have twelve human hearts full of compassion to appeal to—and I can't think it possible a jury of sane men could look at you and condemn you. You must fight for your life; and what is far more to you than life, you must fight for your good name, for your character. Suspicion is not proof of crime, and there is no taint on you yet; for sin alone stains, and if you will only be brave and clear yourself as I know you can, what a grand triumph it will be. If you starve yourself you seal your doom. An empty stomach will do you more harm than the Grand Jury and all the lawyers; for it utterly upsets your nerves, and makes your brain whirl like a top. For three days and nights you have not tasted food: now just to please me, since I have taken so much trouble, sit down here by me, and eat what I have brought. I know you would rather not; I know you don't want it; but, my dear child, take it like any other dose, which will strengthen you for your battle. It is very fine to rant about heroism, but starvation is the best factory for turning out cowards: and even the courage of old Caesar would have had the 'dwindles,' if he had been stinted in his rations."

She removed the napkin, and displayed a tempting luncheon, served in pretty, gilt-banded white china. What a contrast it presented, to the steaming tin platter and dull tin quart cups carried daily to the adjoining cell?

Beryl laid her hand on Mrs. Singleton's shoulder, and her mouth trembled.

"I thank you, sincerely, for your sympathy—and for your confidence; and to show my appreciation of your kindness, I wish I could eat that dainty luncheon; but I think it would strangle me—I have such a ceaseless aching here, in my throat. I feel as if I should stifle."

"See here! I brought you some sweet rich milk in my little boy's cup. He was my first-born, and I lost him. This was his christening present from my mother. It is very precious, very sacred to me. If you will only drink what is in it, I shall be satisfied. Don't slight my angel baby's cup. That would hurt me."

She raised the pretty "Bo-Peep" silver cup to the prisoner's lips, and seeing the kind hazel eyes swimming in tears, Beryl stooped her head and drank the milk.

The warden's wife lifted the cup, looked wistfully at it, and kissed the name engraved on the metal:

"You know now I must think you pure and worthy. I have given you the strongest possible proof; for only the good could be allowed to touch what my dead boy's lips have consecrated. Now come out with me, and get some pure fresh air."

Beryl shrank back.

"These close walls seem a friendly shelter from the horrible faces that cluster outside. You can form no idea how I dread contact with the vile creatures, whose crimes have brought them here for expiation. The thought of breathing the same atmosphere pollutes me. I think the loathsomeness of perdition must consist in association with the depraved and wicked. Not the undying flames would affright me, but the doom of eternal companionship with outcast criminals. No! No! I would sooner freeze here, than wander in the sunshine with those hideous wretches I saw the day I was thrust among them."

"Trust me, and I will expose you to nothing unpleasant. Take your hat and shawl; I shall not bring you back here. There is time enough for cells when you have been convicted and sentenced; and please God, you shall never stay in this one again. Come."

"Stay, madam. What is your purpose? I have been so hunted down, I am growing suspicious of the appearance of kindness. What are you going to do?"

Mrs. Singleton took her hand and pressed it gently.

"I am going to trust, and help, and love you, if you will let me; and for the present, I intend to keep you in a room adjoining mine, where you will have no fear of wicked neighbors."

"That will be merciful indeed. May God bless you for the thought."

Down iron staircases, and through dim corridors bordered with dark cells, gloomy as the lairs of wild beasts whom the besotted inmates resembled, the two women walked; and once, when a clank of chains and a hoarse human cry broke the dismal silence, Beryl clutched her companion's arm, and her teeth chattered with horror.

"Yes, it is awful! That poor woman is the saddest case we have. She waylaid and stabbed her husband to death, and poisoned his mother. We think she is really insane, and as she is dangerous at times, it is necessary to keep her chained, until arrangements can be made to remove her to the insane asylum."

"I don't wonder she is mad! People cannot dwell here and retain their reason; and madness is a mercy that blesses them with forgetfulness."

Beryl shivered, and her eyes glittered with an unnatural and ominous brilliance.

The warden's wife paused before a large door with solid iron panels, and rang a bell. Some one on the other side asked:

"What is the order? Who rang?"

33

"Mrs. Singleton; I want to get into the chapel. Let me out, Jasper."

The door swung slowly back, and the guard touched his hat respectfully.

Through an open arcade, where the sunlight streamed, Mrs. Singleton led her companion; then up a short flight of stone steps, and they found themselves in a long room, with an altar railing and pulpit at one end, and rows of wooden benches crossing the floor from wall to wall. Even here, the narrow windows were iron barred, but sunshine and the sweet, pure breath of the outside world entered freely. Within the altar railing, and at the right of the reading desk where a Bible lay, stood a cabinet organ. Leaving the prisoner to walk up and down the aisle, Mrs. Singleton opened the organ, drew out the stops, and after waiting a few moments, began to play.

At first, only a solemn prelude rolled its waves of harmony through the peaceful sunny room, but soon the strains of the beautiful Motet "Cast thy burden on the Lord," swelled like the voice of some divine consoler. Watching the stately figure of the prisoner who wandered to and fro, the warden's wife noticed that like a magnet the music drew her nearer and nearer each time she approached the chancel, and at last she stood with one hand on the railing. The beautiful face, sharpened and drawn by mental agony, was piteously wan save where two scarlet spots burned on her cheeks, and the rigid lips were gray as some granite Statue's, but the eyes glowed with a strange splendor that almost transfigured her countenance.

On and on glided the soft, subtle variations of the Motet, and gradually the strained expression of the shining eyes relaxed, as if the soul of the listener were drifting back from a far-off realm; the white lids quivered, the stern lines of the pale lips unbent. At that moment, the face of her father seemed floating on the sunbeams that gilded the pulpit, and the tones of her mother's voice rang in her ears. The terrible tension of many days and nights of torture gave way suddenly, like a silver thread long taut, which snaps with one last vibration. She raised her hands:

"My God! Why hast Thou forsaken me?"

The cry ended in a wail. Into her burning eyes merciful tears rushed, and sinking on her knees she rested against the railing, shaken by a storm of passionate weeping.

Mrs. Singleton felt her own tears falling fast, but she played for a while longer; then stole out of the chapel, and sat down on the steps.

Across the grass plot before the door, burnished pigeons cooed, and trod their stately minuet, their iridescent plumage showing every opaline splendor as the sunlight smote them; and on a buttress of the clock tower, a lonely hedge-sparrow poured his heart out in that peculiarly pathetic threnody which no other feathered throat contributes to the varied volume of bird lays. Poised on the point of an iron spike in the line that bristled along the wall, a mocking bird preened, then spread his wings, soared and finally swept downward, thrilling the air with the bravura of the "tumbling song"; and over the rampart that shut out the world, drifted the refrain of a paean to peace:

"Bob White!" "Peas ripe?" "Not quite!"

In the vast epic of the Cosmos, evoked when the "Spirit of God moved upon the face of the waters"—an epic printed in stars on blue abysses of illimitable space; in illuminated type of rose leaf, primrose petal, scarlet berry on the great greenery of field and forest; in the rainbows that glow on tropical humming birds, on Himalayan pheasants, on dying dolphins in purple seas; and in all the riotous carnival of color on Nature's palette, from shifting glory of summer clouds, to the steady fires of red autumn skies—we find no blot, no break, no blurred abortive passages, until man stepped into creation's story. In the material, physical Universe, the divine rhythm flows on, majestic, serene as when the "morning stars sing together" in the choral of praise to Him, unto whom "all seemed good"; but in the moral and spiritual realm evolved by humanity, what hideous pandemonium of discords drowns the heavenly harmony? What grim havoc marks the swath, when the dripping scythe of human sin and crime swings madly, where the lilies of eternal "Peace on earth, good will to man," should lift their silver chalices to meet the smile of God?

A vague conception of this vexing problem, which like a huge carnivorous spectre, flaps its dusky wings along the sky of sociology, now saddened Mrs. Singleton's meditations, as she watched the lengthening shadow cast by the tower upon the court-yard; but she was not addicted to abstract speculation, and the words of her favorite hymn epitomized her thoughts: "Though every prospect pleases, and only man is vile."

The brazen clang of the deep-throated bell rang out on the quiet air, and a moment later, the piercing treble of a child's cry made her spring to her feet. She peeped into the chapel all was still.

On tiptoe she passed swiftly down the aisle to the chancel, and saw the figure crouched at the altar, with one arm twined through the railing. For many days and nights the tortured woman had not known an instant of repose; nervous dread had scourged her to the verge of frenzy, but when the flow of long-pent tears partly extinguished the fire in her brain, overtaxed Nature claimed restitution, and the prisoner yielded to overwhelming prostration. Death might be hovering near, but her twin sister sleep intervened, and compassionately laid her poppies on the snowy eyelids.

Stooping close, Mrs. Singleton saw that tears yet hung on the black lashes which swept the flushed cheeks, but the parted lips were at rest, and the deep regularly drawn breath told her that at last the weary soul reposed in the peaceful domain of dreams. Deftly, and softly as thistledown falls, she spread her own shawl over the drooping shoulders, then noiselessly hurried back to the door. Locking it, she took the key, ran across the grass, into the arcade, and up to the great iron barrier, which the guard opened as she approached. With flying feet she neared her own apartments, whence issued the indignant wail of her implacable baby girl. As she opened the door, her husband held the disconsolate child toward her.

"You are in time for your share of the fun; I have had enough and to spare. How you stand this diabolical din day in, day out, passes my comprehension. You had not been gone fifteen minutes when Missy tuned up. I patted and, 'She-e-d' her, but she got her head above cover, squinted around the room, and not finding you, set up a squall that would have scared a wildcat. The more I patted, the worse she screamed, and her feet and hands flew around like a wind-mill. I took her up, and trotted her on my knee, but bless you! she squirmed like an eel, and her little bald head bobbed up and down faster than a di-dapper. Then I walked her, but I would as soon try to swing to a greased snake. She wriggled and bucked, and tied herself up into a bow knot, and yelled—. Oh! a Comanche papoose is a dummy to her. As if I had not hands full, arms full, and ears full, Dick must needs wake up and pitch head foremost out of the cradle, and turn a double summerset before he landed upside down on the floor, whereupon he lifted up his voice, and the concert grew lively. I took him under one arm, so, and laid Missy over my shoulder, and it struck me I would join the chorus in self defence, so I opened with all my might on 'Hold the Fort'; but great Tecumseh! I only insulted them both, and finding my fifth fiddle was nowhere in the fray, I feared Jarvis would hear the howling and ring the alarm bell, so I just sat down. I spread out Dick in a soft place, where he could not bump his brains out, and laying my lady across my lap, I held her down by main force, while she screamed till she was black in the face. If you had not come just when you did, I should have turned gray and cross-eyed. Hello, Missy! If she is not cooing and laughing! Little vixen! Oh! but—'lambs'!—I believe they are! Hereafter tend your own flock; and in preference I will herd young panthers."

He wiped his forehead where the perspiration stood in drops, and watched with amazement the sudden lull in the tempest.

Clasped in her mother's arms, the baby smiled and gurgled, and Dick, drying his eyes on the maternal bosom, showed the exact spot where she must kiss his bruised head.

"Ned, what have you done? This baby's hair is dripping wet, and so is the neck of her dress."

"Serves her right, too. I sprinkled her, that's all."

"Sprinkled her! Have you lost your senses?"

"Shouldn't wonder if I had; people in bedlam are apt to be crazy. Yes, I sprinkled Missy, because she turned so black in the face, I thought she was strangling; and my step-mother always sprinkled me when I had a fit of tantrums. But let me tell you, Missy will never be a zealous Baptist, she doesn't take to water kindly."

"When I want my children step-mothered I will let you know. Give me that towel, and baby's woollen cap hanging on the knob of the bureau. Bless her precious heart! if she does not keep you up all night, with the croup, you may thank your stars."

"Susie, just tell me how you tame them, so that next time—"

"Next time, sir, I shall not trust you. I just love them, and they know it; that is what tames the whole world."

Edward Singleton stooped over his wife, and kissed her rosy cheek.

"Little woman, what luck had you in No. 19?"

"The best I could wish. I have saved that poor girl from brain-fever, I hope."

"How did you manage it?"

"Just simply because I am a flesh and blood woman, and not a blundering, cast-iron man."

"How does she seem now?"

"She has had a good, hearty spell of wholesome crying; no hysterics, mind you, but floods of tears; and now she is sound asleep with her head on the altar railing, in the chapel. I locked her up there, and here is the key. When she wakes, I want her brought up here, put in that room yonder, and left entirely to me, until her trial is over. I never do things half way, Ned, and you need not pucker your eyebrows, for I will be responsible for her. I have put my hand to the plough, and you are not to meddle with the lines, till I finish my furrow."

CHAPTER VIII.

In one of the "outhouses" which constituted the servants' quarters, in that which common parlance denominated the "back-yard" at "Elm Bluff," an old negro woman sat smoking a pipe.

The room which she had occupied for more than forty years, presented a singular melange of incongruous odds and ends, the flotsam of a long term of service, where the rewards, if intrinsically incommensurate, were none the less invaluable, to the proud recipient. The floor was covered by a faded carpet, once the pride of the great drawing-room, but the velvet pile had disappeared beneath the arched insteps and high heels of lovely belles and haughty beaux, and the scarlet feathers and peacock plumes that originally glowed on the brilliant buff ground, were no longer distinguishable.

An old-fashioned piece of furniture, coeval with diamond shoe-buckles, ruffled shirts and queues, a brass bound mahogany chiffonier, with brass handles and tall brass feet representing cat claws, stood in one corner; and across the top was stretched a rusty purple velvet strip, bordered with tarnished gilt gimp and fringe, a fragment of the cover which belonged to the harp on which General Darrington's grandmother had played.

The square bedstead was a marvel in size and massiveness, and the heavy mahogany posts nearly black with age, and carved like the twisted strands of a rope, supported a tester lined with turkey-red pleatings, held in the centre by the talons of a gilt spread-eagle. So tall was the bed, that three steps were required to ascend it, and the space thus left between the mahogany and the floor, was hidden by a valance of white dimity, garnished with wide cotton fringe. Over this spacious place of repose, a patchwork quilt of the "rising sun" pattern displayed its gaudy rays, resembling some sprawling octopus, rather than the face of Phoebus.

The contents of a wide mantel board flounced with fringed dimity, (venerable prototype of macrame and Arrasene lambrequins), would have filled with covetousness the soul of the bric-a-brac devotee; and graced the counters of Sypher.

There were burnished brass candle-sticks, with extinguishers in the shape of prancing griffins, and snuffers of the same metal, fashioned after the similitude of some strange and presumably extinct saurian; and a Dresden china shepherdess, whose shattered crook had long since disappeared, peeped coquettishly through the engraved crystal of a tall candle shade at the bloated features of a mandarin, on a tea-pot with a cracked spout—that some Darrington, stung by the gad-fly of travel, had brought to the homestead from Nanking. A rich blue glass vase poised on the back of a bronze swan, which had lost one wing and part of its bill in the combat with time, hinted at the rainbow splendors of its native Prague, and bewailed the captivity that degraded its ultra-marine depths into a receptacle for cut tobacco.

The walls, ceiled with curled pine planks, were covered with a motley array of pasted and tacked pictures; some engraved, many colored, and ranging in comprehensiveness of designs, from Bible scenes cut from magazines, to "riots" in illustrated papers; and even the garish glory of circus and theatre posters.

In one corner stood an oak spinning-wheel, more than centenarian in age, fallen into hopeless desuetude, but gay with the strings of scarlet pepper pods hung up to dry, and twined among its silent spokes. On a trivet provided with lizard feet that threatened to crawl away, rested a copper kettle bereft of its top, once the idol of three generations of Darringtons, to whom it had liberally dispensed "hot water tea," in the blessed dead and embalmed era of nursery rule and parental power; now eschewed with its despised use, and packed to the brim with medicinal "yarbs," bone-set, horse mint, life everlasting, and snake-root.

In front of the fire which roared and crackled in the cavernous chimney, "Mam' Dyce" rocked slowly, enjoying her clay pipe, and meditatively gazing up at an engraved portrait of "Our First President," suspended on the wall. It was appropriately framed in black, and where the cord that held it was twined around a hook, a bow and streamers of very brown and rusty crape fluttered, when a draught entered the apartment.

Obese in form, and glossy black in complexion, "Mam' Dyce" retained in old age the scrupulous neatness which had characterized her youth, when promoted to the post of seamstress and ladies' maid, she had ruled the servants' realm at "Elm Bluff" with a sway as autocratic as that of Catherine over the Muscovites. Her black calico dress, donned as mourning for her master, was relieved by a white apron tied about the ample waist; a snowy handkerchief was crossed over the vast bosom, and a checked white and black turban skilfully wound in intricate folds around her gray head, terminated in a peculiar knot, which was the pride of her toilet. A beautiful spotted pointer dog with ears like brown satin, was lying asleep near the fire, but suddenly he lifted his head, rose, stretched himself and went to the door. A moment later it opened, and the whilom major-domo, Abednego, came in; put his stick in one corner, hung his hat on a wooden peg, and approached the fireplace.

"Well, ole man; you know I tole you so."

"You wimmen would ruther say that, than eat pound cake. Supposin' you did tell me, what's the upshot?"

"That gimlet-eyed weasel is snuffing round you and me; but we won't turn out to be spring chickens, ready picked."

"Which is to signify that Miss Angerline smells a mouse? Don't talk parables, Dyce. What's she done now?"

"She is hankering after that hankchiff. 'Pears to me, if she only went on four legs 'sted of two, she would sell high for a bloodhound."

"Great Nebuckadanzer! How did she find out?"

"Don't ax me; ax the witches what she has in cahoot. I always tole you, she had the eyes of a cunjor, and she has sarched it out. Says she saw you when you found it; which ain't true. Eavesdrapping is her trade; she was fotch up on it, and her ears fit a key-hole, like a bung plugs a barrel. She has eavesdrapped that hankchiff chat of our'n somehow. Wuss than that, Bedney, she sot thar this evening and faced me down, that I was hiding something else; that I picked up something on the floor and hid it in my bosom, after the crowner's inquess. Sez I: 'Well, Miss Angerline, you had better sarch me and be done with it, if you are the judge, and the jury, and the crowner, and the law, and have got the job to run this case.' Sez she, a-squinting them venomous eyes of her'n, till they looked like knitting needles red hot: 'I leave the sarching to be done by the cunstable—when you are 'rested and handcuffed for 'betting of murder.' Then my dander riz. Sez I, 'Crack your whip and go ahead! You know how, seeing you is the offspring of a Yankee overseer, what my marster, Gin'l Darrington, had 'rested for beating one of our wimen, on our 'Bend' plantation. You and your pa is as much alike, as two shrivelled cow peas out'en one pod. Fetch your cunstable, and help yourselves.'"

Dyce rose, knocked the ashes out of her pipe, and stood like a dusky image of an Ethiopian Bellona.

"Drat your servigerous tongue! Now the fat's in the fire, to be sho! Ever since I tuck you for better for wuss, I have been trying to larn you 'screshun! and I might as well 'a wasted my time picking a banjo for a dead jackass tu dance by; for you have got no more 'screshun than old Eve had, in confabulating with the old adversary! Why couldn't you temperlize? Sassing that white 'oman, is a aggervating mistake."

Under ordinary circumstances, Bedney and Dyce prided themselves on the purity of their diction, and they usually abstained from plantation dialect; but when embarrassed, frightened or excited, they invariably relapsed into the lingo of the "Quarters."

"Hush! What's that? A screech owull! Bedney, turn your pocket."

With marvellous swiftness she plunged her hand into her dress pocket, and turned it wrong side out, scattering the contents—thimble, thread, two "scalybarks," and some "ground peas" over the floor. Then stooping, she slipped off one shoe, turned it upside down, and hung it thus on a horseshoe fastened to the mantel board.

"Just lem'me know when you have appinted to hold your sarching, and I will make it convenient to have bizness consarning that bunch of horgs and cattle, I am raising on shares in the 'Bend' plantation: and you can have your sarching frolic," said Bedney, too angry to heed the superstitious rites.

Dyce made a warning gesture, and listened intently.

"I am a-thinking you will be chief cook and bottle-washer at that sarching, for the appintment is at hand. Don't you hear Pilot baying the cunstable?"

She sank into her rocking-chair, picked up a gray yarn sock, and began to knit unconcernedly; but in a significant tone, she added, nodding her head:

"Hold your own hand, Bedney; don't be pestered about mine. I'll hoe my row; you 'tend to yourn."

Then she leaned back, plying her knitting needles, and began to chant: "Who will be the leader when the Bridegroom comes?"

Hearing the knock on the door, her voice swelled louder, and Bedney, the picture of perplexity, stood filling his pipe, when the bolt was turned, and a gentleman holding a whip and wearing a long overcoat entered the room.

"Good evening, Bedney. Are you and Dyce holding a camp meeting all by yourselves? I hallooed at the gate till your dog threatened to devour me, and I had to scare him off with my buggy whip."

"Why, how'dy, Mars Alfred? I am mighty glad to see you! Seems like old times, to shake hands with you in my cabin. Lem'me take off your overcoat, sir, and gim'me your hat, and make yourself comfortable, here by the jam of the chimbly."

"No, Bedney, I can't spare the time, and I only want a little business matter settled before I get back to town to my office. Thank you, Dyce, this is an old-time rocker sure enough. It is a regular 'Sleepy Hollow.'"

Mr. Churchill pushed back his hat, and held his gloved hand toward the fire.

"Bedney, I want to see that handkerchief you found in your master's room, the day after he was murdered."

"What hankchuf, Marse Alfred? I done tole everything I know, to the Crowner's inquess."

"I dare say you did; but something was found afterward. I want to see it."

"Who has been villifying of me? You have knowed me ever since you was knee-high to a duck, and I—."

"Nobody has vilified you, but Miss Dobbs saw you examining something, which she says you pushed up your coat sleeve. She thinks it was a handkerchief, but it may have been valuables. Now it is my duty, as District Solicitor, to discover and prosecute the person who killed your master, and you ought to render me every possible assistance. Any unwillingness to give your testimony, or surrender the articles found, will cast suspicion on you, and I should be sorry to have you arrested."

"Fore Gord, Marse Alfred, I—"

"Own up, husband. You did find a hankchef. You see, Marse Alfred, we helped to raise that poor young gal's mother; and Bedney and me was 'votedly attached to our young Mistiss, Miss Ellie, and we thought ole Marster was too hard on her, when she run off with the furrin fiddler; so when this awful 'fliction fell upon us and everybody was cusing Miss Ellie's child of killing her own grandpa, we couldn't believe no such onlikely yarn, and Bedney and me has done swore our vow, we will stand by that poor young creetur, for her ma's sake; for our young mistiss was good to us, and our heart strings was 'rapped round her. We does not intend, if we can help it, to lend a hand in jailing Miss Ellie's child, and so, after the Crowner had 'liced all the facts as he said, and the verdict was made up, Bedney and me didn't feel no crampings in our conscience, about holding our tongues. Another reason why we wanted to lay low in this hiere bizness, was that we didn't hanker after sitting on the anxious seats of witnesses in the court-house; and being called ongodly thieves, and perjured liars, and turned wrong side out by the lie-yers, and told our livers was white, and our hearts blacker than our skins. Marse Alfred, Bedney and me are scared of that court; what you call the law, cuts curous contarabims sometimes, and when the broad axe of jestice hits, there is no telling whar the chips will fly; it's wuss than hull-gull, or pitching heads and tails. You are a lie-yer, Marse Alfred, and you know how it is yourself; and I beg your pardon, sir, for slighting the perfession; but when I was a little gal, I got my scare of lie-yers, and it has stuck to me like a kuckleburrow. One Christmas eve jest before ole Marster got married, he had a egg-nog party; and a lot of gentlemen was standing 'round the table in the dining-room. One of 'em was ole Mr. Dunbar, Marse Lennox' father, and he axed ole Marster if he had saved that game rooster for him, as he promised, Marster told him he was very sorry, but some rogue had done gone and burnt some sulphur the week before in his henhouse, and bagged that 'dentical rooster. Presently Mr. Dunbar axed if Marster would let him have one of the blue hen's roosters, if he would catch the rogue for him before midnight. Of course Marster said he would. Mr. Dunbar (Marse Lennox' pa), he was practicing law then, had a pot full of smut on the bottom, turned upside down on the dining-room flo', and he and Marster went out to the hen-'ouse and got a dominicker rooster and shoved him under the pot. Then they rung the bell, and called every darkey on the place into the dining-room, and made us stand in a line. I was a little gal then, only so high, but I followed my daddy in the house, and I never shall disremember that night, 'cause it broke up our home preachment. Mr. Dunbar made a speech, and the upshot of it was, that every darkey was to walk past the pot and rub his finger in the smut; and he swore a solemn oath, that when the pusson that stole that fine game rooster, touched the pot, the dominicker rooster would crow. As Marster called our names, we every one marched out and rubbed the pot, and when all of us had tried, the rooster hadn't crowed. Mr. Dunbar said there was some mistake somewhere, and he made us step up and show hands, and make prints on his hankcher; and lo, and behold! one darkey had not touched the pot; his forefinger was clean; so Mr. Dunbar says, 'Luke, here is your thief!' and shore 'nuff, it was our preacher, and he owned up. I never forgot that trick, and from that day 'till now, I have been more scared of a lie-yer, than I am of a mad dog. They is the only perfession that the Bible is agin, for you know they jawed our Lord hisself, and he said, 'Woe! woe! to you lie-yers.' Now, Marse Alfred, if you have made up your mind you are gwine to have that hankcher, it will be bound to come; for if it was tied to a millstone and drapped in the sea, you lie-yers would float it into court; so Bedney, jest perduce what you found."

"That is right, Dyce; I am glad your opinion of my profession has forced you to such a sensible conclusion. Come, Bedney, no balking now."

Perplexed by Dyce's tactics, Bedney stood irresolute, with his half-filled pipe slipping from his fingers; and he stared at his wife for a few seconds, hoping that some cue would be furnished.

"Bedney, there's no use in being cantankerous. If you won't perduce it, I will."

Plunging her hand into the blue glass bowl, she pushed aside the tobacco, and extracted a key; then crossed the room, lifted the valance of the patriarchal bed, and dragged out a small, old-fashioned hair trunk, ornamented with stars and diamonds of brass tack heads. Drawing it across the floor, she sat down near Mr. Churchill, and bending over, unlocked and opened it. After removing many articles of clothing, and sundry heirlooms, she lifted from the bottom a bundle, which she laid on her lap, and edging her chair closer to the Solicitor, proceeded to unfold the contents. The outside covering was a richly embroidered Canton crape shawl, originally white, now yellow as old ivory; but when this was unwrapped, there appeared only an ordinary sized brown gourd, with a long and singularly curved handle, as crooked as a ram's horn. Bending one of her knitting needles into a hook, Dyce deftly inserted it in the neck, where it joined the bowl, and after manoeuvring a few seconds, laid down the needle, and with the aid of her thumb and forefinger slowly drew out a long roll, tightly wrapped with thread. Unwinding it, she shook the roll, and a small, gray object, about two inches long, dropped into her lap. Mr. Churchill sat leaning a little forward, as if intent on Dyce's movements, but his elbow rested on the arm of the rocking chair, and holding his hand up to screen his face from the blaze of the fire, he was closely watching Bedney. When Dyce shook out and held up a faded, dingy blue silk handkerchief, the lawyer noted a sudden twinkle in the old man's eyes, but no other feature moved, and he stooped to take a coal of fire from the hearth.

"There is the hankchuf that Bedney found. But mebbe you don't know what this is, that I wrapped up in it, to bring us good luck?"

She spread the handkerchief over his knee, and held up the small gray furry object, which had fallen from its folds.

"Rabbit's foot? Let me see; yes, that is the genuine left hind foot. I know all about it, because when my regiment was ordered to the front, my old colored Mammy—Ma'm Judy—who nursed me, sewed one just like that, inside the lining of my coat skirt. But, Dyce, that rabbit's foot was not worth a button; for the very first battle I was in, a cannon ball killed my horse under me, and carried away my coat tail—rabbit's foot and all. Don't pin your faith to left hind feet, they are fatal frauds. You are positive, this is the handkerchief Bedney found? It smells of asafoetida and camphor, and looks like it had recently been tied around somebody's sore throat."

"Marse Alfred, I will swear on a stack of Bibles high as the 'Piscopal church steeple, that Bedney Darrington gim'me that same blue hankcher, and he said he found it. I wasn't with him when he found it, but I hardly think he would 'a stole a' old rag like that. I have perduced it! now if you want to sarch behind it, you must tackle Bedney."

She resumed her knitting and her lips closed like the spring of a steel trap.

"Dyce, I haven't heard the rooster crow yet. Somebody has fought shy of the pot. See here, I am in earnest now, and I will give you both a friendly word of warning. Your actions are so suspicious, that unless you produce the real article you found, I shall be obliged to send you to jail, and try you for the murder. How do I know that you and Bedney are not the guilty parties, instead of General Darrington's granddaughter? This soiled rag will impose neither upon me, nor upon the court, and I give you five minutes to put into my possession the real genuine handkerchief. I shall know it when I see it, because it is white, with red spots on the border."

"Paddle your own 'dug out,' Bedney, and show your s'creshun. If Marse Alfred wants to set the red-eyed hounds of the Law on an innocent 'oman, let him blow his horn."

She knitted assiduously, and looked composedly at her husband, whose lower jaw had suddenly fallen, while his eyelids blinked nervously, as though attacked by St. Vitus' dance.

"Only five minutes, Bedney."

Mr. Churchill took out his watch, and held it open.

"You see, Marse Alfred, I—"

"I don't see anything but an infernal fraud you two have planned. Only three minutes more. There is a constable waiting at the gate, and if he can not persuade you to—"

"Bedney, step and fetch him in, and let Marse Alfred see the sarching job done up all right."

"No, I don't hunt foxes that way. Instead of searching this cabin, we will just march you both instanter out of these comfortable quarters, and let you try how soft the beds are, at the 'State boarding-house.' You will sleep cold on iron bunks, and miss your feathers and your crazy quilts. Time's up."

He closed his watch, with a snap, and rose as he returned it to his pocket.

"Hold on, Marse Alfred! My head ain't hard enough to run it plum into a wolf's jaws. I ain't 'sponsible for nobody's acts but my own, and if Dyce have committed a pius fraud, in this here hank'cher bizness, to screen Miss Ellie's child, why, you see yourself, I had no hand in it. I did find that blue 'rag,' as you seen fit to call it, but it was nigh on to twenty years ago, when I pulled it out of the breast pocket of a dead Yankee officer, we found lying across a cannon, what my old Marster's regiment captured at the battle of Manassas. I gin it to my wife as a screw-veneer o' the war and she have treasured it accordin'. You are a married man yourself, Marse Alfred, and you are obleedged to know that wedlock is such a tight partnership, that it is an awfully resky thing for a man to so much as bat his eyes, or squint 'em, toward the west, when the wife of his bosom has set her'n to the east. I have always 'lowed Dyce her head, 'pecially in jokes like that one she was playing on you just now, 'cause St. John the Baptist said a man must forsake father and mother and cleave unto his wife; but conjugular harness is one thing, and the law is another, and I don't hanker after forsaking my pine-knot fire, and feather bed, to cleave unto jail bars, and handcuffs. I see you are tired of Dyce's jokes, and you mean bizness; and I don't intend to consume no more of your valuable solicitous time. Dyce, fetch me that plank bottom cher to stand on."

"Fetch it yourself. Paddling your own canoe, means headin' for the mill dam."

Bedney hastened to procure the designated chair, which he mounted in front of the mantel piece, and thence reaching up to the portrait of President Lincoln, took it carefully down from the hook. With the blade of his pocket-knife, he loosened some tacks which secured the thin pine slats at the back of the picture, and removed them. He took everything from the frame, and blank dismay seized him, when the desired object was nowhere visible.

"Marse Alfred, I swear I tacked that hank'cher in the back of this here portrait, between the pasteboard and the brown paper, only yestiddy, and 'fore Gord! I haint seen it since."

Grasping his wife's shoulder, he shook her, until her tall turban quivered and bent over like the Tower of Pisa, and Mr. Churchill saw that in his unfeigned terror, drops of perspiration broke out on his wrinkled forehead.

"Have you turned idjut, that you want us both to be devoured by the roarin' lion of the Law? My mammy named me Bedney, not Dani-yell, and she had oughter, for Gord knows, you have kept me in a fiery furnace ever since I tuck you for better for wurser, mostly wurser. I want that hank'cher, and you'd better believe—I want it quick. I found it, and I'm gwine to give it up; and you have got no right to jeppardy my life, if you are fool enough to resk your own stiff neck. Gim'me that hank'cher! Fantods is played out. I would ruther play leap frog over a buzz-saw than—than—pester and rile Marse Alfred, and have the cunstable clawing my collar."

"You poor, pitiful, rascally, cowardly creetur! Whar's that oath you done swore, to help 'fend Miss Ellie's child? And you a deacon, high in the church! If I had found that hank'cher, I would hide it, till Gabriel's horn blows; and I would go to jail or to Jericho; and before I would give testimony agin my dear young Mistiss's poor friendless gal, I would chaw my tongue into sassage meat. That's the diffunce between a palavering man full of 'screshun, and a 'oman who means what she says; and will stand by her word, if it rains fire and brimstone. Betrayin' and denying the innercent, has been men's work, ever since the time of Judas and Peter. Now, Marse Alfred, Bedney did tack the hank'cher inside the portrait of President Linkum, 'cause we thought that was the saftest place, but I knowed the house would be sarched, so I jest hid it in a better place. Since he ain't showed no more backbone than a saucer of blue-mange, I shall have to give it up; but if I had found it, you would never set your two eyes on it, while my head is warm."

She stooped, lifted the wide hem of her black calico skirt, and proceeded to pick out the stitches which held it securely. When she had ripped the thread about a quarter of a yard, she raised the edge of the unusually deep hem, and drew out a white handkerchief with a colored border.

Bedney snatched it from her, and handed it to the Solicitor, who leaned close to the fire, and carefully examined it. As he held it up by the corners, his face became very grave and stern, and he sighed.

"This is evidently a lady's handkerchief, and is so important in the case, that I shall keep it until the trial is over. Bedney, come to my office by nine o'clock to-morrow, as the Grand Jury may ask you some questions. Good bye, Dyce, shake hands; for I honor your loyalty to your poor young mistress, and her unfortunate child. You remind me of my own old mammy. Dear good soul, she was as true as steel."

As Mr. Churchill left the house, Bedney accompanied him to the gate. When he returned, the door was locked. In vain he demanded admittance; in vain tried the windows; every entrance was securely barred, and though he heard Dyce moving about within, she deigned no answer to his earnest pleadings, his vehement expostulations, or his fierce threats of summary vengeance. The remainder of that night was spent by Pilot and his irate master in the great hay bin of the "Elm Bluff" stables. When the sun rose next morning, Bedney rushed wrathful as Achilles, to resent his wrongs. The door of his house stood open; a fire glowed on the well swept hearth, where a pot of boiling coffee and a plate of biscuit welcomed him; but Dyce was nowhere visible, and a vigorous search soon convinced him she had left home on some pressing errand.

Two hours later, Mrs. Singleton opened the door of the small room adjoining her own bedchamber, to which she had insisted upon removing the prisoner.

Beryl stood leaning against the barred window, and did not even turn her head.

"Here is a negro woman, begging to see you for a few moments. She says she is an old family servant of General Darrington's."

Standing with her back toward the door, the prisoner put out one hand with a repellent gesture:

"I have surely suffered enough from General Darrington and his friends; and I will see nobody connected with that fatal place, which has been a curse to me."

"Just as you please; but old Auntie here, says she nursed your mother, and on that account wants to see you."

Without waiting for permission, Dyce darted past the warden's wife, into the room, and almost before Beryl was aware of her presence, stood beside her.

"Are you Miss Ellie's daughter?"

Listlessly the girl turned and looked at her, and Dyce threw her arms around her slender waist, and falling on her knees hid her face in Beryl's dress, sobbing passionately. In the violence of her emotion, she rocked back and forth, swaying like a reed in some fierce blast the tall form, to whom she clung.

"Oh, my lovely! my lovely! To think you should be shut up here! To see Miss Ellie's baby jailed, among the off-scourings of the earth! Oh, you beautiful white deer! tracked and tore to pieces by wolves, and hounds, and jackalls! Oh, honey! Just look straight at me, like you was facing your accusers before the bar of God, and tell me you didn't kill your grandpa. Tell me you never dipped your pretty hands in ole Marster's blood."

Tears were streaming down Dyce's cheeks.

"If you knew my mother, how can you think it possible her child could commit an awful crime?"

"Oh, God knows—I don't know what to think! 'Peers to me the world is turned upside down. You see, honey, you are half and half; and while I am perfectly shore of Miss Ellie's half of you, 'cause I can always swear to our side, the Darrington in you, I can't testify about your pa's side; he was a—a—"

"He was as much a gentleman, as my mother was a lady; and I would rather be his daughter, than call a king my father."

"I believe you! There ain't no drop of scrub blood in you, as I can see, and if you ain't thoroughbred, 'pearances are deceitful. I loved your ma; I loved the very ground her little feet trod on. I fed her out of my own plate many a time, 'cause she thought her Mammy's vittils was sweeter than what Mistiss 'lowed her to have; and she have slept in my bosom, and these arms have carried her, and hugged her, and—and—oh, Lord God A'mighty! it most kills me to see you, her own little baby here! In this awful, cussed den of thieves and villi-yans! Oh, honey! for God's sake, just gin me some 'surance you are as pure as you look; just tell me your soul is a lily, like your face."

Beryl stooped, put her hand on the turbaned head, and bending it back, so as to look down into the swimming eyes, answered:

"If I had died when I was a month old, my baby soul would not have faced God any more innocent of crime then, than I am to-day. I had no more to do with taking General Darrington's money and his life, than the archangels in Heaven."

"Bless God! Now I am satisfied. Now I see my way clare. But it sets my blood afire to see you here; it's a burning shame to put my dear young Mistiss' child in this beasts' cage. I can't help thinking of that poor beautiful white deer, what Marster found crippled, down at our 'Bend' Plantation, that some vagabond had shot. Marster fotch it up home, and of all the pitifulist sights!"

Dyce had risen, and covering her face with her white apron, she wept for some minutes.

"Are you not the wife of Bedney, who saved my mother's life, when the barn burned?"

"Yes, honey, I am Mam' Dyce, and if I am spared, I will try to save your'n. That is what has brung me here. You are 'cused of the robb'ry and the murder, and you have denied it in the court; but chile, the lie-yers are aworking day and night fur to hang you, and little is made of much, on your side, and much is spun out of little, on theirn. They are more cunning than foxes, and bloodthirstier than panters, and they no more git tired than the spiders, that spin and piece a web as fast as you break it. Three nights ago, I got down on my knees, and I kissed a little pink morocco slipper what your Ma wore the day when she took her first step from my arm to her own mother's knees, and I swore a solemn oath, if I could help free Miss Ellie's child, I would do it. Now I want to ask you one thing. Did you lose anything that day you come to our house, and had the talk with old Marster?"

"Nothing, but my peace and happiness."

"Are you shore you didn't drap your hank'cher?"

"Yes, I am sure I did not, because I wrapped it around some chrysanthemums I gathered as I went away."

"Well, a lady's hank'cher was found in Marster's room, and it did smell of chloryform. Bedney picked it up, and we said nothing and laid low, and hid the thing; but that Godforsaken and predestinated sinner, Miss Angeline, kept sarching and eavesdrapping, and set the lie-yers on the scent, and they have 'strained Bedney on peril of jailing him, to perduce it. When it got into their claws, and I thought it might belonk to you, my teeth chattered, and I felt like the back of my frock was a ice-warehouse. Now, honey, can you testify before God and man, that hank'cher ain't yourn?"

"I certainly can. I had only three handkerchiefs with me when I left home, and I have them still. Here is one, the other two lie yonder. But that handkerchief is worth everything; because it must belong to the vile wretch who committed the crime, and it will help to prove my innocence. Where is it?"

"The Grand Jury is setting on it."

Here Dyce looked cautiously around, and tip-toed to the door; finding it ajar, closed it, then stole back. Putting her lips close to Beryl's ear, she whispered:

"Did you lose a sleeve button?"

"No. I did not wear any."

"Thank God! I feel like all the bricks in the court-house was lifted off my heart, and flung away. I was in fear and trimbling about that button, 'cause I picked it up, just under the aidge of the rug, where ole Marster fell, when he got his death blow; and as sure as the coming of the Judgment Day, it was drapped by the pusson who killed him. I was so afeared it might belonk to you, that I have been on the anxious seat ever since I found it; and I concluded the safest way was to bring it here to you. I am scared to keep it at home, 'cause them yelping wolves as wears the sheepskins of Justice, are on my tracks. I would never give it up, if I was chopped to mince meat; but Bedney ain't got no more than enuff backbone for half of a man, and the lie-yers discomfrizzle him so, I could not trust him, when it comes to the scratch. Now that button is worth a heap, and I am precious careful of it. Look here."

She took from her pocket two large pods of red pepper, which looked exactly alike, but the end of one had been cut out around the stem, then neatly fitted back, and held in place by some colorless cement. Beckoning Beryl to follow, Dyce went closer to the window, and with the aid of her teeth drew out the stem. Into her palm rolled a circular button of some opaque reddish-brown substance, resembling tortoise shell, and enamelled with gilt bunches of grapes, and inlaid leaves of mother-of-pearl. Across the top, embossed in gilt letters ran the word "Ricordo."

The old woman lifted her open palm, and as Beryl saw the button, a gasping, gurgling sound broke from her. She snatched it, stared at it. Then the Gorgon head slipped through her fingers, she threw herself against the window, shook the iron bar frantically; and one desperate cry seemed to tear its way through her clinched teeth, over her ashy lips:

"Oh, Mother! Mother—Mother! You are nailing me to a cross."

CHAPTER IX.

Nowhere in the vast vista of literature is there an episode more exquisitely pathetic than that serene picture of the Grove at Colonus, sacred to the "Semnai Theai;" where the dewy freshness, the floral loveliness, the spicery, and all the warbling witchery of nature pay tribute to the Avenging Goddesses.

Twenty-two centuries have sifted their dust over the immortal figures seated on the marble bench within the precincts consecrated to the Eumenides, but in deathless tenacity, the rich aroma of Sophocles' narcissus, and the soft crocus light linger there still; while from thickets of olive, nightingales break their hearts in song, as thrilling as the melody that smote the ears of doomed and dying Oedipus.

So in all ages, we, born thralls of grief, lift streaming eyes, and chant elegies to stony-hearted Mother-Earth, but her starry orbs shine on, undimmed by sympathetic tears; her smiling lips show only sunshine in their changeless dimples, and her myriad fingers sweeping the keys of the Universal Organ, drown our De Profundis in the rhythmic thunders of her Jubilate. Wailing children of Time, we crouch and tug at the moss-velvet, daisy-sprinkled skirts of the mighty Mater, praying some lullaby from her to soothe our pain; but human woe frets not her sublime serenity, as deaf as desert sphinx, she fronts the future.

Some echo of this maddening mystery sounded in the ears of the lonely woman, who clutched the bars of her dungeon, and stared through its iron lattice, at the peaceful, happy, outside world. At her feet lay X——, divided by the silvery river, which, here rushed with arrowy swiftness under the gray stone arches of the bridge, and there widened into glassy lakelets, as if weary from the mad plunge over a distant rocky ledge in mid-stream, whence the dull steady roar of the "falls" thrilled the atmosphere, like the "tremolo" in a dim cathedral, where fading daylight dies on painted apse and gilded pipes. As a chessboard the squares of buildings were spread out, defined by wide streets, where humanity and its traffic sped, busy as ants. In a green plot, the sombre facade of the court-house surmounted by an eyeless stone statue of Justice, frowned on the frivolous throng below; and along the verge of the common, marble fingers pointed up to the heaven of blue that bent above "God's Acre"; while now and then, bulbous towers, and glittering steeple vanes, caught the sunshine on their polished crests. Beyond the whole, and bounding the valley filled with a billowy sea of bluish-green pine tops, rose a wooded eminence, wearing still its Persian robe of autumn foliage, and on its brow the colonnade and chimneys of "Elm Bluff" blotted the southern sky, like a threatening phantom.

To-day forest, stream, earth and sky, appeared branded with one fatal word, as if the world's wide page held only "Ricordo! Ricordo!"

Beryl shut her eyes and groaned; but the scene merely shifted to a dell under the shadow of Carrara hills, where olives set "Ricordo" among their silver leaves; and lemons painted "Ricordo" in their pale gold; and scarlet pomegranates and nodding violets, burning anemones and tender green of trailing maiden-hair ferns all blazoned "Ricordo."

The fierce tide of wrath, that indignation and her keen sense of outraged innocence had poured like molten lead through her throbbing arteries, was oozing sluggishly, congealing under the awful spell of that one word "Ricordo." Hitherto, the shame of the suspicion, the degradation of the imprisonment had caught and empaled her thoughts; but by degrees, these became dwarfed by the growing shadow of a possibly ignominious death, which spread its sable pinions along the rosy dawn of her womanhood, and devoured the glorious sun of her high hopes. The freezing gloom was creeping nearer, and to-day she could expect no succor, save by one avenue.

Islam believes that only the cimeter edge of Al Sirat divides Paradise from perdition. Beryl realized that in her peril, she trod an equally narrow snare, over yawning ruin, holding by a single thread of hope that handkerchief. Weak natures shiver and procrastinate, shunning confirmation of their dread; but to this woman had come a frantic longing to see, to grasp, to embrace the worst. She was in a death grapple with appalling fate, and that handkerchief would decide the issue.

Physical exhaustion was following close upon the mental agony that had stretched her on the rack, for so many days and nights. To sit still was impossible, yet in her wandering up and down the narrow room, she reeled, and sometimes staggered against the wall, dizzy from weakness, to which she would not succumb.

Human help was no more possible for her, than for Moses, when he climbed Nebo to die; and alone with her God, the brave soul wrestled. Wearily she leaned against the window bars, twining her hot fingers around them, pressing her forehead to the cold barrier; and everywhere "Ricordo" stabbed her eyes like glowing steel.

The door opened, some words were uttered in an undertone, then the bolt clicked in its socket, and Mr. Dunbar approached the window. Mechanically Beryl glanced over her shoulder, and a shiver crept across her.

"I believe you know me. Dunbar is my name."

He stood at her side, and they looked into each other's eyes, and measured lances. Could this worn, pallid woman, be the same person who in the fresh vigor of her youthful beauty, had suggested to him on the steps of "Elm Bluff," an image of Hygeia? Here insouciante girlhood was dead as Manetho's dynasties, and years seemed to have passed over this auburn head since he saw it last. Human faces are Nature's highest type of etchings, and mental anguish bites deeper than Dutch mordant; heart-ache is the keen needle that traces finest lines.

"Yes, I know you only too well. You are Tiberius."

Her luminous deep eyes held his at bay, and despite his habitual, haughty equipoise, her crisp tone of measureless aversion stung him.

"Sarcasm is an ill-selected arbiter between you and me; and your fate for all time, your future weal or woe is rather a costly shuttlecock to be tossed to and fro in a game of words. I do not come to bandy phrases, and in view of your imminent peril, I cannot quite understand your irony."

"Understand me? You never will. Did the bloodthirsty soul of Tiberius comprehend the stainless innocence of the victims he crushed for pastime on the rocks below Villa Jovis? There is but one arbiter for your hatred, the hang-man, to whom you would so gladly hurry me. Hunting a woman to the gallows is fit sport for men of your type."

Unable to withdraw his gaze from the magnetism of hers, he frowned and bit his lip. Was she feigning madness, or under the terrible nervous strain, did her mind wander?

"Your language is so enigmatical, that I am forced to conclude you resort to this method of defence. The exigencies of professional duty compel me to assume toward you an attitude, as painfully embarrassing to me as it is threatening to you. Because the stern and bitter law of justice sometimes entails keen sorrow upon those who are forced to execute her decrees, is it any less obligatory upon the appointed officers to obey the solemn behests?"

"Justice! Into what a frightful mockery have such as you degraded her worship! No wonder justice fled to the stars. You are the appointed officer of a harpy screaming for the blood of the innocent. How dare you commit your crimes, raise your red hands, in the sacred name of justice? Call yourself the priest of a frantic vengeance, for whom some victim must be provided; and libel no more the attribute of Jehovah."

Scorn curled her lips, and beneath her glowing eyes, his grew restless, as panoplied in conscious innocence she seemed to defy attack.

"You evidently credit me with motives of personal animosity, which would alike disgrace my profession and my manhood. For your sake, rather than my own, I should like to remove this erroneous impression from your mind. If you could only understand—"

She threw up her hand, with an imperious gesture of disdain.

"Save your sophistries; they are wasted here. Why multiply cobwebs? I understand you. If doves have a sixth sense that warns them before they hear the hawk's cry, or discern the shadow of his circling wings, and if mice, dumb in a cat's claws, surmise the exact value of the preliminary caresses, the graceful antics, the fatal fondling of the velvet paw, so we, the prey of legal 'Justice' know instinctively what the swinging of censers, and the chanting of her high priest mean, when he draws near us. I understand you. You intend to hang me if you can."

He drew his breath with a hissing sound, and a dark flush Stained his broad smooth brow.

"On my honor as a gentleman, I came here to-day solely to—"

41

"Solely to assure yourself of some doubtful link you must weld into your chain; solely to plunge the scalpel of some double-edged question. If there must be an ante mortem examination, we will wait, if you please, for the legal dissection when I am stretched before the jury-box. Until then, you have no right to intrude upon the misery you have brought on an innocent woman."

They stood so near each other, that he could count the fierce throbbing of the artery in her round snowy throat, and see the shadow of her long lashes; and again some electric current flashed from her feverishly bright eyes, burning its way to the secret chambers of his selfish heart, melting the dross that ambition and greed had slowly cemented, and dropping one deathless spark into a deep adytum, of the existence of which he had never even dreamed. Unconsciously he leaned toward her, but she pressed back against the iron bars, and drew her dress aside as if shunning a leper. There was no petulance in the motion, but its significance pricked him, like a dagger point.

"It was the hope of finding you an innocent woman, that must plead my pardon for what you consider an unwarrantable 'intrusion.' Will you believe me, if I swear to you, that I have come as a friend?"

"As a friend to me? No. As a friend to General Darrington and his adopted son Prince? Yes. Oh, Tiberius! Your rosy apples are flavored like those your forefather offered Agrippina."

"Do you regard me as an unscrupulous, calculating villain, who pretending kindness, plots treachery? Do you deliberately offer me this wanton insult?"

His swart face reddened, and the fine lines of his handsome mouth hardened.

She shrank a few inches closer to the window, and compressed her lips.

"If you were a man, I should swiftly resent the affront you have thrust upon me, and suitable redress would be peculiarly sweet and welcome; but you are a defenceless and unfortunate woman, and my hands are tied. I desire to help you; you repulse me and insult my manhood. I will do my painful duty, because it is sternly and inexorably my duty; but, I wish to God, I had never set my eyes on you."

The sudden passionate ring in his voice surprised her, and she looked searchingly at him, wondering into what pitfall it was intended to lure her.

"If you had never set your eyes on me? Ah, would to God I had died ten thousand times before I encountered their evil spell! If you had never set your eyes on me? I should be now, a happy, hopeful girl, with life beckoning me like the rosy Syrian plains that smiled on the desert-weary. The world looked so bright to me that day, when first I smelled the sweet resinous pines, and dreamed of my work, and all the glory of the victory, I knew that I should win over poverty and want. I was so poor in worldly goods, but oh!—Croesus could not have bought my proud hopes! So rich, so overflowing with high hope! As I think of my feelings that day, among the primroses and pine cones, it seems a hundred years ago, and I recall the image of a girl long dead; such a proud girl; so happy in the beautiful world of the art she loved! Then some strange awful curse that had lain in wait, ambushed among the flowers I gathered that last day of my dead existence, fell upon me—I saw you! No wonder I shivered, when you met me. I saw you. Then my sun sickened and went out, and my hopes crumbled, and my youth shrivelled and perished forever; and the wide world is a rayless dungeon, and the girl Beryl is buried so deep, that the Angels of the Resurrection will never find her!—and I?—I am only a withered, disgraced woman, hurled into a den; trampled, branded; with a soul devoured by despairing bitterness, with a broken heart, a brain on fire! If you had drawn a knife across my throat, or sent a bullet through my temples, my spirit might have rested in the Beyond, and I could have forgiven that which hastened me to heaven; but you strangled my hopes, and mutilated my youth, and dishonored my father's name!—You robbed me of my stainless character, and cast me among outlaws and fiends!—Worse yet, oh! blackest of all your crimes!—you have almost throttled my faith in Christ. You have torn away my hold upon the eternal God! You are the curse of my life. You wish you had never set your eyes on me? Take courage, finish your work; the best of me is utterly dead already, and when you have taken my blood, and laid my polluted body in a convict's shallow grave, your enmity will be satiated. Then I, at least, I shall be free from my hideous curse. If there be any comfort left me, it lurks in the knowledge that when you succeed in convicting me, the same world will no longer hold us both."

Was it the fever of disease, or incipient madness that blazed in her eyes, flamed on her cheeks, and lent such thrilling cadence to her pure clear voice? Was she a consummate actress, or had he made a frightful mistake, and goaded an innocent girl to the verge of frenzy? Some occult influence seemed clouding his hitherto infallible perceptions, melting his heart, paralyzing his will. He walked up and down the floor, with his hands clasped behind him, then came close to the prisoner.

"If I have unjustly suspected and persecuted you, may God forgive me! If I have wronged you by suspicion and accusation of a crime which you did not commit, then my atonement shall be your triumphant vindication. I would give a good deal to know that your hands are as pure as they look, and innocent of theft and murder. Tell me—tell me the truth. I will save you, I will give you back all that you have lost, and tenfold more. For God's sake, for your own sake, and for mine, I entreat you to tell me the truth. Did you go back to 'Elm Bluff' that night, after I met you in the pine woods?"

His dark face was close to hers, and his keen blue eyes seemed to probe the recesses of her soul. If she answered, would the steel springs of some trap close upon her?

"I did not go back to 'Elm Bluff.' My hands, my heart, my soul are as free from crime as they were when God sent them into the world, I am innocent—innocent—innocent as any baby only a week old, lying dead in its little coffin. Innocent—but defiled, disgraced; innocent as the Lord Jesus was of the sins for which He died; but you can not save what you have destroyed. You have ruined my life."

He was a strong man, cold, collected, priding himself upon his superb physique, his nerves of steel; but as he watched and listened, he trembled, and the girl's eyes dilated, sparkled through the sudden moisture that so strangely and unexpectedly gathered in his own.

"Then you must prove the truth of your solemn words; and it was this faint hope that induced me to come here to-day. Only one circumstance stands between the Grand Jury and your indictment for murder; and time presses. Now tell me, do you know this?"

He took from his coat pocket a small parcel wrapped in paper, and tore off the covering. Beryl stood faint and dizzy, resting against the window, but erect, on guard and defiant. He shook out and held up a square of fine linen, daintily hem-stitched. Along the border ran graceful arabesques, swelling into scallops and dotted with stars, embroidered in some rich red thread; and in one corner, enclosed in a wreath of exquisitely designed fuchsias, the large, elaborately ornate capitals "B. B." were worked in fadeless scarlet scrolls to match the wreath. Above the drooping flowers, poised the red wings of a descending butterfly. Artistic instincts had outlined, and deft delicate touches filled in, with the glowing embroidery.

Did she know it? Could she ever forget that serene May day when the air was liquid gold, and the Mediterranean molten sapphire, wreathed with pearls, as the wavelets crested; when the rosy oleanders and silvery flakes of orange blossoms floated down upon the ferny cliff, where sitting by her father's side, she had drawn this design, spreading the linen on the back of her father's worn copy of Theocritus? If she lived a thousand years, would it be possible to forget the thin, almost transparent white hand, with its blue veins swollen like cords, which had gently taken the pencil from her fingers, and retouched and rounded the sweep of the curves; the dear wasted hand that she had stooped and kissed, as it corrected her work?

As on the golden background of a cherished Byzantine picture, memory held untarnished every tint and outline of that blessed day, when she and her father had looked for the last time on the sunny sea they loved so well.

Did fell fate hover, even then, in that sparkling perfumed air, and in sinister prescience trace this tangling web of threads, with grim intent to snare her unwary feet?

Savants tell us, that ages ago, in the dim dawn, primeval rain drops made their pattering print, and left it to harden on the stone pages, awaiting decipherment by human eyes and human brains, not yet

"Born of the brainless Nature,
Who knew not that which she bore."

Is there an analogous iron chain linking the merest trifles, the frivolous accidents, the apparently worthless coincidences that swell the sum of what we are pleased to call the nobly independent life of the "free-agent" Man? In the matrix of time, do human tears and human blood-drops leave their record, to be conned when Nemesis holds her last assize?

As the handkerchief swayed in the lawyer's grasp, Beryl saw the red "B. B." like a bloody brand. At that instant she felt that the death clutch fastened upon her throat; that fate had cast her adrift, on the black waves of despair. In her reeling brain kaleidoscopic images danced; her father's face, the lateen sail of fishing boats rocking on blue billows, white oxen browsing amid purple iris clusters; she heard her mother's voice, her brother's gay laugh; she smelled the prussic acid fragrance of the vivid oleanders, then over all, like tongues of devouring flames, flickered "Ricordo." "B. B."

In the frenzy of her desperation she sprang forward, seized the arms that held up the fatal handkerchief, and shook the man, as if he had been an infant. Her eyes full of horror, were fixed on the scrap of linen, and a frantic cry rang from her lips.

"Father! Father! There is no hereafter for you and me! Prayer is but the mockery of fools! There is no heaven for the pure, because there is no God! No God!—to hear, to save the innocent who trusted in Him. Oh—no God!"

Mr. Dunbar dropped the handkerchief, and as the irresistible conviction of her guilt rolled back, crushing the hope he had cherished a moment before, a spasm of pain seized his heart, and with a groan that would not be repressed, he covered his eyes to shut out the vision of the despairing woman, whose doom seemed sealed. Her right hand which unconsciously clutched his left shoulder, shivered like an aspen, and he knew that for the moment she was entirely oblivious of his presence; blind to everything but the assurance of her ruin.

After all, he had made no mistake; his keen insight was well nigh infallible; but his triumph was costly. The luscious fruit of professional success left an acrid flavor; the pungent dead sea ashes sifted freely. He set his heel on the embroidered butterfly, and in his heart cursed the hour he had first seen it. His coveted bread was petrifying between his teeth.

The grasp on his shoulder relaxed, the hand fell heavily. When he looked in the face of his victim, he caught his breath at the strange, inexplicable change a few minutes had wrought. Protest and resistance had come to an end. Surrender was printed on every feature. The wild fury of the passionate struggle that convulsed her, had spent itself; and as after a violent wintry tempest the gale subsides, and the snow compassionately shrouds the scene, burning the dead sparrows, the bruised flowers, so submission laid her cold touch on this quivering face, and veiled and froze it.

From afar the sound of rushing waters seemed to smite Beryl's ears, to surge nearer, to overflow her brain. She sank suddenly to the floor, clinging with one hand to the window bar, and her auburn head fell forward on the up-lifted arm. Thinking that she had fainted, Mr. Dunbar stooped and raised her face, holding it in his palms. The eyes met his, unflinching but mournful as those of a tormented deer whom the hunters drag from worrying hounds. She writhed, freed herself from his touch; and resting against the window sill, drew a long deep breath.

"You have succeeded in your mission today. You have the only clue you needed. You have no occasion to linger. Now—will you leave me?"

He picked up the handkerchief.

"This is your handkerchief?"

She made no answer. A leaden hand was pressing upon her heart, her brain, her aching eyes.

"You have basely deceived me. You did go back that night, and you left this, to betray you. Saturated with chloroform you laid it over your grandfather's face. Load your soul with no more falsehoods. Confess the deeds of that awful night."

"I did not go back. I never saw 'Elm Bluff' after I met you. I know no more of the chloroform than you do. I have told the truth first and last, and always. I have no confession to make. I am as innocent as you are. Innocent! Innocent! You are going to hang me for a crime I did not commit. When you do, you will murder an innocent woman."

She spoke slowly, solemnly, and at intervals, as if she found it difficult to express her meaning. The passionless tone was that of one, standing where the river of death flowed close to her feet, and her beautiful face shone with the transfiguring light of conscious purity.

"Hold up your hand, and tell me this is not your handkerchief; and I will yet save you."

"It was my handkerchief, but I am innocent. Finish your work."

"How can you expect me to believe your contradictory statements?"

Wearily she turned her head, and looked at him. A strange drowsiness dimmed her vision, thickened her speech.

"I expect nothing from you—but—death."

"Will you explain how your handkerchief chanced to be found on your grandfather's pillow? Trust me, I am trying to believe you. Tell me."

In his eagerness he seized her hand, clasped it tightly, bent over her. She made no reply, and the silky black lashes sank lower, lower till they touched the violet circle suffering had worn under her eyes. Like a lily too heavy for its stem, the glossy head fell upon her breast. Her hot fingers throbbed in his palm, and when he felt her pulse, the rapid bounding tide defied his counting. Kneeling beside her, he laid the head against his shoulder.

"Are you ill? What is the matter? Speak to me."

Her parched lips unclosed, and she muttered with a sigh, like a child falling asleep after long sobbing:

"My handkerchief—Tiberius—my—han—"

She had fought against fearful odds, with sleepless nights and fasting days sapping her strength; and when the battle ended, though the will was unfaltering, physical exhaustion triumphed, and delirium mercifully took the tortured spirit into her cradling arms.

CHAPTER X.

When Leo Gordon celebrated her twenty-second birthday, Judge Dent, appreciating the importance of familiarizing her with the business details and technicalities of commercial usage, incident to the management of her large estate, had insisted upon terminating his guardianship, and transferring to her all responsibility for the future conduct of her financial affairs. New books were placed in her hands, in which he required her to keep systematically and legibly all her accounts; she drew and signed her own checks, and semi-annually furnished for his inspection a neat balance-sheet.

As adviser, and agent for the collection of dividends and rents, the change or renewal of investments, he maintained only a general supervision, and left her untrammelled the use of her income. As a dangerous innovation upon time-honored customs, which under the ante bellum regime, had kept Southern women as ignorant of practical business routine, as of the origin of the Weddas of Ceylon, Miss Patty bitterly opposed and lamented her brother's decision; dismally predicting that the result must inevitably be the transformation of their refined, delicate, clinging "Southern lady", into that abhorred monster—"a strong-minded independent business woman".

Intensely loyal to the social standard, usages and traditions of an aristocracy, that throughout the South had guarded its patrician ranks with almost Brahmin jealousy, she sternly decried every infringement of caste custom and etiquette. Nature and education had combined to deprive her of any adaptability to the new order of things; and she rejected the idea that "a lady should transact business", with the same contemptuous indignation that would have greeted a proposition to wear "machine-sewed garments", that last resort of impecunious plebeianism. However unwelcome Leo had found this assumption of the grave duties of mature womanhood, she met the responsibility unflinchingly, and gathered very firmly the reins transferred to her fair hands for guidance. Judge Dent and Miss Patty were the last of their family, except the orphan niece who had been left to their care, and as their earthly possessions would ultimately descend to her, she had been reared in the conviction that their house was her only home.

Study and travel, potent factors in the march of progress, had so enlarged the periphery of Leo's intellectual vision, that she frequently startled her prim aunt, by the enunciation of views much too extended and cosmopolitan to fit that haughty dame's Procrustean limits of "Southern ladyhood". Blessed with a discriminating governess and chaperon, who while fostering a genuine love of the beautiful, had endeavored to guard her pupil from straying into any of those fashionable "art crazes", which in their ephemeral exaggeration approach caricatures of aestheticism, Leo became deeply imbued with the spirit of classic literature and art; and grew especially fond of the study of Greek and Roman architecture.

Believing that the similarity of climate in her native State, justified the revival of an archaic style of building, she ardently desired and finally obtained her uncle's consent to the erection (as an addition to the Dent mansion), of a suite of rooms, designed in accordance with her taste, and for her own occupancy. Hampered by no prudential economic considerations, and fearless of criticism as regarded archaeological anachronisms, Leo allowed herself a wide-eyed eclecticism, that resulted in a thoroughly composite structure, eminently satisfactory at least to its fastidious owner. A single story in height, it contained only four rooms, and on a reduced scale resembled the typical house of Pansa, except that the flat roof rose in the center to a dome. Constituting a western wing of the old brick mansion which it adjoined, the entrance fronting north, opened from a portico with clustered columns, into a square vestibule; which led directly to a large, octagonal atrium, surrounded by lofty fluted pillars with foliated capitals that supported the arched and frescoed ceiling. In the centre, a circular impluvium was sunk in the marble paved floor, where in summer a jet of spray sprang from the water on whose surface lily pads floated; and in winter, shelves were inserted, which held blooming pot plants, that were arranged in the form of a pyramid. The dome overarching this, was divided into three sections; the lower frescoed, the one above it filled with Etruscan designs in stained glass; the upper, formed of white ground glass sprinkled with gilt stars representing constellations, was so constructed, that it could be opened outward in panels, and thus admit the fresh air.

On the east side of this atrium, Leo's bed-room connected with that occupied by Miss Patty in the old house; and opposite, on the west, was a large square Pompeian library, with dark red dado, daintily frescoed panels, and richly tinted glowing frieze. At the end of this apartment, and concealed by purple velvet curtains lined with rose silk, an arch opened into a small semi-circular chapel or oratory, lighted by stained glass windows, whose brilliant hues fell on a marble altar upheld by two kneeling figures; and here lay the family Bible of Leo's great-grandfather, Duncan Gordon, with tall bronze candelabra on each side, holding wax candles. At the right of two marble steps that led to the altar, was spread a rug, and upon this stood an ebony reading-desk where a prayer-book rested. Filling a niche in the wall on the left side, the gilded pipes of an organ rose to meet a marble console that supported a Greek cross.

In order to secure an unobstructed vista from the front door, that portion of the building which corresponded to the ancient tablinum, was used merely as an aviary, where handsome brass cages of various shapes showed through their burnished wires snowy cockatoos, gaudy paroquets, green and gold canaries, flaming red and vivid blue birds, and one huge white owl, whose favorite perch when allowed his freedom, was a bronze Pallas on a projecting bracket.

Conspicuous among these, was a peculiar cage made of tortoise shell, ivory and silver wire, which Leo had assigned to a scarlet-crested, crimson-throated Australian cockatoo. Beyond this undraped rear vestibule stretched the peristyle, a parallelogram, surrounded by a lofty colonnade. The centre of this space was adorned by a rockery whence a fountain rose; flower beds of brilliant annuals and coleus encircled it like a mosaic, and the ground was studded with orange and lemon trees, banana and pineapple plants; while at the farther side delicate exotic grape vines were trained from column to column.

In summer this beautiful court was entirely open to the sky, but at the approach of winter a movable framework of iron pillars was erected, which supported a glass roof, that sloped southward, and garnered heat and sunshine. Neither chimneys nor fireplaces were visible, but a hidden furnace thoroughly warmed the entire house, and in each apartment the registers represented braziers of classic design.

Except for the external entrances, doors had been abolished; portieres of plush, satin, and Oriental silk closed all openings in winter; and during long sultry Southern summers were replaced by draperies of lace, and wicker-work screens where growing ivy and smilax trained their cool green leaves, and graceful tendrils. Wooden floors had accompanied the doors to Coventry; and everywhere squares of marble, and lemon and blue tiles showed shimmering surfaces between the costly rugs, and fur robes scattered lavishly about the rooms. Surrounded by a gilded wreath of olive leaves, and incised on an architrave fronting the vestibule, the golden "Salve" greeted visitors; just beneath it, on an antique shaped table of topaz-veined onyx, stood a Vulci black bowl or vase, decorated in vermilion with Bacchanal figures; and this Leo filled in summer with creamy roses, in winter, with camellias. Where the shrines and Lares stood in ancient houses, a square, burnished copper pedestal fashioned like an altar had been placed, and upon it rose from a bed of carved lilies, a copy in white marble of Palmer's "Faith".

From the front portico, one could look through the vestibule, the atrium, the aviary, and on into the peristyle, where among vine branches and lemon boughs, the vista was closed by a flight of stone steps with carved cedar balustrade, leading up to the flat roof, where it sometimes pleased the mistress to take her tea, or watch the sunset. In selecting and ordering designs for the furniture, a strict adherence to archaic types had been observed; hence the couches, divans, chairs, and tables, the pottery and bric-a-brac, the mirrors and draperies, were severely classic.

An expensive whim certainly, far exceeding the original estimate of its cost; and Miss Patty bewailed the "wicked extravagance of squandering money that would have built a handsome church, and supported for life two missionaries in mid-China"; but Judge Dent encouraged and approved, reviving his classical studies to facilitate the successful accomplishment of the scheme. When the structure was completed and Leo declared herself perfectly satisfied with the result, it was her uncle who had proposed to celebrate her twenty-fourth birthday by a mask-ball in which every costume should be classic, distinctively Roman or Greek; and where the mulsum dispensed to the guests should be mixed in a genuine Cratera.

To this brilliant fete, one cloudless June night, friends from distant States were invited; and fragrant with the breath of its glowing roses, the occasion became memorable, embalmed forever in Leo's happy heart, because then and there, beside the fountain in the peristyle, she had pledged her hand and faith to Mr. Dunbar.

Sitting to-day in front of the library window, whence she had looped back the crimson curtains, to admit the November sunshine, Leo was absorbed in reading the description of the private Ambar-valia celebrated by Marius at "White Nights". Under the spell of the Apostle of Culture, whose golden precept: "BE PERFECT IN REGARD TO WHAT IS HERE AND NOW," had appealed powerfully to her earnest exalted nature, she failed to observe the signals of her pet ring-doves cooing on the ledge outside. Finally their importunate tapping on the glass arrested her attention, and she raised the sash and scattered a handful of rice and millet seed; whereupon a cloud of dainty wings swept down, and into the library, hovering around her sunny head, and pecking the food from her open palms. One dove seemed particularly attracted by the glitter of the diamond in her engagement ring, and perched on her wrist, made repeated attempts to dislodge the jewel from its crown setting. Playfully she shook it off several times, and amused by its pertinacity, finally closed her hands over it, and rubbed her soft cheek against the delicate silvery plumage.

"No, no, you saucy scamp! I can't afford to feed you on diamonds from my sacred ring! Did you get your greedy nature from some sable Dodonean ancestress? If we had lived three thousand years ago, I might be superstitious, and construe your freak into an oracular protest against my engagement. Feathered augurs survive their shrines. Clear out! you heretic!"

As she tossed it into the garden and closed the window, the portiere of the library was drawn aside, and her maid approached, followed by a female figure draped in a shawl and wearing a lofty turban.

"Miss Leo, Aunt Dyce wants to see you on some particular business."

"Howdy do, Aunt Dyce? It is a long time since you paid us a visit. Justine, push up a chair for her, and then open the cages and let the birds out for an hour. What is the matter, Aunt Dyce, you look troubled? Sit down, and tell me your tribulations."

"Yes, Miss Leo, I am in deep waters; up to my chin in trouble, and my heart is dragging me down; for it's heavier 'an a bushel of lead. You don't remember your own ma, do you?"

"I wish I did; but I was only five months old when I lost her."

"Well, if she was living to-day, she would stretch her two hands and pull me out of muddy waves; and that's why I have come to you. You see, Miss Marcia and my young Mistiss, Miss Ellice, was bosom friends, playmates, and like sisters. They named their dolls after one another, and many a time your ma brought her wax doll to our house, for me to dress it just like Miss Ellice's, 'cause I was the seamstus in our family, and I always humored the childun about their doll clothes. They had their candy pullins, and their birthday frolics, and their shetlan' ponies no bigger 'an dogs, and, oh Lord! what blessed happy times them was! Now, your ma's in glory, and you is the richest belle in the State; and my poor young mistiss is in the worst puggatory, the one that comes before death; and her child, her daughter that oughter be living in style at 'Elm Bluff', like you are here, where is she? Where is she? Flung down among vilyans and mallyfactors, and the very off-scourings of creation, in the penitenchery! Tears to me like, if old mistiss is as high-headed and proud as she was in this world, her speert would tear down the walls and set her grandchild free. When I saw that beautiful young thing beating her white hands agin the iron bars, it went to my heart like a carving knife, and—"

Dyce burst into tears, and covered her face with her apron, Leo patted her shoulder softly, and essayed to comfort her.

"Don't cry so bitterly; try to be hopeful. It is very, very sad, but if she is innocent, her stay in prison will be short."

"There ain't no 'ifs'—when it comes to 'cusing my mistiss' child of stealing and murdering. Suppose the sheriff was to light down here this minute, and grab you up and tell folks 'spectable witnesses swore you broke open your Uncle Mitchell's safe, and brained him with a handi'on? Would you think it friendly for people to say, if she didn't they will soon turn her aloose? Would that be any warm poultice to your hurt feelin's? It's the stinging shame and the awful, disgrace of being 'spicioned, that you never would forgive."

"Yes, it is very dreadful, and I pity the poor girl; but it seems that appearances are all against her, and I fear she will find it difficult to explain some circumstances."

"If your ma was here to-day, she wouldn't say that. When she was a friend, she was stone deaf and mole blind to every evil report agin them she loved. Miss Marcia would go straight to that jail, and put her arms 'round Miss Ellice's child, and stand by her till her last breath; and the more she was pussecuted, the closer she would stick. Miss Leo, you must take your ma's place, you must heir her friendship just like you do her other property. I have come to you, 'cause I am going away to New York, and can't feel easy 'till you promise me you will do what you can. Miss Ellice is laying at the pint of death, and her poor child is so deestracted about her needing comforts, that I tole her I'de go on an' nuss her ma for her, 'till she was sot free and could hurry back. I dreampt last night that ole mistiss called me and Bedney, and said 'Take good care of Ellice'; and I got right out of bed and packed my trunk. I'm just from the penitenchery, and that poor tormented child don't know me, don't know nothing. Trouble have run her plum crazy, and what with brain fever and them lie-yers, God only knows what's to become of her. Handi'ons ain't the only godforsaken things folks are murdered with. Miss Leo, promise me you will go to see her while I am gone, and 'tend to it that she has good nussing."

"I will do what is possible for her comfort; and as it will be an expensive journey to you, I will also help you to pay your passage to New York. How much money—"

"I don't want your money, Miss Leo. Bedney and me never is beholdin' to nobody for money. We was too sharp to drap our savings in the 'Freedman's Bank', 'cause we 'spicioned the bottom was not soddered tight, and Marster's britches' pocket was a good enough bank for us. We don't need to beg, borrow, nor steal. As I tole you, I was the seamstress, and just before Miss Ellice run away from the school, ole mistiss had a fine lot of bran-new clothes made ready for her when she come home to be a young lady. She never did come home, and when ole mistiss died I jist tuck them new clothes I had made, and packed 'em in a wooden chist, and kept 'em hid away; 'cause I was determed nobody but Miss Ellice should wear 'em. I've hid 'em twenty-three years, and now I've had 'em done up, and one-half I tuck to that jail, for that poor young thing, and the rest of 'em I'm gwine to carry to Miss Ellice. They shan't need money nor clothes; for Bedney and me has got too much famly pride to let outsiders do for our own folks; but Miss Leo, you can do what nobody else in this wide world can. I ain't a gwine to walk the devil 'round the stump, and you mustn't take no 'fence when I jumps plum to the pint. Mars Lennox is huntin' down Miss Ellice's child like a hungry hound runs a rabbit, and I want you to call him off. If he thinks half as much of you as he oughter, you can stop him. Oh, Miss Leo, for God's sake—call him off—muzzle him!"

Leo rose haughtily, and a quick flush fired her cheek; but as she looked at the old woman's quivering mouth and streaming eyes, compassion arrested her displeasure.

"Aunt Dyce, there are some things with which ladies should not meddle; and I cannot interfere with any gentleman's business affairs."

"Oh, honey! if Miss Marcia was living, she wouldn't say that! She would just put her arm round Miss Beryl and tell Mars Lennox: 'If you help to hang my friend's child, you shan't marry my daughter!' Your ma had pluck enuff to stop him. Mark what I say; that poor child is innercent, and the Lord will clear up everything some day, and then He will require the blood of them that condemned the innercent. Suppos'n appearances are agin her? Wasn't appearances all agin Joseph's bruthren when the money and the silver cup was found in their bags, and them afleein home? And if the 'Gyptian lie-yers could have got their claws on that case, don't you know they would have proved them innercent boys guilty, and a hung em? Oh, I am afeerd of Mars Lennox, for he favors his pa mightily; he has got the keenest scent of all the pack; and he went up yonder, and 'cused, and 'bused, and browbeat and aggervated and tormented that poor, helpless young creetur,'till she fell down in a dead faint on the jail floor; and sence then, the Doctor says her mind is done clean gone. Don't get mad with me, Miss Leo; I am bound to clare my conscience, and now I have done all I could, I am gwine to leave my poor young mistiss' child in God's hands, and in yourn, Miss Leo; and when I come back, you must gim'me an account of your stewudship. You are enuff like Miss Marcia, not to shirk your duty; and as you do, by that pussecuted child, I pray the Lord to do by you."

She seized Leo's hand, kissed it, and left the room.

For some moments Leo sat, with one finger between the creamy leaves of her favorite book, but the charm was broken; her thoughts wandered far from the stories of Apuleius, and the oration of Aurelius, and after mature deliberation, she put aside the volume and rang the library bell.

"Justine, is Mrs. Graham here?"

"She is coming now; I see the carriage at the gate."

"Do not invite her into Aunt Patty's room, until I have seen her. Tell Andrew to harness Gypsy, and bring my phaeton to the door; and Justine, carry my felt hat, driving gloves and fur jacket to Aunt Patty's room."

Confined to her bed by a severe attack of her chronic foe, inflammatory rheumatism, Miss Dent had sent for her dearest friend and faithful colleague in church work, Mrs. Graham, who came to spend a day and night, and discuss the affairs of the parish.

"Aunt Patty, Mrs. Graham is in the parlor, and as I am well aware you can both cheerfully dispense with my society for the present, I am going into town. Dyce Darrington has been here, and I have promised to go and see that unfortunate girl who is in prison."

"Leo Gordon, you don't mean to tell me that you are going into the penitentiary!"

"Why not?"

"It is highly improper for a young lady to visit such places, and I am astonished that you should feel any inclination to see the countenances of the depraved wretches herded there. I totally disapprove of such an incomprehensible freak."

"Then I will hold the scheme in abeyance, until I ask Uncle Mitchell's advice. I shall call at his office, and request him to go with me."

"Don't you know that the Grand Jury brought in a true bill against that young woman? She is indicted for murder, robbery and the destruction of her grandfather's will. Mitchell tells me the evidence is overwhelming against her, and you know he was disposed to defend her at first."

"Yes, Aunty. I am aware that everything looks black for the unfortunate girl; but I learn she is very ill, and as it cannot possibly injure me to endeavor to contribute to her physical comfort. I shall go and see her, unless Uncle Mitchell refuses his consent to my visit to the prison."

"But, Leo, what do you suppose Mr. Dunbar will think and say, when he hears of this extraordinary procedure?"

"Mr. Dunbar is neither the custodian of my conscience, nor the guardian and dictator of my actions. Good-bye, Aunty dear. Justine, show Mrs. Graham in."

"Mr. Dunbar will never forgive such a step; because, like all other men, no matter how much license he allows himself, he is very exacting and fastidious about the demeanor of his lady-love."

"I shall not ask absolution of Mr. Dunbar, and I hope my womanly intuitions are a safer and more refined guide, than any man's fastidiousness. Remember, Aunt Patty, religion's holiest work consists in ministering to souls steeped in sin. Are we too pure to follow where Christ led the way?"

CHAPTER XI.

"Madam, I ordered the prisoner's head shaved. Did you understand my instructions?"

"Yes, sir."

"Why were my orders not obeyed?"

"Because I don't intend you shall make a convict of her, before she has been tried and sentenced. She has the most glorious suit of hair I ever looked at, and I shall save it till the last moment. Doctor Moffat, you need not swear and fume, for I don't allow even my husband to talk ugly to me. You directed a blister put on the back of the neck, as close as possible to the skull; it is there, and it is drawing fast enough to satisfy any reasonable person. I divided the hair into four braids and plaited them, and you can see I have hung up the ends here just loose enough to save any pulling, and yet the hair is out of the way, so that I keep her head cool with this India-rubber ice-bag. I will be responsible for the blister."

Mrs. Singleton spread her arms over the sick girl, as a hen shelters her brood from a swooping hawk.

"But, Susie, the Doctor knows better what is—"

"Hush, Ned. Perhaps he does; but I 'detailed' myself to nurse this case; and I don't propose to surrender all my common sense, and all my womanly judgment, and maternal experience, in order to keep the Doctor in a good humor. I will have my own head shaved before hers shall be touched."

Mr. Singleton discreetly withdrew from the conference, softly closing the door behind him; and Doctor Moffat bent over the thermometer with which he was testing the temperature. When he raised his head, a kindly smile lurked in his deep set eyes:

"I can't afford to quarrel with you, madam; you are too faithful and watchful a nurse. After all, the chances are, that it will ultimately make very little difference; she grows worse so rapidly. I will come in again before bed-time, and meanwhile make no change in the medicine."

The warden's wife replenished the ice in a bowl, whence a tube supplied the cap or bag on the head of the sufferer, and taking a child's apron from her work-basket on the floor, resumed her sewing. After a while, the door opened noiselessly, and glancing up, she saw Mr. Dunbar.

"May I come in?"

"Yes. You need repentance; and this is a good place to begin."

"Is there any change?"

"Only for the worse. No need now to tip-toe; she is beyond being disturbed by noise. I think the first sound she will notice, will be the harps of the angels."

"I trust the case is not so hopeless?"

"Queer heart you must have! You are afraid she will slip through your fingers, and get to heaven without the help of the gallows and the black cap? Death cheats even the lawyers, sometimes, and seems to be snatching at your prey. You don't believe in prayer, and you have no time to waste that way. I do; and I get down here constantly on my knees, and pray to my God to take this poor young thing out of the world now, before you all convict her, and punish her for crimes she never committed."

"Madam, her conviction would grieve me as much as it possibly could you; and unless she can vindicate herself, I earnestly hope she may never recover her consciousness."

The unmistakable sincerity of his tone surprised the little woman, and scanning him keenly as he stood, hat in hand, at the foot of the cot, her heart relented toward him.

"You still consider her guilty?"

"Since my last interview with her, I have arrived at no conclusion. Whether she be innocent or guilty, is known only by her, and her God. All human judgments in such cases are but guesses at the truth. Is she entirely unconscious, or has she lucid intervals?"

"Mr. Dunbar, on your honor as a gentleman, answer me. Are you here hunting evidence on a death-bed? Would you be so diabolical as to use against her any utterances of delirium?" The flash of his eyes reminded her of the peculiar blue flame that leaps from a glowing bed of anthracite coal; and she had her reply before his lips moved.

"Am I a butcher, madam? Your insinuations are so insulting to my manhood, that it is difficult for me to remember my interrogator is a lady; doubly difficult for me to show you the courtesy your sex demands. Sooner than betray the secrets of a sick room, or violate the sanctity of the confidence which that poor girl's condition enjoins, I would cut off my right arm."

"I intend no discourtesy, sir; but my feelings are so deeply enlisted, that I cannot stop to choose and pick phrases, in talking to the person who caused that child to be shut up here. She thinks you are the most vindictive and dangerous enemy she has; and I had no reason to contradict her. Don't be offended, Mr. Dunbar."

He deigned no answer, but the dilation of his thin nostrils, and the stern contraction of his handsome lips, attested his wrath. Mrs. Singleton rose and laid her fingers on his coat sleeve.

"If I felt sure I could trust you—"

"I decline your confidence. Madam, if I could only tell you, that your vile suspicions are too contemptible to merit the indignation they arouse, I should to some extent feel relieved."

"Then having said it, I will let you off without an apology; and wipe the slate, and start fresh. You are sensitive about your honor, and I am determined to find out just how much it is worth. Trusting you as an honorable gentleman, I am going to ask you to do something for me, which may be of service to my patient; and I ask it, because I have unlimited faith in your skill. Find out who 'Ricordo' is."

"Why? I must thoroughly understand the import of whatever I undertake, and if your reasons are too sacred to be communicated to me, you must select some other agent. I do not solicit your confidence, mark you; but I must know all, or nothing."

"The day she was taken so ill, I was undressing her, and she looked at me very strangely, and said she believed she was losing her mind. Then she raised her hands and prayed:

"'Lord, be merciful! Lord, seal my lips! Seal my lips!'

"Since then she has not known me, but several times she cried out 'Ricordo'! Last night she sat up suddenly, and stared at something she seemed to see right before her in the air. She shook her head at first, and said—'Oh, no! it cannot be possible'. Then she clutched at some invisible object, and a look of horror came into her eyes. She struck her palms together, and I never heard such an agonizing cry, 'There is no help! I must believe it—oh Ricordo!—Ricordo—Ricordo'. She fell back and shivered as if she had an ague. I tried to soothe her, and told her she had a bad dream. She kept saying: 'Oh, horrible—it was, it was Ricordo!' Once, early this morning, she pulled me down to her and whispered: 'Don't tell mother—it would break her heart to know it was Ricordo!' She has not spoken distinctly since, though she mutters to herself. Now, Mr. Dunbar, if I did not feel as sure of her innocence as I am of my own, I should never tell you this; but I want your aid to hunt and catch this 'Ricordo', because I am satisfied it will help to clear her."

"Was it not 'Ricardo'?"

"No, sir—it sounded as if spelled with an o not an a—and it was 'Ricordo'."

"Ricardo is a proper name, but I am under the impression that 'Ricordo' is an Italian word that means simply a remembrance, a souvenir, sometimes a warning. I am glad, however, to have the clue, and I will do all I can to discover what connection exists between that word, and the crime. Can you tell me nothing more?"

"Sometimes she seems to be drawing and painting, and talks to her father about pictures; and once she said: 'Hush! hush—mother is ill. She must not know I died, because I promised her I would bear everything. She made me promise'."

At this moment the keen wail of a young child, summoned the warden's wife to her own apartment, and Mr. Dunbar sat down in the rocking-chair beside the iron cot.

In that strange terra incognita, the realm of psychology, are there hidden laws that defy alike the ravages of cerebral disease, and the intuitions of the moral nature; inexorable as the atomic affinities, the molecular attractions that govern crystallization? Is the day dawning, when the phenomena of hypnotism will be analyzed and formulated as accurately as the symbols of chemistry, or the constituents of protoplasm, or the weird chromatics of spectroscopy? Beryl's head, that hitherto had turned restlessly on its pillow, became motionless; the closed eyes opened suddenly, fastened upon the lawyer's; and some inexplicable influence impelled her to stretch out her hand to him.

"Tiberius, you have come for me."

"I have come to ask if you are better to-day."

Her burning fingers closed tightly over his, and the fever flame lent an indescribable splendor to eyes that seemed to penetrate his heart. Bending over her, he gently lifted a shining fold of hair from her white temple, and still clasping her hand, said in a low voice:

"Beryl, do you know me? Are you better?"

"Wait till I finish the sketch from San Michele. After I am hung, you will sell it. The light is so lovely."

Up and down, her right hand moved through the air, making imaginary strokes as on canvas, but her luminous gaze, held by some powerful fascination, never left his. The gray depths had darkened, swallowed by the widening pupils that made them almost black; and as Mr. Dunbar recognized the complete surrender of physical and mental faculties, her helplessness stirred some unknown sea of tenderness in the man's hard, practical, realistic nature.

Phlegmatic rather than emotional, and wholly secretive, he had accustomed himself to regard romantic ideality, and susceptibility to sentimentality as a species of intellectual anaemia; holding himself always thoroughly in hand, when subjected to the softening influences that now and then invaded professional existence, and melted the conventional selfish crust over the hearts of his colleagues, as the warm lips and balmy breath of equatorial currents kiss away the jagged ledges of drifting icebergs. In his laborious life, that which is ordinarily denominated "love" had been so insignificant a factor, that he had never computed its potentiality; much less realized its tremendous importance in solving the problem of his social, financial, and professional success. Beauty had not allured, nor grace enthralled his fancy; and his betrothal was a mere incident in the quiet tenor of business routine, a necessary means for the accomplishment of a cherished plan.

To-day, while those hot slender fingers clung to his, and he leaned over the pillow, watching his victim, a rising tide surged, rolled up from some unexplored ocean of strange sensations, and its devouring waves threatened to demolish and engulf the stately structure pride and ambition had combined to rear. A brilliant alliance that insured great wealth, that promised a secure stepping-stone to political preferment, was apparently a substantial bulwark against the swelling billows of an unaccountable whim; yet he was impotent to resist the yearning tenderness which impelled him to forget all else, in one determined effort to rescue and shelter the life he had been the chief agent in imperilling. Clear eyed, keen witted, he did not for an instant deceive himself; and he knew that neither compassion for misfortune, nor yet a chivalrous remorse for having consigned a helpless woman to a dungeon, explained this new emotion that threatened to dominate all others.

Cool reason assured him that under existing entanglements, the girl's speedy death would prove the most felicitous solution of this devouring riddle, which so unexpectedly crossed his smooth path; then what meant the vehement protest of his throbbing heart, the passionate longing to snatch her from disease, and disgrace, and keep her safe forever in the close cordon of his arms?

The door was cautiously opened and closed, and noiselessly as a phantom, Leo Gordon stood within the room. One swift survey enabled her to grasp all the details. The small, comfortless, dismal apartment, the barred narrow window, the bare floor, the low iron cot in one corner, with its beautiful burden; the watching attitude of the man, who for years had possessed her heart. Resting one elbow on his knee, his chin leaned on his left hand, but the light fell full on his handsome face, and she started, marvelled at the expression of the brilliant eyes fixed upon the sufferer; eyes suffused and eloquent with tenderness, never before seen in their cold sparkling depths.

Mighty indeed must be the compassion, evocative of that intense yearning look in his usually guarded, irresponsive countenance. A painfully humiliating sense of her own personal incompetence to arouse the feeling, so legibly printed on her lover's features, jarred upon Leo's heart like a twanging dissonance breaking the harmonious flow of minor chords; but a noble pity strangled this jealous thrill, and she softly approached the cot.

The rustle of her dress attracted his attention, and glancing up, he saw his betrothed at his side. One might have counted ten, while they silently regarded each other; and as if conscious of having unmasked some disloyalty, scarcely yet acknowledged to himself, haughty defiance hardened and darkened his face. Involuntarily his hold on Beryl's fingers tightened.

"Prison wards are not proper fields for the cultivation and display of Miss Gordon's amateur kid glove charity. I hope, at least, it was a species of exaggerated high-flown sentimentality, rather than mere feminine curiosity that tempted you to precincts revolting to the delicacy and refinement with which my imagination invested you."

"My motives I shall not submit to the crucible of your criticism; and a little reflection will probably suggest to you, that perhaps you are unduly enlarging the limits, and prematurely exercising the rights of anticipated censorship. There are blunders that trench closely upon the borders of crime, and if professional zeal has betrayed you into the commission of a great wrong upon an innocent woman, it is a sacred duty to your victim, as well as my privilege as your betrothed, to alleviate her suffering as much as possible, and to repair the injury for which you are responsible. When human life and reputation are at stake, hypercritical fastidiousness is less pardonable than the deplorable mistake that endangers both."

"And if I have not blundered; and she be guilty?"

"Then your presence here, can only be explained by motives so malignant and contemptible, that I blush to ascribe them to you."

"If I am morbidly sensitive about your line of conduct you should understand and pardon my jealous espionage."

"If I, realizing that you are act infallible, entertain a nervous dread that unintentionally you may have inflicted an irreparable wrong, you at least should not feel offended, because I am sensitive as regards reflections upon your honor as a gentleman, and your astuteness as a lawyer."

Her fair face had flushed; his grew pale.

"Leo, is this to be our first quarrel?"

"If so, you are entitled to the role of protagonist."

He put out his left hand, and took hers, while his right was closely clasping one that lay upon the chintz coverlid.

What strange obliquity of vision, what inscrutable perversity possessed him, he asked himself, as he looked up at the slight elegant figure, clad in costly camel's-hair garments, with Russian sables wrapped about her delicate throat, with a long drifting plume casting flickering shadows over her sweet flowerlike face; the attractive embodiment of patrician birth and environment of riches, and all that the world values most—then down at the human epitome of wretchedness, represented by a bronze-crowned head, with singularly magnetic eyes, crimsoned cheeks, and a perfect mouth, whose glowing, fever-rouged lips were curved in a shadowy smile, as she muttered incoherently of incidents, connected with the life of a poverty-stricken adventuress? Was friendly fate flying danger signals by arranging and accentuating this vivid contrast, in order to recall his vagrant wits, to cement his wavering allegiance?

He was a brave man, but he shivered slightly, as he confronted his own insurgent and defiant heart; and involuntarily, his fingers dropped Leo's, and his right hand tightened on the hot palm throbbing against it.

On that dark tossing main, where delirium drove Beryl's consciousness to and fro like a rudderless wreck, did some mysterious communion of spirits survive? Did some subtle mesmeric current telegraph her soul, that her foul wrongs were at last avenged? Whatever the cause, certainly a strangely clear, musical laugh broke suddenly from her lovely lips, mingled with a triumphant "Che sara, sara!" The heavy lids slowly drooped, the head turned wearily away.

Smothering a long drawn sigh, which his pride throttled, Mr. Dunbar rose and stood beside his fiancee.

"You have been feeling her pulse, how is the fever?" asked Leo.

"About as high as it can mount. The pulse is frightfully rapid. I did not even attempt to count it."

"Mrs. Singleton tells me she is entirely unconscious—recognizes no one."

"At times, I think she has partly lucid glimpses; for instance, a little while ago she called me 'Tiberius', the same appellation she unaccountably bestowed on me the day of her preliminary examination. Evidently she associates me with every cruel, brutal monster, and even in delirium maintains her aversion."

Miss Gordon's hand stole into his, pressing it gently in mute attestation of sympathy. After a moment, she said in a low tone:

"She is very beautiful. What a noble, pure face? How exquisitely turned her white throat, and wrists, and hands."

He merely inclined his head in assent.

"It seems a profanation to connect the idea of crime with so lovely and refined a woman. Lennox?"

He turned, and looked into her brown eyes, which were misty with tears.

"Well, my dear Leo, what is burdening your generous heart?"

"Do you, can you, believe her guilty? Her whole appearance is a powerful protest."

"Appearances are sometimes fatally false. I think you told me, that the purest and loveliest face, guileless as an angel's, that you saw in Europe, was a portrait of Vittoria Accoramboni; yet she was veritably the 'White Devil', 'beautiful as the leprosy, dazzling as the lightning'. Do I believe her guilty? From any other lips than yours, I should evade the question; but I proudly acknowledge your right to an expression of my opinion, when—"

"I withdraw the question, because I arrogate no 'rights'. I merely desire the privilege of sympathizing, if possible, with your views; of sharing your anxiety in a matter involving such vital consequences. Privilege is the gift of affection; right, the stern allotment of law. Tell me nothing now; I shall value much more the privilege of receiving your confidence unsolicited."

He took both her hands, drew her close to him, and looked steadily down into her frank tender eyes.

"Thank you, my dear Leo. Only your own noble self could so delicately seek to relieve me from a painful embarrassment; but our relations invest you with both rights and privileges, which for my sake at least, I prefer you should exercise. You must allow me to conclude my sentence; you are entitled to my opinion—when matured. As far as I am capable of judging, the evidence against her is—overwhelmingly condemnatory. I thought so before her arrest; believed it when her preliminary examination ended, and subsequent incidents strengthen and confirm that opinion; yet a theory has dawned upon me, that may possibly lighten her culpability. I need not tell you, that I feel acutely the responsibility of having brought her here for trial, and especially of her present pitiable condition, which causes me sleepless nights. If she should live, I shall make some investigation in a distant quarter, which may to some extent exculpate her, by proving her an accessory instead of principal. My—generous Leo, you shall be the first to whom I confide my solution—when attained. I am sorely puzzled, and harassed by conflicting conjectures; and you must be patient with me, if I appear negligent or indifferent to the privileges of that lovely shrine where my homage is due."

"If you felt less keenly the distressing circumstances surrounding you, I should deeply regret my misplaced confidence in your character; and certainly you must acquit me of the selfishness that could desire to engross your attention at this juncture."

Desirous of relieving him of all apprehension relative to a possible misconstruction of his motives and conduct, she left one hand in his, and laid the other with a caressing touch on his arm; an unprecedented demonstration, which at any other time would have surprised and charmed him.

"Ah, what a melancholy sight! So much delicate refined beauty, in this horrible lair of human beasts! Lennox, let us hope that the mercy of God will call her speedily to His own bar of justice, before she suffers the torture and degradation of trial, by earthly tribunals."

She felt the slight shudder that crept over him, the sudden start with which he dropped her hand, and bent once more over the cot.

"God forbid she should die now, leaving the burden of her murder on my soul!"

His countenance was averted, but the fervor of his adjuration filled her with a vague sense of painful foreboding.

"Is it friendly to desire the preservation of a life, whose probable goal seems the gallows, or perpetual imprisonment? Poor girl! In the choice of awful alternatives, death would come here as an angel of mercy."

Leo took Beryl's hand in hers, and tears filled her eyes as she noted the symmetry of the snowy fingers, the delicate arch of the black brows, the exceeding beauty of the waving outline where the rich mahogany-hued hair touched the forehead and temples, that gleamed like polished marble.

"Is it friendly to wish an innocent girl to go down into her grave, leaving a name stained for all time by suspicion, if not absolute conviction of a horrible crime?"

Mr. Dunbar spoke through set teeth, and Leo's astonishment at the expression of his countenance, delayed an answer, which was prevented by the entrance of Mrs. Singleton.

"Miss Gordon, your uncle wishes to know whether you are ready to go home; as he has an engagement that calls him away?"

Did Leo imagine the look of relief that seemed to brighten Mr. Dunbar's face, as he said promptly:

"With your permission, I will see you safely down stairs, and commit you to Judge Dent's care."

Standing beside the cot, she watched Mrs. Singleton measure the medicine from a vial into a small glass. When the warden's wife knelt down, and putting one arm under the pillow elevated it slightly, while she held the glass to the girl's lips, Beryl attempted to push it aside.

"Take it for me, dear child; it will make you sleep, and ease your pain."

The beautiful eyes regarded her wistfully, then wandered to the face of the lawyer and rested, spellbound.

"Here, swallow this. It is not bad to take."

Mrs. Singleton patted her cheek and again essayed to administer the draught, but without success.

"Let me try."

Mr. Dunbar took the glass, but as he bent down, the girl began to shiver as though smitten with a mortal chill. She writhed away, put out her shuddering hands to ward it off; and starting up, her eyes filled with a look of indescribable horror and loathing, as she cried out:

"Ricordo! Oh, mother—it is Ricordo! I see, it! Father—it was my Pegli handkerchief!—with the fuchsias you drew! Father—ask Christ to pity me!"

She sank back quivering with dread, pitiable to contemplate; but after a few moments her hands sought each other, and her trembling lips moved evidently in prayer, though the petition was inaudible. Mrs. Singleton sponged her forehead with iced water, and by degrees the convulsive shivering became less violent. The wise nurse began in a subdued tone to sing slowly, "Nearer my God to Thee," and after a little while, the sufferer grew still, the heavy lids lifted once or twice, then closed, and the laboring brain seized on some new vision in the world of fevered dreams.

Mrs. Singleton took the medicine from the attorney, and put it aside.

"Sleep is her best physic. When these nervous shivers come on, I find a hymn chanted, soothes her as it does one of my babies. Poor child! she makes my heart ache so sometimes, that I want to scream the pain away. How people with any human nature left in them, can look at her and listen to her pitiful cries to her dead father, and her dying mother, and her far-off God, and then believe that her poor beautiful hands could shed blood, passes my comprehension; and all such ought to go on four feet, and browse like other brutes. I am poor, but I vow before the Lord, that I would not stand in your shoes, Mr. Dunbar, for all the gold in the Government vaults, and all the diamonds in Brazil."

Tears were dripping on the costly furs about Leo's neck, as she moved closer to the attorney, and linked her arm in his:

"Mr. Dunbar, we will detain my uncle no longer. Mrs. Singleton has told me, that one of her children is ill, had a spasm last night; and since maternal duties are most imperative, it is impossible for her to give undivided attention to this poor sufferer. If you will kindly take me down stairs, I will call at the 'Sheltering Arms', and secure the services of one of the 'Sisters' who is an experienced nurse. This will relieve Mrs. Singleton, and we shall all feel assured that our poor girl has careful and tender watching, and every comfort that anxious sympathy can provide."

CHAPTER XII.

It was midnight in November, keenly cold, but windless; and in the purplish sky, the wintry crown of stars burned with silvery lustre, unlike the golden glow of constellations throbbing in sultry summer, and their white fires sparkled, flared as if blown by interstellar storms. The large family of Lazarus huddled over dying embers on darkening hearths, and shivered under scanty shreds of covering; but the house of Dives was alight with the soft radiance of wax candles, fragrant with the warm aroma of multitudinous exotics, and brimming with waves of riotous music, on which merry-hearted favorites of fashion swam in measured mazes. The "reception" given by Judge Parkman to the Governor and his staff, on the occasion of a review of State troops at X—, was at its height; and several counties had been skimmed for the creme de la creme of most desirable representatives of wit, wealth and beauty.

Miss Gordon had arrived unusually late, and as she entered the room, leaning on her uncle's arm, she noticed that Mr. Dunbar was the centre of a distinguished group standing under the chandelier. He was gently fanning his hostess, who stood beside the Governor, and evidently he was narrating some spicy incident, or uttering some pungent witticism, whereat all laughed heartily. The light fell full on his fine figure, which rose above all surrounding personages, and was faultlessly apparelled in evening dress; and Leo's heart filled with tender pride, at the consciousness that he was all her own. The exigencies of etiquette prevented for more than an hour any nearer approach, but when Mr. Dunbar had rendered "Caesar's things" to social Caesar, and paid tribute of bows, smiles, compliments and persiflage into the coffer of custom, he made his way through the throng, to the spot where his betrothed stood resting after her third dance.

"Will Miss Gordon grant me a promenade in lieu of the dance, which misfortunes conspired to prevent me from securing earlier in the evening?"

He drew her hand under his arm, and his eyes ran with proprietorial freedom over the details of her costume, pale blue satin, creamy foam of white lace, soft sheen of large pearls, and bouquet of exquisite half blown La France roses.

Since their betrothal, he had claimed the privilege of sending the flowers she wore, on special occasions, and she had invariably expressed her appreciation through the dainty lips of a boutonniere arranged by her own fingers. Now while he recognized the roses resting on her corsage, her eyes dwelt on her favorite double lilac violets, nestling in the buttonhole of his coat.

"You were very late to-night. I loitered in ambush about the precincts of the dressing-room, hoping for the pleasure of conducting you down-stairs; but 'the best laid schemes o' mice and men gang aft aglee', and I became the luckless prey of similar tactics. That marauding Tomyris, Mrs. Halsey, sallied out at the head of her column of daughters, espied me lurking behind the portiere, and proclaiming her embarras de richesse, 'paid me the compliment' of consigning one fair campaigner, Miss Eloise Hermione, to my care. Fancy the strain on courtesy, as I accepted my 'quite unexpected good fortune'!"

He spoke with a nervous rapidity, at variance with his usual imperturbable deliberateness of manner, and she thought she had never seen his eyes so restless and brilliant.

"I was unusually late, owing to the fact that the Governor and staff dined with Uncle Mitchell, and they lingered so long over their cigars and wine, that I was delayed in the drawing-room, waiting for them; consequently was very late in changing my dress. We were sorry you were prevented from joining us. Uncle pronounced the dinner a perfect success; and certainly Governor Glenbeigh was in his happiest mood, and particularly agreeable."

"Given his hostess, and entourage, could he possibly have been less? Rumor's hundred tongues wag with the announcement, that his Excellency is no longer inconsolable for his wife's death; and desires to testify to the happiness of conjugal relations, by a renewal of the sweet bondage; a curiously subtle compliment to the deceased. If I may be pardoned the enormity of the heresy, I think Shakspeare blundered supremely, when he gave Iago's soul to a man. Diabolical cunning, shrewd malevolence pure and simple, armed with myriads of stings for hypodermic incisions that poison a man's blood, should be appropriately costumed in a moss-green velvet robe, should wear frizzled bangs as yellow as yonder bouquet of Marechal Neils, so suggestive of the warning flag flying over pest-houses!"

"It is very evident you are not equally generous in surrendering the amiability of Timon, along with the depravity of Iago, to the arsenal of feminine weapons. What corroding mildew of discontent has fallen from Mrs. Parkman's velvet dress, and rusted the bright blade of your chivalry?"

"The very breath of Iago, filling my ears and firing my heart with the architectural details of her coveted 'castle in Spain.' Glenbeigh is her cousin. The ladder of his preferment is set up before my eyes, and his Excellency springs up the rounds, from Governor to Senatorship, thence to a place in the Cabinet, certainly to an important foreign embassy; where, in the eternal fitness of things, somebody, somebody with tender brown eyes like a thrush's, and the voice of a siren, and the red lips of Hebe—will be invited to reign as l'ambassadrice! If I am not as mad with jealous despair as Othello, attribute my escape either to a sublime faith in your adorable constancy and incorruptibility, or to my own colossal vanity, fatuous beyond absolution."

He pressed her arm closer to his side, and covered with one hand the gloved fingers resting on his sleeve; then added:

"You must permit me to congratulate you upon your beautiful toilette to-night. The harmony of the dress, and the grace of the wearer leave nothing to be desired. Although debarred the pleasure of dining with you, I had hoped to enter, at least, with the coffee, but the freight train upon which I returned, was delayed; and I had no choice but to await your arrival here."

He indulged so rarely in verbal compliments, that she flushed with profound gratification at flip fervor of his tone.

"I am glad you like my dress, to which your roses lend the loveliest garniture. I was not aware that X—could furnish at this season such superb La France buds. Where did you find them?"

"They travelled several hundred miles, for the privilege of nestling against my Leo's heart."

Spartan thieves are not the only heroic sufferers who smile and make no moan, clasping close the hidden fangs ravening on their vitals.

"As you mentioned in your note that very important business had called you unexpectedly away, I hope your mission proved both pleasant and successful."

A shadow drifted over his countenance, like that cast by some summer cloud long becalmed, which sets sail before a sudden gust.

"Only a modicum of success to counterbalance the disagreeable features of a journey in a freight train caboose."

"Why do you hazard that dangerous schedule, instead of waiting for the passenger express?"

"Business exigencies narrow the limits of choice; moreover, had I waited for the express, I should have missed the coveted pleasure of this meeting with you. The rosy glamour of happy anticipation conquers even the discomfort of a freight caboose."

Did she suspect that some sullen undercurrent of intense feeling drove these eddying foam bells of flattery into the stream of conversation; or was her reply merely a chance ricochet shot, more accurately effective than direct fire?

"This afternoon I had a note from Sister Serena, asking for a few articles conducive to the comfort of a sick room; and I really cannot determine whether we should feel regret, or relief at the tidings that that unfortunate girl—can scarcely—"

"Spare me the Egyptian mummy at my feast! The memento mori when I would fain forget. Let me inhale the perfume of your roses, without hearing that possibly a worm battens on their petals. Will you ride with me tomorrow afternoon?"

"I am sorry that an engagement to dine will prevent, as the afternoons are so short."

"Are you going to the Percy's?"

"Yes. Will you not be there?"

"Too bad! I have just declined attending that dinner, because I had planned the horseback ride. Formerly fate seemed to smile upon me; now she shows herself a scowling capricious beldam. I have lost this evening, waiting to see you, and now, I must steal away unnoticed; because of an important matter which admits of no delay. Have you promised to dance with Mayfield? Here he comes. Good-night, my dear Leo, expect to see me at 'The Lilacs' at the earliest possible moment."

Unobserved he made his escape, and hurried away. At a livery stable he stopped to order his horse saddled, and brought to his door, and a few moments later, stood before the grate in his law office, where the red glow of the coals had paled under ashy veils. From the letter-rack over the mantel, he took a note containing only a line:

"She has reached the crisis. We have no hope." "SINGLETON."

In the hot embers, it smoked, shrivelled, disappeared; and the attorney crossed his arms over his chest to crush back the heavy sigh struggling for escape. The long overcoat buttoned from throat to knee, enhanced his height, and upon his stern, handsome features had settled an expression of sorrowful perplexity; while his keen eyes showed the feverish restlessness that, despite his efforts, betrayed heartache. Above the heads of the gay throng he had just left, he had seen all that evening a slender white hand beckoning to him from the bars of a dungeon; and dominating the music of the ball room, the laughter of its dancers, had risen the desperate, accusing cry:

"You have ruined my life!"

Was it true, that his hand had dashed a foul blot of shame upon the fall pure page of a girl's existence, and written there the fatal finis? If she died, could he escape the moral responsibility of having been her murderer? Amid the ebb and flow of conflicting emotions, one grim fact stared at him with sardonic significance. If he had ruined her life, retribution promptly exacted a costly forfeit; and his happiness was destined to share her grave.

He neither analyzed nor understood the nature of the strange fascination which he had ineffectually striven to resist; and he ground his teeth, and clinched his hands with impotent rage, under the stinging and humiliating consciousness that his unfortunate victim had grappled his heart to hers, and would hold it forever in bondage. No other woman had ever stirred the latent and unsuspected depths of his tenderness; but at the touch of her hand, the flood burst forth, sweeping aside every barrier of selfish interest, defying the ramparts of worldly pride. Guilty or innocent, he loved her; and the wretchedness he had inflicted, was recoiling swiftly upon himself.

Unbuttoning his overcoat, he took from an inside pocket, the torn half of a large envelope, and unlocking the drawer of his desk, hunted for a similar fragment. Spreading them out before him, he fitted the zigzag edges with great nicety, and there lay the well-known superscription: "Last Will and Testament of Robert Luke Darrington." One corner of the last found bit was brown and mud-stained, but the handwriting was in perfect preservation. As he stooped to put it all back in a secret drawer, something fell on the floor. He picked up the dainty boutonniere of pale sweet violets, and looked at it, while a frown darkened his countenance, as though he recognized some plenipotentiary pleading for fealty to a sacred compact.

"Poor Leo! how little she suspects disloyalty. How infinite is her trust, and what a besotted ingrate I am!"

He tossed the accusing flowers into the grate, took his riding-whip and went down to the door, where his horse was champing the bit, and pawing with impatience. Along the deserted streets, out of the sleeping town, he rode toward the long stone bridge that spanned the winding river. When he had reached the centre, his horse darted aside, because of the sudden leap of a black cat from the coping of the nearest pier, whence she sped on, keeping just ahead of him. The spectral sickle of a waning moon hung on the edge of the sky, and up and down the banks of the stream floated phantoms of silvery mist, here covering the water with impalpable wreaths, and there drifting away to enable Andromeda to print her starry image on the glassy surface.

Behind stretched the city, marked by lines of gas lamps; in front rose the hill clothed with forests; and frowning down upon the rider, the huge shadow of the dismal dungeon crouched like a stealthy beast ready to spring upon him. Dark as the deeds of its inmates, the mass of stone blotted the sky, save in one corner, where a solitary light shone through iron lattice work. Was it a beacon of hope, or did the rays fall on features cold under the kiss of death?

Spurring his horse up the rocky hill, Mr. Dunbar was greeted by the baying of two bloodhounds within the enclosure; and soon after, Mr. Singleton conducted him up the steps leading to the room where Beryl had been placed.

"She is alive; that is all. The doctor said she could not last till midnight, but it is now half-past one; and my wife has never lost hope. She has sent the nurse off to get some sleep, and you will find Susie in charge."

The hazel eyes of the gaoler's wife were humid with tears, as she glanced up at the attorney, and motioned him to the low chair she vacated.

"I knew you would come, and when I heard you gallop across the bridge, I sent Sister Serena off to bed. There is nothing to be done now, but watch and pray. If she ever wakes in this world she will be rational, and she will get well. The nurse thinks she will pass away in this stupor; but I have faith that she will not die, until she clears her name."

Nature makes some women experts in the fine art of interpreting countenance and character, and by a mysterious and unerring divination, Mrs. Singleton knew that her visitor desired no companion in his vigils; hence, after flitting about the room for a few moments, she added:

"If you will sit here a while, I can look after my babies. Should any change occur, tap at my door; I shall not be long away."

What a melancholy change in the sleeper, during the few days of his absence; how much thinner the hollow cheek, how sunken the closed eyes; how indescribably sharpened the outlines of each feature. The face which had formerly suggested some marble statue, had now the finer tracery as of an exquisite cameo; and oblivion of all earthly ills had set there the seal of a perfect peace. She lay so motionless, with her hands on her breast, that Mr. Dunbar bent his head close to hers, to listen to her respiration; but no sound was audible, and when his ear touched her lips, their coldness sent a shiver of horror through his stalwart frame. Pure as the satin folds of an annunciation lily pearled with dew, was the smooth girlish brow, where exhaustion hung heavy drops; and about her temples the damp hair clung in glossy rings, framing the pallid, deathlike face.

At her wrist, the fluttering thread eluded his grasp, and kneeling beside the cot, he laid his head down on her breast, dreading to find no pulsation; but slow and faint, he felt the tired heart beat feebly against his cheek; and tears of joy, that reason could neither explain nor justify, welled up and filled his eyes. Leaning his head on her pillow, he took one hand between both his, and watched the profound sleep that seemed indeed twin sister of death.

Softened by distance came the deep mellow sound of the city clock striking two. Down among the willows fringing the river bank, some lonely water-fowl uttered its plaintive cry, whereat the bloodhounds bayed hoarsely; then velvet-sandalled silence laid her soothing touch upon the world, and softly took all nature into her restful arms.

In the searching communion which he held with his own heart, during that solemn watch, Mr. Dunbar thrust aside all quibbles and disguises, and accepted as unalterable, two conclusions.

She was innocent of crime, and he loved her; but she knew who had committed the murder, and would suffer rather than betray the criminal. The conjecture that she was shielding a lover, was accompanied by so keen a pang of jealous pain, that it allowed him no room to doubt the nature or intensity of the feeling which she had inspired.

In her wan loveliness, she seemed as stainless as a frozen snowdrop, and while his covetous gaze dwelt upon her he felt that he could lay her in her coffin now, with less suffering, than see her live to give her brave heart to any other man. To lift her spotless and untrampled from the mire of foul suspicion, where his hand had hurled her, was the supreme task to which he proposed to devote his energies; but selfishness was the sharpest spur; she must be his, only his, otherwise he would prefer to see her in the arms of death.

So the night waned; and twice, when the warden's wife stole to the door, he lifted his head and waved her back. When the clock in the tower struck four, he felt a slight quiver in the fingers lying within his palm, and Beryl's face turned on the pillow, bringing her head against his shoulder. Was it the magnet of his touch drawing her unconsciously toward him, or merely the renewal of strength, attested already by the quickened throb of the pulse that beat under his clasp? By degrees her breathing became audible to his strained ear, and once a sigh, such as escapes a tired child, told that nature was rallying her physical forces, and that the tide was turning. Treacherous to his plighted troth, and to the trusting woman whom he had assiduously wooed and won, he yielded to the hungry yearning that possessed him, and suddenly pressed his lips to Beryl's beautiful mouth. Under that fervent touch, consciousness came back, and the lids lifted, the dull eyes looked into his with drowsy wonder. Stepping swiftly to the door which stood ajar, he met Mrs. Singleton, and put his hand on her shoulder.

"She is awake, and will soon be fully conscious, but perfect quiet is the only safeguard against relapse. When she remembers, leave her as much alone as possible, and answer no questions."

Holding her baby on her breast, Mrs. Singleton whispered:

"Put out the lamp, so that she can see nothing to remind her."

As he took his hat, and put his hand on the lamp, he looked back at the cot, and saw the solemn eyes fixed upon him. He extinguished the light, and passed into the room where Susie Singleton stood waiting.

"She will not know Sister Serena, and for a day or two I will keep out of sight when she is awake. Mr. Dunbar, God has done His part, now see that you do yours. Have you found out who 'Ricordo' is?"

"Certainly, it is a thing; not a person. As yet the word has given no aid."

"Then you have discovered nothing new during your absence?"

"Yes, I have found the missing half of the envelope which contained General Darrington's will; but ask me no questions at present. For her sake, I must work quietly. Send me a note at twelve o'clock, that I may know her exact condition, and the opinion of the doctor. Has nothing been heard from Dyce?"

"As far as I know, not a syllable."

They shook hands, and once more Mr. Dunbar sprang into his saddle. Overhead the constellations glowed like crown jewels on black velvet, but along the eastern horizon, where the morning-star burned, the sky had blanched; and the air was keen with the additional iciness that always precedes the dawn. Earth was powdered with rime, waiting to kindle into diamonds when the sun smote its flower crystals, and the soft banners of white fog trailed around the gray arches and mossy piers of the old bridge. At a quick gallop Mr. Dunbar crossed the river, passed through the heart of the city, and slackened his pace only when he found himself opposite the cemetery, on the road leading to "Elm Bluff." As the iron gate closed behind him, he walked his horse, up the long avenue, and when he fastened him to the metal ring in the ancient poplar, which stood sentinel before the deserted House, the deep orange glow that paves the way for coming suns, had dyed all the sky, blotting out the stars; and the new day smiled upon a sleeping world. The peacock perched upon the balustrade of the terrace greeted him vociferously, and after some moments his repeated knock was answered by the cautious opening of the front door, and Bedney's gray head peered out.

"Lord—Mars Lennox! Is it you? What next? 'Pears to me, there's nothing left to happen; but howsomever, if ther's more to come, tell us what's to pay now?"

"Bedney, I want you to help me in a little matter, where your services may be very valuable; and as it concerns your old master's family, I am sure you will gladly enter into my plan—"

"Bless your soul, Mars Lennox, you are too good a lieyer to be shore of anything, but the undertaker and the tax collector. I am so old and broke down in sperrits, that you will s'cuse me from undertaking of any jobs, where I should be obleeged to pull one foot out'en the grave before I could start. I ain't ekal to hard work now, and like the rest of wore-out stock, I am only worth my grabs in old fields."

Sniffing danger, Bedney warily resolved to decline all overtures, by taking refuge in his decrepitude; but the attorney's steady prolonged gaze disconcerted him.

"You have no interest, then, in discovering the wretch who murdered your master? That is rather suspicious."

"What ain't 'spicious to you, Mars Lennox? It comes as natchal to you to 'spicion folks, as to eat or sleep, and it's your trade. You believe I know something that I haven't tole; but I swear I done give up everything to Mars Alfred; and if my heart was turned inside out, and scraped with a fine-tooth comb, it wouldn't be no cleaner than what it is. I know if I was lying you would ketch me, and I should own up quick; 'cause your match doesn't go about in human flesh; but all the lancets and all the doctors can't git no blood out'en a turnup."

"You are quite willing, then, to see General Darrington's granddaughter suffer for the crime?"

"'Fore Gord! Mars Lennox, you don't tote fair! 'Pears to me you are riding two horses. Which side is you on?"

"Always on the side of justice and truth, and it is to help your poor young mistress that I came to see you; but it seems you are too superannuated to stretch out your hand and save her."

"Ain't you aiming to prove she killed old marster? That's what you sot out to do; and tarrapin's claws are slippery, compared to your grip, when you take holt."

The old negro stood with his white head thrown back, and unfeigned perplexity printed on his wrinkled features, while he scanned the swart face, where a heavy frown gathered.

"I set out this morning to find a faithful, old family servant, whose devotion has never before been questioned; but evidently I have wasted my confidence as well as my time. Where is Dyce? She is worth a hundred superannuated cowards."

"Don't call no names, Mars Lennox. If there's one mean thing I nachally despises as a stunnin' insult, it's being named white-livered; and my Confederate record is jest as good as if I wore three gilt stars on my coat collar. You might say I was a liar and a thief, and maybe I would take it as a joke; but don't call Bedney Darrington no coward! It bruises my feelins mor'n I'le stand. Lem'me tell you the Gord's truth; argufying with lie-yers is wuss than shootin' at di-dappers, and that is sport I don't hanker after. I ain't spry enuff to keep up with the devil, when you are whipping him around the stump; and I ain't such a forsaken idjut as to jump in the dark. Tell me straight out what you want me to do. Tote fair, Mars Lennox."

"I am about to offer a reward of two hundred and fifty dollars, and I thought I would allow you privately the opportunity of securing the money, before I made it public. Where is Dyce?"

"You might as well ax the man in the moon. The only satisfaction she gin me when she left home, was—she was gwine to New York to hunt for Miss Ellie. I tole her she was heading for a wild goose chase, and her answer signified she was leaving all of them fowls behind. If she was here, she'd be only a 'clean chip in your homny pot'; for she wouldn't never touch your job with a forty-foot pole, and what's more, she'd tie my hands. I ain't afeard of my ole 'oman, but I respects her too high to cross her; and if ever you git married, you will find it's a mighty good rule to 'let sleeping dogs lay'. Who do you expect me to ketch for two hundred and fifty dollars?"

"A lame negro man, about medium size, who was seen carrying a bundle on the end of a stick, and who was hanging about the railroad station on the night of General Darrington's death. He probably lives on some plantation south of town, as he was travelling in that direction, after the severe storm that night. I want him, not because he had any connection with your master's murder, but to obtain from him a description of a strange white man, whom he directed to the railroad water-tank. If you can discover that lame negro, and bring him to my office, I will pay you two hundred and fifty dollars, and give him a new suit of clothes. The only hope for General Darrington's granddaughter is in putting that man on the witness stand, to corroborate her statement of a conversation which she heard. This is Wednesday. I will give you until Saturday noon to report. If you do not succeed I shall then advertise. If you wish to save Miss Brentano, help me to find that man."

He swung himself into the saddle, and rode away, leaving Bedney staring after him, in pitiable dubiety as to his own line of duty.

"Wimmen are as hard to live peaceable with as a hatful of hornets, but the'r brains works spryer even than the'r tongues; and they do think as much faster 'an a man, as a express train beats er eight ox-team. Dyce is the safest sign-post! If she was only here now, I couldn't botch things, for she sees clare through a mill-stone, and she'd shove me the right way. If I go a huntin', I may flounder into a steel trap; if I stand still, wuss may happen. Mars Lennox is too much for me. I wouldn't trust him no further 'n I would a fat possum. I am afeard of his oily tongue. He sot out to hang that poor young gal, and now he is willing to pay two hundred and fifty dollars to show the court he was a idjut and a slanderer! I ain't gwine to set down on no such spring gun as that! Dyce ought to be here. When Mars Lennox turns summersets in the court, before the judge, I don't want to belong to his circus—but, oh Lord! If I could only find out which side he raily is on?"

<h3 align="center">CHAPTER XIII.</h3>

During the early stages of her convalescence, Beryl, though perfectly rational, asked no questions, made no reference to her gloomy surroundings and maintained a calm, but mournful taciturnity, very puzzling to Mrs. Singleton, who ascribed it at first to mental prostration, which rendered her comparatively obtuse; but ere long, a different solution presented itself, and she marvelled at the silence with which a desperate battle was fought. With returning consciousness, the prisoner had grasped the grievous burden of her fate, unflinchingly lifted and bound it upon her shoulders; and though she reeled and bent under it, made no moan, indulged no regret, uttered no invective.

One cold dismal day, when not a rift was visible in the leaden sky, and a slanting gray veil of sleety rain darkened the air and pelted the dumb, shivering earth, Beryl sat on the side of her cot, with her feet resting on the round of a chair, and her hands clasped at the back of her head. Her eyes remarkably large from the bluish circles illness had worn beneath them, were fixed in a strained, unwinking, far-away gaze upon the window, where black railing showed the outside world as through some grim St. Lawrence's gridiron.

From time to time the warden's wife glanced from her sewing toward the motionless figure, reluctant to obtrude upon her revery, yet equally loath to leave her a prey to melancholy musing. After a while, she saw the black lashes quiver, and fall upon the waxen cheeks, then, as she watched, great tears glittered, rolled slowly, dripped softly, but there was no sigh, no sound of sobs. Leaning closer, she laid her arm across the girl's knee.

"What is it, dearie? Tell me."

There was no immediate reply; when Beryl spoke, her voice was calm, low and measured, as in one where all the springs of youth, hope, and energy are irreparably broken.

"Every Gethsemane has its strengthening Angels. The agony of the Garden brought them to Christ. I thank God, mine did not fail me. If they had not come, I think I could never have borne this last misery that earth can inflict upon me. My mother is dead."

"Why distress yourself with sad forebodings? Weakness makes you despondent, but you must try to hope for the best; and I dare say in a few days, you will have good news from your mother."

"I shook hands with Hope, and in her place sits the only companion who will abide with me during the darkness that is coming on—Patience, pale-browed, meek-eyed, sad-lipped Patience. If I can only keep my hold upon her skirts, till the end. To me, no good news can ever come. As long as mother lived, I had an incentive to struggle; now I am alone, and they who thirst for my blood are welcome to take it speedily. I know my mother is dead; I have seen her."

"Wake up, child. Your brain is weak yet and full of queer delirious visions, and when you doze, realities and dreams are all jumbled together. You have a deal too much sense to harbor any crazy spiritual crankiness. Take your wine, and lie down. You have sat up too long, and tired yourself."

"No. I have wanted to tell you for several days, because you have been so good, and I have heard you praying here at night that God would be merciful to me; but I waited until I had strength to be calm. I have lain here day after day, and night after night, face to face with desolation and despair, and now I have grown accustomed to the horror. I know that in this world there is no escape, no help, no hope; so—the worst is over. When you consent to fate, and stretch out your arms to meet death, there is no more terror, only waiting, weary waiting. I am not superstitious, and unfortunately I am not one of the victims of dementia, whose spectral woes are born of disordered brains. I am sadly sane; and what I am about to tell you is no figment of feverish fancy. I do not know how long I have been sick, but one night great peace and ease came suddenly upon me. I swung in some soft tender arms, close to the gates of Release, and the iron bars melted away, and my soul was borne toward the wonderful light; but suddenly a shock, a strange thrill ran through me, and the bars rose again, and the light faded. Then all at once my father and my mother stood beside me, bent over me. Father said: 'Courage, my daughter, courage! Bear your cross a little longer,' My mother wept, and said, 'My good little girl. So faithful, so true. I died in peace, trusting your promise. For my sake can you endure till the end?' They faded away; and sorrow sat down once more, clutching my heart; and death, the Angel who keeps the key of the Gate of Release, turned his back upon me. I had almost escaped; I was close to the other world, and I was conscious. I saw my mother's spirit; it was no delirious fancy. I know that she is dead. Even in the world of the released, she grieves over the awful consequences of my obedience to her wishes. Mortal agony of body and soul brings us so near to the borderland, that we have glimpses; and those we love, lean across the boundary line and compassionate us. So my Gethsemane called down the one strengthening Angel of all the heavenly hosts, who had most power to comfort my heart, and gird me for my fate, my father, my noble father. God, in pity, sent him to exhort me to bear my cross bravely."

The low solemn voice ceased, and in the silence that followed, only the dull patter of the rain, and the persistent purring of a kitten curled up on the cot were audible. Mrs. Singleton finished the buttonhole in Dick's apron, and threaded her needle.

"If it comforts you at all to believe that, I have no right to say anything."

"You think, however, that I am the victim of some hallucination?"

"Not even that. I think you had a very vivid dream, and being exhausted, you mistook a feverish vision for a real apparition. I can't believe your mother is dead, because if such were the case, Dyce would have returned at once, and told us."

"Dyce has a kind heart, and shrinks from bringing me the sad news; for she knows my cup was already full. I know that my mother is dead. Time will show you that I make no mistake. The veil was lifted, and I saw beyond."

"Maybe so; may be not. I am stubborn in my opinions, and I never could think it possible for flesh to commune with spirits. Don't let us talk about anything that disturbs you, until you regain your strength. Why will you not try a little of this port wine? Miss Gordon brought it yesterday, and insisted I should give it to you, three times a day. It is very old and mellow. Look at things practically. God kept you alive for some wise purpose, and since you are obliged to face trouble, is it not better to arm yourself with all the physical vigor possible? Drink this, and lie down."

As Beryl mechanically drained the glass and handed it back, Mrs. Singleton added:

"I believe I told you, Miss Gordon is Mr. Dunbar's sweetheart. Their engagement is no secret, and he is a lucky man; for she is as good as she is pretty, and as sweet as she is rich. She has shown such a tender interest in you, and manifests so much sympathy, that I am sure she will influence him in your favor, and I feel so encouraged about your future."

A shadowy smile crossed the girl's wan face,

"Invest no hope in my future; for escape is as impossible for me, as for that innocent victim foreordained to entangle his horns in the thicket on Mount Moriah. He could have fled from the sacrificial fire, and from Abraham's uplifted knife, back to dewy green pastures poppy-starred, back to some cool dell where Syrian oleanders flushed the shade, as easily as I can defy these walls, loosen the chain of fate, elude my awful doom."

"It is because you are not yet yourself, that you take such a despairing view of matters. After a while, things will look very different, and you are too plucky to surrender your life without a brave fight. A great change has come over Mr. Dunbar, and there is no telling what he cannot do, when he sets to work. If ever a lawyer's heart has been gnawed by remorse, it is his. He and Miss Gordon together can pull you out of the bog, and I believe they will."

"Mr. Dunbar's professional reputation is more precious in his sight than a poor girl's life; moreover, even if he desired to undo his work, he could not. I am beyond human succor. Fate nails me to a cross, but God consents; so I make no struggle, for behind fate stands God— and my father."

Wearily she leaned back on her pillows, and turned her face to the wall. Mrs. Singleton drew the blankets over her, folded her own shawl about the shoulders, and smoothing away the hair, kissed her on the temple; then stole into the adjoining room, where her children slept.

Before the fire that leaped and crackled in the wide chimney, and leaning forward to rest her turbaned head against the mantelpiece, while she spread her hands toward the blaze, stood a much muffled figure.

"Dyce!"

Mrs. Singleton had left the door ajar, and the old woman turned and pointed to it, laying one finger on her lips; but the warning came too late.

"Hush! I don't want her to know I am here. Your husband told me she was sitting up, and in her right mind, but too weak to stand any more trouble. I wish I could run away, and never see her again, for when I go in there, I feel like I was carrying a knife to cut the heart out of a fawn, what the hounds had barely left life in. I can't bear the thought of having to tell her—"

Dyce covered her face with her shawl, to stifle her sobs, and her large frame shook. Mrs. Singleton whispered:

"Tell me quick. What is it."

"Miss Ellie is dead. I got there three days after she was buried."

The warden's wife sank into a chair, and drew the weeping negro into one beside her.

"Do you know exactly what time she died?"

"Yes—I had it all put down in black and white. She died on Tuesday night, just as the clock struck two; and the hospital nurse says— Lord, amercy, Miss Susan! are you going to faint? You have turned ashy!"

As Mrs. Singleton's thoughts recurred to the fact that it was at that hour that Beryl lay in the stupor of the crisis, from which she awoke perfectly conscious, and recalled the dream that the sick girl held as a vision, she felt a vague but bewildering dread seize her faculties, in defiance of cool reason, and scoffing scepticism.

"Go on, Dyce. I felt a little sick. Tell me—"

She paused and listened to an unusual and inexplicable noise issuing from the next room; the harsh sound of something scraping the bare floor.

"You must pick your time to break this misery to that poor young thing. I can't do it. I would run a mile sooner than face her with the news, that her ma is dead; and I have grieved and cried, till I feel like my brains had been put in a pot and biled. The Lord knows His bizness, of course; yes, of course He knows the best to do; but 'pears to me, His mercy hid its face behind His wrath, when He saw fit to let that poor innercent young creetur in there get well, after her ma was laid in the grave. It will be a harder heart than mine what can stand by, and tell her she is motherless."

"There is no need to tell her. She knows it."

"How? Did she get the letter the Doctor said he wrote?"

"No. She thinks her mother—"

The noise explained itself. Too feeble to walk alone, Beryl had pushed a chair before her, until she reached the door, and now stood grasping it, swaying to and fro, as she endeavored to steady herself. One hand held at her throat the black shawl, whose loosened folds fell like a mourning mantle to her feet, the other clutched the door, against the edge of which she leaned for support.

"Dyce, I have known for some days that I have no mother in this world. I have seen her. Your kind heart dreads giving me pain, but nothing can hurt me now. I cannot suffer any more, because I am bruised and beaten to numbness. I want to see you alone; I want to know everything."

At sight of her, the old woman darted forward and caught the tall, wasted, tottering form in her strong arms. Lifting her as though she had been a child, she bore her back to her small bleak room, laid her softly on her cot, then knelt down, and burst into a fit of passionate crying.

As if to shut out some torturing vision, Beryl clasped her hands over her eyes, and when she spoke, her voice was very unsteady:

"Did you see mother alive?"

"Oh, honey, I was too late! I was three days too late to see her at all. When I got to New York, and found the Doctor's house, he was not at home; had just gone to Boston a half hour before I rung the bell. His folks couldn't tell me nothin', so I had to wait two days. When I give him your note, he looked dreadful cut up, and tole me Miss Ellie had all the care and 'tention in the world, but nothin' couldn't save her. He said she didn't suffer much, but was 'lirious all the time, until the day before she died, when all of a sudden her mind cleared. Then she axed for you, honey—God bless you, my poor lamb! I hate to harrify your heart. The Doctor comforted her all he could, and tole her bizness of importance had done kept you South. Miss Ellie axed how long she could live; he said only a few hours. She begged him to prop her up, so she could write a few words. He says he held the paper for her, and she wrote a little, and rested; and then she wrote a little mere and fell back speechless. He pat the piece of paper in a invellop and sealed it, and axed her if she wished it given to her daughter Beryl. She couldn't talk then, but she looked at him and nodded her head. That was about four o'clock in the evening of Tuesday. She had a sort of spasm, and went to sleep. At two o'clock, she woke up in Heaven. He said he felt so sorry for you—dear lamb! He wouldn't let them burry her where most was hurried that died in the hospital. He had her laid away in his own lot in some graveyard, where his childun was burried, 'till he could hear from you. He tole me, she was tenderly handled, and everything was done as you would have wanted it; and he cut off some of the beautiful hair—and—"

Dyce smothered her sobs in the bedclothes, but Beryl lay like a stone image.

"Oh, honey! It jest splits my heart in two, to tell you all this—"

"Go on, Dyce."

"The doctor gin me a note to the nuss at the hospital, what 'tended the ward Miss Ellie was in, and I got all her clothes, and packed 'em in a box and brought 'em home. She told me pretty much what the doctor had said, only she was shore your ma spoke jest before she died, and called twice—'Ignace! Ignace!' She said she was beautiful as a angel and her hair was a wonder to all who saw her, it was so long and so lovely. She tole me the doctor hissef put a big bunch of white carnations and tuberoses in her hand, after they put her in the coffin, and she looked like a queen. The doctor wrote you a letter 'splainin' everything, and sent it to the postmaster here. He seemed dreadfull grieved and 'stonished when I tole him how I had left you, and said if he could help you, he would be very glad to do it. I tole him we would pay his bill, as soon as this here trial bizness was over; and he answered: 'Tut—tut; bill indeed! That poor unfortunate girl need never worry over any bill of mine. I did all I could for her mother, but the best of us fail sometimes. Tell that poor child to come and see me, as soon as she gets out of the clutches of those fire-eating devils down South.' Honey, I couldn't be satisfied without seeing for myself, where they had laid my dear young mistiss. I got 'rections from the doctor, and I spent good part of a day huntin' the cemetery, and at last a man in a uniform showed me Doctor Grantlin's lot. Oh, my lamb! That was the first and only comfort I had, when I stood in front of that grand lovely marble potico—with great angels kneeling on the four corners, and knew my dear young mistiss was resting in such a beautiful place. I felt so proud that ole mistiss' chile was among the best people, sleeping with flowers in her hands, in that white marble house! I wanted to be shore there warn't no mistake, and the keeper of the graveyard tole me a lady had been put 'temporary' in the vault, four days before. I had bought a bunch of violets from a flower shop, but I could not get nearer than the door, where some brass rods was stretched like a kind of a net; so I laid my little bunch down on the marble steps, close as I could push it agin the rod; and though I couldn't see my dear young mistiss, maybe—up in heaven—she will know her poor ole mammy did not forget her, and—"

The old woman cried bitterly, and one thin hand, white as a snowflake, fell upon her bowed head, and softly stroked her black wrinkled face. After some minutes, when the paroxysm of weeping had spent itself, Dyce took the hand, kissed it reverently, and pressed into it a package.

"The doctor tole me to put that into your hands. He said he knew it would be very precious to you, but he felt shore he could trust me to bring it safe. Now, honey, I know you want to be by yourself, when you read your ma's last words. I will go and set in yonder by the fire, till you call me. My heart aches and swells fit to bust, and I can't stan' no more misery jest now, sech as this."

57

For some moments, Beryl lay motionless, then the intolerable agony clutched her throat with an aching sense of suffocation, and she sat up, with nerveless hands lying on the package in her lap. She was prepared for, expectant of the worst, but the details added keener stings to suffering that had benumbed her. At last, with a shuddering sigh, she broke the seal, and took from folds of tissue paper, a long thick tress of the beautiful black hair. Shaking it out of its satin coil, she held it up, then wrapped it smoothly over her hand, and laid it caressingly against her cheek.

Prison walls melted away; she stood again in the New York attic, and combed, and brushed, and braided those raven locks, and saw the wan face of the beloved invalid, and the jasmine and violets she had pinned at her throat.

What had become of the proud, high-spirited ambitious girl, who laughed at adverse fortune, and forgot poverty in lofty aspirations? How long ago it seemed, since she kissed the dear faded cheek, and knelt for her mother's farewell benediction. Was it the same world? Was she the same Beryl; was the eternal and unchanging God over all, as of yore? She had shattered and ruined the sparkling crystal goblet of her young life, scattering in the dust the golden wine of happy hope, in the effort to serve and comfort that loved sufferer, who, languishing on a hospital cot, had died among strangers; had been shrouded by hirelings. That any other hand than hers had touched her sacred dead, seemed a profanation; and at the thought of the last rites rendered, the loyal child shivered as though some polluting grasp had been laid upon herself. Out of the envelope rolled a broad hoop of reddish gold, her mother's wedding ring; and in zigzag lines across a sheet of paper was written the last message:

"My dear, good little girl, so faithful, so true, my legacy of love is your mother's blessing. You must be comforted to know I am dying in peace, because I trust in your last promise—"

Then a blot, some unintelligible marks, and a space. Lower still, scarcely legible characters were scrawled:

"Tell my darling—to wear my ring as a holy—"

In death as in life, the last word, and the deepest feeling were not for her; the sacred souvenir was left for the hand that had so often stabbed the idolatrous heart, now stilled forever.

In all ages the ninety and nine that go not astray, never feel the caressing touch which the yearning Shepherd lays on the obstinate wanderer, who would not pasture in peace; and from the immemorial dawn of inchoate civilization, prodigals have possessed the open sesame to parental hearts that seemed barred against the more dutiful. By what perverted organon of ethics has it come to pass in sociology, that the badge of favoritism is rarely the guerdon of merit?

To the orphaned, forsaken, disgraced captive, sitting amid the sombre ruins of her life, drinking the bitter lees of the fatal cup a mother's hand had forced to her reluctant lips, there seemed nothing strange in the injustice meted out; for had not the second place in maternal love always been hers? As the great gray eyes darkening behind their tears, like deep lakes under coming rain, read and re-read the blurred lines, the frozen mouth trembled, and Beryl kissed the hair, folded it away in the letter, and pinned both close to her heart. Staggering to her feet, she held up the ring, and said in a broken, half audible voice:

"When I am dead, your darling shall have it; until then lend it to your little girl, as a strengthening amulet. The sight of it will hold me firm, will girdle my soul with fortitude, as it girdles my finger; will set a yet holier seal to the compact whereby I pledged my life, that you might die in peace. If, in the last hour, you had known all my peril, all that my promise entails, would you have released me? Would you have died content knowing that your idol was guarded and safe, behind the cold shield of your little girl's polluted body? The blood in my veins flowed from yours; I slept on your heart, I was the last baby whose lips fed at your bosom. Mother! Mother, if you had known all, could you have seen the load of guilt and shame and woe laid on your innocent child, and bought the life of your first-born, by the sacrifice of a scapegoat? Dear mother, my mother, would you shelter him, and leave your baby to die?"

Slipping the ring on her finger, she kissed it twice. The hot flood of tears overflowed, and she fell on her knees beside the cot, clasping her hands above her bowed head.

"Alone in my desolation! Oh, father! keep close to my soul, and pray that I may have strength to bear my burden, even to the end. My God! My God! sustain me now. Help me to be patient, and when the sacrifice is finished, accept it for Christ's sake, and grant that the soul of my brother may be ransomed, because I die for his sins."

CHAPTER XIV.

"Well, dear child, what is the trouble? Into what quagmire have your little feet slipped? When you invite me so solemnly to a private conference in this distractingly pretty room, the inference is inevitable that some disaster threatens. Have you overdrawn your bank account?"

Judge Dent leaned back, making himself thoroughly comfortable in a deep easy chair in Leo's luxurious library; and taking his niece's hand, looked up into her grave, sweet face.

"I want you to honor my draft for a large amount. I am about to draw upon your sympathy; can I ever overdraw my account with that royal bank?"

"Upon my sympathy, never; but mark you, this does not commit me to compliance with all your Utopian schemes. If you were raving mad, I should sympathize, but nevertheless I should see that the strait-jacket was brought into requisition. When your generosity train dashes recklessly beyond regulation schedules of safety, I must discharge engineer sympathy, and whistle down the brakes. What new hobby do you intend that I shall ride?"

"I have no intention of sharing that privilege even with you; I merely desire you to inspect the accoutrements, to examine reins, and girth, and stirrup. I lend my hobby to no one, and it is far too mettlesome to 'carry double'. Uncle Mitchell, I feel so unhappy about that poor girl, that I must do something to comfort her, and only one avenue presents itself. I want you to have her brought into court on a writ of Habeas Corpus, and to use your influence with Judge Parkman to grant her bail. I desire to give the amount of bond he may require, because I think it would gratify her, to have this public assurance that she possessed the confidence of her own sex; for nothing so strengthens and soothes a true woman as the sympathy and trust of women."

"Looking at the case dispassionately from a professional point of view, I am sorry to tell you that the judge would scarcely be warranted in granting bail. Were I still upon the bench, I could not conscientiously release her, in the face of constantly accumulating evidence against her, although she has my deepest compassion. Conceding, however, for the moment, that Parkman consents to the petition and the girl is set at liberty, are you prepared to pay the large forfeit, if she, realizing the fearful odds against her acquittal, should take permanent bail by absconding before the trial? Abstract sympathy and generous sentiments are one phase of this matter; positively paying a fifteen or a twenty-thousand-dollar-bond is quite another. Weigh it carefully. We pity this unfortunate prisoner, but we know absolutely nothing in her favor, to counterbalance the terrible array of accusing circumstances fate has piled against her. If she be guilty, can she resist the temptation to escape by flight; and if indeed she be innocent, how much more difficult to await all that is involved in this trial, and abide the issue? Because she is beautiful, has a refined and noble air, and seems unsullied as some grand snow image, do not blind yourself to the fact, that for aught we can prove to the contrary, she may have a heart as black as Tullias', hands as bloody as Brunehaut's."

"You believe that as little as I do. I have pondered the matter in all its aspects, and I take the risk."

"You can afford to pay for her flight?"

"I will pay for her flight, no matter what it may cost."

Judge Dent took her hand between both his.

"Let us be frank."

"'The things we do—
We do; we'll wear no mask, as if we blushed!'"

"Are you so assured of the woman's fidelity; or do you deliberately leave the door ajar, foreseeing the result, deeming this the most expedient method of cutting the Gordian knot?"

For a moment she hesitated, then her soft brown eyes looked down bravely into his.

"I believe she is innocent, and that she will be loyal if released on bail; but if I mistake her character, and she should flee for her life from the lifted sword of justice, then I shall gladly pay the expense of playing Alexander's role; and shall feel rejoiced that she lives to repent her crime; and that the man to whom I have promised my hand, has been relieved of the awful responsibility of hunting her to death."

"Have you made him acquainted with this scheme?"

"Certainly not. I owed it to you to secure your approbation and co-operation, before mentioning the matter to him."

"Have you considered the opposition which, without inconsistency, he cannot fail to offer? As prosecuting attorney for the Darringtons he would be recreant to his client, if he consented to release on bail."

"His sympathy is deeply enlisted in her behalf, and I do not anticipate opposition; nevertheless, it would not deter me from the attempt to free her, at least temporarily from prison. As you have no connection with the trial, I can see no impropriety in your telling Judge Parkman, that the girl's health demands a change of air and scene, and that it is my desire to furnish any bond he may deem suitable, and then bring the prisoner under my own roof, until the day fixed for her trial. If you are unwilling to speak to him, will you permit me to mention the subject to him?"

"I fear enthusiasm is hurrying you into a proposal, the possibly grave consequences of which you do not realize. You would run a great risk in bringing here that unfortunate woman, over whose head has gathered so black a cloud of suspicion. In becoming her gaoler, you assume a fearful responsibility."

"I fully comprehend all the hazard, and with your permission, I shall not shrink. I have a conviction, for which I can offer no adequate grounds, that this girl is as innocent as I am; and if all the world hissed and jeered, I should stretch out my hand to her. Do you recollect Ortes' booty when Antwerp fell into Alva's hands? The keys of the dungeons. I would rather swing wide the barred doors of yonder human cage across the river, and lead that woman out under God's free sky, than wear all of Alva's jewels, own his gold. Uncle, will you speak, or shall I?"

"I must first talk with Churchill and Dunbar. Your effort might result only in injury to the prisoner; because if she were brought into Court on writ of Habeas Corpus, and refused bail, as I fear would be the case, the failure would operate very unfavorably for her cause, on public opinion, of which after all, in nineteen cases out of twenty, the jury verdict is a reflection. Some new evidence has been presented since the preliminary examination, and its character will determine the question of bail. If I can see any chance of your success I will speak to Parkman; for, indeed, my dear child, I honor your motive, and share your hope; but unless I find more encouragement than I expect, I will not complicate matters by a futile attempt, which would certainly recoil disastrously."

"Thank you, Uncle Mitchell. Please act promptly. I have set my heart of hearts on having that poor young woman here to spend Christmas. Her freedom to walk about in the sunshine, is the one Christmas gift I covet; and I know you will gratify me if possible. You have only four days in which to secure my present."

"When do you expect to see Dunbar?"

"I promised to ride with him this afternoon; but I prefer not to discuss this subject, as he has earnestly requested me 'to abstain from any reference to that gloomy business during his hours of recreation;' and I have no intention of setting black care en croupe to share our canter to-day. Having told me that when he leaves his office to visit us, he locks his professional affairs in his desk, you can readily understand that good taste enforces respect for his wishes, at least in the matter of avoiding tabooed topics."

"Does it occur to you that he will object very strenuously to seeing the personification of 'that gloomy business' sitting at your hearth-stone? That he may refuse to lock up in his law office the significant and disagreeable reflection, that the woman whom he arrested find prosecutes for a vile crime, is championed and housed by one whom he claims as his promised wife? Dunbar has a keen eye for the 'eternal fitness of things,' and, where you are concerned, is a jealous stickler for social convenance. I warn you he will be bitterly offended, if you bring General Darrington's granddaughter under this roof."

Her delicate flower-like face flushed; and the slight figure became proudly erect.

"It is my house, and I acquit him of the presumption of desiring to dictate to whom its doors shall be opened. If he has no confidence in my discretion, no respect for my motives, no tolerance for difference of opinion in a matter of vital importance, then the sooner our engagement is annulled the better for both of us. When I have taken my vows, I hope I shall steadfastly keep them, but meantime I am still a Gordon. The irrevocable ubi tu Caius, ego Caia, has not yet been uttered, and while it would grieve me very much to wound his feelings, I claim the exercise of my own judgment. I am not indifferent to his wishes; on the contrary, I ardently desire, as far as is consistent with my self-respect, to defer to them; but when I pledged him my faith, I did not surrender my will, nor obliterate my individuality."

Judge Dent rose, put his arm around her shoulders, and drew the sunny head to his breast.

"Leo, listen to me. There is no heaven on earth, but the nearest approach to it, the outlying suburbs whence we get bewildering glimpses of beatitude beyond, is the season of courtship and betrothal. In the magical days of sweetheartdom, a silvery glorifying glamour wraps the world, brims jagged black chasms with glittering mist, paves rugged paths with its shimmering folds, and tenderly covers very deep in rose leaves, the clay feet of our idols. That wonderful light shines only once full upon us, but the memory of it streams all along the succeeding journey; follows us up the arid heights, throws its mellow afterglow on the darkening road, as we go swiftly down the slippery hill of life. It comes to all, as hope's happy prophecy, this sparkling prologue, and we never dream that it is the sweetest and best of the drama that follows; but let me tell you, enjoy it while you may. Beautiful, hallowing sweetheart days, keep them unclouded, guard them from strife; hold them for the precious enchantment they bring, and take an old man's advice, do not quarrel with your sweetheart."

He kissed her cheek, and when the door closed behind him, she sat down and covered her face with her hands.

Was that witching light already fading in her sky? Was the storm even now muttering, that would rudely toss aside the rose leaves that garlanded the feet of her beloved? In the midst of her eloquent prologue would darkness smite suddenly, and end the drama? Life had poured its richest wine into the cup she held to her lips; should she risk spilling the priceless draught? She could turn a deaf ear to teazing whispers of suspicion, she could shut her eyes to the spectre that threw up warning hands, and so drift on; but the dream would be broken perhaps too late, and all time could not repair the possible shipwreck. Into the chill shadow of this problem plunged Miss Patty, bringing through the room the penetrating spicery of an apron full of pinks, which she was sorting and tying in star-shaped clusters.

"An extraordinary and most unexpected thing has happened, and I know you will be surprised."

"What is it, Aunt Patty? Something very pleasant, I hope."

"I have actually changed my opinion; and you know how tenacious I usually am of my well-matured views, because they are always founded on such sound reasons. Quite surprised, aren't you, dear?"

"That is far too mild and inadequate a term to express my sensations. Your views and opinions bear the same royal, inviolable seal as those of the Medes and Persians, and from their unchangeableness must have floated down the stream of Aryan migration, from some infallible fountain in Bactria. I should not be much more astonished to hear that Cynosure had grown giddy, had swung down and waltzed in the arms of Sirius."

"Leo, that sounds very pedantic, and there is nothing I dislike more. A woman bedecked with rags and tags of farfetched learning, is about as attractive an object as if she had turned out a full beard and mustache. I am very sure you have heard me assert more than once, that I verily believe Venus herself would scare all the men into monasteries, if she wore blue stockings. Too much learning in a lady's conversation is as utterly unpardonable as a waste of lemon and nutmeg in a chicken-pie; or a superfluity of cheese in Turbot a la creme; just a hint of the flavor, the merest soupcon is all that is admissible in either. I came in to tell you, that I have experienced quite a change of feeling with reference to that poor young lady, whom Mr. Dunbar with such officious haste arrested and threw into gaol. I am now convinced that a great wrong has been committed."

For a moment Leo stooped to stroke the head of her Siberian hound, crouching on the velvet rug at her feet; then she frankly met the twinkling black eyes that peered over their gold-rimmed spectacles.

"I am glad to hear it; but to what circumstance is so deckled a revulsion of sentiment attributable?"

"You know I have great confidence in Sister Serena's sagacity, and during the past fortnight she has talked frequently with me on the subject of the prisoner. When she undertook to nurse the poor child, she too considered her guilty of the unnatural crime; but by degrees she began to doubt it. About ten days ago, she says she went to the penitentiary, and found the prisoner reading a Bible which she had borrowed from the gaoler's wife. She asked her if she would like her to offer up a prayer, in her behalf, and they knelt down side by side. Sister Serena prayed that God would melt her heart if she was guilty, and help her to repent. While they were still on their knees, Sister Serena put one arm around her and said:

"'God knows whether you are the criminal; and if so, let me beg of you to make a full confession; it will unload your conscience, and may be the means of arousing more sympathy in the public heart.' She says that the poor girl looked at her a moment so reproachfully, and answered: 'When we meet in heaven, you will understand how cruelly your words hurt me. I know that appearances are hopelessly against me, and I expect to die; but I am so innocent, I keep my soul close to God, for He who knows the truth, will help me to bear man's injustice.' Then she prayed aloud for herself, that she might endure patiently and meekly an awful punishment which she did not deserve; and while she prayed, her countenance was so pure, so angelic, and there was such unmistakable fervor and sincerity in her petition, that Sister Serena says she could not help bursting into tears, and she actually begged the girl's pardon for having doubted her innocence. She has fallen completely in love with the poor young creature, and tells me she finds her wonderfully talented and cultivated. This morning she showed me some of the most beautiful designs for decorating our altar on Christmas, which the prisoner sketched for her. She cut all the models for her, and gave her such lovely suggestions, and when Sister Serena thanked her, she says the most touching smile she ever saw came into that child's face, as she answered: 'I ought to thank you for the privilege of decorating my Savior's altar, at the last Christmas I shall spend on earth. Next year, I shall spend Jesus' birthday with Him.' I felt so uncomfortable when I heard all that passed between her and Sister Serena, that I could not be easy until I had seen for myself; and as Sister Serena was going over to carry some letters to be painted and gilded, I went with her. I have seen her, and talked with her, and I pity the hard, bitter, unregenerate and vindictive heart of the man who is prosecuting her for murder. I do not believe that in all the world, Mr. Dunbar can find twelve men idiotic and vicious enough to convict that beautiful orphan girl; and his failure will do as little credit to his intellect, as success would to his moral nature."

"While I prefer to exclude Mr. Dunbar's name from our discussions, I think it merely bare justice to the absent, to assure you that he desires her conviction even less than you or I; and will do all in his power to avert it. I feel more interest in this matter than you can possibly realize, and, believing her innocent, I will befriend her to the last extremity. Did Sister Serena succeed in fitting the black dress I sent?"

"The poor child had on a mourning dress, but I was not aware you sent it. Losing her mother seems almost to have broken her heart. Poor Ellice Darrington! Petted and fostered like a hot-house flower, and then to die a pauper in a hospital! What an awful retribution for her disobedience to her parents? There is the bell."

"Yes, Auntie, and I must ask you to excuse me. Some of my Sunday-school class are coming to practise their carols, and conclude a little holiday preparation, and I hear them now on the steps."

"Did Mitchell show you Leighton's telegram?"

"He told me the good news, that at the last moment Leighton had filled his pulpit for the holidays, and would preach for us on Christmas. How delightfully it will revive the dear old days to have him back? Fancy our hanging up our stockings once more at the foot of Uncle Mitchell's bed! Your letter must have been eloquent, indeed, to entice him from the splendors of the metropolis, to the yule log at our quiet 'Lilacs'; and his coming is a tribute of gratitude to you, for all your loving care of him. I know you are so happy at the thought of taking the Holy Communion from the hand of your dear boy, that it will consecrate this Christmas above all others; and I congratulate you heartily, dear Aunt Patty."

It was late in the afternoon of Saturday, Christmas Eve, when Leo knocked at the door of Mrs. Singleton's room. A dispirited expression characterized the countenance usually serene and happy, and between her brows a perpendicular line marked the advent of anxious foreboding. Her hopeful scheme had dissolved, vanished like a puff of steam on icy air, leaving only a teazing memory of mocking failure. Judge Dent's conference with the District Solicitor, had convinced him of the futility of any attempt to secure bail; moreover, a message from the prisoner earnestly exhorted them to abandon all intercessory designs in her behalf, as she would not accept release on bail, and preferred to await her trial.

"Good evening, Miss Gordon. If you want to see her, Ned will show you the way to the chapel, where I left her a while ago. Since her mother's death, the only comfort she gets, is from the organ; so we let her go there very often. I would go with you, but I want to finish a black shawl I am crocheting for her."

The warden escorted his visitor through the chill dim corridors that had formerly so appalled Beryl's soul, and upon the steps of the chapel, both paused to listen. On the small cabinet organ, a skilful hand was playing a grand and solemn aria, which Leo had heard once before in the cool depths of Freiburg Cathedral. It had impressed her then most powerfully, as the despairing invocation of some doomed Titan; to-day it thrilled her with keen and intolerable pain. Waving the warden back, she softly entered the chapel, closed the door, and sat down.

Through the narrow windows, the afternoon sunlight, fettered by shadowy bars, fell on the bare floor, and the radiance smote the organ and the wan face of the musician, gilding the dark reddish-brown hair coiled loosely on her nobly poised head. Her black dress enhanced the extreme pallor of delicate features, which, outlined against that golden background, bore a strong resemblance to the lovely portrait of Titian's wife in the Louvre. Unmindful of the keys, across which her fingers strayed, she was gazing off into space, as if seeking some friendly face; and to the same sombre, passionate, plaintive melody she sang:

"The way is dark, my Father! Cloud upon cloud
Is gathering thickly o'er my head, and loud
The thunders roar above me. O, see—I stand
Like one bewildered! Father, take my hand—
And through the gloom lead safely home Thy Child!
The day declines, my Father! and the night
Is drawing darkly down. My faithless sight
Sees ghostly visions. Fears like a spectral band
Encompass me. O, Father, take my hand,
And from the night lead up to light Thy Child!
The cross is heavy, Father! I have borne
It long, and still do bear it. I cannot stand
Or go alone. O, Father, take my hand,
And reaching down, lead to the crown Thy Child!"

The voice was wonderfully sweet and rich, vibrating with the intense pathos of minor chords in a mellow old violoncello, and either from physical weakness, or the weight of woe, it quivered at last into a thrilling cry. Tears were dripping over Leo's cheeks, as she went up to the chancel railing, and leaning across, put out her hand. Beryl rose and came forward, and so, with only the pine balustrade between, the two stood palm in palm. No moisture dimmed the prisoner's eyes, but around her beautiful mouth sorrowful curves betokened the fierceness of the ordeal she was enduring; and her lips trembled a little, like rose leaves under a sudden rude gust.

"I have wanted very much to see you, Miss Gordon, to thank you for the great kindness that prompted your effort to help me; and yet, I have no hope of expressing adequately the comfort I derived from this manifestation of your confidence. The knowledge that you offered security for me, above all, that you were willing to take me—an outcast, almost a convicted criminal—into the holy shelter of your own home, oh! you can never realize, unless you stood in my place, how it soothes my heart, how it will always make a bright spot in the blackness of my situation. The full sympathy of a noble woman is the best tonic for a feeble sufferer, who knows the world has turned its back upon her. If I were unworthy, your goodness would be the keenest lash that could scourge me; but forlorn though I seem, your friendship brings me measureless balm, and while I could never have accepted your generous offer, I thank you sincerely."

"Why were you so unwilling that I should try to release you?"

"I have not a dollar to pay my expenses anywhere, and I appreciated too fully all that was involved in your hospitable offer, to take me under your roof, to be willing to avail myself of it. Here I am provided for, by those who believe me guilty; and here I have the kind sympathy of Mr. and Mrs. Singleton, who were my first friends when the storm broke over my doomed head. To go out of prison into the world now, would be torturing, because I am proud and sensitive; and these dark walls screen me from the curious observation from which I shrink, as from being flayed. To the desolate and homeless, change of place brings no relief; and since there is no escape for me, I prefer to wait here for the end, which, after all, cannot be very distant."

"Do you refer to the trial next month?"

"No, to that which yawns behind the trial; a shallow gash out there under the pines, where the sound of the penitentiary bell tolls requiems for the souls of its mangled victims."

"Hush! hush! You wrong yourself by imagining the possibility of such horrible results. Gloomy surroundings, coupled with your great bereavement, render you morbidly despondent; and it was the hope of cheering you, that made me so anxious to get you away. If I could only take you home, even for one week!"

"The wish has cheered me inexpressibly. How good, how noble, how tender you are! Miss Gordon, because I am so grateful, let me now say one thing. You cannot help me in future, and it would grieve me to think that I fell, as an unlifting shadow, between your heart and the sunshine that warms it. In the night of my wretchedness, you have groped your way to me, and in defiance of the circumstances that are so cruelly leagued to strangle me, you throw your confidence like a warm mantle around my shivering soul; you have courageously laid your pure, womanly hands in mine—oh, God bless you! God reward you! Do you think I could bear to know that I had caused even a hand's breadth of cloud to drift over the heavenly blue of your happy sky? The bow of promise that spans your life is no secret. Let no thought of me jar the harmony that reigned before I came here. Leave me to my doom, which human hands cannot avert now; and be happy without questioning. Inexorable fate stands behind men; makes them, sometimes, irresponsible puppets."

A deep flush had risen to Leo's temples, and withdrawing her hand, she shaded her face for a moment. The great bell below the tower clock rang sullenly.

"Good-bye, Miss Gordon. I had permission to stay here only till the bell sounded. Pray for me, but do not come again. Visits to me could bring you nothing but sorrow in return for your compassion, and that would add to my misery. I wish you a pleasant Christmas, a happy New Year, and as cloudless a life as your great goodness deserves."

Once more their hands met, in a long close clasp, then Leo laid on the chancel railing a large square envelope.

"It is only a Christmas card, but so lovely, I know your artistic taste cannot fail to admire it; and it may brighten your cheerless room. It is the three-hundred-dollar-prize-card, and particularly beautiful."

"Thank you, dear Miss Gordon. It may help to deaden the merciless stings of memory, which all day long has tortured me by unrolling the past, where my Christmas days stand out like illuminated capitals on black-letter pages."

Deaden the stings of memory? What spell suddenly evoked the image of her invalid mother, all the details of the attic room, the litter of pencils on the table; the windows of a florist's shop where, standing on the pavement, she had studied hungrily the shapes of the blossoms poverty denied her as models; the interior of the Creche, which she had penetrated in order to sketch the heads of sleeping babies, as a study for cherubs?

Leo had almost reached the door, when a passionate, indescribably mournful cry arrested her steps.

"Too late!—too late! O, God! What a cruel mockery!"

Beryl stood leaning against the railing of the altar, with the light of the setting sun falling aslant on the gilded card she held up in one hand; on her white convulsed face, where tears fell in a scalding flood. Retracing her steps, Leo said falteringly:

"In my efforts to comfort you, have I only wounded more sorely? How have I hurt you? What can I do?"

"No—no! you are an angel of pity, hovering over an abyss of ruin, whose darkest horrors you only imagine faintly. What can you do? Nothing, but pray to God to paralyze my tongue, and grant me death, before I lose my last clutch on faith, and curse my Creator, and drift down to eternal perdition! It was hard enough before, but this mockery maddens."

With a sudden abandonment, she hurled the card away, threw her arms around Leo's neck and sobbed unrestrainedly. Tenderly the latter held her shivering form, as the proud head fell on her shoulder; and after a time, Beryl lifted a face white as an annunciation lily, drenched by tropical rain.

"I thought misfortune had emptied all her vials, and that I was nerved, because there was nothing more to dread. But the worst is always behind, and this is the irony of fate. You think that merely a rhetorical metaphor, a tragic trope? How should you know? That Christmas card is the solitary dove I sent out to hunt a resting-place for mother and for me, when the flood engulfed us. It was my design sent to Boston, to compete for the prizes offered. How I dreamed, how I toiled! Haunting the flower shops for a glimpse of heartsease, and passion flowers, and stars of Bethlehem; begging a butcher at the abattoir to spare a lamb, until I could sketch it; kneeling by cradles in the public Creche to get the full red curve of a baby's sucking lips, as they forsook the bottle, the dimple in the tiny hands, the tendrils of hair on the satin brow! Over that card I sang, and I wept; I worked, hoped, prayed, believed! So much depended upon it! Could the Christ to whom I dedicated it, fail to answer my prayer for success? Three hundred dollars! What a mint! It would pay the doctor, and make mother comfortable, and get her a warm new suit for coming winter. Oh! it is so easy to believe in God, until He denies us; and to trust Christ, till He hurls our prayers back, and the stones crush us. Only three hundred dollars between life and death; between a happy, proud girl with a noble future, and a disgraced, broken-hearted wreck trampled into a convict's grave! It would have saved all; all the awful consequences of the journey here, which only dire extremity of need forced upon me. On the fatal day I started South, I went at the last moment, hoping that some tidings from my card would come on angel wings. The decision had been made, but the awards were not yet published, and so my doom was sealed. To-morrow, happy women, no more innocent than I am, will smile at my Christmas card, and give it with warm kisses and loving words to their dear ones; and to-day, my white dove of hope, flies back in my face, with the talons of a harpy, to devour me with maddening reminders of 'what might have been'. My coveted three hundred dollars! Three hundred taunting fiends! to jeer and torment me. The Christmas sun will shine on a pauper's empty cot in a charity hospital; on a disgraced, insulted, forsaken convict. Take away this last mockery, it is more than I can bear. There on the back in gilt letters—Prize Card—Three Hundred Dollars! Yet a stranger paid for my mother's coffin, and—. Three hundred furies to lash my heart out! Too late! Take it away! too late! oh, too late! This is worse than the pangs of death."

CHAPTER XV.

The Christmas Sabbath dawned cold and dim, and along the eastern sky gray marbled masses of cloud with dun, stratified bases, built themselves into the likeness of vast teocallis to Tonatiuh, over whose apex the struggling rays fell red and presageful. Dulled by the stained glass windows, the light that filled the semi-circular chapel at "The Lilacs", was chill and sombre, until the fair sacristan held a taper over the tall wax candles on each side of the altar, whence a mellow radiance soon streamed over all; flashing along the golden letters under the cross, and upon the gilded pipes of the little organ. On the marble steps in front of the altar were two baskets filled with white camellias, and great spikes of pink and blue hyacinths, that seemed to break their hearts in waves of aromatic incense. The family Bible of the Gordons lay open, on the reading desk, and upon its yellow pages rested a Maltese cross of snowy Roman hyacinths. Looping back the purple velvet portiere over the arch leading into the library, Leo sat down on the organ bench to await the coming of the family, leisurely arranged the stops, and marked in her prayer-book the Collect for Christmas. In her morning robe of crimson cashmere, with its cascade of soft rich lace foaming from throat to feet, and wearing a dainty cluster of double white violets fastened just below one ear, where the wax light kissed her sunny hair, she appeared a St. Cecilia, very fair and sweet, to the eyes of the man who stood a moment unperceived beneath the arch. A figure of medium height, clad in priestly garments, with a white surplice sweeping to the marble floor; a finely modelled head thickly fleeced with light brown hair, a serene pleasant face, with regular features, deep-set black eyes magnified by spectacles, and an expression of habitual placidity, that bespoke a soul consecrated by noble aims, and at perfect peace with his God.

Hearing his step as he crossed the floor, Leo looked over her shoulder, smiled, and began to play softly, while he ascended the steps and knelt before the altar. After some moments Miss Patty rustled in, sank on her knees and finally settled herself comfortably on one of the crescent-shaped, cushioned sofas; then Judge Dent entered, followed by Justine and the aged negro butler, Joel, the two servants finding seats just behind their master. Doctor Leighton Douglass selected his hymns, and the leaves of five prayer-books fluttered, as Collects were found, but Leo continued to play.

Twice she turned and looked around the chapel, seeking some one, delaying the commencement of the service. Finally accepting defeat, her pretty fingers fell from the keys, and with them dropped two tears, forced from her by the keen disappointment that robbed this occasion of all its anticipated pleasure. Singularly free from fashionable elocutionary affectations, and certain declamatory stage tricks, by which the recitation of the Creed and the Lord's Prayer becomes a competitive test of lungs in the race for breath, Leighton Douglass read the morning service, in a well-modulated voice, and with a profound solemnity that left its impress on each heart. The responses were fervent, and the Christmas hymns were sung with joyful earnestness; then priestly arms rose like the wings of a great snowy dove, and from holy, priestly lips fell the mellow music of the benediction:

"The grace of our Lord Jesus Christ, and the love of God, and the fellowship of the Holy Ghost, be with us all evermore. Amen."

Even while he pronounced the words, a whirring rustle filled the beautiful oratory, and two of Leo's pet ring-doves, fluttering round and round the frescoed ceiling, descended swiftly. One perched upon her head, cooing softly, and its mate nestled down with outspread pinions, pecking at the white muslin folds on Doctor Douglass' shoulder.

"Paracletes, dun plumed! Leo, let us accept them as happy auguries, prophetic of divine blessing on our future work in the Master's vineyard. My cousin, I wish you a very happy Christmas."

He had approached the organ where she sat, and held out his hand.

"Happy Christmas, Leighton, and many thanks to you for this consecrating service in my place of prayer. After today, it will always seem a more hallowed shrine, and before you leave us, we will gather here as a family, and join in the celebration of the Holy Communion."

They stood a moment hand in hand, looking into each other's eyes; and watching them, Miss Patty's heart swelled with pardonable pride in the two, whom her loving arms had so tenderly cradled. Pinching her brother's hand, as she walked with him under the velvet draperies, she whispered:

"What a noble match for both! And he's only her second cousin."

Leo's eyes were wet with tears, which Doctor Douglass ascribed to devotional fervor; and withdrawing her hand, she opened one of the windows, and called the doves to the stone ledge, putting them very gently out upon the ivy wreaths that clambered up the wall, and peeped into the chapel.

"I believe you are sacristan here?" he said, pointing to the candles that flared, as the wind rushed in.

"Yes, here I sweep, dust, decorate daily, allowing no other touch; and here I bring my daintiest, rarest flowers, as tribute to Him who tapestried the earth with blossoms, and sprinkled it with perfumes—when? Not until just before the advent of humanity, whose material kingdom was perfected, and furnished in anticipation of his arrival."

Extinguishing the candles, she closed the old Bible, covered it with a square of velvet, and hung the cross of hyacinths upon the folded hands of one of the marble angels that upheld the altar.

"Pure-handed women are natural priestesses, meet for temple ministration; and I have no doubt your exoteric labors here, merely typify the secret daily sweeping out of evil thoughts, the dusting away of motes of selfishness, the decorating with noble beautiful aims, and holy deeds, whereby you sanctify that inner shrine, your own soul."

"Praise from you means so much, that you need not stoop to flatter me. The very vestments of you Levites should exhale infectious humility; and I especially need exhortations against pride, my besetting sin. I built this chapel, not because I am good, but in order to grow better. Every dwelling has its room in which the inmates gather to eat, to study, to work, to sleep; why not to pray, the most important privilege of many that divide humanity from brutes? After all, the pagans were wiser than we, and the heads of families were household priests, setting examples of piety at every rising of the sun."

"Let us see. Greek and Roman fathers laid a cake dripping with wine, a wreath of violets, a heart of honey-comb, a brace of doves on the home altar, and immediately thereafter, set the example of violating every clause in the Decalogue. Mark you, paganism drew fine lines in morals, long anterior to the era of monotheism and of Moses, and furnished immortal types of all the virtues; yet the excess of its religious ceremonial, robbed it of vital fructifying energies. The frequency and publicity of sacerdotal service, usurped the place of daily individual piety. The tendency of all outward symbolical observances, unduly multiplied, is to substitute mere formalism for fervor."

"Leighton, humanity craves the concrete. All the universe is God's temple, yet the chill breath of the abstract freezes our hearts; and we pray best in some pillared niche consecrated and set apart, I recall a day in Umbria, when the wonderful light of sunset fell on ilex and olive, on mountain snows, on valleys billowing between vine-mantled hills, on creamy marble walls, on columned campaniles; and standing there, I seemed verily to absorb, to become saturated as it were, with the reigning essence of beauty. I walked on, a few steps, lifted a worn, frayed leather curtain, and looked into a small gray, dingy church, where a mist of incense blurred the lights on the ancient altar, and the muffled roll of an organ broke into sonorous waves, like reverberations of far-away thunder; and why was it, tell me, that the universal glory thrilled me only as a sensuous chord of color, but in the dark corner consecrated to the worship of our God, my soul expanded, as if a holy finger touched it, and I fell on my knees, and prayed? Each of us comes into this world dowered with the behest to make desperate war against that indissoluble 'Triple Alliance, the World, the Flesh and the Devil,' and needing all the auxiliaries possible, I resort to conscription wherever I can recruit. Since I am two thousand years too young to set up a statue of Hestia yonder in my imitation prostas, I have built instead this small sacred nook for prayer, which helps me spiritually, much as the Ulah aids Islam."

"Your oratory is lovely, and I wish its counterpart adorned every homestead in our land; but are you quite sure that in your individual experience you are not mistaking effect for cause? Your holy heart demands fit shrine for—"

"I am quite sure I will not allow you to stand a moment longer on this cold floor; and I do not intend that you shall pay me undeserved compliments. It is derogatory to your dignity, and dangerous to my modicum of humility. As soon as you are ready for breakfast, come to the dining-room, where Santa Klaus left his remembrances last night. O, Leighton! I had half a mind to hang up two stockings at uncle's bed, for the sake of dear old lang syne. If we could only shut our eyes, and drift back to the magical time of aprons, short clothes, and roundabouts, when a sugar rooster with green wings and pink head, and a doll that could open and shut her eyes, were considered more precious than Tiffany's jewels, or Collamore's Crown Derby! Can Delmonico offer you a repast half as appetizing as the hominy, the tea cakes, the honey and the sweet milk which you and I used to enjoy at our supper just at sunset, at our own little table set under the red mulberry trees in the back yard?"

"Why should my cousin, whose present is so rose-colored, whose future so blissful, turn to rake amid the ashes of the past?"

"Because, like Lot's wife, we are all prone to stare backward. Who lives in the present? Do you? When we are young we pant for the future, that pitches painted tents before us. When we are older, we live in the past, that wraps itself in a sacred gilding glamour, and is vocal with the happy echoes which alone survive. Far-off fields before and behind us are so dewy, so vividly green; and the present is gray and stony, and barren of charm, and we turn fretfully. It is part of the grim tyranny of Time that it is tideless; that the stream bears remorselessly on, and on, never back to the dear old spots; always on, to lose itself in the eternal and unknown. So, to-day's Christmas lacks the zest of its predecessors."

Leo loosened the gilded chain that looped the curtains, and as the purple folds fell behind her, hiding the arch, Doctor Douglass said gently:

"There is a solemn truth and wise admonition in one of Rabbi Tyra's dicta: 'Thy yesterday is thy past; thy to-day is thy future; thy to-morrow is a secret.'"

"Leo, here is a package and a note which arrived during service, and as Mr. Dunbar's servant said there was no answer expected, he did not wait."

As Miss Patty delivered the parcel to her niece, the minister walked away to lay aside his vestments, but he noted the sudden hardening of his cousin's face, the flush of displeasure, the haughty curl of her lips; and on his ears fell his aunt's voice:

"You expected and waited for him at morning prayer?"

"I invited him to join us, if he felt disposed to do so."

"What possible excuse can he offer for such negligence, when he knew that Leighton would read the service?"

An uwonted sparkle leaped into Leo's mild hazel eyes, and without examination she handed the package and note to Justine.

"Lay them in the drawer of my writing-desk, and then call all the servants into the dining-room. Auntie, tardy excuses must wait longer for an audience than we waited for the writer. Come to breakfast; uncle will be impatient, and I want to enjoy his surprise when he sees his Santa Klaus."

She was sorely disappointed, deeply affronted by Mr. Dunbar's failure to present himself on an occasion at which she had especially desired his presence; and as she recalled the affectionate phraseology of her note of invitation, her fair cheek burned with an intolerable sense of humiliation. Was it partition, or total loss, of her precious kingdom? In after years, she designated this Christmas as the era when the "sceptre departed from Judah;" but putting away the chagrin, and sealing the well of bitterness in her heart, she exchanged holiday greetings, and proudly wore her royal robes throughout the day, holding sternly off the spectre, which grimly bided its time—the hour of her abdication.

Through the benevolent and compassionate efforts of Mr. and Mrs. Singleton, some faint reflection of the outside world festivities penetrated the dismal monotony of prison routine; and the hearts of the inmates were softened and gladdened by kind tokens of remembrance, that carried the thoughts of bearded convicts back to Christmas carols in innocent youth, and to the mother's knees where prayers were lisped.

Illness had secured to Beryl immunity from contact with her comrades in misery, and except to visit the little chapel, she never left the sheltering walls of her small comfortless room, grateful for the unexpected boon of silent seclusion. Her Christmas greeting had been little Dick's sweet lips kissing her cheek, as he deposited upon her narrow bed the black and white shawl his mother had knitted, and a box left by Miss Gordon on the previous day, which contained half a dozen pretty handkerchiefs with mourning borders, some delicate perfume and soaps, toilet brushes and a sachet.

An hour later, when Mrs. Singleton and her babies had gone to spend the day with relatives in the city, Beryl went to the window, pushed the sash up, and listened to the ringing of the Sabbath-school bells, as every church beyond the river called its nursery to the altar, to celebrate the day. The metallic clangor was mellowed by distance, rising and falling like rhythmic waves, and the faint echo, filtered through dense pine forests behind the penitentiary, had the ghostly iteration of the Folge Fond.

A gaunt yellow kitten, with a faded red ribbon knotted about its neck, and vicious, amber-colored eyes that were a perpetual challenge, had fled from the tender mercies of Dick to the city of refuge under Beryl's cot; and community of suffering had kindled an attachment that now prompted the lesser waif to spring into the girl's folded arms, and rub its head against her shoulder. Mechanically Beryl's hand stroked the creature's ear, while it purred softly under the caress; but suddenly its back curved into an arch, the tail broadened, the purr became a growl. Had association lifted the brute's instincts to the plane of human antipathies?

The warden had opened the door and quickly closed it, after ushering in a tall figure, who wore an overcoat which was buttoned from throat to knees. At sight of Mr. Dunbar, the cat plunged to the floor, and sped away to the darkest corner under the iron bedstead.

"Good morning. I dare not utter here the greetings of the day, because you would construe it into a heartless mockery."

He came forward hesitatingly, and she turned swiftly away, pressing her face against the bars of the window, waving him back.

"Why will you persist in regarding as an enemy, the one person in all the world who is most anxious to befriend you?"

Still no answer; only the repellent gesture warning him away.

"Will you allow me, this Christmas morning, to comfort myself in some degree, by leaving here a few flowers to brighten your desolate surroundings?"

He held out a bouquet of rare and brilliant hothouse blossoms, whose delicious fragrance had already pervaded the room. They stood side by side, yet she shrank farther, and kept her face averted, shivering perceptibly. Lifting one arm he drew down the sash to shut out the freezing air.

"You are resolved neither to look at nor speak to me? So be it. At least you must listen to me. You may not care to hear that I have been absent, but perhaps it will interest you to know that I went in search of the man for whose crime you are paying the penalty."

If he expected her to wince under the probe, her nerves were taut, and she defied the steel; but the face she now turned fully to him was so blanched by illness, so hopeless in its rigid calm, that he felt a keen pain at his own heart.

"Prisoners, victims of justice, have, it seems, no privileges; else my one request, my earnest prayer to be shielded from your presence, might have protected me from this intrusion. Are you akin to Parrhasius that you come to gloat over the agonies of a moral and mental vivisection? The sight of suffering to which you have brought a helpless woman, is scarcely the recompense I was taught to suppose agreeable to a chivalrous Southern gentleman. If, wearing the red livery of Justice, undue zeal for vengeance betrayed you into the fatal mistake of trampling me into this horrible place, there might be palliation; but for the brutal persistency with which you thrust your tormenting presence upon me, not even heavenly charity could possibly find pardon. Literally you are heaping insult upon awful injury. Is it a refinement of cruelty that brings you here to watch and analyze my suffering, as a biologist looks through lenses at an insect he empales, or Pasteur scrutinizes the mortal throes of the victims into whose veins he has injected poison?"

If she had drawn a lash across his face, it would not have stung more keenly than her words, so expressive of detestation.

"Will you consider for a moment the possibility that other motives actuate me; that ceaseless regret, remorse, if you choose, for a terrible mistake, impels me to come here in the hope of making reparation?"

"Such a supposition is as inconceivable as the idea of reparation. When a reaper goes forth to his ripe harvest, his lawful labor, and wantonly turns aside into a by-path, to try the edge of his sickle on an humble, unoffending stalk that fights for life among the grass and weeds, and struggles to get its head sufficiently in the sunshine to bloom—when he cuts it off unopened, crushes it into the sod, can he make reparation? Although it is neither bearded yellow wheat, nor yet a black tare, it proved the temper of his blade; and all the skill, all the science of universal humanity, cannot re-erect the stem, cannot remove the stains, cannot unfold the bruised petals. There are wrongs that all time will never repair. Your sword of justice needs no whetting; one stroke has laid me low."

"I purpose to file it two-edged, in order to make no more mistakes. Before long I shall cut down the real criminal, the principal, who shall not escape, and for whom you shall not suffer."

"Then 'a life for a life' no longer satisfies? How many are required? The law has need of a sacrificial stone wide as that of the Aztecs. Is justice a 'daughter of the horse-leech'?"

"So help me God—"

"Hush! Take not His name upon your lips. Men like you cannot afford to credit the existence of a holy God. This is Christmas—at least according to the almanac—now as a 'chivalrous Southern gentleman,' will you grant me a very great favor if I humbly crave it? Ah, noblesse oblige! you cannot deny me. I beg of you, then, leave me instantly; come here no more. Never let me see your face again, or hear your voice, except in the court-room, when I am tried for the crime which you have told the world I committed. This boon is the sole possible reparation left you."

She had clasped her hands so tightly, that the nails were bloodless, and the fluttering in her white throat betrayed the throbbing of her heart.

"You are afraid of me, because you dread my discovering your secret, which is—"

"You have done your worst. You have locked me away from a dying mother; disgraced an innocent life; broken a girl's pure, happy heart; what else is there to dread? Although a bird knows full well when it has received its death wound, instinct drives it to flutter, drag itself as far as possible from the gaze of the sportsman, and gasp out its agony in some lonely place."

"When I hunt birds, and a partridge droops its wings, and hovers almost at my feet, inviting capture, I know beyond all peradventure that it is only love's ruse; that something she holds dearer than her own life, is thereby screened, saved. You are guilty of a great crime against yourself, you are submitting tacitly, consenting to an awful doom, in order to spare and protect the real murderer."

He bent closer, watching breathlessly for some change in her white stony face; but her sad eyes met his with no wavering of the lids, and only her delicate nostrils dilated slightly. She raised her locked hands, rested her lips a moment on her mother's ring, as if drinking some needed tonic, and answered in the same low, quiet tone:

"Then, prime minister of justice, set me free, and punish the guilty. Who murdered General Darrington?"

"You have known from the beginning; and I intend to set you free, when that cowardly miscreant has been secured. You would die to save your lover; you, proud, brave, noble natured, would sacrifice your precious life for that wretched, vile poltroon, who flees and leaves you to suffer in his stead! Truly, there is no mystery so profound, so complex, so subtle as a woman's heart. To die for his crimes, were a happier fate than to sully your fair soul by alliance with one so degraded; and, by the help of God, I intend to snatch you from both!"

He had put his hands for an instant upon her shoulders, and his handsome face flushed, eloquent with the feeling that he no longer cared to disguise, was so close to hers, that she felt his breath on her cheek.

Swiftly, unerringly she comprehended everything; and the suddenness of the discovery dazzled, awed her, as one might feel under the blue flash of a dagger when thrust into one's clasp for novice fingers to feel the edge. Was the weapon valued merely because of the possibility of fleshing it in the heart of him who had darkened her life? Did he understand as fully the marvellous change in the beautiful face, that had lured him from his chapel tryst with his betrothed? He was on the alert for signals of distress, of embarrassment, of terror; but what meant the glad light that leaped up in her eyes, the quick flush staining her wan cheek, the triumphant smile curving lips that a moment before might have belonged to Guercino's Mater Dolorosa, the relaxation of figure and features, the unmistakable expression of intense relief that stole into the countenance?

"Will you be so good as to tell me my lover's name, and where the fox terriers of the law unearthed him?"

"I will tell you something which you do not already know; that I have found a clue, that I shall hunt him out, hide, crouch where he may; that here, where he sinned, he shall expiate his crime, and that when your lover is hung, your name, your honor, shall be vindicated. So much, Lennox Dunbar promises you, on his honor as a gentleman."

"Words, vapid words! Empty, worthless as last year's nests. My lover," she laughed scornfully, "is quite safe even from your malevolence. If indeed 'one touch of nature makes the whole world kin,' one might expect some pity from the guild of love swains; and it augurs sadly for Miss Gordon's future, that the spell is so utterly broken."

His dark face reddened, lowered.

"If you please, we will keep Miss Gordon's name out of the conversation, and hereafter when—"

"Enough! I shall keep her image in my grateful heart, the few tedious months I have to live; and there seems indeed a sort of poetic justice in the fact that the bride you covet, has become the truest, tenderest friend of the hapless girl whom you are prosecuting for murder."

"Beryl—"

"I forbid such insolent presumption! You shall not utter the name my father gave me. It is holy as my baptism; it must be kept unsullied for my lover's lips to fondle. This is your last visit here, for if you dare to intrude again, I will demand protection from the warden. I will bear no more."

As he looked at her, the witchery of her youthful loveliness, heightened by the angry sparkle in her deep eyes, by the vivid carnation of her curling lips, mastered him; and when he thought of the brown-haired woman to whom he was pledged, he set his teeth tight, to smother an execration. He moved toward the door, paused, and came back.

"Will it comfort you to know that I suffer even more than you do; that I am plunged into a fiercer purgatory than that to which I have condemned you? I am devoured by regret; but I will atone. I came here as your friend; I can never be less, and in defiance of your hatred, I shall prove my sincerity. Because I bemoan my rash haste, will you say good-bye kindly? Some day, perhaps, you will understand."

He held out his hand, and his blue eyes lost their steely glitter, filled with a prayer for pardon.

She picked up the bouquet which had fallen from the window sill to the floor, and without hesitation put it into his fingers.

"I think I understand all that words could ever explain. My short stream of life is very near the great ocean of rest. I have ceased to struggle, ceased to hope; and since the end is so close, I wish no active warfare even with those who wronged me most foully. If you will spare me the sight of you, I will try to forget the added misery of the visits you have forced upon me, and perhaps some of the bitterness may die out. Take the flowers to Miss Gordon; leave no trace to remind me of your persecution. We bear chastisement because we must, but the sight of the rod renews the sting; so, henceforth, I hope to see you no more. When we meet before our God, I may have a new heart, swept clean of earthly hate, but until then—until then—"

He caught her fingers, crushed his lips against them, and walked from the room, leaving the bouquet a shattered mass of perfume in the middle of the floor.

CHAPTER XVI.

Standing before Leon Gerome's tragic picture, and listening to the sepulchral echo that floats down the arcade of centuries. "Ave, Imperator, morituri te salutant," nineteenth century womanhood frowns, and deplores the brutal depravity which alone explains the presence of that white-veiled vestal band, whose snowy arms are thrust in signal over the parapet of the bloody arena; yet fair daughters of the latest civilization show unblushing flower faces among the heaving mass of the "great unwashed" who crowd our court-rooms—and listen to revolting details more repugnant to genuine modesty, than the mangled remains in the Colosseum. The rosy thumbs of Roman vestals were potent ballots in the Eternal City, and possibly were thrown only in the scale of mercy; but having no voice in verdicts, to what conservative motive may be ascribed the presence of women at criminal trials? Are the children of Culture, the heiresses of "all the ages", really more refined than the proud old dames of the era of Spartacus?

Is the spectacle of mere physical torture, in gladiatorial combats, or in the bloody precincts of plaza de toros, as grossly demoralizing as the loathsome minutiae of heinous crimes upon which legal orators dilate; and which Argus reporters, with magnifying lenses at every eye, reproduce for countless newspapers, that serve as wings for transporting moral dynamite to hearthstones and nurseries all over our land? Is there a distinction, without a difference, between police gazettes and the journalistic press?

If extremes meet, and the march of human progress be along no asymtotic line, is the day very distant when we shall welcome the Renaissance of that wisdom which two thousand years ago held its august tribunal in the solemn hours of night, when darkness hid from the Judges everything save well-authenticated facts? The supreme aim of civil and criminal law being the conservation of national and individual purity, to what shall we attribute the paradox presented in its administration, whereby its temples become lairs of libel, their moral atmosphere defiled by the monstrous vivisection of parental character by children, the slaughter of family reputation, the exhaustive analysis of every species of sin forbidden by the Decalogue, and floods of vulgar vituperation dreadful as the Apocalyptic vials? Can this generation

"—in the foremost files of time—"

afford to believe that a grim significance lurks in the desuetude of typical judicial ermine?

Traditions of ante bellum custom proclaimed that "good society" in the town of X—, formerly considered the precincts of courts as unfit for ladies as the fetid air of morgues, or the surgical instruments on dissecting tables; but the vanguard of cosmopolitan freedom and progress had pitched tents in the old-fashioned place, and recruited rapidly from the ranks of the invaded; hence it came to pass, that on the second day of the murder trial, when the preliminaries of jury empanelling had been completed, and all were ready to launch the case, X— announced its social emancipation from ancient canons of decorum, by the unwonted spectacle of benches crowded with "ladies", whose silken garments were crushed against the coarser fabrics of proletariat. Despite the piercing cold of a morning late in February, the mass of human furnaces had raised the temperature to a degree that encouraged the fluttering of fans, and necessitated the order that no additional spectators should be admitted.

Viewed through the leaden haze of fearful anticipation, the horror of the impending trial had seemed unendurable to the proud and sensitive girl, whom the Sheriff placed on a seat fronting the sea of curious faces, the battery of scrutinizing eyes turned on her from the jury-box. Four months of dread had unnerved her, yet now when the cruel actuality seized her in its iron grasp, that superb strength which the inevitable lends to conscious innocence, so steeled and fortified her, that she felt lifted to some lonely height, where numbness eased her aching wounds.

Pallid and motionless, she sat like a statue, save for the slow strokes of her right hand upon the red gold of her mother's ring; and the sound of a man's voice reading a formula, seemed to echo from an immeasurable distance. She had consented to, had deliberately accepted the worst possible fate, and realized the isolation of her lot; but for one thing she was not prepared, and its unexpectedness threatened to shiver her calmness. Two women made their way toward her: Dyce and Sister Serena. The former sat down in the rear of the prisoner, the latter stood for a few seconds, and her thin delicate hand fell upon the girl's shoulder. At sight of the sweet, placid countenance below the floating white muslin veil, Beryl's lips quivered into a sad smile; and as they shook hands she whispered:

"I believe even the gallows will not frighten you two from my side."

Sister Serena seated herself as close as possible, drew from her pocket a gray woollen stocking, and began to knit. For an instant Beryl's eyes closed, to shut in the sudden gush of grateful tears; when she opened them, Mr. Churchill had risen:

"May it please the Court, Gentlemen of the Jury: If fidelity to duty involved no sacrifice of personal feeling, should we make it the touchstone of human character, value it as the most precious jewel in the crown of human virtues? I were less than a man, immeasurably less than a gentleman, were I capable of addressing you to-day, in obedience to the behests of justice, and in fulfilment of the stern requirements of my official position, without emotions of profound regret, that implacable Duty, to whom I have sworn allegiance, forces me to hush the pleading whispers of my pitying heart, to smother the tender instincts of human sympathy, and to listen only to the solemn mandate of those laws, which alone can secure to our race the enjoyment of life, liberty and property. An extended professional career has hitherto furnished me no parallel for the peculiarly painful exigencies of this occasion; and an awful responsibility scourges me with scorpion lash to a most unwelcome task. When man crosses swords with man on any arena, innate pride nerves his arm and kindles enthusiasm, but alas, for the man! be he worthy the name, who draws his blade and sees before him a young, helpless, beautiful woman, disarmed. Were it not a bailable offence in the court of honor, if his arm fell palsied? Each of you who has a mother, a wife, a lily browed daughter, put yourself in my place, lend me your sympathy; and at least applaud the loyalty that strangles all individuality, and renders me bound thrall of official duty. Counsel for the defence has been repeatedly offered, nay, pressed upon the prisoner, but as often persistently rejected; hence the almost paralyzing repugnance with which I approach my theme.

"The Grand Jury of the county, at its last sitting, returned to this court a bill of indictment, charging the prisoner at the bar with the wilful, deliberate and premeditated murder of Robert Luke Darrington, by striking him with a brass andiron. To this indictment she has pleaded

'Not Guilty,' and stands before her God and this community for trial. Gentlemen of the jury, you represent this commonwealth, jealous of the inviolability of its laws, and by virtue of your oaths, you are solemnly pledged to decide upon her guilt or innocence, in strict accordance with the evidence that may be laid before you. In fulfilling this sacred duty, you will, I feel assured, be governed exclusively by a stern regard to the demands of public justice. While it taxes our reluctant credulity to believe that a crime so hideous could have been committed by a woman's hand, could have been perpetrated without provocation, within the borders of our peaceful community, nevertheless, the evidence we shall adduce must inevitably force you to the melancholy conclusion that the prisoner at the bar is guilty of the offence, with which she stands charged. The indictment which you are about to try, charges Beryl Brentano with the murder.

"In outlining the evidence which will be presented in support of this indictment, I earnestly desire that you will give me your dispassionate and undivided attention; and I call God to witness, that disclaiming personal animosity and undue zeal for vengeance, I am sorrowfully indicating as an officer of the law, a path of inquiry, that must lead you to that goal where, before the altar of Truth, Justice swings her divine scales, and bids Nemesis unsheathe her sword.

"On the afternoon of October the twenty-sixth, about three o'clock, a stranger arrived in X—and inquired of the station agent what road would carry her to 'Elm Bluff', the home of General Darrington; assuring him she would return in time to take the north-bound train at 7.15, as urgent business necessitated her return. Demanding an interview with Gen'l Darrington, she was admitted, incognito, and proclaimed herself his granddaughter, sent hither by a sick mother, to procure a certain sum of money required for specified purposes. That the interview was stormy, was characterized by fierce invective on her part, and by bitter denunciation and recrimination on his, is too well established to admit of question; and they parted implacable foes, as is attested by the fact that he drove her from his room through a rear and unfrequented door, opening into a flower garden, whence she wandered over the grounds until she found the gate. The vital import of this interview lies in the great stress Gen'l Darrington placed upon the statement he iterated and reiterated; that he had disinherited his daughter, and drawn up a will bequeathing his entire estate to his step-son Prince.

"Miss Brentano did not leave X—at 7.15, though she had ample time to do so, after quitting 'Elm Bluff'. She loitered about the station house until nearly half-past eight, then disappeared. At 10 P.M. she was seen and identified by a person who had met her at 'Elm Bluff', crouching behind a tree near the road that led to that ill-fated house, and when questioned regarding her presence there, gave unsatisfactory answers. At half-past two o'clock she was next seen hastening toward the station office, along the line of the railroad, from the direction of the water tank, which is situated nearly a mile north of town. Meanwhile an unusually severe storm had been followed by a drenching rain, and the stranger's garments were wet, when, after a confused and contradictory account of her movements, she boarded the 3.05 train bound north.

"During that night, certainly after ten o'clock, Gen'l Darrington was murdered. His vault was forced open, money was stolen, and most significant of all, the WILL was abstracted. Criminal jurisprudence holds that the absence of motive renders nugatory much weighty testimony. In this melancholy cause, could a more powerful motive be imagined than that which goaded the prisoner to dip her fair hands in her grandfather's blood, in order to possess and destroy that will, which stood as an everlasting barrier between her and the estate she coveted?

"Crimes are referrible to two potent passions of the human soul; malice, engendering thirst for revenge, and the insatiable lust of money. If that old man had died a natural death, leaving the will he had signed, his property would have belonged to the adopted son, to whom he bequeathed it, and Mrs. Brentano and her daughter would have remained paupers. Cut off by assassination, and with no record of his last wishes in existence, the beloved son is bereft of his legacy, and Beryl Brentano and her mother inherit the blood-bought riches they covet. When arrested, gold coins and jewels identified as those formerly deposited in Gen'l Darrington's vault, were found in possession of the prisoner; and as if every emissary of fate were armed with warrants for her detection, a handkerchief bearing her initials, and saturated with the chloroform which she had administered to her victim, was taken from the pillow, where his honored gray head rested, when he slept his last sleep on earth. Further analysis would insult your intelligence, and having very briefly laid before you the intended line of testimony, I believe I have assigned a motive for this monstrous crime, which must precipitate the vengeance of the law, in a degree commensurate with its enormity. Time, opportunity, motive, when in full accord, constitute a fatal triad, and the suspicious and unexplainable conduct of the prisoner in various respects, furnishes, in connection with other circumstances of this case, the strongest presumptive evidence of her guilt. These circumstances, far beyond the realm of human volition, smelted and shaped in the rolling mills of destiny, form the tramway along which already the car of doom thunders; and when they shall have been fully proved to you, by unassailable testimony, no alternative remains but the verdict of guilty. Mournful as is the duty, and awfully solemn the necessity that leaves the issue of life and death in your hands, remember, gentlemen, Curran's immortal words: 'A juror's oath is the adamantine chain that binds the integrity of man to the throne of eternal justice'."

No trace of emotion was visible on the prisoner's face, except at the harsh mention of her mother's name; when a shudder was perceptible, as in one where dentist's steel pierces a sensitive nerve. In order to avoid the hundreds of eyes that stabbed her like merciless probes, her own had been raised and fixed upon a portion of the cornice in the room where a family of spiders held busy camp; but a fascination song resisted, finally drew their gaze down to a seat near the bar, and she encountered the steady, sorrowful regard of Mr. Dunbar.

Two months had elapsed since the Christmas morning on which she had rejected his floral offering, and during that weary season of waiting, she had refused to see any visitors except Dyce and Sister Serena; resolutely denying admittance to Miss Gordon. She knew that he had been absent, had searched for some testimony in New York, and now meeting his eyes, she saw a sudden change in their expression—a sparkle, a smile of encouragement, a declaration of success. He fancied he understood the shadow of dread that drifted over her face; and she realized at that instant, that of all foes, she had most to apprehend from the man who she knew loved her with an unreasoning and ineradicable fervor. How much had he discovered? She could defy the district solicitor, the judge, the jury; but only one method of silencing the battery that was ambushed in those gleaming blue eyes presented itself. To extinguish his jealousy, by removing the figment of a rival, might rob him of the motive that explained his persistent pursuit of the clue she had concealed; but it would simultaneously demolish, also, the barrier that stretched between Miss Gordon's happy heart and the bitter waves of a cruel disappointment. If assured that her own affection was unpledged, would the bare form and ceremonial of honor bind his allegiance to his betrothed?

Absorbed in these reflections, the prisoner became temporarily oblivious of the proceedings; and it was not until Sister Serena touched her arm, that she saw the vast throng was watching her, waiting for some reply. The Judge repeated his question:

"Is it the desire of the prisoner to answer the presentation of the prosecution? Having refused professional defence, you now have the option of addressing the Court."

"Let the prosecution proceed."

There was no quiver in her voice, as cold, sweet and distinct it found its way to the extremity of the wide apartment; yet therein lurked no defiance. She resumed her seat, and her eyes sank, until the long black fringes veiled their depths. Unperceived, Judge Dent had found a seat behind her, and leaning forward he whispered:

"Will you permit me to speak for you?"

"Thank you—no."

"But it cuts me to the heart to see you so forsaken, so helpless."

"God is my helper; He will not forsake me."

The first witness called and sworn was Doctor Ledyard, the physician who for many years had attended General Darrington; and who testified that when summoned to examine the body of deceased, on the morning of the inquest, he had found it so rigid that at least eight hours must have elapsed since life became extinct. Had discovered no blood stains, and only two contusions, one on the right temple, where a circular black spot was conspicuous, and a bluish bruise over the region of the heart. He had visited deceased on the morning of previous day, and he then appeared much better, and almost relieved of rheumatism and pains attributable to an old wound in the right knee. The skull had not been fractured by the blow on the temple, but witness believed it had caused death; and the andiron, which he identified as the one found on the floor close to the deceased, was so unusually massive, he was positive that if hurled with any force, it would produce a fatal result.

Mr. Churchill: "Did you at that examination detect any traces of chloroform?"

"There was an odor of chloroform very perceptible when we lifted the hair to examine the skull; and on searching the room, we found a vial which had contained chloroform, and was beside the pillow, where a portion had evidently leaked out."

"Could death have occurred in consequence of inhaling that chloroform?"

"If so, the deceased could never have risen, and would have been found in his bed; moreover, the limbs were drawn up, and bent into a position totally inconsistent with any theory of death produced by anaesthetics; and the body was rigid as iron."

The foregoing testimony was confirmed by that of Doctor Cranmar, a resident physician, who had been summoned by the Coroner to assist Doctor Ledyard in the examination, reported formally at the inquest.

"Here, gentlemen of the jury, is the fatal weapon with which a woman's hand, supernaturally nerved in the struggle for gain, struck down, destroyed a venerable old man, an honored citizen, whose gray hairs should have shielded him from the murderous assault of a mercenary adventuress. Can she behold without a shudder, this tell-tale instrument of her monstrous crime?"

High above his head, Mr. Churchill raised the old-fashioned andiron, and involuntarily Beryl glanced at the quaint brass figure, cast in the form of a unicorn, with a heavy ball surmounting the horn.

"Abednego Darrington!"

Sullen, crestfallen and woe-begone was the demeanor of the old negro, who had been brought vi et armis by a constable, from the seclusion of a corner of the "Bend Plantation", where he had secreted himself, to avoid the shame of bearing testimony against his mistress' child. When placed on the witness stand, he crossed his arms over his chest, planted his right foot firmly in advance, and fixed his eyes on the leather strings that tied his shoes.

After some unimportant preliminaries, the District Solicitor asked:

"When did you first see the prisoner, who now sits before you?"

"When she come to our house, the evening before ole Marster died."

"You admitted her to your Master's presence?"

"I never tuck no sech libberties. He tole me to let her in."

"You carried her to his room?"

"Yes, sir."

"About what time of the day was it?"

"Don't know."

"Gen'l Darrington always dined at three o'clock. Was it before or after dinner?"

"After."

"How long was the prisoner in the General's room?"

"Don't know."

"Did she leave the house by the front door, or the side door?"

"Can't say. Didn't see her when she come out."

"About how long was she in the house?"

"I totes no watch, and I never had no luck guessing. I'm shore to land wrong."

"Was it one hour or two?"

"Mebbe more, mebbe less."

"Where were you during that visit?"

"Feedin' my game pullets in the backyard."

"Did you hear any part of the conversation between the prisoner and Gen'l Darrington?"

"No, sir! I'm above the meanness of eavesdrapping."

"How did you learn that she was the granddaughter of Gen'l Darrington?"

"Miss Angerline, the white 'oman what mends and sews, come to the back piazer, and beckoned me to run there. She said ther must be a 'high ole fracas', them was her words, agoin' on in Marster's room, for he was cussin' and swearin', and his granddaughter was jawing back very vicious. Sez I, 'Who'? Sez she, 'His granddaughter; that is Ellice's chile'. Sez I, 'How do you know so much'? Sez she, 'I was darning them liberry curtains, and I couldn't help hearing the wrangle'. Sez I, 'You picked a oncommon handy time to tackle them curtains; they must be mighty good to cure the ear-itch'. She axed me if I didn't see the family favor in the 'oman's face; and I tole her no, but I would see for myself. Sez she, to me, 'No yow won't, for the Gen'l is in a tearing rage, and he's done drove her out, and kicked and slammed the doors. She's gone.'"

"Then you did not see her?"

"I went to the front piazer, and I seen her far down the lawn, but Marster rung his bell so savage, I had to run back to him."

"Did he tell you the prisoner was his granddaughter?"

"No, sir."

"Did you mention the fact to him?"

"I wouldn't 'a dared to meddle with his fambly bizness!"

"He appeared very angry and excited?"

"He 'peard to want some ole Conyyac what was in the sideboard, and I brung the bottle to him."

"Do you remember whether his vault in the wall was open, when you answered the bell?"

"I didn't notice it."

"Where did you sleep that night?"

"On a pallet in the middle passage, nigh the star steps."

"Was that your usual custom?"

"No, sir. But the boy what had been sleepin' in the house while ole Marster was sick, had gone to set up with his daddy's corpse, and I tuck his place."

"Did you hear any unusual noise during the night?"

"Only the squalling of the pea-fowul what was oncommon oneasy, and the thunder that was ear-splitting. One clap was so tremenjous it raised me plum off'en the pallet, and jarred me to my backbone, as if a cannon had gone off close by."

"Now, Bedney, state carefully all the circumstances under which you found your master the next morning; and remember you are on your oath, to speak the truth, and all the truth."

"He was a early riser, and always wanted his shavin' water promp'. When his bell didn't ring, I thought the storm had kep' him awake, and he was having a mornin' nap, to make up for lost time. The clock had struck eight, and the cook said as how the steak and chops was as dry as a bone from waitin', and so I got the water and went to Marster's door. It was shet tight, and I knocked easy. He never answered; so I knocked louder; and thinkin' somethin' was shorely wrong, I opened the door—"

"Go on. What did you find?"

"Mars Alfred, sir, it's very harryfyin to my feelins."

"Go on. You are required to state all you saw, all you know."

Bedney drew back his right foot, advanced his left. Took out his handkerchief, wiped his face and refolded his arms.

"My Marster was layin' on the rug before the fireplace, and his knees was all drawed up. His right arm, was stretched out, so—and his left hand was all doubled up. I know'd he was dead, before I tetched him, for his face was set; and pinched and blue. I reckon I hollered, but I can't say, for the next thing I knowed, the horsler and the cook, and Miss Angerline, and Dyce, my ole 'oman, and Gord knows who all, was streamin' in and out and screamin'."

"What was the condition of the room?"

"The front window was up, and the blinds was flung wide open, and a cheer was upside clown close to it. The red vases what stood on the fire-place mantle was smashed on the carpet, and the handi'on was close to Marster's right hand. The vault was open, and papers was strowed plentiful round on the floor under it. Then the neighbures and the Doctor, and the Crowner come runnin' in, and I sot down by the bed and cried like a chile. Pretty soon they turned us all out and hilt the inquess."

"You do not recollect any other circumstance?"

"The lamp on the table was burnin'—and ther' wan't much oil left in it. I seen Miss Angerline blow it out, after the Doctor come."

"Who found the chloroform vial?"

"Don't know."

"Did you hear any name mentioned as that of the murderer?"

"Miss Angerline tole the Crowner, that ef the will was missin', Gen'l Darrington's granddaughter had stole it. They two, with some other gentleman, sarched the vault, and Miss Angerline said everything was higgledy piggledy and no will there."

"You testified before the Coroner?"

"Yes, sir."

"Why did you not give him the handkerchief you found?"

"I didn't have it then."

"When and where did you get it? Be very careful now."

For the first time Bedney raised his eyes toward the place where Dyce sat near the prisoner, and he hesitated. He took some tobacco from his vest pocket, stowed it away in the hollow of his cheek, and re-crossed his arms.

"When Marster was dressed, and they carried him out to the drawing-room, Dyce was standin' cryin' by the fireplace, and I went to the bed, and put my hand under the bolster, where Marster always kep' his watch and his pistol. The watch was ther' but no pistol; and just sorter stuffed under the pillow case—was, a hank'cher. I tuk the watch straight to the gentlemen in the drawin'-room, and they come back and sarched for the pistol, and we foun' it layin' in its case in the table draw'. Of all the nights in his life, ole Marster had forgot to lay his pistol handy."

"Never mind about the pistol. What became of the handkerchief?"

"When I picked it up, an injun-rubber stopper rolled out, and as ther' wan't no value in a hank'cher, I saw no harm in keepin' it—for a'mento of ole Marster's death."

"You knew it was a lady's handkerchief."

"No, sir! I didn't know it then; and what's more, I don't know it now."

"Is not this the identical handkerchief you found?"

"Cant say. 'Dentical is a ticklish trap for a pusson on oath. It do look like it, to be shore; but two seed in a okrey pod is ezactly alike, and one is one, and t'other is t'other."

"Look at it. To the best of your knowledge and belief it is the identical handkerchief you found on Gen'l Darrington's pillow?"

"What I found had red specks sewed in the border, and this seems jest like it; but I don't sware to no dentical—'cause I means to be kereful; and I will stand to the aidge of my oath; but—Mars Alfred—don't shove me over it."

"Can't you read?"

"No, sir; I never hankered after book-larnin' tomfoolery, and other freedom frauds."

"You know your A B C's?"

"No more 'n a blind mule."

As the solicitor took from the table in front of the jury box, the embroidered square of cambric, and held it up by two corners, every eye in the court-room fastened upon it; and a deadly faintness seized the prisoner, whitening lips that hitherto had kept their scarlet outlines.

"Gentlemen of the jury, if the murdered man could stand before you, for one instant only, his frozen finger would point to the fatal letters which destiny seems to have left as a bloody brand. Here in indelible colors are wrought 'B. B.'!—Beryl Brentano. Do you wonder, gentlemen, that when this overwhelming evidence of her guilt came into my possession, compassion for a beautiful woman was strangled by supreme horror, in the contemplation of the depravity of a female monster? If these crimson letters were gaping wounds, could their bloody lips more solemnly accuse yonder blanched, shuddering, conscience-stricken woman of the sickening crime of murdering her aged, infirm grandfather, from whose veins she drew the red tide that now curdles at her heart?"

CHAPTER XVII.

As the third day of the trial wore away, the dense crowd in the court-room became acquainted with the sensation of having been unjustly defrauded of the customary public peruisite; because the monotonous proceedings were entirely devoid of the spirited verbal duels, the microscopic hair splitting, the biting sarcasms of opposing counsel, the brow-beating of witnesses, the tenacious wrangling over invisible legal points, which usually vary and spice the routine and stimulate the interest of curious spectators. When a spiritless fox disdains to double, and stands waiting for the hounds, who have only to rend it, hunters feel cheated, and deem it no chase.

To the impatient spectators, it appeared a very tame, one-sided, and anomalous trial, where like a slow stream the evidences of guilt oozed, and settled about the prisoner, who challenged the credibility of no witness, and waived all the privileges of cross-examination. Now and then, the audience criticised in whispers the "undue latitude" allowed by the Judge, to the District Solicitor; but their "exceptions" were informal, and the prosecution received no serious or important rebuff.

Was the accused utterly callous, or paralyzed by consciousness of her crime; or biding her time for a dramatic outburst of vindicating testimony? To her sensitive nature, the ordeal of sitting day after day to be stared at by a curious and prejudiced public, was more torturing than the pangs of Marsyas; and she wondered whether a courageous Roman captive who was shorn of his eyelids, and set under the blistering sun of Africa, suffered any more keenly; but motionless, apparently impassive as a stone mask, on whose features pitiless storms beat in vain, she bore without wincing the agony of her humiliation. Very white and still, she sat hour by hour with downcast eyes, and folded hands; and those who watched most closely could detect only one change of position; now and then she raised her clasped hands, and rested her lips a moment on the locked fingers, then dropped them wearily on her lap.

Even when a juryman asked two searching questions of a witness, she showed no sign of perturbation, and avoided meeting the eyes in the jury-box, as though they belonged to basilisks. Was it only three days since the beginning of this excruciating martyrdom of soul; and how much longer could she endure silently, and keep her reason?

At times, Sister Serena's hand forsook the knitting, to lay a soft, caressing touch of encouragement and sympathy on the girl's shoulder; and Dyce's burning indignation vented itself in frequent audible grating of her strong white teeth. So passed Monday, Tuesday, Wednesday, in the examination of witnesses who recapitulated all that had been elicited at the preliminary investigation; and each nook and cranny of recollection in the mind of Anthony Burk, the station agent; of Belshazzer Tatem, the lame gardener; of lean and acrid Miss Angeline, the seamstress, was illuminated by the lurid light of Mr. Churchill's adroit interrogation. Thus far, the prosecution had been conducted by the District Solicitor, with the occasional assistance of Mr. Wolverton, who, in conjunction with Mr. Dunbar, had appeared as representative of the Darrington estate, and its legal heir, Prince; and when court adjourned on Wednesday, the belief was generally entertained that no defence was possible; and that at the last moment, the prisoner would confess her crime, and appeal to the mercy of the jury. As the deputy sheriff led his prisoner toward the rear entrance, where stood the dismal funereal black wagon in which she was brought from prison to court, Judge Dent came quickly to meet her.

"My niece, Miss Gordon, could not, of course, come into the court-room, but she is here in the library, with her aunt, and desires to see you for a moment?"

"Tell her I am grateful for her kind motives, but I wish to see no one now."

"For your own sake, consider the—ah! here is my niece."

"I hope you need no verbal assurance of my deep sympathy, and my constant prayers," said Leo, taking one passive hand between hers, and pressing it warmly.

"Miss Gordon, I am comforted by your compassion, and by your unwavering confidence in a stranger whom your townsmen hold up as a 'female monster'. Because I so profoundly realize how good you are, I am unwilling that you should identify yourself with my hopeless cause. My sufferings will soon be over, and then I want no shadowy reflex cast upon the smiling blue sky of your future. I have nothing more to lose, save the burden of a life—that I shall be glad to lay down; but you—! Be careful, do not jeopardize your beautiful dream of happiness."

"Why do you persist in rejecting the overtures of those who could assist, who might successfully defend you? I beg of you, consent to receive and confer with counsel, even to-night."

"You will never understand why I must not, till the earth gives up her dead. You tremble, because only one more link can be added to the chain that is coiling about my neck, and that link is the testimony of the man whose name you expect to bear. Miss Gordon"—she stooped closer, and whispered slowly: "Do not upbraid your lover; be tender, cling to him; and afford me the consolation of knowing that the unfortunate woman you befriended, and trusted, cast not even a fleeting shadow between your heart and his. Pray for me, that I may be patient and strong. God bless you."

Turning swiftly, she hurried on to the officer, who had courteously withdrawn a few yards distant. As he opened the door of the wagon, he handed her a loosely folded sheet of paper.

"I promised to deliver your answer as soon as possible."

By aid of the red glow, burning low in the western sky, she read:

"Mr. Dunbar requests that for her own sake, Miss Brentano will grant him an interview this evening."

"My answer must necessarily be verbal. Say that I will see no one."

To the solitude and darkness of prison she fled for relief, as into some merciful sheltering arms; and not even the loving solicitude of Mrs. Singleton was permitted to penetrate her seclusion, or share her dreary vigil. Another sleepless night dragged its leaden hours to meet the dawn, bringing no rest to the desolate soul, who silently grappled with fate, while every womanly instinct shuddered at the loathsome degradation forced upon her. Face downward on her hard, narrow cot, she recalled the terrible accusations, the opprobrious epithets, and tearless, convulsive sobs of passionate protest shook her from head to foot.

Tortured with indignation and shame, at the insults heaped upon her, yet sternly resolved to endure silently, these nights were veritable stations along her Via Dolorosa; and fortified her for the daily flagellation in front of the jury-box.

On Thursday a slow, sleeting rain enveloped the world in a gray cowl, bristling with ice needles; yet when Judge Parkman took his seat at nine o'clock, there was a perceptible increase in the living mass, packed in every available inch of space.

For the first time, Mr. Dunbar's seat between his colleagues was vacant; and Mr. Churchill and Mr. Wolverton were conversing in an animated whisper.

Clad in mourning garments, and with a long crape veil put back from her face, the prisoner was escorted to her accustomed place; and braced by a supreme effort for the critical hour, which she felt assured was at hand, her pale set features gleamed like those of a marble statue shrouded in black.

Called to the stand, Simon Frisby testified that "he was telegraph operator, and night train despatcher for railway in X—. On October the twenty-sixth, had just gone on duty at 8 P.M. at the station, when prisoner came in, and sent a telegram to New York. A copy of that message had been surrendered to the District Solicitor. Witness had remained all night in his office, which adjoined the ladies' waiting-room, and his attention having been attracted by the unusual fact that it was left open and lighted, he had twice gone to the door and looked in, but saw no one. Thought the last inspection was about two o'clock, immediately after he had sent a message to the conductor on train No. 4. Saw prisoner when she came in, a half hour later, and heard the conversation between her and Burk, the station agent. Was very positive prisoner could not have been in the ladies' waiting-room during the severe storm."

Mr. Churchill read aloud the telegram addressed to Mrs. Ignace Brentano: "Complete success required delay. All will be satisfactory. Expect me Saturday. B. B."

He commented on its ambiguous phraseology, sent the message to the jury for inspection, and resumed his chair.

"Lennox Dunbar."

Sister Serena's knitting fell from her fingers; Dyce groaned audibly, and Judge Dent, sitting quite near, uttered a heavy sigh. The statue throbbed into life, drew herself proudly up; and with a haughty poise of the head, her grand eloquent gray eyes looked up at the witness, and for the first time during the trial bore a challenge. For fully a moment, eye met eye, soul looked into soul, with only a few feet of space dividing prisoner from witness; and as the girl scanned the dark, resolute, sternly chiselled face, cold, yet handsome as some faultless bronze god, a singular smile unbent her frozen lips, and Judge Dent and Sister Serena wondered what the scarcely audible ejaculation meant:

"At the mercy of Tiberius!"

No faintest reflection of the fierce pain at his heart could have been discerned on that non-committal countenance; and as he turned to the jury, his swart magnetic face appeared cruelly hard, sinister.

"I first saw the prisoner at 'Elm Bluff', on the afternoon previous to Gen'l Darrington's death. When I came out of the house, she was sitting bareheaded on the front steps, fanning herself with her hat, and while I was untying my horse, she followed Bedney into the library. The blinds were open and I saw her pass the window, walking in the direction of the bedroom."

Mr. Churchill: "At that time did you suspect her relationship to your client, Gen'l Darrington?"

"I did not."

"What was the impression left upon your mind?"

"That she was a distinguished stranger, upon some important errand."

"She excited your suspicions at once?"

"Nothing had occurred to justify suspicion. My curiosity was aroused. Several hours later I was again at 'Elm Bluff' on legal business, and found Gen'l Darrington much disturbed in consequence of an interview with the prisoner, who, he informed me, was the child of his daughter, whom he had many years previous disowned and disinherited. In referring to this interview, his words were: 'I was harsh to the girl, so harsh that she turned upon me, savage as a strong cub defending a crippled, helpless dam. Mother and daughter know now that the last card has been played; for I gave the girl distinctly to understand, that at my death Prince would inherit every iota of my estate, and that my will had been carefully written in order to cut them off without a cent.'"

"You were led to infer that Gen'l Darrington had refused her application for money?"

"There was no mention of an application for money, hence I inferred nothing."

"During that conversation, the last which Gen'l Darrington held on earth, did he not tell you he was oppressed by an awful presentiment connected with his granddaughter?"

"His words were: 'Somehow I am unable to get rid of the strange, disagreeable presentiment that girl let behind her as a farewell legacy. She stood there at the glass door, and raised her hand: 'Gen'l Darrington, when you lie down to die, may God have more mercy on your poor soul, than you have shown to your suffering child.'

"I advised him to sleep off the disagreeable train of thought, and as I bade him good night, his last words were:

"'I shall write to Prince to come home.'"

"What do you know concerning the contents of your client's will?"

"The original will was drawn up by my father in 187-, but last May, Gen'l Darrington required me to re-write it, as he wished to increase the amount of a bequest to a certain charitable institution. The provisions of the will were, that with the exception of various specified legacies, his entire estate, real and personal, should be given to his stepson Prince; and it was carefully worded, with the avowed intention of barring all claims that might be presented by Ellice Brentano or her heirs."

"Do you recollect any allusion to jewelry?"

"One clause of the will set aside a case of sapphire stones, with the direction that whenever Prince Darrington married, they should be worn by the lady as a bridal present from him."

"Would you not deem it highly incompatible with all you know of the Gen'l's relentless character, that said sapphires and money should have been given to the prisoner?"

"My surmises would be irrelevant and valueless to the Court; and facts, indisputable facts, are all that should be required of witnesses."

"When and where did you next see the prisoner?"

Cold, crisp, carefully accentuated, his words fell like lead upon the ears of all present, whose sympathies were enlisted for the desolate woman; and as he stood, tall, graceful, with one hand thrust within his vest, the other resting easily on the back of the bench near him, his clear cut face so suggestive of metallic medallions, gave no more hint of the smouldering flame at his heart than the glittering ice crown of Eiriksjokull betrays the fierce lava tides beating beneath its frozen crust.

"At 10 o'clock on the same night, I saw the prisoner on the road leading from town to 'Elm Bluff', and not farther than half a mile from the cedar bridge spanning the 'branch', at the foot of the hill where the iron gate stands."

"She was then going in the direction of 'Elm Bluff?'"

"She was sitting on the ground, with her head leaning against a pine tree, but she rose as I approached."

"As it was at night, is there a possibility of your having mistaken some one else for the prisoner?"

"None whatever. She wore no hat, and the moon shone full on her face."

"Did you not question her about her presence there, at such an hour?"

"I asked: 'Madam, you seem a stranger; have you lost your way?' She answered, 'No, sir.' I added: 'Pardon me, but having seen you at "Elm Bluff" this afternoon, I thought it possible you had missed the road.' She made no reply, and I rode on to town."

"She betrayed so much trepidation and embarrassment, that your suspicion was at once aroused?"

"She evinced neither trepidation nor embarrassment. Her manner was haughty and repellent, as though designed to rebuke impertinence. Next morning, when informed of the peculiar circumstances attending Gen'l Darrington's death, I felt it incumbent upon me to communicate to the magistrate the facts which I have just narrated."

"An overwhelming conviction of the prisoner's guilt impelled you to demand her arrest?"

"Overwhelming conviction rarely results from merely circumstantial evidence, but a combination of accusing circumstances certainly pointed to the prisoner; and following their guidance, I am responsible for her arrest and detention for trial. To the scrutiny of the Court I have submitted every fact that influenced my action, and the estimate of their value decided by the jurymen, must either confirm the cogency of my reasoning, or condemn my rash fallibility. Having under oath conscientiously given all the evidence in my possession, that the prosecution would accept or desire, I now respectfully request, that unless the prisoner chooses to exercise her right of cross-examination, my colleagues of the prosecution, and his Honor, will grant me a final discharge as witness."

Turning toward Beryl, Judge Parkman said:

"It is my duty again to remind you, that the cross-examination of witnesses is one of the most important methods of defence; as thereby inaccuracies of statement regarding time, place, etc., are often detected in criminal prosecutions, which otherwise might remain undiscovered. To this invaluable privilege of every defendant, I call your attention once more. Will you cross-question the witness on the stand?"

Involuntarily her eyes sought those of the witness, and despite his locked and guarded face, she read there an intimation that vaguely disquieted her. She knew that the battle with him must yet be fought.

"I waive the right."

"Then, with the consent of the prosecuting counsel, witness is discharged, subject to recall should the necessities of rebuttal demand it."

"By agreement with my colleagues, I ask for final discharge, subject to your Honor's approval."

"If in accordance with their wishes, the request is granted."

The clock on the turret struck one, the hour of adjournment, and ere recess was declared, Mr. Churchill rose.

"Having now proved by trustworthy and unquestioned witnesses, a dark array of facts, which no amount of additional testimony could either strengthen, or controvert, the prosecution here rest their case before the jury for inspection; and feeling assured that only one conclusion can result, will call no other witness, unless required in rebuttal."

Desiring to be alone, Beryl had shut out even Sister Serena, and as the officer locked her into a dark antechamber, adjoining the court-room, she began to pace the floor. One tall, narrow window, dim with inside dust, showed her through filmy cobwebs the gray veil of rain falling ceaselessly outside, darkening the day that seemed a fit type of her sombre-hued life, drawing swiftly to its close, with no hope of rift in the clouds, no possibility of sunset glow even to stain its grave. Oh! to be hidden safely in mother earth—away from the gaping crowd that thirsted for her blood!—at rest in darkness and in silence; with the maddening stings of outraged innocence and womanly delicacy stilled forever. Oh! the coveted peace of lying under the sod, with only nodding daisies, whispering grasses, crystal chimes of vernal rain, solemn fugue of wintry winds between her tired, aching eyes and the fair, eternal heavens! Harrowing days and sleepless, horror-haunted nights, invincible sappers and miners, had robbed her of strength; and the uncontrollable shivering that now and then seized her, warned her that her nerves were in revolt against the unnatural strain. The end was not far distant, she must endure a little longer; but that last battle with Mr. Dunbar? On what ground, with what weapons would he force her to fight? Kneeling in front of a wooden bench that lined one side of the room, she laid her head on the seat, covered her face with her hands, and prayed for guidance, for divine help in her hour of supreme desolation.

"God of the helpless, succor me in my need. Forbid that through weakness the sacrifice should be incomplete. Lead, sustain, fortify me with patience, that I may ransom the soul I have promised to save."

After a time, when she resumed her walk, a strange expedient presented itself. If she sent for Mr. Dunbar, exacted an oath of secrecy, and confided the truth to his keeping, would it avail to protect her secret; would it silence him? Could she stoop so low as to throw herself upon his mercy? Therein lay the nauseous lees of her cup of humiliation; yet if she drained this last black drop, would any pledge have power to seal his lips, when he saw that she must die?

The deputy sheriff unlocked the door, and she mechanically followed him.

"I wish you would drink this glass of wine. You look so exhausted, and the air in yonder is so close, it is enough to stifle a mole. This will help to brace you up."

"Thank you very much, but I could not take it. I can bear my wrongs even to the end, and that must be very near."

As he ushered her into the court-room, Judge Dent met her, took her hand, and led her to the seat where Dyce and Sister Serena awaited her return.

"My poor child, be courageous now; and remember that you have some friends here, who are praying God to help and deliver you."

"Did He deliver His own Son from the pangs of death? Pray, that I may be patient to endure."

One swift glance, showed her that Mr. Dunbar, forsaking his former place beside the district attorney, was sitting very near, just in front of her. The jurymen filed slowly into their accustomed seats, and the judge, who had been resting his head on his hand, straightened himself, and put aside a book. There was an ominous hush pervading the dense crowd, and in that moment of silent expectancy, Beryl shut her eyes and communed with her God. Some mystical exaltation of soul removed her from the realm of nervous dread; and a peace, that this world neither gives nor takes away, settled upon her. Sister Serena untied and took off the crape veil and bonnet, and as she resumed her seat, Judge Parkman turned to the prisoner.

"In assuming the responsibility of your own defence you have adopted a line of policy which, however satisfactory to yourself, must, in the opinion of the public, have a tendency to invest your cause with peculiar peril; therefore I impress upon you the fact, that while the law holds you innocent, until twelve men agree that the evidence proves you guilty, the time has arrived when your cause depends upon your power to refute the charges, and disprove the alleged facts arrayed against you. The discovery and elucidation of Truth, is the supreme aim of a court of justice, and to its faithful ministers the defence of innocence is even more imperative than the conviction of guilt. The law is a Gibraltar, fortified and armed by the consummate wisdom of successive civilizations, as an impregnable refuge for innocence; and here, within its protecting bulwarks, as in the house of a friend, you are called on to plead your defence. You have heard the charges of the prosecution; listened to the testimony of the witnesses; and having taken your cause into your own hands, you must now stand up and defend it."

She rose and walked a few steps closer to the jury, and for the first time during the trial, looked at them steadily. White as a statue of Purity, she stood for a moment, with her wealth of shining auburn hair coiled low on her shapely head, and waving in soft outlines around her broad full brow. Unnaturally calm, and wonderfully beautiful in that sublime surrender, which like a halo illumines the myth of Antigone, it was not strange that every heart thrilled, when upon the strained ears of the multitude fell the clear, sweet, indescribably mournful voice.

"When a magnolia blossom or a white camellia just fully open, is snatched by violent hands, bruised, crushed, blackened, scarred by rents, is it worth keeping? No power can undo the ruin, and since all that made it lovely—its stainless purity—is irrevocably destroyed, why preserve it? Such a pitiable wreck you have made of the young life I am bidden to stand up and defend. Have you left me anything to live for? Dragged by constables before prejudiced strangers, accused of awful crimes, denounced as a female monster, herded with convicts, can you imagine any reason why I should struggle to prolong a disgraced, hopelessly ruined existence? My shrivelled, mutilated life is in your hands, and if you decide to crush it quickly, you will save me much suffering; as when having, perhaps unintentionally, mangled some harmless insect, you mercifully turn back, grind it under your heel, and end its torture. My life is too wretched now to induce me to defend it, but there is something I hold far dearer, my reputation as an honorable Christian woman; something I deem most sacred of all—the unsullied purity of the name my father and mother bore. Because I am innocent of every charge made against me, I owe it to my dead, to lift their honored name out of the mire. I have pondered the testimony; and the awful mass of circumstances that have combined to accuse me, seems indeed so overwhelming, that as each witness came forward, I have asked myself, am I the victim of some baleful destiny, placed in the grooves of destroying fate-foreordained from the foundations of the world to bear the burden of another's guilt? You have been told that I killed Gen'l Darrington, and stole his money and jewels, and destroyed his will, in order to possess his estate. Trustworthy witnesses have sworn to facts, which I cannot deny, and you believe these facts; and yet, while the snare tightens around my feet, and I believe you intend to condemn me, I stand here, and look you in the face—as one day we thirteen will surely stand at the final judgment—and in the name of the God I love, and fear, and trust, I call you each to witness, that I am innocent of every charge in the indictment. My hands are as unstained, my soul is as unsullied by theft or bloodshed, as your sinless babes cooing in their cradles.

"If you can clear your minds of the foul tenants thrust into them, try for a little while to forget all the monstrous crimes you have heard ascribed to me, and as you love your mothers, wives, daughters, go back with me, leaving prejudice behind, and listen dispassionately to my most melancholy story. The river of death rolls so close to my weary feet, that I speak as one on the brink of eternity; and as I hope to meet my God in peace, I shall tell you the truth. Sometimes it almost shakes our faith in God's justice, when we suffer terrible consequences, solely because we did our duty; and it seems to me bitterly hard, inscrutable, that all my misfortunes should have come upon me thick and fast, simply because I obeyed my mother. You, fathers, say to your children, 'Do this for my sake,' and lovingly they spring to accomplish your wishes; and when they are devoured by agony, and smothered by disgrace, can you sufficiently pity them, blind artificers of their own ruin?

"Four months ago I was a very poor girl, but proud and happy, because by my own work I could support my mother and myself. Her health failed rapidly, and life hung upon an operation and certain careful subsequent treatment, which it required one hundred dollars to secure. I was competing for a prize that would lift us above want, but time pressed; the doctor urged prompt action, and my mother desired me to come South, see her father, deliver a letter and beg assistance. As long as possible, I resisted her entreaties, because I shrank from the degradation of coming as a beggar to the man who, I knew, had disinherited and disowned his daughter.

"Finally, strangling my rebellious reluctance, I accepted the bitter task. My mother kissed me good-bye, laid her hands on my head and blessed me for acceding to her wishes; and so—following the finger of Duty—I came here to be trampled, mangled, destroyed. When I arrived, I found I could catch a train going north at 7.15, and I bought a return ticket, and told the agent I intended to take that train. I walked to 'Elm Bluff,' and after waiting a few moments was admitted to Gen'l Darrington's presence. The letter which I delivered was an appeal for one hundred dollars, and it was received with an outburst of wrath, a flood of fierce and bitter denunciation of my parents. The interview was indescribably painful, but toward its close, Gen'l Darrington relented. He opened his safe or vault, and took out a square tin box. Placing it on the table, he removed some papers, and counted down into my hand, five gold coins—twenty dollars each. When I turned to leave him, he called me back, gave me the morocco case, and stated that the sapphires were very costly, and could be sold for a large amount. He added, with great bitterness, that he gave them, simply because they were painful souvenirs of a past, which he was trying to forget; and that he had intended them as a bridal gift to his son Prince's wife; but as they had been bought by my mother's mother as a present for her only child, he would send them to their original destination, for the sake of his first wife, Helena.

"I left the room by the veranda door, because he bade me do so, to avoid what he termed 'the prying of servants.' I broke some clusters of chrysanthemums blooming in the rose garden, to carry to my mother, and then I hurried away. If the wages of disobedience be death, then fate reversed the mandate, and obedience exacts my life as a forfeit. Think of it: I had ample time to reach the station before seven o'clock, and if I had gone straight on, all would have been well. I should have taken the 7.15 train, and left forever this horrible place. If I had not loitered, I should have seen once more my mother's face, have escaped shame, despair, ruin—oh! the blessedness of what 'might have been!'

"Listen, my twelve judges, and pity the child who obeyed at all hazards. Poor though I was, I bought a small bouquet for my sick mother the day that I left her, and the last thing she did was to arrange the flowers, tie them with a wisp of faded blue ribbon, and putting them in my hand, she desired me to be sure to stop at the cemetery, find her mother's grave in the Darrington lot, and lay the bunch of blossoms for her upon her mother's monument. Mother's last words were: 'Don't forget to kneel down and pray for me, at mother's grave.'"

The voice so clear, so steady hitherto, quivered, ceased; and the heavy lashes drooped to hide the tears that gathered; but it was only for a few seconds, and she resumed in the same cold, distinct tone:

"So I went on, and fate tied the last millstone around my neck. After some search I found the place, and left the bunch of flowers with a few of the chrysanthemums; then I hastened toward town, and reached the station too late; the 7.15 train had gone. Too late!—only a half hour lost, but it carried down everything that this world held for me. I used to wonder and puzzle over that passage in the Bible, 'The stars in their courses fought against Sisera!' I have solved that mystery, for the stars in their courses' have fought against me; heaven, earth, man, time, circumstances, coincidences, all spun the web that snared my innocent feet. When I paid for the telegram to relieve my mother's suspense, I had not sufficient money (without using the gold) to enable me to incur hotel bills; and I asked permission to remain in the waiting-room until the next train, which was due at 3.05. The room was so close and warm I walked out, and the fresh air tempted me to remain. The moon was up, full and bright, and knowing no other street, I unconsciously followed the one I had taken in the afternoon. Very soon I reached the point near the old church where the road crosses, and I turned into it, thinking that I would enjoy one more breath of the pine forest, which was so new to me. It was so oppressively hot I sat down on the pine straw, and fanned myself with my hat. How long I remained there, I know not, for I fell asleep; and when I awoke, Mr. Dunbar rode up and asked if I had lost my way. I answered that I had not, and as soon as he galloped on, I walked back as rapidly as possible, somewhat frightened at the loneliness of my position. Already clouds were gathering, and I had been in the waiting-room, I think about an hour, when the storm broke in its fury. I had seen the telegraph operator sitting in his office, but he seemed asleep, with his head resting on the table; and during the storm I sat on the floor, in one corner of the waiting-room, and laid my head on a chair. At last, when the tempest ended, I went to sleep. During that sleep, I dreamed of my old home in Italy, of some of my dead, of my father—of gathering grapes with one I dearly loved—and suddenly some noise made me spring to my feet. I heard voices talking, and in my feverish dreamy state, there seemed a resemblance to one I knew. Only half awake, I ran out on the pavement. Whether I dreamed the whole, I cannot tell; but the conversation seemed strangely distinct; and I can never forget the words, be they real, or imaginary: "'There ain't no train till daylight, 'cepting it be the through freight.'

"Then a different voice asked: 'When it that due?'"

"'Pretty soon I reckon, it's mighty nigh time now, but it don't stop here; it goes on to the water tank, where it blows for the bridge.'"

"'How far is the bridge?'"

"'Only a short piece down the track, after you pass the tank.'"

"When I reached the street, I saw no one but the figure of an old man, I think a negro, who was walking away. He limped and carried a bundle on the end of a stick thrown over his shoulder. I was so startled and impressed by the fancied sound of a voice once familiar to me, that I walked on down the track, but could see no one. Soon the 'freight' came along; I stood aside until it passed, then returned to the station, and found the agent standing in the door. When he questioned me about my movements; I deemed him impertinent; but having nothing to conceal, stated the facts I have just recapitulated. You have been told that I intentionally missed the train; that when seen at 10 P.M. in the pine woods, I was stealing back to my mother's old home; that I entered at midnight the bedroom where her father slept, stupefied him with chloroform, broke open his vault, robbed it of money, jewels and will; and that when Gen'l Darrington awoke and attempted to rescue his property, I deliberately killed him. You are asked to believe that I am 'the incarnate fiend' who planned and committed that horrible crime, and, alas for me! every circumstance seems like a bloodhound to bay me. My handkerchief was found, tainted with chloroform. It was my handkerchief; but how it came there, on Gen'l Darrington's bed, only God witnessed. I saw among the papers taken from the tin box and laid on the table, a large envelope marked in red ink, 'Last Will and Testament of Robert Luke Darrington'; but I never saw it afterward. I was never in that room but once; and the last and only time I ever saw General Darrington was when I passed out of the glass door, and left him standing in the middle of the room, with the tin box in his hand.

"I can call no witnesses; for it is one of the terrible fatalities of my situation that I stand alone, with none to corroborate my assertions. Strange, inexplicable coincidences drag me down; not the malice of men, but the throttling grasp of circumstances. I am the victim of some diabolical fate, which only innocent blood will appease; but though I am slaughtered for crimes I did not commit, I know, oh! I know, that BEHIND FATE, STANDS GOD!—the just and eternal God, whom I trust, even in this my hour of extremest peril. Alone in the world, orphaned, reviled, wrecked for all time, without a ray of hope, I, Beryl Brentano, deny every accusation brought against me in this cruel arraignment; and I call my only witness, the righteous God above us, to hear my solemn asseveration: I am innocent of this crime; and when you judicially murder me in the name of Justice, your hands will be dyed in blood that an avenging God will one day require of you. Appearances, circumstances, coincidences of time and place, each, all, conspire to hunt me into a convict's grave; but remember, my twelve judges, remember that a hopeless, forsaken, broken-hearted woman, expecting to die at your hands, stood before you, and pleaded first and last—Not Guilty! Not Guilty!—"

A moment she paused, then raised her arms toward heaven and added, with a sudden exultant ring in her thrilling voice, and a strange rapt splendor in her uplifted eyes:

"Innocent! Innocent! Thou God knowest! Innocent of this sin, as the angels that see Thy face."

CHAPTER XVIII.

As a glassy summer sea suddenly quivers, heaves, billows under the strong steady pressure of a rising gale, so that human mass surged and broke in waves of audible emotion, when Beryl's voice ceased; for the grace and beauty of a sorrowing woman hold a spell more potent than volumes of forensic eloquence, of juridic casuistry, of rhetorical pyrotechnics, and at its touch, the latent floods of pity gushed; people sprang to their feet, and somewhere in the wide auditory a woman sobbed. Habitues of a celebrated Salon des Etrangers recall the tradition of a Hungarian nobleman who, apparently calm, nonchalant, debonair, gambled desperately; "while his right hand, resting easily inside the breast of his coat, clutched and lacerated his flesh till his nails dripped with blood." With emotions somewhat analogous, Mr. Dunbar sat as participant in this judicial rouge et noir, where the stakes were a human life, and the skeleton hand of death was already outstretched. Listening to the calm, mournful voice which alone had power to stir and thrill his pulses, he could not endure the pain of watching the exquisite face that haunted him day and night; and when he computed the chances of her conviction, a maddening perception of her danger made his brain reel.

To all of us comes a supreme hour, when realizing the adamantine limitations of human power, the "thus far, no farther" of relentless physiological, psychological and ethical statutes under which humanity lives, moves, has its being—our desperate souls break through the meshes of that pantheistic idolatry which kneels only to "Natural Laws"; and spring as suppliants to Him, who made Law possible. We take our portion of happiness and prosperity, and while it lasts we wander far, far away in the seductive land of philosophical speculation, and revel in the freedom and irresponsibility of Agnosticism; and lo! when adversity smites, and bankruptcy is upon us, we toss the husks of the "Unknowable and Unthinkable" behind us, and flee as the Prodigal who knew his father, to that God whom (in trouble) we surely know.

Certainly Lennox Dunbar was as far removed from religious tendencies as conformity to the canons of conventional morality and the habits of an honorable gentleman in good society would permit; yet to-day, in the intensity of his dread, lest the "consummate flower" of his heart's dearest hope should be laid low in the dust, he involuntarily invoked the aid of a long-forgotten God; and through his set teeth a prayer struggled up to the throne of that divine mercy, which in sunshine we do not see, but which as the soul's eternal lighthouse gleams, glows, beckons in the blackest night of human anguish. In boyhood, desiring to please his invalid and slowly dying mother, he had purchased and hung up opposite her bed, an illuminated copy of her favorite text; and now, by some subtle transmutation in the conservation of spiritual energy, each golden letter of that Bible text seemed emblazoned on the dusty wall of the court-room: "God is our refuge and strength, a very present help in trouble."

When a stern reprimand from the Judge had quelled all audible expression of the compassionate sympathy that flowed at the prisoner's story—as the flood at Horeb responded to Moses' touch—there was a brief silence.

Mr. Dunbar rose, crossed the intervening space and stood with his hand on the back of Beryl's chair; then moved on closer to the jury box.

"May it please your Honor, and Gentlemen of the Jury: Sometimes mistakes are crimes, and he who through unpardonable rashness commits them, should not escape 'unwhipped of justice'. When a man in the discharge of that which he deemed a duty, becomes aware that unintentionally he has perpetrated a great wrong, can he parley with pride, or dally, because the haunting ghost of consistency waves him back from the path of a humiliating reparation? Error is easy, confession galling; and stepping down from the censor's seat to share the mortification of the pillory, is at all times a peculiarly painful reverse; hence, powerful indeed must be the conviction which impels a man who prided himself on his legal astuteness, to come boldly into this sacred confessional of truth and justice and plead for absolution from a stupendous mistake. Two years ago, I became Gen'l Darrington's attorney, and when his tragic death occurred in October last, my professional relations, as well as life-long friendship, incited me to the prompt apprehension of the person who had murdered him. After a careful and apparently exhaustive examination of the authenticated facts, I was convinced that they pointed only in one direction; and in that belief, I demanded and procured the arrest of the prisoner. For her imprisonment, her presence here to-day, her awful peril, I hold myself responsible; and now, gentlemen of the jury, I ask you as men having hearts of flesh, and all the honorable instincts of manhood, which alone could constitute you worthy umpires in this issue of life or death, do you, can you wonder that regret sits at my ear, chanting mournful dirges, and remorse like a harpy fastens her talons in my soul, when I tell you, that I have committed a blunder so frightful, that it borders on a crime as heinous as that for which my victim stands arraigned? Wise was the spirit of a traditional statute, which decreed that the author of a false accusation should pay the penalty designed for the accused; and just indeed would be the retribution, that imposed on me the suffering I have entailed on her.

"Acknowledging the error into which undue haste betrayed me, yet confident that divine justice, to whom I have sworn allegiance, has recalled me from a false path to one that I can now tread with absolute certainty of success, I come to-day into this, her sacred temple, lay my hand on her inviolate altar, and claiming the approval of her officiating high-priest, his Honor, appeal to you, gentlemen of the jury, to give me your hearty co-operation in my effort to repair a foul wrong, by vindicating innocence.

"Professors of ophthalmology in a diagnosis of optical diseases, tell us of a symptom of infirmity which they call pseudoblepsis, or 'false sight.' Legal vision exhibits, now and then, a corresponding phase of unconscious perversion of sight, whereby objects are perceived that do not exist, and objects present become transformed, distorted; and such an instance of exaggerated metamorphosia is presented to-day, in the perverted vision of the prosecution. In the incipiency of this case, prior to, and during the preliminary examination held in October last, I appeared in conjunction with Mr. Wolverton, as assistant counsel in the prosecution, represented by the Honorable Mr. Churchill, District Solicitor; the object of said prosecution being the conviction of the prisoner, who was held as guilty of Gen'l Darrington's death. Subsequent reflection and search necessitated an abandonment of views that could alone justify such a position; and after consultation with my colleagues I withdrew; not from the prosecution of the real criminal, to the discovery and conviction of whom I shall dedicate every energy of my nature, but from the pursuit of one most unjustly accused. Anomalous as is my attitude, the dictates of conscience, reason, heart, force me into it; and because I am the implacable prosecutor of Gen'l Darrington's murderer, *I COME TO PLEAD IN DEFENSE OF THE PRISONER*, whom I hold guiltless of the crime, innocent of the charge in the indictment. In the supreme hour of her isolation, she has invoked only one witness; and may that witness, the God above us, the God of justice, the God of innocence, grant me the inspiration, and nerve my arm to snatch her from peril, and triumphantly vindicate the purity of her noble heart and life."

Remembering the important evidence which he had furnished to the prosecution, only a few hours previous, when on the witness stand, people looked at one another questioningly; doubting the testimony of their own senses; and VOX POPULI was not inaptly expressed by the whispered ejaculation of Bedney to Dyce.

"Judgment day must be breaking! Mars Lennox is done turned a double summersett, and lit plum over on t'other side! It's about ekal to a spavinned, ring-boned, hamstrung, hobbled horse clearin' a ten-rail fence! He jumps so beautiful, I am afeered he won't stay whar he lit!"

Comprehending all that this public recantation had cost a proud man, jealous of his reputation for professional tact and skill, as well as for individual acumen, Beryl began to realize the depth and fervor of the love that prompted it; and the merciless ordeal to which he would subject her. Inflicting upon himself the smarting sting of the keenest possible humiliation, could she hope that in the attainment of his aim he would spare her? If she threw herself even now upon his mercy, would he grant to her that which he had denied himself?

Dreading the consequences of even a moment's delay, she rose, and a hot flush crimsoned her cheeks, as she looked up at the Judge.

"Is it my privilege to decide who shall defend me? Have I now the right to accept or reject proffered aid?"

"The law grants you that privilege; secures you that right."

"Then I decline the services of the counsel who offers to plead in my defence. I wish no human voice raised in my behalf, and having made my statement in my own defence, I commit my cause to the hands of my God."

For a moment her eyes dwelt upon the lawyer's, and as she resumed her seat, she saw the spark in their blue depths leap into a flame. Advancing a few steps, his handsome face aglow, his voice rang like a bugle call:

"May it please your Honor: Anomalous conditions sanction, necessitate most anomalous procedure, where the goal sought is simple truth and justice; and since the prisoner prefers to rest her cause, I come to this bar as Amicus Curiae, and appeal for permission to plead in behalf of my clients, truth and justice, who hold me in perpetual retainment. In prosecution of the real criminal, in order to unravel the curiously knitted web, and bring the culprit to summary punishment, I ask you, gentlemen of the jury, to ponder dispassionately the theory I have now the honor to submit to your scrutiny.

"The prisoner, whom I regard as the victim of my culpable haste and deplorably distorted vision, is as innocent of Gen'l Darrington's murder as you or I; but I charge, that while having no complicity in that awful deed, she is nevertheless perfectly aware of the name of the person who committed it. Not particeps crimmis, neither consenting to, aiding, abetting nor even acquainted with the fact of the crime, until accused of its perpetration; yet at this moment in possession of the only clue which will enable justice to seize the murderer. Conscious of her innocence, she braves peril that would chill the blood of men, and extort almost any secret; and shall I tell you the reason? Shall I give you the key to an enigma which she knows means death?

"Gentlemen of the jury, is there any sacrifice so tremendous, any anguish so keen, any shame so dreadful, any fate so overwhelmingly terrible as to transcend the endurance, or crush the power of a woman's love? Under this invincible inspiration, when danger threatens her idol, she knows no self; disgrace, death affright her not; she extends her arms to arrest every approach, offers her own breast as a shield against darts, bullets, sword thrusts, and counts it a privilege to lay down life in defence of that idol. O! loyalty supreme, sublime, immortal! thy name is woman's love.

"All along the march of humanity, where centuries have trailed their dust, traditions gleam like monuments to attest the victory of this immemorial potency, female fidelity; and when we of the nineteenth century seek the noblest, grandest type of merely human self-abnegation, that laid down a pure and happy life, to prolong that of a beloved object, we look back to the lovely image of that fair Greek woman, who, when the parents of the man she loved refused to give their lives to save their son, summoned death to accept her as a willing victim; and deeming it a privilege, went down triumphantly into the grave. Sustained, exalted by this most powerful passion that can animate and possess a human soul, the prisoner stands a pure, voluntary, self-devoted victim; defying the terrors of the law, consenting to condemnation—surrendering to an ignominious death, in order to save the life of the man she loves.

"Grand and beautiful as is the spectacle of her calm mournful heroism, I ask you, as men capable of appreciating her noble self-immolation, can you permit the consummation of this sacrifice? Will you, dare you, selected, appointed, dedicated by solemn oaths to administer justice, prove so recreant to your holy trust as to aid, abet, become accessories to, and responsible for the murder of the prisoner by accepting a stainless victim, to appease that violated law which only the blood of the guilty can ever satisfy?

"In order to avert so foul a blot on the escutcheon of our State judiciary, in order to protect innocence from being slaughtered, and supremely in order to track and bring to summary punishment the criminal who robbed and murdered Gen'l Darrington, I now desire, and request, that your Honor will permit me to cross-examine the prisoner on the statement she has offered in defence."

"In making that request, counsel must be aware that it is one of the statutory provisions of safety to the accused, whom the law holds innocent until proved guilty, that no coercion can be employed to extort answers. It is, however, the desire of the court, and certainly must accrue to the benefit of the prisoner, that she should take the witness stand in her own defence."

For a moment there was neither sound nor motion.

"Will the prisoner answer such questions as in the opinion of the court are designed solely to establish her innocence? If so, she will take the stand."

With a sudden passionate movement at variance with her demeanor throughout the trial, she threw up her clasped hands, gazed at them, then pressed them ring downward as a seal upon her lips; and after an instant, answered slowly:

"Now and henceforth, I decline to answer any and all questions. I am innocent, entirely innocent. The burden of proof rests upon my accusers."

As Mr. Dunbar watched her, noted the scarlet spots burning on her cheeks, the strange expression of her eyes that glowed with unnatural lustre, a scowl darkened his face; a cruel smile curved his lips, and made his teeth gleam. Was it worth while to save her against her will; to preserve the heart he coveted, for the vile miscreant to whom she had irrevocably given it? With an upward movement of his noble head, like the impatient toss of a horse intolerant of curb, he stepped back close to the girl, and stood with his hand on the back of her chair.

"In view of this palpable evasion of justice through obstinate non responsion, will it please the Court to overrule the prisoner's objection?"

Several moments elapsed before Judge Parkman replied, and he gnawed the end of his grizzled mustache, debating the consequences of dishonoring precedent—that fetich of the Bench.

"The Court cannot so rule. The prisoner has decided upon the line of defence, as is her inalienable right; and since she persistently assumes that responsibility, the Court must sustain her decision."

The expression of infinite and intense relief that stole over the girl's countenance, was, noted by both judge and jury, as she sank back wearily in her chair, like one lifted from some rack of torture. Resting thus, her shoulder pressed against the hand that lay on the top of the chair, but he did not move a finger; and some magnetic influence drew her gaze to meet his. He felt the tremor that crept over her, understood the mute appeal, the prayer for forbearance that made her mournful gray eyes so eloquent, and a sinister smile distorted his handsome mouth.

"The spirit and intent of the law, the usages of criminal practice, above all, hoary precedent, before which we bow, each and all sanction your Honor's ruling; and yet despite everything, the end I sought is already attained. Is not the refusal of the prisoner proof positive, 'confirmation strong as proofs of Holy Writ' of the truth of my theory? With jealous dread she seeks to lock the clue in her faithful heart, courting even the coffin, that would keep it safe through all the storms of time. Impregnable in her citadel of silence, with the cohorts of Codes to protect her from escalade and assault, will the guardians of justice have obeyed her solemn commands when they permit the prisoner to light the funeral pyre where she elects to throw herself—a vicarious sacrifice for another's sins? For a nature so exalted, the Providence who endowed it has decreed a nobler fate; and by His help, and that of your twelve consciences, I purpose to save her from a species of suicide, and to consign to the hangman the real criminal. The evidence now submitted, will be furnished by the testimony of witnesses who, at my request, have been kept without the hearing of the Court."

He left Beryl's chair, and once more approached the jury,

"Isam Hornbuckle."

A negro man, apparently sixty years old, limped into the witness stand, and having been sworn, stood leaning on his stick, staring uneasily about him.

"What is your name?"

"Isam Clay Hornbuckle."

"Where do you live?"

"Nigh the forks of the road, close to 'Possum Ridge."

"How far from town?"

"By short cuts I make it about ten miles; but the gang what works the road, calls it twelve."

"Have you a farm there?"

"Yes'ir. A pretty tolerable farm; a cornfield and potato patch and gyarden, and parsture for my horgs and oxin, and a slipe of woods for my pine knots."

"What is your business?"

"Tryin' to make a livin', and it keeps me bizzy, for lans is poor, and seasons is most ginerally agin crops."

"How long have you been farming?"

"Only sence I got mashed up more 'an a year ago on the railroad."

"In what capacity did you serve when working on the road?"

"I was fireman under ingeneer Walker on the lokymotive 'Gin'l Borygyard,' what most ginerally hauled Freight No. 2. The ingines goes now by numbers, but we ole hands called our'n always 'Borygyard'."

"You were crippled in a collision between two freight trains?"

"Yes'ir; but t'other train was the cause of the—"

"Never mind the cause of the accident. You moved out to 'Possum Ridge; can you remember exactly when you were last in town?"

"To be shore! I know exactly, 'cause it was the day my ole 'oman's step-father's granny's funeral sarmont was preached; and that was on a Thursday, twenty-sixth of October, an' I come up to 'tend it."

"Is it not customary to preach the funeral sermons on Sunday?"

"Most generally, Boss, it are; but you see Bre'r Green, what was to preach the ole 'oman's sarmont, had a big baptizin' for two Sundays han' runnin', and he was gwine to Boston for a spell, on the next comin' Saddy, so bein' as our time belonks to us now, we was free to 'pint a week day."

"You are positive it was the twenty-sixth?"

"Oh, yes'ir; plum postiv. The day was norated from all the baptiss churches, so as the kinfolks could gether from fur and nigh."

"At what hour on Thursday was the funeral sermon preached?"

"Four o'clock sharp."

"Where did you stay while in town?"

"With my son Ducaleyon who keeps a barber-shop on Main Street."

"When did you return home?"

"I started before day, Friday mornin', as soon as the rain hilt up."

"At what hour, do you think?"

"The town clock was a strikin' two, jes as I passed the express office, at the station."

"Now, Isam, tell the Court whom you saw, and what happened; and be very careful in all you say, remembering you are on your oath."

"I was atoting a bundle so—slung on to a stick, and it gaided my shoulder, 'cause amongst a whole passel of plunder I had bought, ther was a bag of shot inside, what had slewed 'round oft the balance, and I sot down, close to a lamp-post nigh the station, to shift the heft of the shot bag. Whilst I were a squatting, tying up my bundle, I heered all of a suddent—somebody runnin', brip—brap—! and up kern a man from round the corner of the stationhouse, a runnin' full tilt; and he would a run over me, but I grabbed my bundle and riz up. Sez I: 'Hello! what's to pay?' He was most out of breath, but sez he: 'Is the train in yet?' Sez I: 'There ain't no train till daylight, 'cepting it be the through freight.' Then he axed me: 'When is that due?' and I tole him: 'Pretty soon, I reckon, but it don't stop here; it only slows up at the water tank, whar it blows for the Bridge.' Sez he: 'How fur is that bridge?' Sez I: 'Only a short piece down the track, after you pass the tank.' He tuck a long breath, and kinder whistled, and with that he turned and heeled it down the middle of the track. I thought it mighty curus, and my mind misgive me thar was somethin' crooked; but I always pintedly dodges; 'lie-lows to ketch meddlers,' and I went on my way. When I got nigh the next corner whar I had to turn to cross the river, I looked back and I seen a 'oman standin' on the track, in front of the station-house; but I parsed on, and soon kem to the bridge (not the railroad bridge), Boss. I had got on the top of the hill to the left of the Pentenchry, when I hearn ole 'Bory' blow. You see I knowed the runnin' of the kyars, 'cause that through freight was my ole stormpin-ground, and I love the sound of that ingine's whistle more 'an I do my gran'childun's hymn chunes. She blowed long and vicious like, and I seen her sparks fly, as she lit out through town; and then I footed it home."

"You think the train was on time?"

"Bound to be; she never was cotched behind time, not while I stuffed her with coal and lightwood knots. She was plum punctchul."

"Was the lamp lighted where you tied your bundle?"

"Yes'ir, burnin' bright."

"Tell the Court the appearance of the man whom you talked with."

Mr. Dunbar was watching the beautiful face so dear to him, and saw the prisoner lean forward, her lips parted, all her soul in the wide, glowing eyes fastened on the countenance of the witness.

"He was very tall and wiry, and 'peared like a young man what had parstured 'mongst wild oats. He seemed cut out for a gintleman, but run to seed too quick and turned out nigh kin to a dead beat. One-half of him was hanssum, 'minded me mightly of that stone head with kurly hair what sets over the sody fountin in the drug store, on Main Street. Oh, yes'ir, one side was too pretty for a man; but t'other! Fo' Gawd! t'other made your teeth ache, and sot you cross-eyed to look at it. He toted a awful brand to be shore."

"What do you mean by one side? Explain yourself carefully now."

"I dun'no as I can 'splain, 'cause I ain't never seed nothing like it afore. One 'zact half of him, from his hair to his shirt collar was white and pretty, like I tell you, but t'other side of his face was black as tar, and his kurly hair was gone, and the whiskers on that side—and his eye was drapped down kinder so, and that side of his mouth sorter hung, like it was unpinned, this way. Mebbee he was born so, mebbee not; but he looked like he had jes broke loose from the conjur, and caryd his mark."

For one fleeting moment, the gates of heaven seemed thrown wide, and the glory of the Kingdom of Peace streamed down upon the aching heart of the desolate woman. She could recognize no dreaded resemblance in the photograph drawn by the witness; and judge, jury and counsel who scrutinized her during the recital of the testimony, were puzzled by the smile of joy that suddenly flashed over her features, like ilie radiance of a lamp lifted close to some marble face, dim with shadows.

"Do you think his face indicated that he had been engaged in a difficulty, in a fight? Was there any sign of blood, or anything that looked as if he had been bruised and wounded by some heavy blow?"

"Naw, sir. Didn't seem like sech bruises as comes of fightin'. 'Peared to me he was somehow branded like, and the mark he toted was onnatral."

"If he had wished to disguise himself by blackening one side of his face, would he not have presented a similar appearance?"

"Naw, sir, not by no manner of means. No minstrel tricks fotch him to the pass he was at. The hand of the Lord must have laid too heavy on him; no mortal wounds leave sech terrifyin' prints."

"How was he dressed?"

"Dunno. My eyes never drapped below that curus face of his'n."

"Was he bareheaded?"

"Bar headed as when he come into the world."

"He talked like a man in desperate haste, who was running to escape pursuit?"

"He shorely did."

"Did you mention to any person what you have told here to-day?"

"I tole my ole 'oman, and she said she reckoned it was a buth mark what the man carryd; but when I seen him I thunk he was cunjured."

"When you heard that Gen'l Darrington had been murdered, did you think of this man and his singular behavior that night?"

"I never hearn of the murder till Christmas, 'cause I went down to Elbert County arter a yoke of steers what a man owed me, and thar I tuck sick and kep my bed for weeks. When I got home, and hearn the talk about the murder, I didn't know it was the same night what I seen the branded man."

"Tell the Court how your testimony was secured."

"It was norated in all our churches that a 'ward was offered for a lame cullud pusson of my 'scription, and Deacon Nathan he cum down and axed me what mischief I'de been a doin', that I was wanted to answer fur. He read me the 'vertisement, and pussuaded me to go with him to your office, and you tuck me to Mr. Churchill."

Mr. Dunbar bowed to the District Solicitor, who rose and cross-examined.

"Can you read?"

"Naw, sir."

"Where is your son Deucalion?"

"Two days after I left town he want with a 'Love and Charity' scurschion up north, and he liked it so well in Baltymore, he staid thar."

"When Deacon Nathan brought you up to town, did you know for what purpose Mr. Dunbar wanted you?"

"Naw, sir."

"Was it not rather strange that none of your friends recognized the description of you, published in the paper?"

"Seems some of 'em did, but felt kind of jub'rus 'bout pinting me out, for human natur is prone to crooked ways, and they never hearn I perfessed sanctification."

"Who told you the prisoner had heard your conversation with the man you met that night?"

"Did she hear it? Then you are the first pusson to tell me."

"How long was it, after you saw the man, before you heard the whistle of the freight train?"

"As nigh as I kin rickolect about a half a hour, but not quite."

"Was it raining at all when you saw the woman standing on the track?"

"Naw, sir. The trees was dripping steady, but the moon was shining."

"Do you know anything about the statement made by the prisoner?"

"Naw, sir."

"Fritz Helmetag."

As Isam withdrew, a middle-aged man took the stand, and in answer to Mr. Dunbar's questions deposed: "That he was 'bridge tender' on the railroad, and lived in a cottage not far from the water tank. On the night of the twenty-sixth of October, he was sitting up with a sick wife, and remembered that being feverish, she asked for some fresh water. He went out to draw some from the well, and saw a man standing not far from the bridge. The moon was behind a row of trees, but he noticed the man was bareheaded, and when he called to know what he wanted, he walked back toward the tank. Five minutes later the freight train blew, and after it had crossed the bridge, he went back to his cottage. The man was standing close to the safety signal, a white light fastened to an iron stanchion at south end of the bridge, and seemed to be reading something. Next day, when he (witness) went as usual to examine the piers and under portions of the bridge, he had found the pipe, now in Mr. Dunbar's possession. Tramps so often rested on the bridge, and on the shelving bank of the river beneath it, that he attached no importance to the circumstance; but felt confident the pipe was left by the man whom he had seen, as it was not there the previous afternoon; and he put it in a pigeon-hole of his desk, thinking the owner might return to claim it. On the same day, he had left X—— to carry his wife to her mother, who lived in Pennsylvania, and was absent for several weeks. Had never associated the pipe with the murder, but after talking with Mr. Dunbar, who had found the half of an envelope near the south end of the bridge, he had surrendered it to him. Did not see the man's face distinctly. He looked tall and thin."

Here Mr. Dunbar held up a fragment of a long white em elope such as usually contain legal documents, on which in large letters was written "LAST WILL"—and underscored with red ink. Then he lifted a pipe, for the inspection of the witness, who identified it as the one he had found.

As he turned it slowly, the Court and the multitude saw only a meerschaum with a large bowl representing a death's head, to which was attached a short mouth-piece of twisted amber.

The golden gates of hope clashed suddenly, and over them flashed a drawn sword, as Beryl looked at the familiar pipe, which her baby fingers had so often strained to grasp. How well she knew the ghastly ivory features, the sunken eyeless sockets—of that veritable death's head? How vividly came back the day, when asleep in her father's arms, a spark from that grinning skull had fallen on her cheek, and she awoke to find that fond father bending in remorseful tenderness over her? Years ago, she had reverently packed the pipe away, with other articles belonging to the dead, and ignorant that her mother had given it to Bertie, she deemed it safe in that sacred repository. Now, like the face of Medusa it glared at her, and that which her father's lips had sanctified, became the polluted medium of a retributive curse upon his devoted child. So the Diabolus ex machina, the evil genius of each human life decrees that the most cruel cureless pangs are inflicted by the instruments we love best.

Watching for some sign of recognition, Mr. Dunbar's heart was fired with jealous rage, as he marked the swift change of the prisoner's countenance; the vanishing of the gleam of hope, the gloomy desperation that succeeded. The beautiful black brows met in a spasm of pain over eyes that stared at an abyss of ruin; her lips whitened, she wrung her hands unconsciously; and then, as if numb with horror, she leaned back in her chair, and her chin sank until it touched the black ribbon at her throat. When after a while she rallied, and forced herself to listen, a pleasant-faced young man was on the witness stand.

"My name is Edgar Jennings, and I live at T——, in Pennsylvania. I am ticket agent at that point, of——railway. One day, about the last of October (I think it was on Monday), I was sitting in my office when a man came in, and asked if I could sell him a ticket to St. Paul. I told him I only had tickets as far as Chicago, via Cincinnati. He bought one to Cincinnati and asked how soon he could go on. I told him the train from the east was due in a few minutes. When he paid for his ticket he gave me a twenty-dollar gold piece, and his hand shook so, he dropped another piece of the same value on the floor. His appearance was so remarkable I noticed him particularly. He was a man about my age, very tall and finely made, but one half of his face was black, or rather very dark blue, and he wore a handkerchief bandage-fashion across it. His left eye was drawn down, this way, and his mouth was one-sided. His right eye was black, and his hair was very light brown. He wore a close-fitting wool hat, that flapped down and his clothes were seal-brown in color, but much worn, and evidently old. I asked him where he lived, and he said he was a stranger going West, on a pioneering tour. Then I asked what ailed his face, and he pulled the handkerchief over his left eye, and said he was partly paralyzed from an accident. Just then, the eastern train blew for T——. He said he wanted some cigars or a pipe, as he had lost his own on the way, and wondered if he would have time to go out and buy some. I told him no; but that he could have a couple of cigars from my box. He thanked me, and took two, laying down a silver dime on top of the box. He put his hand in the inside pocket of his coat, and pulled out an empty envelope, twisted it, lit it by the coal fire in the grate, and lighted his cigar. The train rolled into the station; he passed out, and I saw him jump aboard the front passenger coach. He had thrown the paper, as he thought, into the fire, but it slipped off the grate, fell just inside the fender, and the flame went out. There was something so very peculiar in his looks and manner, that I thought there was some mystery about his movements. I picked up the paper, saw the writing on it, and locked it up in my cash drawer. He had evidently been a very handsome man, before his 'accident', but he had a jaded, worried, wretched look. When a detective from Baltimore interviewed me, I told him all I knew, and gave him the paper."

Again Mr. Dunbar drew closer to the jury, held up the former fragment of envelope, and then took from his pocket a second piece. Jagged edges fitted into each other, and he lifted for the inspection of hundreds of eyes, the long envelope marked and underscored:-"LAST WILL AND TESTAMENT OF ROBERT LUKE DARRINGTON." The lower edge of the paper was at one corner brown, scorched, somewhat burned.

"Lucullus Grantlin."

An elderly man of noble presence advanced, and Mr. Dunbar met and shook hands with him, accompanying him almost to the stand. At sight of his white head, and flowing silvery beard, Beryl's heart almost ceased its pulsation. If, during her last illness her mother had acquainted him with their family history, then indeed all was lost. It was as impossible to reach him and implore his silence, as though the ocean rocked between them; and how would he interpret the pleading gaze she fixed upon his face? The imminence of the danger, vanquished every scruple, strangled her pride. She caught Mr. Dunbar's eye, beckoned him to approach.

When he stood before her, she put out her hand, seized one of his, and drew him down until his black head almost touched hers. She placed her lips close to his ear, and whispered:

"For God's sake spare the secrets of a death-bed. Be merciful to me now; oh! I entreat you—do not drag my mother from her grave! Do not question Doctor Grantlin."

She locked her icy hands around his, pressing it convulsively. Turning, he laid his lips close to the silky fold of hair that had fallen across her ear:

"If I dismiss this witness, will you tell me the truth? Will you give me the name of the man whom I am hunting? Will you confess all to me?"

"I have no sins to confess. I have made my last statement. If you laid my coffin at my feet, I should only say I am innocent; I would tell you nothing more."

"Then his life is so precious, you are resolved to die, rather than trust me?"

She dropped his hand, and leaned back in her chair, closing her eyes. When she opened them, Doctor Grantlin was speaking:

"I am on my way to Havana, with an invalid daughter, and stopped here last night, at the request of Mr. Dunbar."

"Please state all that you know of the prisoner, and of the circumstances which induced her to visit X——."

"I first saw the prisoner in August last, when she summoned me to see her mother, who was suffering from an attack of fever. I discovered that she was in a dangerous condition in consequence of an aneurism located in the carotid artery, and when she had been relieved of malarial fever, I told both mother and daughter that an operation was necessary, to remove the aneurism. Soon after, I left the city for a month, and on my return the daughter again called me in. I advised that without delay the patient should be removed to the hospital, where a surgeon—a specialist—could perform the operation. To this the young lady objected, on the ground that she could not assist in nursing, if her mother entered the hospital; and she would not consent to the separation. She asked what amount would be required to secure at home the services of the surgeon, a trained nurse, and the subsequent treatment; and I told her I thought a hundred dollars would cover all incidentals, and secure one of the most skilful surgeons in the city. I continued from time to time to see the mother, and administered such medicines as I deemed necessary to invigorate and tone up the patient's system for the operation. One day in October, the young lady came to pay me for some prescriptions, and asked if a few weeks' delay would enhance the danger of the operation. I assured her it was important to lose no time, and urged her to arrange matters so as to remove the patient to the hospital as soon as possible, offering to procure her admission. She showed great distress, and informed me that she hoped to receive very soon a considerable sum of money, from some artistic designs that she felt sure would secure the prize. A week later she came again, and I gave her a prescription to allay her mother's nervousness. Then, with much agitation, she told me that she was going South by the night express, to seek assistance from her mother's father, who was a man of wealth, but had disowned Mrs. Brentano on account of her marriage. She asked for a written statement of the patient's condition, and the absolute necessity of the operation. I wrote it, and as she stood looking at the paper, she said:

"'Doctor do you believe in an Ahnung?' I said, 'A what?' She answered slowly and solemnly: 'An Ahnung—a presentiment? I have a crushing presentiment that trouble will come to me, if I leave mother; and yet she entreats, commands me to go South. It is my duty to obey her, but the errand is so humiliating I shrink, I dread it. I shall not be long away, and meanwhile do please be so kind as to see her, and cheer her up. If her father refuses to give me the one hundred dollars, I will take her to the hospital when I return.' I walked to the door with her, and her last words were: 'Doctor, I trust my mother to you; don't let her suffer.' I have never seen her again, until I entered this room. I visited Mrs. Brentano several times, but she grew worse very rapidly. One night the ensuing week, my bell was rung at twelve o'clock, and a woman gave me this note, which was written by the prisoner immediately after her arrest, and which enclosed a second, addressed to her mother."

As he read aloud the concluding lines invoking the mother's prayers, the doctor's voice trembled. He took off his spectacles, wiped them, and resumed:

"I was shocked and distressed beyond expression, for I could no more connect the idea of crime with that beautiful, noble souled girl, than with my own sinless daughter; and I reproached myself then, and doubly condemn myself now, that I did not lend her the money. All that was possible to alleviate the suffering of that mother, I did most faithfully. Under my personal superintendence she was made comfortable in the hospital; and I stood by her side when Doctor——operated on the aneurism; but her impaired constitution could not bear the strain, and she sank rapidly. She was delirious, and never knew why her daughter was detained; because I withheld the note. Just before the end came, her mind cleared, and she wrote a few lines which I sent to the prisoner. From all that I know of Miss Brentano, I feel constrained to say, she impressed me as one of the purest, noblest and most admirable characters I have ever met. She supported her mother and herself by her pencil, and a more refined, sensitive woman, a more tenderly devoted daughter I have yet to meet."

"Does your acquaintance with the family suggest any third party, who would be interested in Gen'l Darrington's will, or become a beneficiary by its destruction?"

"No. They seemed very isolated people; those two women lived without any acquaintances, as far as I know, and apared proudly indifferent to the outside world. I do not think they had any relatives, and the only name I heard Mrs. Brentano utter in her last illness was, 'Ignace,—Ignace.' She often spoke of her'darling,' and her 'good little girl'."

"Did you see a gentleman who visited the prisoner? Did you ever hear she had a lover?"

"I neither saw any gentleman, nor heard she had a lover. In January, I received a letter from the prisoner enclosing an order on S—& E—, photographers of New York, for the amount due her, on a certain design for a Christmas card, which had received the Boston first prize of three hundred dollars. With the permission of the Court, I should like to read it. There is no objection?"

"PENITENTIARY CELL, JANUARY 8TH

"In the name of my dead, whom I shall soon join—I desire to thank you, dear Doctor Grantlin, for your kind care of my darling; and especially for your delicate and tender regard for all that remains on earth of my precious mother. The knowledge that she was treated with the reverence due to a lady, that she was buried—not as a pauper, but sleeps her last sleep under the same marble roof that shelters your dear departed ones, is the one ray of comfort that can ever pierce the awful gloom that has settled like a pall over me. I am to be tried soon for the black and horrible crime I never committed; and the evidence is so strong against me, the circumstances I cannot explain, are so accusing, the belief of my guilt is so general in this community, that I have no hope of acquittal; therefore I make my preparations for death. Please collect the money for which I enclose an order, and out of it, take the amount you spent when mother died. It will comfort me to know, that we do not owe a stranger for the casket that shuts her away from all grief, into the blessed Land of Peace. Keep the remainder, and when you hear that I am dead, unjustly offered up an innocent victim to appease justice, that must have somebody's blood in expiation, then take my body and mother's and have us laid side by side in the Potter's field. The law will crush my body, but it is pure and free from every crime, and it will be worthy still to touch my mother's in a common grave. Oh, Doctor! Does it not seem that some terrible curse has pursued me; and that the three hundred dollars I toiled and prayed for, was kept back ten days too late to save me? My Christmas card will at least bury us decently—away from the world that trampled me down. Do not doubt my innocence, and it will comfort me to feel that he who closed my mother's eyes, believes that her unfortunate child is guiltless and unstained. In life, and in death, ever

"Most gratefully your debtor,
"BERYL BRENTANO."

A few moments of profound silence ensued: then Doctor Grantlin handed some article to Mr. Dunbar, and stepping down from the stand, walked toward the prisoner.

She had covered her face with her hands, while he gave his testimony: striving to hide the anguish that his presence revived. He placed his hand on her shoulder, and whispered brokenly:

"My child, I know you are innocent. Would to God I could help you to prove it to these people!"

The terrible strain gave way suddenly, her proud head was laid against his arm, and suppressed emotion shook her, as a December storm smites and bows some shivering weed.

CHAPTER XIX.

Friday, the fifth and last day of the trial, was ushered in by a tempest of wind and rain, that drove the blinding sheets of sleet against the court-house windows with the insistence of an icy flail; while now and then with spasmodic bursts of fury the gale heightened, rattled the sash, moaned hysterically, like invisible fiends tearing at the obstacles that barred entrance. So dense was the gloom pervading the court-room, that every gas jet was burning at ten o'clock, when Mr. Dunbar rose and took a position close to the jury-box. The gray pallor of his sternly set face increased his resemblance to a statue of the Julian type, and he looked rigid as granite, as he turned his brilliant eyes full of blue fire upon the grave, upturned countenances of the twelve umpires:

"Gentlemen of the Jury: The sanctity of human life is the foundation on which society rests, and its preservation is the supreme aim of all human legislation. Rights of property, of liberty, are merely conditional, subordinated to the superlative divine right of life. Labor creates property, law secures liberty, but God alone gives life; and woe to that tribunal, to those consecrated priests of divine justice, who, sworn to lay aside passion and prejudice, and to array themselves in the immaculate robes of a juror's impartiality, yet profane the loftiest prerogative with which civilized society can invest mankind, and sacrilegiously extinguish, in the name of justice, that sacred spark which only Jehovah's fiat kindles. To the same astute and unchanging race, whose relentless code of jurisprudence demanded 'an eye for an eye, a tooth for a tooth, a life for a life,' we owe the instructive picture of cautious inquiry, of tender solicitude for the inviolability of human life, that glows in immortal lustre on the pages of the 'Mechilti' of the Talmud. In the trial of a Hebrew criminal, there were 'Lactees,' consisting of two men, one of whom stood at the door of the court, with a red flag in his hand, and the other sat on a white horse at some distance on the road that led to execution. Each of these men cried aloud continually, the name of the suspected criminal, of the witnesses, and his crime; and vehemently called upon any person who knew anything in his favor to come forward and testify. Have we, supercilious braggarts of this age of progress, attained the prudential wisdom of Sanhedrim?

"The State pays an officer to sift, probe, collect and array the evidences of crime, with which the criminal is stoned to death; does it likewise commission and compensate an equally painstaking, lynx-eyed official whose sole duty is to hunt and proclaim proofs of the innocence of the accused? The great body of the commonwealth is committed in revengeful zeal to prosecution; upon whom devolves the doubly sacred and imperative duty of defence? Are you not here to give judgment in a cause based on an indictment by a secret tribunal, where ex parte testimony was alone received, and the voice of defence could not be heard? The law infers that the keen instinct of self-preservation will force the accused to secure the strongest possible legal defenders; and failing in this, the law perfunctorily assigns counsel to present testimony in defence. Do the scales balance?

"Imagine a race for heavy stakes; the judges tap the bell; three or four superb thoroughbreds carefully trained on that track, laboriously groomed, waiting for the signal, spring forward; and when the first quarter is reached, a belated fifth, handicapped with the knowledge that he has made a desperately bad start, bounds after them. If by dint of some superhuman grace vouchsafed, some latent strain, some most unexpected speed, he nears, overtakes, runs neck and neck, slowly gains, passes all four and dashes breathless and quivering under the string, a whole length ahead, the world of spectators shouts the judges smile, and number five wins the stakes. But was the race fair?

"Is not justice, the beloved goddess of our idolatry, sometimes so blinded by clouds of argument, and confused by clamor that she fails indeed to see the dip of the beam? If the accused be guilty and escape conviction, he still lives; and while it is provided that no one can be twice put in jeopardy of his life for the same offence, vicious tendencies impel to renewal of crime, and Nemesis, the retriever of justice, may yet hunt him down. If the accused be innocent as the archangels, but suffer conviction and execution, what expiation can justice offer for judicially slaughtering him? Are the chances even?

"All along the dim vista of the annals of criminal jurisprudence, stand grim memorials that mark the substitution of innocent victims for guilty criminals; and they are solemn sign-posts of warning, melancholy as the whitening bones of perished caravans in desert sands. History relates, and tradition embalms, a sad incident of the era of the Council of Ten, when an innocent boy was seized, tried and executed for the murder of a nobleman, whose real assassin confessed the crime many years subsequent. In commemoration of the public horror manifested, when the truth was published, Venice decreed that henceforth a crier should proclaim in the Tribunal just before a death sentence was pronounced, 'Ricordatevi del povero Marcolini! remember the poor Marcolini;' beware of merely circumstantial evidence.

"To another instance I invite your attention. A devoted Scotch father finding that his own child had contracted an unfortunate attachment to a man of notoriously bad character, interdicted all communication, and locked his daughter into a tenement room; the adjoining apartment (with only a thin partition wall between) being occupied by a neighbor, who overheard the angry altercation that ensued. He recognized the voices of father and daughter, and the words 'barbarity,' 'cruelty,' 'death,' were repeatedly heard. The father at last left the room, locking his child in as a prisoner. After a time, strange noises were heard by the tenant of the adjoining chamber; suspicion was aroused, a bailiff was summoned, the door forced open, and there lay the dying girl weltering in blood, with the fatal knife lying near. She was asked if her father had caused her sad condition, and she made an affirmative gesture and expired. At that moment the father returned, and stood stupefied with horror, which was interpreted as a consciousness of guilt; and this was corroborated by the fact that his shirt sleeve was sprinkled with blood. In vain he asserted his innocence, and showed that the blood stains were the result of a bandage having become untied where he had bled himself a few days before. The words and groans overheard, the blood, the affirmation of the dying woman, every damning circumstance constrained the jury to convict him of the murder. He was hung in chains, and his body left swinging from the gibbet. The new tenant, who subsequently rented the room, was ransacking the chamber in which the girl died, when, in a cavity of the chimney where it had fallen unnoticed, was found a paper written by this girl, declaring her intention to commit suicide, and closing with the words: 'My inhuman father is the cause of my death'; thus explaining her dying gestures. On examination of this document by the friends and relatives of the girl, it was recognized and identified as her handwriting; and it established the fact that the father had died innocent of every crime, except that of trying to save his child from a degrading marriage.

"Now, mark the prompt and satisfactory reparation decreed by justice, and carried out by the officers of the law. The shrivelled, dishonored body was lowered from the gibbet, given to his relatives for decent burial, and the magistrates who sentenced him, ordered a flag waved over his grave, as compensation for all his wrongs.

"Gentlemen of the jury, to save you from the commission of a wrong even more cruel, I come to-day to set before you clearly the facts, elicited from witnesses which the honorable and able counsel for the prosecution declined to cross-examine. An able expounder of the law of evidence has warned us that: 'The force of circumstantial evidence being exclusive in its nature, and the mere coincidence of the hypothesis with the circumstances, being, in the abstract, insufficient, unless they exclude every other supposition, it is essential to inquire, with the most scrupulous attention, what other hypothesis there may be, agreeing wholly or partially with the facts in evidence.'

"A man of very marked appearance was seen running toward the railroad, on the night of the twenty-sixth, evidently goaded by some unusual necessity to leave the neighborhood of X—before the arrival of the passenger express. It is proved that he passed the station exactly at the time the prisoner deposed she heard the voice, and the half of the envelope that enclosed the missing will, was found at the spot where the same person was seen, only a few moments later. Four days afterward, this man entered a small station in Pennsylvania, paid for a railroad ticket, with a coin identical in value and appearance with those stolen from the tin box, and as if foreordained to publish the steps he was striving to efface, accidentally left behind him the trumpet-tongued fragment of envelope, that exactly fitted into the torn strip dropped at the bridge. The most exhaustive and diligent search shows that stranger was seen by no one else in X—; that he came as a thief in the night, provided with chloroform to drug his intended victim, and having been detected in the act of burglariously abstracting the contents of the tin box, fought with, and killed the venerable old man, whom he had robbed.

"Under cover of storm and darkness he escaped with his plunder, to some point north of X—where doubtless he boarded (unperceived) the freight train, and at some convenient point slipped into a wooded country, and made his way to Pennsylvania. Why were valuable bonds untouched? Because they might aid in betraying him. What conceivable interest had he in the destruction of Gen'l Darrington's will? It is in evidence, that the lamp was burning, and the contents of that envelope could have possessed no value for a man ignorant of the provisions of the will; and the superscription it was impossible to misread. Suppose that this mysterious person was fully cognizant of the family secrets of the Darringtons? Suppose that he knew that Mrs. Brentano and her daughter would inherit a large fortune, if Gen'l Darrington died intestate? If he had wooed and won the heart of the daughter, and believed that her rights had been sacrificed to promote the aggrandizement of an alien, the adopted step-son Prince, had not such a man, the accepted lover of the daughter, a personal interest in the provisions of a will which disinherited Mrs. Brentano, and her child? Have you not now, motive, means, and opportunity, and links of evidence that point to this man as the real agent, the guilty author of the awful crime we are all leagued in solemn, legal covenant to punish? Suppose that fully aware of the prisoner's mission to X—, he had secretly followed her, and supplemented her afternoon visit, by the fatal interview of the night? Doubtless he had intended escorting her home, but when the frightful tragedy was completed, the curse of Cain drove him, in terror, to instant flight; and he sought safety in western wilds, leaving his innocent and hapless betrothed to bear the penalty of his crime. The handkerchief used to administer chloroform, bore her initials; was doubtless a souvenir given in days gone by to that unworthy miscreant, as a token of affection, by the trusting woman he deserted in the hour of peril. In this solution of an awful enigma, is there an undue strain upon credylity; is there any antagonism of facts which the torn envelope, the pipe, the twenty-dollar gold pieces in Pennsylvania, do not reconcile?

"A justly celebrated writer on the law of evidence has wisely said: 'In criminal cases, the statement made by the accused is of essential importance in some points of view. Such is the complexity of human affairs, and so infinite the combinations of circumstances, that the true hypothesis which is capable of explaining and reuniting all the apparently conflicting circumstances of the case, may escape the acutest penetration: but the prisoner, so far as he alone is concerned, can always afford a clue to them; and though he may be unable to support his statement by evidence, his account of the transaction is, for this purpose, always most material and important. The effect may be to suggest a view, which consists with the innocence of the accused, and might otherwise have escaped observation.'

"During the preliminary examination of this prisoner in October, she inadvertently furnished this clue, when, in explaining her absence from the station house, she stated that suddenly awakened from sleep, 'she heard the voice of one she knew and loved, and ran out to seek the speaker'. Twice she has repeated the conversation she heard, and every word is corroborated by the witness who saw and talked with the owner of that 'beloved voice'. When asked to give the name of that man, whom she expected to find in the street, she falters, refuses; love seals her lips, and the fact that she will die sooner than yield that which must bring him to summary justice, is alone sufficient to fix the guilt upon the real culprit.

"There is a rule in criminal jurisprudence, that 'presumptive evidence ought never to be relied on, when direct testimony is wilfully withheld'. She shudders at sight of the handkerchief; did she not give it to him, in some happy hour as a tender Ricordo? When the pipe which he lost in his precipitate flight is held up to the jury, she recognizes it instantly as her lover's property, and shivers with horror at the danger of his detection and apprehension. Does not this array of accusing circumstances demand as careful consideration, as the chain held up to your scrutiny by the prosecution? In the latter, there is an important link missing, which the theory of the defence supplies. When the prisoner was arrested and searched, there was found in her possession only the exact amount of money, which it is in evidence, that she came South to obtain; and which she has solemnly affirmed was given to her by Gen'l Darrington. We know from memoranda found in the rifled box, that it contained only a few days previous, five hundred dollars in gold. Three twenty-dollar gold coins were discovered on the carpet, and one in the vault; what became of the remaining three hundred and twenty dollars? With the exception of one hundred dollars found in the basket of the prisoner, she had only five copper pennies in her purse, when so unexpectedly arrested, that it was impossible she could have secreted anything. Three hundred and twenty dollars disappeared in company with the will, and like the torn envelope, two of those gold coins lifted their accusing faces in Pennsylvania, where the fugitive from righteous retribution paid for the wings that would transport him beyond risk of detection.

"Both theories presented for your careful analysis, are based entirely upon circumstantial evidence; and is not the solution I offer less repugnant to the canons of credibility, and infinitely less revolting to every instinct of honorable manhood, than the horrible hypothesis that a refined, cultivated, noble Christian woman, a devoted daughter, irreproachable in antecedent life, bearing the fiery ordeal of the past four months with a noble heroism that commands the involuntary admiration of all who have watched her—that such a perfect type of beautiful womanhood as the prisoner presents, could deliberately plan and execute the vile scheme of theft and murder? Gentlemen, she is guilty of but one sin against the peace and order of this community: the sin of withholding the name of one for whose bloody crime she is not responsible. Does not her invincible loyalty, her unwavering devotion to the craven for whom she suffers, invest her with the halo of a martyrdom, that appeals most powerfully to the noblest impulses of your nature, that enlists the warmest, holiest sympathies lying deep in your manly hearts? Analyze her statement; every utterance bears the stamp of innocence; and where she cannot explain truthfully, she declines to make any explanation. Hers is the sin of silence, the grievous evasion of justice by non-responsion, whereby the danger she will not avert by confession recoils upon her innocent head. Bravely she took on her reluctant shoulders the galling burden of parental command, and stifling her proud repugnance, obediently came—a fair young stranger to 'Elm Bluff.' Receiving as a loan the money she came to beg for, she hurries away to fulfil another solemnly imposed injunction.

"Gentlemen, is there any spot out yonder in God's Acre, where violets, blue as the eyes that once smiled upon you, now shed their fragrance above the sacred dust of your dead darlings; and the thought of which melts your hearts and dims your vision? Look at this mournful, touching witness, which comes from that holy cemetery to whisper to your souls, that the hands of the prisoner are as pure as those of your idols, folded under the sod. Only a little bunch of withered brown flowers, tied with a faded blue ribbon, that a poor girl bought with her hard earned pennies, and carried to a sick mother, to brighten a dreary attic; only a dead nosegay, which that mother requested should be laid as a penitential tribute on the tomb of the mother whom she had disobeyed; and this faithful young heart made the pilgrimage, and left the offering—and in consequence thereof, missed the train that would have carried her safely back to her mother—and to peace. On the morning after the preliminary examination I went to the cemetery, and found the fatal flowers just where she had placed them, on the great marble cross that covers the tomb of 'Helena Tracey—wife of Luke Darringtun.'

"You husbands and fathers who trust your names, your honor, the peace of your hearts-almost the salvation of your souls—to the women you love: staking the dearest interest of humanity, the sanctity of that heaven on earth—your stainless homes—upon the fidelity of womanhood, can you doubt for one instant, that the prisoner will accept death rather than betray the man she loves? No human plummet has sounded the depths of a woman's devotion; no surveyor's chain will ever mark the limits of a woman's faithful, patient endurance; and only the wings of an archangel can transcend that pinnacle to which the sublime principle of self-sacrifice exalts a woman's soul.

"In a quaint old city on the banks of the Pegnitz, history records an instance of feminine self-abnegation, more enduring than monuments of brass. The law had decreed a certain provision for the maintenance of orphans; and two women in dire distress, seeing no possible avenue of help, accused themselves falsely of a capital crime, and were executed; thereby securing a support for the children they orphaned.

"As a tireless and vigilant prosecutor of the real criminal, the Cain-branded man now wandering in some western wild, I charge the prisoner with only one sin, suicidal silence; and I commend her to your must tender compassion, believing that in every detail and minutiae she has spoken the truth; and that she is as innocent of the charge in the indictment as you or I. Remember that you have only presumptive proof to guide you in this solemn deliberation, and in the absence of direct proof, do not be deluded by a glittering sophistry, which will soon attempt to persuade you, that: 'A presumption which necessarily arises from circumstances,—is very often more convincing and more satisfactory than any other kind of evidence; it is not within the reach and compass of human abilities to invent a train of circumstances, which shall be so connected together as to amount to a proof of guilt, without affording opportunities of contradicting a great part, if not all, of these circumstances.'

"Believe it not; circumstantial evidence has caused as much innocent blood to flow, as the cimeter of Jenghiz Khan. The counsel for the prosecution will tell you that every fact in this melancholy case stabs the prisoner, and that facts cannot lie. Abstractly and logically considered, facts certainly do not lie; but let us see whether the inferences deduced from what we believe to be facts, do not sometimes eclipse Ananias and Sapphira! Not long ago, the public heart thrilled with horror at the tidings of the Ashtabula railway catastrophe, in which a train of cars plunged through a bridge, took fire, and a number of passengers were consumed, charred beyond recognition. Soon afterward, a poor woman, mother of two children, commenced suit against the railway company, alleging that her husband had perished in that disaster. The evidence adduced was only of a circumstantial nature, as the body which had been destroyed by flames, could not be found. Searching in the debris at the fatal spot, she had found a bunch of keys, that she positively recognized as belonging to her husband, and in his possession when he died. One key fitted the clock in her house, and a mechanic was ready to swear that he had made such a key for the deceased. Another key fitted a chest she owned, and still another fitted the door of her house; while strongest of all proof, she found a piece of cloth which she identified as part of her husband's coat. A physician who knew her husband, testified that he rode as far as Buffalo on the same train with the deceased, on the fatal day of the disaster; and another witness deposed that he saw the deceased take the train at Buffalo, that went down to ruin at Ashtabula. Certainly the chain of circumstantial evidence, from veracious facts, seemed complete; but lo! during the investigation it was ascertained beyond doubt, to the great joy of the wife, that the husband had never been near Ashtabula, and was safe and well at a Pension Home in a Western State.

"The fate of a very noble and innocent woman is now committed to your hands, and only presumptive proof is laid before you. 'The circumstance is always a fact; the presumption is the inference drawn from that fact. It is hence called presumptive proof, because it proceeds merely in opinion.' Suffer no brilliant sophistry to dazzle your judgment, no remnant of prejudice to swerve you from the path of fidelity to your oath. To your calm reasoning, your generous manly hearts, your Christian consciences, I resign the desolate prisoner; and as you deal with her, so may the God above us, the just and holy God who has numbered the hairs of her innocent head, deal here and hereafter with you and yours."

That magnetic influence, whereby the emotions of an audience are swayed, as the tides that follow the moon, was in large measure the heritage of the handsome man who held the eyes of the jurymen in an almost unwinking gaze; and when his uplifted arm slowly fell to his side, Judge Dent grasped it in mute congratulation, and Mr. Churchill took his hand, and shook it warmly.

Mr. Wolverton came forward to sum up the evidence for the prosecution, and laboriously recapitulated and dwelt upon the mass of facts which he claimed was susceptible of but one interpretation, and must compel the jury to convict, in accordance with the indictment.

Upon the ears of the prisoner, his words fell as a harsh, meaningless murmur; and above the insistent mutter, rose and fell the waves of a rich, resonant voice, that surrounded, penetrated, electrified her brain; thrilled her whole being with a strange and inexplicable sensation of happiness. For months she had fought against the singular fascination that dwelt in those brilliant blue eyes, and lurked in every line of the swart, stern face; holding at bay the magnetic attraction which he exerted from the hour of the preliminary examination. Of all men, she had feared him most, had shrunk from every opportunity of contact, had execrated him as the malign personification, the veritable incarnation of the evil destiny that had hounded her from the day she first saw X———.

Listening to his appeal for her deliverance, each word throbbing with the fervent beat of a heart that she knew was all her own, an exquisite sense of rest gradually stole over her; as a long-suffering child spent with pain, sinks, soothed at last in the enfolding arms of protective love. That dark, eloquent face drew, held her gaze with the spell of a loadstone, and even in the imminence of her jeopardy, she recalled the strange resemblance he bore to the militant angel she had once seen in a painting, where he wrestled with Satan for possession of the body of Moses. Disgrace, peril, the gaunt spectre of death suddenly dissolved, vanished in the glorious burst of rosy light that streamed into all the chill chambers of her heart; and she bowed her head in her hands, to hide the crimson that painted her cheeks.

How long Mr. Wolverton talked, she never knew; but the lull that succeeded was broken by the tones of Judge Parkman.

"Beryl Brentano, it is my duty to remind you that this is the last opportunity the law allows you, to speak in your own vindication. The testimony has all been presented to those appointed to decide upon its value. If there be any final statement that you may desire to offer in self-defence, you must make it now."

Could the hundreds who watched and waited ever forget the sight of that superb, erect figure, that exquisite face, proud as Hypatia's, patient as Perpetua's; or the sound of that pathetic, unwavering voice? Mournfully, yet steadily, she raised her great grey eyes, darkened by the violet shadows suffering had cast, and looked at her judges.

"I am guiltless of any and all crime. I have neither robbed, nor murdered; and I am neither principal, nor accomplice in the horrible sin imputed to me. I know nothing of the chloroform; I never touched the andiron; I never saw Gen'l Darrington but once. He gave me the gold and the sapphires, and I am as innocent of his death, and of the destruction of his will as the sinless little children who prattle at your firesides and nestle to sleep in your arms. My life has been disgraced and ruined by no act of mine, for I have kept my hands, my heart, my soul, as pure and free from crime as they were when God gave them to me. I am the helpless prey of suspicion, and the guiltless victim of the law. O, my judges! I do not crave your mercy—that is the despairing prayer of conscious guilt; I demand at your hands, justice."

The rushing sound as of a coming flood filled her ears, and her words echoed vaguely from some immeasurably distant height. The gaslights seemed whirling in a Walpurgis maze, as she sat down and once more veiled her face in her hands.

When she recovered sufficiently to listen, Mr. Churchill had risen for the closing speech of the prosecution.

"Gentlemen of the Jury: I were a blot upon a noble profession, a disgrace to honorable manhood, and a monster in my own estimation, if I could approach the fatal Finis of this melancholy trial, without painful emotions of profound regret, that the solemn responsibility of my official position makes me the reluctant bearer of the last stern message uttered by retributive justice. How infinitely more enviable the duty of the Amicus Curiae, my gallant friend and quondam colleague, who in voluntary defence has so ingeniously, eloquently and nobly led a forlorn hope, that he knew was already irretrievably lost? Desperate, indeed, must he deem that cause for which he battles so valiantly, when dire extremity goads him to lift a rebellious and unfilial voice against the provisions of his foster-mother, Criminal Jurisprudence, in whose service he won the brilliant distinction and crown of laurel that excite the admiration and envy of a large family of his less fortunate foster-brothers. I honor his heroism, applaud his chivalrous zeal, and wish that I stood in his place; but not mine the privilege of mounting the white horse, and waving the red flag of the 'Lactees.' Dedicated to the mournful rites of justice, I have laid an iron hand on the quivering lips of pity, that cried to me like the voice of one of my own little ones; and very sorrowfully, at the command of conscience, reason and my official duty, I obey the mandate to ring down the black curtain on a terrible tragedy, feeling like Dante, when he confronted the doomed—

"'And to a part I come, where no light shines.'"

So clearly and ably has my distinguished associate, Mr. Wolverton, presented all the legal points bearing upon the nature and value of the proof, submitted for your examination, that any attempt to buttress his powerful argument, were an unpardonable reflection upon your intelligence, and his skill; and I shall confine my last effort in behalf of justice, to a brief analysis and comparison of the hypothesis of the defence, with the verified result of the prosecution.

"Beautiful and sparkling as the frail glass of Murano, and equally as thin, as treacherously brittle, is the theory so skilfully manufactured in behalf of the accused; and so adroitly exhibited that the ingenious facets catch every possible gleam, and for a moment almost dazzle the eyes of the beholder. In attempting to cast a lance against the shield of circumstantial evidence, his weapon rebounded, recoiled upon his fine spun crystal and shivered it. What were the materials wherewith he worked? Circumstances, strained, well nigh dislocated by the effort to force them to fit into his Procrustean measure. A man was seen on the night of the twenty-sixth, who appeared unduly anxious to quit X—before daylight; and again the mysterious stranger was seen in a distant town in Pennsylvania, where he showed some gold coins of a certain denomination, and dropped on the floor one-half of an envelope, that once contained a will. In view of these circumstances (the prosecution calls them facts), the counsel for the defence PRESUMES that said stranger committed the murder, stole the will; and offers this opinion as presumptive proof that the prisoner is innocent. The argument runs thus: this man was an accepted lover of the accused, and therefore he must have destroyed the will that beggared his betrothed; but it is nowhere in evidence, that any lover existed, outside of the counsel's imagination; yet Asmodeus like he must appear when called for, and so we are expected to infer, assume, presume that because he stole the will he must be her lover. Does it not make your head swim to spin round in this circle of reasoning? In assailing the validity of circumstantial evidence, has he not cut his bridges, burned his ships behind him?

"Gentlemen, fain would I seize this theory were it credible, and setting thereon, as in an ark, this most unfortunate prisoner, float her safely through the deluge of ruin, anchor her in peaceful security upon some far-off Ararat; but it has gone to pieces in the hands of its architect. Instead of rescuing the drowning, the wreck serves only to beat her down. If we accept the hypothesis of a lover at all, it will furnish the one missing link in the terrible chain that clanks around the luckless prisoner. The disappearance of the three hundred and twenty dollars has sorely perplexed the prosecution, and unexpectedly the defence offers us the one circumstance we lacked; the lover was lurking in the neighborhood, to learn the result of the visit, to escort her home; and to him the prisoner gave the missing gold, to him intrusted the destruction of the will. If that man came to 'Elm Bluff' prepared to rob and murder, by whom was he incited and instigated; and who was the accessory, and therefore particeps criminis? The prisoner's handkerchief was the medium of chloroforming that venerable old man, and can there be a reasonable doubt that she aided in administering it?

"The prosecution could not explain why she came from the direction of the railroad bridge, which was far out of her way from 'Elm Bluff'; but the defence gives the most satisfactory solution: she was there, dividing her blood-stained spoils with the equally guilty accomplice—her lover. The prosecution brings to the bar of retribution only one criminal; the defence not only fastens the guilt upon this unhappy woman, by supplying the missing links, but proves premeditation, by the person of an accomplice. Four months have been spent in hunting some fact that would tend to exculpate the accused, but each circumstance dragged to light serves only to swell the dismal chorus, 'Woe to the guilty'. To-day she sits in the ashes of desolation, condemned by the unanimous evidence of every known fact connected with this awful tragedy. To oppose this black and frightful host of proofs, what does she offer us? Simply her bare, solemnly reiterated denial of guilt. We hold our breath, hoping against hope that she will give some explanation, some solution, that our pitying hearts are waiting so eagerly to hear; but dumb as the Sphinx, she awaits her doom. You will weigh that bare denial in the scale with the evidence, and in this momentous duty recollect the cautious admonition that has been furnished to guide you: 'Cosceding that asseverations of innocence are always deserving of consideration by the executive, what is there to invest them with a conclusive efficacy, in opposition to a chain of presumptive evidence, the force and weight of which falls short only of mathematical demonstration?' The astute and eloquent counsel for defence, has cited some well-known cases, to shake your faith in the value of merely presumptive proof.

"I offer for your consideration, an instance of the fallibility of merely bare, unsupported denial of guilt on the part of the accused. A priest at Lauterbach was suspected, arrested and tried for the murder of a woman, under very aggravated circumstances. He was subjected to eighty examinations; and each time solemnly denied the crime. Even when confronted at midnight with the skull of the victim murdered eight years before, he vehemently protested his innocence; called on the skull to declare him not the assassin, and appealed to the Holy Trinity to proclaim his innocence. Finally he confessed his crime; testified that while cutting the throat of his victim, he had exhorted her to repentance, had given her absolution, and that having concealed the corpse, he had said masses for her soul.

"The forlorn and hopeless condition of the prisoner at this bar, appeals pathetically to that compassion which we are taught to believe coexists with justice, even in the omnipotent God we worship; yet in the face of incontrovertible facts elicited from reliable witnesses, of coincidences which no theory of accident can explain, can we stifle convictions, solely because she pleads 'not guilty'? Pertinent, indeed, was the ringing cry of that ancient prosecutor: 'Most illustrious Caesar! if denial of guilt be sufficient defence, who would ever be convicted?' You have been assured that inferences drawn from probable facts eclipse the stupendous falsehood of Ananias and Sapphira! Then the same family strain inevitably crops out, in the loosely-woven web of defensive presumptive evidence—whose pedigree we trace to the same parentage. God forbid that I should commit the sacrilege of arrogating His divine attribute—infallibility—for any human authority, however exalted; or claim it for any amount of proof, presumptive or positive. 'It is because humanity even when most cautious and discriminating is so mournfully fallible and prone to error, that in judging its own frailty, we require the aid and reverently invoke the guidance of Jehovah.' In your solemn deliberations bear in mind this epitome of an opinion, entitled to more than a passing consideration: 'Perhaps strong circumstantial evidence in cases of crime, committed for the most part in secret, is the most satisfactory of any from whence to draw the conclusion of guilt; for men may be seduced to perjury, by many base motives; but it can scarcely happen that many circumstances, especially if they be such over which the accuser could have no control, forming altogether the links of a transaction, should all unfortunately concur to fix the presumption of guilt on an individual, and yet such a conclusion be erroneous.'

"Gentlemen of the jury: the prosecution believes that the overwhelming mass of evidence laid before you proves, beyond a reasonable doubt, that the prisoner did premeditatedly murder and rob Robert Luke Darrington; and in the name of justice, we demand that you vindicate the majesty of outraged law, by rendering a verdict of 'guilty'. All the evidence in this case points the finger of doom at the prisoner, as to the time, the place, the opportunity, the means, the conduct and the motive. Suffer not sympathy for youthful womanhood and wonderful beauty, to make you recreant to the obligations of your oath, to decide this issue of life or death, strictly in accordance with the proofs presented; and bitterly painful as is your impending duty, do not allow the wail of pity to drown the demands of justice, or the voice of that blood that cries to heaven for vengeance upon the murderess. May the righteous God who rules the destinies of the universe guide you, and enable you to perform faithfully your awful duty."

Painfully solemn was the profound silence that pervaded the court-room, and the eyes of the multitude turned anxiously to the grave countenance of the Judge. Mr. Dunbar had seated himself at a small table, not far from Beryl, and resting his elbow upon it, leaned his right temple in the palm of his hand, watching from beneath his contracted black brows the earnest, expectant faces of the jurymen; and his keen, glowing eyes indexed little of the fierce, wolfish pangs that gnawed ceaselessly at his heart, as the intolerable suspense drew near its end.

Judge Parkman leaned forward.

"Gentlemen of the jury: before entering that box, as the appointed ministers of justice, to arbitrate upon the most momentous issue that can engage human attention—the life or death of a fellow creature—you called your Maker to witness that you would divest your minds of every shadow of prejudice, would calmly, carefully, dispassionately consider, analyze and weigh the evidence submitted for your investigation; and irrespective of consequences, render a verdict in strict accordance with the proofs presented. You have listened to the testimony of the witnesses, to the theory of the prosecution, to the theory of the counsel for the defence; you have heard the statement of the accused, her repeated denial of the crime with which she stands charged; and finally you have heard the arguments of counsel, the summing up of all the evidence. The peculiar character of some of the facts presented as proof, requires on your part the keenest and most exhaustive analysis of the inferences to be drawn from them, and you 'have need of patience, wisdom and courage'. While it is impossible that you can contemplate the distressing condition of the accused without emotions of profound compassion, your duty 'is prescribed by the law, which allows you no liberty to indulge any sentiment, inconsistent with its strict performance'. You should begin with the legal presumption that the prisoner is innocent, and that presumption must continue, until her guilt is satisfactorily proved. This is the legal right of the prisoner; contingent on no peculiar circumstances of any particular case, but is the common right of every person accused of a crime. The law surrounds the prisoner with a coat of mail, that only irrefragable proofs of guilt can pierce, and the law declares her innocent, unless the proof you have heard on her trial satisfies you, beyond a reasonable doubt, that she is guilty. What constitutes reasonable doubt, it becomes your duty to earnestly and carefully consider. It is charged that the defendant, on the night of the twenty-sixth of October, did wilfully, deliberately, and premeditatedly murder Robert Luke Darrington, by striking him with a brass andiron. The legal definition of murder is the unlawful killing of another, with malice aforethought; and is divided into two degrees. Any murder committed knowingly, intentionally and wantonly, and without just cause or excuse, is murder in the first degree; and this is the offence charged against the prisoner at the bar. If you believe from the evidence, that the defendant, Beryl Brentano, did at the time and place named, wilfully and premeditatedly kill Robert Luke Darrington, then it will become your duty to find the defendant guilty of murder; if you do not so believe, then it will be your duty to acquit her. A copy of the legal definition of homicide, embracing murder in the first and second degrees, and of manslaughter in the first and second degrees, will be furnished for your instruction; and it is your right and privilege after a careful examination of all the evidence, to convict of a lesser crime than that charged in the indictment, provided all the evidence in this case, should so convince your minds, to the exclusion of a reasonable doubt.

"In your deliberations you will constantly bear in memory, the following long established rules provided for the guidance of jurors:

"'I.—The burden of proof rests upon the prosecution, and does not shift or change to the defendant in any phase or stage of the case.

"'II.—Before the jury can convict the accused, they must be satisfied from the evidence that she is guilty of the offence charged in the indictment, beyond a reasonable doubt. It is not sufficient that they should believe her guilt only probable. No degree of probability merely, will authorize a conviction; but the evidence must be of such character and tendency as to produce a moral certainty of the prisoner's guilt, to the exclusion of reasonable doubt.

"'III.—Each fact which is necessary in the chain of circumstances to establish the guilt of the accused, must be distinctly proved by competent legal evidence, and if the jury have reasonable doubt as to any material fact, necessary to be proved in order to support the hypothesis of the prisoner's guilt, to the exclusion of every other reasonable hypothesis, they must find her not guilty.

"'IV.—If the jury are satisfied from the evidence, that the accused is guilty of the offence charged, beyond reasonable doubt, and no rational hypothesis or explanation can be framed or given (upon the whole evidence in the cause) consistent with the innocence of the accused, and at the same time consistent with the facts proved, they ought to find her guilty. The jury are the exclusive judges of the evidence, of its weight, and of the credibility of the witnesses. It is their duty to accept and be governed by the law, as given by the Court in its instructions.'

"The evidence in this case is not direct and positive, but presumptive; and your attention has been called to some well known cases of persons convicted of, and executed for capital crimes, whose entire innocence was subsequently made apparent. These arguments and cases only prove that, 'all human evidence, whether it be positive or presumptive in its character, like everything else that partakes of mortality, is fallible. The reason may be as completely convinced by circumstantial—as by positive evidence, and yet may possibly not arrive at the truth by either.'

"The true question, therefore, for your consideration, is not the kind of evidence in this case, but it is, what is the result of it in your minds? If it has failed to satisfy you of the guilt of the accused, and your minds are not convinced, vacillate in doubt, then you must acquit her, be the evidence what it may, positive or presumptive; but if the result of the whole evidence satisfies you, it you are convinced that she is guilty, then it is imperatively your duty to convict her, even if the character of the evidence be wholly circumstantial." Such is the law.

"In resigning this case to you, I deem it my duty to direct your attention to one point, which I suggest that you consider. If the accused administered chloroform, did it indicate that her original intention was solely to rob the vault? Is the act of administering the chloroform consistent with the theory of deliberate and premeditated murder? In examining the facts submitted by counsel, take the suggestion just presented, with you, and if the facts and circumstances proved against her, can be accounted for on the theory of intended, deliberate robbery, without necessarily involving premeditated murder, it is your privilege to put that merciful construction upon them.

"Gentlemen of the jury, I commit this mournful and terrible case to your decision; and solemnly adjure you to be governed in your deliberations, by the evidence as you understand it, by the law as furnished in these instructions, and to render such verdict, as your reason compels, as your matured judgment demands, and your conscience unhesitatingly approves and sanctions. May God direct and control your decision."

CHAPTER XX.

Drifting along the stream of testimony that rolled in front of the jury-box, an eager and excited public had with scarcely a dissenting voice arrived at the conclusion, that the verdict was narrowed to the limits of only two possibilities. It was confidently expected that the jury would either acquit unconditionally, or fail to agree; thus prolonging suspense, by a mistrial. It was six o'clock when, the jurors, bearing the andiron, handkerchief, pipe, and a diagram of the bedroom at "Elm Bluff", were led away to their final deliberation; yet so well assured was the mass of spectators, that they would promptly return to render a favorable verdict, that despite the inclemency of the weather, there was no perceptible diminution of the anxious crowd of men and women.

The night had settled prematurely down, black and stormy; and though the fury of the gale seemed at one time to have spent itself, the wind veered to the implacable east, and instead of fitful gusts, a steady roaring blast freighted with rain smote the darkness. The officer conducted his prisoner across the dim corridor, and opened the door of the small anteroom, which frequent occupancy had rendered gloomily familiar.

"I wish I could make you more comfortable, and it is a shame to shut you up in such an ice-box. I will throw my overcoat on the floor, and you can wrap your feet up in it. Yes, you must take it. I shall keep warm at the stove in the Sheriff's room. The Judge will not wait later than ten o'clock, then I'll take you back to Mrs. Singleton. It seems you prefer to remain here alone."

"Yes, entirely alone."

"You are positive, you won't try a little hot punch, or a glass of wine?"

"Thank you, but I wish only to be alone."

"Don't be too down-hearted. You will never be convicted under that indictment, at least not by this jury, for I have a suspicion that there is one man among them, who will stand out until the stars fall, and I will tell you why. I happened to be looking at him, when your Christmas card was shown by Mr. Dunbar. The moment he saw it, he started, stretched out his hand, and as he looked at it, I saw him choke up, and pass his hand over his eyes. Soon after Christmas, that man lost his only child, a girl five years old, who had scarlet fever. To divert her mind, they gave her a Christmas card to play with, that some friend had sent to her mother. She had it in her hand when she died, in convulsions, and it was put in her coffin and buried with her. My wife helped to nurse and shroud her, and she told me it was the card shown in court; it was your card. The law can't cut out the heartstrings of the jury, and I don't believe that man would lift his hand against your life, any sooner than he would strike the face of his dead child."

He locked the door, and Beryl found herself at last alone, in the dreary little den where a single gas burner served only to show the surrounding cheerlessness. The furniture comprised a wooden bench along the wall, two chairs, and a table in the middle of the floor; and on the dusty panes of the grated window, a ray of ruddy light from a lamp post in the street beneath, broke through the leaden lances of the rain, and struggled for admission.

The neurotic pharmacopoeia contains nothing so potent as despair to steady quivering nerves, and steel to superhuman endurance. For Beryl, the pendulum of suspense had ceased to swing, because the spring of hope had snapped; and the complete surrender, the mute acceptance of the worst possible to come, had left her numb, impervious to dread. As one by one the discovered facts spelled unmistakably the name of her brother, allowing no margin to doubt his guilt, the necessity of atonement absorbed every other consideration; and the desire to avert his punishment extinguished the last remnant of selfish anxiety. If by suffering in his stead, she could secure to him life—the opportunities of repentance, of expiation, of making his peace with God, of saving his immortal soul—how insignificant seemed all else. The innate love of life, the natural yearning for happiness, the once fervent aspirations for fame—the indescribable longing for the fruition of youth's high hopes, which like a Siren sang somewhere in the golden mists of futurity—all these were now crushed beyond recognition in the whirlwind that had wrecked her.

Her father slept under silvery olives in a Tuscan dell, her mother within hearing of the waves that broke on the Atlantic shore; and if the wanderer could be purified by penitential tears, what mattered the shattering of the family circle on earth, when in the eternal Beyond, it would be indissolubly reformed? Over the black gulf that yawned in her young, pure life, the wings of her Christian faith bore her steadily, unwaveringly to the heavenly rest, that she knew remained for the people of God; and so, she seemed to have shaken hands with the things of time and earth, and to stand on the border land, girded for departure. To meet her beloved dead, with the blessed announcement that Bertie must join them after a while, because she had ransomed his precious soul; and that the family would be complete under the heavenly

89

roof, was recompense so rich, that the fangs of disgrace, of physical and mental torture were effectually extracted. By day and by night the ladder of prayer lifted her soul into that serene realm, where the fountains of balm are never drained; and into her face stole the reflection of that peace which only communion with the Christian's God can bring to those whom grief has claimed for its own.

To-night, as she listened to the Coronach chanted by the gale, and the dismal accompaniment of the pelting rain, she realized how utterly isolated was her position, and kneeling on the bare floor, crossed her arms on the table, bowed her head upon them, and prayed for patience and strength. The ordeal had been fiery, but the end was at hand, and release must be near.

She heard quick steps in the corridor, and the key was turned in the lock. Had the jury so promptly decided to destroy her? For an instant only, she shut her eyes; and when she opened them, Mr. Dunbar was leaning over her, folding closely about her shoulders some heavy wrap, whose soft fur collar his fingers buttoned around her throat. She had not known that she was cold, until the delicious sensation of warmth crept like a caressing touch over her chilled limbs. She did not stir, and neither spoke; but after a moment he turned toward the door; then she rose.

"There is something I wish to say, and this is my last opportunity, as after to-night we shall not meet again. During the past four months I have said harsh, bitter things to you, and have unjustly judged you. In grateful recognition of all that you have so faithfully essayed to accomplish in my behalf, I ask you now to forget everything but my gratitude for your effort to save me; and I offer my hand to you, as the one friend who sacrificed even his manly pride, and endured humiliation in order to redress my wrongs. I thank you very sincerely, Mr. Dunbar."

He took her outstretched hand, pressed it against his cheek, his eyes, held it to his lips; then a half smothered groan escaped him, and afraid to trust himself, he went quickly out.

Believing that she stood on the confines of another world, she had possessed her soul in patience, waiting for the consummation of the sacrifice; yet at the crisis of her fate, that singular, incomprehensible influence, long resisted, drew her thoughts to him, whom she regarded as the chosen puppet of destiny to hurry her into an untimely grave. She had fought the battle with him, under fearful odds; conscious of sedition in the heart that defied him, warily clutching with one hand the throat of rebellion in her citadel, while with the other, she parried assault.

Keeping lonely vigil, amid the strewn wreck of life and hope, she had waved away one persistent thought, that lit up the blackness with a sudden glory, that came with the face of an angel of light, and babbled with the silvery tongue of sorcery. As far as her future was concerned, this world had practically come to a premature end; but above the roar of ruin, and out of the yawning graves of slaughtered possibilities, rose and rang the challenge: If she had never come South, if she could have been allowed the chance of happiness that seemed every woman's birthright, if she had met and known Mr. Dunbar, before he was pledged to another; what then? If she were once more the Beryl of old, and he were free? If? What necromancy so wonderful, as the potentiality of if? Weighed in that popular balance— appearances—how stood the poor friendless prisoner, loaded with suspicion, tarnished with obloquy, on the verge of an ignominious death; in comparison with the fair, proud heiress, dowered with blue blood, powerful in patrician influence, rich in all that made her the envy of her social world?

In the dazzling zenith of temporal prosperity, Leo Gordon considered the heart of her betrothed her most precious possession; the one jewel which she would gladly have given all else to preserve; and yet, fate tore it from her grasp, and laid it at the feet, nay thrust it into the white hand of the woman who must die for a fiendish crime. A latter-day seer tells us, that in all realms, "Between laws there is no analogy, there is Continuity"; then in the universe of ethical sociology, who shall trace the illimitable ramifications of the Law of Compensation?

Up and down, back and forth, slowly, wearily walked the prisoner; and when the town clock struck eight, she mechanically counted each stroke. As in drowning men, the landmarks of a lifetime rise, huddle, almost press upon the glazing eyes, so the phantasmagoria of Beryl's past, seemed projected in strange luminousness upon the pall of the present, like profiles in silvery flame cast on a black curtain.

Holding her father's hand, she walked in the Odenwald; sitting beside her mother on a carpet of purple vetches, she stemmed strawberries in a garden near Pistoja; clinging to Bertie's jacket, she followed him across dimpling sands to dip her feet in the blue Mediterranean waves, that broke in laughter, showing teeth of foam, where dying sunsets reddened all the beach. Through sunny arcades, flushed with pomegranate, glowing with orange, silvered with lemon blossoms, came the tinkling music of contadini bells, the bleating of kids, the twittering of happy birds, the distant chime of an Angelus; all the subtle harmony, the fragmentary melody that flickers through an Impromptu of Chopin or Schubert. She saw the simulacrum of her former self, the proud, happy Beryl of old, singing from the score of the "Messiah", in the organ loft of a marble church; she heard the rich tenor voice of her handsome brother, as he trilled a barcarole one night, crossing the Atlantic; she smelled the tuberoses at Mentone, the faint breath of lilies her father had loved so well, and then, blotting all else, there rose clear as some line of Morghen's, that attic room; the invalid's bed, the low chair beside it, the wasted figure, the suffering, fever-flushed face of the beloved mother, as she saw her last, with the Grand Duke jasmine fastened at her throat.

The door was thrown open, and the officer beckoned her to follow him. Back into the crowded court-room, where people pressed even into the window sills for standing room, where Judge and counsel sat gravely expectant; where the stillness of death had suddenly fallen. The officer conducted her to the bar, then drew back, and Mr. Dunbar came and stood at her side; resting his hand on the back of her chair.

In that solemn hush, the measured tramp of the jury advancing, and filing into their box, had the mournful, measured beat as of pall bearers, keeping step to a dismal dirge; and when the foreman laid upon the table the fatal brass unicorn, the muffled sound seemed ominous as the grating of a coffin lowered upon the cross bars of a gaping grave. As the roll was called, each man rose, and answered in a low but distinct tone. Then the clerk of the court asked:

"Gentlemen of the jury, have you agreed upon your verdict?"

"We have," replied the foreman.

"What say you! Guilty, or not guilty?"

Beryl had risen, and the gaslight shining full upon her pale, Phidian face, showed no trace of trepidation. Only the pathetic patience of a sublime surrender was visible on her frozen features. The eyes preternaturally large and luminous were raised far above the sea of heads, and their strained gaze might almost have been fixed upon the unveiled face of the God she trusted. Her hands were folded over her mother's ring, her noble head thrown proudly back.

"We the jury, in the case of the State against Beryl Brentano, find defendant not guilty as charged in the indictment; but guilty of manslaughter in the first degree; and we do earnestly commend her to the mercy of the Court."

The girl staggered slightly, as if recoiling from a blow, and Mr. Dunbar caught her arm, steadied her. The long pent tide of popular feeling broke its barriers, and the gates of Pandemonium seemed to swing open. Women sobbed; men groaned. In vain the Judge thundered "Silence", "Order!" and not until an officer advanced to obey the command, to clear the court-room, was there any perceptible lull, in the storm of indignation.

Turning to the Judge, Mr. Dunbar said:

"In behalf of the prisoner, I most respectfully beg that the Court will end her suspense; and render her return to this bar unnecessary by promptly pronouncing sentence."

"Is it the wish of the prisoner, that sentence should not be delayed?"

"She wishes to know her fate."

She had uttered no sound, but the lashes trembled, fell over the tired, aching, strained eyes; and lifting her locked hands she bowed her chin upon them.

Some moments elapsed, before Judge Parkman spoke; then his voice was low and solemn.

"Beryl Brentano, you have been indicted for the deliberate and premeditated murder of your grandfather, Robert Luke Darrington. Twelve men, selected for their intelligence and impartiality, have patiently and attentively listened to the evidence in this case, and have under oath endeavored to discover the truth of this charge. You have had the benefit of a fair trial, by unbiased judges, and finally, the jury in the conscientious discharge of their duty, have convicted you of manslaughter in the first degree, and commended you to the mercy of the Court. In consideration of your youth, of the peculiar circumstances surrounding you, and especially, in deference to the wishes and recommendation of the jury—whose verdict, the Court approves, I therefore pronounce upon you the lightest penalty which the law affixes to the crime of manslaughter, of which you stand convicted; which sentence is—that you be taken hence to the State Penitentiary, and there be kept securely, for the term of five years."

With a swift movement, Mr. Dunbar drew the crape veil over her face, put her arm through his, and led her into the corridor. Hurriedly he exchanged some words in an undertone with the two officers, who accompanied him to the rear entrance of the court-house; and then, in answer to a shrill whistle, a close carriage drawn by two horses drew up to the door, followed by the dismal equipage set apart for the transportation of prisoners. The deputy sheriff stepped forward, trying to shield the girl from the driving rain, and assisted her into the carriage. Mr. Dunbar sprang in and seated himself opposite. The officer closed the door, ordered the coachman to drive on, and then entering the gloomy black box, followed closely, keeping always in sight of the vehicle in advance.

The clock striking ten, sounded through the muffling storm a knell as mournful as some tolling bell, while into that wild, moaning Friday night, went the desolate woman, wearing henceforth the brand of Cain—remanded to the convict's home.

She had thrown back her veil to ease the stifling sensation in her throat, and Mr. Dunbar could see now and then, as they dashed past a street lamp, that she sat upright, still as stone.

At last she said, in a tone peculiarly calm, like that of one talking in sleep:

"What did it mean—that verdict?"

"That you went back to 'Elm Bluff' with no intention of attacking Gen'l Darrington."

"That I went there deliberately to steal, and then to avoid detection, killed him? That was the verdict of the jury?"

She waited a moment.

"Answer me. That was the meaning? That was the most merciful verdict they could give to the world?"

Only the hissing sound of the rain upon the glass pane of the carriage, made reply.

They had reached the bridge, when a hysterical laugh startled the man, who leaned back on the front seat, with his arms crossed tightly over a heart throbbing with almost unendurable pain.

"To steal, to rob, to plunder. Branded for all time a thief, a rogue, a murderess. I!—I—"

A passionate wail told the strain was broken: "I, my father's darling, my father's Beryl! Hurled into a living tomb, herded with convicts, with the vilest outcasts that disgrace the earth—this is worse than a thousand deaths! It would have been so merciful to crush out the life they mangled; but to doom me to the slow torture of this loathsome grave, where death brings no release! To die is so easy, so blessed; but to live—a convicted felon! O, my God! my God! Hast Thou indeed forsaken me?"

In the appalling realization of her fate, she rocked to and fro for a moment only, fiercely shaken by the horror of a future never before contemplated. Then the proud soul stifled its shuddering sigh, lifted its burden of shame, silently struggled up its awful Via Crucis. Mute and still, she leaned back in the corner of the carriage.

"I could have saved you, but you would not accept deliverance. You thwarted every effort, tied the hands that might have set you free; and by your own premeditated course throughout the trial, deliberately dragged this doom down upon your head. You counted the cost, and you elected, chose of your own free will to offer yourself as a sacrifice, to the law, for the crime of another. You are your own merciless fate, decreeing self-immolation. You were willing to die, in order to save that man's life; and you can certainly summon fortitude to endure five years' deprivation of his society; sustained by the hope that having thereby purchased his security, you may yet reap the reward your heart demands, reunion with its worthless, degraded idol. I have watched, weighed, studied you; searched every stray record of your fair young life, found the clear pages all pure; and I have doubted, marvelled that you, lily-hearted, lily-souled, lily-handed, could cast the pearl of your love down in the mire, to be trampled by swinish feet."

The darkness of the City of Dis that seemed to brood under the wings of the stormy night, veiled Beryl's face; and her silence goaded him beyond the limits of prudence, which he had warily surveyed for himself.

"Day and night, I hear the maddening echo of your accusing cry, 'You have ruined my life!' God knows, you have as effectually ruined mine. You have your revenge—if it comfort you to know it; but I am incapable of your sublime renunciation. I am no patient martyr; I am, instead, an intensely selfish man. You choose to hug the ashes of desolation; I purpose to sweep away the wreck, to rebuild on the foundation of one hope, which all the legions in hell cannot shake. Between you and me the battle has only begun, and nothing but your death or my victory will end it. You have your revenge; I intend to enjoy mine. Though he burrow as a mole, or skulk in some fastness of Alaska, I will track and seize that cowardly miscreant, and when the law receives its guilty victim, you shall be freed from suspicion, freed from prison, and most precious of all boons, you shall be freed forever from the vile contamination of his polluting touch. For the pangs you have inflicted on me, I will have my revenge: you shall never be profaned by the name of wife."

Up the rocky hill toiled the horses, arching their necks as they stooped their faces to avoid the blinding rain: and soon the huge blot of prison walls, like a crouching monster ambushed in surrounding gloom, barred the way.

In two windows of the second story, burned lights that borrowed lurid rays in their passage through the mist, and seemed to glow angrily, like the red eyes of a sullen beast of prey. The carriage stopped. A moment after, the deputy-sheriff sprang from his wagon and rang the bell close to the great gate. Two dogs bayed hoarsely, and somewhere in the building an answering bell sounded.

Beryl leaned forward.

"Mr. Dunbar, there is one last favor I ask at your hands. I want my—my—I want that pipe, that was shown in court. Will you ask that it may be given to me? Will you send it to me?"

A half strangled, scarcely audible oath was his only reply.

She put out her hand, laid it on his.

"You dare caused me so much suffering, surely you will not deny me this only recompense I shall ever ask."

His hand closed over hers.

"If I bring it to you, will you confess who smoked it last?"

"After to-night, sir, I think it best I should never see your face again."

The officer opened the carriage door, the warden approached, carrying a lantern in one hand and an umbrella in the other. Mr. Dunbar stepped from the carriage and turning, stretched out his arms, suddenly snatched the girl for an instant close to his heart, and lifted her to the ground.

The warden opened the gate, swinging his lantern high to light the way, and by its flickering rays Lennox Dunbar saw the beautiful white face, the wonderful, sad eyes, the wan lips contracted by a spasm of pain.

She turned and followed the warden; the lights wavered; the great iron gate swung back in its groove, the bolt fell with a sullen clang; the massive key rattled, a chain clanked, and all was darkness as she was locked irrevocably into her living tomb.

CHAPTER XXI.

The annual resurrection had begun; the pulse of Nature quickened, rose, throbbed under the vernal summons; pale, tender grass-blades peeped above the mould, houstonias lifted their blue disks to the March sun, and while the world of birds commenced their preludes where silky young leaves shyly fluttered, earth and sky were wrapped in that silvery haze with which coy Springtime half veils her radiant face. The vivid verdure of wheat and oat fields, the cooler aqua marina of long stretches of rye, served as mere groundwork for displaying in bold relief the snowy tufts of plum, the creamy clusters of pear, and the glowing pink of peach orchards that clothed the hillsides, and brimmed the valleys with fragrant prophecies of fruitful plenty.

Dimmed by distance to fine lines of steel, wavered the flocks of wild geese flying from steaming bayous to icy lakes in the far North, and now and then as the ranks dipped, a white flash lit the vignettes traced against the misty, pearl-gray sky.

Spring sunshine had kissed the lips of death, and universal life sprang palpitating to begin anew the appointed yearly cycle; yet amid the flush and stir of mother earth, there lay hopelessly still and cold some human hopes, which no divine "Come forth" would ever revivify.

Into the face of Leo Gordon had crept that strange and indescribable change, which is analogous to the peculiar aspect of the clear heavens when dark clouds just faintly rim the horizon, below which they heap their sombre, sullen masses, projecting upward weird shadows.

Apparently the sun of prosperity burned in the zenith and gilded her path with happiness, but analyzed by the prism of her consciousness the brightness faded, the colors paled, and grim menace crossed all, like the dark lines of Fraunhofer. To be chosen, loved, wooed and won exclusively for herself, irrespective of all extraneous appurtenances and advantages, is the supreme hope innate in every woman, and the dread that her wealth might invest her with charms not intrinsic, had made Leo unusually distrustful of the motives of her numerous suitors. That Leighton Douglass loved the woman, not the heiress, she knew beyond the possibility of cavil or doubt, and when, after mature deliberation, she promised her hand to Mr. Dunbar, she had felt equally sure that no mercenary consideration biased his choice or inspired his professions of attachment.

For a nature so proudly poised, so averse to all impulsive manifestations of emotion, her affections were surprisingly warm and clinging, and she loved him with all the depth and fervor of her tender, generous heart; hence the slow torture of her humiliation in the hour of disenchantment. To women who love is given a sixth sense, a subtle instinct whereby, as in an occult alembic, they discern the poison that steals into their wine of joy; so Leo was not long in ignorance that her coveted kingdom belonged by right of conquest to another, and that she reigned only nominally and by courtesy.

The evil we most abhor generally espies us afar off, chases tirelessly, crouches at our feet, grimacing triumphantly at our impotence to escape its loathsome clutches; and Leo's pride bled sorely in the realization that she had sold her hand and heart for base counterfeit equivalents. In a crisis of keen disappointment, only very noble natures can remain strictly just, yet in arraigning her lover for disloyalty, this sorrowing woman abstained from casting all the blame upon him. He had not intentionally deceived her, had not deliberately betrayed her trust; he was the unwilling victim of an inexplicable fascination against which she felt assured he had struggled sullenly and persistently; and which, in destroying the beautiful edifice of their mutual hopes, offered him nothing but humiliation in exchange.

Standing to-day beside the pyramid of scarlet geraniums, and velvety, gold-powdered begonias in the centre of the octagonal room, where the warm Spring sun shone down through the dome, falling aslant on the great snowy owl and the rose-colored cockatoo smoothing their plumes on the top of the glittering brass cages—Leo contrasted the luxurious and elegant details of her lovely home with the grim and bleak cell where, in shame and ignominy, dwelt the young stranger who had stolen her throne. A beggar by the road-side had filched from the queen in her palace, her crown and sceptre, and the pomp and splendor of royal surroundings only mocked and emphasized an empty sham. Merely a trifle paler than usual, and somewhat heavy-eyed from acquaintance with midnight vigils, she proudly bore her new burden of grief with her wonted easy grace; but the pretty mouth was compressed into harder, narrower lines, and the delicate nose dilated in a haughtier curve. Sooner or later we all learn the wisdom of the unwelcome admonition: "Fortune sells what we believe she gives."

For two months Leo's relations with Mr. Dunbar had been distinctly strained, and while both carefully avoided any verbal attempt at explanation, her manner had grown more distant, his more scrupulously courteous, but pre-occupied, guarded and cold. Knowing that abdication was inevitable, she slowly revolved the best method of release, which promised the least sacrifice of womanly dignity, and the greatest economy of unpleasantness on the part of her betrothed.

During the week of the trial, she had seen him but twice, and immediately after he had been summoned to attend some suit in New Orleans, and had hurriedly bidden her adieu in the presence of others. With punctilious regularity he wrote studiedly polished, graceful yet merely friendly letters, and like ice morsels they slowly widened the glacier creeping between the two.

To her council she admitted only her bruised pride, her bleeding heart, her relentless incorruptible conscience; and over the conclusion, she shed no tears, made no moan, allowed no margin for pity. Early on that Spring morning, she had received a glowing sheaf of La France and Duchess de Brabant roses, accompanied by a brief note announcing Mr. Dunbar's return, and requesting an interview at noon. The tone of her reply was markedly cordial, and after offering congratulations upon his birthday, she begged his acceptance of a souvenir made for the occasion by her own hands, a dainty "bit of embroidery which she flattered herself, he would value for the sake of the donor."

Who doubts that Vashti made a most elaborate toilette, on that day of humiliation, when discarded and discrowned she trailed her royal robes for the last time across the marble courts of Shushan, going forth to make room for Queen Esther? Amid the loops of lace at her throat, and into the jewelled clasp of her belt, Leo had fastened the exquisite roses, noting the perfect harmony of her costume, as she smoothed the folds of the sapphire velvet robe which she knew that Mr. Dunbar particularly admired. The lofty, beautiful room was aglow with rich color from oriental rugs strewn about the marble floor, from masses of hyacinths and crimson camellias in stands, baskets, vases; from brilliant tropical birds flitting to and fro; and through the gilt wire vista of the aviary, the fountain in the peristyle beyond threw up its silvery hands to arrest attention, and softly beat time to the music of the gold and green canaries. The large white owl with wide, prescient, berylline eyes, rose suddenly, and on slow wings circled round and round, flying gradually to the ceiling of the dome, then swooped back to its perch; and the Siberian hound, a huge, dun-hued creature, lifted his head from the velvet rug and rubbed it against his mistress' dress.

As the sound of a step she knew so well, rang in the vestibule, the blood leaped to Leo's cheeks, but she walked quickly forward, and met her visitor just beneath the "Salve" in the scroll of olives, putting out her hands across the onyx table with its red and black bowl of violets. Thus at arm's length, she held him a moment.

"I am very glad to see you; and I wish you a happy birthday, hoping your new year may be as bright as the sun that ushers it in; and as full of fragrance as these lovely roses, which I wear in honor of the day."

Hand in hand, she smiled up into his handsome face, and certainly he had never looked more kingly, more worthy of her homage.

"Thank you, dear Leo. The light and sweetness of my future can be blotted out, only by losing you. You must be the fulfilment of your own kind wishes."

He raised her left hand, kissed it lightly, and as she withdrew her fingers and resumed her seat, in front of an ottoman ablaze with a tangled mass of brilliant Berlin wool, he sat down at her side.

Ere she was aware of his intention, he pushed the ottoman beyond her reach, and dexterously catching her hand, took the gold thimble from her finger and dropped it into his vest pocket.

"Perish the fetich of needle-work, crochet and knitting! To-day at least it shall not come between us;—and I claim your eyes, your undivided attention. Now tell me how many of my rivals, how many audacious suitors you have held at bay, by these gay Penelope webs woven in my absence?"

"Has Ulysses the right to be curious? Should not memories of Calypso incline him to unlock the fetters of Penelope?"

"Did she ever for one instant deem the silken cords she hugged to her loyal, tender heart—fetters? Sweet, patient incarnation of unquestioning fidelity, she stands the eternal antithesis of Mrs. Caudle. From Kittie's letter, I inferred you were not well; but certainly, my dear Leo, I never saw you look more lovely than to-day."

"Just now Kittie's perceptions are awry, dazzled by the rose light that wrap? her world. Has Prince arrived?"

"Yes, he came yesterday, and my little sister is entirely and overwhelmingly happy, for he is literally her Prince. Physically he is much improved; has developed surprisingly, but has the shy, taciturn manner of a student, and is, I fear, a hopeless bookworm."

"Why should his literary taste disquiet you? He went to Germany to foster his scholarly inclination."

"Why? Why should a man apprentice himself to a carpenter, and become an expert joiner, when he can never obtain the tools requisite to enable him to work successfully? His aspirations run along the grooves of science; and after dear little Kittie, his favorite Goddess is

Biology. Trained in the laboratory of a German scientist, where every imaginable facility for researches in vivisection, and for the investigation of certain biological problems was afforded him, he lands in America empty-handed, and behold my carpenter minus tools."

"Having fitted himself for the profession, you surely will not attempt now to discourage or dissuade him."

"The logic of impecuniosity will doubtless accomplish more than the dissuasion of friends. Microscopic inspection of red and white corpuscles, of virus, tissues, protoplasm and chlorophyl is probably very interesting to lovers of microbes, and students of segmentation, but such abstract pursuits appertain to purple and fine linen. A profession means much; but ability to practise, infinitely more. Just now the paramount problem is, how Prince can best make his bread. Six months ago, he was prospectively so rich that he could indulge the whim of blowing scientific soap-bubbles labelled with abstruse symbols; at present, necessity directs his attention to paying his board bills."

"I thought a liberal allowance had been settled upon him, and ample provision made for his future?"

"So there certainly was, on paper; but the destruction of the record invalidated the gift."

"All the world knows that he has the rights of an adopted son."

"All the world knows equally well, that failing to produce the will, Prince has lost his legacy, and must enlist in the army of 'bread-winners'."

"Then what becomes of 'Elm Bluff' and its fine estate?"

"They descend in the line decreed alike by law and nature, to the nearest blood relation."

Leo felt the blood reddening her throat and cheeks, but under the quick glance of her hazel eyes, his handsome face always en garde showed no embarrassing consciousness. Fearful of silence, she said in a perplexed, inconsequent tone:

"How manifestly unjust. Poor Kittie!"

"Why poor Kittie? Her beaming face is eloquent repudiation of your pity, and she verily believes her blond-headed, scholarly Prince a bountiful equivalent for all Croesus' belongings. Rich little Kittie! After all, where genuine love reigns, worldly environment matters comparatively little; love makes happiness, and happiness is the reconciler."

A throb of pain shook the woman's heart as she realized the bitter truth that he spoke from an experience born out of season: that he was athirst for that which her fortune, her love, her own fair, graceful self could never give him.

She looked at him, with an arch smile lighting her face, but he saw the trembling of her lips, noted the metallic ring in her voice.

"'Et in Arcadia Ego?' Recent associations have rendered you idyllic. I can recall a period when 'love in a cottage' was the target that challenged the keenest arrows of your satire. Rich little Kittie has my warmest congratulations. Will Prince remain in X—?"

"How can he? The demand here for amateur scientists is not sufficiently encouraging; and I rather think he gravitates toward a college professorship, which might at least supply him abundantly with rabbits, turtles, frogs and guinea-pigs for biological manipulation and experiment. One of the gay balloons floating through his mind, is a series of lectures to be delivered in the large cities. Heredity is his pet hobby, and he proposes to canter it under the saddle of Weismann's theory (whatever that may be), expounding it to scientific Americans. As yet no plans have crystallized. His allowance was paid semi-annually, but of course it failed him last January, and no alternative presents itself but some attempt to utilize his technical lore. There is a vacancy in the faculty of C—-University, and I shall write at once to the board of trustees."

Like a moth, Leo flitted closer to the flame.

"Will he make no attempt to secure his rights?"

"He is too wise to waste his time in so fruitless an endeavor."

"Have you advised him to submit tamely to the deprivation of his fortune?"

"He has not consulted me, but Wolverton, who is his cousin, convinced him of the futility of any legal proceedings."

"Does General Darrington's granddaughter understand that Prince's career will be ruined for want of the money to which he is entitled?"

"I am not acquainted with the views Gen'l Darrington's granddaughter entertains concerning Prince, as I have not seen her since the trial ended. Have you?"

Each looked steadily at the other, and under the gleam of his eyes, hers fell, and her color flickered.

"I went once, but was denied admission. Even Sister Serena sees her no longer. You doubtless know that she is recovering slowly from a severe attack of illness."

"I have heard nothing since the night she was convicted and sentenced. To-day I found a message at my office from Singleton, asking me to call at my earliest convenience at the penitentiary, on a matter of legal business. To what it refers, I know not, as I came immediately here."

There was a brief silence, in which his gaze mercilessly searched her fair, proud face; then with a supreme effort she laid her hand suddenly on his, and looked up smiling:

"I believe I was growing very impatient over your prolonged absence in New Orleans. Time dragged dismally, and I was never more rejoiced than when I received your last letter, and knew that I should see you to-day. Lennox, I have set my heart on something, which only your consent and acquiescence will secure to me. I am about to ask for a mammoth sugar-plum that has dangled temptingly before my eyes for nearly a year, and I shall enjoy it the more if you bestow it graciously. Can you be generous and indulge my selfish whim?"

He felt a quiver in the cold fingers over which his warm hand closed, saw the throbbing of the artery in her white throat, the ebbing of the scarlet in lips that bravely held their coaxing, smiling curves, and he knew that the crisis he had long foreseen was drawing near.

Leaning closer, he looked down into her brown eyes. The end must come; but he would not precipitate it. Like Francis at Pavia, he acknowledged to himself that all was lost, save honor.

"Whenever my Leo convinces me she can be selfish, I promise all that she can possibly ask; but the selfishness must first be incontrovertibly established."

He had never been dearer to her than at that moment, when his brilliant eyes seemed to search her soul and magnetize her; yet she did not falter and the aching of her heart was a goad to her will.

"You merely shower lesser sugar-plums, intending they shall surfeit. Lennox, you know how often I have longed to make the journey to Greece, Asia Minor and Egypt; you remember I have repeatedly expressed the wish? You—"

"Pardon me, sweetheart, but this is the first time I ever heard it." "You forget. At last the consummation unfolds itself as smoothly as the fourth act of a melodrama. My friend and schoolmate, Alma Cutting, of New York, invites a small party of ladies and gentlemen to accompany her in a cruise through the Levant, on her father's new and elegant steam yacht 'Cleopatra'. I have pressing letters from Alma and Mr. Cutting, kindly urging me to join them in New York by the first of May, at which time they expect to start on a preliminary cruise through the North and Baltic seas; drifting southward so as to reach Sicily and Malta as soon as cool weather permits. Do you wonder that so charming and picturesque a tour tempts me sorely?"

Unconsciously she had hurried her enunciation, but imperturbable as the bronze he resembled, Mr. Dunbar listened; merely passing his left arm around her, drawing her resisting form closer to him, holding her firmly.

"I am waiting for the selfish aspect of this scheme, else I should answer at once, the coveted sugar-plum is yours, and we will make the tour whenever you like, with the minor difference of mere details; we will go in our own yacht."

She caught her breath, and for an instant the world swam in a burst of dazzling light. Beyond the reach of the usurper's witchery, was it not possible that she might regain the alienated heart? Love chanted, it is worth the trial; take him away, win him back. Pride sternly set foot upon this spark of hope, with cruel insistence answering: his love has never been yours; defrauded of the diamond, will you accept and patiently wear paste? The quick revulsion was tantalizing as would have been the vanishing of the ram from Abraham's gladdened sight; the swift withdrawal of Diana's stag into the miraculous cloud at Aulis.

"That would be too severe a tax upon your good nature and indulgence, and involves a sacrifice of your professional plans, which I certainly am not so intensely and monstrously selfish as to permit you to make. I am so well aware of the reasons that necessitate your remaining in America, in order to secure the appointment you are laboring to obtain, that I refuse the sugar plum if bought with your disappointment."

"Selfishness not established; you must plead on some better ground. Suppose that the happiness of the woman who has done me the honor to promise me her hand, is just now my supreme aim, paramount to every other ambitious scheme; and that to insure it, I hazard all else? Remember the privilege of choice is mine."

It was the instinct not of affection, but of honor straining hard to hold him to his allegiance, and her proud spirit thrilled under the consciousness of his motive in striving to spare her. A crimson spot burned on each cheek, a spark kindled in the soft, tender eyes. She struggled to free herself, but his clasp tightened.

"Conceding the generosity that would impel you to immolate your feelings, in order to gratify my willies, I decline the sacrifice. You must indulge my desire to receive my sugar plum in the bonbonniere of the 'Cleopatra'."

He pressed her sunny head against his shoulder, and rested his cheek on hers.

"Is it my Leo's wish to leave me, to go alone?"

"Yes, to accompany Alma."

"For an absence of indefinite duration?"

"Certainly for a year; possibly longer; but you must be gracious in yielding. If you really desire to promote my happiness, let me go feeling that you consent freely."

He comprehended fully all that he was surrendering, the noble, pure, devoted heart; the refining, elevating companionship, the control of a liberal fortune, the proud distinction of calling her his wife; and yet above the refrain of many mingled regrets, he felt an infinite relief that he had been spared the responsibility of the estrangement.

"Whatever your happiness demands, I cannot refuse to concede, but you can scarcely require me to receive 'graciously' the only construction I can possibly place upon your request; that I am no longer an essential element in your happiness."

Knowing that he owed her every possible reparation, he was resolved to shield her womanly pride from any additional wounds. He withdrew his encircling arm, released her hand, walked to the end of the aviary, and stood watching the shimmer of the fountain, where two of the ring-doves held their wings aslant to catch the spray. After some moments she joined him, and laid her slender fingers on his arm.

"Dear Lennox, I propose at least a temporary change in our relations, and even at the risk of incurring your displeasure, I prefer to be perfectly frank. When you asked me to become your wife, neither of us contemplated the long separation involved in this cruise abroad, which I ardently desire for many reasons to make; and I am unwilling to fetter either you or myself by an engagement during my absence. I want to be entirely free, bound by no promise; and could I ask release, unless you accepted yours?"

He put his palm under her chin, and lifted the sweet, pure face, forcing her to return his gaze.

"Have I forfeited your confidence?"

"No. Lennox. I have an indestructible faith in your honor."

Her clear, truthful eyes assured him she acquitted him of all intention to violate in any jot or tittle the forms of his allegiance.

"You deem me incapable of intentionally betraying your noble trust?"

"I do—indeed I do."

"My peerless Leo, have you ceased to love me?"

She shut her eyes an instant, and the delicate, flower face blanched; the treacherous lips quivered:

95

"No."

"Who has supplanted me in your heart, for once I know it was all my own?"

"Lennox, you are still more to me than all the world beside; but I ask time, I must be free at present. Let me go away untrammelled; consider yourself as unfettered, as before our engagement, and when the year expires, if you deem me absolutely necessary to your happiness, you can readily ask a renewal of your bonds, and I can be sure by that time whether my happiness depends upon becoming your wife. After to-day I shall not wear your ring; and if, while away, I send it back to you, interpret it as a final decision that in the future we can only be very faithful and attached friends. I have sadly mistaken your character if you refuse me release from a compact which I now certainly desire to cancel."

A shadow fell over his face, and he sighed heavily; but whether the utterance of regret or relief she never knew.

"Your heart shall no longer be burdened by bonds which I can loosen. Because your peace and happiness are more to me than my own, I grant you complete release. When my ring affronts you with disagreeable memories of a past, which will always be hallowed and precious to me, as the one beautiful dream that brightened my youth, that crowned me for a season at least with the trust and love of the noblest woman I have ever known, do not return it; let it slip from the hand it made my own, and find in the blue sea a grave as deep as the chasm—that you will—shall divide our lives. I honor you too profoundly to question your course; yet there is an explanation which I owe to myself as well as to you. Leo, no man can ever be worthy to call you wife, but perhaps I am less unworthy than you probably deem me? While in New Orleans, I wrote a long letter, which I afterward decided not to send by mail. I brought it to-day, intending to put it into your hand."

He took from the inside pocket of his coat, an envelope addressed to her, broke the seal and pointed at the head of the sheet to the date, some three weeks earlier. She surmised by that wonderful instinct which God grants women as armor against the slow, ponderous aggressiveness of man's tyranny, the nature of its contents. Had she merely anticipated by an hour his petition for release? Even the bitterness of this conjecture was neutralized by the testimony it bore to his integrity of purpose, his unwillingness to conceal his disloyalty. When temples are shattered and altars crumble, we save our idol and flee into the wilderness, exulting in the assurance that no clay feet defile it.

Leo shook her head and gently put aside the proffered letter.

"You wrote it for the eyes of one who had pledged herself to bear your name; the revocation of that promise annuls my right to read it."

Mr. Dunbar understood the apprehension that made her shiver slightly. She was marching away proudly with flying colors, having dictated the terms of his capitulation. Should he suffer the imputation of treachery and intentional deception, rather than turn the tide of battle, trail her banner in the dust, and add to her pain by mortally stabbing that intense womanly pride which now swallowed up every emotion of her soul?

The more thoroughly chivalrous a man's nature, the keener his craving for the honors of war.

"Because henceforth our paths diverge, I prefer to offer you my exculpation, desiring amid the general wreck, to retain at least your undiminished esteem. Will you read my confession?"

"No; that would entail the necessity of absolution, and I might not be able to command the requisite amiability, should occasion demand it. We have shaken hands with the past, and you owe me nothing now but pardon for any pain I may have given you, and occasional kind thoughts when the ocean divides us. I promise you my unwavering esteem; in exchange grant me your cordial friendship."

She was growing strangely white, and her breath fluttered, but eyes and lips came to the rescue with a steadfast smile.

"You allow me no alternative but submission to your will; yet remember, dear Leo, that in surrendering your pledged faith, I hold myself as free from any intentional forfeiture, as on the day you gave me your promise."

"In token that I believe it, I salute and wear your roses."

She bent her head, touched with her lips the flowers at her throat, and smiling bravely, held out both hands. He took them, joined the palms, and kissed her softly, reverently on the forehead.

"God bless you, dear Leo. To have known so intimately a nature as noble and exalted as yours, has left an indelible impression for good upon my life, which must henceforth be very kinely. Good-bye."

With beat of drum, and blare of bugles, pride claimed the victory; but as Leo watched the tall, fine form pass out from the beautiful home she had fondly hoped to share with him, she clasped her hands across her lips to stifle the cry that told how dearly she had bought the semblance of triumph.

When the quick echo of his horse's hoofs died away, she went swiftly to her writing desk.

"Dear Uncle: Please send the enclosed telegram to Mr. Cutting. I had a sad but decisive interview with Mr. Dunbar, and after obtaining his consent to my tour, we thought it best to annul our engagement. Tell Aunt Patty, and spare me all questions. I have not been hasty, and I asked to be released, because I have deemed it best to leave him entirely free."

Sealing the note she rang for Justine.

"Take this to my uncle's study, and tell Andrew to bring my phaeton to the door at four o'clock. Until then, see that no one disturbs me."

With averted face she held out the envelope, then the curtain fell; and in solitude the aching heart went over the fatal field, silently burying its slain hopes, realizing the bitterness of its Cadmean victory.

CHAPTER XXII.

"Certainly, Prince, I understand your motives and applaud your decision, which is creditable alike to your heart and head. At father's death he confided Kittie to my guardianship, and I cannot consent to her scheme of going abroad with you, until your studies have been completed. She has a few thousands, it is true, but her slim fortune would not suffice to accomplish your scientific object, and even if it were larger, you are quite right to decline with thanks'. Kittie must be patient, and you must be firm, for you are both quite young enough to afford to wait a few years. Loving little heart! She longed to aid you, and this was the only method that presented itself. If we can secure the commission I mentioned last week, your marriage need only be deferred until Kittie is twenty-one. After all, Prince, when you bartered your name and became a Darrington, for sake of this fair heritage, you only accomplished early in life that into which sooner or later all men are betrayed, the sale of a birthright for a mess of pottage; the clutching at the shadowy present, thereby losing the substantial future."

"On that score I indulge no regrets. General Darrington was the only father I ever knew, and since it was his wish, I shall gladly wear the name with which he endowed me, in grateful recognition of the affection, confidence and generous kindness he lavished upon me. That the rich legacy he designed for me has been diverted into the channel of all others most repugnant to him, is my misfortune, not his fault; for ho took every possible precaution to secure my inheritance. Had I been indeed his own son, he could not have done more, and I have a son's right to mourn sincerely over his cruel and untimely end."

The two men sat on the front steps at "Elm Bluff", and as Prince's eyes wandered over the exceeding beauty of the "great greenery" of velvet lawn, the stately, venerable growth of forest trees, wearing the adolescent mask of tender young foliage, the outlying fields flanking the park, the sunny acres now awave with crinkling mantles of grain, he sighed very heavily at the realization of all that adverse fortune had snatched away.

Blond as Baldur of the Voluspa, with a wealth of golden brown beard veiling his lips and chin, he appeared far more than six years the junior of the clear cut, smoothly shaven face that belonged to his prospective brother-in-law; and their countenances contrasted as vividly as the portraiture of bland phlegmatic Norse Aesir, with some bronze image of Mercury, as keenly alert as his sacred symbolic cocks.

Strolling leisurely through the flowery decoying fields, that beckon all around the outskirts of the vast, lonely wilderness of positive Science, the dewy freshness of the youthful amateur still clung to Prince's garments; even as souvenirs gathered by flitting Summer tourists prattle of glimpses of wild, towering fastnesses, where strewn bones of martyr pioneers whiten as monuments of failure. In the guise of a green-kirtled enchantress, with wild poppies and primroses wreathed above her starry eyes, Science was luring him through the borderland of her kingdom, toward that dark, chill, central realm where, transformed as a gnome, she clutches her votaries, plunges into the primeval abyss-the matrix of time—and sets them the Egyptian task of weighing, analyzing the Titanic "potential" energy, the infinitesimal atomic engines, the "kinetic" force, the chemical motors, the subtle intangible magnetic currents, whereby in the thundering, hissing, whirling laboratory of Nature, nebulae grow into astral and solar systems; the prophetic floral forms of crystals become, after disintegration, instinct with organic vegetable germs,—and the Sphinx Life—blur-eyed—deaf, blind, sets forth on her slow evolutionary journey through the wastes of aeons; mounting finally into that throne of rest fore-ordained through groping ages, crowned with the soul of Shakspeare, sceptred with the brain of Newton.

Like a child with some Chinese puzzle far beyond the grasp of his smooth, uncreased baby brain, Prince played in unfeigned delight with his problem: "Given the Universe, to explain the origin and permanence of Law," without any assistance from the exploded hypothesis of a law maker. Equipped with hammer, chisel, microscope, spectroscope and crucibles, he essayed the solution, undismayed by memories of his classics, of Sisyphus and Tantalus; seeing only the nodding poppies, the gilded primroses of his dancing goddess.

Will he discover ere long, that a lesser riddle would have been to stand in the manufactory of the Faubourg St. Marcel, and abolishing the pattern of the designers, the directing touch of Lebrun, the restraint of the heddle, demand that the blind, insensate automatic warp and woof should originate, design and trace as well as mechanically execute the weaving of the marvellous tapestries?

"Prince. I learn from Kittie that you visited the penitentiary last week."

"Yes. I could not resist the curiosity to see the author of my recent misfortunes; but I regret the sight. I am haunted by the painful recurrence of that blanched, hopeless, beautiful face, which reminds me of a pathetic picture I saw abroad—Charlotte Corday peering through the bars of her dungeon window."

"With a difference surely! Marat's murderess gloried in her crime; an innocent prisoner languishes yonder, in that stone cage beyond the river."

Mr. Dunbar pointed over the billowing sea of green tree tops, toward an irregular dark shadow that blurred the northern sky line; and his eagle eyes darkened as they discerned the prison outlines.

"Did you ever see a sketch of Rossetti's 'Pandora'?" asked Prince.

"No."

"The face is somewhat like that young prisoner's; the same mystical, prescient melancholy in the wide eyes, as if she realized she was predestine to work woe. I am heartily glad I was spared the pain of the prosecution, for had I been here, compassion would almost have paralyzed the effort to secure justice; and now, while my loss is irreparable, the law insures punishment for father's wrongs. As I walk about this dear old place, which he intended I should possess, and recall all that we had planned, it seems hard indeed that I find myself so unable to execute his wishes. After a few days, when I shall leave it, I suppose that for the next five years the house will become an owl roost and den of bats and spiders. On Thursday I go temporarily to Charleston to visit my uncle, Doctor Thornton, who offers me a place in his office, and a home at his hearthstone."

"Why specifically for five years?"

"That is the term of her imprisonment. At the expiration of her sentence, I presume Gen. Darringtor's grand-daughter will hasten to take possession of her dearly-bought domain."

A derisive smile unbent the tight lines of the lawyer's mouth.

"Come here to live? She would sooner spring into the jaws of hell!"

Prince Darrington's large light eyes opened wide, in a questioning stare.

"If she is innocent, as you believe, why should she shrink from occupying the family homestead? If she be guilty, which I (having seen her) cannot credit, there is no probability that remorseful scruples would influence her. No conceivable contingency can ever again make it my home, and on Thursday I go away forever."

"That which a man claims and expects, generally deserts and betrays him; it is the unforeseen, the unexpected that comes in the form of benediction. Time is the master magician, and 'Tout vent a qui sait attendre'. Kittie may yet trail her velvet robe as chatelaine through these noble old halls and galleries. Come to my office at ten o'clock tomorrow; I may have an answer to my letter to Doctor Balfour."

Six months before, Mr. Dunbar had walked down these steps, mounted his horse and hurried away to keep tryst with the fair, noble woman, whose promised hand was the guerdon of ambitious schemes, and years of patient, persistent wooing. To-day he rode slowly to a parting interview, which would sever the last link that Bad so long held their lives in tender association. Whatever of regret mingled with the contemplation of his ruined matrimonial castle, lay hidden so deep in the debris, that no faintest reflection was visible in his inscrutable face.

When he reached the railway station where a special car containing a small party, awaited the arrival of the north bound train that would attach it to its sinuous length, a number of friends had assembled to say good-bye to the departing favorite. The announcement of Miss Gordon's extended yachting trip, had excited much comment in social circles, and while people wondered at the prolongation of the engagement, none but her immediate family suspected that the betrothal had been cancelled.

Leo's wonted gracious composure betrayed no hint of the truth, and she greeted Mr. Dunbar with outstretched hand and a friendly smile.

"I am indebted to your kind courtesy, Lennox, for the most auspicious omen at the outset of my long journey; and I shall not attempt to tell you how cordially I appreciate your tasteful souvenir. Your roses are exquisite, and fragrant as the message they bring me."

She glanced up at a large horseshoe made of her favorite pink roses, which had been hung by a silver wire directly over the seat she occupied.

"Will you give me your interpretation of their message?"

He swept aside a shawl and reticule, and sat down beside her.

"It is written legibly all over their lovely petals. You wish me a rose-strewn itinerary, all conceivable forms of 'good luck'; as though you stood on tip-toe and shouted after me: 'Gluck auf.' As a happy augury, I accept it. Like the old Romans, you have offered up for me a dainty sacrifice to propitiate Domiduca—the goddess who grants travellers a safe return home."

"Meanwhile I hope you see quite as clearly, that the thorns have all been stripped off and set thickly along my path?"

Her smiling eyes met his steadily, and the brave heart showed no quailing.

"If I imagine that complimentary inference is written between the lines, is it not pardonable to welcome the assurance that you will sometimes be sharply pricked into remembrance of your absent friend?"

At this moment, with clanging bells and thundering wheels the train swept in, and Leo rose to exchange last greetings with numerous friends Judge Dent and Miss Patty accompanied her as far as New York, and when the car had been coupled at the end of the long line, and all was in readiness, Mr. Dunbar took his companion's hand.

"When we parted last, I was angry and hasty. Now I desire to make one farewell request. You ask a release from our engagement. I grant it. I hold you perfectly free; but I will consider myself bound, pledged to you until the expiration of one year. Nothing you can say shall alter my determination; but twelve months hence, if you can trust your happiness to my hands, send me this message: 'I wear your ring.' Once more I offer you my letter of confession. Will you receive it now; will you look into the heart which I have bared for your scrutiny?"

"No. I voluntarily forfeited that right, when I asked my freedom. If your letter contains aught that would change my high regard, my confidence, my affectionate interest in your happiness, I am doubly anxious to avoid acquaintance with its contents. You have long held the first place in my esteem, why seek to impair my valuation of your character? Let us be friends, now and forever."

"Remember you broke your fetters; I hug mine—a year longer. Forget me if you will; but Leo, when your heart refuses to be strangled, suffer its cry to reach me. Whatever the future may decree, you shall always be my noble ideal of exalted womanhood, my own proud, sensitive, unselfish Leo; and from the depth of my heart I wish you a pleasant tour, and a safe and speedy return."

A premonitory thrill shook the ear, and dropping the fingers that lay cold as marble in his, Mr. Dunbar swung himself to the station platform. The train moved off, but he knew that it would return in switching, and so he stood hat in hand.

As it slowly glided back, he stepped close to the open window, and Leo's last look at the man she had loved so long and well, showed him with the sun shining on his superb form, and coldly locked face. He saw her hazel eyes dim in their mist of unshed tears, and the sweet, blanched lips trembling from the spasm that held her heart. She leaned down, laid her hand on his shoulder.

"Dear Lennox, open your hand carefully; there—hold it close. Good-bye."

Into his palm she dropped something; their faces almost touched, eyes met, heart looked into heart; then Leo smiled and drew back, lowering her veil, and as the cars shivered, lurched, moved on, Mr. Dunbar put on his hat and unclosed his fingers.

The white fire leaping in the diamonds destroyed the last vestige of a betrothal, that he had once regarded as the summum bonum of his successful career; consumed in its incipiency the farewell compact, which his regard for Leo's womanly pride, and an honorable desire to cling as closely as possible to at least the loyal forms of allegiance, had prompted him to impose upon himself.

Apparently unwounded, she would sail away victrix, with gay pennons flying through distant summer seas, while he remained, stranded on the reefs of adverse fate, a target for cynical society batteries, a victim of the condolence of sympathizing friends.

In reality he felt the benignant touch of fortune still upon his head, and thanked her heartily that Leo had taken the initiative; that no overt act of disloyalty blurred his escutcheon, and above all, that he had been spared the humiliation of acknowledging his inability to resist the strange fascination that dragged him from his allegiance, as Auroras swing the needle from the pole. He did not attempt to underrate the vastness of his loss, nor to condone the folly which he designated as "infernal idiocy"; yet conscience acquitted him of intentionally betraying the trust a noble woman had reposed; and his vanity was appeased by the conviction that though Leo had cast him out of her life, she went abroad because she loved him supremely. Putting the ring in his pocket, he turned away as from a grave that had closed forever over that which once held ail the promise of life.

Three hours later, that carefully written letter acknowledging to his fiancee that his heart had rebelliously swung from its moorings, under the magnetic strain of another woman, and asking her tender forbearance to aid him in conquering a weakness for which he blushed, had been reduced to a drab shadow on his office hearth; and the lawyer was engrossed by the preparation of a testamentary document, which embraced several pages of legal cap. Again and again he read it over, pausing now and then as if striving to recall some invisible scroll, and at last as if satisfied with the result, placed it in an envelope, thrust it into his pocket, and once more mounted his horse. The ceaseless and intense yearning to see again the young stranger, who seemed destined to play the role of Ate in so many lives, would no longer be denied; and at a swift gallop he took the road leading to the penitentiary.

Four or five carriages were drawn up in front of the iron gate, and when, in answer to the bell, Jarvis, the underwarden, came forward to admit Mr. Dunbar, he informed him that the State Inspectors were making a tour of investigation through the building.

"I want to see Singleton."

"Just now he is engaged showing the inspectors around, and they generally turn everything upside down, and inside out. If you will step into the office and wait awhile, he will be at leisure."

"Where is Mrs. Singleton?"

"She has just gone into the women's workroom. One of the sewing gang is epileptic, and fell in a fit a few minutes ago, so I sent for her. Come this way and I will find her."

The visitor hesitated, drew back.

"Is Miss Brentano there also?"

"No. She is still on the infirmary list."

Jarvis opened the door of a long, well-lighted but narrow room, in the centre of which was a table extending to the lower end; and on each side of it sat women busily engaged in stitching and binding shoes, and finishing off various articles of clothing; while two were ticketing a pile of red flannel and blue hickory shirts. Four sewing-machines stood near the wall where grated windows admitted sunshine, and their hymn to Labor was the only sound that broke the brooding silence. The room was scrupulously clean and tidy, and the inmates, wearing the regulation uniform of blue-striped homespun, appeared comparatively neat; but sordid, sullen, repulsively coarse and brutish were many of the countenances bent over the daily task, and now and then swift, furtive glances from downcast eyes betrayed close kinship with lower animals.

At one of the machines sat a woman whose age could not have exceeded twenty-eight years, with a figure of the Juno type, and a beautiful dark face where tawny chatoyant eyes showed the baleful fire of a leopardess. Winding a bobbin, she leaned back in her chair, with the indolent, haughty grace of a sultana, and when she held the bobbin up against the light for an instant, her slender olive hand and rounded wrist might have belonged to Cleopatra.

"Who is that woman winding thread?"

"Her name is Iva Le Bougeois, but we call her the 'Bloody Duchess'. She was sent up here two years ago, from one of the lower counties, for wholesale butchery. Seems her husband got a divorce, and was on the eve of marrying again. She posted herself about the second wedding, and managed to make her way into the parlor, where she hid behind the window curtains. Just as the couple stood up to be married, she cut her little boy's throat with a razor, dragged the body in front of the bride, and before any one could move, drew a revolver, blew the top of her husband's head off, and then shot herself. The ball passed through her shoulder and broke her arm, but as you see, she was spared, as many another wildcat has been. Her friends and counsel tried to prove insanity, but the plea was too thin; so she landed here for a term of twenty years, and it will take every day of it to cut her claws. She is as hard as flint, and her heart is as black as a wolf's mouth."

"Medea's wrongs generally end in Medea's crimes," answered the visitor; watching the defiant poise of the small shapely head, covered with crisp, raven locks. Having less acquaintance with the classics than with the details of prison discipline, the under-warden stared.

After a moment he pointed to a diminutive figure standing at the end of the long table, and engaged in folding some white garments.

"See that pretty little thing, with the yellow head? Shouldn't you say she looks like an angel, and ought to be put on the altar to hear the prayers of sinners? Would you believe she is a mother? Arson is her hobby. She is a regular 'fire-bug'. She was adopted by a German couple, and one night, when the old farmer had come home with the money paid him for his sheep and hogs, she stole the last cent he had, pocketed all the oold frau's silver spoons, poured kerosene around the floor, set fire to the house in several places, locked the door and ran for her life. A peddler happened to seek quarters for the night, and finding the place on fire, managed to break through the windows and save the old folks from being roasted alive. When the case came to trial it was proved that she had set fire to two other buildings, but on account of her youth had escaped prosecution. They could not hang her, though she deserved the gallows, and her child was born three months after she came here. Looks innocent as a wax doll doesn't she? Eve Werneth she calls herself; and she is well named after the original mother of all sin. She is Satan's own imp, and we chain her every night, for she boasts that when things grow tiresome to her she always burns her way out. I think she is the worst case we have, except the young mulatto—I don't see her here just now—who was sent up for life, for poisoning a baby she was hired to nurse. There is Mrs. Singleton."

The warden's wife came forward with a vial in one hand, and at sight of the visitor, paused and held out the other.

"How'dy do, Mr. Dunbar. You are waiting to see Ned?"

"I much prefer seeing you, if you have leisure for an interview. Singleton can join us when the inspectors take their leave."

"Very well; come up stairs. Jarvis, send Ned up as soon as you can."

She led the way to the room where her two children were at play, and breaking a ginger cake between them, dragged their toys into one corner, and bade them build block houses, without a riot.

"I have never received even a verbal reply to the note which I requested your husband to place in Miss Brentano's hands."

"Probably you never will. She took cold by being dragged back and forth to court during that freezing weather, and two days after her conviction she was taken ill with pneumonia. First one lung, then the other, and the case took a typhoid form. For six weeks she could not lift her head, and now though she goes about my rooms, and into the yard a little, she is awfully shattered, and has a bad cough, Once when we had scarcely any hope, she asked the doctor to give her no more medicine; said that it would be a mercy to let her die. Poor thing! her proud spirit is as broken as her body, and the thought of being seen seems to torture her. Dyce is the only person whom she allows to come near her."

"Where is she?"

"We were obliged to move her, after she was sentenced, but the doctor said one of those cells down stairs would be certain and quick death for her, with her lungs in such a condition; so we put her in the smallest room on this floor; the last one at the end of the corridor. It is only a closet it is true, but it is right in the angle, and has two narrow slits of windows, one opening south, the other west, and the sunshine gets in. The day after her trial ended, she sent for the sheriff, who happened to be here, and asked him if solitary confinement was not considered a more severe penalty than any other form here? When he told her it was, she said: Then it could not be construed into clemency or favoritism if you ordered me into solitary confinement? Certainly not, he told her. Whereupon she begged him to allow her to be shut up away from the others, as she would sooner sit in the dark and see no human being, than be forced to associate with the horrible, guilty outcasts down stairs. While he and Ned were consulting about her case, she was taken very ill. Of course you know Ned has a good deal of latitude and discretion allowed him, and the doctor is on our side, but even at best, the rules are stern. She takes her meals alone, and the only place where she meets the other convicts—isn't it a shame to call her one!—is the chapel; and even there she is separated, because Ned has given her charge of the organ. Everybody under sentence is obliged to work, but she does not go down into the general sewing room. The superintendent of that department apportions a certain amount of sewing, and her share is sent up daily to her. She really is not able to work, but begged that we should give her some employment."

"She consented to see Mr. Prince Darrington?"

"Oh, no! It was the merest accident that he succeeded in speaking to her. He happened to come the day that I took her out for the first time in the garden, for a little fresh air in the sunshine; and we met him and Ned on the walk. O, Mr. Dunbar! It was pitiful to see her face, when the young man took off his hat, and said:

"'I am General Darrington's adopted son.'

"She was so weak she had been leaning on me, but she threw up her head, and her figure stiffened into steel. 'You imagine that I am the person who robbed you of Gen'l Darrington's fortune? I suffer for crimes I did not commit; and am the innocent victim selected to atone for your injuries. My wrongs are more cruel than yours. You merely lost lands and money. Can you, by the wildest flight of fancy conjecture that aught but disgrace and utter ruin remain for me?' Ned and I walked away; and when we came back she had stepped into the hall, and drawn the inside door between them. He was standing bareheaded, gazing up at her, and she was looking down at him through the open iron lattice, as if he were the real culprit. That night she had a nervous chill that lasted several hours, and we promised that no one should be allowed to see her. Of course the inspectors go everywhere, and when Ned opened her door, I was with her, giving her the tonic the Doctor ordered three times a day. I had prepared her for their visit, but when the gentlemen crowded in, she put her hands over her face and hid it on the table. There was not a syllable uttered, and they walked out quickly."

"Will you do me the kindness to persuade her to see me?"

"I am sure, sir, she will refuse; because she desires most especially to be shielded from your visits."

"Nevertheless, I intend to see her. Please say that I am here, and have brought the papers Mr. Singleton desired me to prepare for her."

Ten minutes elapsed before the warden's wife returned, shaking her head:

"She prefers not seeing you, but thanks you for the paper which she wishes left with Mr. Singleton. When she has read it, Mr. Singleton will probably bring you some message. She hopes you will believe that she is very grateful for your attention to her request."

"Go back and tell her that unless she admits me, she shall never see the paper, for I distinctly decline to put it in any hand but hers; and, moreover, tell her she asked me to obtain for her a certain article which, for reasons best known to herself, she holds very dear. This is her only opportunity to receive it, which must be directly from me. Say that this is the last time I will insist upon intruding, and after to-day she shall not be allowed the privilege of refusing me an audience. I am here solely in her behalf, and I am determined to see her now."

When Mrs. Singleton came back the second time, she appeared unwontedly subdued, perplexed; and her usually merry eyes were gravely fixed with curious intentness upon the face of her visitor.

"The room straight ahead of you, with the door partly open, at the end of this corridor. She sees you 'only on condition that this is to be the final annoyance'. Mr. Dunbar, you were born to tyrannize. It seems to me you have merely to will a thing, in order to accomplish it."

"If that were true, do you suppose I would allow her to remain one hour in this accursed cage of blood-smeared criminals?"

Down the dim corridor he walked slowly, as if in no haste to finish his errand, stepped into the designated cell, and closed the door behind him.

CHAPTER XXIII.

The apartment eight by twelve feet possessed the redeeming feature of a high ceiling, and on either side of the southwest corner wall, a window only two feet wide allowed the afternoon sunshine to print upon the bare floor the shadow of longitudinal iron bars fastened into the stone sills. A narrow bedstead, merely a low black cot of interlacing iron straps, stood against the eastern side, and opposite, a broad shelf, also of iron, ran along the walls and held a tin ewer and basin, a few books, and a pile of clothing neatly folded.

Across the angle niche between the windows a wooden bench had been drawn; in front of it stood a chair and oval table, on which lay some sheets of paper, pen and ink, and a great bunch of yellow jasmine, and wild pink azaleas that lavishly sprinkled the air with their delicate spicery. Pencils, crayons, charcoal and several large squares of cardboard and drawing-paper were heaped at one end of the bench, and beside these sat the occupant of the cell, leaning with folded arms on the table in front of her; and holding in her lap the vicious, ocelot-eyed yellow cat.

Against the shimmering glory of Spring sunshine streaming down upon her, head and throat were outlined like those of haloed martyrs that Mantegna and Sodoma left as imperishable types of patient suffering. She made no attempt to rise, and for a moment both were mute.

When the visitor came forward to the table that barred nearer approach, she made no attempt to rise, and for a moment both were mute. He saw the noble head shorn of its splendid coronal of braids, and covered thickly with short, waving, bronzed tendrils of silky hair, that held in its glistening mesh the reddish lustre of old gold, and the deep shadows of time-mellowed mahogany. That most skilful of all sculptors, hopeless sorrow, had narrowed to a perfect oval the wan face, waxen in its cold purity; and traced about the exquisite mouth those sad, patient curves that attest suffering which sublimates, that belong alone to the beauty of holiness. Eyes unusually large and shadowy now, beneath their black fringes, were indescribably eloquent with the pathos of a complete, uncomplaining surrender to woes that earth could never cure; and the slender wasted fingers, in their bloodless semi-transparency, might have belonged to some chiselled image of death. Every jot and tittle of the degrading external badges of felony had been meted out, and instead of the mourning garment she had worn in court, her dress to-day was of the coarse dark-blue home-spun checked with brown, which constituted the prison uniform of female convicts.

As Mr. Dunbar noted the solemn repose, the pathetic grace with which she endured the symbols that emblazoned her ignominious doom, a dark red glow suffused his face, a flush of shame for the indignity which he had been impotent to avert.

"Who dared to cut your hair—and thrust that garb upon you? They promised me you should be exempt from brands of felony."

"When one is beaten with many stripes, a blow more or less matters little; is not computed. They kindly tell me that illness and the doctor's commands cost me the loss of my hair; and after all, why should I object to the convict coiffure? Nothing matters any more."

"Why not admit at once that, Bernice-like, you freely offered up your beautiful hair as love's sacrifice?"

He spoke hotly, and an ungovernable rage possessed him as he realized that though so near, and apparently so helpless, she was yet so immeasurably removed, so utterly inaccessible. Her drooping white lids lifted; she looked steadily up at him, and the mournful eyes held no hint of denial. He stretched his hand across the table, and all the gnawing hunger at his heart leaped into his voice, that trembled with entreaty.

"For God's sake give me your hand just once, as proof that you forgive my share in this cruel, dastardly outrage."

"Do not touch me. When we shake hands it must be as seal upon a very sacred compact, which you are not yet ready to make."

She straightened herself, and her hands were removed from the table; fell to stroking the cat lying on her knee.

"What conditions would you impose upon me?"

"Sit down, Mr. Dunbar, and let us transact the necessary business which alone made this interview possible."

With an imperious gesture, befitting some sovereign who reluctantly accords audience, she motioned him to the chair, and as he seated himself his eyes gleamed ominously.

"It pleases you to ignore our past relations?"

"Even so. To-day we meet merely as attorney and client to arrange the final QUID PRO QUO. You have brought the paper?"

"I inferred from your message that you desired as exact a copy as memory permitted. Here it is."

He took from his pocket a long legal envelope.

"I believe you stated that your father originally drew up this paper, and that recently you altered and re-wrote it?"

"Those are the facts relative to it."

"Can you recall the date of the revision?"

"Nearly a year ago. Last May it was signed in the presence of Doctor Ledyard and Colonel Powell, who also signed as witnesses, though ignorant of its contents."

"You offer me this as a correct expression of Gen'l Darrington's wishes regarding the distribution of his estate, real and personal?"

"At your request I furnish from memory a copy of Gen'l Darrington's will, which I have faithfully endeavored to recall, and I conscientiously believe this to be strictly accurate. Shall I read it?"

A severe and prolonged fit of coughing delayed her reply; and when she held out her hand for the paper, her breathing was painfully rapid and labored.

"I will not tax you. Let me glance over it."

Spreading the long sheets open before her, she leaned over the table and read.

In the palm of her right hand rested her temple, and the left smoothed and turned the leaves. Crossing his arms on the top of the table, the attorney bent forward and surrendered himself to the coveted delight of studying the face, that had made summary shipwreck of his matrimonial fortune. No slightest detail escaped him; the burnished locks curled loosely around the forehead smooth as a sleeping baby's, the broad arch of the delicately-pencilled black brows, the Madonna droop of the lids whose heavy sable fringes deepened the bluish shadows beneath the eyes, the straight, flawless nose, the perfect chin with its deeply-incised dimple, the remarkably beautiful mouth, which despairing grief had kissed and made its own.

Pale as marble, the proud, patrician face was pure as some bending lily frozen on its graceful, rounded stem: and the tapering fingers with daintily curved, polished nails would have suited better the lace and velvet of royal robes than the rough home-spun sleeves folded back from the white wrists.

Mr. Dunbar had met many lovely, gracious, high-bred women, yet escaped heart whole; and even the nobility and sweetness of his pretty fiancee, enhanced by the surrounding glamour of heiresship, failed to touch the flood gates of tender love that a pauper's hand had suddenly unloosed, to sweep as a destroying torrent through the fair garden of his most cherished hopes. What was the spell exerted by the young convict when she grappled his heart, and in the havoc of her own life carried down all the possibilities of his future peace? Personal ambition, calculating mercenary selfishness had melted away in the volcanic madness that seized him, and to his own soul he acknowledged that his dominant and supreme wish was to gather in his arms and hold forever the condemned woman, who wore with such sublime serenity the livery of felony.

After all, have we misread our classics? Had not Homer a prevision of the faith that Aphrodites' altar belonged in the Temple of the Fates?

Beryl refolded the paper and looked up. In the face so close to hers, she saw all the yearning tenderness, the over-mastering love that had convulsed his nature, and before the pleading magnetic eyes that essayed to probe her soul, hers fell.

As out of a cloud, some burst of sunlight striking through the ruby vestments of apostles in a cathedral window falls aslant and suddenly crimsons the marble features of a sculptured angel guarding the high altar, so unexpectedly a vivid blush dyed the girl's cheeks. Her lips trembled; she swept her hand across her eyes as though blotting out some fascination upon which it was not her privilege to dwell; then the glow faded, she moved back on the bench, and leaned her head against the wall.

"Where are the bonds and other securities described in this paper?"

"In a compartment of the safety deposit vault of the—Bank, of which Gen'l Darrington was a large stockholder and director. His box was opened last week in presence of his adopted son, and we hoped to find perhaps a duplicate of the lost will; but there was not even a memorandum to indicate his last wishes."

"Can you tell me whether Mr. Prince Darrington will take any legal steps to recover the legacy which the loss of the will appears to have cancelled?"

"He certainly has no such intention."

"Are you quite sure of his views?"

"Absolutely sure, having talked with him this morning. I speak authoritatively."

"He was entirely dependent on Gen'l Darrington?"

"Wholly so with regard to pecuniary resources."

"At present he is as much a beggar as I was that day when I first saw X—? Is it true that want of money obliged him to quit Germany before he obtained the university degree, for which his studies were intended to fit him?"

"Strictly true. He sorely laments his inability to complete the course of study, and hopes at some future day to return and reap the distinction which he feels sure awaits him in scientific fields."

A brief silence followed, and the girl's thoughts seemed to drift far from her gloomy surroundings to some lofty plane of peace beyond the ills of time. Once more a spasm of coughing seized her; then she looked at the attorney.

"I learned in court that the destruction of Gen'l Darrington's will would secure to my mother the possession of all his estate. She has entered into Rest; into possession of her heritage in Christ's kingdom. Am I, her child, the lawful heir of Gen'l Darrington's fortune? Are there any legal quibbles that could affect my rights?"

"I am aware of none. The estate is certainly yours, and the law will sustain your claims."

"Claim? I only claim the right to repair as far as possible a wrong for which I suffer, yet am not responsible. I sent for a copy of the will because—"

"May I tell you why? Because in order to execute its provisions, it was essential that you should know them accurately."

The assurance that he interpreted so correctly her motive, brought a quick throb to her tired Heart, and a faint flush of pleasure to her thin cheeks.

"Had you read as accurately my intentions, six months ago, when you woke me from my sleep under the pine trees, how different the current of many lives! Mr. Dunbar, my ignorance of legal forms constrains me to accept your assistance in a matter which I am unwilling to delay—" She hesitated, and he smiled bitterly.

"You need be at no trouble to emphasize your reluctance. I quite understand your ineradicable repugnance. Nevertheless good luck ordains that only I can serve you at present, so be pleased to command me."

"Thank you. I wish you to help me make my will."

"Why?"

"How long do you suppose I can endure this 'death in life?' I am patient because I hope and believe my release is not far distant. Galloping consumption is a short avenue to freedom."

He caught his breath, and the blood ebbed from his lips, but he hurled aside the suggestion as though it were a coiled viper.

"Life has for you one charm which will successfully hold death at bay. Love has sustained you thus far; it will lend wings to the years that must ultimately bring the recompense for which you long, the sight of him whose crime you expiate."

He could not understand the peculiar smile that parted her lips, nor the far-away, preoccupied expression that crept into her sad eyes.

"Nevertheless I have decided to make my will. I desire that in every detail it shall duplicate the provisions of the instrument I am punished for having stolen and destroyed; and I charge you to write it so carefully, that when all the legacies shall have been paid, the residue of the estate cannot fail to reach the hands of the son for whom it was intended. To Mr. Prince Darrington I give and bequeath, mark you now, ALL MY RIGHT AND TITLE to the fortune left by Gen'l Darrington."

"Before I pledge myself to execute this commission, I wish you to know that of such testamentary disposition of your estate, I should become remotely a beneficiary. Mr. Darrington has asked my only sister to be his wife, and their marriage is contingent merely on his financial ability to maintain her comfortably. Mine is scarcely the proper hand to pour the rich stream of your possessions into his empty coffers."

"I am well aware of the tie that binds your sister and Mr. Darrington."

"Since when have you known it?"

"No prison walls are sufficiently thick to turn the stream of gossip; it trickles, oozes through all barriers. Exactly when or how I became acquainted with your family secret is not germane to the subject under consideration."

"Cognizant of the fact that Gen'l Darrington's adopted son was my prospective brother-in-law, you have paid me the compliment of believing that selfish, pecuniary motives incited my zeal in securing your prosecution, for the loss of the fortune I coveted? Your heart garners that insult to me?"

The only storm signal that defied his habitual control, was the intense glow in his eyes where an electric spark rayed out through the blue depths.

"I might tell you, that my heart is a sepulchre too crowded with dead hopes to hold resentment against their slayer; but you have a right to something more. I pay you the just tribute of grateful admiration for the unselfish heroism that prompted you to plead so eloquently in defence of a forsaken woman who, living or dead, defrauded your sister of a brilliant fortune. You fought courageously to save me, and I am quite willing you should know that it is partly due to my recognition of your bravery in leading that forlorn hope, that I am anxious by immediate reparation to restore matters to their original status. Life is so uncertain I can leave nothing to chance; and when my will is signed and sealed, and in your possession, I shall know that even if I should be suddenly set free, Mr. Darrington and your sister will enjoy their heritage. When you will have drawn up the paper send it to Mr. Singleton. I will sign it in his presence and that of the doctor, which will suffice for witnesses."

"In view of the peculiar provisions of the will, I prefer you should employ some other instrument for its preparation. Judge Dent, Churchill or Wolverton, will gladly serve you, and I will send to you whomsoever you select. I decline to become the medium of transferring the accursed money that cost you so dearly, to the man whom my sister expects to marry."

"As you will; only let there be no delay. Ask Judge Dent to prove his friendship for Gen'l Darrington by enabling me to execute his wishes."

"Judge Dent went this morning to New York; but by the latter part of the week you may expect the paper for signature."

"That relieves one anxiety, for while I was so ill I was tortured by the thought that I could not make just restitution to innocent sufferers. Mr. Dunbar, a yet graver apprehension now oppresses me. If I should live, how can I put the rightful owners in immediate possession? What process does the law prescribe for conveying the property directly to Mr. Darrington?"

"Ordinarily the execution of a deed of gift from you to him, would accomplish that object."

"Will you please write out the proper form on the paper in front of you?"

"I certainly will not."

"May I know why?"

"For two reasons. Personally, the deed of gift would embarrass me even more than the will. Professionally, it occurs to me you are not of age; hence the transfer would be invalid at present. Pardon me, how old are you?"

"I was eighteen on the fourth of July last. Grim sarcasm is it not, that the child of Independence Day should be locked up in a dungeon?"

"The law of the State requires the age of twenty-one years to insure the validity of such a transaction as that which you contemplate."

"Do you mean that my hands are tied; that if I should live, I can do nothing for more than two years?"

"Such is the law."

"Then the justice that fled from criminal law, steers equally clear of the civil code? What curious paradoxes, what subtleties of finesse lurk in those fine meshes of jurisprudence, ingeniously spread to succor wary guilt, to tangle and trip the careless feet of innocence! All the world knows that the dearest wish that warmed General Darrington's heart was to disinherit and repudiate his daughter, and to secure his worldly goods to his adopted son; and yet because a sheet of paper expressing that desire could not be produced in court, the will of the dead is defied, and the fortune is thrust into the hated hands which its owner swore should never touch it; hands that the law says murdered in order to steal. When the child of the disowned and repudiated, holding sacred the unfortunate man's wishes, refuses to accept the blood-bought heritage, and attempts to replace the fatal legacy in the possession of those for whom it was notoriously intended—this Tartufe of justice strides forward and forbids righteous restitution; postpones the rendering of 'Caesar's things to Caesar' for two years, in order to save the condemned the additional pang of regretting the generosity of her minority! Human wills, intentions and aims, no matter how laudable and well known, are blandly strangled by judicial red tape, and laid away with pompous ceremonial in the dusty catacombs of legal form. Grimly grotesque, this masquerade of equity! Something must be done for Mr. Darrington, to enable him to finish his studies and embark on the career his father designed."

"He is a man, and can learn to carve his way unaided."

She sighed wearily, and a troubled look crossed her face; while the visitor followed with longing eyes the slow motion of her delicate hand, beautiful as Herses', that softly stroked the cat purring against her shoulder.

"Surely there is an outlet to this snare. You could help me if you would."

"I? Do you imagine that after all the injuries I have inflicted on you, I can consent to help you beggar yourself?"

"You know that I would sooner handle red-hot ploughshares, than touch a dollar, a cent, of that fortune. It would greatly relieve my mind and comfort me, if you would indicate some method by which I can convey to Mr. Darrington that which really belongs to him. Unless he can enjoy it, it might as well be in the grave now with its former owner. Do help me."

The pathetic pleading of face and voice almost unnerved him, but he sat silent.

"Cannot I dispose at least of the income or interest? If a definite amount should be allowed me each year, during my minority, could I do as I please with that sum?"

"Certainly you have that right. I may as well tell you, there is one method of accomplishing your aim, by applying to the Legislature to legalize your acts by declaring you of age. At present the estate is in the hands of Mr. Wolverton, whom the Probate Court has appointed administrator; and at the expiration of eighteen months from the date of Gen'l Darrington's death, the control of the whole will devolve to some extent upon you. Meanwhile the administrator will allow you annually a reasonable amount."

"Do you know what sum Mr. Darrington required while abroad?"

"I am told his allowance was four thousand dollars per annum. Histology, morphology, and aetiology are whims too costly for impecunious students. Prince must reduce his stable of hobbies."

"No, he is entitled to canter as many as he likes, and the money could not be better spent than in promoting the noble work of the advancement of Science. The problem is solved, and my earthly cares are at an end. Leave the copy you brought, and ask Mr. Wolverton to see me to-morrow. He shall write both the will and the deed of gift, which you think can be made valid, and meanwhile the annual allowance must be paid as formerly to the son. Whether I live or die, the wishes of the dead will be respected, and Prince Darrington shall have his own. It is an intense relief to know that two innocent and happy lives will never feel the fatal chill of my shadow; and when your sister enters 'Elm Bluff' as its mistress, the balance-sheet will be complete."

As if some dreaded task had been finally accomplished, she drew a deep sigh of weariness that was cut short by a spell of coughing.

"There is a Scriptural injunction concerning kindness to enemies, which amounts to heaping coals of fire on their heads; and to my unregenerate nature, it savors more of subtle inquisitorial cruelty, than of Christian charity."

"Your sister is not my enemy, I hope, and need I so rank your sister's brother? There is one thing more, which even your sarcasm shall not prevent."

She drew from beneath the cardboard a paper box, placed it on the table and removed the lid.

"I presume the Sheriff meant kindly when he sent me this as my property, which having testified to suit the prosecution, was returned to the burglar in whose possession it was found. The sight of it was as humiliating as a blow on the cheek. Some gifts are fatal; nevertheless, you must ascribe no sinister motive to me, when I fulfil that injunction of Gen'l Darrington's last Will and Testament, which set apart these sapphires for his son's bride. They are just as I received them from his hands. My mother, for whom they were intended, never saw them; I thank God that she wears the eternal jewels that He provides for the faithful and the pure in heart. I wish you to deliver this case, and the gold pieces, one hundred dollars, to Mr. Darrington; and it will be a mercy to rid me of torturing reminders."

She looked at the azure flame leaping from the superb stones, and pushed the box away with a gesture of loathing.

"Beautifully blue as those weird nebulae in the far, far South; that brood over the ocean wastes where cyclones are born; but to me and to mine, the baleful medium of an inherited curse. Having accomplished my doom, may they bring only benison to your sister."

"I would see adders fastened in her ears and twined around her neck sooner than those—"

"At least take them out of my sight; give them to Mr. Darrington. They are maddening reminders of a perished past. Now, to the last iota, I have made all possible restitution, and the account is squared; for in exchange for that life, which I am condemned as having taken, my own is the forfeit. The expiation is complete."

She seemed to have forgotten his presence, as her gaze rested on the ring she wore, and a happy smile momentarily glorified the pale face.

"Beryl!—"

She started, winced, shivered; and threw up her hand with the haughty denial he so well remembered.

"Hush! Only my precious dead ever called me so. You must not dare!"

Something she read in the face that leaned toward her, filled her with vague dread, and despite her efforts, she trembled visibly.

"Mr. Dunbar, I am very weary; tired—oh! how tired, body and soul."

"You dismiss me? Recollect I was warned that this would be the last interview accorded me, and I beg your indulgence. If you knew all, if you could imagine one-half the sorrow you have caused me, you would consider our accounts as satisfactorily balanced as your settlement with the Darringtons. Whether you have ruined my life, or are destined to purify and exalt it, remains to be determined. To see you as you are, is almost beyond my powers of endurance, and for my own sake—mark you—to ease my own heart, I shall redouble my efforts to have you liberated. There is one speedy process, the discovery of the man whom, thus far, you have shielded so effectually; and next week I begin the hunt in earnest by going West."

He saw her fingers clutch each other, and the artery in her throat throb quickly.

"How many victims are required to appease the manes of Gen'l Darrington? Be satisfied with having sacrificed me, and waste no more time in search that can bring neither recompense to you, nor consolation to me. If I can bear my fate, you, sir, have no right to interfere."

"Then, like the selfish man I am, I usurp the right. What damnable infatuation can bind you to that miserable poltroon, who skulks in safety, knowing that the penalty of his evil deeds falls on you? One explanation has suggested itself: it haunts me like a fiend, and only you can exorcise it. Are you married to that brute, and is it loyalty that nerves you? For God's sake do not trifle, tell me the truth."

He leaned across the table, caught her hands. She shook off his touch, and her eyes were ablaze.

"Are you insane? How dare you cherish such a suspicion? The bare conjecture is an insult, and you must know it is false. Married? I?"

"Forgive me if I wound you, but indeed I could conceive of no other solution of the mystery of your self-sacrifice; for it is utterly incredible that unless some indissoluble tie bound you, that cowardly knave could command your allegiance. It maddens me to think that you, so far beyond all other women, can tolerate the thought of that—"

"Hush! hush! You conjure phantoms with which to taunt and torture. You pity me so keenly, that your judgment becomes distorted, and you chase chimeras. Banish imaginary husbands, Western journeys, even the thought of my wretched doom, and try henceforth to forget that I ever saw X—."

"What does this mean? It was not on your hand when I held it so long that day—in my own. Tell me, and quiet my pain."

He pointed to the heavy ring, which was much too large for the wasted finger where it glistened.

"What does it mean? A tale of woe. It means that when my broken-hearted mother was dying among strangers, in a hospital, she kissed her wedding ring, and sent it with her love and blessing to the child—she idolized. It means—" She held up her waxen hand, and into her voice stole immeasurable tenderness: "Shall I tell you all it means? This little gold hoop inscribed inside 'I. B. to E. D.,' girdles all that this world has left for me; memories of father, mother, sunny childhood in a peaceful home, lofty ambitions, happy, happy beautiful hopes that once belonged to the girl Beryl, whom pitiless calamity has broken on her cruel wheel. Walled up, dying slowly in a convict's tomb, the only light that shines into my desolate heart, flickers through this little circle; and clasping it close through the long, long nights, when horrible images brood like vampires, it soothes me, like the touch of the dear hand which it graced so long, and brings me dreams of the fair, sweet past."

Was it the mist in his eyes that showed her almost glorified by the level rays of the setting sun, as like a tired child she leaned her head against the wall, a pale image of resignation?

To lose her was a conjecture so fraught with pain, that his swart face blanched, and his voice quivered under its weight of tender entreaty.

"What is it that sustains you in your frightful martyrdom? Why do you endure these horrors which might be abolished? You hurl me back upon the loathsome thought that love, love for a depraved, brutal wretch is the secret that baffles me. I might be able to see you die, to lay you, stainless snowdrop that you are, in the coffin that would keep you sacred forever; but please God! I will never endure the pain of seeing you leave these sheltering walls to walk into that man's arms. I swear to you by all I hold most precious, that if he be yet alive, I will hand him over to retribution."

He had pushed aside the table, and stood before her, with the one wholly absorbing love of his life glowing in his face. She dared not meet the gaze that thrilled her with an exquisite happiness, and involuntarily rose. Had she not strangled the impulse, her fluttering heart would have prompted her to lean forward, rest her head against his arm, and tell him all; but close as they stood, and realizing that she reigned supreme in his affection, one seemed to rise reproachfully between them; that generous, gentle woman to whom his faith was pledged. No matter at what cost, she must guard Leo's peace of mind; and to dispel his jealous illusion now, would speedily overwhelm the tottering fabric of his allegiance. Folding her arms tightly across her breast, she answered proudly:

"So be it then. Do your worst."

"You admit it!"

"I admit nothing."

"You defy me?"

"Defy? It seems I am always at the mercy of Tiberius."

"Can you look at me, and deny that you are screening your lover?"

She quickly lifted her head, with a peculiar haughty movement that reminded him of a desperate stag at bay, and he never forgot the expression of her eyes.

"I deny that Miss Gordon's accepted lover has any right to catechise me concerning a subject which, were his suspicions correct, should invest it with a sanctity inviolable by wanton curiosity."

He recoiled slightly as from a lash.

"Miss Gordon is on the eve of sailing through the sunny isles of Greece; and while she is absent I purpose finding my nepenthe in my hunt for murderers among Montana wilds. You have defied me, and I will do my worst, nay, my very best to catch and hang that cowardly rogue who adroitly used your handkerchief as the instrument to aid his crime."

She walked a few steps, putting once more between them the table, against which she leaned.

"If you are successful, and the mystery of that awful murder should be unravelled, you will then comprehend something of the desperation that makes me endure even this crucifixion of soul; and in that day, when you discover the fugitive lover, you will blush for the taunts aimed at a defenceless and sorely-stricken woman."

"Nevertheless, I bend my energies henceforth to his capture and punishment."

"Because he is my lover? Or because he may be a criminal? Ask that question of your honor. Answer it to your own conscience, and to the noble heart of the trusting woman you asked to become your wife. Mr. Dunbar, you must leave me now; my strength is almost spent."

Baffled, exasperated, he approached the table and took something from his vest-pocket.

"I hold my honor flawless, and with the sanction of my conscience I prefer to answer to you—you alone—because he is your lover, I will have his life."

She smiled, and her eyes drooped; but there was strange emphasis in her words as she clasped her hands:

"God keep my lover now and forever. Mr. Dunbar, when you discover him, I have no fear that you will harm one hair in his dear head."

"If you knew all you have cost me, you might understand why I will never forego my compensation. I bide my time; but I shall win. You asked me, as a special favor, to preserve and secure for you something which you held very valuable. Because no wish of yours can ever be forgotten, I have complied with your request and brought you this 'precious souvenir' of a tender past."

He tore away the paper wrapping, and held toward her the meerschaum pipe, then dropped it on the table as though it burned his fingers.

At sight of it, a sudden faintness made the girl reel, and she put her hand to her throat, as if to loosen a throttling touch. Her eyes filled, and in a whirling mist she seemed to see the beloved face of the father long dead, of the gay, beautiful young brother who had wrought her ruin. Weakness overpowered her, and sinking to her knees, she drew the pipe closer, laid it against her cheek, folded her arms over it on the table and bowed her head.

What a host of mocking phantoms leaped through the portals of the Bygone—babbling of the glorious golden dawn that was whitening into a radiant morning, when the day-star fell back below the horizon, and night devoured the new-born day. Memory comes, sometimes, in the guise of an angel, wearing fragrant chaplets, singing us the perfect harmonies of a hallowed past; but oftener still, as a fury scourging with serpents; and always over her shoulder peers the wan face and pitying eyes of a divine Regret.

The sun had gone down behind the dense pine forest stretching beyond the prison, but the sky was a vast shifting flame of waning rose and deepening scarlet, and the glow from the West still defied the shadows gathering in the cell. Beryl was so still, that Mr. Dunbar feared she had fainted from exhaustion.

He stepped to her side, and laid his hand on the bronzed head, smoothing caressingly yet reverently the short, silky hair. Ah, the unfathomable tenderness with which he bent over the only woman he ever loved; the intolerable pain of the thought that after all he might lose her. He heard the shuddering sob that broke from her overtaxed and aching heart, and despite his jealous rage he felt unmanned. When she raised her face, tears hung on her lashes.

"I will thank you, Mr. Dunbar, as long as I live, for this last and greatest kindness. If I could tell you what this precious relic represents to me, oh, if you knew! you would pity me indeed."

"Tell me. Trust me. God knows I would never betray your confidence, no matter what it cost me."

It was a powerful temptation to divulge the truth, and her heart whispered that Bertie's safety would be secured by removing all jealous incentive to his pursuit; but she remembered the fair, sweet, heroic woman who had dared her fiance's wrath in order to unbar those prison doors; who had faithfully and delicately thrown over the convict the mantle of her friendship; and the loyal soul of the prisoner strangled its weakness.

Perishing in the desert where scorching sands stifled her, she had surrendered to death, when love sprang to her side, lifted her into the heavenly peace of dewy palms, and held to parched lips the sparkling draught a glimpse of which electrified her. Would starvation entitle her to drink? Over the head of pleading love stretched the arm of stony-eyed duty, striking into the dust the crystal drops, withering the palms; and following her stern beckon, the thirsty pilgrim re-trod the sands of surrender, more intolerable than before, because the oasis was still in sight. Duty! Rugged incorruptible Spartan dame, whose inflexible mandate is ever: "With your shield, or on it."

Beryl put up her hand, drew his from her head to her lips, kissed it softly.

"Good-bye, Mr. Dunbar. I promise you one thing. If I find I cannot live, I will send for you. Upon the border of the grave I will open my heart. You shall see all; and then you will understand, and deliver a message which I must leave in your hands. Give my grateful remembrance to Miss Gordon. Make her happy; and ask her to pray for me, that I may be patient. Now leave me, for I can bear no more."

She put aside his hand, and hid her face once more. He stooped, laid his lips on the shining hair, and walked away. At the door he paused. The long corridor was very dim and gloomy, and the deep-toned bell in the tower was ringing slowly. Looking back into the cell, he saw that Beryl had risen, and against the sullen red glow on the western window, her face and figure outlined a silhouette of hopeless desolation.

CHAPTER XXIV

Each human soul is dowered with an inherent adaptability to its environment, with an innate energy which properly directed, grapples successfully with all assailing ills; and Time, the tireless reconciler, flies always low at our side, hardening the fibre of endurance, stealthily administering that supreme and infallible anaesthetic whereby the torturing throes of human woe are surely stilled. Existence involves strife; mental and moral growth depend upon the vigor with which it is waged, and scorning cowardice, Nature provides the weapons essential to victory. The evils that afflict humanity are meted out with a marvellously accurate reference to the idiosyncrasies of character; and no weight is imposed which cannot by heroic effort be sustained. The Socratic belief that if all misfortunes were laid in a heap, whence every man and woman must draw an equal portion, each would select the burden temporarily laid down and walk away comforted, was merely an adumbration of the sublimer truth, "As thy day, so shall thy strength be."

Very slowly physical health and spiritual patience came back to Beryl; but by degrees she bravely lifted the stained and mutilated wreck of life, and staggered on her lonely way, finding that repose which means the death of hope.

At one time death had smilingly pushed ajar the door that opened into eternal peace, and beckoned her bruised soul to follow; then mockingly barred escape, and left her to renew the battle. From that double window in the second story of the prison, she watched the silver of full moons shining on the spectral white columns that crowned "Elm Bluff", the fire of setting suns that blazed ruby-red as Gubbio wine, along the line of casements that pierced the front facade, a bristling perpetual reminder of the tragedy that cried to heaven for vengeance. She learned exactly where to expect the first glimpse of the slender opal crescent in the primrose west; followed its waxing brilliance as it sailed out of the green bights of the pine forest, its waning pallor, amid the sparkling splendor of planets that lit the far east.

As the constellations trod the mazes of their stately minuet across the distant field of blue, their outlines grew familiar as human countenances; and from the darkness of her cell she turned to the great golden stars throbbing in midnight skies, peering in through the iron bars like pitying eyes of heavenly guardians. Locked away from human companionship, and grateful for the isolation of her narrow cell, the lonely woman found tender compensation in the kindly embrace of Nature's arms, drawn closely about her.

The procession of the seasons became to her the advent of so many angels, who leaned in at her window and taught her the secret of floral runes; the mysterious gamut of bird melodies, the shrill and weird dithyrambics of the insect world; the recitative and andante and scherzo of wind and rain, of hail and sleet, in storm symphonies.

The Angel of Spring, with the snow of dogwood, and the faint pink of apple blossoms on her dimpling cheeks; with violet censers swinging incense before her crocus-sandalled feet, and the bleating of young lambs that nestled in her warm arms.

The Angel of Summer, full blown as the red roses flaunting amid the golden grain and amber silk tassels that garlanded her sunny brow; poised languorously on the glittering apex of salmon clouds at whose base lightning flickered and thunder growled,—watching through drowsy half shut lids the speckled broods of partridges scurrying with frantic haste through the wild poppies of ripe wheat fields, the brown covey of shy doves ambushed among purple morning glories swinging in the dense shade of rustling corn; listening as in a dream to the laughter of reapers, whetting scythes in the blistering glare of meadow slopes, yet hearing all the while, the low, sweet babble of the slender stream that trickled through pine roots, down the hillside, and added its silvery tinkle to the lullaby crooned by the river to its fringe of willows, its sleeping lily pads.

The Angel of Autumn, radiant through her crystal veil of falling rain, as with caressing touches she deepened the crimson on orchard treasures, mellowed the heart of vineyard clusters, painted the leaves with hectic glory that reconciled to their approaching fall, smiled on the chestnuts that burst their burrs to greet her, whispered to the squirrels that the banquet was ready; kissed into starry bloom blue asters crowding about her knees, and left the scarlet of her lips on the kingdom of berries ordained to flush the forest aisles, where wolfish winds howled, when leaves had rustled down to die, and verdure was no more.

The Angel of Winter, a sad, mute image, wan as her robes of snow, stretching white wings to shelter perishing birds huddled on the cold pall that covered a numb world,—crowned with icicles that clasped her silver locks, shedding tears that froze upon her marble cheeks; standing on the universal grave where Nature lay bound in cerements, hearkening to the dismal hooting of the owl at her feet, the sharp insistent cry of gray killdees hovering above icy marshes, the wailing tempest dirge over the dead earth; and while with one benignant hand she tenderly folded her mantle about the sleepers, the other kindled a conflagration along the western sky, that reddened and warmed even the wastes of snow, and when she beckoned, the attendant stars seemed to circle closer and closer, burning with an added lustre that made night glorious. Answering her call, the Auroral arch sprang out of the North, spanning the sky with waving banners of orange and violet flame, that illumined the Niobe of the Seasons, as she hovered with out-stretched glittering pinions, and mournful ice-dimmed eyes above her shrouded dead children.

With returning health, had come to Beryl activity of those artistic instincts, which for a time, had slumbered in the torpor of despair; and when her daily task of work had been accomplished, the prisoner leaned with folded arms on the stone ledge of the window, and studied every changing aspect of earth and atmosphere. By degrees the old ambition stirred, and she began to sketch the slow panorama of July clouds, built of mist and foam into the likeness of domes of burnished copper, and campaniles of silver; the opaque mountain masses, stratified along the horizon, leaden in hue, with sullen bluish gorges where ravening January winds made their lair; the intricate, graceful tracery of gnarled bare boughs and interlacing twigs, that would serve as a framework when May hung up her green portieres to screen the down-lined boudoirs where happy birds nestled; the gray stone arches of the bridge in the valley below, the groups of cattle couched on the rocky hillside, up which the pine forest marched like ranks of giants.

On sultry afternoons she watched lengthening tree-shadows creep across the reddish-brown carpeting of straw, and in the long nights when sleeplessness betrayed her into the clutches of torturing retrospection, she waited and longed for the pearly lustre that paved the east for the rosy feet of dawn; listened to the beating of Nature's heart in the solemn roar of the Falls two miles away, in the strophe and anti-strophe of winds quivering through pine tops, the startled cry of birds dozing in cedar thickets, the shrill droning of crickets, the monotonous recrimination of katydids, the peculiar, querulous call of a family of flying squirrels housed in the cleft of an old magnolia, the Gregorian chant of frogs cradled in the sedge and ferns, where the river lapped and gurgled.

Humanity had turned its back upon her; but the sinless world of creation, with all its glorious chords of beautiful color, and the soothing witchery of the solemn voices of the night, ministered abundantly to eye and ear. She had hoped and prayed to die; God denied her petition; and sent, instead of His Angel of Death, two to comfort her, the Angel of Health and the Angel of Resignation; whereby she understood, that she had not yet earned surcease from suffering, but was needed for future work in the Master's vineyard.

If live she must, through the five years of piacular sacrifice, why vitiate its efficacy by rebellious repining, that seemed an affront to the divine arbiter of human destinies? She could not escape the cross; and bitterness of heart might jeopardize the crown. Beggared by time, could she afford to risk the eternal heritage? The deepest conviction of her soul was, "Behind fate, stands God"; hidden for a season, deaf and blind and mute, it seemed, but always surely there; waiting His own appointed season of rescue, and of recompense. So strong was her faith in His overruling wisdom and mercy, that her soul found rest, through perpetual prayer for patience; and as weeks slipped into months, and season followed season, she realized that though no roses of happiness could ever bloom along her arid path, the lilies of peace kissed her tired feet.

Somewhere in the wicked world, Bertie was astray; and perhaps God has kept her alive, intending she should fulfil her mission years hence, by bringing him out of the snares of temptation, back into the fold of Christ's redeemed. Five years of penal servitude to ransom his soul; was the price exorbitant?

One dull, wintry afternoon as she pressed close to the window, to catch the fading light on the page of her Bible, it chanced to be the chapter in St. Luke, which contained the parable of the Pharisee and the Publican; and while she read, a great compunction smote her; a remorseful sense of having scorned as utterly unclean and debased, her suffering fellow prisoners.

Was there no work to be done for the dear Master, in that moral lazaretto—the long rows of cells down stairs, where some had been consigned for 'ninety-nine years'? Hitherto, she had shrunk from contact, as from leprous contagion; meeting the Penitentiary inmates only in the chapel where, since her restoration to health, she went regularly to sing and play on the organ, when the chaplain held service. The world had cruelly misjudged her; was she any more lenient to those who might be equally innocent?

Next day she went humbly, yet shyly, down to the common work-room, and took her place among the publicans, hoping that the soul of some outcast might be won to repentance. Now and then messages of sympathy reached her from the outside world, in the form of flowers, books, magazines; and two of the jurors who convicted her, sent from time to time generous contributions of dainty articles that materially promoted her comfort; while a third, whose dead child had clung to her Christmas card, eased his regretful pangs by the gift of a box containing paper, canvas, crayons, brushes, paints, and all requisite appliances for artistic work.

Sister Serena had gone on a labor of love, to a distant State; and faithful Dyce, hopelessly crippled by a fall from the mule which she was forcing across the bridge leading to the State dungeon, had been permanently consigned to the wide rocking chair, beside her cabin hearth at "Elm Bluff".

It was a bleak night in January, and intensely cold, when Mrs. Singleton wrapped a shawl about her head, and ran along the dark corridor to the cell, where Beryl was walking up and down to keep herself warm. Only the moonlight illumined it, as the rays fell on the bare floor, making a broad band of silver beneath the window.

"I forgot to tell you, that something very dreadful happened at the 'Lilacs' last week. Judge Dent had a stroke of paralysis and died the same night. As if that were not trouble enough to last for a while at least, the house took fire in that high wind yesterday, and burned to the ground; leaving poor Miss Patty Dent without a roof to cover her. She had gone to the cemetery to carry flowers to her brother's grave, and when she returned, it was too late to save anything. Miss Gordon's new wing cost thousands of dollars and was furnished like a palace, so I am told; but the flames destroyed every vestige of the beautiful house, and the pictures and statues. It seems that it was heavily insured, but money can't buy the old portraits and family silver, the mahogany and glass, and the yellow damask—that have been kept in the Dent family since George Washington was a teething baby; and Miss Patty wails loudest over the loss of an old, old timey communion service, that the Dents boasted Queen Anne gave to one of them, who was an Episcopal minister. The poor old soul is almost crazy, I hear, and Mr. Dunbar carries her to New York to-morrow, where she has a nephew living; and next month she will go to Europe to join Miss Gordon. It is reported in town, that when Judge Dent died so suddenly, Miss Patty sent a cable telegram to her niece to come home; but early yesterday, just before the fire, an answer came by cable, asking Miss Patty to come to Europe. Some people think Mr. Dunbar intends escorting her, and that when he meets Miss Gordon, the marriage will take place over there; but I never will believe that, till it happens."

She peered curiously into the face of her listener, but the light was too dim to enable her to read its expression.

"Why not? Under the circumstances, such a course seems eminently natural and proper."

"Do you really think he intends marrying?"

"I am the confidant of neither the gentleman nor the lady; but you told me long ago, that a marriage engagement existed between them; and since both have shown me much kindness and sympathy, I sincerely hope their united lives may be very happy. If Mr. Dunbar searched the universe, he could scarcely find Miss Gordon's equal, certainly not her superior; and he cannot fail to appreciate his good fortune in winning her."

Mrs. Singleton lifted her shoulder significantly. "Perhaps! but you can never be sure of men. They are about as uncertain calculations as the hatching of guinea eggs, or the sprouting of parsley seed. What is theirs can't be worth much; but what belongs to somebody else, is invaluable; moreover, they are liable to sudden tantrums of sheer obstinacy, that hang on like whooping-cough, or a sprain in one's joints. Did you never see a mule take the sulks on his way to the corn crib and the fodder rack, and refuse to budge, even for his own benefit? Some men are just that perverse. Mr. Dunbar is trailing game, worth more to him at present, than a sweetheart across the Atlantic Ocean; which reminds me of what brought me here. He asked Ned to-day, if you saw Mr. Darrington yesterday when he came here; and learning that you did not, he gave him this paper, which he said would explain what the Legislature did last month, about declaring you of age. Ned told him you signed some document Mr. Wolverton brought here last week, which secured all the property to Mr. Darrington, and he said he had been informed of the transaction, and that Mr. Darrington would soon go back to Germany. Then he added: 'Singleton, present my respects to Miss Brentano and tell her, I am happy to say that my trip West last summer was not entirely unsuccessful. It has furnished me with a very valuable clue. She will understand.' Oh, dear! how bitterly cold it is! Come to my room, and get thoroughly thawed; Ned is down stairs, and the children are asleep."

"No, thank you; I should only feel the cold more, when I came back."

"Then take my shawl and cover your ears and throat. There, you must. Good night."

She closed the door, and fled down the long black passage, to the bright cozy room, where her babes slumbered.

Slowly Beryl resumed her walk from window to door, from bar to bar, but of the stinging cold she grew oblivious; and the blood burned in her cheeks and throbbed with almost suffocating violence at her heart.

She comprehended fully the significance of the message, and dared not comfort herself with the supposition that it was prompted by a spirit of bravado.

To what quarter of the globe was he tracking the desperate culprit, who had fled sorely wounded from his murderous assault? Ignorant of his mother's death, and of his sister's expiatory incarceration, might not Bertie venture back to the great city, where she had last seen him; and be trapped by those wily "Quaestores Paricidii" of the nineteenth century—special detectives?

Fettered, muzzled by the stone walls of her dungeon, she could send him no warning, could only pray and endure, while she and her reckless, wayward brother drifted helplessly down the dark, swift river of doom. At every revival of fears for his safety, up started the mighty temptation that never slumbered, to confess all to Mr. Dunbar; but as persistently she took it by the throat, and crushed it back, resolved at all hazards to secure, if possible, the happiness of the woman who had trusted her.

In the midst of the wreck of her life, out of the depths of the dust of humiliation, had sprung the beautiful blossom of love, shedding its intoxicating fragrance over ruin; yet, because the asp of treachery lurked in the exquisite, folded petals, she shut her eyes to the bewildering loveliness, and loyalty strove to tear it up by the roots, to trample it out; learning thereby, that the fibrous thread had struck deep into her own heart, defying ejectment.

She had forbidden his visits, interdicted letters; but she could not expel the vision of a dear face that haunted her memory; nor exorcise the spell of a voice that had first thrilled her pulses when pleading with the jury in her behalf.

Sometimes she wondered whether she had been created as a mere sentient plummet to sound every gulf of human woe; then humbly recanted the impious repining, and thanked God that, at least, she had been spared that deepest of all abysses, the Hades of remorse. That which comes to most women as the supreme earthly joy—the consciousness of possessing the heart of the man they love, fell upon Beryl like the lash of flagellation; rendering doubly fierce the battle of renunciation, which she fought, knowing that sedition and treason were raising the standard of revolt within the fortress.

During the eight months that had elapsed since Leo sailed for Europe, Beryl had exchanged no word with Mr. Dunbar; but twice a sudden, tumultuous leaping of her heart surprised her at sight of him, standing in the door of the chapel; watching her as she sat within the altar rail, playing the little organ, while the convict congregation stood up to sing. Although no name was ever appended, she knew what hand had directed the various American and foreign art magazines, which brought their argosy of beauty to divert and gladden her sombre meditations.

On Christmas morning, the second of her sojourn within penitentiary walls, the express messenger had brought to the door of her cell, two packages, one a glowing heart of crimson and purple passion flowers, the other an exquisite engraving of Sir Frederick Leighton's "Hercules Wrestling with Death"; and below the printed title, she recognized the bold characters traced in red ink: "The Alcestis you emulate."

To-night, a ray of moonlight crept across the wall, and shivered its silver over the rigid face of the dead wife in the picture; and the prisoner, gazing mournfully at it, comprehended that her own fate was sadder than that of the immortal Greek devotee. To die for Admetus after he had sworn on the altar of his gods, that he would spend alone the remainder of his days, solaced by no fair successor, dedicating his fidelity to appease her manes, was comparatively easy; but to turn away, voluntarily resign the man she loved, and assist in forging the links which she must live to see chaining him to a happy rival, were an ordeal more appalling to Alcestis than premature descent into the dusky realm of Persephone.

To secure to her brother immunity from pursuit, and to Miss Gordon the allegiance of the husband of her choice, was the problem that banished sleep and kept Beryl pacing the floor, until welcome day hung her orange mantle over the quivering splendor of the morning star. One final effort was all that seemed possible now; and kneeling before the table she wrote and sealed a note, to be delivered before the express train bore the lawyer away on his journey:

"Your message was received, and it has so disquieted and alarmed me that I am forced to treat for peace. If you will cancel your police contracts, cease your search, go to Europe with Miss Dent, and pledge me your honor to marry Miss Gordon before you return, I will solemnly promise, bind myself in the sight of the God I serve, to live and to die Beryl Brentano; and never, without your consent and permission, will I look again on the face of the man whom you are hunting to death. The assurance of his safety will atone for all you have made me suffer; will nerve me to bear whatever the future may hold. You will imagine you understand, but it is impossible that you can ever realize the nature of the pain this proposal involves for me; nevertheless, if you accept and keep the compact, I believe you know that, at all costs, I shall never forfeit the pledged word of

"BERYL BRENTANO."

When marriage vows had irrevocably committed Leo's happiness to his honor, it might then be safe to tell him the truth, and solicit release from the self-imposed terms. Five hours later, she received an answer:

"A trifle too late, you unfurled the flag of truce. With my game in sight, I decline to forego the chase. For your solicitude regarding my marriage, I tender my thanks; and the assurance, that no magnet can draw, not all the charms of Circe lure me across the Atlantic, until I have accomplished my purpose. The tardiness of your proposal is unerring appraiser of its costliness; and I were a monster of cruelty to debar you the sight of your idol, though I bring him with the grim garniture of chains and handcuffs. When I consign Miss Dent to her relatives in New York, I go to a miners' camp in Dakota, to identify a man bearing the marks of one who fled from X——, and lost his pipe, on the night he murdered Gen'l Darrington.

"DUNBAR."

To temporize longer would be fatal to Bertie; and no alternative remained but to tell the simple truth.

Without an instant's delay she took up her pen, but ere half a line had been traced on the paper, a hoarse whistle, somewhat muffled by distance, told her the attempt was futile; and through the valley beyond the river a trailing serpent of black smoke showed the express train darting northward. The attorney had left X——, but might linger in New York sufficiently long for a letter to reach him; and doubtless his address could be learned at his office:

"If Mr. Dunbar will give me an opportunity of acquainting him with some facts, he is anxious to discover, he shall find it unnecessary to travel to Dakota; and will thank me for saving him from the long journey he contemplates.

"B. B."

The sun was setting when Mr. Singleton returned from the attorney's office, and held out the note which he had been instructed to address and deposit in the mail.

"If it is a matter of any importance, I am sorry to tell you that this cannot reach Mr. Dunbar immediately. He goes only as far as Philadelphia, where Miss Dent's nephew meets her; then Dunbar travels right on West without stopping, till he reaches Bismarck. He left instructions at his office to retain all mail matter here, for a couple of weeks, then forward to Washington City; as business would detain him there some days after his return from the west. Good gracious! how white your lips are. Sit down. What ails you?"

109

She put her hand over her eyes, and tried to collect her thoughts. To suffer so long, so keenly, and yet lose the victory; could it be possible that her sacrifice would prove utterly futile?

"Mr. Singleton, you have shown me many times your friendly sympathy, and I am again forced to tax your kindness. It is important that I should see or communicate with Mr. Dunbar within the next forty-eight hours. Could you induce the telegraph operator here to have a message delivered to him on the train, before it reaches Washington City?"

"I will certainly do my best; and to insure it I will go to the railroad operator, who understands the stations, and can catch Dunbar more easily than a message from the general office. Write our your telegram, while I order my buggy."

"MR. DUNBAR. On board Train No. 2.

"Please let me see you before you go West. I promise information that will render you unwilling to make the journey to Bismarck."
"B."

Anxiously she computed the time within which an answer might reasonably be expected; and her heart dwelt as a suppliant before God, that the message would avail to arrest pursuit; but hours wore wearily away, tedious days trod upon the slow skirts of dreary nights; and no response lifted the burden of dread. Hope whispered feebly that his failure to send a telegraphic reply, implied his intention of returning to X——from Philadelphia; and she clung to this rope of sand until a week had passed. Then the conviction was inevitable that he regarded her appeal as merely a ruse to divert his course, to delay the seizure of his prey; and that while he misinterpreted the motive that prompted her message, she had merely furnished an additional goad to his jealous hatred.

As helpless wrack borne on the sullen tide of destiny, she struck her trembling hands together, and cried out in the dark solitude of her cell: "Verily! The stars in their courses fought against Sisera."

CHAPTER XXV.

The winter was marked by an unusual severity of cold, which prolonged the rigor of mid-season until late in February, and despite the efforts of penitentiary officials who made unprecedented requisitions upon the board of inspectors, for additional clothing, the pent human herd suffered keenly.

Alarmed by the rapidly increasing rate of sickness within the "walls," Mr. Singleton demanded a sanitary commission, which, after apparently thorough investigation, reported no visible local cause for the mortality among the convicts; but the germs of disease grew swiftly as other evil weeds, and the first week in March saw a hideous harvest of diphtheria of the most malignant type.

At the earliest intimation of the character of the pestilence, the warden's wife fled with her little children to her mother's home in a neighboring county; maternal solicitude having extinguished her womanly reluctance to desert her husband, at a juncture when her presence and assistance would so materially have cheered, and lightened his labors. An attempt was made to isolate the first case in the hospital, but the cots in that spacious apartment filled beyond the limits of accommodation; and soon, a large proportion of the cells on the ground floor held each its victim of the fatal disease, that as the scythe of death cut a wide swath through convict ranks. Consulting physicians walked through the infected ward, altered prescriptions, advised disinfectants which were liberally used, until the building seemed to exhale pungent, wholesome, but unsavory odors; yet there was no abatement in the virulence of the type. When the twenty-third case was entered on the hospital list, the trustees and inspectors determined to remove all who showed no symptom of the contagion, to an old, long-abandoned cotton factory several miles distant; where the vacant houses of former operatives would afford temporary shelter; and to diminish the chances of carrying infection, each prisoner was carefully examined by the attending physician, and then furnished with an entirely new suit of clothing.

When the nature of the epidemic could no longer be concealed from the inmates, instinctive horror drove them from the neighborhood of the victims, and like frightened sheep they huddled in remote corners, removed as far as possible from the infected precincts, and loath to minister to the needs of the sufferers.

Two men, and as many women, selected and detailed as nurses in their respective wards, openly rebelled; and while Doctor Moffat and Mr. Singleton were discussing the feasibility of procuring outside assistance, the door of the dispensary adjoining the hospital, opened, and Beryl walked up to the table, where medicines were weighed and mixed.

"Put me to work among the sick. I want to help you."

"You! What could you do? I should as soon take a magnolia blossom to scrub the pots and pans of a filthy kitchen," answered the doctor, looking up over his spectacles from the powder he was grinding in a glass mortar.

"I can follow your directions; I can obey orders; and physicians deem that the sine qua non in nurses. Closed lips, open ears, willing hands are supposed to outweigh any amount of unlicensed brains. Try me."

"No, I am not willing. Go back up-stairs, and stay there," said the warden.

"Why may I not assist in nursing?"

"In the first place you are not fit to mix with those poor creatures, in yonder; their oaths would curdle your blood; and in the second, you are not strong, and would be sure to take the disease at once."

"I am perfectly well; my lungs are now as healthy as yours, and I am not afraid of diphtheria. You detailed nurses, who refused to serve; I volunteer; have you any right to reject me?"

"Yes, the right to protect and save your life, which is worth twenty of those already in danger," replied Mr. Singleton, pausing in his task of filling capsules with quinine.

"Who made you a judge of the value of souls? My life belongs first to God, who gave it, next to myself; and if I choose to jeopardize it, in work among my suffering comrades in disgrace, you must not usurp the authority to prevent me."

"Has it become so intolerable that you desire to commit suicide, under the specious plea of philanthropic martyrdom?" said Doctor Moffat, whose keen black eyes scanned her closely, from beneath shaggy gray brows.

"I think I may safely say, no such selfish motive underlies my resolution. My heart is full of pity, and of dread for some women here, who admit their guilt, yet have sought no pardon from the Maker their sins insult. Sick souls cry out to me louder than dying bodies; and who dare deny me the privilege of ministering to both? The parable of the sparrows is no fable to me; and if, while trying to comfort my unhappy associates here, God calls me out of this dark stony vineyard, His will alone overrules all; and I can meet His face in peace. We say: 'Lord what wilt Thou have us to do?' and when the answer comes, pointing us to perilous and loathsome labors, will He forget if we shut our eyes, and turn away, coveting the sunny fields into which He sent others to toil? Let me go to my work."

During almost eighteen months, both men had studied her character as manifested in the trying phases of prison existence, finding no flaw; to-day they looked up reverently at the graceful form in its homespun uniform, at the calm, colorless face, wearing its crown of meekness, with an inalienable, proud air of cold repose.

"To keep you here is about as sacrilegious as it would have been to thrust St. Catherine among the chain-gang in the galleys," muttered the doctor.

"No doubt duty called her to much worse places; therefore, when she died, the angels buried her on Sinai," answered the prisoner; before whose wistful eyes drifted the memory of Luini's picture.

"You have set your heart on this; nothing less will content you?"

"While the necessity continues, nothing less will content me."

"Remember, you voluntarily take your life in your own hands."

"I assume the entire responsibility for any risk incurred."

"Then, I wish you God speed; for the harvest is white, the laborers few."

"Why, doctor! I relied on you to help me keep her out of reach. If anything happens, how shall I pacify Susie? She made me promise every possible care of her favorite. Look here, only an hour ago I received a letter and this package marked, 'One for Ned; the other for Miss Beryl.' Two little red flannel safety bags, cure-alls, to be tied around our necks, close to our noses, as if we could not smell them a half mile off? Assafoetida, garlic, camphor, 'jimson weed,' valerian powder—phew! What not? Mixed as a voudoo chowder, and a scent twice as loud!"

"Be thankful your wife is not here to enforce the wearing of the sanitary sachet," said the doctor, allowing himself a grimace of contemptuous disgust.

"So I am! but being a bachelor, answerable only to yourself, you cannot understand how absence does not exonerate me from the promise made when she started away. I would sooner face an 'army with banners,' than that little brown-eyed woman of mine when she takes the lapel of my coat in one hand, raises the forefinger of the other, turns her head sideways like a thrush watching a wriggling worm, and says, in a voice that rises as fast as the sound a mouse makes racing up the treble of the piano keys: 'Ump! whew! Didn't I tell you so? The minute my back was turned, of course you made ducks and drakes of all your promises. Show me a "Flying Jenney," that the tip end of any idiot's little finger can spin around, and I'll christen it Edward McTwaddle Singleton!' Seems funny to you, doctor? Just wait till you are married, and your Susan shuts the door and interviews you, picking a whole flock of crows, till you wonder if it isn't raining black feathers. When I am taken to taw about this nursing business, I shall lose no time in laying the blame on you."

"I will assure Mrs. Singleton that you endeavored to dissuade me; and that you faithfully kept your promise to shield me from danger."

"Which she will not believe, because she knows that I have the power to lock you up indefinitely. Besides, if you live to explain matters, there will be no necessity; but suppose you do not? You are running into the jaws of an awful danger, and if—"

His frank, pleasant countenance clouded, he gnawed his mustache, and the question ended in a long sigh. After a moment, a low, sweet voice completed the sentence:

"If I should die, your tender-hearted wife is so truly and faithfully my friend, that she could not regret to hear I have entered into my rest."

There was a brief silence, during which the physician crossed the floor, opened a glass door and surveyed the stock of drugs. When he came back, and took up the pestle, he spoke with solemn emphasis:

"This is the most malignant type of an always dangerous disease that I have ever encountered; and constant exposure to it, without the careful, persistent use of tonic and disinfectant precautions, would be tantamount to walking unvaccinated into a pest-house, where people were dying of confluent small-pox. I have no desire to frighten, but it is proper that I should warn you; and insist upon the duty of watching your own health as closely as the symptoms of the victims you are desirous of nursing. Will you follow the regimen I shall prescribe for yourself?"

"Implicitly."

The warden finished filling the capsules, rose and looked at his watch.

"As far as the chances go, it is 'heads I win, tails you lose'; and sorry enough I am to see you come down and dare the pestilence; but since you are, I might as well say what I was asked to tell you last night. For your sake I kept silent; now since you persist, I wash my hands of all responsibility for the consequences. You have heard the history of the woman Iva Le Bougeois, better known in the 'walls' as the 'Bloody Duchess'. Two days ago the scourge struck her down; she is very ill, the worst symptoms have appeared, and she is almost frantic with terror. Last night, at 12 o'clock, I was going the rounds of the sick wards, and found her wringing her hands, and running up and down the cell like a maniac. I tried to quiet and encourage her, but she paid no more attention than if stone deaf; and when I started to leave her, she seized my arm, and begged me to ask you to come and stay with her. She thinks if you would sing for her, she could listen, and forget the horrible things that haunt her. It is positively sickening to see her terror at the thought of death. Poor, desperate creature."

"Yet you withheld her message when I might have comforted her?"

111

"It was a crazy whim. In hardened cases like hers, death-bed remorse counts for very little. Her conscience is lashing her; could you quiet that? Could you bleach out the blood that spots her soul?"

"Yes, by leading her to One who can."

"Remember, you asked me as a special favor to keep you as far apart as possible from all of her class."

"At that time, overwhelmed by the misery of my own fate, I was pitiless to the sufferings of others. The rod that smote me was very cruel then; but by degrees it seems to bud like Aaron's with precious promise, that may expand into the immortal flowers of souls redeemed. I dwelt too long in the seat of the Pharisees; I shall live closer to God, walking humbly among the Publicans. Will you show me the way to the woman who wishes to see me?"

"Not yet. There are some instructions that must be carefully weighed before I can install you as nurse, in that dismal mire of moral and physical corruption. Singleton, send the hospital steward to me."

There are spectacles which brand themselves so ineffaceably upon memory, that time has no power to impair their vividness; and of such were some of the scenes witnessed by the new nurse.

Sitting on the side of her cot, from which the gray blanket had been dragged and folded half across her shoulders, where one hand held it, while the other clutched savagely at her throat; with her bare delicate feet beating a tattoo on the white sanded floor, and her thin nostrils dilated in the battle for breath, Iva Le Bougeois moaned in abject terror. The coarse, unbleached "domestic" night-gown that fell to her ankles was streaked across the bosom with some dark brown fluid; and similar marks stained the pillow where her restless head had tossed. The hot eyes and parched red lips seemed to have drained all the tainted blood from her olive cheeks, save where, just beneath the lower lids, ominous terra-cotta rings had been painted and glazed by the disease.

As Beryl pushed open the iron door, and held up the lantern, that its brightness might stream into the cell, where even at five o'clock in the afternoon of a rainy day darkness reigned, the rays flashed back from the glowing eyes chatoyant as a cougar's.

"Your message was not delivered until to-day, and I lost no time in coming."

The small head, where short, straight, blue-black locks, rumpled and disordered, were piled elfishly around the low brow, was thrown up with the swift movement of some startled furry animal, alert even in the throes of death.

"Is all hope over? Did they tell you there is no chance for me?"

The voice was hoarse and thick, the articulation indistinct and smothered.

"No. They think you very ill, but still hope the remedies will save you. The doctor says your fine constitution ought to conquer the disease."

"I am beyond the remedy—because I can't swallow any longer. Since the doctor left me, I have tried and tried. See—"

From a bench within reach, she lifted a small yellow bowl, which contained a dark mixture, put it to her lips, and chafing her swollen glands, attempted several times to swallow the liquid. A gurgling sound betrayed the futility of the effort, the medicine gushed from her nose, the eyes seemed starting from their sockets, and even the husky cry of the sufferer was strangled, as she cowered down.

"Compose yourself; nervousness increases the difficulty. Once I had diphtheria, and could not swallow for two days, yet I recovered. Be quiet, and let me try to help you."

Kneeling in front of her, Beryl turned up the wick of the lantern, and with a small brush attached to a silver wire, finally succeeded in cauterizing and removing a portion of the poisonous growth that was rapidly narrowing the avenue of breath. The spasm of coughing that ensued was Nature's auxiliary effort, and temporarily relieved the tightening clutch.

After a few moments, a dose of the medicine was successfully administered; and then the slender, shapely brown hand of the woman grasped the nurse's blue homespun dress.

"Don't leave me! Save me. Oh, don't let me strangle here alone—in the dark; don't let me die! I'm not fit. I know where I shall go. It's not the devil I dread; I have known many devils in this world,—but God. I am afraid of God!"

"Lie down, and cover your shoulders. If it comforts you to have me, I will stay gladly. The doctor, the warden, all of us will do what we can to cure you; but the help you need most, can come only from one whose pity is greater and tenderer than ours, your merciful God. Lift up your heart in prayer to him; ask him to forgive your sins, and spare you to lead a better life."

"He would not hear, because He knows how black my heart has been all these years; since I gave myself up to hate and cursing. You can't understand—you are not one of us. You are as much out of place here, as one of the angels would be, held over the flames of torment till the wings singed. From the first time we saw you in the chapel, and more and more ever since, we found out you did not belong here. I have been so wicked—so wicked—!"

She paused, panting, then hurried on.

"When the chaplain tried to talk to me, and gave me a book to read, I dashed it back in his face, and insulted him. One Saturday they sent me to sweep out and dust the chapel, and when I finished, I laid down on one of the benches to rest. You went in to practise, not knowing I was there; and began to sing. As I listened, something seemed to stir and wake up in my heart, and somehow the music shook me out of myself. There was one hymn, so solemn, so thrilling, and the end of every verse was, 'Oh, Lamb of God! I come!'—and you sang it with a great cry, as if you were running to meet some one. I had not wept—for oh! I don't know how long—not since—. Then you played on the organ some variations on a tune—'The Sweet By-and-by'—and the tears started, and I seemed but a leaf in a wild storm. That was the song my little boy used to sing! There was a Sunday-school in the basement of a church next to our house, and he would stand at the window, and listen till he caught the tune, and learned the words. Oh, that hymn! Every note stung me like a whip lash when I heard it again. My child's face as I saw him the last time I put him to bed; when he opened his drowsy eyes, and raised up to kiss me good-night, came back to me, and seemed to sing, 'In the sweet by-and-by, we shall meet on that beautiful shore.' No—never—never! Oh, my boy! My beautiful angel Max—there is no room for me, on that heavenly shore! Oh! my darling—there is NO 'Sweet by-and-by' FOR MOTHER NOW."

She had started up, with arms clasped around her knees, and her convulsed face lifted toward the low ceiling of the cell, writhed, as she drew her breath in hissing gasps.

"You loved your little boy?"

"You are not a mother, or you wouldn't ask me that If ever you had felt your baby's sweet warm lips on yours, you would know that it is mother-love that makes tigers of women. Because I idolized my little one, I could not bear the cruel wrong of having him torn from me, taught to despise me; and so I loved him best when I slew him, and I was so mad, with the delirium of pain and rage and despair, that I forgot I was putting the gulf of perdition between us. Rather than submit to separation in this world, than have him raised by them, to turn away from his mother as a thing too vile to wear his father's name, I lost him for ever and ever! My son, my star-eyed darling."

"Listen to me. You loved him so tenderly, that no matter how wilful or disobedient he might have been, you forgave him every offence; and when he sobbed on your bosom, you felt he was doubly dear, and hugged him closer to your heart? Even stronger and deeper is God's love for us. Dare you call yourself more pitiful, more tender than your Father in heaven, who gave you the capacity to love your child, because He so compassionately loves His children? We sin, we go far astray, we think mercy is exhausted, and the door shut against us; but when we truly repent and go back, and kneel, and pray to be forgiven, Christ Himself unbars the door and leads us in; and our Father, loving those whom He created, pardons all; and only requires that we sin no more. God does not follow us; we must humbly go back all the distance we have put between us by our wickedness; but the heavens will fall before He fails to keep His promise to forgive, when we do genuinely repent of our wrongdoing."

"It is easy for the good to believe that. You are innocent of any crime, and you are punished for other people's sins, not for your own; so you can't understand how I dread the thought of God, because I know the blackness of my heart, when, to get my revenge, I sold my soul to Satan. Oh! the horror of feeling that I can't undo the bargain; that pay-day has come! I had the vengeance, I snatched out of God's hands, and for a while I gloated over it; but now the awful price! My little one in heaven with the angels; knowing that his mother is a devil—eternally."

Her head had fallen upon her knees, and in the frenzy of despair she rocked to and fro.

"Don't you remember that the most sinful woman Christ met on earth, was the one of all others that He first revealed Himself to, when He came out of the grave? Because she was so nearly lost, and He had forgiven so much, in order to save her, her purified heart was doubly dear, and he honored her more than the disciples, who had escaped the depth of her wickedness. Try to find comfort in the belief, that if sincere remorse and contrition redeemed the soul of Mary Magdalen, the same Savior who pitied and pardoned her will not deny your prayer."

"God believed her, because she proved her repentance by leading a new, purer life. But I have no chance left to prove mine. If she had been cut off in the midst of her sins, as I am, she would have been obliged to pay in her ruined soul to the Satan she had served so long. When I am called to the settlement, it seems an insult and a mockery to ask God, whom I have defied, to save me. If I could only have a little time to show my penitence."

"Perhaps you may be spared; but if not, God sees your contrition just as fully now as if you lived fifty years to show it in good works. He sees you are sincerely remorseful, and would be a true Christian, if He allowed you an opportunity. That is the blessedness of our religion, that when Christ gives us a new heart, purified by repentance and faith in Him, He says it makes clean hands, in His sight, no matter how black they might have been. One of the thieves was already on the cross, in the agonies of death, with his sins fresh on his soul, and no possible chance of atoning for his past, by future dedication of his life to good; but Christ saw his heart was genuinely repentant, and though the man did not escape crucifixion by humanity, his pardoned soul met Jesus that same day in Paradise. It is not acceptance of our good deeds, though they are required, it is forgiveness of our sins, that makes Christ so precious. Pray from the very bottom of your heart, to God, and try to take hold of the promise to the truly penitent; and trust—trust Him."

For a moment the crouching figure was still, as if the sufferer mentally grasped at some shred of hope; then she fell back on her pillow, and groaned.

"Do you know all I have done? Do you think there is any mercy for—"

"Hush, every word taxes your failing strength. Compose yourself."

"I can't! As long as I have breath let me tell you. If I shut my eyes, horrible things seem to be pouncing upon me; dreadful shapes laugh, and beckon to me, and I see—oh! pity me! I see my murdered child, with the blood spouting, foaming, the velvety brown eyes I loved to kiss, staring and glazed as I dragged his little body to—"

With a gurgling scream she paused, shivered, panted.

"It is a feverish dream. Your child is safe in heaven; ask your Father to let you see his face among the angels."

"It's not fever; it's the past, my own crimes that come to follow me to judgment and accuse me. The hand of my first-born pointing over the last bar at the mother who killed him! Do you wonder I am afraid to die? I don't deny my bloody deeds—but after all it was a foul wrong that drove me to desperation; and God knows, man's injustice brought me to my sin. I was a spoiled, motherless child, married at sixteen to a man whose family despised me, because my pretty face had ruined their scheme of a match with an heiress, whose money was needed to retrieve their fortunes. They never forgave the marriage, and after a few years, mischief began to brew.

"I loved my husband, but his nature was too austere to deal patiently with my freakish, petulant, volcanic temper; and when he lectured me for my frivolity, obstinacy plunged me into excesses of gayety, that at heart I did not enjoy. His mother and sister shunned me more and more, poisoned his mind with wicked and unfounded suspicions, and so we grew mutually distrustful. He tired of me, and he showed it. I loved him. Oh! I loved him better, and better, as I saw him drifting away. He neglected me, spent his leisure where he met the woman he had once intended to marry. I was so maddened with jealous heart-ache, some evil spirit prompted me to try and punish him with the same pangs. That was my first sin of deception; I pretended an attachment I never felt, hoping to rekindle my husband's affection. Like many another heart-sick wife, I was caught in my own snare; and while I was as innocent of any wrong as my own baby boy, his father was glad of a pretext to excuse his alienation. People slandered me; and because I loved Allen so deeply, I was too proud to defend myself, until too late.

"God is my witness, my husband was the only man I ever loved; ah! how dear he was to me! His very garments were precious; and I have kissed and cried over his gloves, his slippers. The touch of his hand was worth all the world to me, but he withheld it. When you know your husband loves you, he may ill treat, may trample you under his feet, but you can forgive him all; you caress the heel that bruises you. Allen ceased to show me ordinary consideration, stung me with sneers, threatened separation; even shrunk from the boy, because he was mine.

"There came a day, when some fiend forged a letter, and the same vile hand laid it in my husband's desk. Only God knows whose is the guilt of that black deed, but I believe it was his sister's work. Allen cursed me as unworthy to be the mother of his child, and swore he would be free. On my knees I begged him to hear, and acquit me. I confessed all my yearning love for him, I assured him I was the victim of a foul plot; and that if he would only take me back to the heaven of his heart, he would find that no man ever had a more devoted wife. He wanted an excuse to put me out of his way; he repulsed me with scorn, and before the sun set, he forsook me, and took up his abode with his mother and sister. Oh! the cruel wrong of that dreadful, parting scene!"

She sprang from the cot, breathless from the passionate recital, beating the air with one small slender hand, while the other tore at the swollen cords of her tortured throat.

Beryl caught the round, prettily turned wrist, and felt the feeble thread of pulse that was only a wild flutter, under the olive satin of the hot skin.

"This excitement only hastens the end you dread. Lie down, and I will pray for you."

"I shall soon lie down for ever. Let me walk a little, before my feet slide into the grave."

She staggered twice across the length of the cell, then tottered and fell back on the cot. At every respiration the thin nostrils flared, and the glazed ring below the eyes lost its sullen red tinge, took on blue shadows.

"I did not know then I was to lose my child also; but before long, all the scheme was made clear. Allen sued for a divorce. He wanted to shake me off; and he persuaded himself all the foul things my enemies had concocted must be true. I had lost his love; I was too proud to show my torn heart to the world; and men make the laws to suit themselves, and they help each other to break chains that gall, so Allen was set free. I shut myself up in two rooms, with my boy, and saw no one. Even then, though my heart was breaking, and I wept away the lonely days—longing for the sight of my husband's face, starving for the sound of his voice—I bore up; because I knew I was innocent, and unjustly censured, and I had my child to comfort me. He slept in my arms and kept me human; and we were all the world to each other.

"Then the last blow fell. There came a note, whose every word bit my heart like an adder. Allen demanded the boy, whom the law gave to his guardianship; and I was warned I must make no attempt to see him after he was taken away, because he would be taught to forget me. I refused. I dared the officer to lay hands on my little one, and I was so frantic with grief, the man had compassion, and left me. Two nights afterward, I rocked him to sleep and put him in bed. His arms fell from my neck; half aroused, he nestled his face to mine—kissed me. I went into the next room, to finish a shirt I was making for him, and I shut the door, fearing the noise of the machine would wake him. I sewed half an hour, and—when I went back, the bed was empty, my child was gone.

"I think I went utterly mad then. I can remember putting my lips to the dent on the little ruffled pillow, where his head had lain, and swearing that I would have my revenge.

"That night turned me to stone; every tender feeling seemed to petrify. When I learned that Allen was soon to marry the woman for whom he had cast me off, and that my boy was to have a new mother to teach him to hate me, it did not grieve me; I had lost all power of suffering; but it woke up a legion of fiends where my heart used to beat, and I bided my time. Happy women in happy homes think me a monster. With their husbands' arms around them, and their babies prattling at their knees, they bear my wrongs so meekly, and shudder at my depravity. When I thought of Allen, who was my first and last and only love, giving my place to some other woman, who was no more worthy than I knew myself to be; and of the baby, who had slept on my heart, and was so dear because he had his father's eyes and his father's brown curls, growing up to deny and condemn his innocent but disgraced mother, it was more than I could bear. I was not insane; oh, no! But I was possessed by more than seven devils; and revenge was all this world could give me. My husband's family had ruined me; so I would spoil their match a second time.

"The wedding was to be very private, but I bribed a servant and got into the house, and stood behind the damask curtains. Allen's mother and sister came in, leading my boy; and they were so close to me I could see the long silky lashes resting against my baby's brow, as his great brown eyes looked wonderingly at a horseshoe of roses dangling from the chandelier. Then my husband, my handsome husband—my darling's father, walked in, with the bride on his arm, and the minister met them, saying: 'Dearly beloved—.' I ceased to be a woman then, I was a fury, a wild beast—and two minutes later my darlings were mine once more, safe from that other woman—dead at my feet. Then the ball I aimed at my own breast missed its destination. I fell on my slaughtered idols; seeing in a bloody mist the wide eyes of my baby boy, and the mangled face of the husband whose kiss was the only heaven I shall ever know. I meant to die with them, but I failed; so they sent me here. That was years ago; but I was a stone until that day in the chapel, when you sang my Max's song, 'By-and-By'."

There was a brief silence, and Beryl's voice wavered as she said very gently:

"Your trials were fiery; and though the crime was frightfully black, God judges us according to the natures we are born with, and the temptations that betray us; and He forgives all, if we are true penitents and throw ourselves trustingly on His mercy. Now take this powder; it will make you sleep."

"Will you stay with me? I shall not trouble anybody much longer. Say a prayer for my sinful soul, that is going down into the eternal night."

"Let us pray together, that your pardoned soul may find blessed and eternal peace."

Coming softly to the door, the doctor looked in through the iron lattice, saw the figure of the nurse kneeling on the sanded floor, with her bronzed head close to the pillow where the moaning victim's lay; and involuntarily he took off his cloth cap, and bowed his gray head to listen to the brief but solemn petition that went up from the dungeon to the supreme and unerring Judge.

When he returned to the same spot an hour later, Beryl sat on the side of the cot, with one hand clasping the brown wrist thrown across her lap, the other pressed gently over the sufferer's hot, aching eyes; and wonderfully sweet was the rich voice that chanted low:

"Just as I am, without one plea,
But that Thy blood was shed for me.
And that Thou bidd'st me come to Thee,
O Lamb of God! I come, I come!
Just as I am, and waiting not
To rid my soul of one dark blot,
To Thee, whose blood can cleanse each spot,
O Lamb of God! I come, I come!"

The noon sun was shining over a wet world, kindling into diamonds the crystal fringe of rain drops hanging from the green lances of willows, where a tufted red bird arched his scarlet throat in madrigal—when four men lifted a cot, and bore it with its apparently dying burden to a spot upon which the warm light fell in a golden flood.

Between the Destroying Angel and his gasping prey, stepped two, anointed with the chrism of the Priesthood of Cure; and undismayed by the strident, sibilant, fitful breath that distorted the blue lips of the victim, they parried the sweep of the scythe of death, with the tiny, glittering steel blade surgery cunningly fashions; and through its silver canula, tracheotomy recalled the vanishing spirit, triumphantly renewed the lease of life.

At sunset on the same day, Beryl followed the warden to the door of the large hospital.

"Of all pitiful sights here, this has harrowed me the most. The doctors did all they could, and the chaplain worked hard to save her soul, but she was like flint, till just before the end, when she raised up, and heard her child crying down in the work-room, where it had been put to sleep. We could scarcely hold her; she fought like a panther to get out of bed, till the blood gushed from her nose, and though she could not speak plainly, she pointed, and we made out: 'Baby—Dovie'. The doctor would not consent that we should expose the child to the risk, but I could not hold out against that poor creature's pleading wild eyes, so I just brought the little one. What a strangling cry she gave, when I put it in her arms, and how the tears poured! She was almost gone, and we saw that she wanted to tell us something about the child, but we could not understand. The doctor put a pencil in her hand, and held a sheet of paper before her, and she tried to scrawl her wishes, but all we can read is: 'Her father won't ever own her. Baptize—her Dovie—Eve Werneth's baby. Don't ever tell her she was born in jail. Raise her a good—good—.' She had a sort of spasm then, and squeezed the child so tight, it screamed. In five minutes, she was dead. Only nineteen years old, and the little one just two years; and not yet weaned! I don't know what to do; so I brought you. If I touch the child, it seems frightened almost to death, but maybe you can coax it away. Poor little thing! What a mercy if it could die!"

"Will you let me have the care of it? Take it, and keep it up in my cell?"

"I shall be only too thankful, if you will lift the load from my shoulders."

"Tell the steward to bring me a cup of warm, sweetened milk and a cracker. The poor little lamb must be almost famished."

Through an open window streamed the radiance of a daffodil sky, flecked with curling plumes of drifting fire, and the glory fell like a benediction on the iron cot, where lay the body of the early dead; a small, slight, blond girl wearing prematurely the crown of maternity, whose thorns had torn and stained the smooth brow of mere childhood. The half-opened eyes, fixed in their filmy blue glaze, seemed a prayer for the pretty infant, whose head, a glistening tangle of yellow curls, was nestled down against the bare white throat of the rigid mother; while the dimpled hands pulled fretfully at the blood-spattered gown, that was buttoned across the breast.

As clusters of wild snowy violets springing up in the midst of mud and mire, in a noxious swamp, look doubly pure and sweet because of fetid surroundings,—so this blossom of the slums, this human bud, with petals of innocence folded close in the calyx of babyhood, seemed supremely and pathetically fair, as she stood leaning against the cot, the little rosy feet on tip-toe, pressing toward her mother; tears on the pink velvet of the round cheeks, on the golden lashes beneath the big blue eyes that grew purplish behind the mist.

The Macedonia of suffering humanity lies always within a stone's throw; and the "cry for help" had found speedy response in more than one benevolent heart.

A gray-haired widow from the "Sheltering Arms," to which Sister Serena belonged, and a Sister of Charity from the hospital in X——, were already ministering tenderly in the crowded ward; and both had essayed to coax away the little figure clutching her mother's gown; but the flaring white cap of one, and the flapping black drapery of the other, frightened the trembling child.

Into the group stole Beryl; followed closely by the yellow cat, which had become her shadow. Kneeling beside the baby, she kissed it softly, took one of the hands, patted her own cheek with it, and lifted the cat to the mattress, where it began to purr. The silky shock of yellow curls was lifted, the wide eyes stared wonderingly first at Beryl's face bending near, then at the cat; and by degrees, the lovely waif suffered an arm to draw her farther and farther, while her rose-red mouth parted in a smile, that showed six little teeth, and with one hand fastened in the cat's fur, she was finally lifted and borne away; Beryl's soft cheek nestled against hers, the bronzed head bent down to the yellow ringlets; one arm holding the baby and the cat, while the other white hand closed warmly over the child's bare, cold, dimpled feet.

CHAPTER XXVI.

Fair and flowery as in the idyllic dawn when Theocritus sang its pafatoral charms, was that sunny Sicilian land where, one May morning, Leo Gordon wandered with a gay party in quest of historic sites, which the slow silting of the stream of time had not obliterated. Viewed from the heights of Achradina, whence all the vestiges of magnificence and luxury have vanished, and only the hideous monument of "man's inhumanity to man" remains, what a vast panorama stretched far as the horizon on every side.

To the north, girding the fire-furrowed plain of Catania where olive, lemon, oleander and orange springing out of black lava, mingled hues like paints on an ebony palette—rose vast, lonely, purple at base, snowy at summit, brooding Etna; dozing in the soft, sweet springtime, with red, wrathful eyes veiled by a silvery haze. An unlimited expanse of crinkling blue sea, shot like Persian silk with gleams of gold, and laced here and there with foam scallops, bounded the east; smiling treacherously above the ghastly wreck sepultured in its coral crypts, that might have told of the crash of triremes, the flames of sinking galleys, which twenty-two centuries ago lit the bloody waves that closed over slaughtered hosts.

Westward lay green, wimpling vales, studded with laurel, arched with vine-draped pergolas, dotted widi flocks, dimpled with reedy marshes where red oxen browsed; and beyond the pale pink flush of almond groves—

"A smoke of blue olives, a vision of towers."

Bucolic paradise of Battus and Bombyce, of Corydon and Daphnis, may it please the hierophants of Sanskrit lore, of derivative Aryan philology, of iconoclastic euhemerism, to spare us yet awhile the lovely myths that dance across the asphodel meads of sunny Sicily.

On the verge of the parapet of the Latomia, where the breath of the sirocco, the gnawing tooth of time, and the slow ravelling of rain had serrated the ledge, stood Leo, gazing into the dizzying depths of the charnel house that swarmed with the ghosts of nine thousand men, who once were huddled within its stony embrace.

As if pitying nature had striven to appease the manes of the unburied dead, a pall of luxuriant ivy and glossy acanthus covered the bottom and sides of the quarry, one hundred feet below; but out of the dust of centuries stared the rayless eyes of corpses, and the gaunt despairing faces seemed still uplifted, now in invocation, anon in imprecation to the overarching sky, where blistering suns mocked them by day, and glittering moons and silver stars paused in their westward march through dewy night, to tell them tantalizing tales of how musically Aegean wavelets broke against the marbles at Piraeus; how loud the nightingales sang in the plane and poplar groves at home; how the white glory of the Parthenon smiled down on violet-crowned Athens, where their wives and children thronged the temples, in sacrificial rites to insure their safety.

In crevices of the perpendicular walls lush creepers tapestried the gray stone, and far down, out of the mould of the subterranean dungeon, sprang slim lemon trees snowed over with fragrant bloom, clumps of oleander waving banners of vivid rose, and golden-green pomegranate bushes, where scarlet flakes glowed like the wings of tropical birds.

"Well, is the game worth the candle? After voyaging thousands of miles, do you feel repaid; or down there, in the heart of the desolation, do you see only the grinning mask of jeering disappointment, which generally follows American realists into the dusty haunts of Old World idealism?"

As she spoke, Alma Cutting stepped back under the cool canopy of a spreading fig-tree, and fanned herself with a tuft of papyrus leaves. She was a tall, handsome woman, pronouncedly brunette in type, with large black eyes whose customary indolent indifference of expression did not entirely veil the fires "banked" under the velvet iris; and a square, firm mouth, around whose full crimson lips lurked a certain haughtiness, that despite the curb of good breeding, bordered at times closely upon insolence. Thirty years had tripped over this dark head, where the hair, innocent of crimp or curl, hung in a straight jet fringe low on her wide forehead; and though no lines marred the smooth, health-tinted skin, she was perceptibly "sun burnt by the glare of life," and the dew of youth had vanished before the vampire lips of ennui.

"Disappointed? Certainly not; and I were exacting and unreasonable indeed, if I did not feel abundantly repaid. Alma, since the days when I pored over Thucydides, Plutarch, Rollin and Grote, this spot has beckoned to my imagination with all the uplifted hands of the nine thousand captives; and the longing of years is to-day completely gratified."

"Am I unusually stupid, or are you rapt, beyond the realm of reason and mid-day common sense? Pray what is the fascination? It is neither so vast, nor so picturesque as the Colosseum. There, one expects to hear the roar of the beasts springing on their human prey; the ring of steel on steel, when the gladiators have bowed like dancing-masters to the bloated old bald-headed Neros and Vespasians; and you fancy that you smell the fountains of perfume that toss their spray from tier to tier; and see the rainbow of the silk awning flapping overhead. Better than all, you imagine you can watch the ravishing toilettes of the Faustinas, and Fulvias and Messalinas who flirt with the handsome, straight-nosed beaux so immensely classical in their togas; and when their thunder-browed husbands unexpectedly step in behind, it is so easy to conjecture the sudden change of theme, as they spread their fans to cover the message just written on their ivory tablets, and straightway fall to clawing the characters of all the Cornelias, and Calpurnias, and Octavias and Julia Domnas, and other respectable wives! All that I quite enjoyed because I understood. Eight years' campaigning in New York, and London and Paris would teach even an idiot that nineteenth century 'best society' can lift you so close to the naughtiness of the golden Roman era, that one only has to strain a very little on tip-toe, to feel at one's ease with the jeunesse doree of dead ages. Here—what do you find in a huge stone well sunk into the bowels of the earth? About as enticing as a plunge into a dry cistern, suddenly unroofed? If spectres we must hunt, do let them be festive, like those Faust danced with on the Brocken!"

"You should be ashamed, Alma! Miss Gordon is the very soul of courteous toleration, or she would resent the teasing goad of your Philistinism," cried the brother, Rivers Cutting, who in his new style yachting suit of blue cloth appeared veritably the jaunty genius of fashionable modernity, confronting the ghost of antiquity

"You forget, Rivers, some of the sage dicta you brought back from the 'Summer School of Philosophy', when you followed your last Boston flame to Concord, where she went poaching on the sacred preserves of the 'Illuminati,' hunting a new sensation. 'We must be as courteous to human beings as we are to a picture, which we are willing to give the advantage of a good light.' Now being Leo's very sincere friend, and knowing that the supreme moment of her facial triumph is when, like a startled fawn, she opens her eyes wide in horrified amazement at some inconceivable heresy, do you suppose I am so recreant to loyalty as to fail in providing her occasionally with the necessary Gorgon, ethical or archaeolegical, as surroundings warrant?

"History was never the fetich of my girlhood, and that quartette of dry-as-dust worthies whom Leo carries around in leash, as other women carry pugs and poodles, came near giving me meningitis in my tender years. My first governess, a Puritan spinster, full of zeal, and conscientiously bent on earning her wages, by exercising my brains to their utmost capacity, undertook to introduce me to all the highly immoral personages and practices that made the Punic Wars famous. By way of making Imilco a lifelong acquaintance, she illustrated the siege of Agrigentum by a huge, hideous image of Phalaris' 'Brazen Bull,' drawn with chalk on the school-room blackboard.

"A wonderful beast it certainly was; that taurus with head lowered, tail lashing the air, one hoof pawing savagely, worthy representative of all the horrors it typified, and which she explained with maddening perspicuity. That night, when papa tore himself away from the club room at one o'clock, and met mamma on the doorstep—just coming home from a supper at Delmonico's after an opera party—they were ascending the stairs, when frantic cries drove from her ears the echoes of 'Traviata's' witching strain. Thinking only a conflagration would justify the din, papa threw up the hall sash and shouted 'fire!' and the police sounded the alarm, and all pandemonium broke loose. Investigation discovered me, wriggled half way down to the foot of my bed, buried under the blankets, and shrieking 'Perillus' Bull! I am roasting in the Brass Bull!' Being not very ardent disciples of Clio, my solicitous parents failed to understand the nightmare; hence cracked ice was folded over my head (mid-winter), and the family physician ordered a mustard plaster half a yard long, down my spine. I vividly remember Imilco, and the bovine fury pawing the blackboard; but of the three Punic Wars, then and there tabooed, I recall only the brass monster at Agrigentum. Leo, when we reach Girgenti, the remaining Mecca of your historic hopes, some time to-morrow, you will understand why, instead of climbing to the temples of the cliff, I shall lock the door of our cabin, and drown the bellowing of the beast in Daudet's new book."

"I wish, indeed I do, that you had staid there to-day, instead of coming ashore to dampen all our ardor and enthusiasm by your constant thin drizzle of scorn. One should suppose that in this idyllic region, some ray of poetic warmth must melt your frigid, scoffing soul. Daudet suits my sister far better than Theocritus," answered her brother, fastening a sprig of orange blossom in his button hole.

Pushing back her sailor hat, Alma looked obliquely at him from beneath her drooping lids.

"Try me. Perhaps infection haunts the air. Spare us the Greek, come down from your Yale and Harvard heights to the level of my ignorance, and warble for me in English some of your Sicilian lark's melodies. At least I have heard of Amaryllis and Simaetha."

Mr. Cutting shook his head.

"What—? Ashamed of your bucolic hobby! No wonder—since after all it's only a goat. I dare you, brother mine, to produce me a Theocritan fragment."

"Take the consequences of your rash levity; though I have a dawning suspicion some 'Imp of the Perverse' has coached you for the occasion."

He stroked his mustache, pondered a moment, then struck an attitude, and declaimed:

"I go a serenading to Amaryllis; what time my flocks browse on the mountains, and Tityrus drives them. Tityrus beloved of me in the highest degree, feed my flocks and lead them to the fountain, etc."

Mimicking his tone exactly, Alma finished the line:

"And mind, Tityrus, that tawny Libyan he-goat lest he butt thee!' Come, Rivers; free translation is allowable, considering surroundings, but not garbling; and every time you know you substituted flocks for goats. Proceed, and do not insult your pet author with emendations."

With his hat on the back of his head, and his thumbs in the armholes of his vest, Mr. Cutting resumed:

"Sweet Amaryllis! though by death defiled,
Thee shall I ne'er forget; dear to my heart
As are my frisking goats, thou did'st depart.
To what a lot—was I, unhappy, born!"

Again the mocking voice responded:

"But see! yon calves devour
The olive branches. Pelt them off I pray.

"Confound the calves! 'St—! you white-skin thief—away!' Thanks, no more at present. Doubtless it sounds very fine in Greek, because then, I could not possibly understand that it is the melody and the rhythmic dance of bleating calves, and capering goats. Here come the stragglers laden with plunder. Oh, papa! Do give me those exquisite acacia clusters."

"My dear, I have ordered luncheon spread down there, in that strange garden. It is the queerest place imaginable; and looking up, the effect is quite indescribable."

"Have you had the skulls polished for drinking cups, and printed the menus on cross-bones? What shocking taste to add insult to injury by spreading all our wealth of canned dainties on the very stones where sit the ghosts of those who perished from hunger and thirst! Eminently Dantesque, but the sacrilege appalls Leo. She would sooner attend an oyster supper, or a clam-bake in the Catacombs, or—" bowing to a young Englishman standing near, "lead a German in the Poets' corner of Westminster Abbey. My dear girl, under which flag do you fight? Athenian, Roman, Carthagenian, Syracusan?

"The child of a man who fell in defence of his own fireside, could scarcely fail to sympathize with the holy cause of the invaded; yet here, in view of the horrors inflicted upon the captives, one almost leans to Athens. It seems to me the most enduring monument of Syracusan glory survives in the eloquent protest of Nicolaus against her cruelty; especially when we recollect that it came from one who, of all others, had most to forgive. Old, decrepit, unable to walk, the venerable sorrow-laden man whose only children, two sons, had died fighting to save Syracuse—was carried on a litter into the midst of the shouting thousands, who were drunk with the wine of victory. 'Behold an unhappy father, who has most cause to detest the Athenians, the authors of this war, the murderers of my children! But I am less sensible of my private afflictions than of the honor of my country, when I see it ready to expose itself to eternal infamy by violating the law of nations, and dishonoring our victory by barbarous cruelty. What! Will you tarnish your glory, and have all the world say that a nation who first dedicated a temple in their city, to Clemency, found none in yours? Triumphs and victories do not give immortal glory to a city; but the use of moderation in the greatest prosperity, the exercise of mercy toward a vanquished enemy, the fear of offending the gods by a haughty and insolent pride.' What a theme for Dore or Munkacsy?"

117

"Thank you ever so much, Miss Gordon, for brushing away the library dust from that historic cameo. I had so utterly forgotten it lay in the musty tomes, that it has all the charm of a curio." Mr. Cutting took off his hat, and bowed.

"Acknowledgments are due rather to my cousin, Dr. Douglass, who called my attention to the passage. The best of all things good abide with him; and out of his overflowing store, he shares with the needy. Only last night he reminded me of an illustration of the vanitas vanitatum of human fame and national gratitude, to be found over yonder in the necropolis. Less than a hundred and forty years after his death, Archimedes was so completely forgotten by the city he had immortalized, that Syracuse denied he was buried on her soil; and a foreigner had the honor of clearing away rubbish and brambles, in order to show the grave to his own countrymen."

Leighton Douglass handed to his cousin a bunch of the delicate lilac blossoms of acanthus, tied with a wisp of some ribbon-like grass, and taking off his spectacles, replied:

"Leo unduly exalts my memory at the expense of her own; and we have all levied heavily on her fund of topographical accuracy."

"If I travel much longer with two such learned and philosophical scholars, I shall inevitably degenerate into an intellectual Dodder," yawned Alma.

"Into a what?" asked her father.

"A Dodder, sir. Pray, papa, be more considerate than to force Doctor Douglass to believe that instead of listening to the sermon he preached us last year, you either slept ignominiously throughout its delivery, or else allowed your unregenerate thoughts to dwell on those devices of Lucifer, 'puts,' 'calls, 'spreads,' 'corners, 'spots' and 'futures'. Of course you remember that he believes in evolution? There was a time, even in my extremely recent day, when that word was more frightful to the orthodox than a ton of nitro-glycerine; was to the elect, a fouler abomination even than opera bouffe and the can can. But 'the thoughts of men are widened with the process of the suns', and now it appears that the immortal soul of us must be evolved, somewhat in the same fashion as protoplasm, and unless we fight for 'survival' elsewhere, we shall not be numbered among the spirited 'fittest', but degenerate into parasites, dodders, backsliders. So, drawing nutriment from the Doctor's historic brains, and from Leo's, I fall back into worse than a dodder, a torpid violator of the Law of Work, a hopeless Sacculina! Doctor Douglass, it was the bravest hour of your life when you stood up in—church pulpit, and told us the scientists whom we were wont to regard as more dreadful than the cannibals and Calmucks, are only a devoted sect of truth seekers, preaching from older texts, and drawing nearer and nearer to the kingdom of Heaven. To throw that ethical bomb, required more courage than Balaklava."

"Mine was merely a feeble attempt to follow out the analogical reasoning of one of the most original and scientific thinkers of our day in Great Britain; but the fact that you recall so correctly the line of argument in a sermon delivered more than a year ago, is certainly complimentary assurance of at least approximate success in my effort."

"After all, I am sorry I humored Leo's whim, and persuaded papa to bring us here."

"Why, my dear? We are enjoying it immensely," said her father.

"Because Syracuse has proved my 'crumpled rose leaf', by destroying the prestige of the 'Cleopatra'. Hitherto, I deemed our yacht quite the most complete and gorgeous floating palace since the days of its highly improper namesake's marauding sails on the Cydnus."

"And so she is; there is nothing afloat comparable to her in speed, appointments, comfort and beauty," interrupted Mr. Cutting.

"Poor papa! How he bristles at the bare suggestion of rivalry. Be comforted, sir, in the knowledge that at least we shall not be run down by a phantom cruiser. It is very humiliating to American pride—after winning the international prizes, and boasting so inordinately, to find out that we are only about—how many centuries, Leo?—twenty-five centuries behind Syracuse in building pleasure crafts. Think of a superb cabin with staterooms containing beds (not bunks) for one hundred and twenty guests, and the floors all covered with agates and other precious stones, that formed a mosaic copy of the Iliad! If you wished to emphasize a discussion on connubial devotion, behold! there on your right, Andromache and Hector; if one's husband objected to a harmless flirtation, lo! on the left, Agamemnon and Briseis; and to point the moral of 'pretty is, as pretty does'—how very convenient to indicate with the tip of your satin slipper, the demure figure of Helen standing on the walls, to watch the duel between Menelaus and Paris! Fancy the consolation a person of my indolent Sacculina temperament might have derived from the untimely fate of Cassandra, oppressed with knowledge in advance of her day and generation! There was the gymnasium for the beaux; and for the belles bona fide gardens, with walks and arbors covered with ivy and flowering vines whose roots rested in great stone vessels filled with earth. Imagine the boudoir and bathrooms paved with precious stones, encrusted with carved ivory and statues—"

"Pooh! Alma. That rigmarole is not in the guide books. Come, Dixon is waving his handkerchief down there, as a signal that luncheon is ready."

"I prefer to wait here. Alma, bring me some anemones, and a sprig of ivy from the circular garden, when you come back," said Leo. Doctor Douglass drew closer, and asked:

"Will you let me stay also, and enjoy with you the wonderful charm of this opalescent air, this beautiful cincturing sea?"

"I would rather be alone. Solitude is a luxury rarely allowed on a yacht cruise; and I want a few quiet moments. By day, poor Aunt Patty has so much to tell me; at night, Alma is a chattering owl."

There are hours when the ghost of a happy past, from which we have persistently fled, constrains us to give audience; and Leo surrendered herself to memories that brought a very mournful shadow into her brave brown eyes. Thirteen months had passed since her departure from X——and despite changing scenes and novel incidents, she could not escape the haunting face that met her on mountains, was mirrored in every sea; the brilliant mesmeric face set in its frame of crisp black locks, with dark blue eyes whose intense lustre had the cold, hard gleam of jewels. Sleeping or waking, always that dear, powerful face daring her to forget.

When Doctor Douglass and Miss Patty joined the yacht party at Palermo, the former had brought a letter and a package, which sorely tested Leo's strength of will. Leaning to-day against the twisted body of an old olive tree, she opened and read once more, the final message.

"When Leighton places this sheet in your hands, the year of release which I could not refuse you, will have expired. Once your noble heart was wholly mine; and the proudest moment of my life was, and will be, that in which you promised to be my wife. All that you ever were, you shall always remain to me; and if you can confide your happiness to my keeping, I will never betray the sacred trust. Life has grown sombre to me, during the past eighteen months; and the only companionship that I can hope to cheer it, you alone can bring me. I have not willingly or intentionally forfeited your confidence; but that I have suffered, I shall not deny. If you love me, as in days gone by, our future rests once more in your hands; and you must renew the pledges that at your request I surrendered. In behalf of our past, I beg that you will retain the ring, hallowed forever by the touch of your hand; and its acceptance will typify, if not a renewal of our engagement, at least the perpetuity of a sacred friendship. Awaiting your final decision, I am, my dear Leo,

"Yours as of yore, LENNOX."

All that she had ever been; no more. The graceful, well-bred heiress whom he admired, who commanded his profoundest respect, whom he had known from his boyhood, and who of all others he had desired should preside over his home and wear his name; but not the woman who reigned in his heart; whose touch had lighted the glowing tenderness that so transfigured his countenance, as she saw it that day, bending over a sick convict in a penitentiary.

He offered her formal allegiance, and that pale phantom of affection grounded in reverence, which is to the ardent love that a true woman demands in exchange for her own, as—

"Moonlight unto sunlight; and as water unto wine."

She knew that he was no willing victim of a fascination, which had audaciously deranged his carefully mapped campaign of life; that he would have set his heel on his own insurgent heart, had it been possible; and she honored him for the stern integrity that forbade his affectation of a warmth of feeling which she was now conscious she had never evoked.

Accepting the theory that the young convict was sustained and animated by her devotion to a guilty lover, Leo fully understood that Lennox, even were he mad enough to sacrifice his pride, could indulge no expectation of ever winning the love of the prisoner; and despite her efforts to regard their rupture as final, she had faintly hoped that he would cross the ocean, and in person urge a renewal of the betrothal. The test of absence had proved as effectual as she intended it should be, and his letter proclaimed the humiliating fact, that while honor inspired him to hold out his wrists for conjugal manacles, honor equally constrained him to spare her the wrong and insult of insincere professions of tenderness.

Had she found it possible to condemn him as unworthy, it would have diminished the pain of surrendering the brightest hope of her life; for contempt is the balm a lofty soul offers a bruised heart, but she was just, even in her anguish; and that when barbed the arrow, was the mortifying consciousness that compassion for her was the strongest motive which dictated the carefully phrased letter. She was far too proud to parley with the temptation to accept the shadow in lieu of the substance; and twenty-four hours after the arrival of the final appeal, her answer was speeding with wings of steam across the ocean.

"DEAR LENNOX:

"My heart overflows with gratitude for all the affectionate interest, the kind solicitude, the innumerable thoughtful attentions you have so indefatigably shown to Aunt Patty, in the sad complication of misfortunes that so suddenly overwhelmed her; and I feel the inadequacy of any attempt to express my thanks. Your letter can only rivet more indissolubly the links of an affectionate friendship that must always bind you and me; but the future can hold no renewal of pledges which I feel assured would conduce neither to your happiness, nor to mine. Let us embalm the past and bury it tenderly; raising no mound to trip our friendly feet in years to come. The serenity of our future might be marred by retrospective gleams of the beautiful ring that once enclosed two lives; hence, I have ordered the diamonds reset in the form of a four-leaved clover, which will be sent to dear Kittie as an auspicious omen.

"With undiminished esteem, and unshaken confidence, and with a prayer for your happiness, which will always be dear to me, I remain,

"Your sincerely attached friend,

"LEO."

The majority of men, and a large class of women, bury their dead, and straightway begin assiduously the cultivation of all that promises oblivion; but Leo's nature was deeper, more intense; and while she made no audible moan, and shed no tears, she accepted the fact that earthly existence had lost its coveted crown, and that her aching heart was the dark grave of a beautiful hope that could know no resurrection. To-day she asked herself: "What shall I do with my life?"

Upon the warm air, sweet with the breath of lemon flowers, floated the peculiar, jeering, yet subdued and musical laughter, which told that Alma had flown straight at some luckless quarry. She held in one hand a cluster of crimson anemones, and purple stars of periwinkle, and walking between two English gentlemen, whose yacht, the "Albatross", lay anchored close to the "Cleopatra" in the harbor below, slowly approached Leo, saying:

"Don't stone your prophets. Especially one hedged about with the triple sanctity of Brasenose! 'Consider that thy marbles are but the earth's callosities, thy gold and silver its faeces; thy silken robe but a worm's bedding; and thy purple an unclean fish.' That is one sugar-coated pill that I administer to my humility now and then to keep it healthy. Hear him again;—'sitting on the marble bench of one of the exhedrea on the edge of the Appian Way, close to the fragrant borders of a rose farm': 'So it is, with the philosophers; all alike are in search of happiness, what kind of thing it is. It is pleasure, it is virtue; what not? All philosophers, so to speak, are but fighting about the ass' shadow. I saw one who poured water into a mortar, and ground it with all his might with a pestle of iron, fancying he did a thing useful; but it remained water only, none the less.' Stoicism, hedonism, the gospel of 'Sweetness and Light'; what is it, may I ask, that your aesthetic priests furnish, to feed immortal British souls? Knee breeches, sun flowers, niello, cretonne, Nanking bowls, lily dados? To us it savors sorrowfully of that which one of your prophets foreshadowed, 'Despair, baying as the poet heard her, in the ruins of old Rome'."

"Beg pardon, Miss Cutting; but you quite surprise me. The tone of many American papers and magazines led us to suppose, really, that the rosy dawn of Culture was beginning to flush the night of Philistinism brooding over your Western world."

"Believe it not. Primeval gloom, raw realism so weigh upon our apathetic souls, that we rub our eyes and stare at sight of your aesthetic catechism: 'Harmony, but no system; instinct, but no logic; eternal growth and no maturity; everlasting movement, and nothing attained; infinite possibilities of everything; the becoming all things, the being nothing.' We have too much Philistine honesty to pretend that we understand that, but like other ambitious parrots we can commit to memory. One of your seers tells us that: 'Renaissance art will make our lives like what seems one of the loveliest things in nature, the iridescent film on the face of stagnant water!' Now it will require at least a decade, to train us to appreciate the subtle symphonies of ditch slime. An English friend compassionating my American stupidity, essayed to initiate me in the cult of 'culture', and gave me a leaf to study, from the latter-day gospel. I learned it after a time, as I did the multiplication table. 'Culture steps in, and points out the grossness of untempered belief. It tells us the beauty of picturesque untruth; the grotesqueness of unmannerly conviction; truth and error have kissed each other in a sweet, serener sphere; this becomes that, and that is something else. The harmonious, the suave, the well bred waft the bright particular being into a peculiar and reserved parterre of paradise, where bloom at once the graces of Panthism, the simplicity of Deism, and the pathos of Catholicism; where he can sip elegances and spiritualities from flowerets of every faith!' Fancy my crass ignorance, when I assure you that I actually laughed over that verbal syllabub, thinking it intended as a famous bit of satire."

"Then it is pathetically true that reverence for the Renaissance has not crossed the Atlantic?" asked one of the "Albatross" party, who with his sketch book half open, was surreptitiously making an "impressionist" view of Leo's profile, as she stood listening to Alma's persiflage, and mechanically arranging her lilac acanthus blossoms.

"Devoted British colporteurs have philanthropically scattered a few art primers and tracts, and there is a possibility that in the near future, our people may search the maps for Orvieto, and the dictionaries for Campo Santo, to compass the mysteries of the 'Triumph of Death', and of 'Symmetria Prisca'. Some of us have even heard of 'Aucassin et Nicolette', and of 'Nencia da Barberino', picking salad in her garden; and I am almost sure a Vassar girl once spoke to me of Delia Quercia's Ilaria; but with all my national pride, candor compels me to admit that it is a 'far cry' to the day when we can devoutly fall on our knees before the bronze Devil of Giovanni da Bologna. Aesthetic paupers, we sit on the lowest bench at the foot of the class, in your Dame's Art School, to learn the alphabet of the wonderful Renaissance; and in our chastened and reverent mood, it almost takes our breath away when your high-priestess unrolls the last pronunciamento, and tells us her startling story of 'Euphorion!' Why? Ah!—don't you know? The Puritan leaven of prudery, and the stern, stolid, phlegmatic decorum of Knickerbockerdom mingle in that consummate flower of the nineteenth century occident, the 'American Girl', who pales and flushes at sight of the carnival of the undraped—in English art and literature. Here, Leo, take your anemones; red, are they not, as the blood once chilled down yonder, in that huge stone kennel? Dr. Douglass has the ivy root; and he and I have concluded, that after all, Syracuse was not more cruel here in the Latomia, than some States in America, where convicts are leased to mining companies, and kept quarrying coal, without even the sweet consolation of staring up at this magical blue sky. We leave hideous moral and physical leprosy at home, and come here to shed dilettante tears over classic tatters twenty-five centuries old! O immortal and ubiquitous Tartufe!"

As Leo walked with her cousin toward the spot, where the "Cleopatra" rose and fell on the crest of waves racing before Libeccio, she suddenly laid her hand on his arm.

"Leighton, I have decided to leave the yacht at Venice and take Aunt Patty to Udine for rest and quiet. When summer is over, I shall be ready to make arrangements for the journey to Syria and Egypt, and you must complete your church mission to England in time to accompany us to Jerusalem."

"Is this your itinerary, or Aunt Patty's?"

"She has set her heart upon it; and it will be agreeable to me."

CHAPTER XXVII.

Is it true that in abstract valuation, "the bird in hand, is worth two in the bush?"

We stand beneath a loaded apricot tree, and would give all the bushel within reach, for one crimson satin globe pendent on the extreme tip of the most inaccessible bough; and the largest, luscious, richest colored orange always glows defiantly, high up, close to the body of the tree, hedged away from our eager grasp by its impenetrable chevaux de frise of bristling thorns. The wonderful water lily we covet is smiling on its green cushion of leaves just beyond the danger line, where death lurks; the rhododendron flame that burned brightest amid surrounding floral fires, and lured us, springs from the crevice of some beetling precipice, waving a challenge over fatal chasms that bar possession; and with fretful dissatisfaction we repine, because the colors of the feathered captives in our gilt cages are so dull, so faded in comparison with their brothers, flashing wings of scarlet, and breasts of vivid blue high in the sunlight of God's free air.

The gold and silver dust that powder velvet butterflies, tarnish at a touch, stain the fingers that clutch them; and the dewy bloom on purple and amber grape clusters, never survives the handling of the vintager.

Leaning back in the revolving chair in front of his office desk, Mr. Dunbar slowly tore into strips a number of notes and letters, and suffered the fragments to fall into a waste basket somewhat faded, yet much too elegant to harmonize with its surroundings.

When Leo quilted the lining of ruby silk and knotted the ribbons that tied it to the wicker lace work, love pelted her cheek with roses, and happy hope sang so loud in her ear, that she could not have divined the cruel fact that she was preparing the dainty coffin, destined to receive the mutilated remains of a betrothal, that typified supreme earthly happiness to her. One by one dropped the shreds of Leo's last message from Palermo, like torn crumpled petals of a once beloved and sacred flower; and the faint, delicate perfume that clung to the fragments, was one which Mr. Dunbar recognized as characteristic of the library at the "Lilacs". The contents of the farewell note had in no degree surprised him; for though fully persuaded that her heart was irrevocably pledged to the past, he was equally sure that only the ardor he scorned to feign, would avail to melt the wall of ice her outraged pride had built between them. There were times when he deplored bitterly the loss of her companionship; at others he exulted in the consciousness of perfect freedom to indulge an overmastering love, amenable to no chastisement by violated loyalty. He had scrupulously endeavored, by careful employment of forms of deference, to spare his betrothed as far as possible, the stinging humiliation and anguish which every woman suffers, when the man whom she loves shows her that she fills only a subordinate and insignificant place in his affection; and yet, while her nobler nature commanded his homage, and the brilliancy of the alliance seems to jeer at his blind fatuity, his heart throbbed and yearned with an intolerable longing for one upon whom the world had set the seal of an ineradicable disgrace.

Nature and education had made him a coldly calculating man, jealous of his honor, but immersed in schemes for his own aggrandizement, and superbly invulnerable to the blandishments of sentimentality; hence his amazement, when the deep and engrossing love of his life burned away that selfishness which was citadel of his affections. Because his infatuation had cost him so much, that was alluring alike to vanity, pride, and ambition, a fierce hunger for revenge possessed him; and herein differs the nature of the love of men and women; the one can sacrifice itself for the happiness of the beloved; the other will crucify its darling to appease jealous pangs in view of happiness it can neither inspire nor share.

"Good morning, Churchill. Come in. Glad to see you. Sit down."

"When did you get back, Lennox?"

"Last night."

"Well, what luck?"

"A rather leaky promise. Kneading slag or cold pig iron into Bessemer steel would be about as easy as pounding the law of evidence into the Governor's brains. I emphasized the moral weight of the petition, by calling his attention to the signatures of the judge, jury, prosecuting counsel and especially of Prince, who presumably has most to forgive. The memorial of the inspectors, warden and physician was appended, and constituted a eulogy upon the behavior and character of the prisoner; especially the heroic service rendered by her during the recent fatal epidemic. Human nature is an infernally vexing bundle of paradoxes, and when a man throws his conscience in your teeth, what then? The argument from which I hoped most, proved a Greek horse, and well-nigh wrought ruin. When I dwelt upon the fact that the prisoner had voluntarily conveyed to Prince all right and title to the fortune, which was supposed to have tempted her to commit the crime, he bristled like a Skye terrier, and grandiloquently assured me he valued his 'prerogative as something too sacred to be prostituted to nepotism!' Prince being his cousin, a readiness to exercise Executive clemency by pardoning the prisoner, might be construed into a species of bargain and sale; and his Excellency could not condone a crime merely because the culprit had relinquished a fortune to his relative. Braying an ordinary fool in a mortar is an unpromising job; but an extraordinary official leatherhead, PLUS thin-skinned conscience, and religious scruples, requires the upper and nether mill stone. You know, Churchill, it is tough work to straighten a crooked ramrod."

"I see; a case of moral curvature of the spine. When he was inaugurated last December, I chanced to be at the Capital, and heard two old codgers from the piney woods felicitating the State upon having a Governor, 'Fit to tie to; honest as the day is long, and walks so straight, he is powerful swaybacked.' Dunbar, did he refuse outright?"

"He holds the matter in abeyance for maturer deliberation; but promises that, unless he sees cogent reasons to the contrary, he may grant a pardon when eighteen months of the sentence have expired. That will be the last week in August, and almost two years since she was thrown into prison. I should have made application to his predecessor, Glenbeigh, had I not been so confident of overtaking the man who killed Gen'l Darrington; but the clue that promised so much merely led me astray. I went with the detective down into the mines, and found the man, who certainly had a hideous facial deformity, but he was gray as a badger, and moreover proved an ALIBI, having been sick with small-pox in the county pest-house on the night of the murder. It is a tedious hunt, but I will not be balked of my game. I will collar that wretch some day, and meantime I will get the pardon."

"I hope so; for I shall never feel easy until that poor girl is set free. The more I hear of her deportment and character, especially of the religious influence she seems to be exerting through some Bible readings she holds among the female convicts, the more painfully am I oppressed with the conviction that we all committed a sad blunder, and narrowly escaped hanging an innocent woman."

"Speak for yourself. I disclaim complicity in the disgraceful wrong of the conviction."

"Well, I confess I would rather stand in your place than mine; especially since my wife's brother Garland was called in as consulting physician, last month at the penitentiary. He has so stirred her sympathies for the woman whom he pronounces a paragon of all the virtues and graces, that I begin to fidget now at the sound of the prisoner's name, and can hardly look my wife straight in the face. When I go up to court next week, I will call on the Governor, and add a personal appeal to the one I have already signed. According to the evidence, she is guilty; but when justice is vindicated, one can afford to listen to the dictates of pity. Now, Dunbar, let me congratulate you on your recent good luck. We hear wonderful accounts of your new fortune."

"Rumor always magnifies such matters; still it is true that I have inherited a handsome estate." "Does your sister share equally?"

"A very liberal legacy was left to her, but you are aware that I was named for my mother's brother, Randall Lennox, and he has for many years regarded me as his heir; hence, gave me the bulk of the property."

"It is rather strange that he never married. I recall him as a very distinguished looking man."

"He had a love affair very early in life, while at college, with the daughter of his Greek professor. Surreptitiously he took her to drive one afternoon, and the horse became frightened, ran away and killed the girl. He was a peculiar man, and seems never to have swerved from his allegiance to her memory."

"I hope it is not true that the conditions of the will require you to remove from X——-and settle in New Orleans? We can't afford to lose you from our bar."

"There are no restrictions in my Uncle Lennox's will; the legacy was unconditional; but the obligation of complying with his urgent desire to have me live in New Orleans will probably induce me to make that my future home. For several years he has associated me with him in the conduct of some important suits; and I understand now, that his motive was to introduce me gradually to a new field of professional labor. Not the least valuable of my new possessions is his superb law library, probably the finest in the South. Of course my business will keep me here, for the present, and I have matured no plans."

"Did you reach New Orleans before his death?"

"No, I was in Dakota, and missed a letter designed to acquaint me with his illness. While in Washington on my return, arguing a case before the Supreme Court, a telegram was forwarded from the office here, and I hurried off by the first train, but arrived about ten hours too late. Another grudge I have to settle with that bloody thief, when I unearth him."

"After all, Dunbar, you are a deucedly lucky fellow,—and—Hello! historic Hebrew! Bedney, have you seen a ghost?"

"Yes—Mars Alfred—two of 'em."

Spent with fatigue, panting, with an ashen pallor on his leathery, wrinkled face, the old negro ran in to the office, and leaned heavily against the oak table.

"What is the matter? Positively, you are turning a grayish white. What is the secret of the bleaching? Police after you? Or does the Sheriff want you?"

"Mars Alfred, this ain't no fitten time to crack your on'-Gawdly jokes, for I am scared all but into fits. I started in a brisk walk, but every step I got more and more afeered to look behind, and I struk a fox trot, and now my wind is clean gone."

"What is the trouble? What are you running from?"

"'Fore Gawd, Mars Alfred, sperrits! Sperrits, sir."

"Do you mean that you want a dram to steady your nerves?"

"I'm that frustrated I couldn't say what I want; but I didn't signify bottle and jimmyjohn liquor, I mean sperrits, sir, ghosts what walk, and make the hair rise like wire all over your head. The ole house is hanted shore 'nuff; and I can't stay there. Lem'me tell you, Lord! Mars Alfred, don't laugh! It's the Gawd's truth, ole Marster's sperrit is fighting up yonder in his room with the man what killed him. I seen him, in the broad daylight, and I have cum for you and Mars Lennox to git there, jest as quick as you kin, so you kin see it fur yourselves. I know you won't believe it till you see it; nuther should I, but it's there. The sperrits have cum back, to show my young mistiss' child never killed her grandpa."

Mr. Dunbar rose quickly, handed a glass of water to the old man, and then placed a chair for him.

"Tell me at once what you saw."

"Ole Marster standin' in the flo' close to the vault, with his arm up so—and the handi'on in his own hand—"

"How dare you come here, with this cock-and-bull story? You are either drunk or in your dotage. Your master has been in his grave for eighteen months, and—"

"Oh! to be shore I know'd what you'd say. Cuss me for an idjut; but I swar, Mars Lennox, I am that scared I dasn't to tell you no lie. The proof of the pudden is jest chawin' the bag, an' I want you both to git a carridge quick, and take me up home; and if you don't see what I tell you is thar, you may kick me from the front door clean down to the big gate. The grave is busted wide open, and the dead walks, for I seen him; and I'll sho' him to you. Come on, I want you to see for yourself."

"You imbecile old nincompoop! Go home, and tell Dyce to give you some catnip tea, and tie you to a chair," laughed Mr. Churchill.

"You'll laugh t'other side of your mouth, Mars Alfred, when you see that awful sight up yonder. Ole Marster has come back, to clare the name of his grandchile, for he and his murderer is a wrastling, and it ain't no 'oman, it's a man! A tall, pretty man, with beard on his face."

Mr. Dunbar struck a bell at his side, and a clerk came promptly from the rear room.

"Nesbitt, step over to the livery stable, and order a carriage sent up at once." Turning to Bedney he continued:

"I suppose the gist of all your yarn-spinning is, that you have found a stranger prowling about the place. How did you discover him?"

"Lem'me tell you, as fur as I can, how I cum to see ole Marster. Mr. Prince gin orders that the house should be opened and arred reglar, and he pintedly enjined us to have that room well cleaned and put in order. We had all pintedly gin it a wide berth, and kep' ourselves on t'other side of the house, 'cause all such places is harryfying; but this morning, I thought I would open the outside blind door on the west gallery, and look in through the glass door. I know'd Mr. Prince had stirred round considerable in there, the day before he left, but I didn't know he had drapped the curting what was looped back the last time I was inside. So I went up the steps and clared away a rose vine what was hanging low down from the i'on pillar of the piazzar, and almost screening the door, and I walked up, I did, and looked in. Lord Gawd Amighty! The red curting was down on the inside, and I seen through it, I swar to Gawd I did, sir! I seen clar spang through into that room, and thar stood Marster in his night clothes, jest so—and thar stood that murdering vil'yan close to him, holding the tin box so—and Marster with the handi'on jest daring him to cum on—and—and oh! I am glad to know my Marster was game to the last, died game! Never show'd no white feather while thar was breath in his body. Mars Lennox, I jest drapped on my knees, and I trimbled, and my teeth chattered, and I felt the hair as it riz straight up. I was afeer'd to stay, and I was afeer'd to move; but I shet my eyes and crawled back'ards easy to the aidge of the steps, and then run as fast as I could. I wanted Dyce to see, too, but the poor cretur is so crippled she can't walk, and as she weighs two hundred and twenty pounds, I couldn't tote her; so I tole her what I seen, and she sent me straight to find Mars Alfred fust, and you next. I run to Mars Alfred's office, and he was out, so I kep' on here. I know'd you lie'yers was barking up the wrong tree, and wrongfully pussecutin' that poor young gal; and now the very sperrits have riz up to testify fur her. If you two can face ole Marster's ghost, and tell him you know better than he did who killed him, you've got better pluck and backbone than I give you credit fur."

"What did you eat last night, Bedney? Baked possum, and fried chitterlings? Evidently you have had a heavy nightmare."

Mr. Churchill drew a match across the heel of his boot, and lighted a cigar; looking quizzically at the old man, who was wiping the perspiration from his face.

"There's the carridg, I hear the wheels. Mars Lennox and Mars Alfred, there is one thing I insists on havin'. The law is all lop-sided from fust to last in this here case, and I want it squoze into shape, till t'other side swells out a little. I want the Crowner to go up yonder now, and hold another inquess. He's done sot all wrong on the body, and now let him set on the sperrit if he kin. I'm in plum earnest. The Crowner swore that poor young gal knocked Marster in the head with the handi'on; and yonder stands Marster, ready to brain that man—with that handi'on hilt tight in his own right hand. Now what I wants to know is, WHAR is the 'delectible corpus' what you lieyers argufied over?"

"You doting old humbug! If you decoy us on a wild goose chase I shall feel like cutting one of your ears off!"

"Slit 'em both and welcome, Mars Alfred, if you don't find I'm telling you the Gawd's truth. I feel all tore up, root and branch, and if folks could be scared to death, I should be stretched out this minute on the west piazzar. I had my doubts about ghosts and sperrits, and I lost my religion when I cotch our preacher brandin' one of my dappled crumple-horned hefers with his i'on; but Bedney Darrington is a changed pusson. Come en, let's see which of you will dar to laugh up yonder."

"Are you really bent on humoring this insane or idiotic vagary?" asked Mr. Churchill, as he saw his companion take his hat and prepare to follow the negro, who had left the room.

"His terror is genuine, and his superstitious tale is probably the outer shell of some kernel of fact that may possibly be valuable. In cases of circumstantial evidence, you and I know the importance of looking carefully into the merest trifles. Come with me; you can spare an hour."

Leaving the carriage at the front entrance of the deserted and stately old house, the attorneys crossed the terrace and walked around to the western veranda, preceded by Bedney, who paused at the steps, and waved them to ascend.

"Go up and see for yourselves. I am nigh as I want to git."

The stone floor was strewn with branches of rose vine, and the pruning shears lay open upon them, just as they had fallen from the old man's hand. The sun had passed several degrees below the meridian, and the shadows of the twisted iron columns were aslant eastward, but the glare of light shone on the plate-glass door, which was rounded into an arch at top, and extended within four inches of the surface of the floor, where it fitted into the wooden frame. It was one wide sheet, unbroken into panes, and on the outside dust had collected, and a family of spiders had colonized in the lower corner, spinning their gray lace quite across the base. It was evident that the Venetian blinds had long been closed, and recently opened, as a line of dust and dried drift leaves attested; and behind the glass hung the dull red, plush curtain, almost to the floor.

Both gentlemen pressed forward, and looked in; but saw nothing.

"Hang your head kinder sideways, down so, and look up, Mars Lennox."

Mr. Dunbar changed his position, and after an instant, started back.

"Do you see it, Churchill? No hallucination; it is as plain as print, just like the negative of a photograph."

"Bless my soul! It beats the Chinese jugglers! What a curious thing!"

"Stand back a little; you obstruct the light. Now, how clearly it comes out."

Printed apparently on the plush background, like the images in a camera, were the distinctly outlined and almost life-size figures of two men. Clad in a long gown, with loose sleeves, Gen'l Darrington stood near the hearth, brandishing the brass unicorn in one hand, the other thrown out and clinched; the face rather more than profile, scarcely three-quarters, was wonderfully distinct, and the hair much dishevelled. In front was the second portrait, that of a tall, slender young man who appeared to have suddenly wheeled around from the open vault, turning his countenance fully to view; while he threw up a dark, square object to ward off the impending blow. A soft wool hat pushed back, showed the curling hair about his temples, and the remarkable regularity of his handsome features; while even the plaid pattern of his short coat was clearly discernible.

As the attorneys came closer, or stepped back from the door, the images seemed to vary in distinctness, and viewed from two angles they became invisible.

Mr. Churchill stared blankly; Mr. Dunbar's gaze was riveted on the face of the burglar, and he took his underlip between his teeth, as was his habit in suppressing emotion.

"Of course there is some infernal trick about this; but how do you account for it? It is beyond Bedney's sleight of hand," said the District Solicitor.

"I think I understand how it came here. Bedney, go around and open the library door leading into this room, and loop back the curtain for a moment."

"No, sir, Mars Lennox. Forty railroad ingines couldn't pull me in there alive. I wouldn't dar tamper with ole Marster's ghost; not for all the money in the bank. Go yourself; I doesn't budge on no sech bizness as prying and spying amongst the sperrits. It would fling me into a fit."

"You miserable coward. Is the house open? Where is the key of this room?"

"Hanging on the horseshoe under my chimbly board. I'll fetch it and unlock the front door, so you kin git in, and hold your inquess inside."

"Will you go, Churchill, or shall I?"

"What is your idea?"

"To ascertain whether the images are on the glass, as I believe, and if they can be seen without the background. Stand just here—and watch. When I pull back the curtain, tell me the effect."

Some moments later, the red folds shook, swayed aside, the curtain was pushed out of sight on its brass rod. The interior of the apartment came into view, the articles of furniture, the face and figure of Mr. Dunbar.

"Is it still there; do you see it?" shouted the latter.

"No. It vanished with the curtain. Drop it back. There! I see it. Now loop it. Gone again. Must be on the curtain," shouted the Solicitor, peering through the glass at his colleague.

Mr. Dunbar turned a key on the inside, pushed back a bolt, and threw open the door, which swung outward on the veranda. Then he carefully let fall the plush curtain once more.

"Do you see it?"

"No. A blank show. I can't see into the trick. Dunbar, change places with me and satisfy yourself."

The solicitor went inside, and Mr. Dunbar watched from the veranda a repetition of the experiment.

"That will do, Churchill. It is all plain enough now, but you cease to wonder at Bedney's superstitious solution. You understand it perfectly, don't you?"

"No, I'll be hanged if I do! It is the queerest thing I ever saw."

"Do you recollect that there was a violent thunder-storm the night of the murder?"

"Since you mention it, I certainly recall it. Go on."

"All the witnesses testified that next morning this door was closed as usual, but the outside blinds were open, and the red curtain was looped back."

"Yes, I remember all that."

"The images are printed on the glass, and were photographed by a flash of lightning."

"I never heard of such a freak. Don't believe it."

"Nevertheless it is the only possible solution; and I know that several similar instances have been recorded. It is like the negative of a common photograph, brought out by a dark background; and do you notice the figures are invisible at certain angles? It is very evident the storm came up during the altercation that night, and electricity printed the whole scene on this door; stamping the countenance of the murderer, to help the instruments of justice. While the blinds were closed, and the curtain was looped aside, of course this wonderful witness could not testify; but Prince let down the folds just before his departure, and the moment Bedney opened the blinds, there lay the truthful record of the awful crime. Verily, the 'irony of fate!' An overwhelming witness for the defence, only eighteen months too late, to save a pure, beautiful life from degradation and ruin. Well may Bedney ask, 'where is your corpus delicti?' Alfred Churchill, I wish you joy of the verdict, you worked so hard to win."

Turning on his heel Mr. Dunbar walked the length of the veranda, and stood gazing gloomily across the tangled mass of the neglected rose garden, taking no cognizance of the garlands of bloom, seeing everywhere only that lithe elegant figure and Hyperion face of the man who reigned master of Beryl's heart.

The Solicitor leaned one shoulder against the door facing, and with his hands in his pockets, and his brows drawn into a pucker, pondered the new fact, and eyed the strange witness.

After a time, he approached his companion.

"If your hypothesis be correct, and it seems plausible, if science asserts that electricity can photograph,—then certainly I am sorry, sorry enough for all I did in the trial; yet I cannot reproach myself, because I worked conscientiously; and the evidence was conclusive against the girl. The circumstantial coincidences were strong enough to have hung her. We all make mistakes, and no doubt I am responsible for my share; but thank God! reparation can be made! I will take the night train and see the Governor before noon to-morrow. The pardon must come now."

"Pardon! He cannot pardon a crime of which she now stands acquitted. The only pardon possible, she may extend to those who sacrificed her. His Excellency need exercise no prerogative of mercy; his aid is superfluous. Churchill, go in as soon as you can, and send out the Sheriff, with as many of the jurors as you can get together; and ask Judge Parkman to drive out this afternoon, and bring Stafford, the photographer, with him. Tell Doctor Graham I want to see him here, as he is an accomplished electrician. I will stay here and guard this door till all X——has seen it."

Winged rumor flew through the length and breadth of the town, and before sunset a human stream poured along the road leading to "Elm Bluff", overflowed the green lawn under the ancient poplars, surged across the terrace, and beat against the railing of the piazza. Men, women, children, lawyers, doctors, newspaper reporters, all pressing forward for a glimpse of the mysterious and weird witness, that, in the fulness of time, had arisen to reprove the world for a grievous and cruel wrong.

The hinges had been removed; the door was set up at a certain angle, carefully balanced against the hanging curtain; and there the curious crowd beheld, in a veritable vision of the dead, torn as it were from the darkness and silence of the grave, the secret of that stormy night, when unseen powers had solemnly covenanted in defence of trusting innocence.

CHAPTER XXVIII.

On Saturday the regulations of prison discipline reduced the working hours much below the daily quota, and at two o'clock the ringing of the tower bell announced that the busy convicts of the various industrial rooms were allowed leisure during the remainder of the afternoon, to give place to the squad of sweepers and scrubbers, who flooded the floors and scoured the benches.

June heat had followed fast upon the balmy breath of May, and though the air at dawn was still iced with crystal dew, the sun that shone through the open windows of the little chapel, burned fiercely on the unpainted pine seats, the undraped reading-desk of the pulpit, the tarnished gilt pipes of the cabinet organ within the chancel railing.

On one of the front benches sat Iva Le Bougeois, with a pair of crutches resting beside her on the arm of the seat, and her hands folded in her lap. Recovering slowly from the paralysis resulting from diphtheria, she had followed Beryl into the chapel, and listened to the hymns the latter had played and sung. The glossy black head was bent in abject despondency upon her breast, and tears dripped over the smooth olive cheeks, but no sound escaped the trembling mouth, once so red and riotous, now drawn into curves of passionate sorrow; and the topaz gleams that formerly flickered in her sullen hazel eyes were drowned in the gloom of dejection. For her, memory was an angel of wrath, driving her into the hideous Golgotha of the past, where bloody spectres gibbered; the present was a loathsome death in life, the future a nameless torturing horror. Helpless victim of her own outraged conscience, she seemed at times sinking into mental apathy more pitiable than that which had seized her physically; and the only solace possible, she found in the encouraging words uttered by the voice that had prayed for her during that long night of mortal agony, in the gentle pressure of the soft hand that often guided her tottering footsteps.

The organ stops had been pushed back, the musical echoes vibrated no longer; and the bare room, filled with garish sunshine, was so still that the drowsy droning of a bee high up on the dusty sash of the barred window, became monotonously audible.

Within the chancel and to the right of the pulpit, a large reversible blackboard had recently been placed, and on a chair in front of it stood Beryl, engrossed in putting the finishing touches to a sketch which filled the entire board; and oblivious for the moment of Eve Werneth's baby, who, having emptied her bottle of milk, had pulled herself up by the chair, and with the thumb of her right hand in her mouth, was staring up at the picture.

The lesson selected for the Sunday afternoon Bible class, which Beryl had so successfully organized among a few of the female convicts, was the fifteenth chapter of Luke; and at the top of the blackboard was written in large letters: "Rejoice with Me, for I have found My sheep which was lost." She had drawn in the foreground the flock couched in security, rounded up by the collie guard in a grassy meadow; in the distance, overhanging a gorge, was a bald, precipitous crag, behind which a wolf crouched, watching the Shepherd who tenderly bore in his arms the lost wanderer. On the opposite side of the blackboard had been carefully copied the Gospel Hymn beginning:—

"There were ninety and nine that safely lay, In the shelter of the fold, But one was out on the hills away, Far off from the gates of gold— Away on the mountains wild and bare, Away from the tender Shepherd's care."

Mental processes are strangely dualistic, and it not unfrequently happens that while one is consciously intent upon a certain train of thought, some secret cunning current of association sets in vibration the coil of ideas locked in the chambers of memory, and long forgotten images leap forth, startling in their pristine vividness.

Absorbed by the text she was illustrating, the artist insensibly followed lines she deemed imaginary, yet when the sketch was completed, the ensemble suddenly confronted her as a miniature reproduction of a very distant scene, that had gladdened her childish heart in the blessed by-gone. Far away from the beaten track of travel, in a sunny cleft of the Pistoian Apennines, she saw the white fleeces grouped under vast chestnuts, the flash of copper buckets plunged by two peasant women into a gurgling fountain, the curly head of Bertie bowed over the rude stone basin, as he gayly coaxed the bearers to let him drink from the beautiful burnished copper; the rocky terraces cut in the beetling cliffs above, where dark ruby-red oleanders flouted the sky with fragrant banners; and the pathetic face of a vagrant ewe tangled among vines, high on a jagged ledge, bleating for the lamb asleep under the chestnuts down in the dell.

Across the chasm of years floated the echo of the tinkling bell, that told where cows climbed in search of herbage; the singular rhythmic cadence of the trescone, danced in a neighboring vineyard; the deep, mellow, lingering tones of a monastery bell, rung by hermit hands in a gray tower on a mountain eyry, that looked westward upon the sparkling blue mirror of the Mediterranean.

Then she was twelve years old, dreaming glorious midsummer day-dreams, as she wandered with parents and brother on one of her father's sketching tours through unfrequented nooks; now—?

A petulant cry, emphasized by the baby hand tugging at the hem of her dress skirt, recalled Beryl's attention; and as she looked down at the waif, whom the chaplain had christened "Dovie" on the day of her mother's burial, the little one held up her arms.

"So tired, Dulce? You can't be hungry; you must want your nap. There don't fret, baby girl. I will take you directly."

She stepped down, turned the side of the blackboard that contained the sketch to the wall; lowered the sash which she had raised to admit fresh air, and lifted the child from the floor. Approaching the figure who sat motionless as a statue of woe, she laid a hand on the drooping shoulder.

"Shall I help you down the steps?"

"No, I'll stay here a while. This is the only place where I can get courage enough to pray. Couldn't you leave her—the child—with me? It has been years since I could bear the sight of one. I hated children, because my heart was so black—so bitter; but now, I yearn toward this little thing. I am so starved for the kiss of—of—," she swept her hand across her throat, where a sob stifled her.

"Certainly, if she will stay contentedly. See whether she will come to you."

At sight of the extended arms, the baby shrank closer to Beryl, nestled her head under the girl's chin, and put up her lower lip in ominous protest. With an indescribably mournful gesture of surrender, the childless mother sank back in the corner of the bench.

"I don't wonder she is afraid; she knows—everybody, everything knows I killed my baby—my own boy, who slept for nearly four years on my heart—oh!—"

"Hush—she was frightened by your crying. She is sleepy now, but when she has had her nap, and wakes good-humored, I will fill her bottle, and bring her down to you. Try not to torment yourself by dwelling upon a distressing past, which you cannot undo; but by prayer anchor your soul in God's pardoning mercy. When all the world hoots and stones us, God is our 'sure refuge'."

"That promise is to pure hearts and innocent hands; not to such as I am, steeped to the lips in crime—black, black—"

"No. One said: 'The whole need not a physician; but they that are sick.' Your soul is sick unto death; claim the pledged cure. Yonder I have copied the hymn for to-morrow's lesson. While you sit here, commit it to memory; and the Shepherd will hear your cry."

Glancing back from the chapel door, she saw that the miserable woman had bowed her face in her hands, and with elbows supported on her knees, was swaying back and forth in a storm of passionate sobs.

"O! my beautiful baby, my angel Max, pray for mother now. Max—Max—there is no 'Sweet By and By'—for mother—"

Hurrying from the wail of anguish that no human agency could lighten, Beryl carried the orphan across the yard, and up the stairs leading to the corridor, whence she was allowed egress at will. She noticed casually, signs of suppressed excitement among some of the convicts, who were lounging in groups, enjoying the half holiday, and three or four men stood around the under-warden who was gesticulating vivaciously; but at her approach he lowered his voice, and she lived so far aloof from the jars and gossip of the lower human strata, that the suspicious indications failed to arouse any curiosity.

The southwest angle of the building was exposed fully to the force of the afternoon sun, and the narrow cell was so hot that Beryl opened the door leading into the corridor, in order to create a draught through the opposite window.

The tired child was fretfully drowsy, but with the innate perversity of toddling babyhood, resented and resisted every effort to soothe her to sleep. Refusing to lie across the nurse's lap, the small tyrant clambered up, wrapped her arms about her neck, and finally Beryl rose and walked up and down, humming softly Chopin's dreamy "Berceuse"; while the baby added a crooning accompaniment that grew fainter and intermittent until the blue eyes closed, one arm fell, and the thumb was plunged between the soft full lips.

Warily the nurse laid her down in a cradle, which consisted of an oval basket mounted on roughly fashioned wooden rockers, and drawing it close to the table, Beryl straightened the white cross-barred muslin slip that was too short to cover the rosy dimpled feet; and smoothed the flossy tendrils of yellow hair crumpled around the lovely face.

The Sister of Charity, who, in the darkest hours of the pestilence had shrouded the poor young mother, did not forget the human waif astray in the world; but having secured a home for it in an "asylum," to which she promised it should be removed so soon as all danger of carrying contagion was over, had appointed the ensuing Monday on which to bear it away from the gloomy precincts, where sinless life had dawned in disgrace and degradation. This pretty toy, dowered with an immortal soul, stained by an inherited criminal strain, had appealed to the feminine tenderness in Beryl's nature, and she stood a moment, lost in admiration of the rounded curves and dainty coloring.

"Poor little blossom. Nobody's baby! A lily bud adrift on a dead sea of sin. Dovie—Eve Werneth's child—but you will always be to me Dulce, my pretty clinging Dulce, my velvet-eyed cherub model."

Turning away, she bathed her face and hands, and leaned for a while against the southern window; listening to the exultant song of a red bird hovering near his brooding brown mate, to the soothing murmur of the distant falls, borne in on the wings of the thievish June breeze that had rifled some far-off garden of the aroma of honeysuckle. The current of air had swung the door back, leaving only a hand's breadth of open space, and while she sang to the baby, her own voice had drowned the sound of footsteps in the corridor.

On the whitewashed wall of the cell, a sheet of drawing paper had been tacked, and taking her crayons, Beryl returned to the cradle, changed the position of the child's left hand, and approaching the almost completed sketch on the wall, retouched the outline of the sleeping figure. Now and then she paused in her work, to look down at the golden lashes sweeping the slumber-flushed cheeks, and pondering the mystery of the waif's future, she chanted in a rich contralto voice, the solemn "Reproaches" of Gounod's "Redemption."

"Oh, my vineyard, come tell me why thy grapes are bitter? What have I done, my People? Wherein hast thou been wronged?"

For weeks the elaboration of this sketch had employed every moment which was not demanded for the execution of her allotted daily task in the convict workroom; and knowing that on Monday she would be bereft of her pretty model, she had redoubled her exertions to complete it.

Beside a bier knelt a winged figure, in act of stealing the rigid form, and to the awful yet strangely beautiful face of the messenger of gloom, she had given the streaming hair, the sunken, cavernous but wonderfully radiant eyes of Moritz Retzsch's weird image of Death. A white butterfly fluttered upward, and in mid-air—neither descending nor drifting, but waiting—poised on outspread pinions, hovered the Angel of the Resurrection holding out his hands. Behind and beneath the Destroyer, rolled dense shadows, and all the light in this picture rayed out from the plumes above, and fell like a glory on the baby's face.

Cut off from all congenial companionship, thrown upon her own mental resources, the prisoner had learned to live in an ideal world; and her artistic tastes proved an indestructible heritage of comfort, while memory ministered lavishly with images from the crowded realm of aesthetics. Victorious over the stony limitations of dungeon walls and dungeon discipline, fetterless imagination soared into the kingdom of beauty, and fed her lonely soul, as Syrian ravens fed God's prophet.

Fourteen months had passed since Mr. Dunbar walked away from this cell, after the interview relative to Gen'l Darrington's will; and though his longing to see the prisoner had driven him twice to the entrance of the chapel, whence he heard the marvellously sweet voice, and gazed at the figure before the organ, no word was exchanged.

To-day, with his hand on the bolt of the door, and his heart in his eyes, he leaned against the facing, and through the opening studied the occupant of the cell that held the one treasure which fate had denied him.

The ravages of disease, the blemish of acute physical suffering had vanished; the clear pallor of her complexion, the full white throat, the rounded contour of the graceful form, bespoke complete restoration of all the vital forces; and never had she appeared so incomparably beautiful.

Oppressed by the heat, she had pushed back the hair from her temples, and though hopeless sadness reigned over the profound repose of her features, the expression of her eyes told that the dream of the artist had borne her beyond surrounding ills.

Where the button of her blue homespun dress fastened the collar, she wore a sprig of heliotrope and a cluster of mignonette, from the shallow box in the window-ledge where they grew together.

How long he stood there, surrendering himself to the happiness of watching the woman whom, against his will, he loved with such unreasoning and passionate fervor, Mr. Dunbar never knew; but a sudden recollection of the face printed on the glass, the face, beautiful as fabled Hylas—of the man for whose sake she was willing to die—stung him like an adder's bite; and setting his teeth hard, he rapped upon the door held ajar; then threw it open.

At sight of him, her arm, lifted to the sketch, fell; the crayon slipped from her nerveless fingers, and a glow rich as the heart of some red June rose stained her cheeks.

126

As he stepped toward her, she leaned against the wall, and swiftly drew the baby's cradle between them. He understood, and for a moment recoiled.

"You barricade yourself as though I were some loathsome monster! Are you afraid of me?"

"What is there left to fear? Have you spared any exertion to accomplish that which you believe would overwhelm me with sorrow?"

"You cannot forgive my rejection of the overtures for a compromise wrung from you by extremity of dread, when I started to Dakota?"

"That rejection freed me from a self-imposed, galling promise; and hence I forgive all, because of the failure of your journey."

"Suppose I have not failed?"

She caught her breath, and the color in her cheeks flickered.

"Had you succeeded, I should not have been allowed so long the comparative mercy of suspense."

"Am I so wantonly cruel, think you, that I gloat over your sufferings as a Modoc at sight of the string of scalps dangling at his pony's neck?"

"When the spirit of revenge is unleashed, Tiberius becomes a law unto himself."

He leaned forward, and his voice was freighted with tenderness that he made no attempt to disguise.

"Once after that long swoon in the court-room, when I held your hand, you looked at me without shrinking, and called me Tiberius. Again, when for hours I sat beside your cot, watching the crisis of your first terrible illness, you opened your eyes and held out your hand, saying: 'Have you come for me, Tiberius?' Why have you told me you were at the mercy of Tiberius?"

Hitherto she had avoided looking at him, and kept her gaze upon the sleeping child, but warned by the tone that made her heart throb, she bravely lifted her eyes.

"When next you write to your betrothed, ask her to go to the Museo Chiaramonti while in Rome, and standing before the crowned Tiberius, she will fancy her future husband welcomes her. Your wife will need no better portrait of you than a copy of that head."

Into his eyes leaped the peculiar glow that can be likened unto nothing but the clear violet flame dancing over a bed of burning anthracite coal, and into his voice an exultant ring:

"Meantime, like my inexorable prototype, 'I hold a wolf by the ears'. Shall I tell you my mission here?"

"As it appears I am indeed always at the mercy of Tiberius, your courtesy savors of sarcasm."

"Oh, my stately white rose! My Rosa Alba, I will see to it, that no polluting hand lays a grasp on you. My errand should entitle me to a more cordial reception, for I bring you good news. Will you lay your hand in mine just once, while I tell you?"

He extended his open palm, but she shook her head and smiled sadly.

"In this world no good news can ever come to me."

"Do you know that recently earnest efforts have been made to induce the Governor to pardon you? That I have just returned from a visit to him?"

"I was not aware of it; but I am grateful for your effort in my behalf."

"I was disappointed. The pardon was not granted. Since then, fate, who frowned so long upon you, has come to your rescue. The truth has been discovered, proclaimed; and I came here this afternoon with an order for your release. For you the prison doors and gates stand open. You are as free as you were that cursed day when first you saw me and robbed my life of peace."

For a moment she looked at him bewildered; then a great dread drove the blood from her lips, and her voice shook.

"What truth has been discovered?"

"The truth that you are innocent has been established to the entire satisfaction of judge and jury, prosecution and Governor, sheriff, warden, and you are free. Not pardoned for that which all the world knows now you never committed; but acquitted without man's help, by the discovery of a fact which removes every shadow of suspicion from your name. You are at liberty, owing no thanks to human mercy; vindicated by a witness subpoenaed by the God of justice, in whom you trusted—even to the end."

"Witness? What witness? You do not mean that you have hunted down—"

She paused, and her white face was piteous with terror, as pushing away the cradle she came close to him.

"I have seen the face of the man who killed Gen'l Darrington."

She threw up her arms, crossing them over her head.

"O, my God! Have I suffered in vain? Shall I be denied the recompense? After all my martyrdom, must I lose the one hope that sustained me?"

Despite the rage which the sight of her suffering woke within his heart, he could not endure to witness it.

"Can you find no comfort in release? No joy in the consciousness of your triumphant vindication?"

"None! If you have robbed me of that which is all I care for on earth, what solace can I find in release? Vindication? What is the opinion of the world to me? Oh! how have I ever wronged you, that you persecute me so vindictively, that you stab the only comfort life can ever hold for me?"

"And you love him so insanely, that to secure his safety, existence here in this moral sty is sweet in comparison with freedom unshared with him? Listen! That belief stirs the worst elements in my nature; it swings the whip of the furies. For your own sake, do not thrust your degrading madness upon my notice. I have labored to liberate you; have subordinated all other aims to this, and now, that I have come to set you free, you repulse and spurn me!"

127

She was so engrossed by one foreboding, that it was evident she had not even heard him, as moving to the bench in front of the window she sat down, shivering. Her black brows contracted till they met, and the strained expression of her eyes told that she was revolving some possibility of succor.

"Where did you see my—my—?"

"Not in Dakota mines, where I expected to find him."

"Mr. Dunbar." She pointed to the chair at her side.

He shook his head, but approached and stood before her.

"I am waiting to hear you."

"I sent you a telegram, promising information that would have prevented that journey."

"It failed to reach me."

Unconsciously she was wringing her hands as her thoughts whirled.

"I will tell you something now, if you will promise me that no harm shall—"

He laughed scornfully.

"As if I had anything to learn concerning that cowardly villain! Thanks for your confidence, which comes much too late."

"You do not know that—"

"Yes, I know all I want to know; more than you shall ever tell me, and I decline to hear a confession that, in my eyes, defiles you; that would only drive me to harsh denunciation of your foul idol. Moreover, I will not extort by torture what you have withheld so jealously. Do not wring your hands so desperately. You are goaded to confession now, because you believe that I have secured your lover? Take courage, he has not yet been arrested; he is still a wanderer hiding from retribution."

She sprang up, trembling.

"But you said you had seen his face?"

"Yes, and I have come to take you where you can identify that face?"

"Then, he is dead." She covered her face with her hands.

"No, I wish to God he was dead! Sit down. I will not see you suffer such agony. He is safe for the present. If you will try to think of yourself for a moment, and pay me the compliment of listening, I will explain. Do you recollect that during the storm on the night of the murder the lightning was remarkably vivid and severe?"

"Yes; can I ever forget any details of that night? Go on."

"Do you recall the position of the glass door on the west veranda; and also that the crimson drapery or curtain was drawn aside?"

"I recall it distinctly because, while Gen'l Darrington was reading my mother's letter, I looked out through the glass at the chrysanthemums blooming in the garden."

"That door was almost opposite the chimney, and the safe or vault in the wall was very near the fireplace. It appears that when the chloroform failed to stupefy Gen'l Darrington, he got up and seized one of the andirons on the hearth, and attacked the thief who was stealing his money. While they were struggling in front of the vault, a burst of electricity, some peculiarly vivid flash of lightning, sent by fate, by your guardian angel, it may have been by God himself—photographed both men, and the interior of the room on the wide glass panel of that door. Forms, faces, features, even the pattern of the cloth coat, are printed plainly there, for the whole world to study. The murderer and the victim in mortal combat over the tin box. Accident—shall I say Providence—unexpectedly brought this witness to light. The curtain so long looped back, was recently lowered, and when, two days ago, the outside blinds were opened, there lay your complete vindication. Crowds have seen it; the newspaper issued an 'extra', and so general was the rejoicing, that a public demonstration would have been made here at the gaol, had not Churchill and I harangued the people and assured them it would only annoy and embarrass you. So you are free. Free to shake the dust of X—forever from your feet; and it must comfort your proud soul to know that you do not owe your liberty to the mercy of a community which wronged you. I forbade Singleton to tell you, to allow any premature hint to reach you; for I claimed the privilege of bringing the glad tidings. Last night I spent in that room at 'Elm Bluff', guarding that door; and the vigil was cheered by the picture hope drew, that when I came to-day you would greet me kindly; would lay your dear hands in mine, and tell me that, at least, gratitude would always keep a place for me warm in your noble heart. I have my recompense in the old currency of scorn. It were well for you if you had shown me your hatred less plainly; now I shall indulge less hesitation in following the clue the lightning lays in my grasp. I warn you that your release only expedites his arrest; for you can never pass beyond my surveillance; and the day you hasten to him, seals his fate. Long imprisoned doves, when set free, fly straight to their distant mates; so—take care—lest the hawk overtake both."

Looking up at him, listening almost breathlessly to the tale of a deliverance that involved new peril for Bertie, the color came slowly back to her blanched face, and her parted lips quivered.

"If the picture means anything, it proves that Gen'l Darrington made the assault with the brass andiron, and in the struggle that followed, the man you saw might have killed him in self defence."

"When he is brought to trial in X—he shall never be allowed the benefit of your affectionate supposition. I promise you, that I will annihilate your tenderly devised theory."

He ground his teeth in view of the transparent fact, that she was too intently considering the bearing of the revelation upon the safety of another, to heed the thought of her own escape from bondage.

The little cluster of flowers fastened at her throat had become loosened, and fell unnoticed into her lap. He stooped, picked them up, and straightened them on his palm. When his eyes returned to Beryl, she had bowed her face in her shielding hands.

How little he dreamed that she was silently praying for strength to deny the cry of her own beating heart, and to keep him from making shipwreck of the honor which she supposed was still pledged to Leo! Security for her brother, and unswerving loyalty to the absent woman who had befriended her in the darkest hours of the accusation, were objects difficult to accomplish simultaneously; yet at every hazard she would struggle on. Because she had learned to love so well this man, who was the promised husband of another, conscience made her merciless to her own disloyalty.

Mr. Dunbar laid on the bench a small package sealed in yellow paper.

"Knowing that your detention here has necessarily forfeited all the industrial engagements by which you maintained yourself, before you came South, I have been requested to ask your acceptance of this purse, which contains sufficient money to defray your expenses until you resume your art labors. It is an offering from your twelve jurors."

"No—no. I could never touch it. Tell them for me that I am not vindictive. I know they did the best they could for me, in view of the evidence. Tell them I am grateful for their offer, but I cannot accept it. I—"

"You imagine I am one of the generous contributors? Be easy; I have not offered you a cent. I am merely the bearer of the gift, or rather the attempt at restitution. Your refusal will grieve them, and add to the pangs of regret that very justly afflict them at present."

"I have some money which Doctor Grantlin collected for my Christmas card. He retained only a portion of the amount, and sent me the remainder. Mr. Singleton keeps it for me, and it is all that I need now."

"The purse contains also a ticket to New York, as it has been supposed that you would desire to return there at once."

"Take all back, with my earnest thanks. I prefer to owe X—only the remembrance of the great kindness which some few have shown me. The officers here have been uniformly considerate and courteous to me; Mr. and Mrs. Singleton will ever be very dear to me for numberless kind deeds; and Sister Serena was a staff of strength during that frightful black week of the trial."

She paused, and her voice betrayed something of the tumult at her heart, as while a sudden wave of scarlet overflowed her cheeks, she rose and held out both hands.

"Mr. Dunbar, if I have seemed unappreciative of your great exertions in my behalf, it is merely because there are some matters which I can never explain in this world. One thing I ask you to believe when I am gone. I will never, so long as I live, cease to remember the debt I owe you. I am and shall be inexpressibly grateful to you, and whenever I think of my terrible sojourn here, be sure I shall recall tenderly— oh! how tenderly! the two friends who trusted and believed in my innocence, when all the world denounced me; the two who generously clung to me when public opinion branded me as an outcast—you two—my best friends, you and Miss Gordon. It makes me proud and happy to know in this hour of my vindication, that in her, and in your good opinion, I needed none. Out of your united lives, let me pass as a fleeting gray shadow."

"Out of my life you can never pass. Into it you have brought disappointment, humiliation, and a keenness of suffering such as I never imagined I was capable of enduring; and some recompense I will have. You hope to plunge into the vortex of a great city, where you can elude observation and obliterate all traces. Do not cherish the ghost of such a delusion. Go where you may, but I give you fair warning, you cannot escape me; and the day you meet that guilty vagabond, you betray him to the scouts of justice."

He held her hands in a close, warm clasp, and a flush crossed his brow, as he looked down into her quivering face where a smile which he could not interpret, seemed only a challenge.

"Would a generous man, worthy of Miss Gordon, harass and persecute a very unhappy and unfortunate woman, who asks at his hands only to be forgotten completely, to be left in peace?"

"I lay no claim to generosity, and, where you are concerned, I am supremely selfish. Miss Gordon has no need of your championship; she is quite equal to redressing her own wrongs, when the necessity presents itself. You are struggling to free your hands, so be it. I have a close carriage at the gate, and to make assurance doubly sure, I have come to take you to 'Elm Bluff'; to show you the face, and ask you to identify it. Understand me, I will harass you with no questions; nor will I intrude upon you there. I have ordered the grounds cleared, have posted police to prevent the possibility of any occurrence unpleasant to you; and all I ask is, that alone, you will examine this witness, produced so strangely for your justification. I shall wait for you in the rose garden, and if you can come down from that gallery and tell me that the face is unknown to you, that the man photographed in the act of stealing, is a stranger, is not the man you love so well that you bore worse than death to save him from punishment, then I will give up the quest; and you may flee unwatched to the ends of the earth."

"Never again will I see that place which has blasted every hope that life held for me."

"Not even to clear away aspersion from his beloved name?"

"I pray God, his beloved and sacred name may never be associated with a crime so awful."

"You will not go to see the face? Remember, I shall ask you neither yea nor nay. I shall need only to look once into your eyes, after you have seen the Gorgon. Beryl, my white rose! Are you ashamed to show me your idol's face?"

"I will never go to 'Elm Bluff'."

"It is no longer necessary. You know already the features printed there, and your avoidance stamps them with infamy. How can your lofty soul, your pure heart, tolerate a creature so craven, so vile?"

"We love not always whom we would, or should, were choice permitted us; and to whom I have given my heart, my whole deep heart, you shall never learn."

The mournful smile that lent such wistful loveliness to her flushed face, seemed to him merely a renewed defiance.

"I bide my time, knowing it will surely come. You are free, but be careful. Once when you lay upon the brink of the grave, unconscious, I knelt at your side and took you in my arms; laid your head on my heart, felt your cheek touch mine. Then and there I made a covenant with my soul; and no other man's arms shall ever enfold you. Ah, my Rosa Alba! I could dig your grave with my own hands, sooner than see that thief claim you. I am a proud man, and you have dragged me through the slough of humiliation, but to-day, as I bid you good-bye, I realize how one felt, who looking at the bust of him she loved supremely, said with her last breath: 'Voila mon univers, mon espoir, et mes dieux!' How soon we meet again depends solely on your future course. You know the conditions; and I promise you I will not swerve one iota."

He took her hand, drew it across his cheek, laid it on his lips; and a moment later walked away, with the faded flowers folded close in his palm.

CHAPTER XXIX.

Conveniently contiguous to the busy centre of a wide and populous city, situated on the shore of one of those great inland fresh-water seas, whose lake line girdles the primeval American upheaval, the Laurentian rocks,—stands in the middle of a square, enclosed by a stone coping and an iron railing, a stately pile of brick and granite several stories high, flanked by wings that enclose in the rear a spacious court. The facade was originally designed in the trabeated style, and still retained its massive entrance, with straight, grooved lintel over the door which was adorned by four round columns; but subsequent additions reflected the fluctuations of popular architectural taste, in the later arched windows, the broad oriel with its carved corbel, and in the new eastern wing, that had flowered into a Tudor tower with bulbous cupola. The strip of velvet sward between the street and the house entrance, was embossed with brilliant coleus set in the form of anchors; and a raised border, running the entire length under the windows of the basement, was ablaze with geraniums of various hues.

On a granite pediment above the portico, a large bronze anchor was supported, and beneath it was cut, in projecting letters: "The Umilta Anchorage".

In front of the building ran a broad, paved boulevard; in the rear, the enclosure was bounded by a stone wall, overgrown with ivy, and built upon the verge of the blue lake, whose waves broke against the base, and rolled away in the distance beyond the northern horizon.

Fully in accord with the liberal eclecticism that characterized its exterior, was the wide-eyed, deep, tender-hearted charity which, ignoring all denominational barriers, opened its doors in cordial welcome to worthy, homeless women, whom misfortune had swept away from family moorings, and whose clean hands and pure hearts sought some avenue to honest work. The institution was a memorial erected and endowed by a wealthy man, whose only child Umilta, just crossing the threshold of womanhood, had been lost in a sudden storm on the lake; whose fair, drowned face had been washed ashore just below the stone wall, and whose statue stood, guarded by marble angels, in the small chapel in the centre of the building, which was designed as an enduring monument to commemorate her untimely fate, and perpetuate her name.

Divided into various industrial departments, the "Anchorage" was maintained almost entirely by the labor of its inmates; and it had rarely been found necessary to draw from the reserve endowment fund, that was gradually accumulating for future contingencies.

Trained nurses, trained housekeepers were furnished on demand; lace curtains mended, laundered; dainty lingerie of every description, from a baby's wardrobe to a bride's trousseau; ornamental needle-work on all fabrics; artificial flowers, card engraving, artistic designs for upholstering, menus, type-writing, all readily supplied to customers; and certain confectionery put up in pretty boxes made by the inmates, and bearing the "Anchor" stamp. A school of drawing, etching, painting, and embroidery attracted many pupils; and a few pensioners who had grown too infirm and dim-eyed for active work, had a warm, bright room where they knitted stockings and underwear of various kinds.

At one end of the long refectory was emblazoned on the wall: "For whosoever shall do the will of my Father which is in Heaven, the same is my brother and sister and mother." At the other: "Bear ye one another's burdens." The chapel contained no pulpit, but on a marble altar stood a life-size figure of a woman clinging to the cross: and on the walls hung paintings representing the Crucifixion, the Descent, the Resurrection and the Mater Dolorosa; while in a niche at the extremity, behind the altar, an Ecce Homo of carved ivory was suspended above a gilt cross, and just beneath it glittered the motto "Faith, Hope, Charity". Every morning and evening the band of women gathered here, and recited the Apostles' Creed, and the Lord's Prayer; but on Sabbath the members attended the church best suited to their individual tenets.

The infirmary was a cheerful, airy room, and here professional nurses were trained under the guidance of visiting physicians; and in an adjoining kitchen were taught to prepare the articles of diet usually belonging to the regimen of sick rooms.

Widows, maidens, Catholics, Protestants, admitted from the age of eighteen to forty, these "Umilta Sisters" were received on probation for eighteen months; then entered upon a term of five years, subject to renewal at will; bound by specified rules, but no irrevocable vow. Yielding implicit obedience to the matron, elected by themselves every four years—subject to approval and ratification by the Chapter of Trustees, they were recognized wherever they went by the gray garb, the white aprons, and snowy mob caps peculiar to the institution.

Fashionable women patronized and fondled the "Anchorage", for much the same reason that led them to pamper their pugs; and since the Chapter of Trustees consisted of men of wealth and prominence, their wives, as magnates in le beau monde, set the seal of "style" upon articles manufactured there, by ordering quilted satin afghans with anchors of pansies embroidered in the centre, for their baby carriages; painted tea gowns; favors for a "German", or fans and bonbonnieres for birthday parties.

If children of the Brahmin caste of millionairdom were seized by the Pariah ills of measles, or chicken-pox, or mumps, it was deemed quite as imperatively the duty of doting parents to provide an "Anchorage" nurse, as to secure an eminent physician, and the most costly brand of condensed milk. In the name of sweet charity, gay gauzy-winged butterflies of fashion harnessed themselves in ropes of roses, and dragged the car of benevolence; as painted papillons drew chariots of goddesses on ancient classic walls; so in the realm of social economy the ubiquitous law of correlation of industrial force—of conservation of energy—transmuted the arrested labor of the rich and idle into the fostering heat that stimulated the working poor.

Scarcely a month previous to her unexpected release from prison, Beryl had received a letter from Doctor Grantlin, enclosing one addressed to "Sister Ruth, Matron of Anchorage". He wrote that his daughter's health demanded some German baths; and on the eve of sailing, he desired to secure for the prisoner a temporary refuge, should the efforts which he had heard were made to obtain her pardon, prove successful. As a nephew of the founder, and a cousin of the young lady for whom the "Anchorage" was intended as a lasting memorial, he had always been accorded certain privileges by the trustees; and the letter, if presented to the matron, would insure at least an entrance into the haven of rest, until the prisoner could mature some plan for her future.

Spurred away from X—by the dread of another interview with the man whom she had assiduously shunned, and of being required to visit "Elm Bluff" and scrutinize the accusing picture, Beryl had shrouded herself in her heavy mourning, and fled from the scene of her suffering, on the 3 A.M. train Sunday morning; ten hours after receiving the certificate of her discharge. Shrinking from observation, she refused Mr. Singleton permission to accompany her to the station house, and bade him good-bye three squares distant; promising to write soon to his still absent wife, and assured by him that a farewell letter of affectionate gratitude should be promptly delivered to Dyce. Fortunately a stranger stood in the office and sold her a ticket; and in the same corner, where twenty months before she had knelt during the storm, she waited once more for the sound of the train. How welcome to her the shuddering shriek that tore its way through the dewy silence of the star-lit summer night, and she hurried out, standing almost on the rails, in her impatience to depart.

Several travellers were grouped near a pile of luggage awaiting the train, but as it rolled swiftly in and jarred itself to a standstill, she saw even through her crape veil a well known figure, leaning against an iron post that held an electric lamp. She sprang up the steps leading to the platform, and took the first vacant seat, which was in front of an open window.

The silvery radiance from the globe just opposite, streamed in, and her heart seemed to cease beating as the tall form moved forward and taking off his hat, stood at the side of the car. Neither spoke. But when the brass bell rang its signal and the train trembled into motion, a hand was thrust in, and dropped upon her lap a cluster of exquisite white roses, with one scarlet passion flower glowing in the centre.

During the three days spent in New York, Beryl's wounds bled afresh, and she felt even more desolate than while sheltered behind prison walls. The six-storied tenement house where she had last seen her mother's face, and kissed her in final farewell, had been demolished to make room for a new furniture warehouse. Strange nurses in the hospital could tell her nothing concerning the last hours of the beloved dead; and the only spot in the wide western world that seemed to belong to her, was a narrow strip of ground in a remote corner of the great cemetery, where a green mound held its square granite slab, bearing the words "Ellice Darrington Brentano."

With her face bowed upon that stone, the lonely woman had wept away the long hours of an afternoon that decided her plan for the future.

Dr. Grantlin had gone abroad for an indefinite period, and no one knew the contents of his last letter. In New York her movements would be subject to the SURVEILLANCE she most desired to escape; but in that distant city where the "Anchorage" was situated, she might disappear, leaving no more trace than that of a stone dropped in some stormy, surging sea.

To find Bertie and reclaim him, was the only goal of hope life held for her, and to accomplish this, the first requisite was to effectually lose herself.

Anxious and protracted deliberation finally resulted in an advertisement, which she carried next morning to the "Herald" office, to be inserted for six months in the personal column, unless answered.

"BERTIE, IF YOU WANT THE LOST BUTTON WE BOUGHT AT LUCCA, WHEN CAN GIGINA HAND IT TO YOU IN ST. CATHERINE'S, CANADA?"

She wore her old blue bunting dress, and a faded blue veil when she delivered the notice at the office of the newspaper, and paid in advance the cost of its publication. Later in the same day, clad in her mourning garments, she went down to the Grand Central Depot and bought a railway ticket; and the night express bore her away on her long journey westward.

It was on the fourth of July, her twenty-first birthday, that she entered the reception room at the "Anchorage", and presented in conjunction with Doctor Grantlin's letter, a copy of the newspaper printed at X—, which contained an article descriptive of the discovery of the picture on the glass door; and expressive of the profound sympathy of the public for the prisoner so unjustly punished by incarceration.

For twenty years a resident of the institution, over which she had repeatedly presided, Sister Ruth was now a woman of fifty-five, whose white hair shone beneath her cap border like a band of spun silver, and whose yellowish, dim eyes seemed unnaturally large behind their spectacles. Thin and wrinkled, her face was nobly redeemed by a remarkably beautiful, patient mouth; and her angular, wiry figure, by small feet and very slender hands, where the veins rose like blue cords lacing ivory satin. Over the shoulders of her gray flannel dress was worn the distinctive badge of her office, a white mull handkerchief pleated surplice fashion into her girdle, whence hung by a silver chain a set of tablets; and the folds of mull were fastened at her throat by a silver anchor.

Having deliberately read letter and paper, she put the former in her pocket, and returned the latter with a stately yet graceful inclination of the head, that would have been creditable in Mdm. Recamier's salon.

"I have expected you for some weeks, an earlier letter from Doctor Grantlin having prepared me for your arrival; but it appears you have not been released from prison by the pardon he anticipated?"

"No, madam; the authorities who caused my arrest and imprisonment, considered the discovery of the printed door a complete refutation of the accusation against me, and ordered my release. I come here not as a pardoned criminal, but as an unfortunate victim of circumstantial evidence; acquitted of all suspicion by a circumstance even stranger than those which seemed to condemn me. In the darkest days of my desolation, Doctor Grantlin believed me innocent, honored me with his confidence and friendship, soothed my mother's dying hour; and he will rejoice to learn that acquittal anticipated the mockery of a pardon. Only his generous encouragement emboldened me to hope for a temporary shelter here."

"Then you have no desire to become a permanent resident?"

"At present, I shall be grateful if allowed to enjoy the privilege of hiding my sore heart for a while from the gaze of a world that has cruelly wronged me. I want to rest where wicked men and women do not pollute the air, where I can try to forget the horrors of convict life; and the rest I need is not idleness, it is labor of some kind that will so fully employ my hands and brain, that when I lie down at night my sad, aching heart and wounded soul can find balm in sleep. Locked at night into a dark cell has made existence for nearly eighteen months a mere hideous vigil, broken by fitful nightmare. To see only pure faces, to listen to sweet feminine voices that never knew the desecration of blasphemy, to exchange the grim, fetid precincts of a penitentiary for a holy haven such as this, is indeed a glimpse of paradise to a tortured spirit."

"Have you special reasons for wishing to shun observation?"

The dim eyes probed like some dull blade that tears the tissues.

"Yes, madam, special cause to want to be forgotten by the public, who have stared me at times almost to frenzy."

"You are an orphan, I am told; with no living relatives in America."

"I am an orphan; and think I have no relative in the United States."

"In the very peculiar circumstances that surround and isolate you, I should imagine you would esteem it a great privilege to cast your lot here, and become one of the permanently located Sisters of the 'Anchorage'. Ours is a noble and consecrated mission."

"Knowing literally nothing of your institution, except that it is a hive of industrious good women, offering a home and honest work to homeless and innocent unfortunates, I could not pledge myself to a life which might not prove suitable on closer acquaintance. Take me in; give me employment that will prevent me from being a tax upon your hospitality and mercifully shelter me from pitiless curiosity and gossip."

"Even were our sympathies not enlisted in your behalf, Doctor Grantlin's request would insure your admission, at least for a season. Where is your luggage?"

"I have only a trunk, for which I have retained the railway check, until I ascertained your willingness to receive me."

"Give it to me."

She crossed the room and pressed the knob of a bell on the opposite wall. Almost simultaneously a door opened, and to a stout, middle-aged woman who appeared on the threshold, the matron gave instructions in an under tone.

Returning to the stranger, she resumed:

"I infer from the Doctor's letter, that you are a gifted person. In what lines do your talents run?"

"Perhaps I should not lay claim to talent, but I am, by grace of study, a good musician; and I draw and paint, at least with facility. At one time I supported my mother and myself by singing in a choir, but diphtheria closed that avenue of work. With the restoration of health, I think I have recovered my voice. I am an expert needle woman, and can embroider well, especially on fine linen."

"Do you feel competent to teach a class in 'water color', in our Art School? Our aquarelle Sister is threatened with amaurosis, and the oculist prohibits all work at present."

"You can form an opinion of my qualifications by examining some sketches which are in my trunk. I have furnished several designs for the 'Society of Decorative Art', and have sold a number of painted articles at the Woman's Exchange."

"Then I think you have only to step into a vacant niche, and supply a need which was beginning to perplex us. During the latter part of September, an International Scientific Congress will be held in this city, and one of our patrons, Mr. Brompton, who expects to entertain the distinguished foreign delegates, has given us an order for dinner cards for eight courses, and each set for twenty-four covers. As nearly as we can comprehend the design, his intention is to represent the order of creation in fish, game, fruits and flowers; and each card will illustrate some special era in geology and zoology. The cream and ices set are expected to show the history of Polar regions as far as known, and at the conclusion of the banquet, each guest will be presented with a velvet smoking cap, to which must be attached a card representing 'scientific soap-bubbles pricked by the last scientists' junta'. Now while the 'Anchorage's' cultured art standard claims to be as high as any, East, we should scarcely venture to fill this order, had not two of the professors in our University, promised to map out the order, and furnish some dots in the way of engravings, which will aid the accomplishment of the work; and we are particularly desirous of pleasing our patron, from whom the 'Anchorage' expects a bequest. If you think you can successfully undertake a portion of this order, given us by Mr. Brompton, we shall make you doubly welcome."

"I think I may safely promise satisfactory work in the line you designate; and at least, I shall be grateful for the privilege of making the attempt."

"You are aware, I presume, that all inmates of the 'Anchorage' are required to wear its regulation uniform."

"I shall be very glad to don it; hoping it may possess some spell to exorcise memories of the last uniform I wore; the blue homespun of penitentiary convicts."

"You must try to forget all that. The 'Anchorage' gates shut fast on the former lives we led; here we dwell in a busy present, hoping to secure a blessed future. Come with me to the cutting room, and be measured for your flannel uniform; then one of the Sisters will show you to your own cell in this consecrated bee-hive, which you will find as peaceful as its name implies."

The first story contained the reception rooms, chapel, schoolroom, apartments for the display of sample articles manufactured; the refectory, kitchen and laundry; and one low wide room with glass on three sides, where orchids and carnations, the floral specialties of the institution, were grown. On the second floor were various workrooms, supplied with materials required for the particular fabric therein manufactured or ornamented; and cut off from communication, was the east wing, used exclusively as an infirmary, and provided with its separate kitchen and laundry. The third story embraced the dormitory, a broad, lofty apartment divided by carved scroll work and snowy curtains, into three sets of sleeves running the entire length of the floor; separated by carpeted aisles, and containing all the articles of furniture needed by each occupant. On the ceiling directly over every bed, was inscribed in gilt letters, some text from the Bible, exhorting to patience, diligence, frugality, humility, gentleness, obedience, cheerfulness, honesty, truthfulness and purity; and mid-way the central aisle, where a chandelier swung, two steps led to a raised desk, whence at night issued the voice of the reader, who made audible to all the occupants the selected chapter in the Bible. At ten o'clock a bell was rung by the Sister upon whom devolved the duty of acting as night watch; then lights were extinguished save in the infirmary. This common dormitory was reserved for Sisters who had spent at least five years in the building; and to probationers were given small rooms on the second story of the west wing.

The third story of the same wing fronted north, and served as a studio where all designs were drawn and painted; and upon its walls hung pictures in oil and water color, engravings, vignettes, and all the artistic odds and ends given or lent by sympathetic patrons.

Each story was supplied with bath-rooms, and the entire work of the various departments was performed by the appointed corps of inmates; the Sisters of the wash tub, and of the broom brigade, being selected for the work best adapted to their physical and intellectual development.

Visitors lingered longest in the great kitchen with its arched recess where the range was fitted; where like organ pipes glittering copper boilers rose, and burnished copper measures and buckets glinted on the carved shelves running along one side. The adjoining pastry room was tiled with stone, furnished with counters covered with marble slabs, and with refrigerators built into the wall; and here the white-capped, white-aproned priestesses of pots, pans and pestles moved quietly to and fro, performing the labor upon which depended in great degree the usefulness of artificers in all other departments.

The refectory opened on a narrow terrace at the rear of the building, which was sodded with turf and starred with pansies and ox-eyed daisies, and on the wide, stone window sills sat boxes and vases filled with maiden-hair ferns and oxalis, with heliotrope and double white violets. Three lines of tables ran down this bright pretty room, and in the centre rose a spiral stair to a cushioned seat, where when "Grace" had been pronounced, the Reader for the day made selections from such volumes of prose or poetry as were deemed by the Matron elevating and purifying in influence; tonic for the soul, stimulant for the brain, balm for the heart.

Close to the rear wall overhanging the lake, ran a treillage of grape vines, and on the small grass sown plat of garden, belated paeonies tossed up their brilliant balls, as play-things for the wind that swept over the blue waves, breaking into a fringe of foam beyond the stone enclosure.

Except at meals, and during the last half hour in the dormitory, night and morning, no restriction of silence was imposed, and one hour was set apart at noon for merely social intercourse, or any individual scheme of labor. Busy, tranquil, cheerful, often merry, they endeavored to eschew evil thoughts; and cultivated that rare charity which makes each tolerant of the failings of the other, which broadens a sympathy that can excuse individual differences of opinion, and that consecrates the harmony of true home life.

The room assigned to Beryl was at the extremity of the second story, just beneath the studio; and as the north end of the wings was built at each corner into projections that were crowned with bell towers, this apartment had a circular oriel window, swung like a basket from the wall, and guarded by an iron balcony. Cool, quiet, restful as an oratory seemed the nest; with its floor covered by matting diapered in blue, its low, wide bedstead of curled maple, with snowy Marseilles quilt, and crisply fluted pillow cases; its book shelves hanging on the wall, surmounted by a copy in oil of Angelico's Elizabeth of Hungary, with rapt face upraised as she lifted her rose-laden skirt.

The lambrequins of blue canton flannel were bordered with trailing convolvulus in pink cretonne, and the diaphanous folds of white muslin curtains held in the centre an embroidered anchor which dragged inward, as the breeze rushed in through open windows. An arched recess in the wall, whence a door communicated with the adjoining chamber, was concealed by a portiere of blue that matched the lambrequins, and the alcove served as a miniature dressing-room, where the brass faucet emptied into a marble basin.

In this apartment the imperial sway of dull maroons, sullen Pompeiian reds, and sombre murky olives had never cast encroaching shadows upon the dainty brightness of tender rose and blue, nor toned down the silvery reflection of the great sea of waters that flashed under the sunshine like some vast shifting mirror.

Travel-worn and very weary, Beryl sat down by the window and looked out over the lake, that far as the eye could reach, lifted its sparkling bosom to the cloudless dim blue of heaven, effacing the sky line; dotted with sails like huge white butterflies, etched here and there with spectral, shadowy ship masts, overflown by gray gulls burnished into the likeness of Zophiels' pinions, as their wings swiftly dipped.

Driven by storms of adversity away from the busy world of her earlier youth, leaving the wrack of hopes behind, she had drifted on the chartless current of fate into this Umilta Sisterhood, this latter day Beguinage; where, provided with work that would furnish her daily bread, she could hide her proud head without a sense of shame. Doctor Grantlin, in compliance with her request, would keep the secret of her retreat; and surely here she might escape forever the scrutiny and the dangerous magnetism of the man who had irretrievably marred her fair, ambitious youth.

To-day, twenty-one, full statured in womanhood, prematurely scorched and scarred in spirit by fierce ordeals, she saw the pale ghost of her girlhood flitting away amid the ruins of the past; and knew that instead of making the voyage of life under silken sails gilded with the light, and fanned by the breath of love and happiness, she had been swept under black skies before a howling hurricane, into an unexpected port,—where, lashed to the deck with "torn strips of hope", she had finally moored a strained, dismasted barque in the "Anchorage", whence with swelling canvas and flying pennons no ships ever went forth.

A rush of grateful tears filled her tired eyes, and soothed by the consciousness of an inviolable security, her trembling lips moved in a prayer of thankfulness to God, upon whom she had stayed her tortured soul, grappling it to the blessed promise: "Lo, I am with you always. I will never leave you nor forsake you."

CHAPTER XXX.

"Why deny it, Leo? Let us at least be frankly realistic, and 'call a spade a spade' when we set ourselves to dig ditches, draining the stagnant pools of life. Each human being has a special goal toward which he or she strains, with nineteen chances out of twenty against reaching it in time; and if it be won, is it worth the race? With some of us it is love, ambition, mundane prosperity; with others, intellectual supremacy, moral perfection, exalted spirituality, sublimated altruism; but after all, in the final analysis, it is only hedonism! Each struggles with teeth and claws for that which gives the largest promise of pleasure to body, mind, or soul, as the individual happens to incline. To Sybarites the race is too short to be fatiguing, and the goal is only an ambuscade for satiety and ennui; to ascetics, the race course stretches to the borders of futurity, but even for them one form of pleasure, spiritual pleasure, lights up eternity. The thing we want, we want; not because of its orthodoxy, or its excellency or beauty PER SE; we want it because it gratifies some idiosyncratic craving of our threefold natures. The good things of this world are very adroitly and ingeniously labelled, but we rummage in the bonbonniere for a certain marron glace, and if it be not there, all the caramels in Venice, all the 'gluko' in Greece, all the rahatlicum in Turkey will not appease us."

With her arms thrown back, and clasped around the satin cushion crushed against her head and shoulders, Miss Cutting lay on a red plush divan in her father's picture gallery at home; and the swathing folds of a topaz-hued surah gown embroidered with scarlet poppies half concealed the feet that beat a tattoo on the polished oak floor.

"Then you have missed your marron glace?" answered Leo, turning from the contemplation of a new picture which Mr. Cutting had recently added to his collection.

"Of course. Do not all of us sooner or later? Where is yours? Safe under lock and key, or hanging on some crag, ripening for the confectioner; or filched by some stealthy white hand, devoured by some eager lips that smile derisively at you while they nibble?"

From beneath drooping lids, Alma's oblique glance noted the result of her Scipio Africanus' tactics.

"Alma, too intemperate and prolonged diet of sweets has ruined your digestion; has rendered you an ethical dyspeptic. A surfeit of sugar betrays itself in fermentation, and you have reached the stage of moral acidulation."

"Ah, don't drift into homiletics! I see your marron grows hard by the vineyard where sour grapes flourish. Leo, I am not so serenely proud as you, but a trifle more honest, and I have cried for my bonbon, never flouting its delicious flavor; hence, when I am ordered back to boiled milk and oatmeal, I make no feint to disguise my wry faces."

Alma's low, teasing laugh stung like some persistent buzzing insect, and a slight flush tinged her companion's cheek as she replied:

"Why plunge to the opposite extreme? You will starve on that porridge you are desperately preparing for yourself."

"What else remains? This world is a huge bazaar, a big church fair, and like other eager-eyed children I promptly set my heart on the great 'bisc' doll with its head turning coquettishly from side to side, singing snatches from 'La Grande Duchcsse', and clad like Sheba's queen! I stake all my pennies on a chance in the raffle, which has a 'consolation prize' hidden away from vulgar gaze. By and by the dice rattle, and over my head, quite out of my reach, is borne the coveted beauty (owned now by a girl I know), bowing and singing to the new owner, who exultantly exhibits her as she departs; and into my outstretched arms falls something hideous enough to play Medusa in a tableau, a rag baby with grinning Senegambian lips, rayless owlish eyes, and a concave nose whose nostrils suggest the Catacombs! Bitter rage and murderous fury possess me, but I am much too wise to show my tempers at the fair; so I hug my 'consolation prize', and get away as fast as possible with my treasure, and once safe from observation, box, deride, trample upon it, and toss it into the garret as suitable prey for dust, cobwebs and mildew! After a time, the keenness of the disappointment dulls, like all other human aches that do not kill, and by degrees I think less vindictively of the despised substitute. Finally comes a day, when all else failing to amuse me, I creep sheepishly into the attic and pick up the rejected, and persuade myself it is at least better than no doll at all, and forthwith adorn it with rags of finery; but the echoes of 'La Grande Duchesse' will always ring in my ears, and through the halo of tears I see ever and anon the prize beauty that was withheld. The two-edged sword in the diablerie of fate is, that we are ordained to fret after 'bisc,' when stuffed rags have been meted out as our share of the fair."

Leo drew a chair near the divan and seated herself; looking steadily into the velvety black eyes that instead of betraying hid, like a domino, the soul of their owner.

"Alma, better cross empty arms forever over empty heart, than mock your womanhood by acceptance of a 'consolation prize'."

"We all say that the day after the fair; but wait a few years as I have done; and like all your sisters in the ranks of the disappointed, you will ultimately crawl back to the attic and kiss the thick lips, and try to persuade yourself the nose is not so formidable, though certainly a trifle less classic than Antinous's! We set out with our eyes fixed on Vega, blazing above, and flaunt our banner—'tout ou rien!'—but when the campaign ends, Vega laughs at us from the horizon, quitting our world; and we console ourselves with a rushlight, and shelter it carefully from the wind with another flag: 'Quand on n'a pas ce qu'on aime, il faut aimer ce qu'on a!' Such is the worldly wisdom that comes with ripening years, like the deep stain on the sunny side of a peach. Moreover, 'folding empty arms,' is only melodrama metaphor, and 'empty hearts' are, begging your pardon, only figments of romantic brains. Our hearts aren't empty, more's the pity! They hold deep, deep, the image of Vega, and the flare of the tallow eandle on the surface serves as cross lights to dazzle the world, and help us to hide the reflection of our star. I saw that metaphor in some novel, and recognize its truth. Do you, my princess?"

"I will never so utterly degrade myself. I could neither lower my standard, nor sacrifice my ideal," said Leo, with a touch of scorn in her usually gentle voice.

"You prefer that your ideal should sacrifice you? One enjoys for a season the wide expanse visible from that lofty emotional pinnacle; but the atmosphere is too rarefied, and we gladly descend to the warm, denser air of the plains of common sense selfishness. If it be lowering your standard to become the wife of a bishop (the youngest ever ordained in his State), clothed with the double distilled odors of sanctity and popularity, then heaven help your standard, which only heaven can fitly house."

"Since you persist in assuming that so flattering an offer has been made me, I will set this subject at rest, by a final assurance that even were your surmise correct, I could never under any imaginable circumstances marry my cousin, Bishop Douglass. Although I trust and reverence him beyond all other men, 'I love my cousin cousinly, no more,' and he is too much absorbed by his holy office and its solemn responsibilities, to waste thought on the frail, sweet, rosy garland of any woman's love. Fret yourself no longer in casting matrimonial horoscopes for me."

The flushed cheeks, and a certain icy curtness in Leo's tone, warned her companion that she was rashly invading sacred precincts.

"Eight years ago I made the solemn asseveration that I would never marry; and I ran as a raw recruit to swell the army of foolish virgins who lost all the wedding splendors, the hypothetical 'cakes and ale', for want of the oil of worldly wisdom. Now I am thirty-three, and my lamp is filled to the brim, and the bridegroom is in sight. Why not? Adverse weather, rain, rust and mildew spoiled my beautiful golden harvest ten years ago, but aftermath is better than bare stubble fields, and though you miss the song of the reapers, you escape starvation. Deny it as we may, we are hopelessly given over to fetichism, and each one of us ties around her stone image some beguiling orthodox label. Leo, yours is pride, masquerading in the dun garb of 'religious duty'. Mine is self-love, pure and simple, the worldly weal of Alma

Cutting; but nominally it is dubbed 'grateful requital of a life of devotion' in my lover! You grieve over my heartlessness? That is the one compensation time brings, when men and women have killed the best in our natures. Teeth ache fiercely; then the nerve dies, and we have surcease from pain, and find comfort in knowing that the darkening wreck can throb no more. There was a time when the pangs of Prometheus seemed only pastime to mine, but all things end; and now I get on as comfortably without a heart, as the victims of vivisection—the frogs, and guinea pigs, and rabbits—do without their brains."

"I do indeed grieve over the fatal step you contemplate; I grieve over your unwomanliness in marrying a man whom you do not even pretend to love; and some terrible penalty will avenge the outrage against feminine nature. Some day your heart will stir in its cold torpor, and then all Dante's visions of horror, will become your realities, scuurging you down to despair."

"Because 'Farleigh Court' may lie dangerously close to 'Denzil Place'? Be easy, Leo; the cold remains of my ossified affection will lie in as decorous repose as the harmless ash heaps of some long buried damosel of the era of Lars Porsenna, dug out of Vulci or Chiusi. To make a safe and brilliant marriage is the acme of social success. What else does the world to which I belong, offer me now?"

"There remains always, Alma, the alternative of listening to the instinctive monitors God set to watch in every woman's nature; and we have the precious and inalienable privilege of being true to ourselves. Better mourn your 'bisc' than stoop to a lower substitute. Be loyal to yourself, be true to your own heart."

"I know myself rather too intimately to offer a tribute of admiration on the altar of ego; and I prefer to make the experiment of trying to be true and loyal to some one else, with whose imperfections I am not so well acquainted. When you meet your adorable 'bisc' in society, with a wife hanging on his arm,—when as pater familias he convoys his flock of small children who tread on your toes at the chrysanthemum shows, what then? The world, my world, is generously and munificently lax, and though the limits of respectable endurance may be as hard to find as the 'fourth dimension of space', or the authenticity of the 'Book of Jasher', still for decency's sake we submit there are limits of decorum; certain proprietorial domains upon which we may not openly poach; and mcum et tuum though moribund, is not yet numbered with belief in the 'grail'. Female emancipation is not quite complete even in America, and noblesse oblige! our code still reads: 'Zeus has unquestioned right to Io; but woe betide Io when she suns her heart in the smiles that belong to Hera!' Some women find exhilaration in the effort to excel, by flying closest to the flame without singeing their satin wings; by executing a pirouette on the extremest ledge of the abyss, yet escape toppling in; female Blondins skipping across the tight rope of Platonic friendship, stretched above the unmentionable. You are shocked?"

"Indeed, I am pained. I can scarcely recognize the Alma of old."

"Wait one moment, I have the floor. In the days when I wept for my—shall I say 'bisc'? for impersonality is hedged about with safety, and the consolation prize had not yet been invited to come back from Coventry, a funny trifle set me to thinking seriously of my sin of covetousness. One summer at a certain fashionable resort, let us call it villeggiatura of the Lepidoptera, the amusement programme had reached the last act, and people yawned for something new, when 'sweet charity' came to the rescue, and proposed an entertainment to raise funds for enlarging an ecclesiastical 'Columbary' where aged, unsightly and repentant doves might moult, and renew their plumage. Musical, dramatic, poetic recitations, and tableaux vivants constituted the method of collecting the money, and the selections would have made Rabelais chuckle. We had the most flagitiously erotic passages (rendered in costume) from opera and opera bouffe, living reproductions of the tragic pose of Paolo and Francesca that would hare inspired Cabanel anew; of 'Ginevra Da Siena,' of 'Vivien,'—a carnival of the carnal! where nurseries were robbed to supply the mimic ballet, and where bald-headed clergyman, and white-haired mothers in Israel clapped and encored. One fair forsaken dame, whose indignant spouse was seeking a divorce, came to the footlights in an artistic garment so decollete that a man sitting behind me whispered to his friend: 'What pictures does she suggest to you? "Phryne before the Judges"—or Long's "Thisbe?" She languorously waved a floral fan of crimson carnations, and recited with all of Siddons' grace and Rachel's fire selections from a book of poems, that were so many dynamite bombs of vice smothered in roses. Amid tumultuous applause, she gave as encore something that contained a fragment of Feydeau, and its closing words woke up my drowsy soul, like a clap of thunder: 'Ce que les poetes appellent l'amour, et les moralistes l'adultere!' Leo, there is a moral somnambulism more frightful than that which leads to midnight promenades on the combs of roofs, and the borders of Goat Island; so I wiped my tears away, and after that day, began to read the billet doux and wear the flowers of my 'consolation prize'."

"You do not love him, and your marriage will degrade you in your own estimation. Your bridal vows will be perjury, an insult to your God, and a foul terrible wrong against the man who trusts your truthfulness. According to our church, wedlock is a 'holy ordinance'; and to me an unloving wife is unhallowed; is a blot on her sex, only a few degrees removed from unmarried mothers. You know the difference between friendship and love, and when you go to the altar, and give the former in exchange for the latter, the base counterfeit for the true gold, you are consciously and premeditatedly dishonest."

"Thanks, for your clearness of diction, your perspicuity which leaves no cobweb of misty doubt wherewith to drape my shivering moral deformity! To 'see ourselves as others see us' is as disappointing as the result of plunging one's hand into the 'grab-bag', but at least it brings the stimulating tingle of a new sensation. Suppose each knows perfectly well that as regards the true gold, both are equally bankrupt? There is a queer moral fungus called 'honesty among thieves', and we both know that we never sang snatches from Offenbach to each other, through pink 'bisc' lips. He loved quite desperately a mignonne of a blonde, with heavenly blue eyes and cherubic yellow hair, who, not knowing his expectations from a California uncle, jilted him for a rich Cuban. Look you, Leo, because I cannot wear Kohinoor, must I disport myself without any diamond necklace? Since he can never own 'La Peregrina,' must he eschew pearl studs in his shield front? We distinctly understand that we are not first prizes; but perhaps we may be something better than total blanks in the lottery, even though we quite realize the difference between love and friendship. Do you? Portia should know every jot and tittle of the law, and all the subtle shades of evidence, before she lifts her voice in court."

Alma pushed away her cushion, sat upright, and the slumbering fire flashed up under her jet lashes.

"If I do, that knowledge which earlier or later comes to all women, is certainly linked with the comforting consciousness that I can trust myself to govern and protect myself, without being tied to a watch-dog, whose baying would serve much the same purpose as that picture in mosaic in the House of the Tragic Poet. I have a very sincere affection for you, Alma, but the day on which you sell yourself in a loveless marriage, will strain hard on the cable of esteem."

"Is it for this reason that you refuse to officiate as my bridesmaid?"

"Solely because I will neither witness nor participate in an act which will give me great pain by lowering my estimate of your character."

Alma's long, supple, tapering fingers were outstretched, and taking Leo's white dimpled hands, drew them caressingly to her face, pressing a palm against each cheek.

"Your good opinion is so precious, I cannot afford to lose it. We accept men's flattery and expect their compliments, because it is a traditional homage that survives the chivalry that inspired it; but we don't mistake chaff for wheat, and the purest, sweetest, noblest and holiest friendship in life is that of a true, good woman. The perfume is as different as the stale odor of a cigar, from the breath of the honeysuckle that bleached all night under crystal dew, floats in at your window like a message from heaven, I love you dearly, my pretty Portia, hence I wince a trifle at your harsh ascription of cave canem motives in my marriage. In the idyllic Arthurian days, the 'Lily Maid of Astolot' made a touching picture, weeping and dying for the man who rode away, marauding on kingly preserves; but this is the era of wise, common sense 'Maud Mullers', and she and the Judge, mating as best they can, lead peaceful lives in a wholesome atmosphere, and cause no scandal by following 'affinities' across the lines of law; as some high in literature, art, and society have done, trusting that the starred mantle of genius would hide their moral leprosy. With all my faults, at least I am honest; and when I bow my stiff neck under the yoke connubial, I promise you I will keep step demurely and sedately. Do you remember a sombre book we read while yachting, which contained this brave confession of a woman, whose marriage made her historic? 'I thought I had done with life. I knew I had now cause to be proud of belonging to this man, and I was proud. At the same time I as little feigned ardent love for him, as he demanded it from me.' Leo, you and I represent different types. You are an eagle brooding in cold eternal solitude upon the heights, rather than be wooed by valley hawks; I am only a very tired wren, who missed a mate on my first Valentine season, and seeing my plumage grows a rusty brown, I accept the overtures of one similarly forlorn, and hope for serene domesticity under the sheltering eaves of some quiet, cosey barn. You are a nobler bird, no doubt; but trust me dear, I shall be the happier."

Leo withdrew her hands, and pushed back her chair, widening the space that divided them.

"You disappoint me keenly. I thought you too brave to crouch before the jeers hurled at 'old maidenism'. Moral cowardice is the last flaw I expected in one of your fibre."

"Wait till you are thirty-three, and stand as a target at Society's archery meeting. Yesterday Celeste was pale with horror when she showed me two white hairs pulled from my 'bangs', and added, 'Helas races! and powdered hair no more the style!' My dear girl—

"'True love, of course, is scarcely in society,
Unless in fancy dress, and masked like one of us—'"

still I really am very proud of my six feet two inches prospective conjugal yoke-fellow; proud of his martial bearing, his brilliant reputation, 'proud of his pride'; and I think I shall grow very fond of him, because in a mild way I think he cares for me'; and we can make a little Indian Summer for each other before the frosts of Winter fall upon us. What else can I do with my life? Think of it. Papa will be married soon, and while I don't propose to tear my hair and insult his bride, nobody can be expected to reach such altitudes of self-abnegation as to want a step-mother. Poor papa, I am sure I hope he may be very happy, but it is superhuman to elect to live under the same roof, and smile benignantly on his bliss. Rivers, too, has slipped under the matrimonial noose, and I am absolutely thrown on my own resources for companionship. What does society offer me? Haggard, weazen old witch, bedizened in a painted mask; don't I know the yellow teeth and bleared eyes behind the paste-board, and the sharp nails in the claws hidden under undressed kid? Have not I gone around for years on her gaudy wheel, like that patient, uncomplaining goat we saw stepping on the broad spokes of the great wheel that churned the butter, and pressed the cheese in that dairy, near Udine? The dizzying circle, where one must step, step—keep time or be lost! In Winter, balls, receptions, luncheons, teas, Germans, theatre parties, opera suppers; a rush for the first glimpse of the last picture that emerges from the custom-house; for a bouquet of the newest rose that took the prize at the London Show. In season, coaching parties, tally ho! Then fox hunting minus the fox, and later, boating and bathing and lawn tennis!—and—always—everywhere heart-burnings, vapid formalities; beaux setting belles at each other like terriers scrambling after a mouse; mothers lying in wait, as wise cats watching to get their paws on the first-class catch they know their pretty kittens cannot manage successfully. Oh! Don't I know it all! I dare say my world is the very best possible of its kind; and I am not cynical, but oh Lord! I am so deadly tired of everything, and everybody."

"No wonder, unless you mercilessly calumniate it; but you have only yourself to blame. You made social success your aim, fashionable life your temple of worship, sham your only God. If you habitually drink poppy juice, can you fail to be drowsy?"

"Oh bless you! I have been polytheistic as any other well-read pagan of my day, and changed the heads and the labels of the fetiches on my altar almost as often as my ball wardrobe. I aspired to 'culture' in all the 'cults', and I improved diligently my opportunities. One year the stylish craze was sesthetics, and I fought my way to the front of the bedlamites raving about Sapphic types, 'Sibylla Palmifera' and 'Astarte Syriaca'; and I wore miraculously limp, draggled skirts, that tangled about my feet tight as the robes of Burne Jones' 'Vivien.' Next season the star of ceramics and bric-a-brac was in the ascendant, and I ran the gamut of Satsuma, Kyoto, de la Robbia, Limoge and Gubbio; of niello, and millchori glass, of Queen Anne brass and Japanese bronze; while my snuff boxes and my 'symphony in fans' graced all the loan exhibitions. Soon after, a celebrated scientist from England who had bowled over all the pins set up by his predecessors, lectured in our Bojotia; and fired with zeal for truth, I swept aside all my costly idealistic rubbish into a 'doomed pyramid of the vanities', and swore allegiance to the Positive, the 'Knowable', whose priests handled hammers, spectroscopes, electric batteries—and who set up for me a whole Pantheon of science fetiches. I bought a microscope and peered into tissues, pollen cells, diatoms, ditch ooze; and pitied my clever and very talented grandmother who died ignorant of the family secrets revealed by 'totemism', ignorant of 'parthenogenesis' which proved so conclusively the truth of her own firm conviction, that the faults she deplored in her son's children were all inherited directly from her daughter-in-law, whom she detested; ignorant of the fact that the sun which she regarded as a dazzling yellow fire was by bolometric measures shown to be in reality of a restful, and refreshing blue color. By the time I was fully convinced that teleology was as dead as the Ptolemaic theory, and that 'wings were not planned for flight, but that flight has produced wings', hence that Haeckel's gospel of

'Dysteleology' or purposelessness in Nature satisfactorily explained creation—a great wave of oriental theosophy overflowed us; and a revival of Buddhism invited me to seek Nirvana as the final beatitude, where—

"'We shall be
Part of the mighty universal whole,
And through all icons mix and mingle with the
Kosmic Soul!'"

Or to make matters clearer still:

"'Om, mani Padma, Om! the dewdrop slips
Into the shining sea!'"

Even a sponge can hold only so much, and I fell back—or shall I say forward—in the path of progress to rest in the dimness of agnosticism. Is it strange, Leo, that I am desperately tired; and willing to plant my feet on the rock of matrimony, which will neither dissolve nor slip away, and to which my vows will moor me firmly?"

"If you had clung to your Bible, and prayed more, you would not have wasted so signally the years that might have brought you enduring happiness. Forgive me, Alma, but you have lived solely for self."

"Yet now, when I propose to live solely for somebody else, you shake me off, and repudiate me? Selfish you think? I dare say I am, but religion now-a-day winks at that, nay fosters it. Each church is an octopus, and the members are laboriously striving to disprove the Saviour's admonition: 'Ye cannot serve God and mammon.' I am no worse than my ritualistic sisters whom I meet and gossip with, under cover of the organ muttering, and sometimes I wonder if after all we are any nearer the kingdom of heaven that Christ preached, than the pagans whose customs we retain under evangelical names. 'They sacrificed a white kid to the propitious divinities, and a black kid to the unpropiticus.' Do not we likewise? The church or one of its pensioners needs money; so instead of denying ourselves some secular amusement, cutting short our chablis, terrapin, pate de foie gras, gateau, Grec, Amontillado; wearing less sealskin and sables, buying fewer pigeon-blood rubies, absolutely mortifying the flesh in order to offer a contribution out of our pockets to God, how ingeniously we devise schemes to extract the largest possible amount of purely personal pleasure from the expenditure of the sum, we call our contribution to charity? We build chapels, and feed orphans, and clothe widows, and endow reformatories, and establish beds in hospitals, how? By a devout, consecrating self-denial which manifests itself in eating and drinking, in singing and dancing, at kirmess, charity balls, amateur theatricals, garden parties; where the cost of our XV. Siecle costume is quadruple the price of the ticket that admits to our sacrifice of black and white kids in the same sanctuary. We serve God with one hand, and we surely serve with the other the Mammon of selfishness and vanity. We have Lenten service, Lenten dietetics, Lenten costumes even; Lenten progressive euchre, Lenten clubs; but where are the Lenten virtues, where the genuine humility, charity, self-dedication of body and soul to true holiness?"

"The church is a school. If pupils will not heed admonition, and defy the efforts of instructors, is the institution responsible for the failure in education? The eradication of selfishness is the mission of the churches; and if we individually practised at home a genuine self-denial for righteousness' sake, we should collectively show the world fewer flaws for scoffing reprimand."

"The Shepherds are too timid to control their flocks. If they only had the nerve to pick us up, turn our hearts inside out, show us the black corners, and the ossifications, and call sin, sin, we should begin to realize what despicable shams we are. Dr. Douglass, the Bishop, is the only one I know who lays us on the dissecting table, and who does not speak of 'human fallibility' when he means vice. He told us one day that the Gospel required a line of demarcation between the godly and the ungodly, between Christians and unbelievers; but that it has become imaginary like the meridian and the equator; and that he very much feared the strongest microscope in the laboratories could not find where the boundary line ran between the World, the Flesh and the Devil, and the Kingdom of God in our souls. I am sorry a distant State called him to her Episcopal chair, for his cold steel is needed among us. Now tell me, Leo, what you intend to do with your life?"

"Spend it for God and my fellow creatures; and enjoy all the pure happiness I can appropriate without wronging others. I have so many privileges granted me, that I ought to accomplish some good in this world, as a thank offering."

"Take care you don't make a fetich of Jerusalem missions, Chinese tracts, and Sheltering Arms; and lose your dear, sweet personality in a goody-goody machine bigot. Forgive me, dear old girl, but sometimes I fear a shadow has fallen in your sunshine."

"Sooner or later they fall into every life, yet mine will pass away I feel assured. 'Pain, suffering, failure are as needful as ballast to a ship, without which it does not draw enough water, becomes a plaything for the winds and waves, travels no certain road, and easily overturns.' If the gloomiest pessimist of this century can extract that comfort, what may I not hope for my future? I am going to rebuild my house at X——and when it is completed, I shall expect the privilege of returning the hospitality you have so kindly shown me. I shall be very busy for at least two years, and I am glad to know that Aunt Patty is beginning to manifest some interest in my plans."

"Leo, may I ask something?"

"If you are quite sure you have the right to ask, and that I can have no reason to decline answering."

"I can't bear that you should live and die without being a happy wife. I don't want you to become a mere benevolent automaton set aside for church work, and charities; getting solemn and thin, with patient curves deepening around your mouth, and loneliness looking out of—

"'Eyes, meek as gentle Mercy's at the throne of heaven.'"

"To be a happy wife is the dream of womanhood, and if the day should ever dawn when God gives me that crown of joy, I shall wear it gladly, proudly, and feel that this world has yielded me its richest blessing; but, Alma, to-day I know no man whom I could marry with the hope of that perfect union which alone sanctions and hallows wedded love. I must be all the world to my husband; and he—next to God—must be the universe to me. There is Gen'l Haughton coming up the stairs, so I considerately efface myself. Good-bye till luncheon."

As she glided away and disappeared behind the curtain leading into the library, Alma looked after her, with very misty eyes, full of tenderness.

137

"Brave, proud soul; deep, sorrowful heart. If she can't drown her star, at least she will admit no lesser light. She will never swerve one iota from her lofty standard, and some day, please God, she may yet wear her coveted crown right royally. Governor Glenbeigh is worthy even of her, but will his devotion win her at last?"

CHAPTER XXXI.

If it be true that the universal Law of Labor, physical or mental, emanated from the Creator as a penal statute, for disobedience which forfeited Eden, how merciful and how marvellous is the delicacy of an adjustment, whereby all growth of body, mind and soul being conditioned by work, humanity converts punishment into benediction; escapes degeneration, attains development solely in accordance with the provisions of the primeval curse, man's heritage of labor? Amid the wreck of sacerdotal systems, the destruction of national gods, the periodical tidal waves of scepticism, the gospel of work maintains triumphantly its legions of evangels; its apostolic succession direct from Adam; its myriad temples always alight with altar fires, always vocal with the sublime hymn swelling from millions of consecrated throats.

The one infallible tonic for weakened souls, the one supreme balm for bruised hearts is the divinely distilled chrism of labor.

Absorbed in the round of duties that employed her hands and thoughts, and necessitated dedication of every waking hour, Beryl found more solace than she had dared to hope; and the artistic fancies which she had supposed extinguished, spread their frail gossamer wings and fluttered shyly into the serene sunshine that had broken rpon her frozen life. The distinctively ornamental character of many of the industrial pursuits at the "Anchorage", demanded originality and variety of designs, and as this department had been assigned to her, she entered with increasing zest the tempting field of congenial employment; yet day by day, bending over her tasks, she never lost sight of the chain that clanked at her wrist, that bound her to a hideous past, to a murky, lowering and menacing future.

Weeks slipped away, months rolled on; Autumn overtook her. Winter snows and sleet blanched the heavenly blue of the dimpling lake, and no tidings reached her from the wanderer, for whom she prayed. The advertisement had elicited no reply, and though it had long ceased to appear, she daily searched the personal column of the "Herald", with a vague expectation of some response. If her brother still lived, was the world so wide, that she could never trace his erring passage through it? Would no instinct of natural affection prompt him to seek news of the mother who had idolized him? After a while she must renew the quest, but for the present, safety demanded her seclusion; and since only Doctor Grantlin knew the place of her retreat, she felt secure from discovery.

One Spring day, when warm South winds had kissed open the spicy lips of lilacs, and yellowed the terrace with crocus flakes, Beryl dismissed her class of pupils in drawing and painting, and was engaged in dusting the plaster casts, and arranging the palettes and pencils left in disorder. The door opened, and a pretty, young German Sister looked in.

"Sister Ruth have need of you to do some errands; and you must go on the street; so you will get your bonnet and veil. Is it that you will be there soon?"

"I will come at once, Sister Elsbeth."

For several days Sister Ruth had been confined to her room by inflammatory rheumatism, and when Beryl entered, the invalid presented the appearance of a mummy swathed in red flannel.

"I am sorry to disturb you, and equally sorry that I feel obliged to exact a reluctant service, because I know you dislike to visit the business part of the city, and there I must send you. This note from Mrs. Vanderdonk will explain the nature of the business, which I can intrust to no one except yourself; and you will see that the commission admits of no delay. Here is your car fare. Go first to No. 100 Lucre Avenue, talk fully with Mrs. Vanderdonk, and then ride down to Jardon & Jackson's and get all the material you think will be required. You will observe, she lays great stress on the superfine quality of the plush. Order the bill delivered with the goods; and if anything be required in your department, you had better leave the list with Kling & Turner."

Three squares south of the "Anchorage" ran a line of street cars which carried her away to the heart of the city; and at the expiration of an hour and a half, Beryl had executed the commission, and was walking homeward, watching for a car which would expedite her return. Dreading identification, she went rarely into the great thoroughfare; and now felt doubly shielded from observation by the Quaker-shaped drab bonnet and veil that covered her white cap. As she was passing the entrance of a dancing academy, a throng of boys and girls poured out, filling the sidewalk, and creating a temporary blockade, through which a gentleman laden with several packages, elbowed his way. A moment later, Beryl's foot struck some obstacle, and looking down she saw a large portfolio lying on the pavement. It was a handsome morocco case, with the initials "G. McI.", stamped in gilt upon the cover, which was tied with well-worn strings. She held it up, looked around, even turned back, thinking that the owner might have returned to search for it; but the gentleman who had hurried through the crowd was no longer visible, and in the distance she fancied she saw a similar figure cross the street, and spring upon a car rolling in the opposite direction.

The human clot had dissolved, the juvenile assembly had drifted away; and as no one appeared to claim the lost article, she signalled to the driver of the car passing just then, entered and took a seat in one corner. The only passengers were two nurses with bands of little ones, seeking fresh air in a neighboring park; and slipping the book under her veil, Beryl began to examine its contents. A glance showed her that it belonged to some artist, and was filled with sketches neatly numbered and dated; while between the leaves lay specimens of ferns and lichens carefully pressed.

The studies were varied, and in all stages of advancement; here two elk heads and a buffalo; there a gaunt coyote crouching in the chaparral; a cluster of giant oaks; far off, a waving line of mountain peaks; a canon with vultures sailing high above it; cow boys, and a shoreless sea of prairie, with no shadows except those cast by filmy clouds drifting against the sun. Slowly turning the leaves, which showed everywhere a master's skilful hand, Beryl found two sheets of paper tied together with a strand of silk; and between them lay a fold of tissue paper, to preserve some delicate lines. She untied the knot, and carefully lifted the tissue, looking at the sketch.

A faint, inarticulate cry escaped her, and she sank back an instant in the corner of the seat; but the chatter of the nurses, and the whimpering wail of one dissatisfied baby mercifully drowned the sound. The car, the trees on the Street, the belfry of a church seemed spinning in some witch's dance, and an icy wind swept over and chilled her. She threw aside her veil, stooped, and her lips whitened.

What was there in the figure of a kneeling monk, to drive the blood in cold waves to her throbbing heart? The sketch represented the head and shoulders of a man, whose cowl had fallen back, exposing the outlines and moulding of a face and throat absolutely flawless in beauty, yet darkened by the reflection of some overpowering and irremediable woe. The features were youthful as St. Sebastian's; the expression that of one prematurely aged by severe and unremitting mental conflict; but neither shaven crown, nor cowl availed to disguise Bertie Brentano, and as his sister's eyes gazed at the sketch, it wavered, swam, vanished in a mist of tears.

In one corner of the sheet a man's hand had written "Brother Luke", August the 10th. Had relenting fate, or a merciful prayer-answering-God placed in her hand the long sought clue? When Beryl recovered from the shock of recognition, and looked around, she found the car empty; and discovered that she had been carried several squares beyond the street where she intended to get out and walk.

Carefully replacing the tissue paper and silk thread, she tied the leathern straps of the portfolio, and left the car, holding the sketches close to her heart as she hurried homeward. When she turned a corner and caught sight of the bronze anchor over the door, she involuntarily slackened her pace, and at the same moment a policeman crossed the street, stood in front of her, and touched his cap. The sight of his uniform thrilled her with a premonition of danger.

"Pardon me, Sister, but something has been lost on the street."

"A portfolio? I have found it."

"It is very valuable to the owner."

"I intend having it advertised in to-morrow's paper."

"The person to whom it belongs, wishes to leave the city; to-night, hence his haste in trying to recover it."

"I picked it up in front of Heilwiggs' Dancing Academy. How did you know who had found it?"

"The owner discovered he had dropped it, soon after he boarded a car, where Captain Tunstall of our force happened to be, and he at once telegraphed to all the stations to be on the look out. A boot-black whose stand is near Heilwiggs', reported that he saw one of the 'Gray Women' pick up something, and get on an upbound car. Our station was telephoned to interview the 'Anchorage', so you see we are prompt. I was just going over to ring the bell, and make inquiries."

"Who lost the book?"

"A man named McIlvane, an Englishman I think, who is obliged to hurry on to-night, in order to catch some New York steamer where his passage is engaged."

"You are sure he is a foreigner?" asked Beryl, who was feverishly revolving the possibility that the sketch belonged to some detective, and was intended for identification of the picture on the glass door at X———.

"You can't be sure of anything that is only lip deep, but that was the account telephoned to us. There is a reward of twenty dollars if the book is delivered by eight P.M.; after that time, ten dollars, and directions left by which to forward it to London. He said it was worthless to anybody else, but contained a lot of pictures he valued."

"I do not want the reward, but before I surrender the portfolio, I must see the owner."

"Why?"

"For reasons that concern only myself. He can come here, and claim his property; or I will take it to him, and restore it, after he has answered some questions. You are quite welcome to the reward, which I am sure you merit because of your promptness and circumspection. Will you notify him that he can obtain his book by calling at the 'Anchorage'?"

"Our instructions are, to deliver the book at Room 213, Hotel Lucullus. It is now four o'clock."

"I will not surrender the book to you; but I will accompany you to the hotel, and deliver it to the owner in your presence. Let us lose no time."

"Very well. Sister, I'll keep a little behind, and jump on the first red star car that passes down. Look out for me on the platform, and I'll stop the car for you."

"Thank you," said Beryl, wondering whether the sanctity of her garb exacted this mark of deference, or whether the instinctive chivalry of American manhood prompted him to spare her the appearance of police surveillance.

Keeping her in sight, he loitered until they found themselves on the same car, where the officer, apparently engrossed by his cigarette, retained his stand on the rear platform. In front of the hotel two omnibuses were discharging their human freight, and in the confusion, Beryl and her escort passed unobserved into the building. He motioned her into one of the reception rooms on the second floor, and made his way to the office.

Drawing her quaint bonnet as far over her face as possible, and straightening her veil, Beryl sat down on a sofa and tried to quiet the beating of her pulses, the nervous tremor that shook her. She had ventured shyly out of her covert, and like all other hunted creatures, trembled at her own daring in making capture feasible. Memory rendered her vaguely apprehensive; bitter experience quickened her suspicions.

Was she running straight into some fatal trap, ingeniously baited with her brother's portrait? Would the Sheriff in X———, would Mr. Dunbar himself, recognize her in her gray disguise? She walked to a mirror set in the wall, and stared at her own image, put up one hand and pushed out of sight every ring of hair that showed beneath the white cap frill; then reassured, resumed her seat. How long the waiting seemed.

Somebody's pet Skye terrier, blanketed with scarlet satin embroidered with a monogram in gilt, had defied the bienseance of fashionable canine and feline etiquette, by flying at somebody's sedate, snowy Maltese cat, whose collar of silver bells jangled out of tune, as the combatants rolled on the velvet carpet, swept like a cyclone through the reception room, fled up the corridor. Two pretty children, gay as paroquets, in their cardinal plush cloaks, ran to the piano and began a furious tattoo, while their nurse gossiped with the bell boy.

With her hands locked around the portfolio, Beryl sat watching the door; and at last the policeman appeared at the threshold, where he paused an instant, then vanished.

A gentleman apparently forty years of age came in, and approached her. He was short in stature, florid, slightly bald; wore mutton chop whiskers, and a traveling suit of gray tweed broadly checked.

Beryl rose, the stranger bowed.

"Ah, you have my sketch book! Madam, I am eternally your debtor. Intrinsically worthless, perhaps; yet there are reasons which make it inestimably valuable to me."

"I picked it up from the pavement, and though I opened and examined it, you will find the contents intact. Will you look through it?"

"Oh! I dare say it is all right. No one cares for unfinished sketches, and these are mere studies."

He untied the thongs, turned over a dozen or more papers, then closed the lid, and put his hand in his pocket.

"I offered a reward to—"

"I wish no fee, sir; but the policeman has taken some trouble in the matter, and without his aid I should probably not have been able to restore it. Pay him what you promised, or may deem proper; and then permit me to ask for some information, which I think you can give me."

She beckoned to the officer who looked in just then; and when the money had been counted into his hand, the latter lifted his cap.

"Sister, shall I see you safe on the car?"

"Thank you, no. I can find my way home. I teach drawing at the 'Anchorage', and desire to ask a few questions of this gentleman, who I am sure is an artist."

When the policeman had left them, Beryl took the portfolio and opened it, while the owner watched her curiously, striving to penetrate the silver gray folds of her veil.

"May I ask whether you expect to leave America immediately?"

"I expect to sail on the steamer for Liverpool next Saturday."

"Have you relatives in this country?"

"None. I am merely a tourist, seeking glimpses of the best of this vast continent of yours."

"Did you make these sketches?"

"I did, from time to time; in fact, mine has been a sketching tour, and this book is one of several I have filled in America."

With trembling fingers she untied the silk, lifted the sketch, and said in a voice which, despite her efforts, quivered:

"I hope, sir, you will not consider me unwarrantably inquisitive, if I ask, where did you see this face?"

"Ah! My monk of the mountains? That is 'Brother Luke'; looks like one of Il Frate's wonderful heads, does he not? I saw him—let me see? Egad! Just exactly where it was, that is the rub! It was far west, beyond Assiniboia; somewhere in Alberta I am sure."

"Was it on British soil, or in the United States?"

"Certainly in British territory; and on one of the excursions I made from Calgary. I think it was while hunting in the mountains between Alberta and British Columbia. Let me see the sketch. Yes—10th of August; I was in that region until 1st of September."

Beryl drew a deep breath of intense relief, as she reflected that foreign territory might bar pursuit; and leaning forward, she asked hesitatingly:

"Have you any objection to telling me the circumstances under which you saw him; the situation in which you found him?"

"None whatever; but may I ask if you know him? Is my sketch so good a portrait?"

"It is wonderfully like one I knew years ago; and of whom I desire to receive tidings. My friend is a handsome man about twenty-four years of age."

"I was camping out with a hunting party, and one day while they were away gunning, I went to sketch a bit of fir wood clinging to the side of a rocky gorge. The day was hot, and I sat down to rest in the shadow of a stone ledge, that jutted over the cove where a spring bubbled from the crag, and made a ribbon of water. Here is the place, on this sheet. Over there, are the fir trees. Very soon I heard a rich voice chanting a solemn strain from Palestrinas' Miserere; the very music I had listened to in the Sistine Chapel, a few months before; and peeping from my sheltered nook, I saw a man clad in monkish garb stoop to drink from the spring. He sat a while, with his arms clasped around his knees, and his profile was so perfect I seized my pencil and drew the outlines; but before I completed it, he suddenly fell upon his knees, and the intense anguish, remorse, contrition—what not—so changed the countenance, that while he prayed, I made rapidly a new sketch. Then the most extraordinary thing happened. He rose, and turning fully toward me, I saw that one-half of his face was nobly regular, classically perfect; while the other side was hideously distorted, deformed. Absolutely he was 'Hyperion and Satyr' combined—with one set of features between them. I suppose my astonishment caused me to utter some exclamation, for he glanced up the cliff, saw me, turned and fled. I shouted and ran, but could not overtake him, and when I reached the open space, I saw a figure speeding away on a white mustang pony, and knew from the fluttering of the black skirts that it was the same man. My sketch shows the right side of his face, the other was drawn down almost beyond the lineaments of humanity. Beg pardon, madam, but would you be so good as to tell me whether this freak of nature was congenital, or the result of some frightful accident?"

Beryl had shut her eyes, and her lips were compressed to stifle the moan that struggled in her throat. When she spoke, the stranger detected a change in her voice.

"The person whose countenance was recalled by your sketch, was afflicted by no physical blemish, when last I saw him."

"His appearance was so singular, that I made sundry inquiries about him, but only one person seemed ever to have encountered him; and that was a half-breed Indian driver, belonging to our party. He told me, 'Brother Luke' belonged to a band of monks living somewhere beyond the mountains; and that he sometimes crossed, searching for stray cattle. That is the history of my sketch, and since I am indebted to you for its recovery, I regret for your sake that it is so meagre."

"It was last August that you made the sketch?"

"Last August. And now may I ask, to whom my thanks are due?"

"I am merely an humble member of a sisterhood of working women, and my name could possess no interest for you. I owe you an apology for trespassing upon your time, and prying into the mysteries of your portfolio; but the beauty of your sketch, and its startling resemblance to one in whom I have long felt an interest, must plead my pardon. I am grateful, sir, for your courtesy, and will detain you no longer."

He bowed profoundly; she bent her head, and walked quickly away, keeping her face lowered, dreading observation.

For the first time since her trial and conviction, a sensation of perfect tranquillity shed rest upon her anxious and foreboding heart. Bertie was safe from capture, on foreign soil; and the testimony of the traveller that he prayed in the solitude of the wilderness, brought her the comforting assurance, that the fires of remorse had begun the purification of his sinful soul from the crime that had blackened so many lives. Trained in his early youth at a Jesuit College, his sympathies had ever been with the priesthood to whom his tutors belonged; and his sister readily understood how swiftly he fled to their penitential, expiatory system, when the blood of his grandfather had stained his hands, and the scouts of the law hunted him to desert wilds.

Vain of the personal beauty that had always distinguished him, she comprehended the keenness of the humiliation, which would goad him to screen in a cloister, the facial mutilation, that punished him more excruciatingly than hair shirt, or flagellation. Beyond the reach of extradition (as she fondly hoped), inviolate beneath the cowl of some Order which, in protecting his body, essayed also to cleanse, regenerate and sanctify his imperilled soul, could she not now dismiss the tormenting apprehension that sleeping or waking had persistently dogged her, since the day when she saw the fuchsias on the handkerchief, and the mother-of-pearl grapes on the sleeve button, in the penitentiary cell?

In a crisis of dire extremity, overborne by adversity, terrified by the realization of human helplessness, we fly to God, and barter by promise all our future, for the boon of temporary succor.

How different, how holy the mood that brings us in tearful gratitude to dedicate our lives to His service, when having abandoned all hope, His healing hand lifts us out of long agony into unexpected rest?

When an ignominious death stared this woman in the face, she had cried to her God: "Though You slay me, yet will I trust You!" and to-night she bowed her head in prayer, thankful that the uplifted hand held no longer a dagger, but had fallen tenderly in benediction.

Far away in the heart of the city, the clock in its granite tower was striking two; yet Beryl knelt at her oriel window, with her arms crossed on the wide sill, and her eyes fixed upon the shimmering sea, where a soft south wind ruffled it into ridges of silver, beneath a full May moon. Beyond those silent waters, hidden in some lonely, snow-girt eyry, where perhaps the muffled thunder of the Pacific responded to the midnight chants of his oratory, dwelt Bertie; and to touch his hand once more, to hear from his own lips that he had made his peace with God, to kiss him good-bye seemed all that was left for accomplishment.

Poor and unknown, she lacked apparently every means requisite for this attainment; but faith, patience, and courage were hers. Daily work for daily wage was the present duty; and in God's good time she would find her brother. How, or when, so expensive and difficult a quest could be successfully prosecuted, disquieted her not; she had learned to labor and to trust; she remembered: "Their strength is to sit still."

The symphony of her life was set in minors, yet subtle and perfect was the harmony that dwelt therein; and because she had sternly shut love out of her lonely heart, she kept votive lights burning ceaselessly on the cold altar of duty. The solitary red rose of happiness that might have brightened and perfumed her thorny path, she had cut off, ere the bud expanded, and offered it as a loyal tribute to broaden the garland that crowned Miss Gordon. At the mandate of conscience, she had unmurmuringly surrendered this precious blossom, but memory was tantalizingly tenacious; and in sorrowful hours of sore temptation, the brave, pure soul came swiftly to the rescue of famishing heart: "What? Is it so hard for us to keep the Ten Commandments? Do we covet our neighbor's lover?"

In the garden of earthly existence, some are ordained to bloom as human plantae tristes, shedding their delicate aroma like the "Pretty-by-nights", only when the glory of the day is done, and twilight shadows coax open their pure hearts.

To-night she seemed cradled in the arms of peace, soothed by an unfaltering trust that whispered:

"Would I could wish my wishes all to rest;
And know to wish the wish, that were the best."

While her lips moved in a prayer for Bertie, she fell asleep; like a child at ease, after long paroxysms of pain. When she awoke, the lilacs were swinging their purple thuribles filled with dew, in honor of the new day; a silvery mist, tinged here and there with the pale pink hue of an almond blossom, wavered and curled over the quiet lake, and a robin red-breast, winging his way from the orange and jasmine boughs of the far sweet South, rested on the ivied wall, and poured out his happy heart in a salutatory to the rising sun.

CHAPTER XXXII.

"I fear, my sister, that you have made a great mistake in refusing an offer of marriage, which almost any woman might be proud to accept."

Sister Ruth closed her writing desk, and looked at Beryl over her spectacles.

"Why should you infer that any such proposal has been made to me?"

"Simply because I know all that has occurred, and my cousin writes me that you decline to marry him. If you had intended to remain here and identify yourself with this institution, I could better understand your motives in rejecting a man who offers you wealth, good looks, a stainless reputation, an honored name, and the best possible social position."

"All of which tempt me in no degree. Mr. Brompton is doubtless everything you consider him; lives in a brown stone palace, is an influential and respected citizen, but comparatively, we are strangers. He bought my pictures, took a fleeting fancy to my face, and to my great surprise, indulged in a romantic whim. What does he comprehend of my past? How little he understands the barrier that shuts me out from the lot of most women."

"He is fully acquainted with every detail of your life that has been confided to me, or discovered by the public; and he has studied and admired you ever since you came to dwell among us. In view of your very peculiar history, you must admit that his affection is certainly strong. If you married him, your past would be effectually blotted out."

"I have no desire to blot it out, and though misfortune overshadowed my name, it is the untarnished legacy my father left me, and I hold it very sacred; wrap it as a mantle about me. When suspicion of any form of disgrace falls upon a woman, it is as though some delicate flower had been thrust too close to a scorching fire; and no matter how quickly or how far removed, no matter how heavy the dews that empearl it, how fresh and cool the wind that sweeps over it, how bright the sun that feeds its pulses,—the curled petals are never smoothed, the hot blasts leaves its ineffaceable blight. To me, the thought of marriage comes no more than to one who knows death sits waiting only for the setting of the sun, to claim his own. That phase of life is as inaccessible and uninviting to me, as Antarctic circumpolar lands; and even in thought, I have no temptation to explore it. My future and my past are so interblended, that I could as easily tear out my heart and continue to breathe, as attempt to separate them. I have a certain work to do, and its accomplishment bars all other paths."

"Does the nature of that work involve vows of celibacy?"

"Sometimes fate decrees for us, allowing no voluntary vows. How soon the path to my work will open before me, I cannot tell; but the day must come, and like a pilgrim girded, I wait and watch."

"Can you find elsewhere a nobler field of work than surrounds you here?"

"Certainly not, and some dross of selfishness mingles with the motives that will ultimately bear me beyond these hallowing precincts; yet a day may come, when having fulfilled a sacred duty, I shall travel back, praying you to let me live, and work, and die among you."

"My sister, your patient submission, your tireless application, have endeared you to me; and I should grieve to lose you from our little gray band, where your artistic labors have reflected so much credit on the 'Home'."

"Thank you, Sister Ruth; praise from fellow toilers is praise indeed, and the greatest blessing one human being can bestow upon another, I owe to you; the blessing of being helped to procure work, which enables me to help myself. If I leave the 'Anchorage' for a season, it will be on an errand such as Noah's dove went forth from refuge to perform; and when I return with my olive branch, the deluge of my life will have spent its fury, and I shall rest in peace where the ark is anchored."

"Do you imagine that desertion from our ranks will be so readily condoned? Drum-head court martial obtains here."

"Would you call it desertion, if seizing the flag of duty that floats over us here, I forsook the camp only long enough to scout on a dangerous outpost, to fight single-handed a desperate battle! If I fell, the folds of our banner would shroud me; if I conquered, would you not all greet me, when weary and worn I dragged myself back to the ranks? Some day, when I tap at the ark window, you will open your arms and take me in; for then my earthly mission will have ended, and the smoke of the accepted sacrifice will linger in my garments."

"Meantime, to-day's duties demand attention. I have a note from Cyril Brompton requesting that special courtesy be shown by us to his friend, the new Bishop, who is in the city, and who desires to inspect the 'Anchorage'. Cyril declines escorting the party, because he finds it painful to meet you now, and he wishes particularly that you should show your own department. I shall not be able to climb to the third story, while my ankles are so swollen, so I must deputize you to do the honors on your floor. Hold yourself in readiness, if I should send for you, and do not forget to give the Bishop a package of the new prospectus of the art school. That basket of orchids must be delivered before five o'clock. Sister Joanna said you detained her to make a sketch of it."

"I had almost finished when you summoned me. Send her up for the basket in half an hour."

The long studio was deserted, and very quiet on that sultry Saturday afternoon in midsummer, and the drowsy air was laden with fragrance from the pots of white carnations, massed on the iron balcony, upon which the tall, plate glass windows opened to the north. Down the centre of the apartment ran a table covered with oil cloth, and on the walls hung pictures in oil, water-color, crayon, while upon brackets and pedestals were mounted plaster casts, terra cotta heads, a few bronzes, and some hammered brass plaques. In the corners of the room, four marvels of taxidermy contributed brilliant colors mixed on the feathered palettes of a pea-fowl, a scarlet flamingo, a gold and a silver pheasant, all perched on miniature mounds, built of curious specimens of rock, of shells, coral and sphagnum.

The slow, languid swish, swish of the waters stirred by a passing steamer, broke on the cliff beyond the wall; and along the sky line where lake and atmosphere melted insensibly into blue distance, great cumulus copper-colored clouds hooded with salmon-tinted folds, tipped here and there with molten silver, shadowed with pearly hollows, hung entranced by their own image, over the inland sea that gleamed like a mirror.

At the end of the studio, near the open windows, Beryl had placed the plateau basket of orchids on the table; and she stood before an easel, transferring to the surface of a concave brass plaque, the fluted outlines of the scarlet and orange ribbons, the vivid green, purple and golden-brown lips, the rose velvet cups, the tender canary-hued calyxes of the glistening floral mass, whose aroma seemed a panting breath from equatorial jungles. Having secured the strange forms of these vegetable simulacra of the insect world, she replaced the sheathing of tissue paper around the gorgeous mosaic of color; and just then, Sister Joanna threw open the door, and ushered in a party of visitors, consisting of two gentlemen and a lady. One was Mr. Kendall, a member of the Chapter of Trustees.

"Good evening, Sister. Bishop Douglass, of our State, and Miss Gordon, from the South. I have been boasting to them of the perfect success of the 'Anchorage', as an industrial institution. Will you show us some of the work done in this department?"

As on a swiftly revolving wheel, Beryl saw the black eyes and gold-rimmed spectacles of Leighton Douglass; the shield-shaped amethyst ring on his broad, white hand; the slender figure by his side, draped in some soft brown tint of surah silk, the blond hair, the wide, startled hazel eyes of Leo, who made a step forward, then paused irresolute.

The gaze of the visitors was fastened upon the superb form wearing the gray garb of flannel, with snowy fluted frills at the rounded wrists and throat, and a ruffled white muslin mob cap crowning rich waves of bronze hair, that framed a beautiful pale face, whose gray eyes kept always the soft shadow of their long jet lashes.

Only half a minute sufficed to gird Beryl, and with no hint of recognition in her tranquil countenance, she moved forward, opened the drawers, and spread out for inspection various specimens of drawing and painting, in all stages of advancement.

A crimson tide overflowed Leo's cheeks, but accepting the cue of silence, she refrained from any manifestation of previous acquaintance; and bending over the pictures, listened to the grave, sweet voice that briefly, though courteously answered all inquiries concerning the school, hours of classes, tuition fees, remunerative rates paid for designs for carpets, wall papers and decorative upholstering. Unrolling from a wooden cylinder a strip of thick paper, two yards long and twenty inches wide, she displayed an elaborate arabesque pattern done in sepia for a sgraffito frieze, sixteenth century, which had been ordered by the architect of the new "Museum of Art".

"A bit of your favorite Florentine facade," said the Bishop, addressing his cousin, and peering closely at the scroll work.

"In this corner of the world, one scarcely expects a glimpse of Andrea Feltrini," answered Leo, avoiding the necessity of looking at Beryl, by glancing at Mr. Kendall.

"What are your sources of information?" inquired Bishop Douglass.

"We have a carefully selected collection of engravings, and a few good sketches and cartoons; moreover, some of our Sisterhood have been in Italy."

In attempting to roll the strip, it slipped from her fingers. Both women stooped to catch it, and their hands met. Looking into Leo's eyes, Beryl whispered: "See me alone." Then she rewound the paper, restored its oil silk cover, and shut the drawer.

"Do you find that the demand for purely ornamental work renders this department self-sustaining?" asked Leighton Douglass.

"I think the experience of the 'Anchorage' justifies that belief; especially since the popularization of so-called 'Decorative Art', which projects the useful into the realm of the beautiful; and by lending the grace of ornament to the strictly utilitarian, dims the old line of demarcation."

"We are particularly interested in acquiring accurate knowledge on this subject, because Miss Gordon hopes to establish a similar institution near her home in the South; where so many of our countrywomen, rendered destitute in consequence of the late war, need training which will enable them to do faithful remunerative work, without compromising their feminine refinement. While in Europe she inspected various industrial organizations; saw Kaiserswerth, and the Training Schools for Nurses, even the Swedish 'Naas Slojd', and her visit here is solely to verify the flattering accounts she has received of the success of the eclectic system of the 'Anchorage'. The South is so rich in fine materials that appear to offer a premium for carving, that we wish to investigate this branch of 'decorative' labor, and hope you can help us by some practical suggestions."

"Within the past twelve months, we have commenced the experiment of wood work; make all the utensils we need, and one of our patrons secured for us some models from the school you mentioned near Gothenburg. As yet we have received only two orders; one for a base in walnut for a baptismal font; the other an oak triptych frame for a choir in a Minnesota church. The carving is a distinct branch, that does not belong to my department; but if you will knock at the arched door on the right hand side of the hall, Sister Katrina, who has charge of that work, will take pleasure in exhibiting the process. Mr. Kendall knows the 'Anchorage' so well, he needs no guide to the work-rooms. Permit me to offer you some copies of our new prospectus, and also a photograph of this building, as a slight souvenir of your visit here."

She fitted papers and picture into a square envelope stamped with an anchor in red ink, and handing it to Miss Gordon, walked to the door and opened it. On the threshold Leo turned, and looked intently into her face:

"Are you sufficiently at leisure to allow me a little further conversation this afternoon; or shall I call again?"

"I am entirely at your service, and shall gladly furnish any information you may desire. Our matron has placed my time at your disposal."

"Mr. Kendall, if you will kindly accompany the Bishop to the wood-carving room, I can remain here a little while, to ask Sister some questions, which would scarcely interest you gentlemen. I will join you there, very soon. Leighton, please get an estimate of the cost of the necessary outfit, and talk with Mr. Kendall concerning the feasibility of sending one of our women here for a year."

Closing the door, Beryl put out both hands, and took Leo's. She stood a moment, holding them in a tight clasp.

"Thank you, for considerately withholding a recognition that would have embarrassed me. I hoped that the habit of our Order would in some degree disguise me, yet, at a glance you knew me."

"Shall I infer that your history is unknown here?"

"Sister Ruth, our Matron, is thoroughly acquainted with my past life, but she kindly respects my sorrows, and deems it unnecessary to publish the details among the Sisterhood. Do you know me so little, that you imagine I am capable of abusing the confidence of the head of an establishment which mercifully shelters an outcast?"

She stepped back, and motioned her visitor to a seat near the balcony.

"I should be very reluctant to ascribe any unworthy motive to you; therefore I fail to understand why you desire to preserve your incognito, especially since the signal vindication of your innocence. The news of the extraordinary discovery of the picture on the glass, and of your complete acquittal, even of suspicion, gave me so much pleasure that I should have written you my hearty congratulations, had I been able to obtain your address."

"I felt assured you would rejoice with me; and because I hold your good opinion so valuable, let me say that my happiness in the unexpected vindication of my character was enhanced by the proud consciousness that in your estimation I needed none. When the blackness of an intolerable shame overshadowed me, you groped your way to the dungeon, and held out your hands in confidence and sympathy. All the world suspected; you trusted me. You offered your noble name as bond, and made a place for me at your own sacred hearthstone. Do you think I can ever forget the blessedness of the balm that your faith in me poured into my crushed, despairing heart? Do you doubt that no sun sets, without seeing me on my knees, praying God's blessing of perfect happiness for you? What would I not do—what would I not suffer—to secure your peace, and to prove my gratitude?"

Her voice vibrated like the silver string of a deep violon-cello, and Leo, gazing up into the misty splendor of the beautiful sad eyes, ceased to wonder at the fascination which she had exerted over Mr. Dunbar. Unintentionally this woman's face had marred her life; had unwittingly stolen her lover's heart; yet she believed no treachery sullied the pure perfection of the soft red lips, and Leo's generous nature rose above the narrow limits of ordinary feminine jealousy. Had she doubted for an instant the theory that Beryl was heroically suffering the penalty of a crime, in order to screen her guilty lover, some suspicion of the truth might have dawned upon her.

"Suppose I intend to put your gratitude to the test? You have exaggerated the debt which you acknowledge; are you prepared to cancel it? If I say to you, because I believed in you, trusted you, will you repay me now, by granting a favor which I shall ask?"

"I think Miss Gordon could express no wish that I would not gladly execute, in order to promote her happiness."

"Will you come back to X——and help me to establish a home for women, who are destitute alike of money and of family ties? When you preside over it I shall be haunted by no fears of failure. Once, I gave you my sympathy; now, when I need help, will you give me yours?"

Beryl shivered, and looked wonderingly at her companion. Was she indeed so unsuspicious of the quicksand on which stood the fair temple of her hopes in marriage?

"O, Miss Gordon! That is the one thing, in all the world, that for your sake as well as mine, I could never do. No, no; impossible."

"Why, not for my sake, since I desire it so earnestly?"

A bright flush had risen in Leo's cheeks, and she threw back her small head challengingly.

For a moment Beryl wavered. Could she bear to wound that proud spirit?

"Go back to X——? To X——! It would be a renewal of my martyrdom, and I should only be a stumbling block in the scheme you contemplate. You do not understand, perhaps; but believe me, I prove my gratitude by refusing your kind offer."

"I think I understand; and if I am willing to run the risk, what then?"

"Do not ask me the impossible. The very atmosphere of X——would numb me, destroy all capability of usefulness, by reviving harrowing memories."

"Had not every shadow of suspicion vanished, and the entire community manifested delight in your triumphant innocence, I should never have suggested a return to the scene of your sufferings. Certainly, I cannot press the payment of a debt, which you volunteered to cancel; but I am sorry your refuse to oblige me."

There was a starry sparkle in the soft hazel eyes, and an involuntary and unconscious hardening of her lips, as Leo rose.

"It is hard, Miss Gordon, to be always misunderstood; but sometimes duty points to lines that subject us to harsh and bitter censure. I bear ever a heavy burden; do not increase my load by condemning me as ungrateful, God knows, you hold a warm and a holy place in my heart, and your happiness is more to me than my own; yet the one thing you ask, my conscience forbids."

"How long have you been here?"

"It will be two years to-morrow since I entered these peaceful walls."

"Then your probation ends, and you become permanently a Sister of the 'Anchorage'?"

"Not yet. I have been permitted to earn my daily bread here, upon conditions somewhat at variance with the regulations that usually govern the institution. I have not applied for admission to permanent membership, because my stay is contingent upon circumstances, which may call me hence to-morrow; which may never arise to beckon me away. Sister Ruth generously allows me the latitude of choice; not for my own sake, but for that of a friend, whose influence secured my admission. After a while, when I have finished my work, I hope to come back; to spend the residue of my earthly days, and to die here, a faithful Umilta Sister of the 'Anchorage', which opened its arms when I was a needy and desolate waif."

"The peace of your new life is certainly reflected in your face. Patience has had its perfect work; and that 'peace that passeth all understanding' is the reward granted you."

Leo held out her hand, and Beryl took it between both hers.

"Dear Miss Gordon, grapes yield no wine until they are crushed, trampled, bereft of bloom, of rounded symmetry, of beautiful color; but the Lord of the Vineyard is entitled to His own. I was a very proud, self-reliant girl, impatient of poverty, daringly ambitious; and what I deemed a cruel fate, threw me into the vat, to be trodden under foot. It may be, that when the ferment ends, and time mellows all, the purple wine of my bruised and broken life may be accounted worthy the seal of a sacramental sacrifice. I have ceased to question, to struggle, to plan. Like a blind child, fearing to stumble into ruin, I stand, and stretch out my hands to Him, who has led me safely through deep waters, along frightful gorges. Each day brings its work, which I strive worthily to accomplish; but my aim is to lay my heart, mind, soul, my stubborn will, all in God's hands. You think peace the summum bonum? Sometimes we obtain it by an ignominious surrender, when we should possess it by conquest. 'Peace of mind is a beautiful and heavenly thing; but even peace of mind may become an idol; and there is perhaps no idol to which women bow down more passionately.' For this reason, I am waiting for the drum beat of duty, and my march may begin at any moment. I asked to see you alone, in order to beg that you will increase my debt of obligations, by promising to reveal to no one the place of my retreat. Accident has betrayed to you that which I am anxious to keep secret; and I trust you will tell no one where you met me."

"Why should you hide, as though you were a culprit? You have been so completely exonerated from the imputation of guilt which once hung over you, that you owe it to yourself to front the gaze of the world fearlessly. What have you to dread?"

"The failure of something, which, though its accomplishment costs me very dear, I shall not relax my efforts to promote. I am trying to be loyal to my duty, even when the command is to strangle my own weak heart. You do not, cannot understand. God grant you never will. There are reasons why it is best for me to live in strict seclusion, for the present. Those reasons I can explain neither to you, nor to any other human being; and yet, I ask you to respect them, and to keep my secret. You trusted me in the terrible exigencies of the past; and you must trust me now, for—oh! God knows—I do indeed deserve your confidence."

She raised the hand folded in her own, and bowed her head upon it.

"You have my promise. Without your permission, I will mention our meeting to no one. I trust you; and perhaps if you would trust me, I might render you some aid."

"The day may come, when I can find it compatible with duty to tell you the secret of my life. In future years, when you are a happy wife, I shall by God's help be able to seek you and your husband, and thank you both for many kindnesses. I pray that you may be as happy as you deserve."

There was no tremor in the voice that answered quickly.

"If you refer to Mr. Dunbar, you have been led astray by the gossip in X——. Once, there seemed a probability that our lives might be united; but long ago, we found that ardent friendship could not take the place of love; and rather more than three years have passed since we have even seen each other."

With a startled movement Beryl dropped her companion's fingers, and laid a hand on her shoulder.

"Oh! do not tell me that you have broken your engagement!"

The two looked steadily at each other, and while Leo's proud face gave no hint of pain or embarrassment, Beryl's blanched, quivered.

"How did you know that any engagement ever existed?"

"All X——knew it. Mrs. Singleton and Sister Serena told me."

"I dissolved that engagement before I went to Europe."

"Then you rashly wrecked your beautiful future. Why did you cast him off? He would have made you happy; he is worthy, I think, even of you."

"Yes, he is worthy, I believe, of any woman whom he may really love; but my happiness is not in his keeping, and my future holds, I trust, something much brighter than our marriage would hate proved to me."

"You have thrown away the substance for the shadow. Before it is too late, reconsider your decision; give him an opportunity to reinstate himself in your affection. You have both been so kind to me, that I have hoped you would find life long happiness in each other."

"Dismiss that delusion. His path and mine diverge more and more, and we no longer dwell in the same State. He has inherited a large amount of property in Louisiana, and now lives in New Orleans; hence you can readily perceive how far apart the currents of our lives have drifted. I rejoice in my freedom; and he, I suspect, is not inconsolable for my loss."

Through Beryl's whirling brain darted the recollection of a rumor, that Leighton Douglass was suitor for his cousin's hand; and that Miss Dent favored the alliance. Was the solution of Miss Gordon's cold, calm indifference to be found in the presence and devotion of the Bishop? Could he have supplanted Mr. Dunbar in her affection? Had the world swung from its moorings? What meant the light that broke upon her, as if the walls of heaven had fallen, and let all the glory out?

After a moment she said, solemnly:

"I pray God to overrule all earthly things, for your welfare, for your heart's truest happiness; and for the realization of your dearest hopes. When my mission has been accomplished, and duty lifts her seal from my lips, I may try to see you once more, and explain the necessity that forced me to seek seclusion."

"I believe I understand; and I trust your reward will not be delayed. You and I can lean with confidence upon the wisdom and the mercy of the God we worship; but each must serve out His appointed time of bondage in the Egypt of suffering, in the famine of the desert; and must drink at Marah, before the blessing of the manna, the grapes of Eshcol, the roses of Sharon. If ever you should need an earthly friend, remember me; and if all other refuge fail you, my home can be always yours."

Hand in hand they walked to the door, and Leo pitied the future of this woman, whose lover was a wandering outlaw, with a price set upon his head; and beneath her gray flannel habit, Beryl's heart was torn with conflicting emotions, as she watched the placid, proud face, that showed no vestige of the storm of disappointment which had stranded her sweetest hope in life.

"Good-bye, Beryl; God keep you in His tender care."

"Good-bye, dear Miss Gordon. I will pray for your happiness, so long as I live."

She stooped, drew Leo's hands to her face, pressed her trembling lips twice upon them; then turned quickly, and locked herself in the studio.

Is it true, that "Orestes and Pylades have no sisters?"

CHAPTER XXXIII.

A Persian proverb tells us: "A stone that is fit for the wall is not left in the way." Strong artistic aspirations will plough through arid sands, leap across bottomless chasms, toil over bristling obstacles, climb bald, freezing crags to reach that shining plateau, where "beauty pitches her tents", and the Ideal beckons. Favorable environment is the steaming atmosphere that fosters, forces and develops germs which might not survive the struggle against adverse influences, in uncongenial habitat; but nature moulds some types that attain perfection through perpetual elementary warfare which hardens the fibre, and strengthens the hold; as in those invincible algx towering in the stormy straits of Tierra del Fuego, swept from Antartic homes toward the equator,—defying the fierce flail of surf that pulverizes rock, "Breed is stronger than pasture; and no matter how savage a stepmother the circumstances of life may prove, the inherited psychological strain will sometimes dominate, and triumph." According to the Talmud: "A myrtle, even in a desert, remains a myrtle".

From her tenth year, Beryl had begun to build her castle in the Spain of Art; daubed its walls with wonderful frescoes, filled its echoing corridors with heroic men and lovely women of the classic ages; and through its mullioned windows looked into an enchanted land, clothed with that witching "light that never was on sea or land". When all else on earth was sombre and dun-hued, sunlight and moonlight still gilded those magical towers. In darkest nights, through hissing rain and hurtling hail, she caught the glitter of its starry vanes smiling through murkiness, and above the wail and sob of the storms that had swept over the waste places of her youth, she heard the divine melodies which the immortal harper, Hope, played always in the marvellous palace of the Muses.

In early girlhood she had followed her father into the solemn mysteries of Greek Tragedy; and in that vast white temple dedicated to the inexorable Fates, where predestined victims moved like marble images to their immolation, her own plastic nature had been moulded in unison with the classic cult. Among the throng of Attic types, an immortal statue of filial devotion and sisterly love had attracted her irresistibly, and to Antigone she rendered the homage of a boundless admiration, an unwavering fealty.

Intellectually, humanity cleaves to idolatry; and each of us worships in the Pantheon, where our favorite divinities in literature crowd the niches. To become a skilful artist, and paint the portrait of Antigone, vas the ambition that had shaped and colored Beryl's young dreams, long ere she suspected that a mournful parallelism in fate would consign her to a living tomb more intolerable than that devised by Theban Creon.

Our grandest pictures, statues, poems, are not the canvas, the marble, the bronze, and the gilded vellum, that the world handles, criticises, weighs, buys and sells, accepts with praise, or rejects with anathema. Invisible and inviolate, imagination, keeps our best, our ideals, locked in the cerebrum cells of "gray matter", which we are pleased to call our workshop.

What art gallery, what library can rival the sublime and beautiful images that crowd the creased and folded labyrinth of the human brain; as far beyond the ken and analysis of the biologist's microscope, as some remote nebulae shining in blue gulfs of interstellar space, that no telescopic Jense can ever discover, even as a faint blur of silvery mist upon the black velvet vault that suns and planets spangle?

In some degree, Beryl's artistic dream had been realized; and the study of years slowly flowered into a large painting, which represented Antigone standing beside the heap of dust, strewn reverently to sepulchre the form dimly outlined at her feet. The sullen red sunset of a tempestuous day flared from the horizon, across a desolate plain; showed the city walls in the background, the hungry vultures poised high above the dead, the marauding dogs crouched in the wind-swept sand, watching their banquet, decreed by the king. The dust had been scattered from a black vase that bore on its front, in a circular medallion, the lurid head of grinning Hecate; and the last rite to appease the unquiet manes was performed by the uplifted right arm that poured libations from a burnished brass urn, held aloft over the pall of earth that denned the figure beneath. The left hand was stretched, not heavenward, but shieldingly over the mound, and in the beautiful, stern face bent a little downward in invocation of the infernal gods, one read sublime self-surrender, grief for Oedipus, regret for Hasmon, farewell to life,—mingled with exultant consciousness that a successful sacrifice had been accomplished for Polynices, and that the spirit of the brother rested in peace.

The soul of the artist seemed to look triumphantly through the solemn, purplish blue eyes of the young martyr, and Beryl knew that her own heart beat under the pamted folds of the diploidion; that she had epitomized in a symbolic picture, the history of her own joyless youth.

The canvas had been framed and hung at the art exhibition of the new "Museum", opened in September; and only the "U" traced in one corner beneath an anchor, indicated that it was the work of the Umilta Sisters' "Anchorage".

The public peered, puzzled, shook its sapient head, shrugged its authoritative shoulders, and sundry criticisms crept into the journals; but the prophet was judged in "his own country"; and home work, according to universal canons, rarely finds favor among home awarding committees, whose dulness its uncomprehended excellence affronts.

One censured vehemently the masonry of the city wall; another deplored pathetically the "defective foreshortening of a dog's shoulders"; the picture "lacked depth of tone"; the "coloring was too bizarre", the "tints too neutral".

Like chemicals tested in a laboratory, or like Pharaoh's lean kine, each objection devoured the preceding one; and unanimity of blame assaulted only one salient point on the entire canvas: the red sandals of the Greek girl—upon which outraged good taste fell with pitiless fury.

Undismayed, Beryl withdrew her picture, erased the ciphers in the corner, and shipped it to New York to Doctor Grantlin, who had recently returned from Europe; requesting him to place it at a picture dealer's on Broadway, and to withhold the name of its birth-place.

Two weeks later, a popular journal published an elaborate description of "A painting supposed to have been obtained abroad by a New York collector, who merited congratulation upon possession of a masterpiece, which recalled the marvellous technique of Gerome, the atmosphere of Jules Breton, the rich, mellow coloring, and especially the scrupulous fidelity of archaic detail, which characterized Alma Tadema; and was conspicuously manifest in the red shoes so distinctively typical of Theban women".

Mr. Kendall caused this article to be copied into the leading newspaper of his own city; and the first mail, thereafter, carried to New York an offer of eight hundred dollars for the painting, from the President of the "Museum" Directors, who had been so shocked by the unknown significance of the "red shoes". After a few days, it was generally known, but mentioned with bated breath, that the "Antigone" had been bought by a wealthy Philadelphian, who paid for it two thousand dollars, and hung it in his gallery, where Fortunys, Madrazos, and Diazs ornamented the walls.

Why should journeying abroad to render "Caesar's things" to foreign Caesars, demand such total bankruptcy that we must needs repudiate the just debts of home creditors, whose chimneys smoke just beyond the fence that divides us? De mortuis nil nisi bonum is a traditional and sacred duty to departed workers; but does it exhaust human charity, or require contemptuous crusade against equally honest, living toilers? Are antiquity and foreign birthplace imperatively essential factors in the award of praise for even faithful and noble work? We lament the caustic moroseness of embittered Schopenhauer, brooding savagely over his failure to secure contemporaneous recognition; yet after all, did he malign his race, or his age, when, in answer to the inquiry where he desired to be buried, he scornfully exclaimed: "No matter where; posterity will find me."

It was on the 26th of October, a week subsequent to the receipt of the letter which contained the check sent in payment for the picture, that Beryl sat down on the stone sill of her oriel window, to rest in the seclusion of her room, after the labors of the day.

It was the anniversary of her ill-starred visit to X——, and melancholy memories had greeted her at dawn, clung to her skirts, chanted their dismal refrain, and renewed the pain which time had in some degree dulled. Four years ago she had felt her mother's feverish lips on hers, in a parting kiss, and four years ago to-day the sun of her girlhood had passed suddenly into total eclipse. Since then, moving in a semi-twilight, suffering had prematurely aged her, and she had schooled herself to expect no star, save that of duty, to burn along her lonely path. To-day, she thought of the pride her picture would have aroused in her devoted father; of the comforts the money would have purchased for her invalid mother; of the pleasure, success as an artist would have brought to her own ambitious soul, if only it had not come so many years too late. What crown could fame bring to one, dwelling always in the chill shadow of a terrible shame? The glory of noble renown could never gild a name that had answered at the convicts' roll call; a name which, at any moment, Bertie's arrest might drag back to the disgrace of established felony.

Of all mocking fiends, the arch torturer is that hand which draws aside the black curtain of grim actuality, and shows us the wonderful realm of "might have been", where lost hopes blossom eternally, and the witchery of hallowed illusions is never dispelled.

Wearily Beryl closed her eyes, as though the white lids availed to shut out visions, tantalizing as the dream of bubbling springs, and palm-fringed isles of dewy verdure, to the delirious traveller dying of thirst, in the furnace blasts of mid-desert.

If she had defied her mother's wishes, and refused to go to X——? How different the world would seem to her; but, what was a world worth, that had never known Mr. Dunbar?

Over burning ploughshares she had walked to meet one destined to stir to its depths the slumbering sea of her tenderest love; and to forego the pain, would she relinquish the recompense?

During the months that elapsed after Leo's visit to the "Anchorage", Beryl had surrendered her heart to the great happiness of dwelling, unrebuked by conscience, upon the precious assurance that the love of the man whom she had so persistently defied and shunned, was irrevocably hers. The sharpest pain that can horrow womanhood, springs from the contemplation of the superior right of another to the object of her affection; and though honor coerces submission to the just claims of a rival, renunciation of the beloved entails pangs that no anaesthetic has power to quiet.

After the long struggle to aid Miss Gordon's accepted lover in keeping his vows of loyalty, the discovery of his freedom, and the belief that Bishop Douglass had supplanted him in the affection of her generous benefactress, had brought to Beryl an exquisite release; sweet as the spicy breath of the tropics wafted suddenly to some stranded, frozen Arctic voyager. Heroic and patient, keeping her numb face steadfastly turned to the pole star of duty, where the compass of conscience pointed—was the floe ice on which she had been wrecked, drifting slowly, imperceptibly, yet surely down to the purple warmth of the Gulf Stream, dotted with swelling sails of rescue? Like oceanic streams meeting, running side by side, freighted with cold for the equatorial caldrons, with heat for the poles, are not the divinely appointed currents of mercy and of affliction, God's agents of compensation, to equalize the destinies of humanity?

We rail at Fate as triple monsters; but sometimes it happens, that the veil of inscrutability floats aside, for an instant, and we catch a glimpse of the radiant smile of an infinite love.

Hope had set in Beryl's sky, but a tender afterglow held off the coming night, when she thought of the face that had bent so yearningly above her, of the passionate voice and the thrilling touch that were now her most precious memories. The pearl which Miss Gordon had cast away as worthless, the discarded convict might surely, without sin, claim as her own for ever. To-day an intense longing to see him once more, to hear from his lips praise of her "Antigone", disturbed the tranquillity that was spreading its robes of minever over a stony path; but she put aside the temptation.

To the Sisterhood of the "Anchorage" she had given one-half the proceeds of the picture sale; and the remainder would enable her at last to renew the search for her unhappy brother. So vague were the topographical lines furnished by the English tourist, that prosecuting her quest in the remote wilderness of mountains, which wore their crown of snow, seemed a reckless waste of hope, time and money; nevertheless, she must make the attempt. She knew that a gigantic railway system was crawling like an anaconda under rocky ranges, over foaming rivers, stretching its sinuous steel trail from Bay of Chaleur to Georgia Gulf; with termini that saw the sun rise from the Atlantic Ocean, and watched its setting in the red glory of the far Pacific; and perhaps steam shovels, and iron tight-ropes might furnish her facilities on her long journey.

Winter would soon overtake her, and in the inhospitable region where her brother had been surprised at his prayers, how could a lonely woman travel without protection? Doubt, apprehension flitted as ill-boding birds of night, flapping dusky wings to hide the signal beacon, which love and duty swung to and fro; yet the yearning to see her brother's face again, dwarfed all barriers, and she trusted God's guidance.

On a chair near her, lay, on this afternoon, a map which for many days she had been studying; and opening it once more, she ran a finger along the dotted lines, mentally debating whether it would be best to go by rail to Ottawa, by water to Sault St. Marie, whence the new railway could be easily reached, or whether the most direct route would be via St. Paul to Winnepeg. When she left the "Anchorage", her destination must remain a secret; hence she could ask no counsel. In view of approaching cold weather, economy of time seemed imperative; and she resolved to buy a railway ticket to Fargo, where she could elude suspicion, should the threatened invisible detective "shadow" her; and whence another Pacific highway offered egress to western wilds. With this definite conclusion she closed the map, and a moment later, some one knocked at her door.

"Come in."

She went forward, and met Sister Katrina, a robust dame of forty years, blond as Gerda; with the "light of the glowworm's tails" in her golden-lashed violet eyes, and the "ruby spots of the cowslip's leaves" on her full, frank lips.

"Will you sit a while with me? There is still a half hour, before your evening work begins in the carving shop. Come in."

"I am sorry I have not time now, to indulge myself in such luxury as a chat with you always proves. I came to beg the loan of your India ink copy of the marble screens at Agra; which I have an idea would be very effective done in cherry, for the panels under the new bookcases we are designing for the library."

"The copy is up stairs in the studio; but I shall be glad to get it for you."

"No; with your permission I can help myself, and I am going up there now, for some red chalk. I know exactly where to find the picture, because I was examining it two days ago. What think you of my idea?"

"I am afraid you will find cherry too dark. A lighter wood, I think, would be better adapted to the exceeding delicacy of the design."

"Wait till I cut out a sample scroll, and we will talk it over. Sister Ruth asked me to hand to you this paper, which contains a very complimentary notice of your lovely picture. I read it as I came up, and congratulate you on all the fine things said. You scarcely know how proud we feel of our Sister's work. Thanks for the use of the drawing."

She smiled, nodded and closed the door; and when her bright cheery countenance vanished, it seemed as though a film of cloud had drifted across the sun.

Beryl went back to a low chair in front of the window, and opened the paper, which chanced to be the New York "Herald." Unfolding it to hunt the designated article, her glance fell accidentally upon the personal column. Her heart leaped, then almost ceased beating, as she read:

"Important. Bertie will meet Gigina in the Museum at Niagara Falls, Canada side, any day during the last week in October."

Two years and a half had almost gone by since she inserted the advertisement, to which this was evidently a reply. Long ago she had ceased to expect any tidings through this channel; but the seed sown in faith, watered by tears, and guarded by continual prayer had stirred to life; blossomed in the sunshine of God's pitying smile, and after weary waiting, the ripe fruit fell at her feet. How fair and smooth, rosy and fragrant it appeared to her famishing heart? How opportune the guiding hand that pointed her way, when cross roads baffled her. Two days later, she would have been journeying away from the coveted goal. Now the tide of battle was turning. Had the stars rolled back on their courses to rescue Sisera?

How long the happy woman sat there, exulting in the mellowness of the perfect fruit of patience, she never knew.

Day died slowly; the vivid crimson and dazzling gold that fired the West were reflected in the tranquil bosom of the lake, faded into the tender pale rose of the sacred lotus, into the exquisite tints that gild the outer petals of a daffodil, the heart of buttercups; and then, robed in faintest violet powdered with silvery dust, the vast pinions of Crepuscule spread over sky and water, fanning into full flame the glittering sparks of planets and constellations that lighted the chariot course of the coming moon.

Across the sleeping lake hurried a north wind, on its long journey to blow open the snowy camellias folded close in the heart of the South, and under his winged sandals the waters crimped, rippled, swelled into wavelets that played their minor adagio in nature's nocturn, as their foam fingers fell on the pebbles that fringed the beach. From the deck of a schooner anchored off shore, floated the deep voice of a man singing Schubert's "Ave Maria"; and far, far away over the weird waste of waters, where a buoy marked a sunken wreck, its red beacon burned like the eye of Polyphemus, crouching in darkness, watching to surprise Galatea.

The penetrating chill of the night air aroused Beryl from her profound trance; and lighting the gas over her dressing table, she re-read the magical words that had transformed her narrow world. This was Monday the 26th, and next Saturday was the limit of the proposed interview. One day must suffice for necessary preparation, and starting by early morning express on Wednesday, she would arrive in time to keep the tryst that involved so much. She cut out the notice that was merely a sentence in the page of social hieroglyphics, where no key fitted more than one paragraph, and forgetting the criticism on her picture, she went swiftly down stairs.

The members of the Sisterhood were at supper, and she waited at the refectory door for an opportunity to meet the matron.

On the platform raised in the centre of the long room, sat the reader for the day, Sister Agatha; a plump, florid young woman, with bright black eyes, and a voice sweet and strong as the flute stop of an organ. The selection that evening had been from "Agate Windows" and "Ice Morsels", and the closing words were:

"Alpine flowers are warmed by snow; the summer beauty of our hills, and the autumn fertility of our valleys, have been caused by the cold embrace of the glacier; and so, by the chill of trial and sorrow, are the outlines of Christian character moulded and beautified. And we, who recognize the loving kindness as well as the power of God in what may seem the harsher and more forbidding agencies of nature, ought not to be weary and faint in our minds, if over our own warm human life, the same kind pitying Hand should sometimes cause His snow of disappointment to fall like wool, and cast forth His ice of adversity like morsels; knowing that even by these unlikely means, shall ultimately be given to us also, as to nature, the beauty of Sharon, and the peace of Carmel!"

Somewhere in the apartment, a bell tapped. All rose, and each head in the gray ranks bowed, while "thanks" were offered; then amid a subdued murmur of conversation, the Sisterhood filed out, gathered in groups, separated for various duties.

"Sister Ruth, may I see you alone?" asked Beryl, touching her arm in the hall.

"This is the night for the examination of accounts, of last week's expenses, and I shall be busy with Sister Elena, our book-keeper; moreover, I promised to look over the linen closet of the Infirmary, with Sister Consuelo, whose demands are like those of the daughter of the horse-leech. Is your business urgent?"

"Yes; but I will not detain you more than ten minutes."

"Very well, come to my cabinet."

The place designated was a pigeon box in size, and adjoined the reception room on the first floor. Two desks packed with papers, three chairs and a picture of Elijah and the ravens, constituted the furniture. The matron brightened the light, seated herself and looked at her companion.

"Well. What can I do for you? Why, Sister? Something has happened; your face is all aglow, your eyes are great stars."

"Yes; a heavy burden I have long borne is slipping from my heart, and after the pressure it rebounds. I have told you that my stay here was contingent on events which I could not control; that at any moment I might consider it incumbent upon me to go away into the world; therefore, I could bind myself by no compact to remain permanently in the 'Anchorage'. The time has come; the drum taps, I must march away."

"And you are so glad to leave us?" said the matron, gazing in wonder at the radiant face, usually so impassive and cold with its locked lips, and grave, sad, downcast eyes.

"No, glad only in the occasion that calls me; regretting that duty separates me temporarily from the Sisterhood, who so mercifully opened their arms, when I had no spot in all the wide world where I could lay my head, but the sod on my mother's grave. This blessed haven is for those whose first duty in life summons them nowhere beyond its walls. If conscience bade you leave these peaceful and hallowed halls, for work far more difficult, would you hesitate to obey? It is safer and less arduous to keep step with the main army; but some must perish on picket duty, and is the choice ours, when an order details us?"

"Who signed your order?"

Sister Ruth took off her spectacles, and bent closer, with a keenness of scrutiny, that was unflatteringly suspicious.

"My dear mother."

"I understood that you had been an orphan for years?"

"Yes, for four wretched, lonely and terrible years; but no tomb is deep enough to shut in the voice that uttered our mother's last wishes; and all time cannot hush the sound of the command, cannot hide the beloved hand that pointed to the path she asked us to follow. When my mother kissed me good-bye, she blessed me, because of a promise I gave her; and Heaven means to me the place where I can look into her sainted face, and tell her 'Hold me close to your tender heart, for oh! I have indeed kept my word. Your little girl obeyed your last command.'" Her voice trembled, and she passed one hand over her eyes for an instant.

"Sister Ruth, the opportunity has arrived, and I go to execute the last clause of a sacred order. When I shall have finished my mission, I shall want to come back home. Oh! you see? I call it home. For where else can I ever have a home, till I join my father and mother? If I should come back and ask you to take me for the remainder of my life, as a sister worker, will you let me die with the 'anchor' on my breast? I shall be as worthy of your confidence then, as I am now."

"Where are you going?"

"I hoped that you would not ask me, because I cannot tell you now. Will you not trust me?"

"Your extremely cautious reticence makes it difficult; and I have always known that some distressing mystery brought you here."

"Confidence that defies suspicious appearances is precious indeed; but confidence that crumbles like Jericho's walls at the blast of Joshua's trumpets, is as worthless a sham as a cable whose strands part at the first taut strain. Sister Ruth, there are reasons why I go away alone, to an unknown destination; and I am about to tax your trust yet more severely, when I tell you that I need the disguise of the 'Umilta' uniform. I ask your permission to wear it during my absence."

The matron shook her head.

"Surely, Sister Ruth, you cannot think it possible that I should bring discredit upon this dear gray flannel, which I hold as sacred as priestly vestments?"

She laid her cheek against her own shoulder, with a caressing motion, and passed her fingers softly across her sleeve.

"My young sister, to some extent I am responsible for those who wear the 'Umilta' gray. If I allowed you to carry our badge under such peculiar circumstances beyond the limits of my supervision, I should hazard too much; should deserve the severity of the censure I most certainly should receive, if any disaster brought reproach upon our spotless record as an institution. It was not designed as a disguise in which to masquerade for unknown purposes."

Beryl put up both hands, pressing her pretty white cap close to her ears; and her lips trembled, as was their wont, when she was wounded.

"Do not discrown me. My father's Beryl will never sully your pure record; and it would be as impossible for me to disgrace your uniform, as defile my mother's shroud. Grant me the protection of this consecrated garb."

"No. The 'Anchorage' must remain as heretofore, like Caesar's wife."

"Although I have lived here so long, how little you know me."

"Very true, my Sister; therefore, as custodian of the interests of our little community, I must not put them in jeopardy. When do you expect to take your departure?"

"Wednesday, at 6 A.M., on the express for New York."

"Have you received letters?"

"No, Sister. Doctor Grantlin is the only person who writes to me, and as his letters are always addressed to your care, I receive them from your hands."

"How long do you propose to stay in New York?"

"I am not going to New York, and I know not how long I may be detained; but I desire to return without needless delay."

"Then you want your money."

"Give me to-morrow five hundred dollars, and keep the remainder until I come, or until you hear from me. Please say that I have gone on a journey to fulfil a pledge made years ago; and try not to show the Sisters that you have no confidence in me. That—would rob my home-coming of half its pleasure. If any unforeseen accident should keep me away, should cut short a life which has overflowed with great sorrow, then retain the money and the pictures I leave behind; and believe that I died, as I have lived, not unworthy of all thy kindness and true charity this dear sacred 'Anchorage' has shown to me. Sister Elena is impatient; I hear her walking up and down the floor. While I am absent, Sister Katrina, and especially Sister Anice, can take my place in the Art School; and all my orders were finished last week, except the mirror for Mrs. St. Clair. She wished it framed in scarlet bignonias, and as the painting is more than half done, Sister Anice can easily complete it. I will not detain you longer. Good-night, Sister Ruth."

No sleep visited Beryl, and as she lay at two o'clock, watching the shimmer of the moonlight reflected from the tossing waves upon the panes of her wide window, where the tangled mesh of quivering rays coiled, uncoiled, glided hither and yon like golden serpents, she heard the click of the key, and the turning of the knob in a door, which opened from the alcove into an adjoining room. That apartment was reserved as a guest chamber; had been unoccupied for months; and puzzled by the sound, Beryl sat up in her bed and listened. The blue folds of the drapery hanging over the alcove arch, were drawn aside, and Sister Ruth, wrapped in a trailing dressing-gown, held up a small lamp and peered cautiously around.

"What is the matter, Sister?"

"Did I frighten you? I came this way rather than knock at the other door, because Sister Frances is on watch to-night; and though she is a dear good soul, she is afflicted with an undue share of the feminine frailty, curiosity, and I prefer that no one should canvass my unseasonable visit to you. Do not get up."

She put the brass lamp on a chair, and sat down on the edge of the bed.

"Our conversation has disquieted me, and I cannot sleep. Long ago, for my own sake, I made a rule by which to govern my judgment of my fellow beings; and it amounts to this: where I cannot be sure of evil in others, I give them the benefit of the doubt, and sincerely endeavor to think the best. I have watched you very closely. There is much that I cannot understand; much that it appears strange you should hesitate to explain; yet in these years I have had no cause to question your truthfulness, and that is the basis of all human worth. We profess to live here as one family, as sisters, holding each other in love, charity and trust; yet in searching myself to-night, I fear I have gone astray. I have pondered and prayed over this matter, and my heart yearns toward you. I feel as I fancy a mother might, who had too hastily slapped the face of her child; and, my sister, I have come to say, forgive me, if I too harshly refused your request, if I wounded you."

She held out her hand, but Beryl did not see it; she had covered her face, and unable to speak she leaned forward and laid her head on the matron's lap. Gently the thin fingers stroked the shining hair, until they were drawn down and pressed to the girl's lips.

"Again, I asked myself, whether my decision had not been inspired by an overweening pride in the public estimation of our home; rather than by an unselfish regard for the welfare and peace of mind of one of its members? What will the world think of us, must be subordinated to, what is the best for my young sister, whose cross it is my duty to lighten? I cannot bear to give you up; and I shall, I will trust you. Wear the 'gray' armor, and remember, if any blot stain it, you will bring disgrace upon a holy cause; you will be the first to stain the Umilta uniform; and I shall be blamed, for reposing confidence in one who betrayed us to public scorn. My Sister Beryl, I give you 'the gray'. God grant it may shelter you from harm, and bring you home to fill my place with honor, when I have passed into the eternal Anchorage."

CHAPTER XXXIV.

Over the region of the great lakes, her favorite haunt, hung the enchanted stillness, the misty glamour of the purple-cloaked witch—Indian Summer; whose sorcery veiled the dazzling face of the sun, and changed the silver lustre of Selene into the vast, solemn red blot that stared wonderingly at its own weird image in the glassy waters.

Wrapped in that soft, sweet haze, which like the eider down of charity smooths all roughness, rounds all angles, the world of shore and lake presented a magical panorama of towns and villages, herds of cattle, flocks of sheep, spires of churches, masts of vessels,—all flashing past the open window of the car, where Beryl sat, watching the shadows lengthen as the long train thundered eastward, and the tree dials marked the hour record on the golden brown stubble fields.

When the goal is in sight, do we dwell on the hazard, the strained muscles, the blistered feet, and the fierce thirst the long race-course cost us? Who know that they are weary and spent, while the prize brightens, nears as they stretch panting to grasp it?

The certainty of meeting her brother, the anticipation of all that she felt assured he would promise concerning his future, when he learned the severity of the ordeal which she had endured in his behalf, blotted out the costliness of the accomplishment. Like that glorious violet haze of Indian Summer, which was drawing its opalescent drapery along the vanishing iron railway track blackened with cinders, and softly shrouding the grim outlines of wreck, that told where a vessel had foundered on the lake in the early autumn gale, an overruling Providence seemed shedding peace even upon her troubled past. In the swift flash of the divine fire that sanctified the accepted sacrifice, she was too dazzled to remember the moan of the slaughtered victim, the agony of the death struggle; and now, her thoughts spanned the gulf of time, and painted the eternal reunion of the broken and dishonored family group.

From these comforting reflections she was aroused by a piercing cry that made her spring forward, and scan the crowd of human faces collected close to the rails, at a small town where the cars had halted.

On a side track in front of her window, was a train which had just dashed in from Buffalo, and amid the surging mass of jeering spectators, two officers stepped down from the platform, each with a hand on the arm of a man, who was heavily handcuffed. At the sight, a white-haired, withered woman leaning from a carriage and staring with horror-haunted eyes, had screamed, and was falling back insensible.

"That is his mother. Poor thing, why did they let her come? He is her only boy," said a man to his comrade, who stood near Beryl's seat.

"What is the matter?" asked a gentleman, sitting immediately in front of her.

"Two of our officers winged a bird, who thought it was safe flying over yonder, with the lake between him and the county jail. Canada is handy hunting-ground, when the game happens to be runaway thieves; and we have bagged one. He was the cashier of our Savings Bank, and not satisfied with tampering with the books, and forcing balances, he finally robbed the vault of a lot of gold, and flew across the line. His wife met him at St. Catherine's, and he met the iron bracelets he was dodging."

The train moved on, and once more Beryl heard the howling of the wolves, that she had hoped were left forever behind; that now seemed in full cry bearing down upon their prey. Should she return to the "Anchorage", and advertise Bertie's danger? So vague were her ideas relative to the limits of extradition, that she had regarded Canada as a city of refuge; considered its protection of United States' criminal fugitives as efficacious, as meeting a Vestal Priestess on the way to his execution, proved in rescuing a Roman malefactor from the penalty of violated law; but this shred of comfort had parted, when most she required its aid.

"Yes, I understand extradition provisions have been arranged, which are bound to have a wholesome effect; especially in this section, where it is so easy to slip across the lakes any dark night. I am told nearly all felonies will be embraced now—from murder to burglary—and that Her Majesty's Secretaries are more willing to aid our officers, than was the case a few years ago, when no end of quibbling tied up justice."

The gentlemen on the seat in front of her, moved away to the smoking car; and the woman in gray listened to the creak and whirr of the wheel of torturing dread, upon which some malignant fate once more bound her. Bertie had been safe in his mountain fastness, until her ill-starred advertisement coaxed him within reach of the police Briareus. Could she discern the hand of merciful warning in this fortuitous meeting with a captured culprit; which so vividly recalled the maddening incidents of her return to X——, when the sheriff had hurried her from the car? A sickening terror seized her, and along the expanse of pearly mist that united earth and sky, in tke snowy fringe of ripples breaking their teeth on the shelving beach, she seemed to read the doom of her stratagem written in words of menace:

"Go where you may, but I give you fair warning you cannot escape me; and the day on which you meet that guilty vagabond, you betray him to the scouts of justice."

Far away, among the orange groves of Louisiana, would he forget his threat, or fail to execute it? On and on darted the train; people laughed and talked; a tired baby swayed from side to side on the nurse's knees, crooned herself to sleep; and a canary in a cage covered with pink net, broke suddenly into a spasm of trills and roulades.

It was almost four o'clock when the dull roar of Niagara set the air a tremble, and the few remaining passengers left the train. The little town was unusually quiet and deserted, the tide of summer travel having ebbed; and not until the crystal fingers of the ice fairy had built her wonderful Giralda out of foam and spray, would that of Winter tourists begin to flow.

Leaving her trunk at the "baggage room" of the station, Beryl engaged a carriage driver to take her to the Suspension Bridge. Drawing her gray bonnet and veil as far as possible over her face, she paid the toll, and noticed that the keeper peered curiously at her, and muttered something in an undertone to a man wearing a uniform, who turned and stared at her.

She hurried away along that iron mesh swinging high in air like a vast spider web, spun from shore to shore across the swirling, snarling caldron of hissing waters. Was the officer the wary spider watching her movements, waiting to slip down the metal snare, and devour her hopes? Her heart beats sounded as the heavy thuds of a drum; the rush of dire forebodings drowned even the roar of the Falls, and the magnificence of the spectacle vanished before the awful realization of the danger to which she had invited Bertie.

The bridge was deserted; no human being was visible; and now and then she glanced back over her shoulder, dreading she knew not what form of pursuit. At last her flying feet touched British soil, but she knew now, that neither Bezer nor yet Shechcm lay before her; and no sign-post rose to welcome her, with the "Refuge—Refuge"—the water and the bread appointed of old, for spent fugitives. Canada was an ambush that, despite all caution, might betray her. Against the last rail of the bridge she leaned, tried to steady her nerves; and put up one passionate prayer:

"Turn not Thy face from me, O my God! in this last hour! Guide me aright. Overrule all my mistakes, and save my repentant brother."

On the wide gallery of the "Clifton House" stood a gardener engaged in removing the flower baskets that hung between the columns; and as he paused in his work, to observe the quaint gray figure below, she asked, in a voice that was strained beyond its customary sweetness:

"Please direct me to the Museum."

"Follow the street along the cliff, and you can't miss it. Behind those trees yonder, on the right hand side. To the best of my belief, it is shut up this week."

Turning south, she walked more leisurely, lest undue haste should excite suspicion; and all the solemn sublimity of the scene confronted her. The green crescent of the Horseshoe blanched to foam, as it leaped to the stony gulf below, the wreaths of mist floating up, gilded by the sunshine; the maddened rush of the tossing, frothing, whirling rapids seething like melted gold as the western radiance smote the bubbling surface; the scarlet flakes of foliage clinging to the trees on Goat Island, and far above, on the wooded height beyond, the picturesque outlines of the Convent, lifting its belfry against the azure sky. As doomed swimmers lost in those rapids, swept head downward to destruction, nearing the last wild plunge catch the glimmer of that consecrated tower held aloft, so to Beryl's eyes it now seemed a symbol of comfort; and faith once more girded her.

A woman wearing a blue plaid handkerchief tied over her head and knotted under her chin, and carrying a basket of red apples on one arm, while with the other she led a lowing cow along the dusty road, paused at a signal, in front of the gray clad stranger.

"Which is the Museum?"

"Yonder, where the goats are huddled."

The building was closed, but in those days a garden lay to the north of it; and a small gate that gave admittance to seats and flowers connected with the Museum, now stood open.

151

The walks were strewn with pale yellow poplar leaves, and bordered with belated pink hollyhocks, and crimson chrysanthemums blighted by frost, shivering in their death chill; and from a neighboring willow stripped of curtaining foliage, a lonely bird piped its plaintive threnody, for the loss of one summer's mate. At the extremity of the little garden, under shelter of an ancient, gnarled tree, that screened a semicircular seat from the observation of those passing on the street, Beryl sat down to rest; to collect her thoughts.

In the solitude, she threw back her veil, leaned her head against the trunk of the tree where wan lichens made a pearly cushion, and shut her eyes. The afternoon was wearing away; a keen wind shook the bare boughs; only the ceaseless, unchanging chant of waters rose from the vast throat of nature, invoking its God.

She heard no footsteps; but some strange current attacked her veins, thrilled along her nerves, strung as taut as the wires of a harp, and starting up she became aware that a man was standing on the clover sward close to her. A dark brown overcoat, a broad brimmed, soft wool hat, drawn as a mask down to the bridge of the nose, and a bare hand covering the mouth, was all she saw.

Stretching out her arms, she sprang to meet him:

"O Bertie! At last! At last!"

The figure drew back slightly, lifted his hat; and where she had expected to see her brother's golden curls, the crisp, black locks of Mr. Dunbar met her gaze.

"You! Here?"

She staggered, and sank back on the bench; the realization of Bertie's peril throttling the joy that leaped up in her heart, at sight of the beloved features.

"I am here. I come as promptly to fulfil my promise as you to keep your tryst. Do you understand me so little, that you doubted my word?"

Her bonnet had slipped back, and as all the chastened beauty of her face framed in the dainty cap, became fully exposed, a heavy sigh escaped him, and he set his teeth, like one nerved to endure torture.

For months he had nourished the germ of a generous purpose, had tried to accustom himself to the idea of ultimately surrendering her; but in her presence, a certain bitter fury swept away the wretched figment, and he remembered only how fair, how holy, how dear she was to him. Once more the cry of his famishing heart was: "Death may part us. I swear no man's arms ever shall."

"Why waylay and torment me? Have I not suffered enough at your hands? Between me and mine not even you can come."

"Take care! For your sake I am here, hoping to spare you some pangs; to allow you at least an opportunity to see him—"

"What have you done? Don't tell me I am too late. Where is he? Oh! where—where is he?"

She had sprung up, and her hands closed around his arm, shaking it in the desperation of her dread; while her voice quivered under the strain of a conjecture that Bertie had already been arrested.

"Where is your chivalrous, courageous, unselfish, devoted lover? To ascertain exactly where he skulks, is my mission to Canada; for I thought I had schooled myself to bear the pain of—"

"What do you mean? What have you done with my Bertie? Oh—"

She threw herself suddenly on her knees, held up her hands, and a wailing cry broke the stillness:

"Save him, Mr. Dunbar! You will break my heart if you bring ruin upon his dear head. He is all I have on earth, he is my own brother! My brother! my brother!"

The blood ebbed from his face; the haughty mouth twitched in a sudden spasm, and he put his hand over his eyes.

Could she adopt this ruse to thwart pursuit of the man whom she idolized? For half a moment he stood, with whitened lips; then stooped, took the face of the kneeling woman in his palms, and scanned it.

"Your brother?"

"My brother. Do you understand at last, why I must save him? Why you must help me to screen him from ruin?"

"Great God! After all, what a blind fool I have been!"

He raised her, placed her on the bench; sat down and leaned his head on his hand. To Beryl, the silence that followed was an excruciating torture, beyond even her power of endurance.

"Do not keep me in suspense. Where is Bertie? Let me see him, if he is here."

"He is not here. It was to assist you in finding him, that I enticed you here."

"You enticed me?"

"I put the advertisement in the 'Herald', knowing that if you chanced to see it, all the legions of Satan could not keep you away. I have been here since Sunday, waiting and watching. I was obliged to see you, for your own sake, as well as to satisfy my longing to look once more into your face; and I felt assured the magnetic name of 'Bertie' would draw you here swiftly."

"Then it was only a snare, that advertisement? Oh! you are cruel!"

"Not to you. It was to promote your peace of mind, by enabling you to meet the man who, I supposed was your lover, that I invited you to this place. Mark you, only to see, never to marry him."

"Where is he?"

"Exactly where, I do not yet know; but very soon you shall learn."

"Is he in peril?"

"Not from arrest at present, by human officers of retributive justice."

"He is not coming here?"

"Certainly not."

"How did you learn his name?"

"I suspected that the advertisement you published in the "Herald" after leaving X——, was a clue that would aid me. I clung to it, for I was sure it referred to the man whom I have hunted so persistently."

"You have something to tell me. Be merciful, and end my suspense."

"First, answer one question. Why did you conceal from me the fact that you had a brother? Why did you allow me to suffer from a false theory, that you knew made my life a slow torture?"

He leaned nearer, and under the blue fire of his eager eyes, the blood mounted into her pale cheeks.

"My motive belongs to a past, with which I trust I have done forever; and you have no right to violate its buried ashes."

"I must, and I will have all the truth, cost what it may. Between you and me, no spectre of mystery shall longer stalk. If you had trusted me, and confessed the facts before the trial, you would have muzzled me effectually, and prevented the employment of detectives whom I have hissed on your brother's track. Why did you lead me astray, and confirm my suspicion that you were shielding a lover?"

"I was innocent; but my name, my father's honored name, was in jeopardy of dishonor, and to protect it, I would not undeceive you. Had my brother been convicted, the established guilt would have tarnished forever our only legacy, all that father left to Bertie and to me—his spotless name."

"You are quibbling. Did you shield the family name by enduring the purgatory of seeing your own on the list of penitentiary convicts? You deliberately fastened the odium of the crime upon your father's daughter; and you knew, you understood perfectly, that by strengthening my erroneous supposition, you were lashing me to a pursuit of the person, whom you could have best protected by frankly telling me all. If he is really your brother, what did you expect to accomplish by fostering my belief that he was your lover?"

"Mr. Dunbar, spare me this inquisition. Release me from the rack of suspense. Tell me why you set this snare, baited with Bertie's name?"

"I must first end my own suspense. If you wish to find the man, you tell me is your brother, I will aid you only when you have bared your heart to me. You had some powerful incentive unrevealed. I will know exactly, why you made me suffer all these years, the pangs of a devouring jealousy, keener than a vulture's talons."

With crimson cheeks, and shy, averted eyes, she sat trembling; unconsciously locking and unlocking her fingers. Her head drooped, and the voice was a low flutter:

"If I had told you that the handkerchief was one I gave to my brother, because he fancied the gay border, and that the pipe belonged to my dear father, and if you had known that for more than a year before I went to X——no tidings from that brother had reached me, would you have kept my secret, when you saw my life laid in the scales held by the jury? Suppose they had condemned me to death? I expected that fate; but knowing the truth, would you have permitted the execution of that sentence?"

"Certainly not; and you understand why I should never have allowed it."

"I knew that in such an emergency I could not trust you."

Five minutes passed, while he silently sought to unravel the web; and Beryl dared not meet his gaze.

"You had some stronger motive, else you would have confessed all, when I started to Dakota. Anxiety for your brother's safety would have unsealed your lips. What actuated you then? I mean to know everything now."

"Miss Gordon was my friend. She showed me kindness which I could never forget."

"Miss Gordon is a very noble woman, kinder to all the world than to herself; but did gratitude to her involve sacrifice of me?"

"You were betrothed. I owed it to her, to keep you loyal to your vows, as far as my power extended. I tried faithfully to guard her happiness, while endeavoring to shield my brother."

"Knowing you had all my heart, you dared not let me learn that the rival existed only in my imagination? loyal soul! Did you deem it a kindness to aid in binding her to an unloving husband? Her womanly instincts saved her from that death in life; and years ago, she set us both free. She wears no willows, let me tell you; and those who should know best, think that before very long she will sail for Europe as wife of Governor Glenbeigh, the newly appointed minister to Z——, a brilliant position, which she will nobly grace. She will be happier as Glenbeigh's wife than I could possibly have made her; for he loves her as she deserves to be loved. So, for Miss Gordon's sake, you immolated me?"

Only the pathetic piping of the lonely bird made answer.

Like the premonitory thrill that creeps through forest leaves, before the coming burst of a tempest, he seemed to tremble slightly; his tone had a rising ring, and a dark flush stained his swarthy face, deepened the color in his brilliant eyes.

"Oh, my white rose! A wonderful fragrance of hope steals into the air; a light breaks upon my dreary world that makes me giddy! Can it be possible that you—"

He paused, and she covered her face with her hands.

"Beryl, you are the only woman I have ever loved. You came suddenly into my life, as an irresistible incarnation of some fateful witchery that stole and fired my heart, subverted all my plans, made havoc of lifelong hopes, dominated my will, changed my nature; overturned the cool selfishness on the altar of my worship, and set up your own image in a temple, swept, garnished, and sanctified forever by your in-dwelling. You have cost me stinging humiliation, years of regret, of bitter disappointment; and the ceaselessly gnawing pain of a jealous dread that despite my vigilance, another man might some day possess you. I have money, influence, professional success, gratified ambition, and enviable social eminence; I have all but that which a man wants most, the one woman in the great wide world whom he loves truly, loves better than he loves himself; and who holds his heart in the hollow of her hand. I want my beautiful, proud, pure, stately white rose. I want my Beryl. I will have my own."

He had risen, stood before her; took the hands that veiled her countenance, and drew her to her feet.

"You have been loyal to parents, to brother, to friends, to duty; be loyal now to your own heart; answer me truly. What did you mean when you once said, with a mournful pathos I cannot forget: 'We love not always whom we should, or would, were choice permitted us?' You defied me that day, and prayed God to bless your lover; taunted me with words that have made days dreary, nights hideous: 'To whom I have given my whole deep heart, you shall never know.' Did you mean—ah—will you tell me now?"

She bent her head till it almost touched him, but no answer came.

"You will not? I swear you shall; else I shall hope, believe, know beyond all doubt, that during these years, I have not been the only sufferer; and that loyal as was your soul, your rebel heart is as truly mine, as all my deathless love is surely yours."

She tried to withdraw her hands; but his hold tightened, and infinite exultation rang in his voice.

"My darling! My darling—you dare not deny it? I shall wear my white rose to make all the future sweet with a blessed love; but have you no word of assurance for my hungry ears? Is my darling too proud?"

He raised her hands, laid her arms around his neck, and folded very close to his heart, the long coveted prize.

"My Beryl, it was a stubborn battle, but Lennox Dunbar claims his own; and will hold her safe forever. Will you be loyal to your tyrant?"

Was it a white or a crimson rose that hid its lovely petals against his shoulder, and whispered with lips that his kiss had rouged:

"Have I ever been allowed a choice? Was I not foredoomed to be always at the mercy of Tiberius?"

The little garden was growing dusky, the gilded mist waving its spectral banners over the thundering cataract, had whitened as the sun went down behind the wooded crest that barred the western sky line; and the shimmering gold on the heaving, whirling current of the Rapids faded to leaden tints, flecked with foam, as like a maddened suitor, parted by Goat Island from its beloved, it rushed to plunge into the abyss, where the silvery bridal veil shook her signal, and all the roaring gorge filled with purple gloom.

Mr. Dunbar drew his companion's hand under his arm, and led her toward the Clifton House.

"You and I have done with shadows. On the heights yonder, the sun still shines. Up there waits one, who will tell you that which he refuses to divulge to any one else. Ten days ago my agents notified me that a man was searching for Mrs. Brentano and her daughter Beryl in New York; and that he had gone to X——, where he spent several days in consultation with the Catholic priest. Singleton sent me a telegram, and I reached X——in time to accompany the stranger back to New York. To me he admits only, that he lives in Montreal; and is the bearer of a message, the import of which, sacred promises prevent him from revealing to any one but Miss Brentano. He is an elderly man, and so wary, no amount of dexterity can circumvent his caution. Very complex and inexplicable motives brought me here; chiefly the longing to see you, to learn your retreat, your mode of existence; and also the intention to exact one condition, before I made it possible for you to find the object of your search. When you had given me your promise not to marry him, it was my purpose to allow you one final meeting; and if you forfeited your compact, the dungeon and the gallows awaited him. Love makes women martyrs; they are the apostles of the gospel of altruism. Love revives in men of my stamp, the primeval and undifferentiated tiger. When I think of all that you have endured, of how nearly I lost you, my snowdrop, do you wonder I shall hasten to set you in the garden of my heart, and shelter your dear head from every chill wind of adversity?"

They had passed through a gate, crossed a lawn, and reached a long, steep flight of steps leading straight up the face of a cliff, to the grounds attached to a villa. With her hand clasped tightly in his, Mr. Dunbar and Beryl slowly mounted the abrupt stairway, and when they gained the elevated terrace, a man who was walking up and down the sward, came quickly forward.

Pressing her fingers tenderly, Mr. Dunbar released her hand.

"When your interview is ended, come to me yonder at the side gate, where I have a carriage to take you over the bridge. Father Beckx, this is Miss Brentano. I leave her in your care."

The sun was sending his last level shafts of light from the edge of the sky, when a man dressed in long black vestments, a raven-haired, raven-eyed, thin lipped and clean shaven personage, with a placid countenance as coldly irresponsive as a stone mask, sat down on the top step of the long stairs, beside the woman in gray, whose eager white face was turned to meet his, in breathless and mute expectancy.

The lingering twilight held at bay slowly marching night; the sunset glory streamed up almost to the zenith in bands of amethyst and faint opaline green, like the far reaching plumes of an archangel's pinions beating the still, crystal air. Later, the vivid orange of the afterglow burned with a transient splendor, as the dying smile of a day that had gone to its eternal grave; and all the West was one vast evening primrose of palest gold sprinkled with star dust, when Beryl went slowly to join the figure pacing restlessly in front of the gate.

Across the grassy lawn he came to meet her. In mute surrender she lifted her arms, laid her proud head, with its bared wealth of burnished bronze hair, down on his shoulder, and wept passionately.

When he had placed her in the carriage, and held her close to his heart, with his dark cheek resting on hers, where tears still trickled, he whispered:

"How much are you willing to tell me?"

"Only that I must start at once on a long, lonely journey to a desolate retreat, in mountain solitudes; far away in the wilderness of the Northwest. Bertie is there; and I must see him once more."

"How soon do you wish to start?"

"Within the next three days."

"You must wait one week. I cannot go before that time."

"You—?"

"Do you suppose I shall allow you to travel there without me? Do you imagine I shall ever lose sight of you, till the vows are uttered that make you my wife? You cannot see your brother's face, until you have first looked into your husband's. In one week I can arrange to go, to the ends of the earth if you will; but you will meet your brother only when you are Beryl Dunbar."

"No—no! You forget, ah!—You forget. I have worn the penitentiary homespun, and the brand of the convict seared my fair name, scarred all my life. The wounds will heal, but time can never efface the hard lines of the cicatrice; and I could not bear to mar the lustre of your honored name by—"

"Hush!—hush. It is ungenerous in you to wound me so sorely. When I remember the fiery furnace through which my wife walked unscorched, with such sublime and patient heroism, is it possible that I should forget whose rash hand, whose besotted idiocy consigned her to the awful ordeal? Out of the black shadow where I thrust you, sprang the halo that glorifies you. How often, in the silence of my sleepless nights, have I heard the echo of your wild, despairing cry: 'You have ruined my life!' Oh, my darling! If you withhold yourself, if you cast me away, you will indeed ruin mine. If you could realize how I wince at the recollection of your suffering, you would not cruelly remind me of my own accursed work."

"If the soul of my brother be ransomed thereby, I shall thank you, even for all that X——cost me. The world knows now, that no suspicion clings to me; but, Mr. Dunbar, the disgrace blots forever the dear name I tried to shield; and my vindication only blackens Bertie."

"The world will never know. Your sad secret shall be kept, and my name shall wrap you in ermine, and my love make your future redeem the past. Having found my darling, can I afford to run the risk of losing her? You belong to me, and I will not trust you out of my sight, until the law gives me a husband's claim. The mother of one of my oldest friends is boarding here in Niagara. I will commit you to her care until to-morrow; then some church will furnish an altar where you shall pledge me your loyalty."

"Impossible! To-night a train will take me to Buffalo, where I can catch the express going West. There are reasons why I must make no delay; must hasten back to explain many things to the Matron of the Sisterhood, where I have dwelt so safely and so peacefully since I left X——."

"Give me the reasons. 'Impossible' ne me dites jamais ce bete de mot!' Give me your reasons."

His arm tightened around her.

"Not now."

"Then you shall not leave me. I will endure no more mysteries."

"Mr. Dunbar, I wear the uniform of a celibate Order of Gray Sisters; and the matron trusted me in an unusual degree, when she consented that I should undertake this journey on a secret mission. I came to Niagara, as I supposed, to keep an appointment with my brother, and I met you. If I lingered one instant here, it might reflect some discredit upon this dear gray garb, which all hold so irreproachable. Sister Ruth trusted me. I cannot, I will not, even in the smallest iota, appear to betray her confidence; and I must go at once, and go as I came—alone. Bid the driver take me to the railway station, and you must remain in the carriage. I can have no escort. Your presence would subject me to criticism, and I will guard the 'gray' that so mercifully guarded me."

"Beryl, are you trying to elude me?"

"I am faithfully trying to keep my compact with Sister Ruth. Here is a card bearing the exact address of the 'Anchorage'. I am going there as quickly as possible, to make speedy arrangements for my long journey West, to that place almost within sound of the Pacific Ocean."

"Put your hand in mine. Promise me before God, that you will not vanish from me; that you will not leave the 'Anchorage' until I come and see you there."

"I promise; but time presses. I must hasten to find Bertie."

"Do you know exactly where to go?"

"Yes. I have minute directions written down."

"Wait until I come. I trust you to keep your promise. Ah! after to-day, I could not bear to lose my 'Rosa Alba.' God make me more worthy of my loyal and beautiful darling. After all, not Alcestis, but Antigone!"

CHAPTER XXXV.

White and still, lay the world of the far Northwest, wrapped in peace as profound as that which reigned in primeval ages; when ancestral Nahuas, dragging their sleds across frozen Behring Straits, or cast amid other drift of the Japanese current upon the strange new Pacific shore, climbed the mountains, and fell on their faces before the sun, whose worshippers have sacrificed in all hemispheres.

If civilization be the analogue of geologic accretion, how tortuous is the trend and dip of the ethnological strata, how abrupt the overlapping of myths. How many aeons divided the totem coyote from the she-wolf of Romulus and Remus? Which is the primitive and parent flame, the sacred fire of Pueblo Estufas, of Greek Prytaneum, of Roman Vesta, of Persian Atish-khudahs? If the Laurentian system be the oldest upheaval of land, and its "dawn animal" the first evolution of life that left fossil footprints, where are all the missing links in ethnology, which would save science that rejects Genesis—the paradox of peopling the oldest known continent by immigration from those incalculably younger?

Winter had lagged, loath to set his snow shoes upon the lingering, diaphanous train of Indian Summer, but December was inexorable, and the livery of ice glittered everywhere in the mid-day sun.

Along a well-worn bridle trail, now slippery as glass, winding around the base of crags, through narrow gorges that almost overarched, leaving a mere skylight of intense blue to mark the way, moved a party of four persons in single file, slowly ascending a steep spiral. In advance, mounted on a black pony, was a cowled monk, whose long, thin profile suggested that of Savonarola; and just behind him rode a Canadian half-breed guide, with the copperish red of aboriginal America on his high cheek bones, and the warm glow of sunny France in his keen black eyes. Guiding his horse with the left hand, his right led the dappled mustang belonging to the third figure; a tall, broad-shouldered man wearing an overcoat that reached to his knees, who walked with his hand on the bridle bit of a white mule, whereon sat a woman, wrapped in silver fox furs from throat to feet. A cap or hood of the same soft, warm material was worn over her head, where a roll of dark auburn hair coiled at the back; and around her white temples clustered rings and tendrils of the glossy bronze locks that contrasted so singularly with the black arch of the brows, and the fringe that darkened the luminous gray eyes.

One month had elapsed since the Umilta Sisters of the "Anchorage", following Sister Ruth, walked in the star-lit dawn of a November day, to a neighboring church, and watched Doctor Grantlin lead down the aisle, a pale, trembling woman whose hand he placed in that of the man, waiting in front of the altar. The Sisterhood had listened to the solemn words of the marriage service, the interchange of vows, and the benediction, while priestly hands were laid tapon two bowed heads.

When the rising sun greeted the husband and wife, they were speeding westward, on the first stage of their long journey.

To-day, the quest would end; and into Beryl's face had crept the wistful yearning that was a reflection of that strange blending of patience and longing, which made her so beautiful in her husband's eyes; so strong in faith, so serene in waiting resignation. Suddenly the monk drew rein, threw up his drooping head, and listened. Clear and sweet as the silvery chime of bells ringing in happy dreams, floated through the crystal air the sound of the Angelus; and fainter and fainter fell the echoes, dying in immeasurable distance. Low bent the shaven head, and through brown, fingers stole the consecrated beads, while with closed eyes the prayers were uttered; and in the pause, the guide made the sign of the cross, and Mr. Dunbar instinctively took off his hat.

"Six hours' steady climbing is a severe tax. Are you very tired?" he whispered, laying his arm around Beryl's waist, and lifting his brilliant eyes eloquent with an infinite tenderness.

With one hand on his shoulder as he stood beside her, she leaned down until her lips touched the black hair tossed back from his forehead.

"After waiting so many terrible years, what are a few more hours of suspense? Since I have you, can I ever again feel tired?"

Behind them lay a dark undulating line, where oak and cedar had made their last stand on the upward march; nearer, the spectral ranks of stunted firs showed the outposts of forest advance; and a few feet from the narrow path, a perpendicular cliff formed one wall of a deep canon, where a glittering ribbon of water hurried to leap into the Pacific, ere pursuing Winter arrested and bound it with icy manacles to its stony bed. To the north dazzling white peaks cut strange solemn shapes, like silver cameos on a ground of indigo sky; and overhead, burnished lines of snow geese printed their glittering triangles on the paler blue of the zenith, as the winged host dipped southward.

The monk moved on, and after a while his companions perceived that the way descended rapidly until they reached the face of a rock that rose straight and smooth as a wall of human masonry, and apparently barred further progress. Taking from his bosom the twisted section of a polished horn, only a finger's length, the cowled figure raised it to his lips, and blew three whistles, that ended in a rising inflection which waked all the wolfish pack of mountain echoes into fitful barking. Two moments later, an answering signal seemed to issue from the invisible jaws of Hades; a wild, quivering sepulchral cry, as of a monster half throttled. Twenty feet beyond the spot where the party had halted, a steep descent led them to a shelving canon, once the bed of a broad mountain torrent, whose course some seismic upheaval had diverted to other channels. Following for a few yards the sinuous stony way, worn here and there into smooth circular cavities like miniature wells, by the eddying of the ancient current and the grinding of pebbles, the travellers turned a sharp angle, and found themselves at the mouth of Tartarus.

The force of the stream had originally cut a low arch in its egress, which human needs and ingenuity had broadened, heightened and closed by heavy iron bars, slipped into stone slots. Behind this gateway glimmered a faint light that brightened into a red star; and soon, a figure clad in the long, black monastic gown, and bearing a huge torch of blazing pitch pine, emerged from the bowels of the earth. There was the rattle of a chain, the creak of a pulley, and the bars were lowered.

So vividly did the scene recall that black, stormy night in February, when Mr. Dunbar had seen the lantern of the gaoler flash through the penitentiary gates closing on the young convict, that he drew his breath now through clinched teeth, and quickly laid his hand upon that of his wife, which grasped the bridle resting upon the neck of her mule. Silently the procession filed in, and with little delay the torch bearer replaced the bars, advanced to the head of the column, and with long, swift strides led the way down a wide tunnel. Between the monks no salutation was exchanged; and only the ringing tramp of the horses' feet on the stone pavement, jarred the profound stillness. The lurid glare of the torch danced on the rocky vault, and the shadows projected by men and beasts were gigantic and grotesque. Very soon a gray twilight stole to meet them; an arch of light like a window opening into heaven brightened, glared, and the party emerged into a courtyard that seemed an entrance to some vast amphitheatre.

Opposite the mouth of the tunnel, and distant perhaps two hundred yards, lay an oval lake, bordered on the right by a valley running southeast, while its northern shore rose abruptly in a parapet of rock, that patient cloistered workmen had cut into broad terraces; and upon which opened rows of cells excavated from the mountain side, and resembling magnified swallow nests, or a huge petrified honeycomb sliced vertically.

A legend so hoary, that "the memory of man runneth not to the contrary", had assigned the outlines of this stone cutting to that dim dawn of primeval tribal life, which left its later traces in the Watch Tower of the Mancos, the Casa del Eco, and the "niche stairway of the Hovenweep".

In the slow deposition of the human strata, cliff dwellers disappeared beneath predatory, nomadic modern savages, who, hunting and fishing in this lonely fastness, had increased its natural fortifications, and made it an impregnable depot of supplies, until Hudson Bay trappers wrenched it from their grasp, and appropriated it as a peltry magazine. To the dynasty of traders had succeeded the spiritual rule of a Jesuit Mission; then miners kindled camp fires in the deserted excavations, as they probed the mountain for ores; and more recently the noiseless feet of a band of holy celibates belonging to an austere Order, went up and down the face of the cliff, with cross and bell and incense exorcising haunting aboriginal spectres; while holy water sprinkled the uncanny, dismal precincts of a circular room hollowed behind and beneath all other apartments, the monumental, sacred Estufa.

At a signal from the monk who had escorted them, Mr. Dunbar lifted Beryl from her saddle, and hand in hand they followed him across the courtyard, mounted a flight of steps cut in the rock, and passed into a low, dim room, where the ceiling was crossed in squares by heavy, red cedar beams. The floor was paved with diamond-shaped slabs of purple slate, the whitewashed wall adorned with colored lithographs of the Passion; and above the cavernous chimney arch, where cedar logs blazed, ran the inscription: "Otiositas inimica est animae."

Noiselessly as the wings of a huge bat, a leathern screen was folded back from the corner of the room, and a venerable man advanced from the gloom.

A fringe of white hair surrounded his head like a laurel chaplet in old statues, and the heavy, straight brows that almost met across the nose, hung as snowflakes over the intensely black eyes as glowing as lamps set in the sockets of an ivory image. Scholarly and magnetic as Abelard, with a certain innate proud poise of the head and shoulders, that ill accorded with the Carlo-Borromeo expression of seraphic serenity and meekness, set like a seal on the large square mouth, he looked a veritable type of the ecclesiastical cenobites who, since the days of Pachomius at Tabennae, have made their hearts altars of the Triple Vows, and girdled the globe with a cable of scholastic mysticism. The pale, shrunken hand he laid on the black serge that covered his breast, was delicate as a woman's, and checkered with knotted lines where the blood crept feebly.

Bowing low, he spoke in a carefully modulated voice, deep and resonant as a bass viol:

"Welcome to such hospitality as our poverty permits. A cipher telegram forwarded from the nearest station, sixty miles hence, prepared us to expect a newly-married woman searching for a man, known to the secular world as Robert Luke Brentano. You claim to be his nearest blood relative?"

"I am his sister. How is he?"

"Alive, but sinking fast; sustained beyond all human calculation by the hope of seeing you. You have not come one moment too soon. The man you seek is only a lay brother here. The rules of our Order forbid the admission of women to the cloister, but in articulo mortis! can I deny him now the confession he wishes to offer you? Our holy ordinances have done their divine work; the last rites of the Church have soothed and consecrated the heart of Brother Luke, and an hour ago, extreme unction was administered. Follow me."

"He knows that I am coming?" asked Beryl, raising her white, tear-drenched face from her husband's shoulder.

"He knows; and holds death back to see you. His self-imposed penance makes him steadfastly refuse the comparative comfort of our meagre infirmary, and it is his wish to die, where he has spent so many nights in penitential prayer. For several days, the paralysis of years has been gradually loosening its fetters, and this morning, the distressing and ghastly distortion of one side of his face almost disappeared. Though his voice is well nigh gone, it returns fitfully, and his strength seems supernatural. Fearing that you might not arrive in time, I have written down his last confession, and here commit it to you."

He placed a roll of paper in her hand, and drawing his cowl over his head, led them up an easy stairway cut in the stone, to a second terrace four feet wide, that projected as a roof beyond the lower tier of cells.

A hundred feet below lay the lakelet, shining as a mirror; to the southeast stretched a valley bounded by buttes crowned with cedar, and in the undulating field, locked from fierce winds, cattle and goats sunned themselves, where in summer time grain waved, fruit ripened, and bees hummed.

From the parapet of a low wall facing west, rose a round tower heavily buttressed, where swung the bell; and through an open arch in the side, under the uplifted cross, the eye swept on and on, over a world of snowy peaks, dark canons, mountain minarets girding the northern horizon; and far, far away a scintillating thread of white fire marked where the Pacific smiled behind the fiords that channelled the rock-ribbed coast.

In that still, cold and brilliant atmosphere, how dazzling the snow blink, how sharp the outline of projected shadows, how close the bending heavens seemed; but to the yearning soul of Beryl, the silent, solemn sublimity of the mighty panorama made no appeal.

Through slowly dripping tears she saw only the spectral flitting of her mother's sad face, as in their last interview she had committed the soul of the son to the guardianship of the daughter.

The monk paused, and pointed to the third cell from the spot where he stood.

"It is but a step farther. Yonder, where the skull is set over the entrance."

"I will wait here," said Mr. Dunbar, relinquishing with a tight pressure, his wife's cold hand.

"No, come. Are we not one?"

She hurried along the terrace, and reached the low open doorway fronting the South, where the sunshine streamed in like God's smile of forgiveness.

On the stone floor was a straw pallet covered with coarse brown blankets, whereon, half propped by one elbow, with head against the gray rocky wall, lay the emaciated wreck of a man, whose pallid face might have been mistaken for that of a corpse, but for the superhuman splendor of the wide, deep brown eyes.

Beryl sprang into the cave-like recess, and fell on her knees. She snatched him to her heart, laid his head on her shoulder.

"Bertie! My darling! my darling!—"

He tried to raise one arm to her neck, but it fell back. She lifted it, held it close, and face to face with her lips on his, she broke into passionate sobbing, rocking herself to and fro, in the tempest of grief.

"Give me, give—me—air—" He struggled for breath, which her tight clasp denied him; and for some minutes he panted, while Mr. Dunbar fanned him with his hat. Then the heaving chest grew more quiet, and after a moment, his eyes lighted with a happy smile as they fastened on Beryl's face, bent over him.

"Gigina, sweet, faithful sister, it is almost heaven to see you once more. God is good, even to me."

"If I could have found you sooner! All these dreadful years I have lived at God's feet—with one prayer: let me help my Bertie, let me see my brother's face," moaned Beryl, pressing her lips to the clammy, fleshless hand she held against her throat.

"I was too unworthy. I dreaded your pure eyes, and mother's, as I would an accusing angel's. I did not know, then, that mother was already one of the Beatified. I know now, that neither life nor death, nor sin nor shame, nor the brand of disgrace can change mother's love; for I see her to-day, smiling at the door, beckoning me to follow where the sun shines forever. My sainted mother."

"Her last breath was a blessing for you. See, Bertie! this was her wedding ring. Her final message was, 'Give this to my darling!' Be comforted, dear Bertie, she loved you even to the end—supremely. You were her idol in death as in life. Our father's ring was the most sacred relic she owned, and she left it to you."

She attempted to place the gold band on one of his fingers, but he closed that hand, and the dark eyes so like his mother's, were for an instant dimmed by tears.

"Keep it; no sin of theft soils your hands. You can wear it without a blush. You never robbed an old man of his gold. That was my crime, I am a thief."

"Our God sees you have repented bitterly; and He has pardoned your sins for His dear Son's sake. Tell me, Bertie, have you made your eternal salvation sure? Are you, in your soul, at peace with God?"

"At perfect peace. I want to die, because now I am no longer afraid to meet Him, who forgives even thieves. Gigi, wait a little—"

He seemed to make a desperate effort to rally his strength, and the thin, fine nostril flared, in the battle for breath.

"There has been a terrible mistake, and they made you suffer for what they imagined happened. When I found I had only a few months to live, I wrote to Father Beckx, whom I had known in Montreal, and asked him to tell mother where I was. I never knew till he went to X—and wrote us about the trial, that you were suspected and punished for a crime that was never committed. I thought you and mother were safe in New York, all those years, and I knew that you would be sure to take care of her. I have it all written down—and I can't tell you now—but I want to look straight into your dear eyes—my brave sister, my loving sister—and let you learn first from me—the reward you have won—your Bertie is not a murderer. I did take the money from the vault which was wide open, when first I saw it. I did steal and destroy the will, which I thought unjustly robbed us all of our right to the Darrington estate, but that was my sole offence. I am a thief, before God and man, but there is no more stain of blood on my hands than on yours. General Darrington was not murdered. He died by the hand of God alone—"

A bluish shadow settled around his parted lips, and he panted.

Mr. Dunbar raised him, fanned him, rested his head more comfortably against his sister's shoulder; and again he looked intently into her eyes, as though his soul, plumed for departure, must right itself in the presence of hers, before the final flight.

"He struck me with the andiron, and broke my wrist here—then before I ever touched him—as he raised it to assault me the second time—there came an awful blinding glare—the world was wrapped in a blue fire—and God struck us both down. When I became conscious, my senses were all stunned, but after a while I knew I was lying on the floor, with a cold hand resting like lead on my face. I got up; the figure didn't move, and I supposed that like myself he was stunned by the shock. As I passed a mirror on my way to the window—I saw myself—for the lamp was burning bright. God had branded me a thief. Do you see here—drawn—paralyzed, oh, Gina! All these years I have worn the dark streak, and one eye was blind, one ear stone deaf. I was a walking shadow of my own sin; horrible to look upon—and I fled to avoid the gaze of my race. Somewhere, in Illinois I think, I heard two men on a train speak of a large reward offered for the recovery of Gen'l Darrington's will, which had been stolen by one of his heirs, whom the police were hunting. I was branded—and on my breast here was printed the face of the dead man—for he had torn my shirt open as he seized me with one hand, and struck me with the other. I hid in mines, crossed the plains, secreted myself in a bee ranche. Then the Canadian railroad was partly built, and I joined the grading party and worked—until the curse of my sin was more than I could bear. I heard of the holy Brothers here, made my last journey, confessed my theft, and entered on my penance. Gina, General Darrington was killed instantly by the lightning."

As the burden Beryl had long borne slipped suddenly from her heart, the joy of release from blood-stain was so unexpected, so intense, that her face blanched to a deadly pallor, and the glad eyes she lifted to her husband's shone as those of an angel.

"Bertie—Bertie—" Words failed her. She could only kiss the wasted cold hands that were innocent of bloodshed.

After some moments, the dying man said almost in a whisper:

"I never knew you were punished for my sin, until it was too late to save you, but God's witness cleared your pure name. The lightning that scorched me, printed its testimony to set you free. My sister—my sister—God will surely recompense your faithful—" The voice died in a quivering gurgle.

"I have my reward, dear Bertie. Oh, how much more than I deserve! I have you in my arms, innocent of murder, thank God! thank God! I have the blessed absurance that your pardoned soul goes to meet mother's in Eternal Peace; and to secure that, I would have willingly died an ignominious death. It was through the fiery flames of prison, and trial and convict shame, that God led me to the most precious crown any woman ever wore, my husband's confidence and love. Only behind dungeon bars could I have won my husband's heart, which holds for me the whole wide world of earthly peace and hope. For your sin, you have suffered. Its consequences to others from the destruction of the will, have been averted by the prompt transfer of all the property which Gen'l Darrington left, to his chosen heir Prince. Pecuniarily no one was injured by your act. Dear Bertie—Bertie, are you listening?"

He smiled but made no answer, and his eyes had a strained and exultant expression. After a long silence, he cried huskily:

"The curse is taken away—out of my blinded eye I see—Agnus Dei qui tollis peccata mundi—"

A slight spasm shook him, and feeling his cheek grow colder, Beryl threw off the fur cloak, and folded it closely around the wasted body which leaned heavily against her. The sunny short rings of hair clung to his sunken, blue veined temples, where cold drops gathered; and a gray seal was set about the wan lips that writhed in the fight for breath.

"Bertie, kiss me—tell me you are not afraid."

She fancied he nestled his face closer, but the wide eyes were fixed on the golden light that was fading fast across the narrow doorway.

Pressing her quivering lips to his, she sobbed:

"Tell mother, her little girl was faithful—"

Another spasm shook the form, and after a little while, the eyes closed; the panting ceased, and the tired breath was drawn in long, shuddering sighs.

Mr. Dunbar beckoned to the cowled form who, rosary in hand, paced the terrace, and the two laid the dying man back on his pallet of straw.

Fainter grew the slow breath, and the voice of the monk rolled through the silence, like the tremolo swell of an organ:

"Delicta juventutis, et ignorantias ejus, quoesumus, ne memineris, Domine; sed secundum magnam misericordiam tuam memor esto illius in gloria claritatis tuoe."

On the stone floor Beryl knelt, with her brother's icy hand clasped against her cheek, and as she watched, the twitching of the muscles ceased, the lips so long distorted, took on their old curves of beauty. A marble pallor blanched the dark stain of the branded cheek, and the Bertie of innocent youth came slowly out of the long eclipse.

Death, God's most tender angel, laid her divine lips upon the scars of sin, that vanished at her touch; drew her white fingers across the lines and shadows of suffering time, and leaving the halo of eternal peace upon the frozen features, gave back to Beryl her beautiful Bertie of old.

The sun was setting; and far away the ice domes and minarets of immemorial mountains took on the burnished similitude of the New Jerusalem, which only the exiled saw from lonely Patmos.

Lennox Dunbar lifted his wife from the form of the sleeper, whose ransomed soul had entered early into Rest; and folded her tenderly to the heart that henceforth was her refuge from all earthly woes.

At midnight, the brooding silence of the snow-hooded solitude was broken by the tolling of the monastery bell; and while all the mountain echoes responded to the slow knell for the departed soul, there rose from the chapel under the cliffs, the solemn chant of the monks for their dead:

"Requiem aeternam dona eis, Domine, et lux perpetua luceat eis."

"Give them eternal rest, O Lord, and let perpetual light shine upon them."

THE END.

Made in the USA
Las Vegas, NV
09 March 2025

19314477R00090